EVERYMAN'S LIBRARY

EVERYMAN,
I WILL GO WITH THEE,
AND BE THY GUIDE,
IN THY MOST NEED
TO GO BY THY SIDE

JOHN UPDIKE

The Complete Henry Bech
Twenty Stories

Bech: A Book   Bech Is Back
Bech at Bay   His Oeuvre

with an Introduction by
Malcolm Bradbury

EVERYMAN'S   LIBRARY

Alfred A. Knopf New York Toronto

264

THIS IS A BORZOI BOOK
PUBLISHED BY ALFRED A. KNOPF

First included in Everyman's Library, 2001
Bech: A Book Copyright © 1965, 1966, 1968, 1970 by John Updike
Copyright renewed 1993, 1995, 1998 by John Updike
Bech Is Back Copyright © 1975, 1979, 1982 by John Updike
Bech at Bay Copyright © 1998 by John Updike
'His Oeuvre' Copyright © 2000 by John Updike

Introduction Copyright © 2000 by Malcolm Bradbury
Bibliography and Chronology © 2001 by Everyman Publishers plc
Typography by Peter B. Willberg

The New Yorker first published 'The Bulgarian Poetess', 'Bech in
Rumania', 'Rich in Russia' (without appendices), 'Bech Takes Pot
Luck', 'Bech Swings?' (in shorter form), 'Three Illuminations in the
Life of an American Author', 'Bech in Czech', 'His Oeuvre' and
most of 'Bech Noir'. The rest of 'Bech Noir' appeared in *New York
Stories*. *Playboy* magazine first published 'Australia and Canada', 'Bech
Third-Worlds It' and 'The Holy Land'.

All rights reserved under International and Pan-American Copyright
Conventions. Published in the United States by Alfred A. Knopf,
a division of Random House, Inc., New York, and simultaneously in
Canada by Random House of Canada Limited, Toronto. Distributed
by Random House, Inc., New York.

www.randomhouse.com/everymans

ISBN 0-375-41176-3

Library of Congress Cataloging-in-Publication Data
Updike, John.
The complete Henry Bech: twenty stories / John Updike;
with an introduction by Malcolm Bradbury.
p.   cm.—(Everyman's library; 264)
Includes bibliographical references (p.) and index.
Contents: Bech: a book—Bech is back—Bech at bay—His oeuvre.
ISBN 0-375-41176-3 (alk. paper)
1. Bech, Henry (Fictitious character)—Fiction. 2. Humorous
stories, American. 3. Jewish authors—Fiction. I. Title.
PS3571.P4 A6 2001   00-053488
813'.54—dc21   CIP

Book Design by Barbara de Wilde and Carol Devine Carson

Printed and bound in Germany
by GGP Media, Pössneck

THE COMPLETE
HENRY BECH

———

CONTENTS

THE COMPLETE HENRY BECH

INTRODUCTION

In the huge and wonderfully prolix world of what now starts to look like a quite heroic lifetime of writing – no contemporary American writer has written more fully about his own fascinating nation, his wide-ranging observations and insights, his own generous and eclectic bookishness, and this in nineteen novels, nearly as many volumes of short fiction, six collections of poetry, several huge tomes of essays, amounting to just over fifty books in all – John Updike has succeeded in creating for himself two remarkable alter egos. One of them – the friendlier one, the more familiar, the right-hand one, we could say – is Harry 'Rabbit' Angstrom, surely his most famous single character, from his most visible, successful and belaureled sequence of novels. The athletic, hefty, ordinary, mainstream, suburbanized and unliterary American who, as Updike has explained, became 'a way in – a ticket to the America all around me', Rabbit is *l'homme moyen sensuel*, and not in character all that closely tied to his author. A day-to-day user of the familiar, totally caught up in his domesticated world, he has granted Updike, an instinctive social realist and an historian of the rich detail of his own culture, ways of recording the mainstream of American life not readily accessible to contemporary American fiction, much of which is angular to and critical of mainstream society. 'What I saw through Rabbit's eyes was more worth telling than what I saw through my own,' Updike observes. And what he saw, highlighted through those ordinary eyes, was indeed the commonplace, the regular, the ordinary American quiddities – the things which Updike, for all his aesthetic sense of writing, has always written about, poetically, vividly and well. As chronicler of the supermarket and the hamburger joint, the used car lot and the Toyota franchise, the basketball court and the movie theatre, the city and the suburban tract, the rolling superhighway and the wooded and winding back road, Updike found in Rabbit Angstrom his world's natural inhabitant. In his own words, Rabbit became his American Everyman.

Rabbit appeared first in 1960, in *Rabbit, Run*, very near the beginning of Updike's career, and in a time of relative national innocence, the later part of the 'guiltless Fifties', when the post-war novel was taking shape, and when many of the greater enormities of post-war American and superpower culture had not become visible. But he ran and ran, returning in *Rabbit Redux* in 1971, after the cultural radicalizations of the Sixties. By the end it took a tetralogy – the four hefty books published between 1960 and 1990 and now gathered together, re-edited, in Everyman's Library as *Rabbit Angstrom: The Four Novels* – to contain him and complete his life-cycle. Together the four volumes form a sufficient and vivid record of the thirty years of American experience over which Updike was writing. Growing and changing, fleeing and ageing, Rabbit came to confront the future of his own physical simplicity and innocence, and, directly or indirectly, many of the prime incidents of his time: the era of McLuhan's global village, inflation, the Apollo moonshot and Civil Rights, the oil crisis and the Three Mile Island disaster, the growth of the Tiger Economies, Reaganite America, the dawn of the Clinton age. From life to death, and from running to rest, he became the hero of a long tale of middle-American life in the second half of the twentieth century, when America became a superpower, commercialism became an outright ideology, sex became a sport, goods and shopping became the only real culture. Rabbit began close to Babbitt, not so far from the boostering spirit of the 1920s and the depression anxieties of the Thirties; he ended as the age of American innocence was replaced by the age of consumerist exoticism, as not just Rabbit but America itself became superfluously rich. His long tale became what John Galsworthy, another specialist in the history of the ordinary, would have called a Saga, and what Updike himself has called a Mega-Novel. Whatever we call it, it will probably take its place as the most typical, the most mainstream and the most American of his works.

*

But ordinary Rabbit never did encompass all of extraordinary Updike, a writer's writer after all. A realist of his era, he has been one of its literary aestheticians as well; a precise recorder of social change, he has also been an explorer of the strange luminosities that illuminate or make fantastic the commonplace scene. A social historian, he has been even more a literary one: a serious critic, a lover of writerly play and intertext, he has written across most of the genres – poetry, essays, short stories, mega-novels, parodies, prequels and sequels, books on golf. He has written classic fictions, books that take up and confront the grand themes of American writing, remodelling Hawthorne, amending Melville, playing with American culture's Adamic mythologies and its radical yesses and nos. It's not surprising that Updike needed a second alter ego, rather less wholesome, a writer who is both like and unlike himself – a left-handed alter ego, as it were.

So emerges Henry Bech, wandering Jew in an era of American cultural mission work, visiting campus writer and serial lecher, anti-Semitic Semite, latter-day modernist and a man of historical and personal angst, whose literary, psychological and sexual adventures, a number of them taking place in Eastern Europe in the icy snows of the Cold War, were first delineated in *Bech: A Book* (1970). In one of his many interviews, Updike has told the story of Bech's devising, as the literary surrogate for himself he decided to acquire following a six-week tour in Eastern Europe, Commieland, in late 1964. Bech first began life in a *New Yorker* short story, and was revived largely because the story won the O. Henry Prize. 'Distrusting writers as heroes, I made Bech as unlike myself as I could,' Updike explained. 'Instead of being married with four children, he's a bachelor; instead of being a gentile, he's a Jew – of course, a Jewish writer is almost as inevitable as an Italian gangster.'* Bech is no simple American innocent, and he comes from a very different world from Rabbit. Updike has always been very recognizably a WASP writer, a novelist of the white eastern middle class, a social observer and chronicler, a moralist and an aesthete, his novels emerging from the same cultural stream as John Cheever and John O'Hara ('all the

*See Updike, 'One Big Interview', in *Picked-Up Pieces* (New York, 1975), pp. 486–8.

Johns'); the *New Yorker*, where Bech first saw light, has always been his magazine of first resort. Bech by contrast is in the tradition of Jewish-American modernism, in line with the fiction of angst, alienation and protest. His literary culture is the world of *Partisan Review* and *Commentary*; he comes from the counter-strand of American fiction, the dissenting, immigrant, anguished and extreme.

As his character grew and got rounder over the various stories of *Bech: A Book*, Updike clearly relished the opportunity for satire. Bech comes to us complete with writer's full c.v. and bibliography, and an extensive cod apparatus surrounds him ('To be candid, the bibliography was also a matter of working off various grudges... I've never been warmly treated by the *Commentary* crowd – insofar as it is a crowd – and I made Bech its darling.') From all this we know he was born in 1923, making him nearly a decade older than his creator. He grew up in an immigrant family on the Upper West Side, went to P.S. 87 at Seventy-Seventh and Amsterdam, served in the army through the Battle of the Bulge, and then went on to edit an army newspaper in post-war occupied Berlin. After the war he refused the GI Bill in order to write, according to one account; though (forgetfulness or improvement? – at any rate such confusions are adjusted in this re-edited volume) he did attend NYU on its provisions according to another. He made his name in the Fifties in the age of the liberal imagination and the climate of revived Modernism. His early novels, the Kerouackian *Travel Light* (1955) and *Brother Pig* (1957), gave him a serious academic and critical reputation. His more ambitious and Jewish next, *The Chosen* (1963), was an 'honorable failure'. He published a book of (Leslie Fiedlerish) essays, and from his British publisher there appeared the handy anthology *The Best of Bech*, now alas long out of print. Then, though fame and reputation pursued him, along with travel invitations, literary awards, Korean students and the shiksa girls on campus, writer's block set in ('Am I blocked? I'd just thought of myself as a slow typist.') A new novel is so long in coming that he wins the Melville Prize for an author who has not produced anything lately. It takes eighteen or so difficult (or just possibly lazy) years to produce his exotic (and overwritten) magnum opus *Think Big* ('Not quite as *vieux chapeau* as I had every reason to fear', Gore Vidal, *New York Review of Books*), once titled *Easy Money*, which lifts him from modest critical fame to best-selling success. A couple more books (the collection *Biding Time*, 1985, and *Going South*, 1992, which takes in the Vietnam war) make up the writing record, which eventually (gratifying the grandiose dreams of fame that have haunted him since high school) carries him to the highest prizewinning eminence.

As Rabbit is a straight-arrow hero, Bech is a comic one. Updike once said it was not his aim to be satirical, and that he gave Bech his fullest empathy, but this does less than justice to the pleasures of the Bechian world. Bech after all is perfectly well aware – see his teasing and yet in the circumstances extremely generous foreword addressed to his own creator in *Bech: A Book* – that he seems to be compounded out of Singer, Bellow, Mailer, Malamud, Roth and Heller, not to say Kerouac, Salinger and even at times Updike himself. Like his author he shares a heavy and WASPish burden of American literary responsibility, and therefore spends a good deal of time lecturing on the American tradition. He is an habitual traveller, a mostly unmarried man, a serious Manhattanite, the dissident type. He is also a natural member of literary academies, seminars on the state of the novel, creative writing courses, publishers' offices and parties, bookstore readings, book launches, TV arts interview shows, writing festivals, prizegiving ceremonies and the like. His career goes both high and low, and quite often it follows the journeys and even the career of his far more productive author. Updike has always acknowledged his delight in sequels and his pleasure in testing his characters against the changes of contemporary history. So Rabbit is redux, and Bech comes back. We first meet him, living his way through various episodes from the Sixties, in *Bech: A Book*, in 1970. He returns, his career, his ambitions and his love life all developing, in *Bech Is Back* in 1982; here he is wedded and separated, and arrives at bestselling success. He returns, just as troublesome and randy as ever, though now in his lively seventies, in *Bech at Bay* in 1998, where he plumbs the depths of literary revenge – and also achieves his long-dreamt-of literary apotheosis.

But where Rabbit is mega-novel material, and his reappear-
ances are regular, consistent, even stately, Bech belongs in
more casual, ambiguous and eclectically chosen forms. The
short story, the vignette, the parody, the cod bibliography, the
literary fantasy, the tale noir, even something odd called the
'quasi-novel', which appears to start from a nest of short
stories, is his natural habitat. He appears in twenty stories,
written in various manners, and several times he emerges
from his various Manhattan fastnesses to head north to Massachusetts, on journalistic assignment to interview his sometimes
half-tongue-tied, sometimes decidedly rhetorical creator.* As
a result of this wide variety of appearances, in different frames,
settings and narrative codes, it is far from the fiction of an
author who may or may not be himself. He exists, exactly, at
the Bech and call of his own creator. He is fully aware of the
fact, and on occasion reaches a point of crisis when he wonders
if he has exhausted his creator's tolerance completely. At other
times he seems to think his creator's more intimate thoughts
and feel many of his irritations and desires. His appearances,
over the three books, are both irregular and quite often
inconsistent. Sometimes we like him, sometimes we despise
him. Sometimes he is little more than an author's seeing eye;
sometimes, his guts spilling, he groans to us from the depths
of literary, Jewish and human anguish. We can piece together
his story, his temperament, but not exactly his character.
Truth is that although over time his personality, character and

---

*Bech interviews his creator in 'Bech Meets Me' (1971) in *Picked-Up
Pieces* (New York, 1975), pp. 27–30 ('Updike, at first sight, seems
bigger than he is, perhaps because the dainty stitchwork of his prose
style readies one for an apparition of elfin dimensions'; in 'On One's
Own Oeuvre' (1981), in *Hugging the Shore: Essays and Criticism* (New
York, 1983), pp. 870–75 ('He gives the impression, reciting his
responses into the tape recorder with many a fidget and static pause,
of a word processor with some slipped bits'); and in 'Henry Bech
interviews Updike apropos of his fifteenth novel', in *More Matter:
Essays and Criticism* (New York, 1999), pp. 821–5 ('His tousled locks
have grown whiter, his eyes smaller, and his teeth straighter, as
the miracles of cosmetic dentistry pile up'). Overall, it is quite a
relationship.

INTRODUCTION

literary qualities do grow somewhat clearer, we are never fully
sure whether we are dealing with an honest man or a rogue,
a good writer or a bad one, a genius or a clown, a lover or a
lecher, a hero of ideas or a malevolent serial killer, a Bellow
or a squeak, a friend or an enemy, a character that the author
empathizes with or one he can freely parody – just as, quite
plainly, Updike can parody himself. Bech is a writer's writer,
and many of the scenes and characters we meet in his company
are *à clef*. Likewise Updike is frank about the elevations
and the nastinesses of literature, and the power of writerly
jealousies, needs, vanities, desires and envies. Indeed, in the
Bech stories, as in the character of Bech himself, we can often
pick up a definite smell of literary malice and sweetly-taken
revenge.

*

Bech too has been long-lived as Rabbit, a writer for late
modern, postmodern, minimalist and multi-culturalist times.
But he was indeed born long ago, amid the Cold War (that
forty-odd-year freeze that shaped the spirits and dominated
the ideological and literary experience of a whole long generation), in Bulgaria, in an early short story 'The Bulgarian
Poetess'. As Updike explains of that story: 'I have generally
avoided writing about the literary life, and my plunge into it
here has a certain exhilaration. Like Bech, I was a cultural
ambassador to the Communist world in 1964, and for Americans a country like Bulgaria was almost the dark side of the
moon. An early title was "Through the Looking-Glass". Out-
of-the-way places seem to excite me to my best and brightest
prose. One of fiction's basic and ancient functions, after all, is
bringing news to armchair travellers.'* In those days, amid
the Old World Order, the literary traveller on such tours –
with an officially provided guide interpreter no doubt reporting
to the security services on the one hand, a State Department
or a British Council spook on the other – encountered not just

*John Updike, 'Introduction' to *Self-Selected Stories of John Updike*
(Tokyo, 1996), reprinted in Updike, *More Matter: Essays and Criticism*
(New York, 1999, p. 768).

that extraordinary, repressive, political, guilt-making climate that showed that, in another part of the world, the writer's anguish, persecution and suffering was a good deal more intense than our own. At the same time they showed the conditions that allowed western literature to dominate – political freedom, capitalism, commerce, and the desire to promote western values – were themselves no less political, and often quite as ambiguous. The writer felt like a political innocent in the looking-glass world; at the same time writing mattered, or almost mattered, because it was performed in the light of history, and because it was an instrument for the cleansing of false fictions, an instrument of humane decencies, because it sometimes even told the truth.

For those of us who followed the same trail through the Eastern European countries – some urbane and bearing the traces of a once-refined cultural order, some blatant puppet-regimes following a Moscow hard line – these early Bech tales are not just crucial vignettes from real history; they are wonderfully well observed. The difficulties of spending unexportable and unexpendable literary royalties from your translated volumes ('Rich in Russia') were great. The grim-faced state chauffeurs in their Zils, aggressively honking their authority over other traffic and the peasants wandering on Balkan country roads ('Bech in Rumania') were real enough, and as frightening as the story says. The emissaries from the Writers' Union, speaking their patter of progressivism and socialist realism round endless official tables, were real enough too ('The Bulgarian Poetess').* So were the ambassadors and the embassy minders who trusted the quite often dissident and maverick western writer to peddle the cause of freedom or in other words democratic consumer capitalism in the wilderness lands that lay, strange and wonderful as their lives and cultures unfolded, on the further side of the moon. Other tales display the various rewards of literary fame. There are those admiring former writing students, now happy to supply the new

*So, it seems, was the Bulgarian poetess herself – real enough, in fact, to acquire a second literary existence as source to Katya Princip in a novel of my own, *Rates of Exchange*.

pharmacological thrills of the tripping American Sixties ('Bech Takes Pot Luck'), and the sexual confusions they seem to induce, especially in randy Bech. There is the Manhattanite writer's well-funded trip to the balmy campuses of the American South ('Bech Panics'), where amid nature and innocence Bech has to confront the irritable worm of anguish and literariness that devours him ('Who was he? A Jew, a modern man, a writer, a bachelor, a loner, a loss. A con artist in the days of academic modernism undergoing a Victorian shudder. A white monkey hung far out on a spindly heaventree of stars. A fleck of dust condemned to know it is a fleck of dust. A mouse in a furnace. A smothered scream.') In a well-described Sixties Swinging London that Bech visits as the guest of his British publisher, he comes under intricate examination ('Bech Swings?'), and he finds that writers do not just write but are written about, and he becomes a character constructed out of his own fiction. In the final story the schoolboy Bech finds, with his mother, a writers' heaven, a wondrous uptown literary academy or pantheon filled with the rabbis and chieftains of American literature, the immortals under their scroll of stars. This is the heaven he has been chasing, the heaven he is at last, on the strength of his writing, invited to enter, hoping to find the high, calm pool of immortality that is the dream of writing, only to glimpse at once it more closely resembles the foul rag-and-bone shop of the heart.

*

Life in the literary pantheon is the theme of *Bech Is Back*. Now the time is, mostly, the sagging Seventies, and Henry is now the middle-aged angel, bearing the marks of fame but still struggling to touch that elusive immortality. His fiftieth birthday is due; he is a literary backslider. His production has declined almost to nothing, in a kind of laziness; despite that, maybe even because, his fame has grown. Yet critical reputation and a place amid the masters is an ambiguous affair. His signed books are now collected – but collected, he discovers, without fondness, and more for profit than love. The characters in his ever more exotic fictions conflict with, are even silenced by, the more complex characters of real life.

When, as the price of his fame, he is asked to sign thousands of copies of his work for a special edition, he finds his written name has become an absurdity, so that he can no longer seriously write it. In a set of cross-cut tales (these are post-modern times) he goes through various topical versions of literary travelling. He appears here and there in the Third World (one moment it's Ghana, now Venezuela, now Korea), in flashing incidents and half-illuminating moments that emphasize the gap between obscure historical realities and brute American power. He reappears slipping between the doubled British dominion cities of Toronto and Sydney, where one television interview is rather like another, one sexual encounter almost the same as another. The fate that seems to lie beyond fifty is matrimony. And in the event Bech does get himself married, to the most domesticated of his serial lovers, Bea, sister to the more vital Norma, whose maternal embraces he has bedruggedly solicited, a decade or so earlier, when he chose to take pot luck.

Soon Bech is an obessively metropolitan Upper West Side Jew married to a suburban Episcopalian divorcee of Scots descent, and living the life of husband and stepfather to three in Ossining, N.Y., once better known as Sing Sing. On honeymoon in Israel, it is Bea, his wife, who adopts the land of Zion, far more enthusiastically than he ever can. Robbed of half his identity, he takes his revenge travelling in the Scottish Highlands; he turns himself into a tartaned victim of the clearances, a Scots MacBech. Updike's familiar brilliance at turning vignette into story and travel impressions into narrative – and we can often sense the notes he has made, the scenes he has rendered, the impressions soaked up – shades into another drama. Bech needs to write. His new life, worrying about the sex lives of his stepchildren, storm windows, money, his own being and becomingness, seems to have brought him to the end of the road. In one of the splendidly seen paradoxes of writing, Bech, restless upstate, wedded, bedded and tied to the domestic and familiar, is driven upstairs, to the typewriter. Nature sits beyond the windows, children down below. Money would be welcome, fame would be even better. New York City glows from afar, sexy and enticing, far more so than when he lived in it. It becomes an exotic and soapy fiction, and, falling in love with the grand extravagances of metropolitan best-sellerdom, Bech writes again. As usual, some of the most brilliant scenes are those that are set at the centre of the literary world: the scenes in the modernized publishing house, with a new breed of editor, for whom Bech is grand but ancient history, his manners from another world. Yet the book, *Think Big*, a piece of metropolitan exotica, as overwritten as a novel by Tom Wolfe (and what more can one say?), is a best-seller. The reviews (mostly) glow. Even Gore Vidal is almost kind. The book makes a millon dollars. Bech is back. The problem is that the domesticity that created his best-seller is also destroying him; Bech at the end has his fame and his book, but no longer his wife.

*

Bech's last return belongs to another era and another mood. The Cold War is over, or almost over, for the first story in this 'quasi-novel' is set in the Prague of 1986, in the dying days of Communism, when the game is not quite over but the end is nigh. Here Bech returns to the lands that first created him, now riding on a wave of American confidence and triumphalism. His work is widely taught and translated, though some old desires, ambitions and ancient lecheries keep him travelling; he stays grandly at the American Embassy and reads from a Czech translation of 'Bech Panics' in bed. The Prague he visits is already a well-written city, not just at the hands of Kafka and Hašek, but those Jewish-American writers like Philip Roth onto whose territory Bech quite frequently treads. There are the statutory occasions: the visit to Kafka's grave just outside the city (greeted as famous author), the official literary gatherings where apparatchiks, dissidents, publishers, translators gather, to hear his lecture, test his opinions, sing their praises of the postmoderns, dirty realists and minimalists, the writers of the Barthian literature of exhaustion who will one day crowd Bech out. Meanwhile Bech's sense of Europe, the civilized charnel-house, has grown grimmer, but in Reaganite America the times are changing too. Bech is coming up to seventy now, and he still panics, just as he is still the site of strong lecheries, strange fantasies and jealous resentments. He is at bay, jealous and fearful that, along with Kafka, he too belongs in the Jewish cemetery, about to be silenced or written out.

In the rest of the stories of this volume, which explore the landscape of literary senescence, the time is the postmodern Nineties and Bech is energetically attempting to ensure he will be written in again. He experiences life among the Olympians as it is: as jealous, mean and malign as it ever was. He is asked (it's part of a cunning plot) to become the president of 'the Forty,' a century-old artistic academy with a select and now almost entirely geriatric membership, who are incapable of believing in any new art that lies beyond the end of the Gutenberg Galaxy. Should they elect new members, delay till the millennium, or simply close down and cash their assets? Bech tries to hold the fort for literature, against his ironic better judgement. For Bech, for all his speeches, has not been solely a lover of literature, rather a slavish lover of self, engaged only with his own fame and writing. And many trials attend the ageing writer in his closing gallop, not least the postmodern, consumptionist age of towering condos and office blocks, litigation, the computer, of the dying of the Gutenberg Galaxy and the reign of the book. Bech is caught up (as was, in fact, his author) in a long-running Californian court case, arising when Bech, momentarily the crusading journalist, has castigated a notorious Hollywood agent as an 'arch-gouger'. For the moment Bech risks losing all, though a strange sympathy for his extortionate accuser marks a shock of recognition.

The two oddest tales are the two last in *Bech at Bay*: fantastic and wonderful indulgencies that take Bech floating off into the literary empyrean. In 'Bech Noir', gratifying what must be many a writer's greatest fantasy, Updike sets his cape-wearing, rejuvenated, computer-age hero-villain off on an exotic murder spree. Through many ingenious devices – and with the aid of the latest computer-hacking technology, not to say that of a computer expert, his lovely Robin – Bech murders a number of the critics (British aesthetes, Jewish renegades, twee west coast reviewers) whose barbs and cavils, over the long years, have hurt him most. He survives this purge or critical holocaust reinvigorated, to father at the age of seventy-five a late-life child, Golda, on his computer-literate sidekick: possibly his most creative act so far. And his dream-like gratifications are not yet done. All that can be left now is to ascend, onward and upward, to the final prize: it's the Nobel Prize for Literature, of course. Now we learn that for some reason the 1999 was not, as the textbooks say, awarded to Günter Grass, but went against the odds to Henry Bech. This gives Bech – or should we say his creator? – the opportunity to script the greatest text of all: the writer's acceptance speech. This, surprisingly, produces a crisis of writer's block: but then, who, however wise or foolish, can finally tell us what writing, and the passion behind it, is? Bech, almost rendered silent, comes up with an ingenious solution. I will not here say what it is, but simply observe that Updike, who in these stories is often barbed and satiric, can also be a very sentimental romantic, with a soft spot in his heart for the universe, the magic of creation, and even for his selfish, roguish and we now know homicidal alter ego. Bech at any rate hands on the creative torch; and so winds down a sequence of splendid books about writers and writing, about the magic, the malice, the jealousy, the impropriety, the seediness, the commercial-ism, the political importance, the mysterious and unaccount-able wonder of it all. Writers in particular must surely love the Bech sequence, with its cunning of observation, its acid cultural and literary portraits, its knowingness, its characters *à clef*, its frankness about literary greeds and envies, its sheer familiarity. Indulging himself, Updike here lets loose a bitter comic vigour and some striking shafts of malice and mockery, alongside his characteristic sense of literature's magical fasci-nations. But others beside writers will love the Bech books too. It's all Updike at his most left-handed; but that itself is pleasure indeed.

Malcolm Bradbury

SELECT BIBLIOGRAPHY

CLARKE TAYLOR, C., *John Updike: A Bibliography*, Kent State University Press, Kent, Ohio, 1968.

DE BELLIS, JACK, *John Updike: A Bibliography, 1967–1993*, Greenwood Press, Westport, Connecticut, 1994.

UPDIKE, JOHN, *Picked-Up Pieces*, Alfred A. Knopf, New York, 1975.

UPDIKE, JOHN, *Hugging the Shore: Essays and Criticism*, Alfred A. Knopf, New York, 1983.

UPDIKE, JOHN, *More Matter: Essays and Criticism*, Alfred A. Knopf, New York, 1999.

INTERVIEWS WITH JOHN UPDIKE

Life (4 November 1968); *Paris Review* (Winter 1968); *New York Times Book Review* (10 April 1977); *Salmagundi* 57 (1982).

PLATH, JAMES, ed., *Conversations with John Updike*, University Press of Mississippi, Jackson, Mississippi, 1994.

CRITICISM

BAKER, NICHOLAS, *U & I: A True Story*, Random House, New York, 1991.

BLOOM, HAROLD, ed., *Modern Critical Views of John Updike*, Chelsea House, New York, 1987.

DE BELLIS, JACK, *The John Updike Encyclopedia*, Greenwood Press, Westport, Connecticut, 2000.

DETWEILER, ROBERT, *John Updike*, Twayne, Boston, 1984.

GREINER, DONALD, *John Updike's Novels*, Ohio University Press, Athens, Ohio, 1984.

HAMILTON, ALICE and KENNETH, *The Elements of John Updike*, William B. Eerdmans, Grand Rapids, Michigan, 1970.

HUNT, GEORGE, *John Updike and the Three Great Secret Things: Sex, Religion, and Art*, William B. Eerdmans, Grand Rapids, Michigan, 1980.

MACNAUGHTON, WILLIAM R., ed., *Critical Essays on John Updike*, G. K. Hall, Boston, 1982.

MARKLE, JOYCE B., *Fighters and Lovers: Theme in the Novels of John Updike*, New York University Press, New York, 1973.

NEWMAN, JUDIE, *John Updike*, Macmillan, London, 1988.

PRITCHARD, WILLIAM, *Updike: America's Man of Letters*, Steerforth Press, South Royalton, Vermont, 2000.

SCHIFF, JAMES A., *John Updike Revisited*, Twayne, New York, 1998.

SEARLES, GEORGE J., *The Fiction of Philip Roth and John Updike*, Southern Illinois University Press, Carbondale, Illinois, 1984.

TALLENT, ELIZABETH, *Married Men and Magic Tricks: John Updike's Erotic Heroes*, Creative Arts Book Company, Berkeley, California, 1982.

TANNER, TONY, *City of Words: American Fiction, 1950–1970*, Jonathan Cape, London, 1971.

THORBURN, DAVID, and EILAND, HOWARD (eds), *John Updike: A Collection of Critical Essays*, Prentice Hall, Englewood Cliffs, New Jersey, 1979.

UPHAUS, SUZANNE H., *John Updike*, Ungar, New York, 1980.

YERKES, JAMES, ed., *John Updike and Religion*, William B. Eerdmans, Grand Rapids, Michigan, 1999.

MALCOLM BRADBURY was Emeritus Professor of American Studies at the University of East Anglia, and author of *The Modern American Novel* and *The Modern British Novel*. His novels include *The History Man*, *Rates of Exchange*, *Doctor Criminale* and *To The Hermitage*. In 1991 he was awarded the CBE and in 1999 was honoured with a knighthood. He died in November 2000.

CHRONOLOGY

―――

DATE	AUTHOR'S LIFE	LITERARY CONTEXT
1932	Birth of John Hoyer Updike at Shillington, Pennsylvania (18 March).	1932 Huxley: *Brave New World*. Faulkner: *Light in August*.
		1934 Fitzgerald: *Tender is the Night*. Miller: *Tropic of Cancer*. Waugh: *A Handful of Dust*. 1935 Lewis: *It Can't Happen Here*. 1936 Faulkner: *Absalom, Absalom!* Eliot: *Collected Poems*.
		1937 Steinbeck: *Of Mice and Men*. Hemingway: *To Have and Have Not*. 1938 Sartre: *Nausea*. 1939 Steinbeck: *The Grapes of Wrath*. Joyce: *Finnegans Wake*. 1940 Hemingway: *For Whom the Bell Tolls*. Greene: *The Power and the Glory*. 1941 Fitzgerald: *The Last Tycoon*. 1942 Eliot: *Four Quartets*. Camus: *The Stranger*.
1945	Moves with family to old Hoyer farm, eleven miles away.	1945 Orwell: *Animal Farm*. Waugh: *Brideshead Revisited*. Borges: *Fictions*. 1948 Greene: *The Heart of the Matter*. 1949 Orwell: *Nineteen Eighty-Four*. de Beauvoir: *The Second Sex*.
1950	Graduates as co-valedictorian from Shillington High School.	
		1951 Frost: *Complete Poems*. Salinger: *The Catcher in the Rye*. 1952 Beckett: *Waiting for Godot*.
1953	Marries Mary Pennington.	1953 Bellow: *The Adventures of Augie March*.

1932 Election of Roosevelt in US. Nazis become largest party in German Reichstag.

1933 Roosevelt announces 'New Deal.' Hitler becomes German Chancellor.

1936 Outbreak of Spanish Civil War. Hitler and Mussolini form Rome–Berlin Axis. Edward VIII abdicates; George VI crowned in UK. Stalin's 'Great Purge' of the Communist Party (to 1938).
1937 Japanese invasion of China.

1938 Germany annexes Austria; Munich crisis.
1939 Nazi–Soviet Pact; Hitler invades Poland. World War II beings.

1940 Fall of France; Battle of Britain.

1941 Japan attacks Pearl Harbor; US enters war. Hitler invades the Soviet Union.

1944 Allied landings in Normandy.
1945 Unconditional surrender of Germany. Roosevelt dies; Truman becomes President. US drops atomic bombs on Hiroshima and Nagasaki. End of World War II. United Nations founded.
1948 Jewish state of Israel comes into existence. Russian blockade of West Berlin.
1949 Communists win Chinese civil war. North Atlantic Treaty signed.

1950 Korean War begins.

1952 Eisenhower elected US President. Accession of Elizabeth II in UK.
1953 Korean War ends. Death of Stalin.

DATE	AUTHOR'S LIFE	LITERARY CONTEXT
1954–5	Harvard College *summa cum laude* (1954). Attends Ruskin School of Drawing and Fine Art, Oxford, on Knox Fellowship.	1954 Amis: *Lucky Jim*.
		1955 Nabokov: *Lolita*.
1955–7	Staff reporter for *The New Yorker*. Birth of daughter, Elizabeth (1955) and son, David (1957). Moves to Ipswich, Massachusetts (1957).	
		1956 Osborne: *Look Back in Anger*.
		1957 Kerouac: *On the Road*.
1958	*The Carpentered Hen* (in UK as *Hoping for a Hoopoe*) (poetry).	1958 Pasternak: *Doctor Zhivago*. Achebe: *Things Fall Apart*.
1959	*The Poorhouse Fair* (wins Rosenthal Award in 1960). *The Same Door* (stories). Birth of second son, Michael.	1959 Burroughs: *Naked Lunch*. Bellow: *Henderson the Rain King*.
1960	*Rabbit, Run*. Birth of second daughter, Miranda.	
		1961 Heller: *Catch-22*. Naipaul: *A House for Mr Biswas*.
1962	*Pigeon Feathers* (stories).	1962 Nabokov: *Pale Fire*. Solzhenitsyn: *One Day in the Life of Ivan Denisovich*.
1963	*The Centaur* (wins National Book Award). *Telephone Poles* (poetry).	
1964	*Olinger Stories*. Elected to National Institute of Arts and Letters. 'The Bulgarian Poetess' (first Bech story).	1964 Bellow: *Herzog*.
1965	*Of the Farm. Assorted Prose*.	1965 Calvino: *Cosmicomics*.
1966	*The Music School* (stories).	
		1967 Márquez: *One Hundred Years of Solitude*.
1968–9	Lives with family in London. *Couples* (1968). *Midpoint* (poetry, 1969).	1968 Solzhenitsyn: *Cancer Ward*.
1970	*Bech: A Book*.	
1971	*Rabbit Redux*.	
1972	Father dies. *Museums and Women* (stories).	

CHRONOLOGY

HISTORICAL EVENTS

1954 Vietnam War begins.

1956 Soviets invade Hungary. Suez crisis.

1957 Civil Rights Commission established in US to safeguard voting rights.

1959 Castro seizes power in Cuba.

1960 Kennedy elected US President.

1961 Erection of Berlin Wall.

1962 Cuban missile crisis.

1963 Assassination of Kennedy. Johnson becomes US President.

1964 Civil Rights Act prohibits discrimination in US. Brezhnev becomes Communist Party General Secretary in USSR.

1968 Student unrest in US and throughout Europe. Assassination of Martin Luther King, Jr. Soviet invasion of Czechoslovakia. Nixon elected US President.
1970 Death of de Gaulle.

DATE	AUTHOR'S LIFE	LITERARY CONTEXT
		1973 Pynchon: *Gravity's Rainbow*. Solzhenitsyn: *The Gulag Archipelago* (to 1975).
1974	Lives alone in Boston. *Buchanan Dying* (play).	
1975	*A Month of Sundays. Picked-Up Pieces* (essays).	1975 Levi: *The Periodic Table*.
1976	Divorced. Moves to Georgetown, Massachusetts. *Marry Me*. Elected to Academy of Arts and Letters.	
1977	Marries Martha Bernhard. *Tossing and Turning* (poetry).	1977 Morrison: *Song of Solomon*.
1978	*The Coup*.	
1979	*Too Far to Go* and *Problems* (stories).	1979 Calvino: *If on a Winter's Night a Traveler*.
1981	*Rabbit Is Rich* (wins American Book Award for Fiction, Pulitzer Prize, and National Book Critics Circle Award in 1982).	1981 Rushdie: *Midnight's Children*.
1982	Moves to Beverly Farms, Massachusetts. *Bech Is Back*.	1982 Levi: *If Not Now, When?* Márquez: *Chronicle of a Death Foretold*.
1983	*Hugging the Shore* (wins National Book Critics Circle Award for Criticism in 1984).	
1984	*The Witches of Eastwick*.	
1985	*Facing Nature* (poetry).	1985 Márquez: *Love in the Time of Cholera*.
1986	*Roger's Version*.	1986 Levi: *The Drowned and the Saved*.
1987	*Trust Me* (stories).	1987 Morrison: *Beloved*.
1988	*S.*	1988 Rushdie: *The Satanic Verses*.
1989	Mother dies. *Self-Consciousness* (memoirs). *Just Looking* (art criticism). Awarded the National Medal of Arts.	1989 DeLillo: *Libra*. M. Amis: *London Fields*. Márquez: *The General in His Labyrinth*.
1990	*Rabbit at Rest* (wins Pulitzer Prize and National Book Critics Circle Award in 1991).	1990 Walcott: *Omeros*.
1991	*Odd Jobs* (essays).	1991 M. Amis: *Time's Arrow*.
1992	*Memories of the Ford Administration*.	
1993	*Collected Poems*.	1993 Roth: *Operation Shylock*.

CHRONOLOGY

HISTORICAL EVENTS

1974 Nixon resigns in wake of Watergate scandal; Ford becomes US President.
1975 Vietnam War ends.

1976 Death of Mao Tse-Tung. Carter elected US President.

1978 P. W. Botha comes to power in South Africa.
1979 Margaret Thatcher first woman Prime Minister in UK. Carter and Brezhnev sign SALT-2 arms limitation treaty. Soviets occupy Afghanistan.
1980 Lech Walesa leads strikes in Gdansk, Poland. Reagan US President.
1981 Mitterand elected President of France.

1984 Famine in Ethiopia. Indira Gandhi assassinated.
1985 Gorbachev becomes General Secretary in USSR.

1986 Gorbachev–Reagan summit.

1988 Gorbachev announces big troop reductions, suggesting end of Cold War.
1989 Collapse of Communism in Eastern Europe. Fall of the Berlin Wall. First democratic elections in USSR. Tiananmen Square massacre in China.

1990 End of Communist monopoly in USSR. Yeltsin elected first leader of Russian Federation. Nelson Mandela released from jail after 27 years' imprisonment. John Major becomes Prime Minister in UK.
1991 Gulf War. Central government in USSR suspended. War begins in former Yugoslavia.
1992 Clinton elected US President.
1993 Palestinian leader Arafat and Israeli Prime Minister Rabin sign peace agreement in US. Maastricht Treaty (creating European Union) ratified.

DATE	AUTHOR'S LIFE	LITERARY CONTEXT
1994	*Brazil. The Afterlife and Other Stories.*	1994 Heller: *Closing Time.*
1995	Awarded Howells Medal from American Academy of Arts and Letters for *Rabbit at Rest.* Four Rabbit novels published in one volume, *Rabbit Angstrom.*	1995 M. Amis: *The Information.* Rushdie: *The Moor's Last Sigh.*
1996	*In the Beauty of the Lilies. Golf Dreams.*	
1997	*Toward the End of Time.*	1997 Roth: *American Pastoral.* McEwan: *Enduring Love.* Bellow: *The Actual.*
1998	*Bech at Bay. A Century of Arts and Letters* (editor). Awarded the National Book Foundation Lifetime Achievement Award.	1998 Morrison: *Paradise.* DeLillo: *Underworld.* Heller: *Now and Then.* McEwan: *Amsterdam.*
1999	*More Matter* (essays). *The Best American Short Stories of the Century* (editor).	1999 Rushdie: *The Ground Beneath Her Feet.*
2000	*Gertrude and Claudius. Licks of Love.*	2000 Bellow: *Ravelstein.* Roth: *The Human Stain.*

CHRONOLOGY

1994 Mandela and ANC sweep to victory in South African elections. Civil war in Rwanda. Russian military action against Chechen republic. IRA ceasefire announced.

1995 Rabin assassinated.

1996 President Clinton re-elected.

1997 Tony Blair elected Prime Minister (first Labour government in the UK since 1979).

1998 President Clinton impeached in December (acquitted February 1999). Referendum in Northern Ireland accepts Good Friday agreement; an assembly elected.

1999 Serbs attack ethnic Albanians in Kosovo; US leads NATO in bombing of Belgrade.

2000 Putin succeeds Yeltsin as Russian President. Further violence in Chechen republic. Milosevic's regime in the former Yugoslavia collapses; Vojislav Kostunica elected President.

BECH: A BOOK
(1970)

CONTENTS

FOREWORD

DEAR JOHN,

Well, if you must commit the artistic indecency of writing about a writer, better I suppose about me than about you. Except, reading along in these, I wonder if it *is* me, enough me, purely me. At first blush, for example, in Bulgaria (eclectic sexuality, bravura narcissism, thinning curly hair), I sound like some gentlemanly Norman Mailer; then that London glimpse of *silver* hair glints more of gallant, glamorous Bellow, the King of the Leprechauns, than of stolid old homely yours truly. My childhood seems out of Alex Portnoy and my ancestral past out of I. B. Singer. I get a whiff of Malamud in your city breezes, and am I paranoid to feel my "block" an ignoble version of the more or less noble renunciations of H. Roth, D. Fuchs, and J. Salinger? Withal, something Waspish, theological, scared, and insulatingly ironical that derives, my wild surmise is, from you.

Yet you are right. This monotonous hero who disembarks from an airplane, mouths words he doesn't quite mean, has vaguely to do with some woman, and gets back on the airplane, is certainly one Henry Bech. Until your short yet still not unlongish collection, no revolutionary has concerned himself with our oppression, with the silken mechanism whereby America reduces her writers to imbecility and cozenage. Envied like Negroes, disbelieved in like angels, we veer between the harlotry of the lecture platform and the torture of the writing desk, only to collapse, our five-and-dime Hallowe'en priests' robes a-rustle with economy-class jet-set tickets and honorary certificates from the Cunt-of-the-Month Club, amid a standing crowd of rueful, Lilliputian obituaries. Our language degenerating in the mouths

5

of broadcasters and pop yellers, our formal designs crumbling like
sand castles under the feet of beach bullies, we nevertheless and
incredibly support with our desperate efforts (just now, I had to
look up "desperate" in the dictionary for the ninety-ninth time,
forgetting again if it is spelled with two "a"s or three "e"s) a
flourishing culture of publishers, agents, editors, tutors, *Time*niks,
media personnel in all shades of suavity, *chic*, and sexual gusto.
When I think of the matings, the moaning, jubilant fornica-
tions between ectomorphic oversexed junior editors and svelte
hot-from-Wellesley majored-in-English-minored-in-philosophy
female coffee-fetchers and receptionists that have been engi-
neered with the lever of some of my poor scratched-up and
pasted-over pages (they arrive in the editorial offices as stiff with
Elmer's glue as a masturbator's bedsheet; the office boys use
them for tea-trays), I could mutilate myself like sainted Origen,
I could keen like Jeremiah. Thank Jahweh these bordellos in the
sky can soon dispense with the excuse of us entirely; already the
contents of a book count as little as the contents of a breakfast-
cereal box. It is all a matter of the premium, and the shelf site, and
the amount of air between the corn flakes. Never you mind. I'm
sure that when with that blithe goyish brass I will never cease to
test with my teeth you approached me for a "word or two by way
of preface," you were bargaining for a benediction, not a curse.

Here it is, then. My blessing. I like some of the things in these
accounts very much. The Communists are all good – good
people. There is a moment by the sea, I've lost the page, that
rang true. Here and there passages seemed overedited, constip-
ated; you prune yourself too hard. With prose, there is no way
to get it out, I have found, but to let it run. I liked some of the
women you gave me, and a few of the jokes. By the way, I never
– unlike retired light-verse writers – make puns. But if you [*here
followed a list of suggested deletions, falsifications, suppressions, and
rewordings, all of which have been scrupulously incorporated* – ED.],
I don't suppose your publishing this little *jeu* of a book will do
either of us drastic harm.

HENRY BECH

Manhattan,
Dec. 4th–12th, 1969

RICH IN RUSSIA

STUDENTS (not unlike yourselves) compelled to buy paperback copies of his novels – notably the first, *Travel Light*, though there has lately been some academic interest in his more surreal and "existential" and perhaps even "anarchist" second novel, *Brother Pig* – or encountering some essay from *When the Saints* in a shiny heavy anthology of mid-century literature costing $12.50, imagine that Henry Bech, like thousands less famous than he, is rich. He is not. The paperback rights to *Travel Light* were sold by his publisher outright for two thousand dollars, of which the publisher kept one thousand and Bech's agent one hundred (10% of 50%). To be fair, the publisher had had to remainder a third of the modest hard-cover printing and, when *Travel Light* was enjoying its vogue as the post-Golding pre-Tolkien fad of college undergraduates, would amusingly tell on himself the story of Bech's given-away rights, at sales meetings upstairs in "21." As to anthologies – the average permissions fee, when it arrives at Bech's mailbox, has been eroded to $64.73, or some such suspiciously odd sum, which barely covers the cost of a restaurant meal with his mistress and a medium wine. Though Bech, and his too numerous interviewers, have made a quixotic virtue of his continuing to live for twenty years in a grim if roomy Riverside Drive apartment building (the mailbox, students should know, where his pitifully nibbled checks arrive has been well scarred by floating urban wrath, and his last name has been so often ballpointed by playful lobby-loiterers into a somewhat assonant verb that Bech has left the name plate space blank and depends upon the clairvoyance of mailmen), he in truth lives there because he cannot afford to leave. He was rich just once in his life, and that was in Russia, in 1964, a thaw or so ago.

Russia, in those days, like everywhere else, was a slightly more innocent place. Khrushchev, freshly deposed, had left an atmosphere, almost comical, of warmth, of a certain fitful openness, of inscrutable experiment and oblique possibility. There seemed no overweening reason why Russia and America, those lovable paranoid giants, could not happily share a globe so big and blue; there certainly seemed no reason why Henry Bech, the recherché but amiable novelist, artistically blocked but socially fluent, should not be flown into Moscow at the expense of our State Department for a month of that mostly imaginary activity termed "cultural exchange." Entering the Aeroflot plane at Le Bourget, Bech thought it smelled like his uncles' backrooms in Williamsburg, of swaddled body heat and proximate potatoes, boiling.* The impression lingered all month; Russia seemed Jewish to him, and of course he seemed Jewish to Russia. He never knew how much of the tenderness and hospitality he met related to his race. His contact man at the American Embassy – a prissy, doleful ex-basketball-player from Wisconsin, with the all-star name of "Skip" Reynolds, – assured him that two out of every three Soviet intellectuals had suppressed a Jew in their ancestry; and once Bech did find himself in a Moscow apartment whose bookcases were lined with photographs (of Kafka, Einstein, Freud, Wittgenstein) pointedly evoking the glory of pre-Hitlerian *Judenkultur*. His hosts, both man and wife, were professional translators, and the apartment was bewilderingly full of kin, including a doe-eyed young hydraulics engineer and a grandmother who had been a dentist with the Red Army, and whose dental chair dominated the parlor. For a whole long toasty evening, Jewishness, perhaps also pointedly, was not mentioned. The subject was one Bech was happy to ignore. His own writing had sought to reach out from the ghetto of his heart toward the wider expanses across the Hudson; the artistic triumph of American Jewry lay, he thought, not in the novels of the Fifties but in the movies of the Thirties, those gargantuan, crass contraptions

* See Appendix A, section I.

whereby Jewish brains projected Gentile stars upon a Gentile nation and out of a simple immigrant joy gave a formless land dreams and even a kind of conscience. The reservoir of faith, in 1964, was just going dry; through depression and world convulsion the country had been sustained by the *arriviste* patriotism of Louis B. Mayer and the brothers Warner. To Bech, it was one of history's great love stories, the mutually profitable romance between Jewish Hollywood and bohunk America, conducted almost entirely in the dark, a tapping of fervent messages through the wall of the San Gabriel Range; and his favorite Jewish writer was the one who turned his back on his three beautiful Brooklyn novels and went into the desert to write scripts for Doris Day. This may be, except for graduate students, neither here nor there. There, in Russia five years ago, when Cuba had been taken out of the oven to cool and Vietnam was still coming to a simmer, Bech did find a quality of life – impoverished yet ceremonial, shabby yet ornate, sentimental, embattled, and avuncular – reminiscent of his neglected Jewish past. Virtue, in Russia as in his childhood, seemed something that arose from men, like a comforting body odor, rather than something from above, which impaled the struggling soul like a moth on a pin. He stepped from the Aeroflot plane, with its notably hefty stewardesses, into an atmosphere of generosity. They met him with arms heaped with cold roses. On the first afternoon, the Writers' Union gave him as expense money a stack of ruble notes, pink and lilac Lenin and powder-blue Spasskaya Tower. In the following month, in the guise of "royalties" (in honor of his coming they had translated *Travel Light*, and several of his *Commentary* essays ["M-G-M and the U.S.A."; "The Moth on the Pin"; "Daniel Fuchs: An Appreciation"] had appeared in *I Nostrannaya Literatura*, and since no copyright agreements pertained the royalties were arbitrarily calculated, like showers of manna), more rubles were given to him, so that by the week of his departure Bech had accumulated over fourteen hundred rubles – by the official exchange rate, fifteen hundred and forty dollars. There was nothing to spend it on. All his hotels, his plane fares, his meals were paid for. He was a guest of the Soviet state. From morning to night he was never alone. That first afternoon, he had also been given, along with

the rubles, a companion, a translator–escort: Ekaterina Alexandrovna Ryleyeva. She was a notably skinny red-headed woman
with a flat chest and paper-colored skin and a translucent mole
above her left nostril. He grew to call her Kate.

"Kate," he said, displaying his rubles in two fistfuls, letting
some drift to the floor, "I have robbed the proletariat. What can I
do with my filthy loot?" He had developed, in this long time in
which she was always with him, a clowning super-American
manner that disguised all complaints as "acts." In response,
she had strengthened her original pose – of schoolteacherish
patience, with ageless peasant roots. Her normal occupation
was translating English-language science fiction into Ukrainian,
and he imagined this month with him was relatively a holiday.
She had a mother, and late at night, after accompanying him to a
morning-brandy session with the editors of *Yunost*, to lunch at
the Writers' Union with its shark-mouthed chairman,* to Dos-
toevski's childhood home (next to a madhouse, and enshrining
some agonized crosshatched manuscripts and a pair of oval tin
spectacles, tiny, as if fashioned for a dormouse), a museum of folk
art, an endless restaurant meal, and a night of ballet, Ekaterina
would bring Bech to his hotel lobby, put a babushka over her
bushy orange hair, and head into a blizzard toward this ailing
mother. Bech wondered about Kate's sex life. Skip Reynolds
solemnly told him that personal life in Russia was inscrutable. He
also told Bech that Kate was undoubtedly a Party spy. Bech was
touched, and wondered what in him would be worth spying out.
From infancy on we all are spies; the shame is not this but that the
secrets to be discovered are so paltry and few. Ekaterina was
perhaps as old as forty, which could just give her a betrothed
killed in the war. Was this the secret of her vigil, the endless
paper-colored hours she spent by his side? She was always translating for him, and this added to her neutrality and transparence.
He, too, had never been married, and imagined that this was
what marriage was like.

She answered, "Henry" – she usually touched his arm, saying
his name, and it never ceased to thrill him a little, the way the

* See Appendix A, section II.

"H" became a breathy guttural sound between "G" and "K" – "you must not joke. This is your money. You earned it by the sweat of your brain. All over Soviet Union committees of people sit in discussion over *Travel Light*, its wonderful qualities. The printing of one hundred thousand copies has gone *poof!* in the bookstores." The comic-strip colors of science fiction tinted her idiom unexpectedly.

"Poof!" Bech said, and scattered the money above his head; before the last bill stopped fluttering, they both stooped to retrieve the rubles from the rich red carpet. They were in his room at the Sovietskaya, the hotel for Party bigwigs and import- ant visitors; all the suites were furnished in high czarist style: chandeliers, wax fruit, and brass bears.

"We have banks here," Kate said shyly, reaching under the satin sofa, "as in the capitalist countries. They pay interest, you could deposit your money in such a bank. It would be here, enlarged, when you returned. You would have a numbered bankbook."

"What?" said Bech, "And help support the Socialist state? When you are already years ahead of us in the space race? I would be adding thrust to your rockets."

They stood up, both a little breathless from exertion, betraying their age. The tip of her nose was pink. She passed the remainder of his fortune into his hands; her silence seemed embarrassed.

"Besides," Bech said, "when would I ever return?"

She offered, "Perhaps in a space-warp?"

Her shyness, her pink nose and carroty hair, her embarrass- ment were becoming oppressive. He brusquely waved his arms. "No, Kate, we must spend it! Spend, spend. It's the Keynesian way. We will make Mother Russia a consumer society."

From the very still, slightly tipped way she was standing, Bech, bothered by "space-warp," received a haunted impression – that she was locked into a colorless other dimension from which only the pink tip of her nose emerged. "Is not so simple," she omin- ously pronounced.

For one thing, time was running out. Bobochka and Myshkin, the two Writers' Union officials in charge of Bech's itinerary, had

crowded the end of his schedule with compulsory cultural
events. Fortified by relatively leisured weeks in Kazakhstan and
the Caucasus,* Bech was deemed fit to endure a marathon of war
movies (the hero of one of them had lost his Communist Party
member's card, which was worse than losing your driver's
license; and in another a young soldier hitched rides in a maze
of trains only to turn around at the end ["See, Henry," Kate
whispered to him, "now he is home, that is his mother, what a
good face, so much suffering, now they kiss, now he must leave,
oh –" and Kate was crying too much to translate further]) and
museums and shrines and brandy with various writers who uniformly adored Gemingway. November was turning bitter, the
Christmassy lights celebrating the Revolution had been taken
down, Kate as they hurried from appointment to appointment
had developed a sniffle. She constantly patted her nose with a
handkerchief. Bech felt a guilty pang, sending her off into the
cold toward her mother before he ascended to his luxurious hotel
room, with its parqueted foyer stacked with gift books and its
alabaster bathroom and its great brocaded double bed. He would
drink from a gift bottle of Georgian brandy and stand by the
window, looking down on the golden windows of an apartment
building where young Russians were Twisting to Voice of
America tapes. Chubby Checker's chicken-plucker's voice
carried distinctly across the crevasse of sub-arctic night. In an
adjoining window, a couple courteously granted isolation by the
others was making love; he could see knees and hands and then a
rhythmically kicking ankle. To relieve the pressure, Bech would
sit down with his brandy and write to distant women boozy,
reminiscent letters that in the morning would be handed
solemnly to the ex-basketball-player, to be sent out of Russia
via diplomatic pouch.† Reynolds, himself something of a spy, was
with them whenever Bech spoke to a group, whether of translators (when asked who was America's best living writer, Bech said
Nabokov, and there was quite a silence before the next question)
or of students (whom he assured that Yevtushenko's *Precocious*

---

* See Appendix A, section III.
† See Appendix A, section IV.

Autobiography was a salubrious and patriotic work that instead of being banned should be distributed free to Soviet school-children). "Did I put my foot in it?" Bech would ask anxiously afterward – another "act."

The American's careful mouth twitched. "It's good for them. Shock therapy."

"You were charming," Ekaterina Alexandrovna always said loyally, jealously interposing herself, and squeezing Bech's arm. She could not imagine that Bech did not, like herself, loathe all officials. She would not have believed that Bech approached Reynolds with an intellectual's reverence for the athlete, and that they exchanged in private not anti-Kremlin vitriol but literary gossip and pro football scores, love letters and old copies of *Time*. Now, in her campaign to keep them apart, Kate had been given another weapon. She squeezed his arm smugly and said, "We have an hour. We must rush off and *shop*."

For the other thing, there was not much to buy. To begin, he would need an extra suitcase. He and Ekaterina, in their chauf-feured Zil, drove to what seemed to Bech a far suburb, past flickerings of birch forest, to sections of new housing, perforated warehouses the color of wet cement. Here they found a vast store, vast though each salesgirl ruled as a petty tyrant over her domain of shelves. There was a puzzling duplication of suitcase sections; each displayed the same squarish mountain of dark cardboard boxes, and each pouting princess responded with negative insouciance to Ekaterina's quest for a leather suitcase. "I know there have been some," she told Bech.

"It doesn't matter," he said. "I want a cardboard one. I love the metal studs and the little chocolate handle."

"You have fun with me," she said. "I know what you have in the West. I have been to Science-Fiction Writers' Congress in Vienna. This great store, and not one leather suitcase. It is a disgrace upon the people. But come, I know another store." They went back into the Zil, which smelled like a cloakroom, and in whose swaying stuffy depths Bech felt squeamish and chastened, having often been sent to the cloakroom as a child at P.S. 87, on West 77th Street and Amsterdam Avenue. A dozen stuffy miles and three more stores failed to produce a leather suitcase; at last Kate permitted him to buy a paper one – the biggest, with gay plaid sides, and as long as an oboe. To console her, he also bought an astrakhan hat. It was not flattering (when he put it on, the haughty salesgirl laughed aloud) and did not cover his ears, which were cold, but it had the advantage of costing all of fifty-four rubles. "Only a *boyar*," said Kate, excited to flirtation by his purchase, "would wear such a wow of a hat."

"I look like an Armenian in it," Bech said. Humiliations never come singly. On the street, with his suitcase and hat, Bech was stopped by a man who wanted to buy his overcoat. Kate translated and then scolded. During what Bech took to be a lengthy threat to call the police, the offender, a morose bleary-eyed man costumed like a New York chestnut vender, stared stubbornly at the sidewalk by their feet.

As they moved away, he said in soft English to Bech, "Your shoes. I give forty rubles."

Bech pulled out his wallet and said, "*Nyet, nyet.* For your shoes I give fifty."

Kate with a squawk flew between them and swept Bech away. She told him in tears, "Had the authorities witnessed that scene we would all be put in jail, biff, bang."

Bech had never seen her cry in daylight – only in the dark of projection rooms. He climbed into the Zil feeling especially sick and guilty. They were late for their luncheon, with a cherubic museum director and his hatchet-faced staff. In the course of their tour through the museum, Bech tried to cheer her up with praise of Socialist realism. "Look at that turbine. Nobody in America can paint a turbine like that. Not since the thirties. Every part so distinct you could rebuild one from it, yet the whole thing romantic as a sunset. Mimesis – you can't beat it." He was honestly fond of these huge posterish oils; they reminded him of magazine illustrations from his adolescence.

Kate would not be cheered. "It is stupid stuff," she said. "We have had no painters since Rublyov. You treat my country as a picnic." Sometimes her English had a weird precision. "It is not as if there is no talent. We are great, there are millions. The young are burning up with talent, it is annihilating them." She pronounced it *anneeheel* – a word she had met only in print, connected with ray guns.

"Kate, I *mean* it," Bech insisted, hopelessly in the wrong, as with a third-grade teacher, yet also subject to another pressure, that of a woman taking sensual pleasure in refusing to be consoled. "I'm telling you, there is artistic passion here. This bicycle. Beautiful impressionism. No spokes. The French paint apples, the Russians paint bicycles."

The parallel came out awry, unkind. Grimly patting her pink nostrils, Ekaterina passed into the next room. "Once," she informed him, "this room held entirely pictures of *him*. At least that is no more."

Bech did not need to ask who *he* was. The undefined pronoun had a constant value. The name was unspeakable. In Georgia Bech had been shown a tombstone for a person described simply as Mother.

The next day, between lunch with Voznesensky and dinner with Yevtushenko (who both flatteringly seemed to concede to him a hemispheric celebrity equivalent to their own, and who feigned enchantment when he tried to explain his peculiar status, as not a lion, with a lion's confining burden of symbolic portent, but as a graying, furtively stylish rat indifferently permitted to gnaw and roam behind the wainscoting of a firetrap about to be demolished anyway), he and Kate and the impassive chauffeur managed to buy three amber necklaces and four wooden toys and two very thin wristwatches. The amber seemed homely to Bech – melted butter refrozen – but Kate was proud of it. The wristwatches he suspected would soon stop; they were perilously thin. The toys – segmented Kremlins, carved bears chopping wood – were good, but the only children he knew were his sister's in Cincinnati, and the youngest was nine. The Ukrainian needlework that Ekaterina hopefully pushed at him his imagination could not impose on any woman he knew, not even his mother; since his "success," she had her hair done once a week and wore her hems just above the knee. Back in his hotel room, in the ten minutes before an all-Shostakovich concert, while Kate sniffled and sloshed in the bathroom (how could such a skinny woman be displacing all that water?), Bech counted his rubles. He had spent only a hundred and thirty-seven. That left one thousand two hundred and eighty-three, plus the odd kopecks. His heart sank; it was hopeless. Ekaterina emerged from the bathroom with a strange, bruised stare. Little burnt traces, traces of ashen tears, lingered about her eyes, which were by nature a washed-out blue. She had been trying to put on eye makeup, and had kept washing it off. Trying to be a rich man's wife. She looked blank and wounded. Bech took her arm; they hurried downstairs like criminals on the run.

The next day was his last full day in Russia. All month he had wanted to visit Tolstoy's estate, and the trip had been postponed until now. Since Yasnaya Polyana was four hours from Moscow, he and Kate left early in the morning and returned in the dark. After miles of sleepy silence, she asked, "Henry, what did you like?"

"I liked the way he wrote *War and Peace* in the cellar, *Anna Karenina* on the first floor, and *Resurrection* upstairs. Do you think he's writing a fourth novel in Heaven?"

This reply, taken from a little *Commentary* article he was writing in his head (and would never write on paper), somehow renewed her silence. When she at last spoke, her voice was shy. "As a Jew, you believe?"

His laugh had an ambushed quality he tried to translate, with a shy guffaw at the end, into self-deprecation. "Jews don't go in much for Paradise," he said. "That's something you Christians cooked up."

"We are not Christians."

"Kate, you are saints. You are a land of monks and your government is a constant penance." From the same unwritten article – tentatively titled "God's Ghost in Moscow." He went on, with Hollywood, Martin Buber, and his uncles all vaguely smiling in his mind, "I think the Jewish feeling is that wherever they happen to be, it's rather paradisiacal, because they're there."

"You have found it so here?"

"Very much. This must be the only country in the world you can be homesick for while you're still in it. Russia is one big case of homesickness."

Perhaps Kate found this ground dangerous, for she returned to earlier terrain. "It is strange," she said, "of the books I translate, how much there is to do with supernature. Immaterial creatures like angels, ideal societies composed of spirits, speeds that exceed that of light, reversals of time – all impossible, and perhaps not. In a way it is terrible, to look up at the sky, on one of our clear nights of burning cold, at the sky of stars, and think of creatures alive in it."

"Like termites in the ceiling." Falling so short of the grandeur Kate might have had a right to expect from him, his simile went unanswered. The car swayed; dark gingerbread villages swooped by; the back of the driver's head was motionless. Bech idly hummed a bit of "Midnight in Moscow," whose literal title, he had discovered, was "Twilit Evenings in the Moscow Suburbs." He said, "I also liked the way Upton Sinclair was in his bookcase, and how his house felt like a farmhouse instead of a mansion, and his grave."

"So super a grave."

"Very graceful, for a man who fought death so hard." It had been an unmarked oval of earth, rimmed green with frozen turf, at the end of a road in a birchwood where night was sifting in. It had been here that Tolstoy's brother had told him to search for the little green stick that would end war and human suffering. Because her importunate silence had begun to nag unbearably, Bech told Kate, "That's what I should do with my rubles. Buy Tolstoy a tombstone. With a neon arrow."

"Oh those rubles!" she exclaimed. "You persecute me with those rubles. We have shopped more in one week than I shop in one year. Material things do not interest me, Henry. In the war we all learned the value of material things. There is no value but what you hold within yourself."

"O.K., I'll swallow them."

"Always the joke. I have one more desperate idea. In New York, you have women for friends?"

Her voice had gone shy, as when broaching Jewishness; she was asking him if he were a homosexual. How little, after a month, these two knew each other! "Yes. I have *only* women for friends."

"Then perhaps we could buy them some furs. Not a coat, the style would be wrong. But fur we have, not leather suitcases, no, you are right to mock us, but furs, the world's best, and dear enough for even a man so rich as you. I have often argued with Bobochka, he says authors should be poor for the suffering, it is how capitalist countries do it; and now I see he is right."

Astounded by this tirade, delivered with a switching head so that her mole now and then darted into translucence – for they had reached Moscow's outskirts, and street lamps – Bech could only say, "Kate, you've never read my books. They're *all* about women."

"Yes," she said, "but coldly observed. As if extraterrestrial life."

To be brief (I saw you, in the back row, glancing at your wristwatch, and don't think that glance will sweeten your term grade), fur it was. The next morning, in a scrambled hour before the ride to the airport, Bech and Ekaterina went to a shop on Gorky Street where a diffident Mongolian beauty laid pelt after pelt into his hands. The less unsuccessful of his uncles had been for a time a furrier, and after this gap of decades Bech again greeted the frosty luxuriance of silver fox, the more tender and playful and amorous amplitude of red fox, mink with its ugly mahogany assurance, svelte otter, imperial ermine tail-tipped in black like a writing plume. Each pelt, its soft tingling mass condensing acres of Siberia, cost several hundred rubles. Bech bought for his mother two mink still wearing their dried snarls, and two silver fox for his present mistress, Norma Latchett, to trim a coat collar in (her firm white Saxon chin *drowned* in fur, is how he pictured it), and some ermine as a joke for his house-slave sister in Cincinnati, and a sumptuous red fox for a woman he had yet to meet. The Mongolian salesgirl, magnificently unimpressed, added it up to over twelve hundred rubles and wrapped the furs in brown paper like fish. He paid her with a salad of pastel notes and was clean. Bech had not been so exhilarated, so aërated by prosperity, since he sold his first short story – in 1943, about boot camp, to *Liberty*, for a hundred and fifty dollars. It had been humorous, a New York Jew floundering among Southerners, and is omitted from most bibliographies.*

He and Ekaterina rushed back to the Sovietskaya and completed his packing. He tried to forget the gift books stacked in the foyer, but she insisted he take them. They crammed them into his new suitcase, with the furs, the amber, the wristwatches, the infuriatingly knobby and bulky wooden toys. When they were done, the suitcase bulged, leaked fur, and weighed more than his two others combined. Bech looked his last at the chandelier and the empty brandy bottle, the lovesick window and the bugged walls, and staggered out the door. Kate followed with a book and a sock she had found beneath the bed.

Everyone was at the airport to see him off – Bobochka with his silver teeth, Myshkin with his glass eye, the rangy American with his air of lugubrious caution. Bech shook Skip Reynolds's hand goodbye and abrasively kissed the two Russian men on the cheek. He went to kiss Ekaterina on the cheek, but she turned her face so that her mouth met his and he realized, horrified, that he should have slept with her. He had been expected to. From the complacent tiptoe smiles of Bobochka and Myshkin, they assumed he had. She had been provided to him for that purpose. He was a guest of the state. "Oh Kate, forgive me; of course," he said, but so stumblingly she seemed not to have understood him. Her kiss had been colorless but moist and good, like a boiled potato.

Then, somehow, suddenly, he was late, there was panic. His suitcases were not yet in the airplane. A brute in blue seized the two manageable ones and left him to carry the paper one himself. As he staggered across the runway, it burst. One catch simply tore loose at the staples, and the other sympathetically let go. The books and toys spilled; the fur began to blow down the concrete, pelts looping and shimmering as if again alive. Kate broke past the gate guard and helped him catch them; together they scooped all the loot back in the suitcase, but for a dozen fluttering books. They were heavy and slick, in the Cyrillic alphabet, like

* See Appendix B.

high-school yearbooks upside down. One of the watches had cracked its face. Kate was sobbing and shivering in excitement; a bitter wind was blowing streaks of grit and snow out of the coming long winter. "Genry, the books!" she said, needing to shout. "You must have them! They are souvenirs!"

"Mail them!" Bech thundered, and ran with the terrible suitcase under his arm, fearful of being burdened with more responsibilities. Also, though in some ways a man of our time, he has a morbid fear of missing airplanes, and of being dropped from the tail-end lavatory.

Though this was six years ago, the books have not yet arrived in the mail. Perhaps Ekaterina Alexandrovna kept them, as souvenirs. Perhaps they were caught in the cultural freeze-up that followed Bech's visit, and were buried in a blizzard. Perhaps they arrived in the lobby of his apartment building, and were pilfered by an émigré vandal. Or perhaps (you may close your notebooks) the mailman is not clairvoyant after all.

BECH IN RUMANIA;
OR, THE RUMANIAN CHAUFFEUR

DEPLANING IN BUCHAREST wearing an astrakhan hat purchased in Moscow, Bech was not recognized by the United
States Embassy personnel sent to greet him, and, rather than
identify himself, sat sullenly on a bench, glowering like a Soviet
machinery importer, while these young men ran back and forth
conversing with each other in dismayed English and shouting at
the customs officials in what Bech took to be pidgin Rumanian.
At last, one of these young men, the smallest and cleverest,
Princeton '51 or so, noticing the rounded toes of Bech's American shoes, ventured suspiciously, "I beg your pardon, *pazhalusta*,
but are you – ?"

"Could be," Bech said. After five weeks of consorting with
Communists, he felt himself increasingly tempted to evade, confuse, and mock his fellow Americans. Further, after attuning
himself to the platitudinous jog of translatorese, he found rapid
English idiom exhausting. So it was with some relief that he
passed, in the next hours, from the conspiratorial company of his
compatriots into the care of a monarchial Rumanian hotel and a
smiling Party underling called Athanase Petrescu.

Petrescu, whose oval face was adorned by constant sunglasses
and several round sticking plasters placed upon a fresh blue shave,
had translated into Rumanian *Typee*; *Pierre*; *Life on the Mississippi*;
Sister Carrie; *Winesburg, Ohio*; *Across the River and Into the Trees*;
and *On the Road*. He knew Bech's work well and said, "Although
it was *Travel Light* that made your name illustrious, yet in my
heart I detect a very soft spot for *Brother Pig*, which your critics
did not so much applaud."

Bech recognized in Petrescu, behind the blue jaw and sinister glasses, a man humbly in love with books, a fool for literature. As, that afternoon, they strolled through a dreamlike Bucharest park containing bronze busts of Goethe and Pushkin and Victor Hugo, beside a lake wherein the greenish sunset was coated with silver, the translator talked excitedly of a dozen things, sharing thoughts he had not been able to share while descending, alone at his desk, into the luminous abysses and profound crudities of American literature. "With Hemingway, the difficulty of translating – and I speak to an extent of Anderson also – is to prevent the simplicity from seeming simple-minded. For we do not have here such a tradition of belle-lettrist fancifulness against which the style of Hemingway was a rebel. Do you follow the difficulty?"

"Yes. How did you get around it?"

Petrescu did not seem to understand. "Get around, how? Circumvent?"

"How did you translate the simple language without seeming simple-minded?"

"Oh. By being extremely subtle."

"Oh. I should tell you, some people in my country think Hemingway *was* simple-minded. It is actively debated."

Petrescu absorbed this with a nod, and said, "I know for a fact, his Italian is not always correct."

When Bech got back to his hotel – situated on a square rimmed with buildings made, it seemed, of dusty pink candy – a message had been left for him to call a Mr. Phillips at the U.S. Embassy. Phillips was Princeton '51. He asked, "What have they got mapped out for you?"

Bech's schedule had hardly been discussed. "Petrescu mentioned a production of *Desire Under the Elms* I might see. And he wants to take me to Braşov. Where is Braşov?"

"In Transylvania, way the hell off. It's where Dracula hung out. Listen, can we talk frankly?"

"We can try."

"I know damn well this line is bugged, but here goes. This country is hot. Anti-Socialism is busting out all over. My inkling is they want to get you out of Bucharest, away from all the liberal writers who are dying to meet you."

"Are you sure they're not dying to meet Arthur Miller?"

"Kidding aside, Bech, there's a lot of ferment in this country, and we want to plug you in. Now, when are you meeting Taru?"

"Knock knock. Taru. Taru Who?"

"Jesus, he's the head of the Writers' Union – hasn't Petrescu even set up an appointment? Boy, they're putting you right around the old mulberry bush. I gave Petrescu a list of writers for you to latch on to. Suppose I call him and wave the big stick and ring you back. Got it?"

"Got it, tiger." Bech hung up sadly; one of the reasons he had accepted the State Department's invitation was that he thought it would be an escape from agents.

Within ten minutes his phone rasped, in that dead rattly way it has behind the Iron Curtain, and it was Phillips, breathless, victorious. "Congratulate me," he said. "I've been making like a thug and got *their* thugs to give you an appointment with Taru tonight."

"This very night?"

Phillips sounded hurt. "You're only here four nights, you know. Petrescu will pick you up. His excuse was he thought you might want some rest."

"He's extremely subtle."

"What was that?"

"Never mind, *pazhalusta*."

Petrescu came for Bech in a black car driven by a hunched silhouette. The Writers' Union was housed on the other side of town, in a kind of castle, a turreted mansion with a flaring stone staircase and an oak-vaulted library whose shelves were twenty feet high and solid with leather spines. The stairs and hallways were deserted. Petrescu tapped on a tall paneled door of black-ish oak, strap-hinged in the sombre Spanish style. The door opened soundlessly, revealing a narrow high room hung with tapestries, pale brown and blue, whose subject involved masses of attenuated soldiery unfathomably engaged. Behind a huge polished desk quite bare of furnishings sat an immaculate mini-ature man with a pink face and hair as white as a dandelion poll. His rosy hands, perfectly finished down to each fingernail, were folded on the shiny desk, reflected like water flowers; and his face wore a smiling expression that was also, in each neat crease, beyond improvement. This was Taru.

He spoke with magical suddenness, like a music box. Petrescu translated his words to Bech as, "You are a literary man. Do you know the works of our Mihail Sadoveanu, of our noble Mihai Beniuc, or perhaps that most wonderful spokesman for the people, Tudor Arghezi?"

Bech said, "No, I'm afraid the only Rumanian writer I know at all is Ionesco."

The exquisite white-haired man nodded eagerly and emitted a length of tinkling sounds that was translated to Bech as simply "And who is he?"

Petrescu, who certainly knew all about Ionesco, stared at Bech with blank expectance. Even in this innermost sanctum he had kept his sunglasses on. Bech said, irritated, "A playwright. Lives in Paris. Theatre of the Absurd. Wrote *Rhinoceros*," and he crooked a forefinger beside his heavy Jewish nose, to represent a horn.

Taru emitted a dainty sneeze of laughter. Petrescu translated, listened, and told Bech, "He is very sorry he has not heard of this man. Western books are a luxury here, so we are not able to follow each new nihilist movement. Comrade Taru asks what you plan to do while in the People's Republic of Rumania."

"I am told," Bech said, "that there are some writers interested in exchanging ideas with an American colleague. I believe my embassy has suggested a list to you."

The musical voice went on and on. Petrescu listened with a cocked ear and relayed, "Comrade Taru sincerely wishes that this may be the case and regrets that, because of the lateness of the hour and the haste of this meeting urged by your embassy, no secretaries are present to locate this list. He furthermore regrets that at this time of the year so many of our fine writers are bathing at the Black Sea. However, he points out that there is an excellent production of *Desire Under the Elms* in Bucharest, and that our Carpathian city of Braşov is indeed worthy of a visit. Comrade Taru himself retains many pleasant youthful memories concerning Braşov."

Taru rose to his feet — an intensely dramatic event within the reduced scale he had established around himself. He spoke, thumped his small square chest resoundingly, spoke again, and smiled. Petrescu said, "He wishes you to know that in his youth he published many books of poetry, both epic and lyric in manner. He adds, 'A fire ignited here'" – and here Petrescu struck his own chest in flaccid mimicry – "'can never be quenched.'"

Bech stood and responded, "In my country we also ignite fires *here*." He touched his head. His remark was not translated and, after an efflorescent display of courtesy from the brilliant-haired little man, Bech and Petrescu made their way through the empty mansion down to the waiting car, which drove them, rather jerkily, back to the hotel.

"And how did you like Mr. Taru?" Petrescu asked on the way.

"He's a doll," Bech said.

"You mean – a puppet?"

Bech turned curiously but saw nothing in Petrescu's face that betrayed more than a puzzlement over meaning. Bech said, "I'm sure you have a better eye for the strings than I do."

Since neither had eaten, they dined together at the hotel; they discussed Faulkner and Hawthorne while waiters brought them soup and veal a continent removed from the cabbagy cuisine of Russia. A lithe young woman on awkwardly high heels stalked among the tables singing popular songs from Italy and France. The trailing microphone wire now and then became entangled in her feet, and Bech admired the sly savagery with which she would, while not altering an iota her enameled smile, kick herself free. Bech had been a long time without a woman. He looked forward to three more nights sitting at this table, surrounded by traveling salesmen from East Germany and Hungary, feasting on the sight of this lithe chanteuse. Though her motions were angular and her smile was inflexible, her high round bosom looked soft as a soufflé.

But tomorrow, Petrescu explained, smiling sweetly beneath his sad-eyed sunglasses, they would go to Braşov.

Bech knew little about Rumania. From his official briefing he knew it was "a Latin island in a Slavic sea," that during World

War II its anti-Semitism had been the most ferocious in Europe, that now it was seeking economic independence of the Soviet bloc. The ferocity especially interested him, since of the many human conditions it was his business to imagine, murderousness was among the more difficult. He was a Jew. Though he could be irritable and even vengeful, obstinate savagery was excluded from his budget of emotions.

Petrescu met him in the hotel lobby at nine and, taking his suitcase from his hand, led him to the hired car. By daylight, the chauffeur was a short man the color of ashes – white ash for the face, gray cigarette ash for his close-trimmed smudge of a mustache, and the darker residue of a tougher substance for his eyes and hair. His manner was nervous and remote and fussy; Bech's impression was of a stupidity so severe that the mind is tensed to sustain the simplest tasks. As they drove from the city, the driver constantly tapped his horn to warn pedestrians and cyclists of his approach. They passed the prewar stucco suburbs, suggestive of southern California; the postwar Moscow-style apartment buildings, rectilinear and airless; the heretical all-glass exposition hall the Rumanians had built to celebrate twenty years of industrial progress under Socialism. It was shaped like a huge sailor's cap, and before it stood a tall Brancusi column cast in aluminum.

"Brancusi," Bech said. "I didn't know you acknowledged him."

"Oh, much," Petrescu said. "His village is a shrine. I can show you many early works in our national museum."

"And Ionesco? Is he really a non-person?"

Petrescu smiled. "The eminent head of our Writers' Union," he said, "makes little jokes. He is known here but not much produced as yet. Students in their rooms perhaps read aloud a play like *The Singer Devoid of Hair*."

Bech was distracted from the conversation by the driver's incessant mutter of tooting. They were in the country now, driving along a straight, slightly rising road lined with trees whose trunks were painted white. On the shoulder of the road walked bundle-shaped old women carrying knotted bundles, little boys tapping donkeys forward, men in French-blue work clothes sauntering empty-handed. At all of them the driver sounded his horn. His stubby, gray-nailed hand fluttered on the contact rim, producing an agitated stammer beginning perhaps a hundred yards in advance and continuing until the person, who usually moved only to turn and scowl, had been passed. Since the road was well traveled, the noise was practically uninterrupted, and after the first half hour nagged Bech like a toothache. He asked Petrescu, "Must he do that?"

"Oh, yes. He is a conscientious man."

"What good does it do?"

Petrescu, who had been developing an exciting thought on Mark Twain's infatuation with the apparatus of capitalism, which had undermined his bucolic genius, indulgently explained, "The bureau from which we hire cars provides the driver. They have been precisely trained for this profession."

Bech realized that Petrescu himself did not drive. He reposed in the oblivious trust of an airplane passenger, legs crossed, sunglasses in place, issuing smoother and smoother phrases, while Bech leaned forward anxiously, braking on the empty floor, twitching a wheel that was not there, trying to wrench the car's control away from this atrociously unrhythmic and brutal driver. When they went through a village, the driver would speed up and intensify the mutter of his honking; clusters of peasants and geese exploded in disbelief, and Bech felt as if gears, the gears that regulate and engage the mind, were clashing. As they ascended into the mountains, the driver demonstrated his technique with curves: he approached each like an enemy, accelerating, and at the last moment stepped on the brake as if crushing a snake underfoot. In the jerking and swaying, Petrescu grew pale. His blue jaw acquired a moist sheen and issued phrases less smoothly. Bech said to him, "This driver should be locked up. He is sick and dangerous."

"No, no, he is a good man. These roads, they are difficult."

"At least please ask him to stop twiddling the horn. It's torture."

Petrescu's eyebrows arched, but he leaned forward and spoke in Rumanian.

The driver answered; the language clattered in his mouth, though his voice was soft.

Petrescu told Bech, "He says it is a safety precaution."

"Oh, for Christ's sake!"

Petrescu was truly puzzled. He asked, "In the States, you drive your own car?"

"Of course, everybody does," Bech said, and then worried that he had hurt the feelings of this Socialist, who must submit to the aristocratic discomfort of being driven. For the remainder of the trip, he held silent about the driver. The muddy lowland fields with Mediterranean farmhouses had yielded to fir-dark hills bearing Germanic chalets. At the highest point, the old boundary of Austria-Hungary, fresh snow had fallen, and the car, pressed ruthlessly through the ruts, brushed within inches of some children dragging sleds. It was a short downhill distance from there to Braşov. They stopped before a newly built pistachio hotel. The jarring ride had left Bech with a headache. Petrescu stepped carefully from the car, licking his lips; the tip of his tongue showed purple in his drained face. The chauffeur, as composed as raked ashes no touch of wind has stirred, changed out of his gray driving coat, checked the oil and water, and removed his lunch from the trunk. Bech examined him for some sign of satisfaction, some betraying trace of malice, but there was nothing. His eyes were living smudges, and his mouth was the mouth of the boy in the class who, being neither strong nor intelligent, has developed insignificance into a character trait that does him some credit. He glanced at Bech without expression; yet Bech wondered if the man did not understand English a little.

In Braşov the American writer and his escort passed the time in harmless sightseeing. The local museum contained peasant costumes. The local castle contained armor. The Lutheran cathedral was surprising; Gothic lines and scale had been wedded to clear glass and an austerity of decoration, noble and mournful, that left one, Bech felt, much too alone with God. He felt the Reformation here as a desolating wind, four hundred years ago. From the hotel roof, the view looked sepia, and there was an empty swimming pool, and wet snow on the lacy metal chairs. Petrescu shivered and went down to his room. Bech changed neckties and went down to the bar. Champagne music bubbled from the walls. The bartender understood what a Martini was, though he used equal parts of gin and vermouth. The clientele was young, and many spoke Hungarian, for Transylvania had been taken from Hungary after the war. One plausible youth, working with Bech's reluctant French, elicited from him that he was *un écrivain*, and asked for his autograph. But this turned out to be the prelude to a proposed exchange of pens, in which Bech lost a sentimentally cherished Esterbrook and gained a nameless ball-point that wrote red. Bech wrote three and a half postcards (to his mistress, his mother, his publisher, and a half to his editor at *Commentary*) before the red pen went dry. Petrescu, who neither drank nor smoked, finally appeared. Bech said, "My hero, where have you been? I've had four Martinis and been swindled in your absence."

Petrescu was embarrassed. "I've been shaving."

"Shaving!"

"Yes, it is humiliating. I must spend each day one hour shaving, and even yet it does not look as if I have shaved, my beard is so obdurate."

"Are you putting blades in the razor?"

"Oh, yes, I buy the best and use two upon each occasion."

"This is the saddest story I've ever heard. Let me send you some decent blades when I get home."

"Please, do not. There are no blades better than the blades I use. It is merely that my beard is phenomenal."

"When you die," Bech said, "you can leave it to Rumanian science."

"You are ironical."

In the restaurant, there was dancing – the Tveest, the Hully Gullee, and chain formations that involved a lot of droll hopping. American dances had become here innocently birdlike. Now and then a young man, slender and with hair combed into a parrot's peak, would leap into the air and seem to hover, emitting a shrill palatal cry. The men in Transylvania appeared lighter and more fanciful than the women, who moved, in their bell-skirted cock-tail dresses, with a wooden stateliness perhaps inherited from their peasant grandmothers. Each girl who passed near their table was described by Petrescu, not humorously at first, as a "typical Rumanian beauty."

"And this one, with the orange lips and eyelashes?"

"A typical Rumanian beauty. The cheekbones are very classical."

"And the blonde behind her? The small plump one?"

"Also typical."

"But they are so different. Which is more typical?"

"They are equally. We are a perfect democracy." Between spates of dancing, a young chanteuse, more talented than the one in the Bucharest hotel, took the floor. She had learned, probably from free-world films, that terrible mannerism of strenuousness whereby every note, no matter how accessibly placed and how flatly attacked, is given a facial aura of immense accomplishment. Her smile, at the close of each number, combined a conspiratorial twinkle, a sublime humility, and an element of dazed self-congratulation. Yet, beneath the artifice, the girl had life. Bech was charmed by a number, in Italian, that involved much animated pouting and finger-scolding and placing of the fists on the hips. Petrescu explained that the song was the plaint of a young wife whose husband was always attending soccer matches and never stayed home with her. Bech asked, "Is she also a typical Rumanian beauty?"

"I think," Petrescu said, with a purr Bech had not heard before, "she is a typical little Jewess."

The drive, late the next afternoon, back to Bucharest was worse than the one out, for it took place partly in the dark. The chauffeur met the challenge with increased speed and redoubled honking. In a rare intermittence of danger, a straight road near Ploeşti where only the oil rigs relieved the flatness, Bech asked, "Seriously, do you not feel the insanity in this man?" Five minutes before, the driver had turned to the back seat and, showing even gray teeth in a tight tic of a smile, had remarked about a dog lying dead beside the road. Bech suspected that most of the remark had not been translated.

Petrescu said, crossing his legs in the effete and weary way that had begun to exasperate Bech, "No, he is a good man, an extremely kind man, who takes his work too seriously. In that he is like the beautiful Jewess whom you so much admired."

"In my country," Bech said, " 'Jewess' is a kind of fighting word."

"Here," Petrescu said, "it is merely descriptive. Let us talk about Herman Melville. Is it possible to you that *Pierre* is a yet greater work than *The White Whale*?"

"No, I think it is yet not so great, possibly."

"You are ironical about my English. Please excuse it. Being prone to motion sickness has discollected my thoughts."

"Our driver would discollect anybody's thoughts. Is it possible that he is the late Adolf Hitler, kept alive by Count Dracula?"

"I think not. Our people's uprising in 1944 fortunately exterminated the Fascists."

"That is fortunate. Have you ever read, speaking of Melville, *Omoo*?"

Melville, it happened, was Bech's favorite American author, in whom he felt united the strengths that were later to go the separate ways of Dreiser and James. Throughout dinner, back at the hotel, he lectured Petrescu about him. "No one," Bech said – he had ordered a full bottle of white Rumanian wine, and his tongue felt agile as a butterfly – "more courageously faced our native terror. He went for it right between its wide-set little pig eyes, and it shattered his genius like a lance." He poured himself more wine. The hotel chanteuse, who Bech now noticed had buck teeth as well as gawky legs, stalked to their table, untangled her feet from the microphone wire, and favored them with a French version of "Some Enchanted Evening."

"You do not consider," Petrescu said, "that Hawthorne also went between the eyes? And the laconic Ambrose Bierce?"

"*Quelque soir enchanté*," the woman sang, her eyes and teeth and earrings glittering like the facets of a chandelier.

"Hawthorne blinked," Bech pronounced, "and Bierce squinted."

"*Vous verrez l'étranger . . .*"

"I worry about you, Petrescu," Bech continued. "Don't you ever have to go home? Isn't there a Frau Petrescu, Madame, or

whatever, a typical Rumanian, never mind." Abruptly he felt
steeply lonely.

In bed, when his room had stopped the gentle swaying motion
with which it had greeted his entrance, he remembered the driver,
and the man's neatly combed death-gray face seemed the face of
everything foul, stale, stupid, and uncontrollable in the world. He
had seen that tight tic of a smile before. Where? He remembered.
West 86th Street, coming back from Riverside Park, Mickey
Schwartz, a child with whom he always argued, and was always
right, and always lost. Their ugliest quarrel had concerned comic
strips, whether or not the artist – Segar, say, who drew Popeye, or
Harold Gray of Little Orphan Annie – whether or not the artist, in
duplicating the faces from panel to panel, day after day, traced
them. Bech had maintained, obviously, not. Mickey had insisted
that some mechanical process had to be used. Bech tried to explain
that it was not such a difficult feat, that just as a person's handwriting is always the same – Mickey, his face clouding, said it
wasn't possible. Bech explained, what he saw so clearly, that
everything was possible for human beings with a little training
and talent, that the ease and variation of each panel proved his
point. Just learn to look, you dummy. Mickey's face had become
totally closed, with a pig-eyed density quite inhuman, as it steadily shook "No, no, no," and Bech, becoming frightened and
furious, tried to behead the other boy with his fists, and the boy
in turn pinned him and pressed his face into the bitter grit of
pebbles and glass that coated the cement passageway between two
apartment buildings. These unswept jagged bits, a kind of city
topsoil, had enlarged under his eyes, and this experience, the
magnification amidst pain of those negligible mineral flecks, had
formed, perhaps, a vision. At any rate, it seemed to Bech, as he
skidded into sleep, that his artistic gifts had been squandered in the
attempt to recapture that moment of stinging precision.

The next day was his last full day in Rumania. Petrescu took
him to an art museum where, amid many ethnic posters posing as
paintings, a few sketches and sculpted heads by the young Brancusi smelled like saints' bones. The two men went on to the

twenty years' industrial exhibit and admired rows of brightly painted machinery – gaudy counters in some large international game. They visited shops, and everywhere Bech felt a desiccated pinkish elegance groping, out of eclipse, through the murky hardware of Sovietism, toward a rebirth of style. Yet there had been a tough and heroic naïveté in Russia that he missed here, where something shrugging and effete seemed to leave room for a vein of energetic evil. In the evening, they went to *Patima de Sub Ulmi*.

Their driver, bringing them to the very door of the theatre, pressed his car forward through bodies, up an arc of driveway crowded with pedestrians. The people caught in the headlights were astonished; Bech slammed his foot on a phantom brake and Petrescu grunted and strained backward in his seat. The driver continually tapped his horn – a demented, persistent muttering – and slowly the crowd gave way around the car. Bech and Petrescu stepped, at the door, into the humid atmosphere of a riot. As the chauffeur, his childish small-nosed profile intent, pressed his car back through the crowd to the street, fists thumped on the fenders.

Safe in the theatre lobby, Petrescu took off his sunglasses to wipe his face. His eyes were a tender bulging blue, with jaundiced whites; a scholar's tremor pulsed in his left lower lid. "You know," he confided to Bech, "that man our driver. Not all is well with him."

"That's what I keep telling you," Bech said.

O'Neill's starveling New England farmers were played as Russian muzhiks; they wore broad-belted coats and high black boots and kept walloping each other on the back. Abbie Cabot had become a typical Rumanian beauty, ten years past her prime, with a beauty spot on one cheek and artful bare arms as supple as a swan's neck. Since their seats were in the center of the second row, Bech had a good if infrequent view down the front of her dress, and thus, ignorant of when the plot would turn her his way, he contentedly manufactured suspense for himself. But Petrescu, his loyalty to American letters affronted beyond endurance, insisted that they leave after the first act. "Wrong, wrong," he complained. "Even the pitchforks were wrong."

"I'll have the State Department send them an authentic American pitchfork," Bech promised.

"And the girl – the girl is not like that, not a coquette. She is a religious innocent, under economic stress."

"Well, scratch an innocent, find a coquette. Scratch a co-quette, you find economic stress."

"It is your good nature to joke, but I am ashamed you saw such a travesty. Now our driver is not here. We are undone."

The street outside the theatre, so recently jammed, was empty and dark. A solitary couple walked slowly toward them. With surrealistic suddenness, Petrescu fell into the arms of the man, walloping his back, and then kissed the calmly proffered hand of the woman. The couple was introduced to Bech as "a most brilliant young writer and his notably ravishing wife." The man, stolid and forbidding, wore rimless glasses and a bulky checked topcoat. The woman was scrawny; her face, potentially handsome, had been worn to its bones by the nervous activity of her intelligence. She had a cold and a command, quick but limited, of English. "Are you having a liking for this?" she asked.

Bech understood her gesture to include all Rumania. "Very much," he answered. "After Russia, it seems very civilized."

"And who isn't?" she snapped. "What are you liking most?"

Petrescu roguishly interposed, "He has a passion for night-club singers."

The wife translated this for her husband; he took his hands from his overcoat pockets and clapped them. He was wearing leather gloves, so the noise was loud on the deserted street. He spoke, and Petrescu translated: "He says we should therefore, as hosts, escort you to the most celebrated night club in Bucharest, where you will see many singers, each more glorious than the preceding."

"But," Bech said, "weren't they going somewhere? Shouldn't they go home?" It worried him that Communists never seemed to go home.

"For why?" the wife cried.

"You have a cold," Bech told her. Her eyes didn't compre-hend. He touched his own nose, so much larger than hers. "*Un rhume.*"

"Poh!" she said. "Itself takes care of tomorrow."

The writer owned a car, and he drove them, with the gentleness of a pedal boat, through a maze of alleys overhung by cornices suggestive of cake frosting, of waves breaking, of seashells, lion paws, unicorn horns, and cumulus clouds. They parked across the street from a blue sign, and went into a green doorway, and down a yellow set of stairs. Music approached them from one direction and a coat-check girl in net tights from the other. It was to Bech as if he were dreaming of an American night club, giving it the strange spaciousness of dreams. The main room had been conjured out of several basements — a cave hollowed from the underside of jeweler's shops and vegetable marts. Tables were set in shadowy tiers arranged around a central square floor. Here a man with a red wig and mascaraed eyes was talking into a microphone, mincingly. Then he sang, in the voice of a choirboy castrated too late. A waiter materialized. Bech ordered Scotch, the other writer ordered vodka. The wife asked for cognac and Petrescu for mineral water. Three girls dressed as rather naked bicyclists appeared with a dwarf on a unicycle and did some unsmiling gyrations to music while he pedalled among them, tugging bows and displacing straps. "Typical Polish beauties," Petrescu explained in Bech's ear. He and the writer's wife were seated on the tier behind Bech. Two women, one a girl in her teens and the other a heavy old blonde, perhaps her mother, both dressed identically in sequined silver, did a hypnotic, languorous act with tinted pigeons, throwing them up in the air, watching them wheel through the shadows of the night club, and holding out their wrists for their return. They juggled with the pigeons, passed them between their legs, and for a climax the elderly blonde fed an aquamarine pigeon with seeds held in her mouth and fetched, one by one, onto her lips. "Czechs," Petrescu explained. The master of ceremonies reappeared in a blue wig and a toreador's jacket, and did a comic act with the dwarf, who had been fitted with papier-mâché horns. An East German girl, flaxen-haired and apple-cheeked, with the smooth columnar legs of the very young, came to the microphone dressed in a minimal parody of a cowgirl outfit and sang, in English, "Dip in the Hot of Texas" and "Allo Cindy Lou, Gootbye Hot." She pulled guns from her hips and received much pro-American applause, but Bech was on his third Scotch and needed his hands to hold cigarettes. The Rumanian writer sat at the table beside him, a carafe of vodka at his elbow, staring stolidly at the floor show. He looked like the young Theodore Roosevelt, or perhaps McGeorge Bundy. His wife leaned forward and said in Bech's ear, "Is just like home, hey? Texas is ringing bells?" He decided she was being sarcastic. A fat man in a baggy maroon tuxedo set up a long table and kept eight tin plates twirling on the ends of flexible sticks. Bech thought it was miraculous, but the man was booed. A touching black-haired girl from Bulgaria hesitantly sang three atonal folk songs into a chastened silence. Three women behind Bech began to chatter hissingly. Bech turned to rebuke them and was stunned by the size of their wristwatches, which were man-sized, as in Russia. Also, in turning he had surprised Petrescu and the writer's wife holding hands. Though it was after midnight, the customers were still coming in, and the floor show refused to stop. The Polish girls returned dressed as ponies and jumped through hoops the dwarf held for them. The master of ceremonies reappeared in a striped bathing suit and black wig and did an act with the dwarf involving a stepladder and a bucket of water. A black dancer from Ghana twirled firebrands in the dark while slapping the floor with her bare feet. Four Latvian tumblers performed on a trampoline and a seesaw. The Czech mother and daughter came back in different costumes, spangled gold, but performed the identical act, the pigeons whirring, circling, returning, eating from the mother's lips. Then five Chinese girls from Outer Mongolia –

"My God," Bech said, "isn't this ever going to be over? Don't you Communists ever get tired of having fun?"

The writer's wife told him, "For your money, you really gets."

Petrescu and she conferred and decided it was time to go. One of the big wristwatches behind Bech said two o'clock. In leaving, they had to pass around the Chinese girls, who, each clad in a snug beige bikini, were concealing and revealing their bodies amid a weave of rippling colored flags. One of the girls glanced sideways at Bech, and he blew her a pert kiss, as if from a train

window. Their golden bodies looked fragile to him; he felt that
their bones, like the bones of birds, had evolved hollow, to save
weight. At the mouth of the cave, the effeminate master of
ceremonies, wearing a parrot headdress, was conferring with
the hat-check girl. His intent was plainly heterosexual; Bech's
head reeled at such duplicity. Though they added the weight of
his coat to him, he rose like a balloon up the yellow stairs,
bumped out through the green door, and stood beneath the
street lamp inhaling volumes of the blue Rumanian night.

He felt duty-bound to confront the other writer. They stood,
the two of them, on the cobbled pavement, as if on opposite sides
of a transparent wall one side of which was lacquered with
Scotch and the other with vodka. The other's rimless glasses
were misted and the resemblance to Teddy Roosevelt had been
dissipated. Bech asked him, "What do you write about?"

The wife, patting her nose with a handkerchief and struggling
not to cough, translated the question, and the answer, which was
brief. "Peasants," she told Bech. "He wants to know, what do *you*
write about?"

Bech spoke to him directly. "*La bourgeoisie*," he said; and that
completed the cultural exchange. Gently bumping and rocking,
the writer's car took Bech back to his hotel, where he fell into
the deep, unapologetic sleep of the sated.

The plane to Sofia left Bucharest the next morning. Petrescu
and the ashen-faced chauffeur came into the tall *fin-de-siècle*
dining room for Bech while he was still eating breakfast – *jus
d'orange, des croissants avec du beurre* and *une omelette aux fines herbes*.
Petrescu explained that the driver had gone back to the theatre,
and waited until the ushers and the managers left, after midnight. But the driver did not seem resentful, and gave Bech, in
the sallow morning light, a fractional smile, a *risus sardonicus*, in
which his eyes did not participate. On the way to the airport, he
scattered a flock of chickens an old woman was coaxing across
the road, and forced a military transport truck onto the shoulder,
while its load of soldiers gestured and jeered. Bech's stomach
groveled, bathing the fine herbs of his breakfast in acid. The

ceaseless tapping of the horn seemed a gnawing on all of his nerve ends. Petrescu made a fastidious mouth and sighed through his nostrils. "I regret," he said, "that we did not make more occasion to discuss your exciting contemporaries."

"I never read them. They're too exciting," Bech said, as a line of uniformed schoolchildren was narrowly missed, and a field-worker with a wheelbarrow shuffled to safety, spilling potatoes. The day was overcast above the loamy sunken fields and the roadside trees in their skirts of white paint. "Why," he asked, not having meant to be rude, "are all these tree trunks painted?"

"So they are," Petrescu said. "I have not noticed this before, in all my years. Presumably it is a measure to defeat the insects."

The driver spoke in Rumanian, and Petrescu told Bech, "He says it is for the car headlights, at night. Always he is thinking about his job."

At the airport, all the Americans were there who had tried to meet Bech four days ago. Petrescu immediately delivered to Phillips, like a bribe, the name of the writer they had met last night, and Phillips said to Bech, "You spent the evening with *him*? That's fabulous. He's the top of the list, man. We've never laid a finger on him before; he's been inaccessible."

"Stocky guy with glasses?" Bech asked, shielding his eyes. Phillips was so pleased it was like a bright light too early in the day.

"That's the boy. For our money he's the hottest Red writer this side of Solzhenitsyn. He's *waaay* out. Stream of conscious-ness, no punctuation, everything. There's even some sex."

"You might say he's Red hot," Bech said.

"Huh? Yeah, that's good. Seriously, what did he say to you?"

"He said he'll defect to the West as soon as his shirts come back from the laundry."

"And we went," Petrescu said, "to La Caverne Bleue."

"Say," Phillips said, "you really went underground."

"I think of myself," Bech said modestly, "as a sort of low-flying U-2."

"All kidding aside, Henry" – and here Phillips took Bech by the arms and squeezed – "it sounds as if you've done a sensational job for us. Sensational. Thanks, friend."

Bech hugged everyone in parting – Phillips, the chargé d'affaires, the junior chargé d'affaires, the ambassador's twelve-year-old nephew, who was taking archery lessons near the airport and had to be dropped off. Bech saved Petrescu for last, and walloped his back, for his escort had led him to remember, what he was tempted to forget in America, that reading can be the best part of a man's life.

"I'll send you razor blades," he promised, for in the embrace Petrescu's beard had scratched.

"No, no, I already buy the best. Send me books, any books!"

The plane was roaring to go, and only when safely, or fatally, sealed inside did Bech remember the chauffeur. In the flurry of formalities and baggage handling there had been no goodbye. Worse, there had been no tip. The leu notes Bech had set aside were still folded in his wallet, and his start of guilt gave way, as the runways and dark fields tilted and dwindled under him, to a glad sense of release. Clouds blotted out the country. He realized that for four days there; in that driver's care, he had been afraid. The man next to him, a portly Slav whose bald brow was beaded with apprehensive sweat, turned and confided something unintelligible, and Bech said, "*Pardon, je ne comprends pas. Je suis Américain.*"

THE BULGARIAN POETESS

"YOUR POEMS. Are they difficult?"

She smiled and, unaccustomed to speaking English, answered carefully, drawing a line in the air with two delicately pinched fingers holding an imaginary pen. "They are difficult – to write."

He laughed, startled and charmed. "But not to read?"

She seemed puzzled by his laugh, but did not withdraw her smile, though its corners deepened in a defensive, feminine way. "I think," she said, "not so very."

"Good." Brainlessly he repeated "Good," disarmed by her unexpected quality of truth. He was, himself, a writer, this fortyish young man, Henry Bech, with his thinning curly hair and melancholy Jewish nose, the author of one good book and three others, the good one having come first. By a kind of oversight, he had never married. His reputation had grown while his powers declined. As he felt himself sink, in his fiction, deeper and deeper into eclectic sexuality and bravura narcissism, as his search for plain truth carried him further and further into treacherous realms of fantasy and, lately, of silence, he was more and more thickly hounded by homage, by flat-footed exegetes, by arrogantly worshipful undergraduates who had hitchhiked a thousand miles to touch his hand, by querulous translators, by election to honorary societies, by invitations to lecture, to "speak," to "read," to participate in symposia trumped up by ambitious girlie magazines in shameless conjunction with venerable universities. His very government, in airily unstamped envelopes from Washington, invited him to travel, as an ambassador of the arts, to the other half of the world, the hostile, mysterious half. Rather automatically, but with some faint hope

of shaking himself loose from the burden of himself, he consented, and found himself floating, with a passport so stapled with
visas it fluttered when pulled from his pocket, down into the dim
airports of Communist cities.

He arrived in Sofia the day after a mixture of Bulgarian and
African students had smashed the windows of the American legation and ignited an overturned Chevrolet. The cultural officer,
pale from a sleepless night of guard duty, tamping his pipe with
trembling fingers, advised Bech to stay out of crowds and escorted
him to his hotel. The lobby was swarming with Negroes in black
wool fezzes and pointed European shoes. Insecurely disguised, he
felt, by an astrakhan hat purchased in Moscow, Bech passed
through to the elevator, whose operator addressed him in German. "*Ja, vier*," Bech answered, "*danke*," and telephoned, in his
bad French, for dinner to be brought up to his room. He remained
there all night, behind a locked door, reading Hawthorne. He had
lifted a paperback collection of short stories from a legation
window sill littered with broken glass. A few curved bright
crumbs fell from between the pages onto his blanket. The image
of Roger Malvin lying alone, dying, in the forest – "Death would
come like the slow approach of a corpse, stealing gradually
towards him through the forest, and showing its ghastly and
motionless features from behind a nearer and yet a nearer tree" –
frightened him. Bech fell asleep early and suffered from swollen,
homesick dreams. It had been the first day of Hanukkah.

In the morning, venturing downstairs for breakfast, he was
surprised to find the restaurant open, the waiters affable, the eggs
actual, the coffee hot, though syrupy. Outside, Sofia was sunny
and (except for a few dark glances at his big American shoes)
amenable to his passage along the streets. Lozenge-patterns of
pansies, looking flat and brittle as pressed flowers, had been set in
the public beds. Women with a touch of Western *chic* walked
hatless in the park behind the mausoleum of Georgi Dimitrov.
There was a mosque, and an assortment of trolley cars salvaged
from the remotest corner of Bech's childhood, and a tree that
talked – that is, it was so full of birds that it swayed under their
weight and emitted volumes of chirping sound like a great leafy
loudspeaker. It was the inverse of his hotel, whose silent walls

presumably contained listening microphones. Electricity was somewhat enchanted in the Socialist world. Lights flickered off untouched and radios turned themselves on. Telephones rang in the dead of the night and breathed wordlessly in his ear. Six weeks ago, flying from New York City, Bech had expected Moscow to be a blazing counterpart and instead saw, through the plane window, a skein of hoarded lights no brighter, on that vast black plain, than a girl's body in a dark room.

Past the talking tree was the American legation. The sidewalk, heaped with broken glass, was roped off, so that pedestrians had to detour into the gutter. Bech detached himself from the stream, crossed the little barren of pavement, smiled at the Bulgarian militiamen who were sullenly guarding the jewel-bright heaps of shards, and pulled open the bronze door. The cultural officer was crisper after a normal night's sleep. He clenched his pipe in his teeth and handed Bech a small list. "You're to meet with the Writers' Union at eleven. These are writers you might ask to see. As far as we can tell, they're among the more progressive."

Words like "progressive" and "liberal" had a somewhat reversed sense in this world. At times, indeed, Bech felt he had passed through a mirror, a dingy flecked mirror that reflected feebly the capitalist world; in its dim depths everything was similar but left-handed. One of the names ended in "-ova." Bech said, "A woman."

"A poetess," the cultural officer said, sucking and tamping in a fury of bogus efficiency. "Very popular, apparently. Her books are impossible to buy."

"Have you read anything by these people?"

"I'll be frank with you. I can just about make my way through a newspaper."

"But you always know what a newspaper will say anyway."

"I'm sorry, I don't get your meaning."

"There isn't any." Bech didn't quite know why the Americans he met behind the mirror irritated him – whether because they garishly refused to blend into this shadow-world or because they were always so solemnly sending him on ridiculous errands.

*　*　*

At the Writers' Union, he handed the secretary the list as it had been handed to him, on U.S. legation stationery. The secretary, a large stooped man with the hands of a stonemason, grimaced and shook his head but obligingly reached for the telephone. Bech's meeting was already waiting in another room. It was the usual one, the one that, with small differences, he had already attended in Moscow and Kiev, Yerevan and Alma-Ata, Bucharest and Prague: the polished oval table, the bowl of fruit, the morning light, the gleaming glasses of brandy and mineral water, the lurking portrait of Lenin, the six or eight patiently sitting men who would leap to their feet with quick blank smiles. These men would include a few literary officials, termed "critics," high in the Party, loquacious and witty and destined to propose a toast to international understanding; a few selected novelists and poets, mustachioed, smoking, sulking at this invasion of their time; a university professor, the head of the Anglo-American Literature department, speaking in a beautiful withered English of Mark Twain and Sinclair Lewis; a young interpreter with a clammy handshake; a shaggy old journalist obsequiously scribbling notes; and, on the rim of the group, in chairs placed to suggest that they had invited themselves, one or two gentlemen of ill-defined status, fidgety and tieless, maverick translators who would turn out to be the only ones present who had ever read a word by Henry Bech.

Here this type was represented by a stout man in a tweed coat leather-patched at the elbows in the British style. The whites of his eyes were distinctly red. He shook Bech's hand eagerly, made of it almost an embrace of reunion, bending his face so close that Bech could distinguish the smells of tobacco, garlic, cheese, and alcohol. Even as they were seating themselves around the table, and the Writers' Union chairman, a man elegantly bald, with very pale eyelashes, was touching his brandy glass as if to lift it, this anxious red-eyed interloper blurted at Bech, "Your *Travel Light* was so marvelous a book! The motels, the highways, the young girls with their lovers who were motorcyclists, so marvelous, so American, the youth, the adoration for space and speed, the barbarity of the advertisements in neon lighting, the very poetry. It takes us truly into another dimension."

Travel Light was the first novel, the famous one. Bech disliked discussing it. "At home," he said, "it was criticized as despairing."

The man's hands, stained orange with tobacco, lifted in amazement and plopped noisily to his knees. "No, no, a thousand times. Truth, wonder, terror even, vulgarity, yes. But despair, no, not at all, not one iota. Your critics are dead wrong."

"Thank you."

The chairman softly cleared his throat and lifted his glass an inch from the table, so that it formed with its reflection a kind of playing card.

Bech's admirer excitedly persisted. "You are not a *wet* writer, no. You are a dry writer, yes? You have the expressions, am I wrong in English, dry, hard?"

"More or less."

"I want to translate you!"

It was the agonized cry of a condemned man, for the chairman coldly lifted his glass to the height of his eyes, and like a firing squad the others followed suit. Blinking his white lashes, the chairman gazed mistily in the direction of the sudden silence, and spoke in Bulgarian.

The young interpreter murmured in Bech's ear. "I wish to propose now, ah, a very brief toast. I know it will seem doubly brief to our honored American guest, who has so recently enjoyed the, ah, hospitality of our Soviet comrades." There must have been a joke here, for the rest of the table laughed. "But in seriousness permit me to say that in our country we have seen in years past too few Americans, ah, of Mr. Bech's progressive and sympathetic stripe. We hope in the next hour to learn from him much that is interesting and, ah, socially useful about the literature of his large country, and perhaps we may in turn inform him of our own proud literature, of which perhaps he knows regrettably little. Ah, so let me finally, then, since there is a saying that too long a courtship spoils the marriage, offer to drink, in our native plum brandy *slivovica*, ah, firstly to the success of his visit and, in the second place, to the mutual increase of international understanding."

"Thank you," Bech said and, as a courtesy, drained his glass. It was wrong; the others, having merely sipped, stared. The purple burning revolved in Bech's stomach and a severe distaste for himself, for his role, for this entire artificial and futile process, were focused into a small brown spot on a pear in the bowl so shiningly posed before his eyes.

The red-eyed fool smelling of cheese was ornamenting the toast. "It is a personal honor for me to meet the man who, in *Travel Light*, truly added a new dimension to American prose."

"The book was written," Bech said, "ten years ago."

"And since?" A slumping, mustached man sat up and sprang into English. "Since, you have written what?"

Bech had been asked that question often in these weeks and his answer had grown curt. "A second novel called *Brother Pig*, which is St. Bernard's expression for the body."

"Good. Yes, and?"

"A collection of essays and sketches called *When the Saints*."

"I like the title less well."

"It's the beginning of a famous Negro song."

"We know the song," another man said, a smaller man, with the tense, dented mouth of a hare. He lightly sang, "Lordy, I just want to be in that number."

"And the last book," Bech said, "was a long novel called *The Chosen* that took five years to write and that nobody liked."

"I have read reviews," the red-eyed man said. "I have not read the book. Copies are difficult here."

"I'll give you one," Bech said.

The promise seemed, somehow, to make the recipient unfortunately conspicuous; wringing his stained hands, he appeared to swell in size, to intrude grotesquely upon the inner ring, so that the interpreter took it upon himself to whisper, with the haste of an apology, into Bech's ear, "This gentleman is well known as the translator into our language of *Alice in Wonderland*."

"A marvelous book," the translator said, deflating in relief, pulling at his pockets for a cigarette. "It truly takes us into another dimension. Something that must be done. We live in a new cosmos."

The chairman spoke in Bulgarian, musically, at length. There was polite laughter. Nobody translated for Bech. The professorial type, his hair like a flaxen toupee, jerked forward. "Tell me, is it true, as I have read" – his phrases whistled slightly, like rusty machinery – "that the stock of Sinclair Lewis has plummeted under the Salinger wave?"

And so it went, here as in Kiev, Prague, and Alma-Ata, the same questions, more or less predictable, and his own answers, terribly familiar to him by now, mechanical, stale, irrelevant, untrue, claustrophobic. Then the door opened. In came, with the rosy air of a woman fresh from a bath, a little breathless, having hurried, hatless, a woman in a blond coat, her hair also blond. The secretary, entering behind her, seemed to make a cherishing space around her with his large curved hands. He introduced her to Bech as Vera Something-ova, the poetess he had asked to meet. None of the others on the list, he explained, had answered their telephones.

"Aren't you kind to come?" As Bech asked it, it was a genuine question, to which he expected some sort of an answer.

She spoke to the interpreter in Bulgarian. "She says," the interpreter told Bech, "she is sorry she is so late."

"But she was just called!" In the warmth of his confusion and pleasure Bech turned to speak directly to her, forgetting he would not be understood. "I'm terribly sorry to have interrupted your morning."

"I am pleased," she said, "to meet you. I heard of you spoken in France."

"You speak English!"

"No. Very little amount."

"But you *do*."

A chair was brought for her from a corner of the room. She yielded her coat, revealing herself in a suit also blond, as if her clothes were an aspect of a total consistency. She sat down opposite Bech, crossing her legs. Her legs were visibly good; her face was perceptibly broad. Lowering her lids, she tugged her skirt to the curve of her knee. It was his sense of her having hurried, hurried to *him*, and of being, still, graciously flustered, that most touched him.

He spoke to her very clearly, across the fruit, fearful of abusing and breaking the fragile bridge of her English. "You are a poetess. When I was young, I also wrote poems."

She was silent so long he thought she would never answer; but then she smiled and pronounced, "You are not old now."

"Your poems. Are they difficult?"

"They are difficult – to write."

"But not to read?"

"I think – not so very."

"Good. Good."

Despite the decay of his career, Bech had retained an absolute faith in his instincts; he never doubted that somewhere an ideal course was open to him and that his intuitions were pre-dealt clues to his destiny. He had loved, briefly or long, with or without consummation, perhaps a dozen women; yet all of them, he now saw, shared the trait of approximation, of narrowly missing an undisclosed prototype. The surprise he felt did not have to do with the appearance, at last, of this central woman; he had always expected her to appear. What he had not expected was her appearance here, in this remote and abused nation, in this room of morning light, where he discovered a small knife in his fingers and on the table before him, golden and moist, a precisely divided pear.

Men traveling alone develop a romantic vertigo. Bech had already fallen in love with a freckled embassy wife in Russia, a buck-toothed chanteuse in Rumania, a stolid Mongolian sculptress in Kazakhstan. In the Tretyakov Gallery he had fallen in love with a recumbent statue, and at the Moscow Ballet School with an entire roomful of girls. Entering the room, he had been struck by the aroma, tenderly acrid, of young female sweat. Sixteen and seventeen, wearing patchy practice suits, the girls were twirling so strenuously their slippers were unraveling. Demure student faces crowned the unconscious insolence of their bodies. The room was doubled in depth by a floor-to-ceiling mirror. Bech was seated on a bench at its base. Staring above his head, each girl watched herself with frowning eyes frozen, for an instant in the turn, by the imperious delay and snap of her head. Bech tried to remember the lines of Rilke that expressed it, this snap and delay: *did not the drawing remain/that*

*the dark stroke of your eyebrow/swiftly wrote on the wall of its own
turning?* At one point the teacher, a shapeless old Ukrainian lady
with gold canines, a *prima* of the thirties, had arisen and cried
something translated to Bech as, "No, no, the arms free, *free!*"
And in demonstration she had executed a rapid series of pirou-
ettes with such proud effortlessness that all the girls, standing this
way and that like deer along the wall, had applauded. Bech had
loved them for that. In all his loves, there was an urge to rescue –
to rescue the girls from the slavery of their exertions, the statue
from the cold grip of its own marble, the embassy wife from her
boring and unctuous husband, the chanteuse from her nightly
humiliation (she could not sing), the Mongolian from her stolid
race. But the Bulgarian poetess presented herself to him as needing nothing, as being complete, poised, satisfied, achieved. He
was aroused and curious and, the next day, inquired about her of
the man with the vaguely contemptuous mouth of a hare – a
novelist turned playwright and scenarist, who accompanied him
to the Rila Monastery. "She lives to write," the playwright said.
"I do not think it is healthy."

Bech said, "But she seems so healthy." They stood beside a
small church with whitewashed walls. From the outside it looked
like a hovel, a shelter for pigs or chickens. For five centuries the
Turks had ruled Bulgaria, and the Christian churches, however
richly adorned within, had humble exteriors. A peasant woman
with wildly snarled hair unlocked the door for them. Though the
church could hardly ever have held more than thirty worship-
pers, it was divided into three parts, and every inch of wall was
covered with eighteenth-century frescoes. Those in the narthex
depicted a Hell where the devils wielded scimitars. Passing
through the tiny nave, Bech peeked through the iconostasis
into the screened area that, in the symbolism of Orthodox
architecture, represented the next, the hidden world – Paradise.
He glimpsed a row of books, an easy chair, a pair of ancient oval
spectacles. Outdoors again, he felt released from the unpleasantly
tight atmosphere of a children's book. They were on the side of a
hill. Above them was a stand of pines whose trunks were shelled
with ice. Below them sprawled the monastery, a citadel of
Bulgarian national feeling during the years of the Turkish

Yoke. The last monks had been moved out in 1961. An aimless soft rain was falling in these mountains, and there were not many German tourists today. Across the valley, whose little silver river still turned a water wheel, a motionless white horse stood silhouetted against a green meadow, pinned there like a brooch.

"I am an old friend of hers," the playwright said. "I worry about her."

"Are the poems good?"

"It is difficult for me to judge. They are very feminine. Perhaps shallow."

"Shallowness can be a kind of honesty."

"Yes. She is very honest in her work."

"And in her life?"

"As well."

"What does her husband do?"

The other man looked at him with parted lips and touched his arm, a strange Slavic gesture, communicating an underlying racial urgency, which Bech no longer shied from. "But she has no husband. As I say, she is too much for poetry to have married."

"But her name ends in '-ova.'"

"I see. You are mistaken. It is not a matter of marriage; I am Petrov, my unmarried sister is Petrova. All females."

"How stupid of me. But I think it's such a pity, she's so charming."

"In America, only the uncharming fail to marry?"

"Yes, you must be very uncharming not to marry."

"It is not so here. The government indeed is alarmed; our birth rate is one of the lowest in Europe. It is a problem for economists."

Bech gestured at the monastery. "Too many monks?"

"Not enough, perhaps. With too few of monks, something of the monk enters everybody."

The peasant woman, who seemed old to Bech but who was probably younger than he, saw them to the edge of her domain. She huskily chattered in what Petrov said was very amusing rural slang. Behind her, now hiding in her skirts and now darting away, was her child, a boy not more than three. He was faithfully chased, back and forth, by a small white pig, who moved, as pigs do, on tiptoe, with remarkably abrupt changes of direction. Something in the scene, in the open glee of the woman's parting smile and the unself-conscious way her hair thrust out from her head, something in the mountain mist and spongy rutted turf into which frost had begun to break at night, evoked for Bech a nameless absence to which was attached, like a horse to a meadow, the image of the poetess, with her broad face, her good legs, her Parisian clothes, and her sleekly brushed hair. Petrov, in whom he was beginning to sense, through the wraps of foreignness, a clever and kindred mind, seemed to have overheard his thoughts, for he said, "If you would like, we could have dinner. It would be easy for me to arrange."

"With her?"

"Yes, she is my friend, she would be glad."

"But I have nothing to say to her. I'm just curious about such an intense conjunction of good looks and brains. I mean, what does a soul do with it all?"

"You may ask her. Tomorrow night?"

"I'm sorry, I can't. I'm scheduled to go to the ballet, and the next night the legation is giving a cocktail party for me, and then I fly home."

"Home? So soon?"

"It does not feel soon to me. I must try to work again."

"A drink, then. Tomorrow evening before the ballet? It is possible? It is not possible."

Petrov looked puzzled, and Bech realized that it was his fault, for he was nodding to say Yes, but in Bulgarian nodding meant No, and a shake of the head meant Yes. "Yes," he said. "Gladly."

The ballet was entitled *Silver Slippers*. As Bech watched it, the word "ethnic" kept coming to his mind. He had grown accustomed, during his trip, to this sort of artistic evasion, the retreat from the difficult and disappointing present into folk dance, folk tale, folk song, with always the implication that, beneath the embroidered peasant costume, the folk was really one's heart's own darling, the proletariat.

"Do you like fairy tales?" It was the damp-palmed interpreter who accompanied him to the theatre.

"I *love* them," Bech said, with a fervor and gaiety lingering from the previous hour. The interpreter looked at him anxiously, as when Bech had swallowed the brandy in one swig, and throughout the ballet kept murmuring explanations of self-evident events on the stage. Each night, a princess would put on silver slippers and dance through her mirror to tryst with a wizard, who possessed a magic stick that she coveted, for with it the world could be ruled. The wizard, as a dancer, was inept, and once almost dropped her, so that anger flashed from her eyes. She was, the princess, a little redhead with a high round bottom and a frozen pout and beautiful free arm motions, and Bech found it oddly ecstatic when, preparatory to her leap, she would dance toward the mirror, an empty oval, and another girl, identically dressed in pink, would emerge from the wings and perform as her reflection. And when the princess, haughtily adjusting her cape of invisibility, leaped through the oval of gold wire, Bech's heart leaped backward into the enchanted hour he had spent with the poetess.

Though the appointment had been established, she came into the restaurant as if, again, she had been suddenly summoned and had hurried. She sat down between Bech and Petrov slightly breathless and fussed, but exuding, again, that impalpable warmth of intelligence and virtue.

"Vera, Vera," Petrov said.

"You hurry too much," Bech told her.

"Not so very much," she said.

Petrov ordered her a cognac and continued with Bech their discussion of the newer French novelists. "It is tricks," Petrov said. "Good tricks, but tricks. It does not have enough to do with life, it is too much verbal nervousness. Is that sense?"

"It is an epigram," Bech said.

"There are just two of their number with whom I do not feel this: Claude Simon and Samuel Beckett. You have no relation, Bech, Beckett?"

"None."

Vera said, "Nathalie Sarraute is a very modest woman. She felt motherly to me."

"You have met her?"

"In Paris I heard her speak. Afterward there was the coffee. I liked her theories, of the, oh, *what*? Of the *little* movements within the heart." She delicately measured a pinch of space and smiled, through Bech, back at herself.

"Tricks," Petrov said. "I do not feel this with Beckett; there, in a low form, believe it or not, one has human content."

Bech felt duty-bound to pursue this, to ask about the theatre of the absurd in Bulgaria, about abstract painting (these were the touchstones of "progressiveness"; Russia had none, Rumania some, Czechoslovakia plenty), to subvert Petrov. Instead, he asked the poetess, "Motherly?"

Vera explained, her hands delicately modeling the air, rounding into nuance, as it were, the square corners of her words. "After her talk, we – talked."

"In French?"

"And in Russian."

"She knows Russian?"

"She was born Russian."

"How is her Russian?"

"Very pure but – old-fashioned. Like a book. As she talked, I felt in a book, safe."

"You do not always feel safe?"

"Not always."

"Do you find it difficult to be a woman poet?"

"We have a tradition of woman poets. We have Elisaveta Bagriana, who is very great."

Petrov leaned toward Bech as if to nibble him. "Your own works? Are they influenced by the *nouvelle vague*? Do you consider yourself to write anti-*romans*?"

Bech kept himself turned toward the woman. "Do you want to hear about how I write? You don't, do you?"

"Very much yes," she said.

He told them, told them shamelessly, in a voice that surprised him with its steadiness, its limpid urgency, how once he had written, how in *Travel Light* he had sought to show people skimming the surface of things with their lives, taking tints from things the way that objects in a still life color one another,

and how later he had attempted to place beneath the melody of
plot a countermelody of imagery, interlocking images which had
risen to the top and drowned his story, and how in *The Chosen* he
had sought to make of this confusion the theme itself, an epic
theme, by showing a population of characters whose actions
were all determined, at the deepest level, by nostalgia, by a desire
to get back, to dive, each, into the springs of their private
imagery. The book probably failed; at least, it was badly received.
Bech apologized for telling all this. His voice tasted flat in his
mouth; he felt a secret intoxication and a secret guilt, for he had
contrived to give a grand air, as of an impossibly noble and
quixotically complex experiment, to his failure when at bottom,
he suspected, a certain simple laziness was the cause.

Petrov said, "Fiction so formally sentimental could not be
composed in Bulgaria. We do not have a happy history."

It was the first time Petrov had sounded like a Communist. If
there was one thing that irked Bech about these people behind
the mirror, it was their assumption that, however second-rate
elsewhere, in suffering they were supreme. He said, "Believe it
or not, neither do we."

Vera calmly intruded. "Your personae are not moved by
love?"

"Yes, very much. But as a form of nostalgia. We fall in love,
I tried to say in the book, with women who remind us of our first
landscape. A silly idea. I used to be interested in love. I once
wrote an essay on the orgasm – you know the word? –"

She shook her head. He remembered that it meant Yes.

"– on the orgasm as perfect memory. The mystery is, what are
we remembering?"

She shook her head again, and he noticed that her eyes
were gray, and that in their depths his image (which he could
not see) was searching for the thing remembered. She composed her finger tips around the brandy glass and said, "There
is a French poet, a young one, who has written of this. He
says that never else do we, do we so gather up, collect
into ourselves, oh –" Vexed, she spoke to Petrov in rapid Bulgarian.

He shrugged and said, "Concentrate our attention."

"– concentrate our attention," she repeated to Bech, as if the words, to be believed, had to come from her. "I say it foolish – foolishly – but in French it is very well put and – *correct*."

Petrov smiled neatly and said, "This is an enjoyable subject for discussion, love."

"It remains," Bech said, picking his words as if the language were not native even to him, "one of the few things that still deserve meditation."

"I think it is good," she said.

"Love?" he asked, startled.

She shook her head and tapped the stem of her glass with a fingernail, so that Bech had an inaudible sense of ringing, and she bent as if to study the liquor, so that her entire body borrowed a rosiness from the brandy and burned itself into Bech's memory – the silver gloss of her nail, the sheen of her hair, the symmetry of her arms relaxed on the white tablecloth, everything except the expression on her face.

Petrov asked aloud Bech's opinion of Dürrenmatt.

Actuality is a running impoverishment of possibility. Though he had looked forward to seeing her again at the cocktail party and had made sure that she was invited, when it occurred, though she came, he could not get to her. He saw her enter, with Petrov, but he was fenced in by an attaché of the Yugoslav Embassy and his burnished Tunisian wife; and, later, when he was worming his way toward her diagonally, a steely hand closed on his arm and a rasping American female told him that her fifteen-year-old nephew had decided to be a writer and desperately needed advice. Not the standard crap, but real brass-knuckles advice. Bech found himself balked. He was surrounded by America: the voices, the narrow suits, the watery drinks, the clatter, the glitter. The mirror had gone opaque and gave him back only himself. He managed, in the end, as the officials were thinning out, to break through and confront her in a corner. Her coat, blond, with a rabbit collar, was already on; from its side pocket she pulled a pale volume of poems in the Cyrillic alphabet. "Please," she said. On the flyleaf she had written, "to H. Beck, sincerelly, with bad spellings but much" – the last word looked like "leave" but must have been "love."

"Wait," he begged, and went back to where his ravaged pile of presentation books had been and, unable to find the one he wanted, stole the legation library's jacketless copy of *The Chosen*. Placing it in her expectant hands, he told her, "Don't look," for inside he had written, with a drunk's stylistic confidence,

Dear Vera Glavanakova –
It is a matter of earnest regret for me that you and I must live on opposite sides of the world.

BECH TAKES POT LUCK

THOUGH HENRY BECH'S few persistent admirers among the critics praised his "highly individual and refractory romanticism," his "stubborn refusal to mount, in this era of artistic coup d'état and herd movement, any bandwagon but that of his own quixotic, excessively tender, strangely anti–Semitic Semitic sensibility," the author nevertheless had a sneaking fondness for the fashionable. Each August, he deserted his shabby large apartment at 99th and Riverside and rented a cottage on a Massachusetts island whose coves and sandy lanes were crammed with other writers, television producers, museum directors, undersecretaries of State, movie stars whose Forties films were now enjoying a camp revival, old *New Masses* editors possessively squatting on seaside acreage bought for a song in the Depression, and hordes of those handsome, entertaining, professionless prosperous who fill the chinks between celebrities. It innocently delighted Bech, a child of the urban middle class, to see these luxurious people padding in bare feet along the dirty sidewalks of the island's one town, or fighting for overpriced groceries in the tiny general store of an up-island hamlet. It gratified him to recognize some literary idol of his youth, shrunken and frail, being tumbled about by the surf; or to be himself recognized by some faunlike bikinied girl who had been assigned *Travel Light* at the Brearley School, or by a cozy Westchester matron, still plausible in her scoop-back one-piece, who amiably confused Bech's controversial chef-d'œuvre *The Chosen* with a contemporary best-seller of the same title. Though often thus accosted, Bech had never before been intercepted by a car. The little scarlet Porsche, the long blond hair of its driver flapping, cut in front of

Bech's old Ford as he was driving to the beach, and forced him to brake within inches of two mailboxes painted with flowers and lettered, respectively, "Sea Shanty" and "Avec du Sel." The boy – it was a boy's long blond hair – hopped out and raced back to Bech's window, extending a soft hand that, as Bech docilely shook it, trembled like a bird's breast. The boy's plump face seemed falsified by the uncut mane; it engulfed his ears and gave his mouth, perhaps because it was unmistakably male, an assertive quarrelsome look. His eyebrows were sun-bleached to invisibility; his pallid blue eyes were all wonder and love.

"Mr. Bech, hey. I couldn't believe it was you."

"Suppose it hadn't been me. How would you explain forcing me into this ditch?"

"I bet you don't remember who I am."

"Let me guess. You're not Sabu, and you're not Freddie Bartholomew."

"Wendell Morrison, Mr. Bech. English 1020 at Columbia, 1963." For one spring term Bech, who belonged to the last writing generation that thought teaching a corruption, had been persuaded to oversee – it amounted to little more than that – the remarkably uninhibited conversations of fifteen undergraduates and to read their distressingly untidy manuscripts. Languid and clever, these young people had lacked not only patriotism and faith but even the coarse morality competitiveness imposes. Living off fathers they despised, systematically attracted to the outrageous, they seemed ripe for Fascism. Their politics burlesqued the liberal beliefs dear to Bech; their literary tastes ran to chaotic second-raters like Miller and Tolkien and away from those austere, prim saints – Eliot, Valéry, Joyce – whose humble suppliant Bech had been. Bech even found fault with them physically: though the girls were taller and better endowed than the girls of his youth, with neater teeth and clearer skins, there was something doughy about their beauty; the starved, conflicted girls of Bech's generation had had distinctly better legs. He slowly remembered Wendell. The boy always sat on Bech's left, a fair-haired young Wasp from Stamford, crewcut – a Connecticut Yankee, more grave and respectful than the others, indeed so courteous Bech wondered if some kind of irony were intended.

He appeared to adore Bech; and Bech's weakness for Wasps was well known. "You wrote in lower case," Bech said. "An orgy with some girls in a house full of expensive furniture. Glints of pink flesh in a chandelier. Somebody defecated on a polar-bear rug."

"That's right. What a great memory."

"Only for fantasies."

"You gave it an A, you said it really shook you up. That meant a hell of a lot to me. I couldn't tell you then, I was playing it cool, that was my hang-up, but I can tell you now, Mr. Bech, it was real encouragement, it's really kept me going. You were *great*."

As the loosening of the boy's vocabulary indicated a prolonged conversation, the woman beside Bech shifted restlessly. Wendell's clear blue eyes observed the movement, and obligated Bech to perform introductions. "Norma, this is Wendell Morris. Miss Norma Latchett."

"Morrison," the boy said, and reached in past Bech's nose to shake Norma's hand. "He's beautiful, isn't he, Ma'am?"

She answered dryly, "He'll do." Her thin brown hand rested in Wendell's white plump one as if stranded. It was a sticky day.

"Let's *go*," a child exclaimed from the back seat, in that dreadful squeezed voice that precedes a tantrum. Helplessly Bech's hands tightened on the steering wheel, and the hairs on the back of his neck stiffened. After two weeks, he was still unacclimated to the pressures of surrogate paternity. The child grunted, stuffed with fury; Bech's stomach sympathetically clenched.

"Hush," the child's mother said, slow-voiced, soothing. "Uncle Harry's talking to an old student of his. They haven't seen each other for years."

Wendell bent low to peer into the back seat, and Bech was obliged to continue introductions. "This is Norma's sister, Mrs. Beatrice Cook, and her children – Ann, Judy, Donald."

Wendell nodded four times in greeting. His furry plump hand clung tenaciously to the sill of Bech's window. "Quite a scene," he said.

Bech told him, "We're trying to get to the beach before it clouds over." Every instant, the sky grew less transparent. Often the island was foggy while the mainland, according to the radio, blissfully baked.

"Where's everybody staying?" The boy's assumption that they were all living together irritated Bech, since it was correct.

"We've rented a shoe," Bech said, "from an old lady who's moved up to a cigar box."

Wendell's eyes lingered on the three fair children crammed, along with sand pails and an inflated air mattress, into the back seat beside their mother. He asked them, "Uncle Harry's quite a card, huh, kids?"

Bech imagined he had hurt Wendell's feelings. In rapid atonement he explained, "We're in a cottage rented from Andy Spofford, who used to be in war movies – before your time, he played sidekicks that got killed – and lives mostly in Corsica now. Blue mailbox, third dirt road past the Up-Island Boutique, take every left turning except the last, when you go right, not *hard* right. Mrs. Cook is up from Ossining visiting for the week." Bech restrained himself from telling Wendell that she was going through a divorce and cried every evening and lived on pills. Bea was an unspectacular middle-sized woman two years younger than Norma; she wore dull clothes that seemed designed to set off her sister's edgy beauty.

Wendell understood Bech's apologetic burst as an invitation, and removed his hand from the door. "Hey, I know this is an imposition, but I'd love to have you just glance at the stuff I'm doing now. I'm out of that lower-case bag. In fact I'm into something pretty classical. I've seen the movie of *Ulysses* twice."

"And you've let your hair grow. You're out of the barbershop bag."

Wendell spoke past Bech's ear to the children. "You kids like to Sunfish?"

"Yes!" Ann and Judy chorused; they were twins.

"What's Sunfish?" Donald asked.

Going to the beach had been the children's only entertainment. Their mother was drugged and dazed, Norma detested physical activity before dark, and Bech was frightened of the water. Even the ferry ride over to the island felt precarious to him. He never sailed, and rarely swam in water higher than his hips. From his apartment on Riverside Drive, he looked across to New Jersey as if the Hudson were a wide flat black street.

"Let's do it tomorrow," Wendell said. "I'll come for them around one, if that's O.K., ma'am."

Bea, flustered to find herself addressed – for Bech and Norma had almost enforced invisibility upon her, staging their fights and reconciliations as if she were not in the cottage – answered in her melodious grief-slowed voice, "That would be lovely of you, if you really want to bother. Is there any danger?"

"Not a bit, ma'am. I have life jackets. I used to be a camp counselor."

"That must have been when you shot your polar bear," Bech said, and pointedly restarted the motor.

They arrived at the beach just as the sun went behind one of those irregular expanding clouds whose edges hold blue sky at bay for hours. The children, jubilant at freedom and the prospect of Sunfishing, plunged into the surf. Norma, as if unwrapping a fragile gift in faintly poor taste, removed her beach robe, revealing a mauve bikini, and, inserting plastic eyecups in her sockets, arranged herself in the center of a purple towel the size of a double bed. Bea, disconsolate in a loose brown suit that did not do her figure justice, sat down on the sand with a book – one of Bech's, curiously. Though her sister had been his mistress for two and a half years, she had just got around to doing her homework. Embarrassed, fearful that the book, so near his actual presence, would somehow detonate, Bech moved off a few strides and stood, bare-chested, gazing at his splendid enemy the sea, an oblivious hemisphere whose glitter of whitecaps sullenly persisted without the sun. Shortly, a timid adolescent voice, the voice he had been waiting for, rustled at his shoulder. "I beg your pardon, sir, but by any chance are you . . . ?"

Wendell found Bech's diffident directions no obstacle and came for the children promptly at one the next day. The expedition was so successful Beatrice prolonged her visit another week. Wendell took the children clamming and miniature-golfing; he took them to an Indian burial ground, to an abandoned windmill, to grand beaches fenced with No Trespassing signs. The boy had that Wasp knowingness, that facility with things: he knew how to insert a clam knife, how to snorkle (just to put on the mask made Bech gasp for breath), how to bluff and charm his way onto private beaches (Bech believed everything he read), how to excite children with a few broken shell bits that remotely might be remnants of ceremonially heaped conch shells. He was connected to the land in a way Bech could only envy. Though so young, he had been everywhere – Italy, Scandinavia, Mexico, Alaska – whereas Bech, except for Caribbean holidays and a State Department-sponsored excursion to some Communist countries, had hardly been anywhere. He lived twenty blocks north of where he had been born, and couldn't sleep for nervousness the night before he and Norma and his rickety Ford risked the journey up the seaboard to the ferry slip. The continent-spanning motorcyclists of *Travel Light* had been daydreams based upon his Cincinnati sister's complaints about her older son, a college dropout. Wendell, a mere twenty-three, shamed Bech with his Yankee ingenuity, his native woodcraft – the dozen and one tricks of a beach picnic, for instance: the oven of scooped sand, the corn salted in seawater, the fire of scavenged driftwood. It all seemed adventurous to Bech, as did the boy's removal, in the amber summer twilight, of his bathing suit to body-surf. Wendell was a pudgy yet complete Adonis stiff-armed in the waves, his buttocks pearly, his genitals distinctly visible when he stood in the wave troughs. The new generation was immersed in the world that Bech's, like a foolish old bridegroom full of whiskey and dogma, had tried to mount and master. Bech was shy of things, and possessed few, not even a wife; Wendell's room, above a garage on the summer property of some friends of his parents, held everything from canned anchovies and a Bible to pornographic photographs and a gram of LSD.

Ever since Bech had met her, Norma had wanted to take LSD. It was one of her complaints against him that he had never got her any. He, who knew that all her complaints were in truth that he would not marry her, told her she was too old. She was thirty-six; he was forty-three, and, though flirting with the senility that comes early to American authors, still absurdly wary of anything that might damage his brain. When, on their cottage porch, Wendell let slip the fact that he possessed some LSD, Bech recognized Norma's sudden new mood. Her nose sharpened, her wide mouth rapidly fluctuated between a heart-melting grin and a severe down-drawn look almost of anger. It was the mood in which, two Christmases ago, she had come up to him at a party, ostensibly to argue about *The Chosen*, in fact to conjure him into taking her to dinner. She began to converse exclusively with Wendell.

"Where did you get it?" she asked. "Why haven't you used it?"

"Oh," he said, "I knew a turned-on chemistry major. I've had it for a year now. You just don't take it, you know, before bedtime like Ovaltine. There has to be somebody to take the trip with. It can be very bad business" – he had his solemn whispering voice, stashed behind his boyish naïve one – "to go on a trip alone."

"You've been," Bech said politely.

"I've been." His shadowy tone matched the moment of day. The westward sky was plunging toward rose; the sailboats were taking the final tack toward harbor. Inside the cottage, the children, happy and loud after an expedition with Wendell to the lobster hatchery, were eating supper. Beatrice went in to give them dessert, and to get herself a sweater.

Norma's fine lean legs twitched, recrossing, as she turned to Wendell with her rapacious grin. Before she could speak, Bech asked a question that would restore to himself the center of attention. "And is this what you write about now? In the classic manner of *Ulysses* movies?"

Under the embarrassment of having to instruct his instructor, Wendell's voice dropped another notch. "It's not really writable. Writing makes distinctions, and this breaks them down. For example, I remember once looking out my window at Columbia. Someone had left a green towel on the gravel roof. From sunbathing, I suppose. I thought, Mmm, pretty green towel, nice shade of green, *beau*tiful shade of green – and the color at*tacked* me!"

Norma asked, "How attacked you? It grew teeth? Grew bigger? What?" She was having difficulty, Bech felt, keeping herself out of Wendell's lap. The boy's innocent eyes, browless as a Teddy bear's, flicked a question toward Bech.

"Tell her," Bech told him. "She's curious."

"I'm *horribly* curious," Norma exclaimed. "I'm *so* tired of being myself. Liquor doesn't do anything for me anymore, sex, *any*thing."

Wendell glanced again toward Bech, worried. "It – attacked me. It tried to become me."

"Was it wonderful? Or terrible?"

"It was borderline. You must understand, Norma, it's not a playful experience. It takes everything you have." His tone of voice had become the unnaturally, perhaps ironically, respectful one he had used in English 1020.

"It'll even take," Bech told her, "your Saks charge-a-plate."

Bea appeared in the doorway, dim behind the screen. "As long as I'm on my feet, does anybody want another drink?"

"Oh, *Bea*," Norma said, leaping up, "stop being a martyr. It's my turn to cook, let me help you." To Bech, before going in, she said, "*Please* arrange my trip with Wendell. He thinks I'm a nuisance, but he *adores* you. Tell him how good I'll be."

Her departure left the men silent. Sheets of mackerel shards were sliding down the sky toward a magenta sunset; Bech felt himself being sucked into a situation where nothing, neither tact nor reason nor the morality he had learned from his father and Flaubert, afforded leverage. Wendell at last asked, "How stable is she?"

"Very un-."

"Any history of psychological disturbance?"

"Nothing but the usual psychiatry. Quit analysis after four months. Does her work apparently quite well – layout and design for an advertising agency. Likes to show her temper off but underneath has a good hard eye on the main chance."

"I'd really need to spend some time alone with her. It's very important that people on a trip together be congenial. They last at least twelve hours. Without rapport, it's a nightmare." The boy was so solemn, so blind to the outrageousness of what he was proposing, that Bech laughed. As if rebuking Bech with his greater seriousness, Wendell whispered in the dusk, "The people you've taken a trip with become the most important people in your life."

"Well," Bech said, "I want to wish you and Norma all the luck in the world. When should we send out announcements?"

Wendell intoned, "I feel you disapprove. I feel your fright."

Bech was speechless. Didn't he know what a mistress was? No sense of private property in this generation. The early Christians; Brook Farm.

Wendell went on carefully, considerately, "Let me propose this. Has she ever smoked pot?"

"Not with me around. I'm an old-fashioned father figure. Two parts Abraham to one part Fagin."

"Why don't she and I, Mr. Bech, smoke some marijuana together as a dry run? That way she can satisfy her female curiosity and I can see if we could stand a trip together. As I size her up, she's much too practical-minded to be a head. She just wants to make the Sixties scene, and maybe to bug you."

The boy was so hopeful, so reasonable, that Bech could not help treating him as a student, with all of a student's purchased prerogatives, a student's ruthless power to intrude and demand. Young American minds. The space race with Russia. Bech heard himself yield. "O.K. But you're not taking her over into that sorcerer's-apprentice cubbyhole of yours."

Wendell puzzled; he seemed in the half light a blameless furry creature delicately nosing his way through the inscrutable maze of the older man's prejudices. At last he said, "I think I see your worry. You're wrong. There is absolutely no chance of sex. All these things of course are sexual depressants. It's a medical fact."

Bech laughed again. "Don't you dare sexually depress Norma. It's all she and I have any more." But in making this combination of joke and confession, he had waved the maze away and admitted the boy more deeply into his life than he had intended – all because, Bech suspected, at bottom he was afraid of being out-of-date. They agreed that Wendell would bring back some marijuana and they would give him supper. "You'll have to take pot luck," Bech told him.

Norma was not pleased by his arrangements. "How ridiculous of you," she said, "not to trust me alone with that child. You're so immature and proprietorial. You don't own me. I'm a free agent, by your preference."

"I wanted to save you embarrassment," he told her. "I've read the kid's stories; you don't know what goes on in his mind."

"No, after keeping you company for three years I've forgotten what goes on in any normal man's mind."

"Then you admit he *is* a normal man. *Not* a child. O.K. You stay out of that bastard's atelier, or whatever he thinks it is. A pad."

"My, aren't *you* the fierce young lover? I wonder how I survived thirty-odd years out from under your wing."

"You're so self-destructive, I wonder too. And by the way it's not been three years we've been keeping company, it's two and a half."

"You've been counting the minutes. Is my time about up?"

"Norma, *why* do you want to cop out with all these drugs? It's so insulting to the world, to me."

"I want to have an *experience*. I've never had a *ba*by, the only wedding ring I've ever worn is the one you loan me when we go to St. Croix in the winter, I've never been to Pakistan, I'm *never* going to get to Antarctica."

"I'll buy you a freezer."

"That *is* your solution, isn't it? – buy another box. You go from box to box, each one snugger than the last. Well I for one *don't* think your marvelous life-style, your heady mixture of art for art's sake and Depression funk, entirely covers the case. My life is closing in and I hate it and I thought this way I could open it up a little. Just a *little*. Just a teeny *crack*, a splinter of sunshine."

"He's coming back, he's coming back. Your fix is on the way."

"How can I *pos*sibly get high with you and Bea sitting there watching with long faces? It's too grotesque. It's too limiting. My kid sister. My kindly protector. I might as well call my mother – she can fly up from West Orange with the smelling salts."

Bech was grateful to her, for letting her anger, her anguish, recede from the high point reached with the wail that she had never had a baby. He promised, "We'll take it with you."

"Who will? You and Bea?" Norma laughed scornfully. "You two nannies. You're the two most careful people I've ever met."

"We'd *love* to smoke pot. Wouldn't we, Bea? Come on, take a holiday. Break yourself of Nembutal."

Beatrice, who had been cooking lamb chops and setting the table for four while Bech and her sister were obstructively gesturing in the passageway between the kitchen and the dining area, stopped and considered. "Rodney would have a fit."

"Rodney's divorcing you," Bech told her. "Think for yourself."

"It makes it *too* ridiculous," Norma protested. "It takes *all* the adventure out of it."

Bech asked sharply, "Don't you love us?"

"Well," Bea was saying. "On one condition. The children must be asleep. I don't want them to see me do anything wild."

It was Wendell's ingenious idea to have the children sleep on the porch, away from what noise and fumes there might be. He had brought from his magical cache of supplies two sleeping bags, one a double, for the twins. He settled the three small Cooks by pointing out the constellations and the area of the sky where they might, according to this week's newspapers, see shooting stars. "And when you grow tired of that," Wendell said, "close your eyes and listen for an owl."

"Are there owls?" one twin asked.

"Oh, sure."

"On this island?" asked the other.

"One or two. Every island has to have an owl, otherwise the mice would multiply and multiply and there would be no grass, just mice."

"Will it get us?" Donald was the youngest, five.

"You're no mouse," Wendell whispered. "You're a man."

Bech, eavesdropping, felt a pang, and envied the new Americans their easy intermingling with children. How terrible it seemed for him, a Jew, not to have children, to lack a father's dignity. The four adults ate a sober and unconversational meal. Wendell asked Bech what he was writing now, and Bech said nothing, he was proofreading his old books, and finding lots of typos. No wonder the critics had misunderstood him. Norma had changed into a shimmering housecoat, a peacock-colored silk kimono Bech had bought her last Christmas – their second anniversary. He wondered if she had kept on her underclothes, and finally glimpsed, as she bent frowning over her overcooked lamb chop, the reassuring pale edge of a bra. During coffee, he cleared his throat. "Well, kids. Should the séance begin?"

Wendell arranged four chairs in a rectangle, and produced a pipe. It was an ordinary pipe, the kind that authors, in the corny days when Bech's image of the literary life had been formed, used to grip in dust-jacket photographs. Norma took the best chair, the wicker armchair, and impatiently smoked a cigarette while Beatrice cleared away the dishes and checked on the children. They were asleep beneath the stars. Donald had moved his sleeping bag against the girls' and lay with his thumb in his mouth and the other hand on Judy's hair. Beatrice and Bech sat down, and Wendell spoke to them as if they were children, showing them the magic substance, which looked like a residue of pencil shavings in a dirty tobacco pouch, instructing them how to suck in air and smoke simultaneously, how to "swallow" the smoke and hold it down, so the precious narcotic permeated the lungs and stomach and veins and brain. The thoroughness of these instructions aroused in Bech the conviction that something was going to go wrong. He found Wendell as an instructor pompous. In a fury of puffing and expressive inhaling, the boy got the pipe going, and offered first drag to Norma. She had never smoked a pipe, and suffered a convulsion of coughing. Wendell leaned forward and greedily inhaled from midair the smoke she had wasted. He had become, seen sidewise, with his floppy blond hair, a baby lion above a bone; his hungry quick movements were padded with a sinister silence. "Hurry," he hoarsely urged Norma, "don't waste it. It's all I have left from my last trip to Mexico. We may not have enough for four."

She tried again – Bech felt her as tense, rebellious, all too aware that, with the pipe between her teeth, she became a sharp-nosed crone – and coughed again, and complained, "I'm not *get*ting any."

Wendell whirled, barefoot, and, stabbing with the pipestem, said, "Mr. Bech."

The smoke was sweet and circular and soft, softer than Bech could have imagined, ballooning in his mouth and throat and chest like a benevolent thunderhead, like one of those valentines from his childhood that unfolded into a three-dimensional tissue-paper fan. "More," Wendell commanded, thrusting the pipe at him again, ravenously sniffing into himself the shreds of smoke that escaped Bech's sucking. This time there was a faint burning – a ghost of tobacco's unkind rasp. Bech felt himself as a domed chamber, with vaults and upward recesses, welcoming the cloud; he shut his eyes. The color of the sensation was yellow mixed with blue yet in no way green. The base of his throat satisfyingly burned.

While his attention was turned inward, Beatrice was given the pipe. Smoke leaked from her compressed lips; it seemed intensely poignant to Bech that even in depravity she was wearing no lipstick. "Give it to *me*," Norma insisted, greedily reaching. Wendell snatched the pipe against his chest and, with the ardor of a trapped man breathing through a tube, inhaled marijuana. The air began to smell sweetish, flowery, and gentle. Norma jumped from her chair and, kimono shimmering, roughly seized the pipe, so that precious sparks flew. Wendell pushed her back into her chair and, like a mother feeding a baby, insinuated the pipestem between her lips. "Gently, gently," he crooned, "take it in, feel it press against the roof of your mouth, blossoming inside you, hold it fast, fast." His "s"'s were extremely sibilant.

"What's all this hypnosis?" Bech asked. He disliked the deft way Wendell handled Norma. The boy swooped to him and eased the wet pipe into his mouth. "Deeper, deeper, that's it, good...good..."

"It burns," Bech protested.

"It's supposed to," Wendell said. "That's beautiful. You're really getting it."

"Suppose I get sick."

"People never get sick on it, it's a medical fact."

Bech turned to Beatrice and said, "We've raised a generation of amateur pharmacologists."

She had the pipe; handing it back to Wendell, she smiled and pronounced, "Yummy."

Norma kicked her legs and said savagely, "Nothing's *hap*pening. It's not *do*ing anything to me."

"It will, it will," Wendell insisted. He sat down in the fourth chair and passed the pipe to Norma. Fine sweat beaded his plump round face.

"Did you ever notice," Bech asked him, "what nifty legs Norma has? She's old enough to be your biological mother, but condescend to take a gander at her gams. We were the Sinewy Generation."

"What's this generation bag you're in?" Wendell asked him, still rather respectfully English 1020. "Everybody's people."

"*Our* biological mother," Beatrice unexpectedly announced, "thought actually *I* had the better figure. She used to call Norma nobby."

"I *won't* sit here being discussed like a piece of meat," Norma said. Grudgingly she passed the pipe to Bech.

As Bech smoked, Wendell crooned, "Yes, deeper, let it fill you. He really has it. My master, my guru."

"Guru you," Bech said, passing the pipe to Beatrice. He spoke with a rolling slowness, sonorous as an idol's voice. "All you flower types are incipient Fascists." The "a"'s and "s"'s had taken on a private richness in his mouth. "Fascists *manqués*," he said.

Wendell rejected the pipe Beatrice offered him. "Give it back to our teacher. We need his wisdom. We need the fruit of his suffering."

"*Manqué* see, *manqué* do," Bech went on, puffing and inhaling. What a woman must feel like in coitus. More, more.

"*Mon maître*," Wendell sighed, leaning forward, breathless, awed, loving.

"Suffering," Norma sneered. "The day Henry Bech lets himself suffer is a day I'm dying to see. He's the safest man in America, since they retired Tom Dewey. Oh, this is horrible. You're all being so silly and here I sit perfectly sober. I hate it. I hate *all* of you, absolutely."

"Do you hear music?" Bech asked, passing the pipe directly across to Wendell.

"Look at the windows, everybody people," Beatrice said. "They're coming into the room!"

"*Stop* pretending," Norma told her. "You *always* played up to Mother. I'd rather be nobby Norma than bland Bea."

"She's beautiful," Wendell said, to Norma, of Beatrice. "But so are you. The Lord Krishna bestows blessings with a lavish hand."

Norma turned to him and grinned. Her tropism to the phony like a flower's to the sun, Bech thought. Wide warm mouth wherein memories of pleasure have become poisonous words.

Carefully Bech asked the other man, "Why does your face resemble the underside of a colander in which wet lettuce is heaped?" The image seemed both elegant and precise, cruel yet just. But the thought of lettuce troubled his digestion. Grass. All men. Things grow in circles. Stop the circles.

"I sweat easily," Wendell confessed freely. The easy shamelessness purchased for an ingrate generation by decades of poverty and war.

"And write badly," Bech said.

Wendell was unabashed. He said, "You haven't seen my new stuff. It's really terrifically controlled. I'm letting the things dominate the emotions instead of vice versa. Don't you think, since the *Wake*, emotions have about had it in prose?"

"Talk to *me*," Norma said. "*He's* absolutely self-obsessed."

Wendell told her simply, "He's my god."

Beatrice was asking, "Whose turn is it? Isn't anybody else worried about the windows?" Wendell gave her the pipe. She smoked and said, "It tastes like dregs."

When she offered the pipe to Bech, he gingerly waved it away. He felt that the summit of his apotheosis had slipped by, replaced by a widespread sliding. His perceptions were clear, he felt them all trying to get through to him, Norma seeking love, Wendell praise, Beatrice a few more days of free vacation; but these arrows of demand were directed at an object in metamorphosis. Bech's chest was sloping upward, trying to lift his head into steadiness, as when, thirty years ago, carsick on the long subway ride to his Brooklyn uncles, he would fix his eyes in a death grip on his own reflection in the shuddering black glass. The funny wool Buster Brown cap his mother made him wear, his pale small face, old for his age. The ultimate deliverance of the final stomach-wrenching stop. In the lower edge of his vision Norma leaped up and grabbed the pipe from Beatrice. Something fell. Sparks. Both women scrambled on the floor. Norma arose in her shimmering kimono and majestically complained, "It's out. It's all gone. Damn you, greedy Bea!"

"Back to Mexico," Bech called. His own voice came from afar, through blankets of a gathering expectancy, the expanding motionlessness of nausea. But he did not know for a certainty that he was going to be sick until Norma's voice, a few feet away in the sliding obfuscation, as sharp and small as something seen in reversed binoculars, announced, "Henry, you're absolutely yellow!"

In the bathroom mirror he saw that she was right. The blood had drained from his face, leaving like a scum the tallow of his summer tan, and a mauve blotch of sunburn on his melancholy nose. Face he had glimpsed at a thousand junctures, in barbershops and barrooms, in subways and airplane windows above the Black Sea, before shaving and after lovemaking, it witlessly smiled, the eyes very tired. Bech kneeled and submitted to the dark ecstasy of being eclipsed, his brain shouldered into nothingness by the violence of the inversion whereby his stomach emptied itself, repeatedly, until a satisfying pain scraped tears from his eyes, and he was clean.

Beatrice sat alone in the living room, beside the dead fireplace. Bech asked her, "Where is everybody?"

She said, unmoving, uncomplaining, "They went outside and about two minutes ago I heard his car motor start."

Bech, shaken but sane, said, "Another medical fact exploded."

Beatrice looked at him questioningly. Flirting her head, Bech thought, like Norma. Sisters. A stick refracted in water. Our biological mother.

He explained, "A, the little bastard tells me it won't make me sick, and B, he solemnly swears it's a sexual depressant."

"You don't think – they went back to his room?"

"Sure. Don't you?"

Beatrice nodded. "That's how she is. That's how she's always been."

Bech looked around him, and saw that the familiar objects –
the jar of dried bayberry; the loose shell collections, sandy and ill-
smelling; the damp stack of books on the sofa – still wore one
final, gossamer thickness of the mystery in which marijuana had
clothed them. He asked Bea, "How are you feeling? Do the
windows still worry you?"

"I've been sitting here watching them," she said. "I keep
thinking they're going to tip and fall into the room, but I guess
they won't really."

"They might," Bech advised her. "Don't sell your intuitions
short."

"Please, could you sit down beside me and watch them with
me? I know it's silly, but it would be a help."

He obeyed, moving Norma's wicker chair close to Bea, and
observed that indeed the window frames, painted white in
unpainted plank walls, did have the potentiality of animation,
and a disturbing pressingness. Their center of gravity seemed to
shift from one corner to the other. He discovered he had taken
Bea's hand – limp, cool, less bony than Norma's – into his. She
gradually turned her head, and he turned his face away, embarrassed that the scent of vomit would be still on his breath. "Let's
go outside on the porch," he suggested.

The stars overhead were close and ripe. What was that sentence in *Ulysses*? Bloom and Stephen emerging from the house
to urinate, suddenly looking up – *The heaventree of stars hung
with humid nightblue fruit*. Bech felt a sadness, a terror, that
he had not written it. And never would. A child whimpered
and rustled in its sleep. Beatrice was wearing a loose pale dress
luminous in the air of the dark porch. The night was moist, alive;
lights along the horizon pulsed. The bell buoy clanged on a
noiseless swell. She sat in a chair against the shingled wall and
he took a chair facing her, his back to the sea. She asked, "Do
you feel betrayed?"

He tried to think, scanned the scattered stars of his decaying
brain for the answer. "Somewhat. But I've had it coming to me.
I've been getting on her nerves deliberately."

"Like me and Rodney."

He didn't answer, not comprehending and marveling instead

how, when the woman crossed and recrossed her legs, it could have been Norma – a gentler, younger Norma.

She clarified, "I forced the divorce."

The child who had whimpered now cried aloud; it was little Donald, pronouncing hollowly, "Owl!"

Beatrice, struggling for control against her body's slowness, rose and went to the child, kneeled and woke him. "No owl," she said. "Just Mommy." With that ancient strange strength of mothers she pulled him from the sleeping bag and carried him back in her arms to her chair. "No owl," she repeated, rocking gently, "just Mommy and Uncle Harry and the bell buoy."

"You smell funny," the child told her.

"Like what funny?"

"Like sort of candy."

"Donald," Bech said, "we'd never eat any candy without telling you. We'd never be so mean."

There was no answer; he was asleep again.

"I admire you," Beatrice said at last, the lulling rocking motion still in her voice, "for being yourself."

"I've tried being other people," Bech said, fending, "but nobody was convinced."

"I love your book," she went on. "I didn't know how to tell you, but I always rather sneered at you, I thought of you as part of Norma's phony crowd, but your writing, it's terribly tender. There's something in you that you keep safe from all of us."

As always when his writing was discussed to his face, a precarious trembling entered Bech's chest: a case of crystal when heavy footsteps pass. He had the usual wild itch to run, to disclaim, to shut his eyes in ecstasy. More, more. He protested, "Why didn't anybody at least knock on the door when I was dying in the bathroom? I haven't whoopsed like that since the army."

"I wanted to, but I couldn't move. Norma said it was just your way of always being the center of attention."

"That bitch. Did she really run off with that woolly little prep-school snot?"

Beatrice said, with an emphatic intonation dimly, thrillingly familiar, "You *are* jealous. You *do* love her."

Bech said, "I just don't like creative-writing students pushing me out of my bed. I make a good Tiresias but I'm a poor Fisher King."

There was no answer; he sensed she was crying. Desperately changing the subject, he waved toward a distant light, whirling, swollen by the mist. "That whole headland," he said, "is owned by an ex-member of the Communist Party, and he spends all his time putting up No Trespassing signs."

"You're nice," Beatrice sobbed, the child at rest in her arms.

A motor approached down the muffling sandy road. Headlights raked the porch rail, and doubled footsteps crashed through the cottage. Norma and Wendell emerged onto the porch, Wendell carrying a messy thickness of typewriter paper. "Well," Bech said, "that didn't take long. We thought you'd be gone for the night. Or is it dawn?"

"Oh, Henry," Norma said, "you think *every*thing is sex. We went back to Wendell's place to flush his LSD down the toilet, he felt so guilty when you got sick."

"Never again for me, Mr. Bech. I'm out of that subconscious bag. Hey, I brought along a section of my thing, it's not exactly a novel, you don't have to read it now if you don't want to."

"I couldn't," Bech said. "Not if it makes distinctions."

Norma felt the changed atmosphere and accused her sister, "Have you been boring Henry with what an awful person I am? How could the two of you i*mag*ine I'd misbe*have* with this *boy* under your noses? Surely I'm subtler than *that*."

Bech said, "We thought you might be high on pot."

Norma triumphantly complained, "I never got *any*thing. And I'm *pos*itive the rest of you faked it." But, when Wendell had been sent home and the children had been tucked into their bunks, she fell asleep with such a tranced soundness that Bech, insomniac, sneaked from her side and safely slept with Beatrice. He found her lying awake waiting for him. By fall the word went out on the literary circuit that Bech had shifted mistresses again.

BECH PANICS

THIS MOMENT in Bech's pilgrimage must be approached reverently, hesitantly, as befits a mystery. We have these few slides: Bech posing before a roomful of well-groomed girls spread seraglio-style on the floor, Bech lying awake in the frilly guest room of a dormitory, Bech conversing beside a granite chapel with a woman in a purple catsuit, Bech throwing himself like a seed upon the leafy sweet earth of Virginia, within a grove of oaks on the edge of the campus, and mutely begging Someone, Something, for mercy. Otherwise, there is semi-darkness, and the oppressive roar of the fan that cools the projector, and the fumbling, snapping noises as the projectionist irritably hunts for slides that are not there. What made Bech panic? That particular March, amid the ripening aromas of rural Virginia, in that lake of worshipful girls?

All winter he had felt uneasy, idle, irritable, displaced. He had broken with Norma and was seeing Bea. The train ride up to Ossining was dreary, and the children seemed, to this bachelor, surprisingly omnipresent; the twin girls sat up watching television until "Uncle Harry" himself was nodding, and then in the heart of the night little Donald would sleepwalk, sobbing, into the bed where Bech lay with his pale, gentle, plump beloved. The first time the child, in blind search of his mother, had touched Bech's hairy body, he had screamed, and in turn Bech had screamed. Though Donald, who had few preconceptions, soon grew adept at sorting out the muddle of flesh he sometimes found in his mother's bed, Bech on his side never quite adjusted to the smooth transition between Bea's lovemaking and her mothering. Her tone of voice, the curve of her gestures, seemed the same. He, Bech, forty-four and internationally famous, and this towheaded male toddler depended parallel from the same broad body, the same silken breasts and belly, the same drowsy croons and intuitive caresses. Of course, abstractly, he knew it to be so – Freud tells us, all love is one, indivisible, like electricity – but concretely this celibate man of letters, who had been an only son and who saw his sister's family in Cincinnati less than once a year, felt offended at his immersion in the ooze of familial promiscuity. It robbed sex of grandeur if, with Bech's spunk still dribbling from her vagina and her startled yips of pleasure still ringing in his dreams, Bea could rouse and turn and almost identically minister to a tot's fit of night-fright. It made her faintly comical and unappetizing, like the giant milk dispenser in a luncheonette. Sometimes, when she had not bothered to put on her nightie, or had been unable to find where their amorous violence had tossed it, she nestled the boy to sleep against her naked breasts and Bech would find himself curled against her cool backside, puzzled by priorities and discomfited by the untoward development of jealousy's adamant erection.

His attempts to separate her from her family were not successful. Once he stayed at a motel near the railroad station, and took her out, in her own car, on a "date" that was to proceed, after dinner, to his hired room, and was to end with Bea's return home no later than midnight, since the babysitter was the fifteen-year-old daughter of the local Methodist minister. But the over-filling meal at a boorish roadside restaurant, and their furtive decelerated glide through the crackling gravel courtyard of the motel (where a Kiwanis banquet was in progress, and had hogged all the parking spaces), and his fumbly rush to open the tricky aluminoid lock-knob of his door and to stuff his illicit guest out of sight, and the macabre interior of oak-imitating wallboard and framed big-eyed pastels that embowered them proved in sum withering to Bech's potency. Though his suburban mistress gra-ciously, following less her own instincts than the exemplary drift of certain contemporary novels, tried to bring his weakling member to strength by wrapping it in the velvet bandages of her lips, Bech couldn't achieve more than a two-thirds hard-on, which diminished to an even less usable fraction whenever the starchy fare within their stomachs rumbled, or his gaze met that of a pastel waif, or the Kiwanis broke into another salvo of applause, or Bea's beginning yips frightened him up from the primordial level where he was, at last, beginning to thrive. Who, as a rabbi once said, by taking thought can add a cubit to his height? Not Bech, though he tried. The minister's freckle-faced daughter was asleep on the sofa when he and Bea, as caked with dried sweat as a pair of squash players, finally returned.

In Manhattan, on Bech's cozy turf, the problem was different: Bea underwent a disquieting change. At home in Bech's drab large rooms at Riverside and 99th, she became slangy, bossy, twitchy, somewhat sluttish, too much at home – she became in short like her rejected sister Norma. The Latchett blood ran tart at the scent of marriage; old Judge Latchett, when alive, had been one of the hanginger magistrates in Jersey City. Bea, as her underwear and Bech's socks dried together on the bathroom radiator, tended to pontificate. "You should get out of these dreary rooms, Henry. They're half the reason you're blocked."

"Am I blocked? I'd just thought of myself as a slow typist."

"What do you do, hit the space bar once a day?"

"Ouch."

"I'm sorry, that did sound bitchy. But it makes me *sad*, to see someone of your beautiful gifts stagnating."

"Maybe I have a beautiful gift for stagnation."

"Come live with me."

"What about the neighbors? What about the children?"

"The neighbors don't care. The children love you. Come live with us and see in the spring. You're dying of carbon monoxide down here."

"I'd drown in flesh up there. You pin me down and the others play pile-on."

"Only Donald. And aren't you funny about that? Rodney and I absolutely agreed, a child shouldn't be excluded from *any*thing physical. We thought *noth*ing of being nude in front of them."

"Spare me the picture, it's like a Grünewald. You and Rodney, as I understand it, agreed about everything."

"Well at least neither of us were squeamish old maids."

"Unlike a certain *écrivain juif, n'est-ce pas?*"

"You're very good at making me sound like a bitch. But I honestly *do* believe, Henry, you need to do something different with yourself."

"Such as integrating Suburbia. Henry Bech, Ossining's one-man ghetto."

"It's not like that. It's not like a Polish village. Nobody thinks in these categories any more."

"Will I be asked to join the Kiwanis? Does a mama's lover qualify to join the P.-T.A.?"

"They don't call it the P.-T.A. any more."

"Bea baby, here I stand, I can do no other. I've lived here twenty years."

"That is precisely your problem."

"Every shop on Broadway knows me. From the Chinese laundry to the Swedish bakery. From Fruit House to Japanese Foodland. There he goes, they say, Old Man Bech, a legend in his lifetime. Or, as the colored on the block call me, Cheesecake Charley, the last of the Joe Louis liberals."

"You're really terrified, aren't you," Bea said, "of having a serious conversation?"

The telephone rang. Without the telephone, Bech wondered, how would we ever avoid proposing marriage? The instrument sat by a window, on a table with a chessboard inlaid into veneer warped by years of disuse and steam heat. A dust-drenched shaft of four o'clock sun dwelt tepidly upon a split seam in the sofa cover, a scoop-shaped dent in the lampshade, and a yellowing stack of unread presentation copies of once-new novels, arranged to lend stability to the chess table's rickety, dried-out legs. The phone directory was years old and its cover was scrawled with numbers that Bech no longer called, including, in happy crimson greedily inked early one morning, Norma's. The receiver, filmed by air pollution, held a history of fingerprints. "Hello?"

"Mistah Bech? Is that Hainry Bech the authuh?"

"Could be," Bech said. The Southern voice, delightfully female, went on, with a lacy interweave of cajoling and hysterical intonations, to propose that he come and speak or read, whicheveh he prefuhhed, to a girls' college in Virginia. Bech said, "I'm sorry, I don't generally do that sort of thing."

"Oh Mistah Bech, Ah *knew* you'd say that, ouah English instructah, a Miss Eisenbraun, ah don't suppose you know heh, *sayd* you were immensely hard to gait, but you hev *so* many fayuns among the girls heah, we're all just hopin' against hope."

"Well," Bech said – a bad word choice, in the situation.

The voice must have sensed he found the accent seductive, for it deepened. "Oueh countrehsaad round heah is eveh so pretteh, the man who wrote *Travel Laaht* owes it to himself to see it, and though to be shooah we all know moneh is no temptation foh a man of yoh statchuh, we have a *goood* speakeh's budget this ye-ah and kin offeh you –" And she named a round figure that did give Bech pause.

He asked, "When would this be?"

"Oh!" – her yip was almost coital – "oh, Misteh Bech, you mean you *maaht*?" Before she let him hang up he had agreed to appear in Virginia next month.

Bea was indignant. "You've lost all your principles. You let yourself be sweet-talked into that."

Bech shrugged. "I'm trying to do something different with myself."

Bea said, "Well I didn't mean letting yourself be cooed at by an auditorium full of fluffy-headed racists."

"I think of it more as being an apostle to the Gentiles."

"You won't speak at Columbia when it's two subway stops away and full of people on your own wavelength, but you'll fly a thousand miles to some third-rate finishing school on the remote chance you can sack out with Scarlett O'Hara. You are sick, Henry. You are weak, and sick."

"Actually," Bech told Bea, "I'll be there two nights. So I can sack out with Melanie too."

Bea began to cry. The inner slump he felt, seeing her fair face sag, was perhaps a premonition of his panic. He tried to joke through it: "Bea baby, I'm just following your orders, I'm going to see spring in in the Southland. They offered me an even grand. I'll buy a triple bed for you, me, and Donald."

Her blue eyes went milky; her lips and lids became the rubbed

pink color of her nipples. She had washed her hair and was
wearing only his silk bathrobe, one Norma had given him in
response to the gift of a kimono, and when Bea bowed her head
and pressed the heels of her hands into her eyes, the lapels parted
and her breasts hung lustrous in his sight. He tried to fetch up
some words of comfort but knew that none would be comfort
enough but the words, "Marry me." So he looked away, past the
dented lampshade, at the framed rectangle of city that he knew
better than he knew his own soul – the fragile forest of television
aerials, the stunted courtyards of leafless ailanthus, the jammed
clockwork of fire escapes. His soul felt nervously suspended
within him, like a snagged counterweight.

Two petite, groomed, curried girls met him at the airport and
drove him in a pink convertible, at great speed, through the
rolling, burgeoning landscape. Spring had arrived here. New
York had been windy and raw. The marzipan monuments of
Washington, seen from the airport, had glittered above cherry
blossoms. Piedmont Air Lines had lifted him and rocked him
above hills dull evergreen on the ridges and fresh deciduous
green in the valleys, where streams twinkled. The shadow of
the plane crossed racetrack ovals and belts of plowed land. Dot-
sized horses slowly traced lines of gallop within fenced diagrams.
Looking down, Bech was dizzy; twice they bounced down
into small airports cut into hillsides. On the third stop, he
alighted. The sun stood midway down the sky, as it had the
day the phone had rung and Bea had mocked his acceptance, but
now the time stood an hour later in the day; it was after five. The
two girls, giggling, gushing, met him and drove him, in a deaf-
ening rush of speed (if the convertible flipped, his head would be
scraped from his shoulders; he foresaw the fireman hosing his
remains from the highway) to a campus, once a great plantation.
Here many girls in high heels and sheer stockings and, Bech felt,
girdles strolled across acres of hilly lawn overswept by the powerful smell of horse manure. In his citified nostrils, the stench
rampaged, but nothing in the genteel appearance of the place
acknowledged it – not the scrubbed and powdered faces of the

girls, nor the brick-and-trim façades of the buildings, nor the magnolia trees thick and lumpy with mauve-and-cream, turnip-shaped buds. It was as if one of his senses had short-circuited to another channel, or as if a school of deaf-mutes were performing a minuet to the mistaken accompaniment of a Wagnerian storm. He felt suddenly, queasily hollow. The declining sun nubbled the lawn's texture with shadowed tufts, and as Bech was led along a flagstone path to his first obligation (an "informal" hour with the Lanier Club, a branch of budding poetesses) profound duplicity seemed to underlie the landscape. Along with the sun's reddening rays and the fecal stench a devastating sadness swept in. He knew that he was going to die. That his best work was behind him. That he had no business here, and was frighteningly far from home.

Bech was uncomfortable in colleges. War had come when he was eighteen, and a precocious acceptance from *Liberty* two years later. He stayed in Germany a year after V-E Day, editing a news-sheet for the U.S. occupation forces in Berlin, and returned home to find his mother dying. She was not quite fifty. When, having surrendered both breasts to the surgeon's knife, she had beat her way back from the underworld of anaesthesia for the final time, Bech felt he knew too much to submit to a college curriculum. He used the GI Bill to take courses at NYU but evaded graduation. He joined the army of vets who believed they had earned the right to invent their lives. He entered a tranced decade of abstract passions, of the exhilarations of type and gossip and nights spent sitting up waiting for the literary renaissance that would surely surpass that of the Twenties by just as much as this war had surpassed, in nobility and breadth and conclusiveness, its predecessor. But it was with the gaunt Titans of modernism, with Joyce and Eliot and Valéry and Rilke, that one must begin. *Make it new. The intolerable wrestle with words and meanings.* Bech weaned himself from the slicks and wormed his way into the quarterlies. *Commentary* let him use a desk. As he confessed to Vera Glavanakova, he wrote poems: thin poems scattered on the page like soot on snow. He reviewed books, any books, history, mysteries, almanacs, memoirs – any-thing printed had magic. For some months he was the cinema critic for an ephemeral journal titled *Displeasure*. Bech was unpre-possessing then, a scuttler, a petty seducer, a bright-eyed bug of a man in those days before whiskey and fame fleshed him out, his head little more than a nose and a cloud of uncombable hair. He was busy and idle, melancholy and happy. Though he rarely crossed the water necessary to leave Manhattan, he was conscious of freedom – his freedom to sleep late, to eat ham, to read the *Arabian Nights* in the 42nd Street library, to sit an hour in the Rembrandt room at the Metropolitan, to chisel those strange early paragraphs, not quite stories, which look opaque when held in the lap but held up to the window reveal a symmetrical pattern of intended veins. In the years before *Travel Light*, he paced his gray city with a hope in his heart, the expectation that, if not this day the next, he would perfectly fuse these stone rectangles around him with the gray rectangles of printed prose. Self-educated, street-educated, then, he was especially vulnerable to the sadness of schools. They stank of country cruelty to him – this herding, this cooping up of people in their animal prime, stunning them with blunt classics, subjecting them to instructors deadened and demented by the torrents of young blood that pass through their terms; just the lip-licking reverence with which professors pronounce the word "students" made Bech recoil.

Our slide shows him posturing in a sumptuous common room whose walls are padded with leatherbound editions of Scott and Carlyle and whose floor is carpeted with decorously arranged specimens of nubility. He was, possibly, as charming and witty as usual – the florid letter of thanks he received in New York from the Lanier Club's secretary suggested so. But to himself his tongue seemed to be moving strangely, as slowly as one of those galloping horses he had seen from a mile in the air, while his real attention was turned inward toward the swelling of his dread, his unprecedented (not even in the freezing, murderous hell of the Battle of the Bulge, endured when he was twenty-one) recognition of horror. The presences at his feet – those seriously sparkling eyes, those earnestly flushed cheeks, those demurely displayed calves and knees – appalled him with the abyss of their innocence. He felt dizzy, stunned. The essence of matter, he saw, is dread. Death hangs behind everything, a real skeleton about to leap through a door in these false walls of books. He saw himself, in this nest of delicate limbs, limbs still ripening toward the wicked seductiveness Nature intended, as a seed among too many eggs, as a gross thrilling intruder, a genuine male intellectual Jew, with hairy armpits and capped molars, a man from the savage North, the North that had once fucked the South so hard it was still trembling – Bech saw himself thus, but as if in a *trompe-l'œil* box whose painted walls counterfeit, from the single perspective of the peephole, three-dimensional furnishings and a succession of archways. He felt what was expected of him, and felt himself performing it, and felt the fakery of the performance, and knew these levels of perception as the shifting sands of absurdity, nullity, death. His death gnawed inside him like a foul parasite while he talked to these charming daughters of fertile Virginia.

One asked him, "Suh, do you feel there is any place left in modern poetry for *rhaam*?"

"For what?" Bech asked, and educed a gale of giggles.

The girl blushed violently, showing blood suddenly as a wound. "For rhy-em," she said. She was a delicate creature, with a small head on a long neck. Her blue eyes behind glasses seemed to be on stalks. The sickness in Bech bit deeper as he apologized, "I'm sorry, I simply didn't hear what you said. You ask about rhyme. I write only prose –"

A sweet chorus of mutters protested that No, his prose was a poet's, was poetry.

He went on, stooping with the pain inside him, amazed to hear himself making a kind of sense, "– but it seems to me rhyme is one of the ways we make things hard for ourselves, make a game out of nothing, so we can win or lose and lighten the, what?, the *indeterminacy* of life. Paul Valéry, somewhere, discusses this, the first line that comes as a gift from the gods and costs nothing, and then the second line that we make ourselves, word by word, straining all our resources, so that it harmonizes with the supernatural first, so that it *rhymes*. He thought, as I remember, that our lives and thoughts and language are all a 'familiar chaos' and that the arbitrary tyranny of a strict prosody goads us to feats of, as it were, rebellion that we couldn't otherwise perform. To this I would only add, and somewhat in contradiction, that rhyme is very ancient, that it marks rhythm, and that much in our natural lives is characterized by rhythm."

"Could you give us an example?" the girl asked.

"For example, lovemaking," Bech said, and to his horror beheld her blush surging up again, and beheld beyond her blush an entire seething universe of brainless breeding, of moist interpenetration, of slippery clinging copulation, of courtship dances and come-on signals, of which her hapless blush, unknown to her, was one. He doubted that he could stand here another minute without fainting. Their massed fertility was overwhelming; each body was being broadened and readied to generate from its own cells a new body to be pushed from the old, and in time to push bodies from itself, and so on into eternity, an ocean of doubling and redoubling cells within which his own conscious moment was soon to wink out. He had had no child. He had spilled his seed upon the ground. Yet we are all seed spilled upon the ground. These thoughts, as Valéry had predicated, did not come neatly, in chiming packets of language, but as slithering, overlapping sensations, microörganisms of thought setting up in sum a panicked sweat on Bech's palms and a palpable nausea behind his belt. He attempted to grin, and the pond of young ladies shuddered, as if a pebble had been dropped among them. In rescue an unseen clock chimed the half-hour, and a matronly voice, in the accents of Manhattan, called, "Girls, we must let our guest eat!"

Bech was led to a cathedral-sized dining room and seated at a table with eight young ladies. A colored girl sat on his right. She was one of two in the school. The student body, by its own petition, in the teeth of parental protests and financial curtailments from the state legislature, had integrated itself. The girl was rather light-skinned, with an Afro hair-do cut like an upright loaf of bread; she spoke to Bech in a voice from which all traces of Dixie had been clipped. "Mr. Bech," she said, "we admire your gifts of language but wonder if you aren't, now and then, somewhat racist?"

"Oh? When?" The presence of food – shrimp salad nested in lettuce, in tulip glasses – had not relieved his panic; he wondered if he dared eat. The shrimp seemed to have retained their legs and eyes.

"In *Travel Light*, for example, you keep calling Roxanne a Negress."

"But she was one." He added, "I loved Roxanne."

"The fact is, the word has distinctly racist overtones."

"Well, what should we call them?"

"I suppose you might say 'black women.'" But her tone implied that she, like a spinster lecturing on male anatomy, would rather not call certain things anything at all. Bech was momentarily roused from his funk by this threat, that there were holes in language, things that could not be named. He told her, "Calling you a black woman is as inexact as calling me a pink man."

She responded promptly. "Calling me a Negress is as insulting as calling you a kike."

He liked the way she said it. Flat, firm, clear. Fuck you. Black is beautiful. Forced by the argument to see her color, he saw that her loaf of hair was cinnamon-tinted and a spatter of freckles saddled the bridge of her nose. Through this he saw, in a sliding succession of imagery that dumped him back into terror, an Irish overseer raping a slave, vomiting slaves packed beneath the deck of a bucking ship, Africans selling Africans, tribes of all colors torturing one another, Iroquois thrusting firebrands down the throats of Jesuits, Chinese skinning each other in careful strips, predation and cruelty reaching back past Man to the dawn of life, paramecia in a drop of water, aeons of evolution, each turn of beak or stretch of toe shaped by a geological patter of individual deaths. His words echoed weakly in the deep well of this vision. "A black woman could be a woman who's painted herself black. 'Negro' designates a scientific racial grouping, like Caucasian or Mongolian. I use it without prejudice."

"How do you feel then about 'Jewess'?"

Bech lied; the word made him wince. "Just as I do about 'duchess.'"

"As to your love," the girl went on, still with deliberate dignity, holding her head erect as if balancing something upon it and addressing the entire table in full consciousness of dominating, "we've had enough of your love. You've been loving us down in Georgia and Mississippi for hundreds of years. We've been loved to death, we want now to be respected."

"By which you mean," Bech told her, "you want to be feared."

A white girl at the table broke in with hasty politeness. "Pahdon me, Lana Jane, but Misteh Bech, do you *realleh* believe in races? The school I went to befoh, they made us read a Misteh Carleton Coon? He says, I don't believe a word of it but he says, black folks have longer *heels*, thet's whah the men run fastuh in *sprints*?"

"Black *people*, Cindy," Lana Jane corrected. "Not black 'folks.'" At her prim shudder the ring of pink faces broke into relieved, excessive laughter.

Cindy blushed but was not deflected; she continued, "Also he says, Misteh Bech, that they have thinneh *skulls*, thet's whah so many dah in the prahz ring? We used to be told they had *thick*eh!"

Puzzled by the intensity of her blush, Bech saw that for this excited young convert to liberalism anthropology was as titillating as pornography. He saw that even in an age of science and unbelief our ideas are dreams, styles, superstitions, mere animal noises intended to repel or attract. He looked around the ring of munching females and saw their bodies as a Martian or a mollusc might see them, as pulpy stalks of bundled nerves oddly pinched to a bud of concentration in the head, a hairy bone knob holding some pounds of jelly in which a trillion circuits, mostly dead, kept records, coded motor operations, and generated an excess of electricity that pressed into the hairless side of the head and leaked through the orifices, in the form of pained, hopeful noises and a simian dance of wrinkles. Impossible mirage! A blot on nothingness. And to think that all the efforts of his life – his preening, his lovemaking, his typing – boiled down to the attempt to displace a few sparks, to bias a few circuits, within some random other scoops of jelly that would, in less time than it takes the Andreas Fault to shrug or the tail-tip star of Scorpio to crawl an inch across the map of Heaven, be utterly dissolved. The widest fame and most enduring excellence shrank to nothing in this perspective. As Bech ate, mechanically offering votive bits of dead lamb to the terror enthroned within him, he saw that the void should have been left unvexed, should have been spared this trouble of matter, of life, and, worst, of consciousness.

Slide Two. His bedroom was the corner first-floor room of a large new neo-Georgian dorm. Locked glass doors discreetly separated his quarters from the corridors where virginity slept in rows. But frilly touches whispered and giggled in the room – the beribboned lampshade, the petticoat curtains of dotted swiss beneath the velvet drapes, the abundance of lace runners and china figurines on dainty tables. His bed, with its two plumped pillows one on top of the other like a Pop Art sandwich, its brocaded coverlet turned down along one corner like an Open Here tab on a cereal box, seemed artificially crisp and clean: a hospital bed. And indeed, like an infirm man, he discovered he could lie only in one position, on his back. To turn onto either side was to tip himself toward the edge of a chasm; to roll over onto his belly was to risk drowning in the oblivion that bubbled up from the darkness heated by his own body. The college noises beyond his windows drifted into silence. The last farewell was called, the last high heels tapped down a flagstone path. Chapel bells tolled the quarter hours. The land beyond the campus made itself heard in the sounds of a freight train, a whippoorwill, a horse faintly whinnying in some midnight meadow where manure and grass played yin and yang. Bech tried concentrating on these noises, pressing from them, by sheer force of attention, the balm of their undeniability, the innocence that somehow characterized their simple existence, considered apart from their attributes. All things have the same existence, share the same atoms, reshuffled: grass into manure, flesh into worms. But there was a blackness beneath this thought like that of a midnight pane from which frost is rubbed. He tried to relive pleasantly his evening triumph, his so warmly applauded reading: he had read a long section from *Brother Pig*, the part where the hero seduces his stepdaughter in the bowling alley, behind the pin-setting machine, and had been amazed, as he read, by the coherence of the words, by their fearless

onward march. The blanket of applause, remembered, oppressed
him. He tried word games. He went through the alphabet with
world saviors: Attila, Buddha, Christ, Danton . . . Woodrow Wilson, Xerxes the Great, Brigham Young, Zoroaster. There was
some slight comfort in the realization that the world had survived
all its saviors, but Bech had not put himself to sleep. His panic, like
a pain which intensifies when we dwell upon it, when we inflame
it with undivided attention, felt worse away from the wash of
applause; yet, like a wound tentatively defined by the body's
efforts of asepsis and rejection, it was revealing a certain shape. It
felt pasty and stiff. Mixed with the fear, a kind of coagulant, was
shame: shame at his having a "religious crisis" that, by all standard
psychology, should have been digested in early adolescence, along
with post-masturbatory guilt; shame at the degradation of a onetime disciple of those great secreters Flaubert and Joyce into a slick
crowd-pleaser at whistle-stop colleges; shame at having argued
with a Negress, at having made Bea cry, at having proved himself,
in his relations with all women from his mother on, a thin-
skinned, fastidious, skittish, slyly clowning, cold-blooded ingrate.
His mother. He had taken her death as a bump in his road, an
inconvenience in his busy postwar reconstruction of himself. He
had seen death in war, and had learned to sneer at its perennial
melodrama. He had denied his mother's death the reality it must
have had to her, this chasm that numbed as it swallowed; and now
it was swallowing him. He had scarcely mourned. No one sat
shivah. No Kaddish had been said. Six thousand years of obser-
vance had been overturned in Bech. He was cold, as Flaubert and
Joyce were cold. He denied his characters the final measure of
love, that would enable them to break free of his favorite tropes,
the ruts of his phrases, the chains that rattled whenever he sat down
at the typewriter.

     He tried to analyze himself. He reasoned that since the id
cannot entertain the concept of death, which by being not-
being is nothing to be afraid of, his fear must be of something
narrower, more pointed and printed. He was afraid that his critics
were right. That his works were indeed flimsy, unfelt, flashy, and
centrifugal. That the proper penance for his artistic sins was
silence and reduction; that his id, in collaboration with the

superego figures of Alfred Kazin and Dwight Macdonald, had successfully reduced him to artistic impotence and was now seeking, in its rambling, large-hearted way, his personal extinction: hence his pipsqueak ego's present flutter of protest. As soon sleep in a cement mixer as amid these revelations. Sleep, the foreshadow of death, the dab of poison we daily take to forestall convulsion, became impossible. The only position in which Bech could even half-relax was on his back, his head propped on both pillows to hold him above smothering, his limbs held steady in the fantasy that he was a china figurine, fragile, cool, and miniature, cupped in a massive hand. Thus Bech tricked himself, a moment after the chapel bells had struck three, into sleep – itself a devastating testimony to the body's power to drag us down with it. His dreams, strange to report, were light as feathers, and blew this way and that. In one of them, he talked fluid French with Paul Valéry, who looked like the late Mischa Auer.

He awoke stiff. He moved from bed to suitcase to bathroom with an old man's self-dramatizing crouch. By the light of this new day, through the murky lens of his panic, objects – objects, those atomic mirages with edges that hurt – appeared mock-heroic in their persistence, their quixotic loyalty to the shapes in which chance has cast them. They seemed to be watching him, to be animated by their witness of his plight. Thus, like primitive Man, he began to personify the universe. He shat plenteously, hot gaseous stuff acidified into diarrhoea, he supposed, by his fear. He reflected how, these last unproductive years, his output of excrement had grown so that instead of an efficient five minutes he seemed to spend most of his work morning trapped on the toilet, leafing sadly through *Commentary* and *Encounter*. Elimination had become Bech's forte: he answered letters with the promptness of a backboard, he mailed his loose-paper files to the Library of Congress twice a year. He had become a compulsive wastebasket-emptier. Toilets, mailboxes, cunts were all the receptacles of a fanatic and incessant attempt to lighten himself, as if to fly. Standing at the basin of lavender porcelain (which, newly installed, boasted one of those single faucet controls that blends hot and cold like a joy stick on the old biplanes) Bech, far from his figurine fantasy of last night, felt precariously tall: a

sky-high prodigy about to topple, or crumple. His ministrations to himself – brushing his teeth, wiping his anus, shaving
his jaw – seemed laid upon his body from a cosmic distance, amid
the held breath of inert artifacts, frozen presences he believed
were wishing him well. He was especially encouraged, and
touched, by the elfin bar of motel-size mauve soap his fingers
unwrapped across an interstellar gap.

But stepping, dressed, into the sunshine, Bech was crushed by
the heedless scale of outdoors. He was overwhelmed by the
multiple transparent signs – the buds, the twittering, the spring-
tide glisten – of growth and natural process, the inhuman mutual
consumption that is Nature. A zephyr stained by manure recalled
his first flash of terror. He ate breakfast stunned, with a tickling in
his nose that might have been the wish to cry. Yet the eight girls
seated with him – eight new ones, all Caucasian – pretended to
find his responses adequate, even amusing. As he was being led to
his first display case of the day, a seminar in the postwar American
novel, a *zaftig* woman in a purple catsuit accosted him by the
chapel. She was lithe, rather short, in her thirties, with brushed-
back black hair of which some strands kept drifting onto her
temple and cheeks and needed to be brushed back with her
fingers, which she did deftly, cleverly, continuously. Her lips
were long; the upper bore a faint mustache. Her nose too was
long, with something hearteningly developed and intelligent
about the modulations from tip to nostril wing. When she
spoke, it was not with a Southern accent but with Bech's own,
the graceless but rapid and obligingly enunciatory accent of New
York Jews.

She said, "Henry—may I?—I know you're being rushed to
some important destination, but my girls, the girls you spoke to last
night, the Lanier Club, were so, I guess the word is 'impressed,'
that they cooked up a rather impertinent, not to say importunate,
request that none of them had the nerve to deliver. So they asked
me to. I'm their adviser. I was impressed, too, by the way. The
name is Ruth Eisenbraun." She offered her hand.

Bech accepted the offer. Her hand was warmer than porcelain,
yet exact, and firm. He asked, "What are you doing amid all this
alien corn, Ruth?"

The woman said, "Don't knock it, it's a living. This is my fourth year, actually. I like it here. The girls are immensely sweet, and not all of them are dumb. It's a place where you can see things happening, you can actually *see* these kids loosening up. Your consenting to come down here is a tremendous boost to the cause." She took her hand back from his to make the gestures needed to dramatize "loosening up" and "tremendous." In the sunshine glare reflected from the granite chapel Bech could admire the nimble and even flow of her expressiveness; he enjoyed the sensation, as of a tailor's measurements, of her coolly sizing him up even as she maintained a screen of patter, every dry and rapid turn of phrase a calibrated, unembarrassed offer of herself. "In fact," she was saying, "the society as a whole is loosening up. If I were a black, the South is where I'd prefer to be. Nobody in the North believes now in integration because they've never had it, but here, in an economic and social way, they've had integration all along, though of course entirely on the Man's terms. My girls, at least until they marry the local sheriff or Coke distributor, are really very naïvely" – again, arabesques with her hands – "sin*cere*ly excited about the idea that black people are *people*. I find them sweet. After five years at CCNY, this has been a gigantic breath of fresh air. You can honestly tell yourself you're *teach*ing these girls." And by repeating "girls" so often, she was burning into Bech's fogged brain awareness that she, something of a girl herself, was also something more.

"What did they want to ask me?"

"Oh, yes. And that seminar is waiting. You know what their nickname for it is? – 'Bellow's Belles.' Now *that's* been turned into 'Bellow's Balls.' Isn't that a good sign, that they can be obscene? *My* girls delegated me to ask *you*" – and Bech inwardly questioned the source of that delegation – "if you'd please, please, *pretty* please be willing to judge a poetry contest of theirs. I got your schedule from Dean Coates and see you have a big empty slot late this afternoon; if you could *pos*sibly make it over to Ruffin Hall at five, they will recite for you in their best Sunday School manner some awful doggerel you can take back to your room, and give us the verdict before you go tomorrow. It is an imposition, I know. I know, I know. But they'll be so thrilled they'll *melt*."

The zipper of her catsuit was open three inches below the base of her throat. If he pulled the zipper down six inches more, Bech estimated, he would discover that she was wearing no bra. Not to mention no girdle. "I'd be pleased to," he said. "Honored, you can tell them."

"God, that's swell of you," Miss Eisenbraun responded briskly. "I hope you weren't hoping to have a nap this afternoon."

"In fact," he told her, "I didn't get much sleep. I feel very strange."

"In what way strange?" She looked up into his face like a dentist who had asked him to open his mouth. She was interested. If he had said hemorrhoids, she would still be interested. A Jewish mother's clinical curiosity. Abigail Bech had always been prying, poking.

"I can't describe it. *Angst*. I'm afraid of dying. Everything is so implacable. Maybe it's all these earth-smells so suddenly."

She smiled and deeply inhaled. When she sniffed, her upper lip broadened, furry. The forgotten downiness of Jewish women. Their hairy thighs. "It's worst in spring," she said. "You get acclimated. May I ask, have you ever been in analysis?"

His escort of virgins, which had discreetly withdrawn several yards when Miss Eisenbraun had pulled her ambush, rustled nervously. Bech bowed. "I am awaited." Trying to rise to jauntiness from in under her implication that he was mad, he added, "See you later, alligator."

"In a while, crocodile": streetcorner yids yukking it up in the land of milk and honey, giving the gentle indigenes something to giggle about. But with her he had been able to ignore, for an absent-minded moment, the gnawing of the worm inside.

How strange, really, his condition was! As absorbing as pain, yet painless. As world-transforming as drunkenness, yet with no horizon of sobriety. As debilitating, inwardly, as a severed spine yet permitting him, outwardly, a convincing version of his usual performance. Which proved, if proof were needed, how much of a performance it was. Who was he? A Jew, a modern man, a writer, a bachelor, a loner, a loss. A con artist in the days of academic modernism undergoing a Victorian shudder. A white monkey hung far out on a spindly heaventree of stars. A fleck of dust condemned to know it is a fleck of dust. A mouse in a furnace. A smothered scream.

His fear, like a fever or deep humiliation, bared the beauty veiled by things. His dead eyes, cleansed of healthy egotism, discovered a startled tenderness, like a virgin's whisper, in every twig, cloud, brick, pebble, shoe, ankle, window mullion, and bottle-glass tint of distant hill. Bech had moved, in this compressed religious evolution of his, from the morning's raw animism to an afternoon of natural romanticism, of pantheistic pangs. Between lunch (creamed asparagus, French fries, and meatloaf) and the poetry contest he was free; he took a long solitary walk around the edges of the campus, inhaling the strenuous odors, being witness to myriad thrusts of new growth through the woodland's floor of mulching leaves. Life chasing its own tail. Bech lifted his eyes to the ridges receding from green to blue, and the grandeur of the theatre in which Nature stages its imbecile cycle struck him afresh and enlarged the sore accretion of fear he carried inside him as unlodgeably as an elastic young wife carries within her womb her first fruit. He felt increasingly hopeless; he could never be delivered of this. In a secluded, sloping patch of oaks, he threw himself with a grunt of decision onto the damp earth, and begged Someone, Something, for mercy. He had created God. And now the silence of the created universe acquired for Bech a miraculous quality of willed reserve, of divine tact that would let him abjectly pray on a patch of mud and make no answer but the familiar ones of rustle, of whisper, of invisible growth like a net sinking slowly deeper into the sea of the sky; of gradual realization that the earth is populated infinitely, that a slithering slug was slowly causing a dead oak leaf to lift and a research team of red ants were industriously testing a sudden morsel, Bech's thumb, descended incarnate.

Eventually the author arose and tried to brush the dirt from his knees and elbows. To his fear, and shame, was added anger, anger at the universe for having extracted prayer from him. Yet his head felt lighter; he walked to Ruffin Hall in the mood of a condemned spy who, entering the courtyard where the firing squad waits, at least leaves behind his dank cell. When the girls read their poetry, each word hit him like a bullet. The girl with the small head and the long neck read:

> Air, that transparent fire
> our red earth burns
> as we daily expire,
> sing! As water in urns
> whispers of rivers and wharves,
> sing, life, within the jar
> each warm soul carves
> from this cold star.

There was more to this poem, about Nature, about fine-veined leaves and twigs sharp as bird feet, and more poems, concerning meadows and horses and Panlike apparitions that Bech took to be college boys with sticks of pot, and then more poets, a heavy mannish girl with an unfortunate way of rolling her lips after each long Roethkësque line, and a nun-pale child who indicted our bombing of thatched villages with clotted Lowellian tropes, and a budding Tallulah swayed equally by Allen Ginsburg and Edna St. Vincent Millay; but Bech's ears closed, his scraped heart flinched. These youthful hearts, he saw, knew all that he knew, but as one knows the rules of a game there is no obligation to play; the sealed structure of naturalism was a school to them, a prison to him. In conclusion, a splendid, goggle-eyed beauty incanted some Lanier, from "The Marshes of Glynn," the great hymn that begins

> As the marsh-hen secretly builds on the watery sod,
> Behold I will build me a nest on the greatness of God:

and goes on

> And the sea lends large, as the marsh: lo, out of his plenty the sea
> Pours fast: full soon the time of the flood-tide must be:

and ends

The tide is in his ecstasy.
The tide is at his highest height:
And it is night.

Something filmed Bech's eyes, less full-formed tears than the blurry reaction pollen excites in the allergic.

After the poetry reading, there was supper at Madame President's – you know her: hydrangea hair and sweeping manners and a listening smile as keen and neat as an ivory comb. And then there was a symposium, with three students and two members of the English faculty and Bech himself, on "The Destiny of the Novel in a Non-Linear Future." And then a party at the home of the chairman of the department, a bluff old Chaucerian with a flesh-colored hearing aid tucked behind his ear like a wad of chewing gum. The guests came up and performed obeisances, jocular or grave, to Bech, their distinguished interloper, and then resumed seething among each other in the fraught patterns of rivalry and erotic attraction that prevail in English departments everywhere. Amid them Bech felt slow-witted and paunchy; writers are not scholars but athletes, who grow beerbellies after thirty. Miss Eisenbraun detached herself and walked him back across the campus. A pandering Southern moon rode above the magnolias and the cupolas.

"You were wonderful tonight," she told him.

"Oh?" Bech said. "I found myself very lumpish."

"You're just marvelously kind to children and bores," she pursued.

"Yes. Fascinating adults are where I fall down."

A little pause, three footsteps' worth, as if to measure the depth of the transaction they were contemplating. One, two, three: a moderate reading. Yet to lift them back over the sill of silence into conversation, a self-conscious effort, something kept in a felt-lined drawer, was needed. She pulled out French.

"*Votre malaise – est-il passé?*" The language of diplomacy.

"*Il passe, mais très lentement,*" Bech said. "It's becoming part of me."

"Maybe your room has depressed you. Their guest accommodations are terribly little-girly and sterile."

"Exactly. Sterile. I feel I'm an infection. I'm the only germ in a porcelain universe."

She laughed, uncertain. They had reached the glass doors of the dormitory where he slept. An owl hooted. The moon frosted with silver a distant ridge. He wondered if in his room his fear would make him pray again. A muffled radio somewhere played country rock.

"Don't worry," he reassured her. "I'm not catching."

Her laugh changed quality; it became an upwards offer of her throat, followed by her breasts, her body. She was not wearing the catsuit but a black cocktail dress with a square neckline, yet the effect was the same, of a loose slipperiness about her that invited a peeling. She was holding to her breasts a manilla envelope full of poems awaiting his verdict. "I think your room is underfurnished," she told him.

"My rooms in New York are too."

"You need something to sleep beside."

"An oxygen tent?"

"Me."

Bech said, "I don't think we should," and cried. He seemed to mean, to himself, that he was too hideous, too sick; yet also in his mind was the superstition that they must not defile the sleeping dormitory, this halcyon Lesbos, with copulation. Ruth Eisenbraun stared amazed, her hands tightening on the envelope of poems, at the moonlight making ice of Bech's impotent tears. Her firm willing body, silhouetted against the dewy smell of sleeping grass, seemed to him another poem abysmal in its ignorance, deceitful in its desire to mitigate the universe. Poetry and love, twin attempts to make the best of a bad job. Impotent: yet in his stance, his refusal to embrace a hasty cure, we must admire a type of rigidity, an erect pride in his desolation, a determination to defend it as his territory. A craven pagan this morning, he had become by midnight a stern monk.

This is all speculation. Truly we are in the dark here. Knowing Bech on other, better lit occasions, we doubt that, given this importunate woman, the proximity of the glass doors, and the key in his pocket, he did not for all his infirmity take her inside to his sickbed and let her apply to his wound the humid poultice of her flesh. Also, on her side, Ruth was a professor of literature; she would not have misread the works so badly as to misjudge the man. Picture them then. Above Bech and Ruth hangs the black dome of their sepulchre; the nipples of her breasts also appear black, as they swing above him, teasing his mouth, his mouth blind as a baby's, though his eyes, when he shuts them, see through the succulent padding to the calcium xylophone of her rib cage. His phallus a counterfeit bone, a phantasmal creature, like Man, on the borderline of substance and illusion, of death and life. They establish a rhythm. Her socket becomes a positive force, begins to suck, to pound. Enough. Like Bech, we reach a point where words seem horrible, maggots on the carcass of reality, feeding, proliferating; we seek peace in chaste silence.

Wait, wait. Here is another slide, a fifth, found hiding under a stack of gold domes from Russia. It shows Bech the next morning. Again, he has slept on his back, his head held high by two pillows, a china figurine through which dreams idly blow. The pillows having been piled one on top of the other prevent our knowing whether or not two heads lay down on the bed. He rises grudgingly, stiffly. Again, he is wonderfully productive of excrement. His wound feels scabbier, drier; he knows now he can get through a day with it, can live with it. He performs his toilet – washes, wipes, brushes, shaves. He sits down at the little pseudo-Sheraton desk and shuffles the sheaf of poems as if they are physically hot. He awards the first prize, a check for $25, to the girl with the small head and blue eyes on stalks, writing as his citation:

> Miss Haynsworth's poems strike me as technically accomplished, making their way as good loyal citizens under the tyranny of rhyme, and as precociously rich in those qualities we associate with poetesses from Sappho on – they are laconic, clear-eyed, gracious toward the world, and in their acceptance of our perishing frailty, downright brave.

Bech suspected that "poetess" wasn't quite right any more, but arranged to have the envelope delivered to Miss Eisenbraun anyway – delivered by someone else. He was driven to the airport by a homely, tall, long-toothed woman whose voice, he realized, was the voice that beguiled him over the telephone. "Ah'm *so* sorreh, Misteh Bech, evrehbodeh saiys you were *dahl*in, but Ah had to attend mah sisteh's weddin in Roanoke, it was one of those sudden affaihs, and jes got back this mawnin! Believe me, suh, Ah am *moht*ifahd!"

"Neveh you mind," Bech told her, and touched his inside breast pocket to make sure his check was in it. The landscape, unwinding in reverse, seemed greener than when he arrived, and their speed less dangerous. Bea, who with much inconvenience had hired a babysitter so she could meet him at La Guardia, sensed, just seeing him emerge from the giant silver thorax and scuttle across the tarmac in the rain, that something had happened to him, that there wasn't enough of him left for her to have any.

BECH SWINGS?

BECH ARRIVED in London with the daffodils; he knew that he must fall in love. It was not his body that demanded it, but his art. His first novel, *Travel Light*, had become a minor classic of the Fifties, along with *Picnic*, *The Search for Bridey Murphy*, and the sayings of John Foster Dulles. His second novel, a lyrical gesture of disgust, novella-length, called *Brother Pig*, did his reputation no harm and cleared his brain, he thought, for a frontal assault on the wonder of life. The assault, surprisingly, consumed five years, in which his mind and work habits developed in circles, or loops, increasingly leisurely and whimsical; when he sat down at his desk, for instance, his younger self, the somehow fictitious author of his earlier fictions, seemed to be not quite displaced, so that he became an uneasy, blurred composite, like the image left on film by too slow an exposure. The final fruit of his distracted struggles, *The Chosen*, was universally judged a failure – one of those "honorable" failures, however, that rather endear a writer to the race of critics, who would rather be reassured of art's noble difficulty than cope with a potent creative verve. Bech felt himself rise from the rubble of bad reviews bigger than ever, better known and in greater demand. Just as the id, according to Freud, fails to distinguish between a wish-image and a real external object, so does publicity, another voracious idiot, dismiss all qualitative distinctions and feast off good and bad alike. Now five – no, six – years had passed, and Bech had done little but pose as himself, and scribble reviews and "impressionistic" journalism for *Commentary* and *Esquire*, and design a series of repellent rubber stamps:

**HENRY BECH REGRETS THAT HE
DOES NOT SPEAK IN PUBLIC.**

**SORRY, PETITIONS
AREN'T MY METIER.**

**HENRY BECH IS TOO OLD AND ILL
AND DOUBTFUL TO SUBMIT TO
QUESTIONNAIRES AND INTERVIEWS.**

**IT'S YOUR PH.D. THESIS;
PLEASE WRITE IT YOURSELF.**

By appropriately stamping the letters he received and returning them to the sender, Bech simplified his correspondence. But six years had passed, and his third stamp pad had gone dry, and the age of fifty was in sight, and it was high time to write something to justify his sense of himself as a precious and useful recluse. A stimulus seemed needed.

Love? Travel? As to love, he had been recently processed by a pair of sisters, first the one, and then the other; the one was neurotic and angular and harsh and glamorous and childless and exhausting, and the other had been sane and soft and plain and maternal and exhausting. Both had wanted husbands. Both had mundane, utilitarian conceptions of themselves that Bech could not bring himself to corroborate. It was his charm and delusion to see women as deities – idols whose jewel was set not in the center of their foreheads but between their legs, with another between their lips, and pairs more sprinkled up and down, from ankles to eyes, the length of their adorable, alien forms. His transactions with these supernatural creatures imbued him, more keenly each time, with his own mortality. His life seemed increasingly like that sinister fairy story in which each granted wish diminishes a magic pelt that is in fact the wisher's life. But perhaps, Bech thought, one more woman, one more leap would bring him safe into that high calm pool of immortality where Proust and Hawthorne and Catullus float, glassy-eyed and belly up. One more wasting love would release his genius from the bondage of his sagging flesh.

As to travel: his English publisher, J. J. Goldschmidt, Ltd., who had sidestepped Bech's collected essays (published in the United States and Canada as *When the Saints*) and had remaindered *Brother Pig* with the haste usually reserved for bishops' memoirs and albums of Pharaonic art, now, possibly embarrassed by the little novel's creeping success in its Penguin edition, and guilty over the minuscule advances and scrimped printings with which he had bound Bech's thriving name, decided to bring out a thirty-shilling anthology called, all too inevitably, *The Best of Bech*. To support this enterprise he asked the author to come to London for the week before publication and permit himself to "be lionized." The phrase snaked in less time than an eyeblink along three thousand miles of underwater cable.

"I'd rather be lambified," Bech answered.

"What, Henry? Sorry, I can hardly hear you."

"Forget it, Goldy. It was a hard word."

"You heard what?"

"Nothing. This is a very wet connection."

"Dead?"

"Not yet, but let's kill it. I'll come." He arrived with the daffodils. The VC-10 banked over Hampton Court, and the tinge of their yellow was visible from the air. In Hyde Park beside the Serpentine, along Birdcage Walk in St. James's, in Grosvenor Square beneath the statue of Roosevelt and in Russell Square beneath the statue of Gandhi, in all the fenced squares from Fitzroy to Pembroke, the daffodils made a million golden curtseys to those tourists who, like our hero, wandered dazed by jet-lag and lonely as a cloud. *A poet could not but be gay*, Bech recalled, *In such a jocund company*. And the people in the streets, it seemed to him, whether milling along Oxford Street or saunter-ing from lion to lion in Trafalgar Square, formed another golden host, beautiful in the antique cold-faced way of Blake's pastel throngs, pale Dionysiacs, bare thighs and gaudy cloth, lank hair and bell-bottoms, *Continuous as the stars that shine / And twinkle on the milky way*. And, the next morning, watching Merissa move nude to the window and to her closet, he felt her perfections — the parallel tendons at the backs of her knees, the kisslike leaps of shadow among the muscles of her shoulders — flow outdoors and merge with the lacy gauze of the gray British air. A VC-10 hung in silent descent above the treetops of Regent's Park. He rose and saw that this park too had its pools of gold, its wandering beds of daffodils, and that under the sunless noon sky lovers, their heads androgynous masses of hair, had come to lie entwined on the cold greening grass. *Cold greening grass*, Bech heard. The echo disturbed and distracted him. The papery daytime world, cluttered with books he had not written, cut into the substantial dreams of drunkenness and love.

Jørgen Josiah Goldschmidt, a bustling small anxious man with an ambitiously large head and the pendulous profile of a Florentine banker, had arranged a party for Bech the very evening of his arrival. "But, Goldy, by your time I've been awake since two this morning."

They had met several times in New York. Goldschmidt had evidently sized up Bech as a clowner to be chuckled and shushed into line. In turn Bech had sized up Goldschmidt as one of those self-made men who have paid the price (for not letting God make them) of minor defects like inner deafness and constant neuralgia. Goldschmidt's was a success story. A Danish Jew, he had arrived in England in the late Thirties. In twenty years, he had gone from the Ministry of Information to the B.B.C. to an editorship in a venerable publishing house to the founding, in the mid-Fifties, of one of his own, specializing in foreign avant-garde writers no one else wanted and dainty anthologies of poetic matter lapsed from copyright. A lucky recipe book (health food soups) and a compendium of Prayers for Humanists staved off bankruptcy. Now he was prosperous, thanks mostly to his powers of persuading his lawyers and printers to let him publish increasingly obscene American authors. Though devoid of any personal taste for obscenity, he had found a wave and was riding it. His accent and dress were impeccably British. In tune with the times he had sprouted bushy sideburns. His face was always edged with the gray of nagging pain. He said, his brown eyes (in repose, they revealed lovely amber depths, lit by the fire of his brain, but were rarely in repose) flicking past Bech's shoulder toward the next problem, "Henry, you must come. Everyone is dying to meet you. I've invited just the very dearest nicest people. Ted Heath might drop in later, and Princess Margaret was so sorry she must be in Ceylon. You can have a nice nap in your hotel. If the room is too noisy, we can change it. I thought from your books you would enjoy a view of the traffic. Your interview isn't until five, a terribly nice intelligent boy, a compatriot of yours. If you don't like him, just give him a half hour of the usual and he'll be on his way."

Bech protested, "I have no usual," but the other man said deafly, "Bless you," and left.

Too excited by the new city, and by having survived another airplane flight, Bech instead of sleeping walked miles looking at the daffodils, at the Georgian rows plastered with demolition notices and peace slogans, at the ruffled shirts and Unisex pants in the shop windows, at the bobbies resembling humorless male models, at the dingy band of hippies sharing Eros's black island in Piccadilly Circus with pigeons the color of exhaust fumes. On Great Russell Street, down from the British Museum, past a Hindu luncheonette, a plaque marked the site of a Dickens novel as if the characters had occupied the same time-space in which Bech walked. Back in his hotel lobby, he was offended by the American voices, the pseudo-Edwardian decor, the illustrated chart of acceptable credit cards. A typical Goldschmidt snap decision, to stuff him into a tourist trap. A pale young man, plainly American from his round-headed haircut and his clever hangdog way of sidling forward, came up to Bech. "My name is Tuttle, Mr. Bech. I guess I'm going to interview you."

"Your guess is as good as mine," Bech said.

The boy tipped his head slightly, like a radar dish, as if to decipher the something acerb in Bech's tone, and said, "I don't generally do this sort of thing, actually I have as low an opinion of interviews as you do —"

"How do you know I have a low opinion?" Jet-lag was getting to Bech; irritability was droning in his ears.

"You've said so" — the boy smiled shyly, cleverly — "in your other interviews." He went on hastily, pursuing his advantage: "But this wouldn't be like your others. It would be all you, I have no ax to grind, no ax at all. A friend of mine on the staff of the Sunday *Observer* begged me to do it; actually I'm in London researching a thesis on eighteenth-century printers. It would be a sort of full spread to go with *The Best of Bech*. Let me frankly confess, it seemed a unique opportunity. I've written you letters in the past, in the States, but I suppose you've forgotten."

"Did I answer them?"

"You hit them with a rubber stamp and sent them back." Tuttle waited, perhaps for an apology, then went on. "What I have in mind now is a chance for you to explain yourself, to say everything you want to say. *You* want to say. Your *name* is known over here, Mr. Bech, but they don't really know *you*."

"Well, that's their privilege."

"I beg your pardon, sir, I think it's their loss."

Bech felt himself slippingly, helplessly relenting. "Let's sit over here," he said. To take the young man up to his room would, he thought groggily, simulate pederasty and risk the fate of Wilde.

They sat in facing lobby chairs; Tuttle perched on the edge of his as if he had been called into the principal's office. "I've read every word you've written five or six times. Frankly, I think you're *it*." This sounded to Bech like the safest praise he had ever heard; one appetite that had not diminished with the years was for unambiguous, blood-raw superlatives.

He reached over and tagged the boy. "Now you're it," he said.

Tuttle blushed. "I mean to say, what other people *say* they're doing, you really *do*." An echo troubled Bech; he had heard this before, but not applied to himself. Still, the droning had ceased. The blush had testified to some inner conflict, and Bech could maintain his defenses only in the face of a perfectly simple, resolute attack. Any sign of embarrassment or self-doubt he confused with surrender.

"Let's have a drink," he said.

"Thank you, no."

"You mean you're on duty?"

"No, I just don't ever drink."

"Never?"

"No."

Bech thought, They've sent me a Christer. That's what Tuttle's pallor, his sidling severity, his embarrassed insistence reminded Bech of: the Pentecostal fanatic who comes to the door. "Well, let me frankly confess, I sometimes do. Drink."

"Oh, I know. Your drinking is famous."

"Like Hitler's vegetarianism."

In his haste to put Bech at ease, Tuttle neglected to laugh. "Please go ahead," the boy insisted. "If you become incoherent, I'll just stop taking notes, and we can resume another day."

Poor Henry Bech, to whom innocence, in its galoshes of rudeness and wet raincoat of presumption, must always appear as possibly an angel to be sheltered and fed. He ordered a drink ("Do you know what a whiskey sour is?" he asked the waiter, who said "Absolutely, sir" and brought him a whiskey-and-soda) and tried for one more degrading time to dig into the rubbish of his "career" and come up with lost baubles of wisdom. Encouraged by the fanatic way the boy covered page after page of his notebook with wildly oscillating lines, Bech talked of fiction as an equivalent of reality, and described how the point of it, the justification, seemed to lie in those moments when a set of successive images locked and then one more image arrived and, as it were, superlocked, creating a tightness perhaps equivalent to the terribly tight knit of reality, e.g., the lightning ladder of chemical changes in the body cell that translates fear into action, or the implosion of subatomic mathematics consuming the heart of a star. And the down-grinding thing is the realization that no one, not critics or readers, ever notices these tight moments but instead prattles, in praise or blame, with an altogether insolent looseness. That it is neces-sary to begin by believing in an ideal reader and that slowly he is proved not to exist. He is not the daily reviewer skimming a plastic-bound set of raggedy advance proofs, nor the bulk-loving housewife who buys a shiny new novel between the grocer's and the hairdresser's, nor the diligent graduate student with his heap of index cards and grant applications, nor the plump-scripted young ballpointer who sends a mash note via *Who's Who*, nor, in the weary end, even oneself. In short, one loses heart in the discovery that one is not being read. That the ability to read, and therefore to write, is being lost, along with the abilities to listen, to see, to smell, and to breathe. That all the windows of the spirit are being nailed shut. Here Bech gasped for air, to dramatize his point. He said, then, that he was sustained, insofar as he was sustained, by the memory of laughter, the specifically Jewish, sufficiently desperate, not quite belly laughter of his father and his father's brothers, his beloved Brooklyn uncles; that the American Jews had kept the secret of this embattled laughter a generation longer than the Gentiles, hence their present domination of American lit; and that in the world today only the Russians still had it, the Peruvians possibly, and Mao Tse-tung but not any of the rest of the Chinese. In his, Bech's, considered judgment.

Tuttle scribbled another page and looked up hopefully. "Mao-ism does seem to be the coming mood," he said.

"The mood of t'mao," Bech said, rising. "Believe it or not, my lad, I must take a shower and go to a party. Power corrupts."

"When could we resume? I think we've made a fascinating beginning."

"Beginning? You want *more*? For just a little puff in the *Observer*?"

When Tuttle stood, though he was skinny, with a round head like a newel knob, he was taller than Bech. He got tough. "I want it to be much more than that, Mr. Bech. Much more than a little puff. They've promised me as much space as we need. You have a chance here, if you *use* me hard enough, to make a d-definitive t-t-testament."

If the boy hadn't stammered, Bech might have escaped. But the stammer, those little spurts of helpless silence, hooked him. Stalling, he asked, "You never drink?"

"Not really."

"Do you smoke?"

"No."

"Matter of principle?"

"I just never acquired the taste."

"Do you eat between meals?"

"I guess once in a while."

"Call me sometime," Bech conceded, and hated himself. Strange, how dirty the attempt to speak seriously made him feel. Comparable to his sensation when he saw someone press an open book flat and complacently, irreparably crack the spine.

Bech's tuxedo over the years had developed a waxen sheen and grown small; throughout Goldy's party, his waist was being cruelly pinched. The taxicab, so capacious that Bech felt like ballast, turned down a succession of smaller and smaller streets and stopped on a dead-end loop, where, with the mystic menace of a Christmas tree, a portico blazed. The doorknocker was a goldsmith's hammer inscribed with a florid double "J." A servant in blue livery admitted Bech. Goldy bustled forward in a red velvet jacket and flopping ruffles. Another servant poured Bech a warm Scotch. Goldy, his eyes shuttling like a hockey player's, steered Bech past a towering pier glass into a room where beautiful women in cream and saffron and magenta drifted and billowed in soft slow motion. Men in black dinner clothes stood like channel markers in this sea. "Here's a lovely person you must meet," Goldy told Bech. To her he said, "Henry Bech. He's very shy. Don't frighten him away, darling."

She was an apparition – wide powdery shoulders, long untroubled chin ever so faintly cleft, lips ghostly in their cushioned perfection, gray eyes whose light flooded their cages of false lash and painted shadow. Bech asked her, "What do you do?"

She quivered; the corners of her lips trembled wryly, and he realized that the question had been consummately stupid, that merely to rise each morning and fill her skin to the brim with such loveliness was enough for any woman to do.

But she said, "Well, I have a husband, and five children, and I've just published a book."

"A novel?" Bech could see it now: robin's-egg-blue jacket, brisk adultery on country weekends, comic relief provided by precocious children.

"No, not really. It's the history of labor movements in England before 1860."

"Were there many?"

"Some. It was very uphill for them."

"How lovely of you," Bech said, "to care; that is, when you look so" – he rejected "posh" – "unlaborious."

Again, her face underwent, not a change of expression, which was unvaryingly sweet and attentive, but a seismic tremor, as if her composure restrained volcanic heat. She asked, "What are your novels about?"

"Oh, ordinary people."

"Then how lovely of *you*; when you're so extraordinary."

A man bored with being a channel marker came and touched her elbow, and she turned away, leaving Bech her emanations, as an astronomer is flooded by radio waves from a blank part of the sky. He tried to take a fix on her flattery by looking, as he went for another drink, into a mirror. His nose with age had grown larger and its flanges had turned distinctly red; his adoption of the hair style of the young had educed woolly bursts of gray above his ears and a tallowish mass of white curling outwards at the back of his collar: he looked like a mob-controlled congressman from Queens hoping to be taken for a Southern senator. His face was pasty with fatigue, though his eyes seemed frantically alive. He observed in the mirror, observing him, a slim young African woman in see-through pajamas. He turned and asked her, "What *can* we do about Biafra?"

"*Je le regrette, Monsieur,*" she said, "*mais maintenant je ne pense jamais. Je vis, simplement.*"

"*Parce que,*" Bech offered, "*le monde est trop effrayant?*"

She shrugged. "*Peut-être.*" When she shrugged, her silhouetted breasts shivered with their weight; it took Bech back to his avid youthful perusals of the *National Geographic*. He said, "*Je pense, comme vous, que le monde est difficile à comprendre, mais certainement, en tout cas, vous êtes très sage, très belle.*" But his French was not good enough to hold her, and she turned, and was wearing bikini underpants, with tiger stripes, beneath the saffron gauze of her pantaloons. Blue servants rang chimes for dinner. He gulped his drink, and avoided the sideways eye of the congressman from Queens.

On his right was seated a middle-aged Lady of evident importance, though her beauty could never have been much more than a concentrate of sharpness and sparkle. "You

American Jews," she said, "are so romantic. You think every little dolly bird is Delilah. I hate the 'pity me' in all your books. Women don't want to be complained at. They want to be screwed."

"I'll have to try it," Bech said.

"Do. Do." She pivoted toward a long-toothed gallant waiting grinning on her right; he exclaimed "Darling!" and their heads fell together like bagged oranges. On Bech's left sat a magenta shape his first glance had told him to ignore. It glittered and was young. Bech didn't trust anyone under thirty; the young now moved with the sacred and dangerous assurance of the old when he had been young. She was toying with her soup like a child. Her hand was small as a child's, with close-cut fingernails and endearing shadows around the knuckles. He felt he had seen the hand before. In a novel. *Lolita*? *Magic Mountain*? Simple etiquette directed that he ask her how she was.

"Rotten, thanks."

"Think of me," Bech said. "By the time I woke up in, it's four o'clock in the morning."

"I hate sleep. I don't sleep for days sometimes and feel wonderful. I think people sleep too much, that's why their arteries harden." In fact, he was to discover that she slept as the young do, in long easy swings that gather the extra hours into their arc and override all noise – though she had every woman's tendency to stir at dawn. She went on, as if politely, "Do you have hard arteries?"

"Not to my knowledge. Just impotence and gout."

"That sounds come-ony."

"Forgive me. I was just told women don't like being complained to."

"I heard the old tart say that. Don't believe her. They love it. Why are you impotent?"

"Old age?" A voice inside him said, *Old age? he tentatively said.*

"Come off it." He liked her voice, one of those British voices produced halfway down the throat, rather than obliquely off the sinuses, with alarming octave jumps. She was wearing gold granny glasses on her little heart-shaped face. He didn't know if her cheeks were flushed or rouged. He was pleased to observe

that, though she was petite, her breasts pushed up plumply from
her dress, which was ornamented with small mirrors. Her lips,
chalky and cushioned, with intelligent tremulous corners,
seemed taken from the first woman he had met, as if one had
been a preliminary study for the other. He noticed she had a little
mustache, faint as two erased pencil lines. She told him, "You
write."

"I used to."

"What happened?"

A gap in the dialogue. Fill in later. "I don't seem to know."

"I used to be a wife. My husband was an American. Still is,
come to think of it."

"Where did you live?" The girl and Bech simultaneously
glanced down and began to hurry to finish the food on their
plates.

"New York."

"Like it?"

"Loved it."

"Didn't it seem dirty to you?"

"Gloriously." She chewed. He pictured sharp small even teeth
lacerating and compressing bloody beef. He set down his fork.
She swallowed and asked, "Love London?"

"Don't know it."

"You don't?"

"Been here only long enough to look at daffodils."

"I'll show it to you."

"How can you? How can I find you again?" Victorian novel?
Rewrite.

"You're in London alone?"

A crusty piece of Yorkshire pudding looked too good to leave.
Bech picked up his fork again, agreeing, "Mm. I'm alone everywhere."

"Would you like to come home with me?"

The lady on his right turned and said, "I must say, you're a
stinker to let this old fag monopolize me."

"Don't complain. Men hate it."

She responded, "Your hair is smashing. Are the curls induced?"

"Tell me, love, who's this, what do you say, bird on my left?"

"She's Little Miss Poison. Her father bought himself a peerage from Macmillan."

The girl at Bech's back tickled the hairs of his neck with her breath and said, "I withdraw my invitation."

"Let's all," Bech said loudly, "have some more wine," pouring. The man with long teeth put his hand over the top of his glass. Bech expected a magician's trick but was disappointed.

And at the door, as Bech tried to sneak past the voracious pier glass with the girl, Goldy seemed disappointed. "But did you meet *ev*erybody? These are the nicest people in London."

Bech hugged his publisher. Waxy old tux, meet velvet and ruffles. Learn how the other half lives. "Goldy," he said, "the party was nice, nicey, niciest. It couldn't have been nicer. Like, wow, out of sight." He saw drunken noise as the key to his exit. Otherwise this velvet gouger would milk him for another hour of lionization. Grr.

Goldy displayed the racial gracefulness in defeat. His limpid eyes, as busy as if he were playing blitz chess, flicked past Bech's shoulder to the girl. "Merissa dear, *do* take decent care of our celebrity. My fortune rides on his genius." Thus Bech learned her first name.

The taxi, with two in it, felt less like a hollow hull and more like a small drawing room, where voices needn't be raised. They did not, perhaps oddly, touch. *Perhaps oddly?* He had lost all ability to phrase. He was in a decadent Old World metropolis in a cab with a creature whose dress held dozens of small mirrors. Her legs were white like knives, crossed and recrossed. He proofread the triangular bit of punctuation where her thighs ended. The cab moved through empty streets, past wrought-iron gates inked onto the sky and granite museums frowning beneath the weight of their entablatures; it moved across the bright loud gulch of Hyde Park Corner and Park Lane, into darker quieter streets. It passed a shuttered building that Merissa identified as the Chinese Communist Embassy. They entered a region where the shaggy heads of trees seemed to be dreaming of fantastically long colonnades and of high white wedding-cake façades receding to infinity. The cab stopped. Merissa paid. She let him in by a door whose knob,

knocker, and mail slot were silken with polishings. Marble stairs.
Another door. Another key. The odors of floor wax, of stale
cigarette smoke, of narcissi in a pebbled bowl. Brandy with its
scorched, expensive smell was placed beneath his nose. Obediently he drank. He was led into a bedroom. Perfume and powder,
leather and an oil-clothy scent that took him back into English
children's books that his mother, bent on his "improvement,"
used to buy at the Fifth Avenue Scribner's. A window opened.
Chill April smells. *Winter kept us warm.* She brushed back curtains.
A slice of slate night yellowish above the trees. The lights of an
airplane winking in descent. A rustling all around him. The candy
taste of lipstick. Clean air, warm skin. *Feeding a little life with dried
tubers.* Her bare back a lunar surface beneath his hands. The
forgotten impression of intrusion, of subtle monstrous assault,
that the particularities of a new woman's body make upon us.
Summer surprised us. Must find out her last name. There are rings of
release beyond rings, Bech discovered in the bliss – the pang of
relief around his waist – of taking off his tuxedo. Must see a tailor.

"When you were writing *The Chosen*," Tuttle asked, "did you
deliberately set out to create a more flowery style?" This time he
had brought a tape recorder. They were in Bech's hotel rooms,
an extensive corner suite with a fake fireplace and a bed that
hadn't been slept in. The fireplace was not entirely fake; it held a
kind of crinkly plastic sculpture of a coal fire that glowed when
plugged in and even gave off an imitation of heat.

"I never think about style, about creating one," Bech dictated
into the baby microphone of the tape recorder. "My style is
always as simple as the subject matter permits. As you grow
older, though, you find that few things are simple."

"For example?"

"For example, changing a tire. I'm sorry, your question seems
inane to me. This interview seems inane."

"Let me try another approach," Tuttle said, as maddeningly
patient as a child psychiatrist. "In *Brother Pig*, were you conscious
of inserting the political resonances?"

Bech blinked. "I'm sorry, when you say 'resonances' all I see is dried grapes. *Brother Pig* was about what its words said it was about. It was not a mask for something else. I do not write in code. I depend upon my reader for a knowledge of the English language and some acquired vocabulary of human experience. My books, I hope, would be unintelligible to baboons or squid. My books are human transactions – flirtations, quarrels."

"You're tired," Tuttle told him.

He was right. Last night, Merissa had taken him to a restaurant along Fulham Road and then to Revolution, where big posters of Ho and Mao and Engels and Lenin watched from the walls as young people dressed in sequins and bell-bottoms jogged up and down within a dense, throbbing, coruscating fudge of noise. Bech knew something was happening here, a spiritual upthrusting like Christianity among the slaves of Rome or cabalism among the peasant Jews of stagnant Slavic Europe, but his old-fashioned particularizing vision kept dissolving the mob into its components: working girls resigned to a groggy tomorrow at their typewriters; neutered young men in fashion or photography to whom coming here was work; the truly idle, the rich and the black, escaping from the empty-eye-socket stare of spooked hours; the would-be young like himself, ancient lecherous curly-haired Yanks whose willy-nilly charm and backwards success had prevented their learning ever to come in out of the rain; enigmatic tarty birds like Merissa, whose flat, he had discovered, held a room full of electric toys and teddy bears, with a bed where a child slept, her child, she confessed, a son, eight years old, born in America, when Merissa was nineteen, a child sent off to boarding school and even on vacations, Bech suspected, mostly taken to the park and the zoo by Isabella, Merissa's Spanish maid, an old round woman who peeked at Bech through doorways and then quickly, quietly shut the door. It was confusing. Revolution was the cave of a new religion but everyone had come, Bech saw, for reasons disappointingly reasonable and opportunistic. To make out. To be seen. To secure advancement. To be improved. That girl in the chain-link tunic and nothing else was working off her Yorkshire accent. That man flicking his arm like a dervish under the blue battering of the strobe lights was swinging a real-estate deal in his head.

Bech doubted that the men on the wall approved what they saw. They were simple failed librarians like himself, schooled in the pre-Freudian verities. Hunger and pain are bad. Work is good. Men were made for the daylight. Orgasms are private affairs. *Down in Loo-siana/Where the alligators swim so mean...* Opposite him Merissa, who had a way of suddenly looking tall, though her smallness was what enchanted him, twinkled through the holes of her dress and moved her limbs and turned to him a shuddering profile, eyes shut as if better to feel the beat between her legs, that fluttering elusive beat: *What we are witnessing*, Bech announced inside his own head, in his role of college circuit-rider, *is the triumph of the clitoral, after three thousand years of phallic hegemony.* She called over to him, through the flashing din, "It gets to be rather same-y, doesn't it?" And he felt then his heart make the motion he had been waiting for, of love for her; like the jaws of a clam when the muscle is sliced, his heart opened. He tasted it, the sugary nip of impossibility. For he was best at loving what he could never have.

"Lord, you're lovely," he said. "Let's go home."

She accused him: "You don't love London, only me."

His conversations with Merissa did have a way of breaking into two-liners. For example,

MERISSA: "I'm terribly tired of being white."

BECH: "But you're so good at it."

Or:

BECH: "I've never understood what sex is like for a woman."

MERISSA (*thinking hard*): "It's like – fog."

The phone rang at nine the next morning. It was Tuttle. Goldschmidt had given him Merissa's number. Bech thought of expostulating but since the boy never drank he would have no idea how Bech's head felt. With some dim idea of appeasing those forces of daylight and righteous wrath that he had seen mocked on the walls of Revolution last night, he consented to meet Tuttle at his hotel at ten. Perhaps this stab at self-abnegation did him good, for, on his way to the West End in the lurching, swaying upstairs of a 74 bus, nauseated by the motion, having breakfasted on unbuttered toast and reheated tea (Merissa had observed his departure by sighing and rolling over onto her

stomach, and her refrigerator held nothing but yogurt and champagne), gazing down upon the foreshortened shoppers in Baker
Street – shimmering saris, polka-dot umbrellas – Bech was visited
by inspiration. The title of his new novel abruptly came to him:
Think Big. It balanced the title of his first, *Travel Light*. It held in
the girders of its consonants, braced by those two stark "i"s,
America's promise, pathos, crassness, grandeur. As *Travel Light*
had been about a young man, so *Think Big* must be about a
young woman, about openness and confusion, coruscation and
the loss of the breeding function. Merissa could be the heroine.
But she was British. Transposing her into an American would
meet resistance at a hundred points, as for instance when she
undressed, and was as white as an Artemis of marble, whereas any
American girl that age carries all winter the comical ghost of last
summer's bikini, emphasizing her erogenous zones like a diagram. And Merissa's enchanting smallness, the manner in which
her perfection seemed carried out on an elfin scale, so that Bech
could study by lamplight the bones of an ankle and foot as he
would study an ivory miniature, a smallness excitingly violated
when her mouth swam into the dimensions of the normal – this
too was un-American. Your typical Bennington girl wore a $9\frac{1}{2}$
sneaker and carried her sex as in a knapsack, to be unpacked at
night. A rugged Boy/Girl Scout was the evolutionary direction,
not the perfumed, faintly treacherous femininity Merissa exuded
from each dear pore. Still, Bech reasoned while the bus man-
euvered into Oxford Street and the shoppers danced in psychedelic foreshortening, she was not quite convincing as she was
(what did she *do*? for instance, to warrant that expensive flat, and
Isabella, and a dinner invitation from Goldy, and the closets full
of swinging clothes, not to mention riding chaps and mud-
crusted golf shoes), and Bech was sure he could fill in her gaps
with bits of American women, could indeed re-create her from
almost nothing, needing less than a rib, needing only the living
germ of his infatuation, of his love. Already small things from
here and there, kept alive by some kink in his forgetting mechanism, had begun to fly together and fit. A dance hall he had once
walked upstairs to, off of war-darkened Broadway. A rabid but
deft Trotskyite barber his father had patronized. The way New

York's side streets seek the sunset, and the way on Fifth Avenue
hard-shinned women in sunglasses hurry past languorous mannequins in gilded robes, black-velvet cases of jewels wired to
burglar alarms, shopwindows crying out ignored. But what
would be the action of the book? It was a big book, he saw,
with a blue jacket of coated stock and his unsmiling photo full on
the back, bled top and bottom. What were its conflict, its issue,
its outcome? The answer, like the title, came from so deep within
him that it seemed a message from beyond: Suicide. His heroine
must kill herself. Think big. His heart trembled in excitement, at
the enormity of his crime.

"You're tired," Tuttle said, and went on, "I've seen the point
raised about your work, that the kind of ethnic loyalty you
display, loyalty to a narrow individualistic past, is divisive, and
encourages war, and helps account for your reluctance to join the
peace movement and the social revolution. How would you
rebut this?"

"Where did you see this point raised, did you say?"

"Some review."

"*What* review? Are you sure you just didn't make it up? I've
seen some dumb things written about me, but never anything
quite that vapid and doctrinaire."

"My attempt, Mr. Bech, is to elicit from you your opinions. If
you find this an unfruitful area, let's move on. Maybe I should
stop the machine while you collect your thoughts. We're wasting
tape."

"Not to mention my lifeblood." But Bech groggily tried to
satisfy the boy; he described his melancholy feelings in the go-go
place last night, his intuition that self-aggrandizement and entrepreneurial energy were what made the world go and that slogans
and movements to the contrary were evil dreams, evil in that
they distracted people from particular, concrete realities, whence
all goodness and effectiveness derive. He was an Aristotelian and
not a Platonist. Write him down, if he must write him down as
something, as a disbeliever; he disbelieved in the Pope, in the
Kremlin, in the Vietcong, in the American eagle, in astrology,
Arthur Schlesinger, Eldridge Cleaver, Senator Eastland, and East-
man Kodak. Nor did he believe overmuch in his disbelief. He

thought intelligence a function of the individual and that groups of persons were intelligent in inverse proportion to their size. Nations had the brains of an amoeba whereas a committee approached the condition of a trainable moron. He believed, if this tape recorder must know, in the goodness of something vs. nothing, in the dignity of the inanimate, the intricacy of the animate, the beauty of the average woman, and the common sense of the average man. The tape spun out its reel and ran flapping.

Tuttle said, "That's great stuff, Mr. Bech. One more session, and we should have it."

"Never, never, never, never," Bech said. Something in his face drove Tuttle out the door. Bech fell asleep on his bed in his clothes. He awoke and found that *Think Big* had died. It had become a ghost of a book, an empty space beside the four faded spines that he had already brought to exist. *Think Big* had no content but wonder, which was a blankness. He thought back through his life – so many dreams and wakings, so many faces encountered and stoplights obeyed and streets crossed, and there was nothing solid. He had rushed through his life as through a badly chewed meal, leaving an ache of indigestion. In the beginning, the fresh flame of his spirit had burned everything clean – the entire gray city, stone and soot and stoops. Miles of cracked pavement had not been too much. He had gone to sleep on the sound of sirens and woken to the cries of fruit carts. There had been around him a sheltering ring of warm old tall bodies whose droning appeared to be wisdom, whose crooning and laughter seemed to be sifted down from the Great I Am presiding above the smoldering city's lights. There had been classrooms smelling of eraser crumbs, and male pals from whom to learn loyalty and stoicism, and the first dizzying drag on a cigarette, and the first girl who let his hands linger, and the first joys of fabrication, of invention and completion.

Then unreality had swept in. It was his fault; he had wanted to be noticed, to be praised. He had wanted to be a man in the world, a "writer." For his punishment they had made from the sticks and mud of his words a coarse large doll to question and torment, which would not have mattered except that he was trapped inside the doll, shared a name and bank account with it. And the life that touched and brushed other people, that played across them like a saving breeze, could not break through the crust to him. He was, with all his brave talk to Tuttle of individual intelligence and the foolishness of groups, too alone.

He telephoned Goldschmidt, Ltd., and was told Goldy was out to lunch. He called Merissa but her number did not answer. He went downstairs and tried to talk to the hotel doorman about the weather. "Well, sir, weather is weather, I find to be the case generally. Some days is fine, and others a bit dim. This sky today you'll find is about what we generally have this time of the year. It'll all average out when we're in the grave, isn't that the truth of it, sir?" Bech disliked being humored, and the gravedigger scene had never been one of his favorites. He went walking beneath the dispirited, homogenized sky, featureless but for some downward wisps of nimbus promising rain that never arrived. Where were the famous English clouds, the clouds of Constable and Shelley? He tried to transplant the daffodils to Riverside Park, for his novel, but couldn't see them there, among those littered thickets hollowed by teen-aged layabouts bloodless with heroin, these British bulbs laid out in their loamy bed by ancient bowed men, the great-grandchildren of feudalism, who swept the paths where Bech walked with brooms, yes, and this was cheering, with brooms fashioned of twigs honestly bound together with twine. It began to rain.

Bech became a docile tourist and interviewee. He bantered on the B.B.C. Third Programme with a ripe-voiced young Welshman. He read from his works to bearded youths at the London School of Economics, between strikes. He submitted to a cocktail party at the U.S. Embassy. He participated in a television discussion on the Collapse of the American Dream with an edgy homosexual historian whose toupee kept slipping; a mug-shaped small man who thirty years ago had invented a donnish verse form resembling the limerick; a preposterously rude young radical with puffed-out lips and a dominating stammer; and, chairing their discussion, a tall B.B.C. girl whose elongated hands kept arresting Bech in mid-sentence – she had pop eyes and a wild way of summing up, as if all the while she had been attending to angel-voices entirely her own. Bech let Merissa drive him, in her beige Fiat, to Stonehenge and Canterbury. At Canterbury she got into a fight with a verger about exactly where Becket had been stabbed. She took Bech to a concert in the Albert Hall, whose cavernous interior Bech drowsily confused with Victoria's womb, and where he fell asleep. Afterward they went to a club with gaming rooms where Merissa, playing two blackjack hands simultaneously, lost sixty quid in twenty minutes. There was a professional fierceness about the way she sat at the green felt table that requickened his curiosity as to what she *did*. He was sure she did something. Her flat held a swept-off desk, and a bookcase shelf solid with reference works. Bech would have snooped, but he felt Isabella always watching him, and the daylight hours he spent here were few. Merissa told him her last name – Merrill, the name of her American husband – but fended off his other inquiries with the protest that he was being "writery" and the disarming request that he consider her as simply his "London episode." But how did she live? She and her son and her maid. "Oh," Merissa told him, "my father owns things. Don't ask me what things. He keeps buying different ones."

He had not quite given up the idea of making her the heroine of his masterpiece. He must understand what it is like to be young now. "The other men you sleep with – what do you feel toward them?"

"They seem nice at the time."

"At the time; and then afterward not so nice?"

The suggestion startled her; from the way her eyes widened, she felt he was trying to insert evil into her world. "Oh yes, then too. They're so grateful. Men are. They're so grateful if you just make them a cup of tea in the morning."

"But where is it all going? Do you think about marrying again?"

"Not much. That first go was pretty draggy. He kept saying things like, 'Pick up your underwear,' and, 'In Asia they live on ninety dollars a year.'" Merissa laughed.

Her hair was a miracle, spread out on the pillow in the morning light, a lustrous mass, every filament the same lucid black, a black that held red light within it as matter holds heat – whereas even of the hairs on his toes some had turned white. Gold names on an honor roll. As a character, Merissa would become a redhead, with that vulnerable freckled pallor redheads have and overlarge, uneven, earnest front teeth. Merissa's teeth were so perfectly spaced they seemed machined. Like her eyelashes. *Stars with a talent for squad-drill.* As she laughed, divulging the slippery grotto beyond her palate, Bech felt abhorrence rising in his throat. He looked toward the window; an airplane was descending from a ceiling of gray. He asked, "Do you take drugs?"

"Not really. A little grass to be companionable. I don't believe in it."

Her American counterpart would, of course. Bech saw this counterpart in his mind: a pale Puritan, self-destructive, her blue eyes faded like cotton work clothes too often scrubbed. Merissa's green eyes sparkled; her hectic cheeks burned. "What do you believe in?" he asked.

"Different things at different times," she said. "You don't seem all that pro-marriagey yourself."

"I am, for other people."

"I know why sleeping with you is so exciting. It's like sleeping with a dirty monk."

"Dear Merissa," Bech said. He tried to crush her into himself. To suck the harlot's roses from her cheeks. He slobbered on her wrists, pressed his forehead against the small of her spine. He did all this in ten-point type, upon the warm white paper of her sliding skin. Poor child, under this old ogre, who had chewed his life so badly his stomach hurt, whose every experience was harassed by a fictional version of itself, whose waking life was a weary dream of echoes and erased pencil lines; he begged her forgiveness, while she moaned with anticipated pleasure. It was no use; he could not rise, he could not love her, could not perpetuate a romance or *roman* without seeing through it to the sour parting and the mixed reviews. He began, in lieu of performance, to explain this.

She interrupted: "Well, Henry, you must learn to replace ardor with art."

The cool practicality of this advice, its smug recourse to millennia of peasant saws and aristocratic maxims, to all that civilized wisdom America had sought to flee and render obsolete, angered him. "Art *is* ardor," he told her.

"Bad artists hope that's true."

"Read your Wordsworth."

"In tran*quil*lity, darling."

Her willingness to debate was beginning to excite him. He saw that wit and logic might survive into the lawless world coming to birth. "Merissa, you're so clever."

"The weak must be. That's what England is learning."

"Do you think I'm necessarily impotent? As an artist?"

"Unnecessarily."

"Merissa, tell me: what do you *do*?"

"You'll see," she said, pressing her head back into the pillow and smiling in assured satisfaction, as his giant prick worked back and forth. The tail wagging the dog.

Tuttle caught him at his hotel the day before he left and asked him if he felt any affinity with Ronald Firbank. "Only the affinity," Bech said, "I feel with all Roman Catholic homosexuals."

"I was hoping you'd say something like that. How are you feeling, Mr. Bech? The last time I saw you, you looked awful. Frankly."

"I feel better now that you've stopped seeing me."

"Great. It was a real privilege and delight for me, I tell you. I hope you like the way the piece shaped up; I do. I hope you don't mind my few reservations."

"No, you can't go anywhere these days without reservations."

"Ha ha." It was the only time Bech ever heard Tuttle laugh.

Merissa didn't answer her telephone. Bech hoped she'd be at the farewell party Goldy threw for him – a modest affair, without blue livery, and Bech in his altered tuxedo the sole man present in formal dress – but she wasn't. When Bech asked where she was, Goldy said with a twinkle, "Working. She sends her love and regrets." Bech called her at midnight, at one in the morning, at two, at five when the birds began singing, at seven when the earliest church bells rang, at nine and at ten, while packing to catch his plane. Not even Isabella answered. She must be off on a country weekend. Or visiting the boy at school. Or vanished like a good paragraph in a book too bulky to reread.

Goldschmidt drove him to the airport in his maroon Bentley, and with an urgent prideful air pressed a number of Sunday newspapers upon him. "The *Observer* gave us more space," he said, "but the *Times* seemed to like it more. All in all, a very fine reception for a – let's be frank – a rather trumped-up mishmash of a book. Now you must do us a blockbuster." He said this, here at Heathrow, in the second-class passenger lounge, but his eyes were darting over Bech's shoulder toward the stream of fresh arrivals.

"I have just the title," Bech told him. He saw that he must put Goldy into it, as a Jewish uncle. A leatherworker, his right palm hard as a turtle shell from handling an awl. That heavy pampered Florentine head bent full of greedy dreams beneath a naked light bulb, as pocketbooks, belts, and sandals tumbled from the slaughter of screaming calves. The baroque beauty of the scraps piled neglected at his feet. A fire escape out the window. Some of the panes were transparent wire-glass and others, unaccountably, were painted opaque.

Goldschmidt added a folded tabloid to Bech's supply of airplane reading.

PEER, BRIDE NABBED
IN DORSET DOPE RAID

the headline said. Goldschmidt said, "Page seventeen might amuse you. As you know, this is the paper Merissa's father bought last year. Millions read it."

"No, I didn't know. She told me nothing about her father."

"He's a dear old rascal. Almost the last of the true Tories."

"I could have sworn she was a Lib-Lab."

"Merissa is a very clever lamb," Goldschmidt stated, and pinched his lips shut. In our long Diaspora we have learned not to tattle on our hosts. Goldy's right hand, shaken farewell, was unreally soft.

Bech saved page seventeen for the last. The *Times* review was headlined "More Ethnic Fiction from the New World" and lumped *The Best of Bech* with a novel about Canadian Indians by Leonard Cohen and a collection of protest essays and scatalogical poems by LeRoi Jones. The long *Observer* piece was titled "Bech's Best Not Good Enough" and was signed L. Clark Tuttle. Bech skimmed, as a fakir walks on hot coals, pausing nowhere long enough to burn the moisture from the soles of his feet. Almost none of the quotes he had poured into the boy's notebook and tape recorder were used. Instead, an aggrieved survey of Bech's *œuvre* unfolded, smudged by feeble rebuttals.

> ... Queried concerning the flowery, not to say fruity, style of *The Chosen*, Bech shrugged off the entire problem of style, claiming (facetiously?) that he never thinks about it.... Of the book's profound failure, the crippling irreconcilability of its grandiose intentions and the triviality of its characters' moral concerns, Bech appears blissfully unaware, taking refuge in the charming, if rather automatically gnomic, disclaimer that "as you grow older, life becomes complicated" ... This interviewer was struck, indeed, by the defensive nature of Bech's breezy garrulousness; his charm operates as a screen against others – their menacing opinions, the raw *stuff* of their life – just as, perhaps, drink operates within him as a screen against his own deepest self-suspicions ... counter-revolutionary nostalgia ... possibly ironical faith in "entrepreneurism" ... nevertheless, undoubted verbal gifts ... traumatized by the economic collapse of the 1930s ... a minor master for the space of scattered pages ... not to be classed, Bech's faithful *New York Review* claque to the contrary, with the early Bellow or the late Mailer ... reminded, in the end, after the butterfly similes and overextended, substanceless themes of this self-anointed "Best," of (and the comparison may serve English readers as an index of present relevance) Ronald Firbank!

Bech let the paper go limp. The airplane had taxied out and he braced himself for the perilous plunge into flight. Only when aloft, with Hampton Court securely beneath him, a delicate sepia diagram of itself, and London's great stone mass dissolved into a cloud on the surface of the receding earth, did Bech turn to page seventeen. A column there was headed MERISSA'S WEEK. The line drawing of the girl recalled to Bech the spaces in her face – the catlike span between her eyes, the oval granny glasses, the V-shaped little chin, the sudden moist gap of her mouth, which in the caricature existed as a wry tilde, a ∼.

> Merissa had a tamey week ★ ★ ★ The daffodils were just like olde tymes, eh, W. W.? ★ ★ ★ Beware: the blackjack dealer at L'Ambassadeur draws to sixteen and always makes it ★ ★ ★ A verger down at Canterbury C. is such an ignoramus I took him for a Drugs Squad agent ★ ★ ★ The new acoustics in the Albert Hall are still worse than those on Salisbury Plain ★ ★ ★ John & Yoko will cut their next record standing on their heads, their bottoms painted to resemble each other's faces ★ ★ ★ Swinging L. was a shade more swingy this week when the darling American author Henry (*Travel Light, Brother Pig* and don't look blank they're in Penguins) Bech dropped in at Revolution and other In spots. The heart of many a jaded bird beat brighter to see Bech's rabbinical curls bouncing in time to "Poke Salad Annie" and other Yank-y hits. Merissa says: Hurry Back, H. B., transatlantic men are the most existential ★ ★ ★ He was visiting Londinium to help push la crème of his crème, *Bech's Best*, a J. J. Goldschmidt release, with a dull, dull jacket – the author's pic is missing. Confidentially, his heart belongs to dirty old New York ★ ★ ★

Bech closed his eyes, feeling his love for her expand as the distance between them increased. Entrepreneurism rides again. *Rabbinical curls:* somehow he had sold her that. *Automatically gnomic:* he had sold that too. *As a screen against others.* Firbank dead at forty. Still gaining altitude, he realized he was not dead; his fate was not so substantial. He had become a character by Henry Bech.

BECH ENTERS HEAVEN

WHEN HENRY BECH was an impressionable pre-adolescent of
twelve, more bored than he would admit with the question of
whether or not the 1935 Yankees could wrest the pennant back
from a Detroit led by the heroic Hank Greenberg, his mother
one May afternoon took him out of school, after consultation
with the principal; she was a hardened consulter with the principal. She had consulted when Henry entered the first grade, when
he came back from the second with a bloody nose, when he
skipped the third, and when he was given a 65 in Penmanship in
the fifth. The school was P.S. 87, at 77th and Amsterdam – a
bleak brick building whose interior complexity of smells
and excitement, especially during a snowstorm or around
Hallowe'en, was tremendous. None but very young hearts
could have withstood the daily strain of so much intrigue,
humor, desire, personality, mental effort, emotional current, of
so many achingly important nuances of prestige and impersona-
tion. Bech, rather short for his age, yet with a big nose and big
feet that promised future growth, was recognized from the first
by his classmates as an only son, a mother's son more than a
father's, pampered and bright though not a prodigy (his voice had
no pitch, his mathematical aptitude was no Einstein's); naturally
he was teased. Not all the teasing took the form of bloody noses;
sometimes the girl in the adjacent desk-seat tickled the hair on his
forearms with her pencil, or his name was flaunted through the
wire fence that separated the sexes at recess. The brownstone
neighborhoods that supplied students to the school were in those
years still middle-class, if by middle-class is understood not a level
of poverty (unlike today's poor, they had no cars, no credit cards,

and no delivery arrangements with the liquor store) but of self-esteem. Immersed in the Great Depression, they had kept their families together, kept their feet from touching bottom, and kept their faith in the future – their children's future more than their own. These children brought a giddy relief into the sanctum of the school building, relief that the world, or at least this brick cube carved from it, had survived another day. How fragile the world felt to them! – as fragile as it seems sturdy to today's children, who wish to destroy it. Predominately Jewish, Bech's grammar school classes had a bold bright dash of German Gentiles, whose fathers also kept a small shop or plied a manual craft, and some Eastern Europeans, whose fey manners and lisped English made them the centers of romantic frenzy and wild joking attacks. All studied, by the light of yellowish overhead globes and of the 48-star flag nailed above the blackboard, penmanship, the spice routes, the imports and exports of the three Guianas, the three cases of percentage, and other matters of rote given significance by the existence of breadlines and penthouses, just as the various drudgeries of their fathers were given dignity, even holiness, by their direct connection with food and survival. Although he would have been slow to admit this also, little Bech loved the school; he cherished his citizenship in its ragged population, was enraptured by the freckled chin and cerulean eyes of Eva Hassel across the aisle, and detested his mother's frequent interference in his American education. Whenever she appeared outside the office of the principal (Mr. Linnehan, a sore-lidded spoiled priest with an easily mimicked blink and stammer), he was teased in the cloakroom or down on the asphalt at recess; when she had him skip a grade, he had become the baby of the class. By the age of twelve, he was going to school with girls that were women. That day in May, he showed his anger with his mother by not talking to her as they walked from the scarred school steps, down 78th past a mock-Tudor apartment house like some evilly enlarged and begrimed fairy-tale chalet, to Broadway and 79th and the IRT kiosk with its compounded aroma of hot brakes, warm bagels, and vomit.

Extraordinarily, they took a train *north*. The whole drift of their lives was *south* – south to Times Square and to the Public

Library, south to Gimbels, south to Brooklyn where his father's two brothers lived. North, there was nothing but Grant's Tomb, and Harlem, and Yankee Stadium, and Riverdale where a rich cousin, a theatre manager, inhabited an apartment full of glass furniture and an array of leering and scribbled photographs. North of that yawned the foreign vastness, first named New York State but melting westward into other names, other states, where the *goyim* farmed their farms and drove their roadsters and swung on their porch swings and engaged in the countless struggles of moral heroism depicted continuously in the Hollywood movies at the Broadway RKO. Upon the huge body of the United States, swept by dust storms and storms of Christian conscience, young Henry knew that his island of Manhattan existed as an excrescence; relatively, his little family world was an immigrant enclave, the religion his grandfathers had practiced was a tolerated affront, and the language of this religion's celebration was a backwards-running archaism. He and his kin and their kindred were huddled in shawls within an overheated back room while outdoors a huge and beautiful wilderness rattled their sashes with wind and painted the panes with frost; and all the furniture they had brought with them from Europe, the footstools and phylacteries, the copies of Tolstoy and Heine, the ambitiousness and defensiveness and love, belonged to this stuffy back room.

Now his mother was pointing him north, into the cold. Their reflections shuddered in the black glass as the express train slammed through local stops, wan islands of light where fat colored women waited with string shopping bags. Bech was always surprised that these frozen vistas did not shatter as they pierced them; perhaps it was the multi-leveled sliding, the hurtling metal precariously switched aside from collision, more than the odors and subterranean claustrophobia, that made the boy sick on subways. He figured that he was good for eight stops before nausea began. It had just begun when she touched his arm. High, high on the West Side they emerged, into a region where cliffs and windy hilltops seemed insecurely suppressed by the asphalt grid. A boisterous shout of spring rolled upward from the river, and trolley cars clanged along Broadway. Together they walked, the boy and his mother, he in a wool knicker suit that scratched and sang between his legs, she in a tremulous hat of shining black straw, up a broad pavement bordered with cobblestones and trees whose bark was scabbed brown and white like a giraffe's neck. His sideways glance reaped a child's cowing impression of, beneath the unsteady flesh of his mother's jaw, the rose splotches that signaled excitement or anger. He had better talk. "Where are we going?"

"So," she said, "the cat found his tongue."

"You know I don't like your coming into the school."

"Mister Touch-Me-Not," she said, "so ashamed of his mother he wants all his blue-eyed shiksas as to think he came out from under a rock, I suppose. Or better yet lives in a tree like Siegfried."

Somewhere in the past she had wormed out of him his admiration of the German girls at school. He blushed. "Thanks to you," he told her, "they're all a year older than me."

"Not in their empty golden heads, they're not so old. Maybe in their pants, but that'll come to you soon enough. Don't hurry the years, soon enough they'll hurry you."

Homily, flattery, and humiliation: these were what his mother applied to him, day after day, like a sculptor's pats. It deepened his blush to hear her mention Eva Hassel's pants. Were they what would come to him soon enough? This was his mother's style, to mock his reality and stretch his expectations.

She went on, "There's nothing one of those fräuleins would like better than fasten herself to some smart little Jewish boy. Better that than some sausage-grinding Fritz who'll go to beer and beating her before he's twenty-five. You keep your nose in your books."

"That's where it was, before you busted into school. Where are you taking me?"

"To see something more important than where to put your you-know-what."

"Mother, don't be vulgar."

"Vulgar is what I call a boy who wants to put his mother under a rock. His mother and his people and his brain, all under a rock."

"Now I understand. You're taking me to look at Plymouth Rock."

"Something like it. If you have to grow up American, at least let's not look only at the underside. Arnie" – the Riverdale cousin – "got me two tickets from Josh Glazer, to I don't know quite what it is. We shall see."

The hill beneath their feet flattened; they arrived at a massive building of somehow unsullied granite, with a paradoxical look of having been here forever yet having been rarely used. Around its top ran a ribbon of carved names: PLATO · NEWTON · AESCHY-LUS · LEONARDO · AQUINAS · SHAKESPEARE · VOLTAIRE · COPERNI-CUS · ARISTOTLE · HOBBES · VICO · PUSHKIN · LINNAEUS · RACINE and infinitely on, around cornices and down the receding length of the building's two tall wings. Courtyard followed courtyard, each at a slightly higher level than the last. Conical evergreens stood silent guard; an unseen fountain played. For entrance, there was a bewildering choice of bronze doors. Bech's mother pushed one and encountered a green-uniformed guard; she told him, "My name is Abigail Bech and this is my son Henry. These are our tickets, it says right here this is the day, they were obtained for us by a close associate of Josh Glazer's, the playwright. I'm sure you've heard of him. Nobody forewarned me it would be such a climb from the subway, that's why I'm out of breath like this." The guard, and then another guard, for they several times got lost, directed them (his mother receiving and repeating a full set of directions each time) up a ramifying series of marble stair-ways into the balcony of an auditorium whose ceiling, the child's impression was, was decorated with plaster toys – scrolls, masks, seashells, tops, and stars.

A ceremony was already in progress. Their discussions with the guards had consumed time. The bright stage far below them supported a magical tableau. On a curved dais composed of six or seven rows a hundred persons, mostly men, were seated. Though some of the men could be seen to move – one turned his head, another scratched his knee – their appearance in sum had an iron unity; they looked engraved. Each face, even at the distance of the balcony, displayed the stamp of extra precision that devout attention and frequent photography etch upon a visage; each had suffered the crystallization of fame. Young Henry saw that there were other types of Heaven, less agitated and more elevated than the school, more compact and less tragic than Yankee Stadium, where the scattered players, fragile in white, seemed about to be devoured by the dragon-shaped crowd. He knew, even before his mother, with the aid of a diagram provided on her program, began to name names, that under his eyes was assembled the flower of the arts in America, its rabbis and chieftains, souls who while still breathing enjoyed their immortality.

The surface of their collective glory undulated as one or another would stand, shuffle outward from his row, seize the glowing lectern, and speak. Some rose to award prizes; others rose to accept them. They applauded one another with a polite rustle eagerly echoed and thunderously amplified by the anonymous, perishable crowd on the other side of the veil, a docile cloudy multitude stretching backwards from front rows of corsaged loved ones into the dim regions of the balcony where mere spectators sat, where little Bech stared dazzled while his mother busily bent above the identifying diagram. She located, and pointed out to him, with that ardor for navigational detail that had delayed their arrival here, Emil Nordquist, the Bard of the Prairie, the beetle-browed celebrant in irresistible *vers libre* of shocked corn and Swedish dairymaids; John Kingsgrant Forbes, New England's dapper novelist of manners; Fenella Anne Collins, the wispy, mystical poet of impacted passion from Alabama, the most piquant voice in American verse since the passing of the Amherst recluse; the massive Jason Honeygale, Tennessee's fabled word-torrent; hawk-eyed Torquemada Langguth, lover and singer of California's sheer cliffs and sere unpopulated places; and Manhattan's own Josh Glazer, Broadway wit, comedy-wright, lyricist, and Romeo. And there were squat bald sculptors with great curved thumbs; red-bearded painters like bespattered prophets; petite, gleaming philosophers who piped Greek catch-words into the microphone; stooped and drawling historians from the border states; avowed Communists with faces as dry as paper and black ribbons dangling from their *pinces-nez*; atonal composers delicately exchanging awards and reminiscences of Paris, the phrases in French nasally cutting across their speech

like accented trombones; sibylline old women with bronze faces
– all of them unified, in the eyes of the boy Bech, by not only the
clothy dark mass of their clothes and the brilliance of the stage
but by their transcendence of time: they had attained the fixity of
lasting accomplishment and exempted themselves from the nagging nuisance of growth and its twin (which he precociously felt
in himself even then, especially in his teeth), decay. He childishly
assumed that, though unveiled every May, they sat like this
eternally, in the same iron arrangement, beneath this domed
ceiling of scrolls and stars.

At last the final congratulation was offered, and the final
modest acceptance enunciated. Bech and his mother turned to
re-navigate the maze of staircases. They were both shy of speaking, but she sensed, in the abstracted way he clung to her side,
neither welcoming nor cringing from her touch when she
reached to reassure him in the crowd, that his attention had
been successfully turned. His ears were red, showing that an
inner flame had been lit. She had set him on a track, a track
that must be – Abigail Bech ignored a sudden qualm, like a rude
jostling from behind – the right one.

Bech never dared hope to join that pantheon. Those faces of
the Thirties, like the books he began to read, putting aside baseball
statistics forever, formed a world impossibly high and apart, an
immutable text graven on the stone brow – his confused impression was – of Manhattan. In middle age, it would startle him to
realize that Louis Bromfield, say, was no longer considered a
sage, that van Vechten, Cabell, and John Erskine had become as
obscure as the famous gangsters of the same period, and that an
entire generation had grown to wisdom without once chuckling
over a verse by Arthur Guiterman or Franklin P. Adams. When
Bech received, in an envelope not so unlike those containing
solicitations to join the Erotica Book Club or the Associated
Friends of Apache Education, notice of his election to a society
whose title suggested that of a merged church, with an invitation
to its May ceremonial, he did not connect the honor with his
truant afternoon of over three decades ago. He accepted, because

in his fallow middle years he hesitated to decline any invitation, whether it was to travel to Communist Europe or to smoke marijuana. His working day was brief, his living day was long, and there always lurked the hope that around the corner of some impromptu acquiescence he would encounter, in a flurry of apologies and excitedly mis-aimed kisses, his long-lost mistress, Inspiration. He took a taxi north on the appointed day. By chance he was let off at a side entrance in no way reminiscent of the august frontal approach he had once ventured within the shadow of his mother. Inside the bronze door, Bech was greeted by a mini-skirted administrative assistant who, licking her lips and perhaps unintentionally bringing her pelvis to within an inch of his, pinned his name in plastic to his lapel and, as a tantalizing afterthought (the tip of her tongue exposed in playful concentration), adjusted the knot of his necktie. Other such considerate houris were supervising arrivals, separating antique *belle-lettrists* from their overcoats with philatelic care, steering querulously nodding poetesses toward the elevator, administering the distribution of gaudy heaps of name tags, admission cards, and coded numerals.

Bech asked his assistant, "Am I supposed to do anything?"

She said, "When your name is announced, stand."

"Do I take the elevator?"

She patted his shoulders and tugged one of his earlobes. "I think you're a young enough body," she judged, "to use the stairs."

He obediently ascended a thronged marble stairway and found himself amid a cloud of murmuring presences; a few of the faces were familiar — Tory Ingersoll, a tireless old huckster, his androgynous features rigid in their carapace of orangish foundation, who had in recent years plugged himself into hipsterism and become a copious puffist and anthologist for the "new" poetry, whether concrete, non-associative, neo-gita, or plain protest; Irving Stern, a swarthy, ruminative critic of Bech's age and background, who for all his strenuous protests of McLuhanite openness had never stopped squinting through the dour goggles of Leninist aesthetics, and whose own prose style tasted like aspirin tablets being chewed; Mildred Belloussovsky-Dommergues, her name as

polyglot as her marriages, her weight-lifter's shoulders and generous slash of a wise whore's mouth perversely dwindled in print to a
trickle of elliptic dimeters; Char Ecktin, the revolutionary young
dramatist whose foolish smile and high-pitched chortle consorted
oddly with the facile bitterness of his dénouements – but many
more were half-familiar, faces dimly known, like those of bit
actors in B movies, or like those faces which emerge from obscur-
ity to cap a surprisingly enthusiastic obituary, or those names
which figure small on title pages, as translator, co-editor, or "as
told to," faces whose air of recognizability might have been a
matter of ghostly family resemblance, or of a cocktail party ten
years ago, or a P.E.N. meeting, or of a moment in a bookstore, an
inside flap hastily examined and then resealed into the tight bright
row of the unpurchased. In this throng Bech heard his name softly
called, and felt his sleeve lightly plucked. But he did not lift his eyes
for fear of shattering the spell, of disturbing the penumbral de-
corum and rustle around him. They came to the end of their
labyrinthine climb, and were ushered down a dubiously narrow
corridor. Bech hesitated, as even the dullest steer hesitates in the
slaughterer's chute, but the pressure behind moved him on, outward, into a spotlit tangle of groping men and scraping chairs. He
was on a stage. Chairs were arranged in curved tiers. Mildred
Belloussovsky-Dommergues waved an alabaster, muscular arm:
"Yoo-hoo, Henry, over here. Come be a B with me." She even
spoke now – so thoroughly does art corrupt the artist – in
dimeters. Willingly he made his way upwards toward her. Always,
in his life, no matter how underfurnished in other respects, there
had been a woman to shelter beside. The chair beside her bore his
name. On the seat of the chair was a folded program. On the back
of the program was a diagram. The diagram fitted a memory, and
looking outward, into the populated darkness that reached backwards into a balcony, beneath a ceiling dimly decorated with
toylike protrusions of plaster, Bech suspected, at last, where he
was. With the instincts of a literary man he turned to printed
matter for confirmation; he bent over the diagram and, yes,
found his name, his number, his chair. He was here. He had joined
that luminous, immutable tableau. He had crossed to the other
side.

Now that forgotten expedition with his mother returned to him, and their climb through those ramifications of marble, a climb that mirrored, but profanely, the one he had just taken within sacred precincts; and he deduced that this building was vast twice over, an arch-like interior meeting in this domed auditorium where the mortal and the immortal could behold one another, through a veil that blurred and darkened the one and gave to the other a supernatural visibility, the glow and precision of Platonic forms. He studied his left hand – his partner in numerous humble crimes, his delegate in many furtive investigations – and saw it partaking, behind the flame-blue radiance of his cuff, joint by joint, to the quicks of his fingernails, in the fine articulation found less in reality than in the Promethean anatomical studies of Leonardo and Raphael.

Bech looked around; the stage was filling. He seemed to see, down front, where the stage light was most intense, the oft-photographed (by Steichen, by Karsh, by Cartier-Bresson) profile and vivid cornsilk hair of – it couldn't be – Emil Nordquist. The Bard of the Prairie still lived! He must be a hundred. No, well, if in the mid-Thirties he was in his mid-forties, he would be only eighty now. While Bech, that pre-adolescent, was approaching fifty: time had treated him far more cruelly.

And now, through the other wing of the stage, from the elevator side, moving with the agonized shuffle-step of a semi-paralytic but still sartorially formidable in double-breasted chalkstripes and a high starched collar, entered John Kingsgrant Forbes, whose last perceptive and urbane examination of Beacon Hill mores had appeared in World War II, during the paper shortage. Had Bech merely imagined his obituary?

"Arriveth our queen," Mildred Belloussovsky-Dommergues sardonically murmured on his left, with that ambiguous trace of a foreign accent, the silted residue of her several husbands. And to Bech's astonishment in came, supported on the courtly arm of Jason Honeygale, whose epic bulk had shriveled to folds of veined hide draped over stegosaurian bones, the tiny tottering figure of Fenella Anne Collins, wearing the startled facial expression of the blind. She was led down front, where the gaunt figure of Torquemada Langguth, his spine bent nearly double, his falconine crest now white as an egret's, rose to greet her and feebly to adjust her chair.

Bech murmured leftwards, "I thought they were all dead."

Mildred airily answered, "We find it better, not to die."

A shadow plumped brusquely down in the chair on Bech's right; it was – O, monstrous! – Josh Glazer. His proximity seemed to be a patron's, for he told Bech windily, "Jesus Christ, Bech, I've been plugging you for years up here, but the bastards always said, 'Let's wait until he writes another book, that last one was such a flop.' Finally I say to them, 'Look. The son of a bitch, he's *never* going to write another book,' so they say, 'O.K., let's let him the hell in.' Welcome aboard, Bech. Christ I've been a raving fan of yours since the Year One. When're you gonna try a comedy, Broadway's dead on its feet." He was deaf, his hair was dyed black, and his teeth were false too, for his blasts of breath carried with them a fetid smell of trapped alcohol and of a terrible organic something that suggested to Bech – touching a peculiar fastidiousness that was all that remained of his ancestors' ortho- doxy – the stench of decayed shellfish. Bech looked away and saw everywhere on this stage dissolution and riot. The furrowed skulls of philosophers lolled in a Bacchic stupor. Wicked smirks flickered back and forth among faces enshrined in textbooks. Eustace Chubb, America's poetic conscience throughout the Cold War, had holes in his socks and mechanically chafed a purple sore on his shin. Anatole Husač, the Father of Neo- Figurism, was sweating out a drug high, his hands twitching like suffocating fish. As the ceremony proceeded, not a classroom of trade-school dropouts could have been more impudently inattentive. Mildred Belloussovsky-Dommergues persistently tickled the hairs on Bech's wrist with the edge of her program; Josh Glazer offered him a sip from a silver flask signed by the Gershwin brothers. The leonine head – that of a great lexico- grapher – directly in front of Bech drifted sideways and emitted illegible snores. The Medal for Modern Fiction was being awarded to Kingsgrant Forbes; the cello-shaped presenter (best known for his scrupulous editorship of the six volumes of Hamlin Garland's correspondence) began his speech, "In these sorry days of so-called Black Humor, of the fictional apotheosis of the underdeveloped," and a tall black man in the middle of Bech's row stood, spoke a single expletive, and, with much scraping of chairs, made his way from the stage. A series of grants was bestowed. One of the recipients, a tiptoeing fellow in a mauve jump suit, hurled paper streamers toward the audience and bared his chest to reveal painted there a psychedelic pig labeled Milhaus; at this, several old men, an Arizona naturalist and a New Deal muralist, stamped off, and for a long time could be heard buzzing for the elevator. The sardonic hubbub waxed louder. Impatience set in. "Goddammit," Josh Glazer breathed to Bech, "I'm paying a limousine by the hour downstairs, and I've got a helluva cute little fox waiting for me at the Plaza."

At last the time came to introduce the new members. The citations were read by a farsighted landscape painter who had trouble bringing his papers, the lectern light, and his reading glasses into mutual adjustment at such short focus. "Henry Bech," he read, pronouncing it "Betch," and Bech obediently stood. The spotlights dazzled him; he had the sensation of being microscopically examined, and of being strangely small. When he stood, he had expected to rear into a man's height, and instead rose no taller than a child.

"A native New Yorker," the citation began, "who has chosen to sing of the continental distances —"

Bech wondered why writers in official positions were always supposed to "sing"; he couldn't remember the last time he had even hummed.

" — a son of Israel loyal to Melville's romanticism —"

He went around telling interviewers Melville was his favorite author, but he hadn't gotten a third of the way through *Pierre*.

" — a poet in prose whose polish precludes pre- — pro- — pardon me, these are new bifocals —"

Laughter from the audience. Who was out there in that audience?

" — let me try again: whose polish precludes prolificacy —"

His mother was out there in that audience!

" — a magician of metaphor —"

She was there, right down front, basking in the reflected stagelight, an orchid corsage pinned to her bosom.

" – and a friend of the human heart."

But she had died after the war, in Brooklyn's Interfaith Medical Center. As the applause washed in, Bech saw that the old lady with the corsage was applauding only politely, she was not his mother but somebody else's, maybe of the boy with the pig on his stomach, though for a moment, a trick of the light, something determined and expectant in the tilt of her head, something hopeful . . . The light in his eyes turned to warm water. His applause ebbed away. He sat down. Mildred nudged him. Josh Glazer shook his hand, too violently. Bech tried to clear his vision by contemplating the backs of the heads. They were blank: blank shabby backs of a cardboard tableau lent substance only by the credulous, by hopeful mothers and their children. His knees trembled, as if after an arduous climb. He had made it, he was here, in Heaven. Now what?

APPENDICES

APPENDIX A

We are grateful for permission to reprint corroborating excerpts from the unpublished Russian journal of Henry Bech. The journal, physically, is a faded red Expenses diary, measuring 7 ⅜" by 4 ¼", stained by Moscow brandy and warped by Caucasian dew. The entries, of which the latter are kept in red ballpoint pen, run from October 20, 1964, to December 6, 1964. The earliest are the fullest.

I

Oct. 20. Flight from NY at midnight, no sleep, Pan Am kept feeding me. Beating against the sun, soon dawn. Paris strange passing through by bus, tattered tired sepia sets of second-rate opera being wheeled through, false cheer of café awnings, waiting for chorus of lamplighters. Orly to Le Bourget. Moscow plane a new world. Men in dark coats waiting bunched. Solemn as gangsters. Overhead first understood Russian word, *Americanski*, pronounced with wink toward me by snaggle-toothed gent putting bulky black coat in overhead rack. Rack netted cord, inside ribs of plane show, no capitalist plastic. Stewardesses not our smoothly extruded tarts but hefty flesh; served us real potatoes, beef sausage, borsch. Aeroflot a feast afloat. Crowded happy stable smell, animal heat in cold stable, five miles up. Uncles' back rooms in Wmsburg. Babble around me, foreign languages strangely soothing, at home in Babel. Fell asleep on bosom of void, grateful to be alive, home. Woke in dark again. Earth's revolution full in my face. Moscow dim on ocean of blackness, delicate torn veil, shy of electricity, not New York, that rude splash. Premonition: no one will meet. Author Disappears

Behind Iron Curtain. Bech Best Remembered for Early Work. A delegation with roses waiting for me on other side of glass pen, wait for hours, on verge of Russia, decompressing. Time different here, steppes of time, long dully lit terminal, empty of ads. Limousine driven by voiceless back of head, sleigh driver in Tolstoy, long haul to Moscow, a wealth of darkness, gray birches, slim, young, far from gnarled American woods. In hotel spelled out этаж waiting for elevator, French hidden beneath the Cyrillic. Everywhere, secrets.

II

Oct. 23. Met Sobaka, head of Writers' U. Building Tolstoy's old manse, dining room baronial oak. Litterateurs live like aristocrats. Sobaka has lipless mouth, wild bark, must have strangled men with bare hands. Tells me long story of love of his poetry expressed by coalminers in the Urals. Skip translating: "...then, here in...the deepest part of the mine...by only the light of, uh, carbon lights in the miners' caps...for three hours I recited...from the works of my youth, lyrics of the fields and forests of Byelorussia. Never have I known such enthusiasm. Never have I possessed such inspiration, such, ah, powers of memory. At the end...they wept to see me depart...these simple miners...their coal-blackened faces streaked, ah, veined with the silver of tears."

"Fantastic," I say.

"*Fantastichni*," Skip translates.

Sobaka makes Skip ask me if I like the image, their faces of coal veined with silver.

"It's good," say I.

"*Korosho*," says Skip.

"The earth weeps precious metal," I say. "The world's working people weep at the tyranny of capital."

Skip guffaws but translates, and Sobaka reaches under table and seizes my thigh in murderous pinch of conspiracy.

Nov. 12. Back in Moscow, lunch at W.U. Sobaka in fine form, must have chopped off somebody's index finger this morning.

Says trip to Irkutsk hazardous, airport might get snowed in. Hee hee hee. Suggests Kazakhstan instead, I say why not? – *nichyvo*. Eyeball to eyeball. He toasts Jack London, I toast Pushkin. He does Hemingway, I do Turgenev. I do Nabokov, he counters with John Reed. His mouth engulfs the glass and crunches. I think of what my dentist would say, my beautiful gold caps. . . .

Nov. 19. . . . I ask Kate where Sobaka is, she pretends not to hear. Skip tells me later he was friend of Khrush., hung on for while, now non-person. I miss him. My strange weakness for cops and assassins: their sense of craftsmanship?

III

Nov. 1. Off to Caucasus with Skip, Mrs. R., Kate. Fog, no planes for twenty-four hours. Airport crammed with hordes of sleeping. Soldiers, peasants, an epic patience. Sleeping on clothy heaps of each other, no noise of complaint. Many types of soldier uniform, long coats. Kate after twelve hours bullies way onto plane, pointing to me as Guest of the State, fierce performance. Engines screaming, officials screaming, she screaming. Get on plane at 2 A.M., amid bundles, chickens, gypsies, sit opposite pair of plump fortune tellers who groan and (very discreetly) throw up all the way to Tbilisi. Ears ache in descent; no pressurization. Birds in airport, in and out, remind me of San Juan. Happy, sleepless. Sun on hills, flowers like oleanders. Hotel as in Florida Keys in Bogart movies, sour early morning service, a bracing sense of the sinister. Great fist-shaking Lenin statue in traffic circle. Flies buzz in room.

Nov. 2. Slept till noon. Reynolds wakes with phone call. He and Mrs. caught later plane. Cowboys and Indians, even my escorts have escorts. We go in two cars to Pantheon on hill, Georgian escort lantern-jawed professor of aesthetics. Cemetery full of funny alphabet, big stone he says with almost tear in eye called simply "Mother." Reynolds clues me sotto voce it's Stalin's mother. Had been statue of S. here so big it killed two workmen when they pulled it down. Supper with many Georgian poets, toasts in white wine, my own toasts keep calling them "Russians" which Kate corrects in translation to "Georgians." Author of epic infatuated with Mrs. R., strawberry blonde from Wisconsin. Puts hands on thighs, kisses throat, Skip grins sheepishly, what he's here for, to improve relations. Cable car down the mountain, Tbilisi a-spangle under us, all drunk, singing done in pit of throat, many vibrations, hillbilly mournfulness, back to bed. Same flies buzz.

Nov. 3. Car ride to Muxtyeta, oldest church in Christendom, professor of aesthetics ridicules God, chastity, everybody winces. Scaldingly clear blue sky, church a ruddy octagonal ruin with something ancient and pagan in the center. Went to lunch with snowy-haired painter of breasts. These painters of a sleazy ethnic softness, of flesh like pastel landscapes, landscapes like pastel flesh. Where are the real artists, the cartoonists who fill *Krokodil* with fanged bankers and cadaverous Adenauers, the anonymous Chardins of industrial detail? Hidden from me, like missile sites and working ports. Of the Russian cake they give me only frosting. By train to Armenia. We all share a four-bunk sleeper. Ladies undress below me, see Kate's hand dislodge beige buttoned canvasy thing, see circlet of lace flick past Ellen Reynolds's pale round knee. Closeted with female flesh and Skip's supercilious snore expect to stay awake, but fall asleep in top bunk like child among nurses. Yerevan station at dawn. The women, puffy-eyed and mussed, claim night of total insomnia. Difficulty of women sleeping on trains, boats, where men are soothed. Distrust of machinery? Sexual stimulation, Claire saying she used to come just from sitting on vibrating subway seat, never the IRT, only the IND. Took at least five stops.

Nov. 4. Svartz-Notz. Armenian cathedral. Old bones in gold bands. Our escort has withered arm, war record, dear smile, writing long novel about 1905 uprising. New city pink and mauve stone, old one Asiatic heaped rubble. Ruins of Alexander's palace, passed through on way to India. Gorgeous gorge.

Nov. 5. Lake Sevan, grim gray sulphuric beach, lowered lake six feet to irrigate land. Land dry and rosy. Back at hotel, man stopped in lobby, recognized me, here from Fresno visiting relatives, said he couldn't finish *The Chosen*, asked for autograph. Dinner with Armenian science fiction writers, Kate in her element, they want to know if I know Ray Bradbury, Marshall McLuhan, Vance Packard, Mitchell Wilson. I don't. Oh. I say I know Norman Podhoretz and they ask if he wrote *Naked and Dead*.

Nov. 6. Long drive to "working" monastery. Two monks live in it. Chapel carved from solid rock, bushes full of little strips of cloth, people make a wish. Kate borrows my handkerchief, tears off strip, ties to bush, make a wish. Blushes when I express surprise. Ground littered with sacrificial bones. In courtyard band of farmers having ceremonial cookout honoring birth of son. Insist we join them, Reynoldses tickled pink, hard for American diplomats to get to clambake like this, real people. Priest scruffy sly fellow with gold fangs in beard. Armenians all wearing sneakers, look like Saroyan characters. Flies in wine, gobbets of warm lamb, blessings, toasts heavily directed toward our giggling round-kneed strawberry-blonde Ellen R. As we leave we glimpse real monk, walking along tumbledown parapet. Unexpectedly young. Pale, expressionless, very remote. A spy? Dry lands make best saints. Reynoldses both sick from effects of people's feast, confined to hotel while Kate and I, hardened sinners, iron stomachs, go to dinner with white-haired artist, painter of winsome faces, sloe eyes, humanoid fruit, etc.

Nov. 7. Woke to band music; today Revolution Day. Should be in Red Square, but Kate talked me out of it. Smaller similar parade here, in square outside hotel. Overlook while eating breakfast of blini and caviar parade of soldiers, red flags, equipment enlarging phallically up to rockets, then athletes in different colors like gumdrops, swarm at end of children, people, citizens, red dresses conspicuous. Kate kept clucking tongue and saying she hates war. Reynoldses still rocky, hardly eat. Ellen admires my digestive toughness, I indifferent to her praise. Am I falling in love with Kate? Feel insecure away from her side, listen to her clear throat and toss in hotel room next to me. We walk in sun, I jostle to get between her and withered arm, jealous when they talk in Rooski, remember her blush when she tied half my torn hanky to that supernatural bush. What was her wish? Time to leave romantic Armenia. Back to Moscow by ten, ears ache fearfully in descent. Bitter cold, dusting of snow. Napoleon trembles.

IV

This sample letter, never sent, was found enclosed in the journal. "Claire" appears to have been the predecessor, in Bech's affections, of Miss Norma Latchett. Reprinted by permission, all rights © Henry Bech.

Dear Claire:

I am back in Moscow, after three days in Leningrad, an Italian opera set begrimed by years in an arctic warehouse and populated by a million out-of-work baritone villains. Today, the American Ambassador gave me a dinner to which no Russians came, because of something they think we did in the Congo, and I spent the whole time discussing shoes with Mrs. Ambassador, who hails originally, as she put it, from Charleston. She even took her shoe off so I could hold it – it was strange, warm, small. How are you? Can you feel my obsolete ardor? Can you taste the brandy? I live luxuriously, in the hotel where visiting pleni-potentiaries from the Emperor of China are lodged, and Arabs in white robes leave oil trails down the hall. There may be an entire floor of English homosexual defectors, made over on the model of Cambridge digs. Lord, it's lonely, and bits of you – the silken depression beside each anklebone, the downy rhomboidal small of your back – pester me at night as I lie in exiled majesty, my laborious breathing being taped by threescore OGPU rookies. You were so beautiful. What happened? Was it all me, my fearful professional gloom, my Flaubertian syphilitic impo-tence? Or was it your shopgirl go-go brass, that held like a pornographic novel in a bureau (your left nipple was the drawer pull) a Quaker A-student from Darien? We turned each other inside out, it seemed to me, and made all those steak restaurants in the East Fifties light up like seraglios under bombardment. I will never be so young again. I am transported around here like a brittle curio; plug me into the nearest socket and I spout red, white, and blue. The Soviets like me because I am redolent of the oppressive Thirties. I like them for the same reason. You, on the other hand, were all Sixties, a bath of sequins and glowing pubic tendrils. Forgive my unconscionable distance, our preposterous prideful parting, the way our miraculously synchronized climaxes came to nothing, like novae. Oh, I send you such airmail lost love, Claire, from this very imaginary place, the letter may beat the plane home, and jump into your refrigerator, and nestle against the illuminated parsley as if we had never said unforgivable things.

H.

Folded into the letter, as a kind of postscript, a picture postcard. On the obverse, in bad color, a picture of an iron statue, male. On the reverse, this message:

> Dear Claire: What I meant to
> say in my unsent letter was that
> you were so good to me, good for
> me, there was a goodness in me you
> brought to birth. Virtue is so rare,
> I thank you forever. The man on the
> other side is Mayakovsky, who shot
> himself and thereby won Stalin's un-
>   dying love. Henry

Gay with Sputnik stamps, the card passed through the mails uncensored and was waiting for him when he at last returned from his travels and turned the key of his stifling, airless, unchanged apartment. It had been strenuously canceled. The lack of any accompanying note was eloquent. He and Claire never communicated again, though for a time Bech would open the telephone directory to the page where her number was encircled and hold it on his lap. – ED.

APPENDIX B

Bibliography

1. Books by Henry Bech (b. 1923, d. 19——)

Travel Light, novel. New York: The Vellum Press, 1955. London: J. J. Goldschmidt, 1957.

Brother Pig, novella. New York: The Vellum Press, 1957. London: J. J. Goldschmidt, 1958.

When the Saints, miscellany. [*Contents*: "Uncles and Dybbuks," "Subway Gum," "A Vote For Social Unconsciousness," "Soft-Boiled Sergeants," "The Vanishing Wisecrack," "Graffiti," "Sunsets Over Jersey," "The *Arabian Nights* at Your Own Pace," "Orthodoxy and Orthodontics," "Rag Bag" (collection of book reviews), "Displeased in the Dark" (collection of cinema reviews), forty-three untitled paragraphs under the head of "Tumblers Clicking."] New York: The Vellum Press, 1958.

The Chosen, novel. New York: The Vellum Press, 1963. London: J. J. Goldschmidt, 1963.

The Best of Bech, anthology. London: J. J. Goldschmidt, 1968. [Contains *Brother Pig* and selected essays from *When the Saints*.]

Think Big, novel. [In progress.]

2. Uncollected Articles and Short Stories

"Stee-raight'n Yo' Shoulduhs, Boy!", *Liberty*, XXXIV.33 (August 21, 1943) 62–63.

"Home for Hannukah," *Saturday Evening Post*, CCXVII.2 (January 8, 1944) 45–46, 129–133.

"Kosher Konsiderations," *Yank*, IV.4 (January 26, 1944) 6.

"Rough Crossing," *Collier's*, XLIV (February 22, 1944) 23–25.

"London Under Buzzbombs," *New Leader*, XXVII.11 (March 11, 1944) 9.

"The Cockney Girl," *Story*, XIV.3 (May–June, 1944) 68–75.

"V-Mail from Brooklyn," *Saturday Evening Post*, CCXVII.25 (June 30, 1944) 28–29, 133–137.

"Letter from Normandy," *New Leader*, XXVII.29 (July 15, 1944) 6.

"Hey, Yank!", *Liberty*, XXXV.40 (September 17, 1944) 48–49.

"Letter from the Bulge," *New Leader*, XXVIII.1 (January 3, 1945) 6.

"Letter from the Reichstag," *New Leader*, XXVIII.23 (June 9, 1945) 4.

"Fräulein, kommen Sie hier, bitte," *The Partisan Review*, XII (October, 1945), 413–431.

"Rubble" [poem], *Tomorrow*, IV.7 (December, 1945) 45.

"Soap" [poem], *The Nation*, CLXII (June 22, 1946) 751.

"Ivan in Berlin," *Commentary*, I.5 (August, 1946) 68–77.

"Jig-a-de-Jig," *Liberty*, XXVII.47 (October 15, 1946) 38–39.

"Novels from the Wreckage," *New York Times Book Review*, LII (January 19, 1947) 6.

☞ *The bulk of Bech's reviews, articles, essays, and prose-poems 1947–58 were reprinted in* When the Saints (*see above*). *Only exceptions are listed below.*

"My Favorite Reading in 1953," *New York Times Book Review*, LXVII (December 25, 1953) 2.

"Smokestacks" [poem], *Poetry*, LXXXIV.5 (August, 1954) 249–50.

"*Larmes d'huile*" [poem], *Accent*, XV.4 (Autumn, 1955) 101.

"Why I Will Vote for Adlai Stevenson Again" [part of paid political advertisement printed in various newspapers], October, 1956.

"My Favorite Salad," *McCall's*, XXXIV.4 (April, 1957) 88.

"Nihilistic? Me?" [interview with Lewis Nichols], *New York Times Book Review*, LXI (October 12, 1957) 17–18, 43.

"Rain King for a Day," *New Republic*, CXL.3 (January 19, 1959) 22–23.

"The Eisenhower Years: Instant Nostalgia," *Esquire*, LIV.8 (August, 1960) 54–61.

"Lay Off, Norman," *The New Republic*, CXLI.22 (May 14, 1960) 19–20.

"Bogie: The Tic That Told All," *Esquire*, LV.10 (October, 1960) 44–45, 108–111.

"The Landscape of Orgasm," *House and Garden*, XXI.3 (December, 1960) 136–141.

"The Moth on the Pin," *Commentary*, XXXI (March, 1961) 223–224.

"Iris and Muriel and Atropos," *New Republic*, CXLIV.20 (May 15, 1961) 16–17.

"Superscrew," *Big Table*, II.3 (Summer, 1961), 64–79.

"M-G-M and the U.S.A.," *Commentary*, XXXII (October, 1961) 305–316.

"My Favorite Christmas Carol," *Playboy*, VIII.12 (December, 1961) 289.

"The Importance of Beginning with a B: Barth, Borges, and Others," *Commentary*, XXXIII (February, 1962) 136–142.

"Down in Dallas" [poem], *New Republic*, CXLVI.49 (December 2, 1963) 28.

"My Favorite Three Books of 1963," *New York Times Book Review*, LXVII (December 19, 1963) 2.

"Daniel Fuchs: An Appreciation," *Commentary*, XLI.2 (February, 1964) 39–45.

"Silence," *The Hudson Review*, XVII (Summer, 1964) 258–275.

"Rough Notes from Tsardom," *Commentary*, XLI.2 (February, 1965) 39–47.

"Frightened Under Kindly Skies" [poem], *Prairie Schooner*, XXXIX.2 (Summer, 1965) 134.

"The Eternal Feminine As It Hits *Me*" [contribution to a symposium], *Rogue*, III.2 (February, 1966) 69.

"What Ever Happened to Jason Honeygale?" *Esquire*, LXI.9 (September, 1966) 70–73, 194–198.

"The Romantic Agony Under Truman: A Reminiscence," *New American Review*, III (April, 1968) 59–81.

"My Three Least Favorite Books of 1968," *Book World*, VI (December 20, 1968) 13.

3. Critical Articles Concerning (Selected List)

Prescott, Orville, "More Dirt," *New York Times*, October 12, 1955.

Weeks, Edward, "*Travel Light* Heavy Reading," *Atlantic Monthly*, CCI.10 (October, 1955) 131–132.

Kirkus Service, Virginia, "Search for Meaning in Speed," XXIV (October 11, 1955).

Time, "V-v-vrooom!", LXXII.17 (October 12, 1955) 98.

Macmanaway, Fr. Patrick X., "Spiritual Emptiness Found Behind Handlebars," *Commonweal*, LXXII.19 (October 12, 1955) 387–388.

Engels, Jonas, "Consumer Society Justly Burlesqued," *Progressive*, XXI.35 (October 20, 1955) 22.

Kazin, Alfred, "Triumphant Internal Combustion," *Commentary*, XXIX (December, 1955) 90–96.

Time, "Puzzling Porky," LXXIV.3 (January 19, 1957) 75.

Hicks, Granville, "Bech Impressive Again," *Saturday Review*, XLIII.5 (January 30, 1957) 27–28.

Callagan, Joseph, S. J., "Theology of Despair Dictates Dark Allegory," *Critic*, XVII.7 (February 8, 1957) 61–62.

West, Anthony, "Oinck, Oinck," *New Yorker*, XXXIII.4 (March 14, 1957) 171–173.

Steiner, George, "Candide as Schlemiel," *Commentary*, XXV (March, 1957) 265–270.

Maddocks, Melvin, "An Unmitigated Masterpiece," *New York Herald Tribune Book Review*, February 6, 1957.

Hyman, Stanley Edgar, "Bech Zeroes In," *New Leader*, XLII.9 (March 1, 1957) 38.

Poore, Charles, "Harmless Hodgepodge," *New York Times*, August 19, 1958.

Marty, Martin, "Revelations Within the Secular," *Christian Century*, LXXVII (August 20, 1958) 920.

Aldridge, John, "Harvest of Thoughtful Years," Kansas City *Star*, August 17, 1958.

Time, "Who Chose Whom?" LXXXIII.26 (May 24, 1963) 121.

Klein, Marcus, "Bech's Mighty Botch," *Reporter*, XXX.13 (May 23, 1963) 54.

152   BECH: A BOOK

Thompson, John, "So Bad It's Good," *New York Review of Books*, II.14 (May 15, 1963) 6.

Dilts, Susan, "Sluggish Poesy, Murky Psychology," Baltimore *Sunday Sun*, May 20, 1963.

Miller, Jonathan, "Oopsie!", *Show*, III.6 (June, 1963) 49–52.

Macdonald, Dwight, "More in Sorrow," *Partisan Review*, XXVIII (Summer, 1963) 271–279.

Kazin, Alfred, "Bech's Strange Case Reopened," *Evergreen Review*, VII.7 (July, 1963) 19–24.

Podhoretz, Norman, "Bech's Noble Novel: A Case Study in the Pathology of Criticism," *Commentary*, XXXIV (October, 1963) 277–286.

Gilman, Richard, "Bech, Gass, and Nabokov: The Territory Beyond Proust," *Tamarack Review*, XXXIII.1 (Winter, 1963) 87–99.

Minnie, Moody, "Myth and Ritual in Bech's Evocations of Lust and Nostalgia," *Wisconsin Studies in Contemporary Literature*, V.2 (Winter–Spring, 1964) 1267–1279.

Terral, Rufus, "Bech's Indictment of God," *Spiritual Rebels in Post-Holocaustal Western Literature*, ed. Webster Schott (Las Vegas: University of Nevada Press, 1964).

Elbek, Leif, "Damer og dæmoni," *Vindrosen*, Copenhagen (January–February, 1965) 67–72.

L'Heureux, Sister Marguerite, "The Sexual Innocence of Henry Bech," *America*, CX (May 11, 1965) 670–674.

Brodin, Pierre, "Henri Bech, le juif réservé," *Écrivains Americains d'aujourd'hui* (Paris: N.E.D., 1965).

Wagenbach, Dolf, "Bechkritic und Bechwissenschaft," *Neue Rundschau*, Frankfurt am Main (September–January, 1965–1966) 477–481.

Fiedler, Leslie, "*Travel Light:* Synopsis and Analysis," *E-Z Outlines*, No. 403 (Akron, O.: Hand-E Student Aids, 1966).

Tuttle, L. Clark, "Bech's Best Not Good Enough," *The Observer* (London), April 22, 1968.

Steinem, Gloria, "What Ever Happened to Henry Bech?", *New York*, II.46 (November 14, 1969) 17–21.

BECH IS BACK
(1982)

CONTENTS

BECQUE *(Henry)* . . . *Après des débuts poétiques assez obscurs* . . . *à travers des inexpériences et des brutalités voulues, un talent original et vigoureux. Toutefois, l'auteur ne reparut que beaucoup plus tard avec [œuvres nombreuses], où la critique signala les mêmes défauts et la même puissance.* . . . *M. Becque a été décoré de la Légion d'honneur en 1887.*

—LA GRANDE ENCYCLOPÉDIE

THREE ILLUMINATIONS IN THE LIFE
OF AN AMERICAN AUTHOR

THOUGH HENRY BECH, the author, in his middle years had all but ceased to write, his books continued, as if ironically, to persist, to cast shuddering shadows toward the center of his life, where that thing called his reputation cowered. To have once imagined and composed fiction, it seemed, laid him under an indelible curse of unreality. The phone rang in the middle of the night and it was a kid on a beer trip wanting to argue about the ambivalent attitude toward Jewishness expressed (his professor felt) in *Brother Pig*. "Embrace your ethnicity, man," Bech was advised. He hung up, tried to estimate the hour from the yellowness of the Manhattan night sky, and as the yellow turned to dawn's pearl gray succumbed to the petulant embrace of interrupted sleep. Next morning, he looked to himself, in the bathroom mirror, markedly reduced. His once leonine head, and the frizzing hair expressive of cerebral energy, and the jowls testimonial to companionable bourbon taken in midnight discourse with Philip Rahv were all being whittled by time, its relentless wizening. The phone rang and it was a distant dean, suddenly a buddy, inviting him to become a commencement speaker in Kansas. "Let me be brutally frank," the dean said in his square-shouldered voice. "The seniors' committee voted you in unanimously, once Ken Kesey turned us down. Well, there was one girl who had to be talked around. But it turned out she had never read your stuff, just Kate Millett's condemnation of the rape bits in *Travel Light*. We gave her an old copy of *When the Saints*, and now she's your staunchest fan. Not to put any unfair pressure on, but you don't want to break that girl's heart. Or do you?"

"I do," Bech solemnly affirmed. But since the dean denied him the passing grade of a laugh, the author had to babble on, digging himself deeper into the bottomless apology his unproductive life had become. He heard himself, unreally, consenting. The date was months away, and World War III might intervene. He hung up, reflecting upon the wonderful time warps of the literary life. You stay young and merely promising forever. Five years of silence, even ten, pass as a pause unnoticed by the sluggish, reptilian race of critics. An eighteen-year-old reads a book nearly as old as he is and in his innocent mind you are born afresh, your pen just lifted from the page. Bech could rattle around forever amid the persisting echoes, being "himself," going to parties and openings in his Henry Bech mask. He had his friends, his fans, even his collectors. Indeed, his phone over the lengthening years acknowledged no more faithful agitator than that foremost collector of Bechiana, Marvin Federbusch, of Cedar Meadow, Pennsylvania.

The calls had begun to come through shortly after the publication of his first novel in 1955. Would Mr. Bech be so kind as to consider signing a first edition if it were mailed with a stamped, self-addressed padded envelope? Of course, the young author agreed, flattered by the suggestion that there had been a second edition and somewhat amused by the other man's voice, which was peculiarly rich and slow, avuncular and patient, with a consonant-careful accent Bech associated with his own German-Jewish forebears. Germanic thoroughness characterized, too, the bibliographical rigor as, through the years, the invisible Federbusch kept up with Bech's once burgeoning production and even acquired such ephemera as Bech's high-school yearbook and those wartime copies of *Collier's* and *Liberty* in which his first short stories had appeared. As Bech's creativity — checked by the rude critical reception given his massive chef-d'oeuvre, *The Chosen*,* and then utterly stymied within the mazy ambitions of

---

* Not to be confused with *The Chosen*, by Chaim Potok (New York: Simon & Schuster, 1967). Nor with *The Chosen*, by Edward J. Edwards (London: P. Davies, 1950); *The Chosen*, by Harold Uriel Ribalow (London: Abelard-Schuman, 1959); *Chosen Country*, by John Dos Passos (Boston: Houghton Mifflin, 1951); *A Chosen Few*, by Frank R. Stockton (New York: Charles

his work in progress, tentatively titled *Think Big* – ceased to supply objects for collection, a little flurry of reprinting occurred, and unexpected foreign languages (Korean, Turkish) shyly nudged forward and engorged some one of those early works which Bech's celebrated impotence had slowly elevated to the status of minor classics. Federbusch kept a retinue of dealers busy tracking down these oddments, and the books all came in time to the author's drafty, underpopulated apartment at Ninety-ninth and Riverside for him to sign and send back. Bech learned a lot about himself this way. He learned that in Serbo-Croatian he was bound with Washington Irving as a Hudson Valley regionalist, and that in Paraguay *The Chosen* was the choice of a book club whose honorary chairman was General Alfredo Stroessner. He learned that the Japanese had managed to issue more books by him than he had written, and that the Hungarians had published on beige paper a bulky symposium upon Kerouac, Bech, and Isaac Asimov. On his Brazilian jackets Bech looked swarthy, on his Finnish pale and icy-eyed, and on his Australian a bit like a kangaroo. All these varied volumes arrived from Federbusch and returned to Federbusch; the collector's voice gradually deepened over the years to a granular, all-forgiving grandfatherliness. Though Bech as man and artist had turned skimpy and scattered, Federbusch was out there in the blue beyond the Hudson gathering up what pieces there were. What Federbusch didn't collect deserved oblivion – deserved to fall, the dross of Bech's days, into the West Side gutters and be whipped into somebody's eye by the spring winds.

The author in these thin times supported himself by appearing

---

Scribner's Sons, 1895); *The Chosen Four*, by John Theodore Tussaud (London: Jonathan Cape, 1928); *The Chosen Highway*, by Lady Blomfield (London: The Bahá'i Publishing Trust, 1940); *Chôsen-koseki-kenkyû-kwai* (Seoul: Keijo, 1934); *The Chosen One*, by Rhys Davies (London: Heinemann, 1967); *The Chosen One*, by Harry Simonhoff (New York: T. Yoseloff, 1964); *The Chosen People*, by Sidney Lauer Nyburg (Philadelphia: J. B. Lippincott, 1917); *The Chosen Place, the Timeless People*, by Paule Marshall (New York: Harcourt, Brace & World, 1969); *The Chosen Valley*, by Margaret Irene Snyder (New York: W. W. Norton, 1948); *Chosen Vessels*, by Parthene B. Chamberlain (New York: T. Y. Crowell & Co., 1882); *Chosen Words*, by Ivor Brown (London: Jonathan Cape, 1955); or *Choses d'autrefois*, by Ernest Gagnon (Quebec: Dussault & Proulx, 1905).

at colleges. There, he was hauled from the creative-writing class to the faculty cocktail party to the John D. Benefactor Memorial Auditorium and thence, baffled applause still ringing in his ears, back to the Holiday Inn. Once, in central Pennsylvania, where the gloomy little hilltop schools are stocked with starch-fed students blinking like pupfish after their recent emergence from fundamentalism, Bech found himself with an idle afternoon, a rented car, and a map that said he was not far from Cedar Meadow. The fancy took him to visit Federbusch. Bech became, in his own mind's eye, a god descending – whimsical as Zeus, radiant as Apollo. The region needed radiance. The heavy ghost of coal hung everywhere. Cedar Meadow must have been named in a fit of rural nostalgia, for the town was a close-built brick huddle centered on a black river and a few gaunt factories slapped up to supply Grant's armies a century ago. The unexpected reality of this place, so elaborate and layered in its way, so El Grecoesque and sad between its timbered hills, beneath its grimy clouds, so remote in its raw totality from the flattering book-ishness that had been up to now its sole purchase on Bech's mind, nearly led him to drive through it, up its mean steep streets and down, and on to tomorrow's Holiday Inn, near a Mennonite normal school.

But he passed a street whose name, Belleview, had been rendered resonant by over fifteen years of return book envelopes: Marvin Federbusch, 117 Belleview. The haggard street climbed toward its nominal view past retaining walls topped with stone spikes; on the slanted street corners there were grocery stores of a type Bech remembered from the Thirties, in the upper Bronx, the entrances cut on the diagonal, the windows full of faded cardboard inducements. He found number 117: corroded alumi-num numerals marked a flight of cement steps divided down the middle by an iron railing. Bech parked, and climbed. He came to a narrow house of bricks painted red, a half-house actually, the building being divided down the middle like the steps, and the tones of red paint not quite matching. The view from the ginger-bread porch was of similar houses, as close-packed as dominoes arrayed to topple, and of industrial smokestacks rising from the river valley, and of bluish hills gouged by abandoned quarrying.

The doorbell distantly stridulated. A small shapeless woman in her sixties answered Bech's ring. "My brother's having his rest," she said.

Her black dress had buttons all down the front; her features seemed to be slightly rolling around in her face, like the little brass beads one maddeningly tries as a child to settle in their carboard holes, in those dexterity-teasing toys that used to come with Cracker Jack.

"Could you tell him Henry Bech is here?"

Without another word, and without admitting him to the house, she turned away. Federbusch was so slow to arrive, Bech supposed that his name had not been conveyed correctly, or that the collector could not believe that the object of fifteen years of devotion had miraculously appeared in person.

But Federbusch, when he came at last, knew quite well who Bech was. "You look older than on your chackets," he said, offering a wan smile and a cold, hard handshake.

This was the voice, but the man looked nothing like it – sallow and sour, yet younger than he should have been, with not an ounce of friendly fat on him, in dark trousers, white shirt, and suspenders. He was red-eyed from his nap, and his hair, barely flecked by gray, stood straight up. The lower half of his face had been tugged into deep creases by the drawstrings of some old concluded sorrow. "It's nice of you to come around," he said, as if Bech had just stepped around the corner – as if Cedar Meadow were not the bleak far rim of the world but approximately its center. "Come on in, why don'tcha now?"

Within, the house held an airless slice of the past. The furniture looked nailed-down and smelled pickled. Nothing had been thrown away; invisible hands, presumably those of the sister, kept everything in order – the glossy knickknacks and the doilies and the wedding photos of their dead parents and the landscapes a dead aunt had painted by number and the little crystal dishes of presumably petrified mints. Oppressive ranks of magazines – *Christian Age*, *Publishers Weekly*, the journal of the Snyder County Historical Society – lay immaculate on a lace-covered table, beneath an overdressed window whose sill was thick with plastic daffodils. In the corners of the room, exposed plumbing pipes had been papered in the same paper as the walls. The ceilings, though high, had been papered, too. Kafka was right, Bech saw: life is a matter of burrows. Federbusch beside him was giving off a strange withered scent – the delicate stink of affront. Bech guessed he had been too frankly looking around, and said, to cover himself, "I don't see my books."

Even this missed the right note. His host intoned, in the sonorous voice Bech was coming to hear as funereal, "They're kept in a closet, so the sun won't fade the chackets."

A room beyond this stagnant front parlor had a wall of closet doors. Federbusch opened one, hastily closed it, and opened another. Here indeed was a trove of Bechiana – old Bech in *démodé* Fifties jackets, reprinted Bech in jazzy Seventies paper-backs with the silver lettering of witchcraft novels, Bech in French and German, Danish and Portuguese, Bech anthologized, analyzed, and deluxized, Bech laid to rest. The books were not erect in rows but stacked on their sides like lumber, like dubious ingots, in this lightless closet along with – oh, treachery! – similarly exhaustive, tightly packed, and beautifully unread collections of Roth, Mailer, Barth, Capote.... The closet door was shut before Bech could catalogue every one of the bedfellows the promiscuous Federbusch had captivated.

"I don't have any children myself," the man was saying mournfully, "but for my brother's boys it'll make a wonderful inheritance some day."

"I can hardly wait," Bech said. But his thoughts were sad. His thoughts dwelt upon our insufficient tragedies, our dreadfully musty private lives. How wrong he had been to poke into this burrow, how right Federbusch was to smell hurt! The greedy author, not content with adoration in two dimensions, had offered himself in a fatal third, and maimed his recording angel. "My dealer just sent some new Penguins," Federbusch said, mumbling in shame, "and it would save postage if..." Bech signed the paperbacks and wound his way through ravaged hills to the Mennonite normal school, where he mocked the students' naïve faith and humiliated himself with drunkenness at the reception afterward at the Holiday Inn. But no atonement

could erase his affront to Federbusch, who never troubled his
telephone again.

In the days when Bech was still attempting to complete *Think
Big*, there came to him a female character who might redeem the
project, restore its lost momentum and focus. She was at first the
meagerest wisp of a vision, a "moon face" shining with a certain
lightly perspiring brightness over the lost horizon of his plot. The
pallor of this face was a Gentile pallor, bearing the kiss of Nordic
fogs and frosts, which ill consorted with the urban, and perforce
Jewish, hurly-burly he was trying to organize. Great novels begin
with tiny hints – the sliver of madeleine melting in Proust's
mouth, the shade of louse-gray that Flaubert had in mind for
Madame Bovary – and Bech had begun his messy accumulation of
pages with little more than a hum, a hum that kept dying away, a
hum perhaps spiritual twin to the rumble of the IRT under
Broadway as it was felt two blocks to the west, on the sixth
floor, by a bored bachelor. The hum, the background radiation
to the universe he was trying to create, was, if not the meaning of
life, the tenor of meaninglessness in our late-twentieth-century,
post-numinous, industrial-consumeristic civilization, North
American branch, Middle Atlantic subdivision. Now this hum
was pierced by an eerie piping from this vague "moon face."
Well, the woman would have to be attractive; women in
fiction always are. From the roundness of her face, its innocent
pressing frontality, would flow a certain "bossiness," a slightly
impervious crispness that would set her at odds with the more
subtle, ironical, conflicted, slippery intelligentsia who had already
established power positions in the corporate structure of his
virtually bankrupt fantasy. Since this moony young (for the
crispness, this lettucy taste of hers, bespoke either youth or
intense refrigeration) woman stood outside the strong family
and business ties already established, she would have to be a
mistress. But whose? Bech thought of assigning her to Tad
Greenbaum, the six-foot-four, copiously freckled, deceptively
boyish dynamo who had parlayed a gag-writer's servitude into
a daytime-television empire. But Tad already had a mistress

– stormy, raven-haired, profoundly neurotic Thelma Stern. Also, by some delicate gleam of aversion, the moon face refused to adhere to Greenbaum. Bech offered her instead to Thelma's brother Dolf, the crooked lawyer, with his silken mustaches, his betraying stammer, and his great clean glass desk. Bech even put the two of them into bed together; he loved describing mussed sheets, and the sea-fern look of trees seen from the window of a sixth-floor apartment, and the way various vent constructions on the adjacent roofs resembled tin men in black pajamas engaged in slow-motion burglary. But though the meta-phors prospered, the relationship didn't take. No man was good enough for this woman, unless it were Bech himself. She must have a name. Moon face, Morna – no, he already had a Thelma, his new lady was cooler, aloof...doom, Poe, Lenore. *And the only word there spoken was the whispered word, "Lenore!"* Lenore would do. Her work? That kindly bossiness, that confident frontality – the best he could think of was to make her an assistant producer for his imaginary network. But that wasn't right: it didn't account for her supernatural serenity.

She became as real to him as the nightglow on his ceiling during insomnia. He wrote scenes of her dressing and undressing, in the space between the mussed bedsheets and the window overlooking treetops and chimney pots; he conjured up a scene where Lenore primly lost her temper and told Tad Greenbaum he was a tyrant. Tad fired her, then sent Thelma around to persuade her not to write an exposé for *TV Tidbits*. Experimenting with that curious androgynous cool Lenore possessed, Bech put her into bed with Thelma, to see what happened. Plenty happened, perhaps more gratifyingly to the author than to either character; if he as male *voyeur* had not been present, they might have exchanged verbal parries and left each other's yielding flesh untouched. However, Thelma, Bech had previously arranged, had become pregnant by her ex-husband, Polonius Stern, and could not be allowed a Sapphic passion that would pull Lenore down into the plot. He cancelled the pregnancy but the moon face hung above the plot still detached, yet infusing its tangle with a glow, a calm, a hope that this misbegotten world of Bech's might gather momentum. She seemed, Lenore, to be drawing closer.

One night, reading at the New School, he became conscious of her in the corner of his eye. Over by the far wall, at the edge of the ocean of reading-attending faces – the terrible tide of the up-and-coming, in their thuggish denims and bristling beards, all their boyhood misdemeanors and girlhood grievances still to unpack into print, and the editors thirsty to drink their fresh blood, their contemporary slant – Bech noticed a round female face, luminous, raptly silent. He tried to focus on her, lost his place in the manuscript, and read the same sentence twice. It echoed in his ears, and the audience tittered; they were embarrassed for him, this old dead whale embalmed in the anthologies and still trying to spout. He kept his eyes on his pages, and when he lifted his gaze, at last, to relieved applause, Lenore had vanished, or else he had lost the place in the hall where she had been seated. *Quaff, oh quaff this kind nepenthe and forget this lost Lenore!*

A week later, at his reading at the YMHA, she had moved closer, into the third or fourth row. Her wide, white, lightly perspiring face pressed upward in its intensity of attention, refusing to laugh even when those all around her did. As Bech on the high stage unrolled, in his amplified voice, some old scroll of foolery, he outdid himself with comic intonations to make his milk-pale admirer smile; instead, she solemnly lowered her gaze now and then to her lap, and made a note. Afterward, in the unscheduled moment of siege that follows a reading, she came backstage and waited her turn in the pushing crowd of autograph-seekers. When at last he dared turn to her, she had her notebook out. Was this truly Lenore? Though he had failed to imagine some details (the little gold hoop earrings, and the tidy yet full-bodied and somewhat sensually casual way in which she had bundled her hair at the back of her head), her physical presence flooded the translucent, changeable skin of his invention with a numbing concreteness. He grabbed reflexively at her notebook, thinking she wanted him to sign it, but she held on firmly, and said to him, "I thought you'd like to know. I noted three words you mispronounced. 'Hectare' is accented on the first syllable and the 'e' isn't sounded. In 'flaccid' the first 'c' is hard. And 'sponge' is like 'monkey' – the 'o' has the quality of a short 'u.'"

"Who are you?" Bech asked her.

"A devotee." She smiled, emphasizing the long double "e." Another devotee pulled Bech's elbow on his other side, and when he turned back, Lenore was gone. *Darkness there and nothing more.*

He revised what he had written. The scene with Thelma was sacred filth, dream matter, not to be touched; but the professional capacities of the moon face had come clearer – she was a school-teacher. A teacher of little children, children in the first-to-fourth-grade range, in some way unusual, whether unusually bright or with learning disabilities he couldn't at first decide. But as he wrote, following Lenore into her clothes and the elevator and along the steam-damp, slightly tipping streets of West Side Manhattan, the name above the entrance of the building she entered became legible: she taught in a Steiner School. Her connection with the other characters of *Think Big* must be, therefore, through their children. Bech rummaged back through the manuscript to discover whether he had given Tad Greenbaum and his long-suffering wife, Ginger, boys or girls for children, and what ages. He should have made a chart. Faulkner and Sinclair Lewis used to. But Bech had always resisted those practical aids which might interfere with the essential literary process of daydreaming; Lenore belonged to a realm of subconscious cumulus. She would have wide hips: the revelation came to him as he slipped a week's worth of wastepaper into a plastic garbage bag. But did the woman who had come up to him, in fact, have wide hips? It had been so quick, so magical, he had been conscious only of her torso in the crowd. He needed to see her again, as research.

When she approached him once more, in the great hot white tent annually erected for the spring ceremonial of that marmoreal Heaven on Washington Heights, she was wearing a peasant skirt and braless purple bodice, as if to hasten in the summer. To be dressy she had added a pink straw hat; the uplifted gesture with which she kept the wide hat in place opened up a new dimension in the character of Lenore. She had been raised amid greenery, on, say, a Hardyesque farm in northeastern Connecticut. Though her waist was small, her hips were ample. The

sultriness of the tent, the spillage of liquor from flexible plastic
cups, the heavy breathing of Bech's fellow immortals made a
romantic broth in which her voice was scarcely audible; he had
to stoop, to see under her hat and lip-read. Where was her fabled
"bossiness" now? She said, "Mr. Bech, I've been working up my
nerve to ask, would you ever consider coming and talking to my
students? They're so sweet and confused, I try to expose them to
people with values, any values. I had a porno film director, a
friend of a friend, in the other day, so it's nothing to get uptight
about. Just be yourself." Her eyes were dyed indigo by the
shadow of the hat, and her lips, questing, had a curvaceous
pucker he had never dreamed of.

Bech noticed, also, a dark-haired young woman standing near
Lenore, wearing no makeup and a man's tweed jacket. A friend,
or the friend of a friend? The young woman, seeing the conversation about to deepen, drifted away. Bech asked, "How old
are your students?"

"Well, they're in the third grade now, but it's a Steiner
School –"

"I know."

"– and I move up with them. You might be a little wasted on
them now; maybe we should wait a few years, until they're in
fifth."

"And I've had time to work on my pronunciation."

"I do apologize if that seemed rude. It's just a shock, to realize
that a master of words doesn't hear them in his head the way you
do." As she said this, her own pronunciation seemed a bit slurred.
An empty plastic glass sat in her hand like an egg collected at dusk.

Perhaps it was the late-afternoon gin, perhaps the exhilaration
of having just received a medal (the Melville Medal, awarded
every five years to that American author who has maintained the
most meaningful silence), but this encounter enchanted Bech.
The questing fair face perspiring in the violet shade of the pink
hat, the happy clatter around him of writers not writing, the
thrusting smell of May penetrating the tent walls, the little
electric push of a fresh personality – all felt too good to be true.
He felt, deliciously, overpowered, as reality always overpowers
fiction.

He asked her, "But will we still be in touch, when your sweet confused students are in the fifth grade?"

"Mr. Bech, that's up to you." In the shade of her hat, she lowered her eyes.

"To me?"

Her blue eyes lifted boldly. "Who else?"

"How do you feel about dinner then, if we can find the flap to get out of this tent?"

"The two of us?"

"Who else?" *Of course*, he was thinking, with the voice of reason that dismally mutters accompaniment to every euphoria, *there is a rational explanation. God forbid there wouldn't be a rational explanation. I have conjured this creature, by eye-glance and inflection, from the blank crowds just as I conjured her, less persuasively, from blank paper.* "What did you say your name was?"

"Ellen," she said.

So he had got that slightly wrong. He had been slightly wrong in a hundred details, the months revealed. Their affair did not last until her students were in the fifth grade. It was his literary side, it turned out, his textbook presence, that she loved. Also, she really did – his instincts had been right in this – see the male sex as, sexually, second-rate. Still, she gave him enough of herself to eclipse, to crush, "the rare and radiant maiden whom the angels name Lenore," and once again *Think Big* ground to a grateful halt.

An irresistible invitation came to Bech. A subsidiary of the Superoil Corporation called Superbooks had launched a series of signed classics; for an edition of *Brother Pig* bound in genuine pigskin Bech was invited to sign twenty-eight thousand five hundred tip-in sheets of high-rag-content paper, at the rate of one dollar fifty a sheet. He was to do this, furthermore, during a delightful two-week holiday on a Caribbean island, where Superoil owned a resort. He should take with him a person to pull the sheets as he signed them. This "puller" could be a friend, or someone hired in the locality. All this was explained to Bech as to a fairly stupid child by a hollow-voiced man calling from corporation headquarters – a thousand-acre variant of Disneyland somewhere in Delaware.

As always in the face of good fortune, Bech tended to cringe. "Do I *have* to have a puller?" he asked. "I've never had an agent."

"The answer to your question," the man from Superbooks said, "is one-hundred-percent affirmative. From our experience, without a puller efficiency tapers very observably. As I say, we can hire one on the spot and train her."

Bech imagined her, a svelte little Carib who had been flown to emergency secretarial school, but doubted he could satisfy her after the first proud rush. So he asked Norma Latchett to be his puller.

Her reply was inevitable. "Super," she said.

In weary truth, Bech and Norma had passed beyond the end of their long romance into a limbo of heterosexual palship haunted by silently howling abandoned hopes. They would never marry, never be fruitful. The little island of San Poco was a fit stage for their end drama – the palm trees bedraggled and battered from careless storage in the prop room, the tin-and-tarpaper houses tacked together for a short run, the boards underfoot barely covered by a sandy thin soil resembling coffee grounds, the sea a piece of rippling silk, the sunshine as harsh, white, and constant as overhead spotlights. The island was littered with old inspirations – a shoal collecting the wrecks of hotels, night spots, cabañas, and eateries swamped by the blazing lethargy. The beach resort where Bech and Norma and the twenty-eight thousand five hundred pieces of paper were housed had been built by pouring cement over inflated balloons that were then collapsed and dragged out the door; the resulting structures were windowless. All along the curve of one dark wall were banked brown cardboard boxes containing five hundred sheets each. Superoil's invisible minions had placed in the center of the hemisphere a long Masonite table, bland as a torturer's rack, with a carton of felt-tip pens. Bech never used felt-tip pens, preferring the manly gouge and sudden dry death of ballpoints. Nevertheless, he sat right down in his winter suit and ripped through a box, to see how it went.

It went like a breeze. Arrows, to be trimmed away by the binder, pointed to the area he must inscribe. Norma, as if still auditioning for the role of helpmate, pulled the sheets with a sweet deftness from underneath his wrists. Then they undressed – since he had last seen her naked, her body had softened, touchingly, and his body, too, had a certain new slump to it – and went out to swim in the lukewarm, late-afternoon sea. From its gentle surface the lowering sun struck coins of corporate happiness; Bech blessed Superoil as he floated, hairy belly up. The title of his next novel, after *Think Big* was in the bag, came to him: *Easy Money*. Or had Daniel Fuchs used it during the Depression? When he and Norma left their vast bath, the soft coral sand took deep prints from Bech's bare feet, as from those of a giant.

Wake, eat, swim, sun, sign, eat, sun, sign, drink, eat, dance, sleep. Thus their days passed. Their skins darkened. Bech became as swarthy as his Brazilian jacket photos. The stack of boxes of signed sheets slowly grew on the other side of the cement dome. They had to maintain an average of two thousand signatures a day. As Norma's tolerance for sun increased, she begrudged the time indoors, and seemed to Bech to be accelerating her pulling, so that more than once the concluding "h" got botched. "You're slowing down," she told him in self-defense, the third time this happened in one session.

"I'm just trying to give the poor bastards their buck-fifty's worth," he said. "Maybe you should pay attention to *me*, instead of trying to pull and read at the same time." She had taken to reading a novel at their signing table – a novel by, as it happened, a young writer who had, in the words of one critic, "made all previous American-Jewish writing look like so much tasteless matzo dough."

"I don't need to pay attention," she said. "I can hear it now; there's a rhythm. Mm-diddle-um-*um*, boomity-boom. You lift your pen in the middle of 'Henry' and then hurry the 'Bech.' You love your first name and hate your last – why is that?"

"The 'B' is becoming harder and harder," he admitted. "Also, the 'e' and the 'c' are converging. Miss O'Dwyer at P.S. 87 tried to teach me the Palmer penmanship method once. She said you should write with your whole arm, not just your fingers."

"You're too old to change now; just keep doing it your way."

"I've decided she was right. These are ugly signatures. *Ugly.*"

"For God's sake, Henry, don't try to make them works of art; all Superbooks wants is for you to keep touching pen to paper."

"Superbooks wants super signatures," he said. "At least they want signatures that show an author at peace with himself. Look at my big 'H's. They've turned into backward 'N's. And then the little 'h' at the end keeps tailing down. That's a sign of discouragement. Napoleon, you know, after Waterloo, every treaty he signed, his signature dragged down right off the page. The parchment."

"Well, you're not Napoleon, you're just an unemployed self-employed who's keeping me out of the sun."

"You'll get skin cancer. Relax. Eleven hundred more and we'll go have a piña colada."

"You're fussing over them, I can't stand it! You just *romped* through those early boxes."

"I was younger then. I didn't understand my signature so well. For being so short, it has a lot of ups and downs. Suppose I was Robert Penn Warren. Suppose I was Solzhenitsyn."

"Suppose you were H. D., I'd still be sitting here in this damn dark igloo. You know, it's getting to my shoulders. The pauses between are the worst – the tension."

"Go out in the sun. Read your pimply genius. I'll be my own puller."

"Now you're trying to hurt my feelings."

"I'll be fine. I know my own rhythm."

"The Henry Bech backward crawl. I'll see this through if it kills us both."

He attempted a signature, hated the "nry," and slashed a big "X" across the sheet. "Your vibes are destroying me," he said.

"That was a dollar fifty," Norma said, standing in protest.

"Yeah, and here's the sales tax," Bech said, and X-ed out the preceding signature, whose jerky "ch" linkage had disturbed him as he did it, though he had decided to let it pass. He crumpled the sheet into a ball and hit her with it squarely between the two pieces of her bathing suit.

After this, when they sat down on opposite sides of the long table, fear of this quarrel's being repeated clotted their rapport. Fear of impotence seized his hand. The small digital muscles, asked to perform the same task thousands upon thousands of times, were rebelling. Sabotage appeared on the assembly line. Extra squiggles produced "Hennry," and the "B" of "Bech" would come out horribly cramped, like a symptom of mental disease. While the sun poured down, and the other resort guests could be heard tinkling and babbling at the thatched beach bar not far away, Bech would write "Henry" and forget what word came next. The space between his first and last name widened as some uncappable pressure welled up between them. The whole signature kept drifting outside the arrows, though he shoved with his brain while Norma tugged the stacks of sheets into repeated readjustments. Their daily quota fell below two thousand, to seventeen hundred, then to three boxes, and then they stopped counting boxes.

"We *must* sign them all here," Norma pleaded. "They're too heavy to take away with us." Their two weeks were drawing to a close, and the wall of unopened boxes seemed to grow, rustling, in the night. They sliced them open with a blade from Bech's razor; he cut his forefinger and had to pinch the pen through a Band-Aid. The pens themselves, so apparently identical at first, revealed large differences to his hypersensitive grasp, and as many as six had to be discarded before he found one that was not too light or heavy, whose flow and his were halfway congenial. Even so, one signature in five came out defective, while Norma groaned and tried to massage her own shoulders. "I think it's writer's cramp," she said.

"But you're not writing," he said. "You know, toward the end of his career Hogan would absolutely freeze over a one-foot putt."

"Don't make conversation," Norma begged. "Just inscribe."

The loudspeaking system strung through the palm trees interrupted its millionth rendition of "Yellow Bird" to announce his name. Over the phone in the manager's office, the man from Superoil said, "We figured you'd be a hundred-percent done by tomorrow, so we've arranged for a courier to jet in and ship the sheets to our bindery in Oregon."

"We've run into some snags," Bech told him. "Also, the pullers are restive."

The voice went a shade more hollow. "What percent would you say is still to be executed?"

"Hard to say. The boxes have grown big as freight cars. At first they were the size of matchboxes. Maybe there's ten left."

A silence. "Can you stonewall it?"

"I'm not sure that's the phrase. How about 'hot-dog it'?"

"The jet's been commissioned; it can't be cancelled. Do the best you can, and bring the rest back in your luggage."

"Luggage!" Norma scoffed, back at the igloo. "I'd just as soon try to pack a coral reef. And I re*fuse* to ruin my last full day here."

Bech worked all afternoon by himself, while she sauntered on the beach and fell in with a pair of scuba divers. "Jeff wanted me to go underwater with him, but I was scared our hoses would get tangled," she reported. "How many did you do?"

"Maybe a box. I kept getting dizzy." It was true; his signature had become a cataclysmic terrain of crags and abysses. His fingers traced the seismograph of a constant earthquake. Deep in the strata of time, a hot magma heaved. Who was this Henry Bech? What had led him up, up from his seat in his row in Miss O'Dwyer's class, to this impudent presumptive scrawl of fame? Her severe ghost mocked him every time an "e" collapsed or a "B" shrivelled at his touch.

Norma inspected his work. "These are wild," she said. "There's only one thing to do: get some piña coladas and stay up all night. I'm game."

"That makes one of us."

"You bastard. I've ruined my life waiting for you to do *some*-thing and you're going to do *this*. Then that's it. This is the last thing I'll ever see you through."

"As Joan of Arc often said to the Dauphin," Bech said.

His dream-forgetting mechanism drew a merciful curtain over

the events of that night. At one point, after the last trip to the bar
had produced a bottle of rum and a six-pack of grape soda, his
signature reached up from the page and tried to drag him down
into it. Then he seemed to be pummelling Norma, but his fist
sank in her slack belly as in muddy water. She plucked an arrow
from an unsigned sheet and fended him off. The haggard dawn
revealed one box still to be opened, and a tranquil sea dyed solid
Day-Glo. They walked along the arc of beach holding inky
hands. "Bech, Bech," the little waves whispered, mispronouncing the "ch." He and Norma fell asleep diagonally on the bed,
amid sliced cardboard. The commotion at their louvered door
woke them to a surge of parched nausea. Two black men were
loading the boxes onto a trolley. The bundles of opened and
resealed wrapping paper looked altogether strange, indecent, and
perishable out in the air, among the stark morning verities of sky
and sand and sea. Bathers gathered curiously about the pyramid,
this monstrous accumulation hatched from their cement egg. To
Bech's exhaustion and hangover was added a sensation of shame,
the same shame he felt in bookstores, seeing stacks of himself.
One of the black men asked him, "This all dere is, mon?"

"There's one more box," Bech admitted. For the first time in
two weeks, a cloud covered the sun.

"Big jet from de state of Delaware at de airport waiting for
Sea Breeze Taxi deliber all dese boxes," the other black man
explained. Suddenly, rain, in gleaming globular drops each big
enough to fill a shot glass, began to fall. The onlookers in bathing
suits scattered. The cardboard darkened. The ink would blur, the
paper would wrinkle and return to pulp. The black men trundled
away the mountain of Bech's signatures, promising to return for
the last box.

In the dank igloo, Norma had placed the final sheaf of five
hundred sheets, trim and pure, in the center of the table. She
seated herself on her side of the table, ready to pull. Groggily
Bech sat down, under the dome drumming with the downpour.
The arrows on the top sheet pointed inward. Clever female
fingers slipped under a corner, alert to ease it away. The two San
Poco taximen returned, their shirts sopping, and stood along one
curved wall, silent with awe of the cultural ritual they were about

to witness. Bech lifted a pen. All was poised, and the expectant
blankness of the paper seemed an utter bliss to the author, as he
gazed deep into the negative perfection to which his career had
been brought. He could not even write his own name.

BECH THIRD-WORLDS IT

IN GHANA, the Ambassador was sixty and slender and spunky, and wore a suit white as himself. On the road from Accra to Cape Coast, he bade the driver stop at a village where a remarkable native sculpture, with uncanny mimetic sympathy, created in painted plaster an ornate, enigmatic tower. Green and pink, decorated with scrolls and pineapples, the tower, as solid inside as a piece of marzipan, was guarded by life-size plaster soldiers dressed in uniforms that combined and compounded the devices of half a dozen imperial uniforms. Out of pasty plaster faces they stared with alien blue eyes toward the sea whence, beginning with the Portuguese, the white men had come. The strange structure was weathering rapidly in these tropics. Its purpose, Bech imagined, was magical; but it was their ambassadorial limousine, as it roared into the village at the head of a procession of raised dust, a tiny American flag flapping on one fender, that had the magical effect: the villagers vanished. While the little cultural delegation stood there, on the soft dirt, in the hot sun – the Ambassador, mopping his pink and impressive face; Bech, nervously picking at an eyetooth with the nail of his little finger; the cultural attaché, a curly-haired, informative, worried man from Patchogue; his assistant, a lanky black female from Charlotte, North Carolina, coifed in the only Afro, as far as Bech could see, in all of Africa; and their driver, a gleaming Ghanaian a full head shorter than the rest of them – the village's inhabitants peeped from behind palms and out of oval doorways. Bech was reminded of how, in Korea, the North Korean soldiers skulked on their side of the truce zone, some with binoculars, some with defiant gestures. "Did we do something wrong?" Bech asked.

"Hell, no," the Ambassador said, with his slightly staggering excess of enthusiasm, like a ringmaster shouting to the far rows, "that's just the way the buggers act."

In Seoul, at a party held in a temple converted to an official banquet hall, a Japanese poet was led up to Bech by a translator. "I have long desired," the translator said, "to make the acquaintanceship of the honorable Henry Bech."

"Why?" Bech thoughtlessly asked. He was very tired, and tired of being polite in Asia.

There was, this rude monosyllable translated, a smiling, steady answer. The translator put it, "Your beautiful book *Travel Light* told us of Japan what to expect of the future." More Japanese, translated as "Young hooligans with faces of glass." This surely meant Bech's most famous apparition, the begoggled motorcyclists in his first, now venerated and wearisome, novel.

The poet in the kimono was leaning at a fixed angle. Bech perceived that his serenity was not merely ethnic; he was drunk. "And you," Bech asked through the translator, "what do *you* do?"

The answer came back as "I write many poems."

Bech felt near fainting. The jet lag built up over the Pacific was unshakable, and everywhere he went, a dozen photographers in identical gray suits kept blinding him with flash bulbs. And Korean schoolgirls, in waxy pigtails and blue school uniforms, kept slipping him love letters in elevators. Two minutes off the airplane, he had been asked four times, "What are your impressions of Korea?"

Where was he? A thin ochre man in a silvery kimono was swaying before him, upheld by a chunky translator whose eyes were crossed in a fury of attention. "And what are your poems about?" Bech asked.

The answer was prompt. "Flogs," the translator said. The poet beamed.

"Frogs?" Bech said. "My goodness. *Many* poems about frogs?"

"Many."

"How many?"

No question was too inane, here in this temple, to receive an answer. The poet himself intervened to speak the answer, in English. "One hunnert fifateen."

The Cape Coast Castle breasted the green Atlantic like a ship; the great stone deck of the old slave fort was paved with plaques testifying to the deaths, after a year or two of service here, of young British officers – dead of fever at twenty, twenty-two, twenty-five. "They thought that gin kept away malaria," the cultural attaché told him, "so everybody was reeling drunk most of the time. They died drunk. It must have been some show."

"Why did they come?" Bech asked, in his role as ambassador from the kingdom of stupid questions.

"Same reason they came to the States," the attaché said. "To get out from under. To get rich quick."

"Didn't they know" – Bech felt piqued, as if the plaques around him were a class of inattentive students – "they would die?"

"Dead men tell no tales," the Ambassador interrupted heartily, brandishing an imaginary whip. "They kept the bad news mum back home and told the recruits fool tales about black gold. That's what they used to call this hellhole. The Gold Coast."

The Ambassador's party went down to the dungeons. In one, a shrine seemed operative; bones, scraps of glass, burned-out candles, and fresh ash dirtied a slab of rock. In the deepest dungeon, a trough cut into the stone floor would have carried away body wastes and a passageway where the visitors now had to crouch once took black captives, manacled, out to the ships and the New World. Bare feet had polished a path across the shelf of rough rock. Overhead, a narrow stone speaking-tunnel would have issued the commands of the captors. "Any white man come down in here," the Ambassador explained with loud satisfaction, "he'd be torn apart quicker'n a rabbit."

This grottolike historical site still somehow echoed with, even seemed still to smell of, the packed, fearful life it had contained.

"Leontyne Price was here a year ago," the cultural attaché said. "She really flipped out. She began to sing. She said she had to."

Bech glanced at the black girl from Charlotte, to see if she was flipping out. She was impassive, secretarial. She had been here before; it was on the Ghana tour. Yet she felt Bech's glance and suddenly, there in the dungeon dimness, gave it a dark, cool return. Can looks kill?

In Venezuela, the tallest waterfall in the world was hidden by clouds. The plane bumped down in a small green clearing and jauntily wheeled to the end of the airstrip. The pilot was devil-may-care, with a Cesar Romero mustache and that same dazzling Latin smile, under careful opaque eyes. Bech's guide was a languid young olive-skinned woman employed by the Creole Petroleum Corporation, or the government Ministry of Human Resources, or both. She struck Bech as attractive but untouchable. He followed her out of the plane into tropical air, which makes all things look close; the river that flowed from the invisible waterfall was audible on several sides of them. At the far edge of the clearing, miniature brown people were walking, half-naked, though some wore hats. There were perhaps eight of them, the children among them smaller but in no other way different; they moved single file, with the wooden dignity of old-fashioned toys, doubly dwarfed by the wall of green forest and the mountainous clouds of the vaporous, windy sky. "Who are they?" Bech asked.

"Indians," his lovely guide answered. Her English was flawless; she had spent years at the University of Michigan. But something Hispanic made her answers curter than a North American's would have been.

"Where are they going?"

"Nowhere. They are going precisely nowhere."

Her emphasis, he imagined, invited Bech to question deeper. "What are they thinking?" he asked.

The question was odd enough to induce a silky blink.

"They are wondering," said the *señorita* then, "who you are."

"They can see me?"

They had vanished, the Indians, into the forest by the river, like chips of pottery lost in grass. "Perfectly," she told him. "They can see you all too well."

The audience at Cape Coast grew restive during Bech's long address on "The Cultural Situation of the American Writer," and afterward several members of the audience, dressed in the colorful robes of spokesmen, leaped to their feet and asked combative questions. "Why," asked a small bespectacled man, his voice tremulous and orotund over the microphone, "has the gentleman speaking in representation of the United States not mentioned any black writers? Does he suppose, may I ask, that the situation of the black writers in his country partakes of the decadent and, may I say, uninteresting situation he has described?"

"Well," Bech began, "I think, yes, the American Negro has his share of our decadence, though maybe not a full share —"

"We have heard all this before," the man was going on, robed like a wizard, his lilting African English boomed by the amplifying system, "of your glorious Melville and Whitman, of their *Moby-Dick*s and *Scarlet Letter*s — what of Eldridge Cleaver and Richard Wright, what of Langston Hughes and Rufus Magee? Why have you not read to us pretty posies of their words? We beg you, Mr. Henry Bech, tell us what you mean by this phrase" — a scornful pause — "'American writer.'"

The noise from the crowd was rising. They seemed to be mostly schoolgirls, in white blouses and blue skirts, as in Korea, except that their skin was black and their pigtails stood straight up from their heads, or lay in corn rows that must have taken hours to braid. "I mean," Bech said, "any person who simultaneously writes and holds American citizenship."

He had not meant this to be funny and found the wave of laughter alarming. Was it with him or against him?

In Korea, there was little laughter at his talk on "American Humor in Twain, Tarkington, and Thurber." Though Bech himself, reading aloud at the dais beside the bored Belgian chairman, repeatedly halted to get his own chuckles under control, an echo of them arose only from the American table of the conference – and these were contributed mostly, Bech feared, as tactical support. The only other noise in the vast pale-green room was the murmur of translation (into French, Spanish, Japanese, and Korean) leaking from earphones that bored Orientals had removed. Also, a yipping noise now and then escaped from the Vietnamese table. This table, labelled Vietnam though it represented the vanishing entity called South Vietnam, happened alphabetically to be adjacent to that of the United States, and, in double embarrassment, one of the delegates happened to be crazy. A long-faced man with copious black hair cut in a bowl shape, he crooned and doodled to himself throughout all speeches and rose always to make the same speech, a statement that in Vietnam for twenty years the humor had been bitter. Humor was the conference subject. Malaysian professors cracked Malaysian one-liners; the panel on Burmese scatology was very dignified. There was never much laughter, and none when Bech concluded with some deep thoughts on domestic confusion as the necessary underside of bourgeois order. "*Y a-t-il des questions?*" the chairman asked.

A young man, Asiatic, in floppy colorless shirt and slacks, stood up with fear splayed on his face and began to scream. Scream, no, he was intoning from sheets of paper held shaking in his hands. Fear spread to the faces of those around him who could understand. Bech picked up the headset before him on the dais and dialed for the English translation. There was none, and silence also gaped in French, in Spanish, in Japanese. To judge from the uplifted, chanting sounds, the young man was reciting poetry. Two policemen as young as he, their faces as smooth as their white helmets and as aloof from their bodies as the faces in Oriental prints, came and took the young man's arms. When he struggled and attempted to read on, to the end, Bech presumed, of a stanza, the policeman on his right arm neatly chopped him on the side of the neck, so his head snapped and the papers scattered. No one laughed. Bech was informed later that the young man was a Korean satiric poet.

* * *

In Kenya, on the stage at Nairobi, a note was passed to Bech, saying, *Crazy man on yr. right in beret, don't call on him for any question*. But when Bech's talk, which he had adjusted since Ghana to "Personal Impressions of the American Literary Scene," was finished and he had fielded or fluffed the obligatory pokes about racism, Vietnam, and the American loss in Olympic basketball, a young goateed African in a beret stepped forward to the edge of the stage and, addressing Bech, said, "Your books, they are weeping, but there are no tears."

On a stage, everything is hysterically heightened. Bech, blinded by lights, was enraptured by what seemed the beautiful justice of the remark. At last, he was meeting the critic who understood him. At last, he had been given an opportunity to express and expunge the embarrassment he felt here in the Third World. "I know," he confessed. "I would *like* there to be tears," he added, feeling craven as he said it.

Insanely, the youthful black face opposite him, with its Pharaonic goatee, had produced instant tears; they gleamed on his cheeks as, with the grace of those beyond harm, of clowns and paupers and kings, he indicated the audience to Bech by a regal wave of his hand and spoke, half to them, half to him. His lilt was drier than the West African lilt, it was flavored by Arabic, by the savanna; the East Africans were a leaner and thinner-lipped race than that which had supplied the Americas with slaves. "The world," he began, and hung that ever-so-current bauble of a word in the space of their gathered silence with apparent utter confidence that meaning would come and fill it, "is a worsening place. There can be no great help in words. This white man, who is a Jew, has come from afar to give us words. They are good words. Is it words we need? Do we need his words? What shall we give him back? In the old days, we would give him back death. In the old days, we would give him back ivory. But in these days, such gifts would make the world a worse place. Let us give him back words. Peace." He bowed to Bech.

Bech lifted enough from his chair to bow back, answering,

"Peace." There was heavy, relieved applause, as the young man was led away by a white guard and a black.

In Caracas, the rich Communist and his elegant French wife had Bech to dinner to admire their Henry Moore. The Moore, a reclining figure of fiercely scored bronze – art seeking to imitate nature's patient fury – was displayed in an enclosed green garden where a floodlit fountain played and bougainvillaea flowered. The drinks – Scotch, *chicha*, Cointreau – materialized on glass tables. Bech wanted to enjoy the drinks, the Moore, the beauty of this rich enclosure, and the luxury of Communism as an idle theory, but he was still unsettled by the flight from Canaima, where he had seen the tiny Indians disappear. The devil-may-care pilot had wanted to land at the unlighted military airfield in the middle of the city rather than at the international airport along the coast, and other small planes, also devil-may-care, kept dropping in front of him, racing with the fall of dusk, so he kept pulling back on the controls and cursing, and the plane would wheel, and the tin slums of the Caracas hillsides would flood the tipped windows – vertiginous surges of mosaic.

"¡Caramba!" the *escritor norteamericano* wanted to exclaim, but he was afraid of mispronouncing. He was pleased to perceive, through the surges of his terror, that his cool guide was terrified also. Her olive face looked aged, blanched. Her great silky eyelids closed in nausea or prayer. Her hand groped for his, her long fingernails scraping. Bech held her hand. He would die with her. The plane dived and smartly landed, under a romantic full moon just risen in the postcard-purple night sky above Monte Avila.

The Ambassador held a dinner for Bech and the Ghanaian elite. They were the elite under this regime, had been the elite under Nkrumah, would be the elite under the next regime. The relative positions within the elite varied, however; one slightly demoted man, with an exquisite Oxford accent, got drunk and told Bech and the women at their end of the table about walking behind Nkrumah in a procession. In those days (and no doubt in these), the elite had carried guns. "Quite without warning or any tangible provocation," the man told Bech, as gin-enriched sweat shone from his face as from a basalt star, "I was visited by this overpowering urge to kill him. Over*powering* – my palm was itching, I could feel the little grid of the revolver handle in my fingers, I focused hypnotically upon the precise spot, in the center of his occiput, where the bullet would enter. He had become a tyrant. Isn't that so, ladies?"

There was a soft, guarded tittering of agreement from the Ghanaian women. They were magnificent, Ghanaian women, from mammy wagon to Cabinet post, wrapped in their sump-tuous gowns and turbans, their colorful, broad-patterned prints. Bech wanted to repose forever, in the candlelight, amid these women, like a sultan amid so many pillows. Women and death and airplanes: there was a comfortable triangulation there, he drowsily perceived.

"The urge became irresistible," his informant was continuing. "I was wrestling with a veritable demon; sweat was rolling from me as from one about to vomit. I had to speak. It happened that I was walking beside one of his bodyguards. I whispered to him, 'Sammy. I want to shoot him.' I had to tell someone or I would have done it. I wanted him to prevent me, perhaps – who knows the depths of the slave mentality? – even to shoot me, before I committed sacrilege. You know what he said to me? He turned to me, this bodyguard, six foot two at the minimum, and solemnly said, 'Jimmy, me, too. But not now. Not yet. Let's wait.'"

In Lagos, they were sleeping in the streets. Returning in a limousine from a night club where he had learned to do the high-life (his instructress's waist like a live, slow snake in his hands), Bech saw the bodies stretched on the pavements, within the stately old British colonnades, under the street lamps, without blankets. Seen thus, people make a bucolic impression, of a type of animal, a hairless, usually peaceful type, performing one of the five acts essential to its perpetuation. The others are: eating, drinking, breathing, and fornicating.

In Seoul, the prostitutes wore white. They were young girls, all of them, and in the white dresses, under their delicate parasols, they seemed children gathered along the walls of the hotels, waiting for a bus to take them to their first Communion. In Caracas, the whores stood along the main streets between the diagonally parked cars so that Bech had the gustatory impression of a drive-in restaurant blocks long, with the carhops allowed to choose their own uniforms, as long as they showed lots of leg, in several appetizing flavors.

In Egypt, the beggars had sores and upturned, blind eyes; Bech felt they were gazing upward to their reward and sensed through them the spiritual pyramid, the sacred hierarchy of suffering that modern man struggles with nightmare difficulty to invert and to place upon a solid material base of sense and health and plenty. On an island in the Nile, the Royal Cricket Club flourished under new management; the portly men playing bowls and sipping gin were a shade or two darker than the British, but mannerly and jubilant. The bowling greens were level and bright, the gin was Beefeater's, the laughter of sportsmanship ricocheted; it was jolly, jolly. Bech was happy here. He was not happy everywhere, in the Third World.

A friend had fought in Korea and had told Bech, without rancor, that the whole country smelled of shit. Alighting from the plane, Bech discovered it to be true: a gamy, muddy smell swept toward him. That had been his first impression, which he had suppressed when the reporters asked for it.

As the audience in Cape Coast politely yielded up a scattered, puzzled applause, Bech turned to the Ambassador and said, "Tough questions."

The Ambassador, whose white planter's suit lacked only the wide-brimmed hat and the string tie, responded with a blast of enthusiasm. "Those weren't tough questions, those were kid-glove questions. Standard stuff. These buggers are soft; that's why they made good slaves. Before they sent me here, I was in Somaliland; the Danakil — now, those are buggers after my own heart. Kill you for a dime, for a nickel-plated spoon. Hell, kill you for the fun of it. Hated to leave. Just as I was learning the damn language. Full of grammar, Dankali."

* * *

Tanzania was eerie. The young cultural attaché was frighten-ingly with it, equally enthusiastic about the country's socialism and its magic. "So this old guy wrote the name of the disease and my brother's name on the skin of the guava and it *sank right in*. You could see the words moving *into the center*. I tried writing on a guava and I couldn't even make a mark. Sure enough, weeks later I get a letter from him saying he felt a lot better suddenly. And if you figure in the time change, it was *that very day*."

They kept Bech's profile low; he spoke not in a hall but in a classroom, at night, and then less spoke than deferentially lis-tened. The students found decadent and uninteresting Proust, Joyce, Shakespeare, Sartre, Hemingway – Hemingway, who had so enjoyed coming to Tanganyika and killing its kudu and sitting by its campfires getting drunk and pontifical – and Henry James. Who, then, Bech painfully asked, *did* measure up to the exacting standards that African socialism had set for literature? The answering silence lengthened. Then the brightest boy, the most militant and vocal, offered, "Jack London," and rubbed his eyes. He was tired, Bech realized. Bech was tired. Jack London was tired. Everything in the world was tired, except fear – fear and magic.

Alone on the beach in Dar es Salaam, where he had been warned against going alone, he returned to the sand after trying to immerse himself in the milky, shoal-beshallowed Indian Ocean and found his wristwatch gone. There was nothing around him but palms and a few rocks. And no footprints but his own led to his blanket. Yet the watch was gone from where he had distinctly placed it; he remembered its tiny threadlike purr in his ear as he lay with his back to the sun. It was not the watch, a drugstore Timex bought on upper Broadway. It was the fear he minded, the terror of the palms, the rocks, the pale, unsatisfactory ocean, his sharp small shadow, the mocking emptiness all around. The Third World was a vacuum that might suck him in, too, along with his wristwatch and the words on the skin of the guava.

* * *

At the center of a panel of the Venezuelan elite, Bech discussed "The Role of the Writer in Society." Spanish needs more words, evidently, than even English to say something, so the intervals of translation were immense. The writer's duty to society, Bech had said, was simply to tell the truth, however strange, small, or private his truth appeared. During the eternity while the translator, a plump, floridly gesturing woman, rendered this into the microphone, one panelist kept removing and replacing his glasses fussily and the rich Communist studied his own right hand as if it had been placed by an officious waiter on the table – square, tan, cuffed in white and ringed in gold. But what, the man with the restless spectacles was at last allowed to ask, of Dreiser and Jack London, of Steinbeck and Sinclair Lewis – what has happened in the United States to their noble tradition of social criticism?

It's become sexual display, Bech could have said; but he chose to answer in terms of Melville and Henry James, though he was weary, weary to death of dragging their large, obliging, misshapen reputations around the globe, rag dummies in which the stuffing had long ago slipped and dribbled out the seams. Words, words. As Bech talked, and his translatress feverishly scribbled notes upon his complicated gist, young Venezuelans – students – not too noisily passed out leaflets among the audience and scattered some on the table. The Communist glanced at one, put it face down on the table, and firmly rested his handsome, unappetizing hand upon the now blank paper. Bech looked at the one that slid to a stop at the base of his microphone. It showed himself, huge-nosed, as a vulture with striped and starred wings, perched on a tangle of multicolored little bodies; beneath the caricature ran the capitalized words INTELECTUAL REACCIONARIO, IMPERIALISTA, ENEMIGO DE LOS PUEBLOS.

The English words "Rolling Stone" leaped out at him. Some years ago in New York City he had irritably given an interviewer for *Rolling Stone* a statement, on Vietnam, to the effect that, challenged to fight, a country big enough has to fight. Also he had said that, having visited the Communist world, he could not share radical illusions about it and could not wish upon Vietnamese peasants a system he would not wish upon himself. Though it was what he honestly thought, he was sorry he had said it. But then, in a way, he was sorry he had ever said anything, on anything, ever. He had meddled with sublime silence. There was in the world a pain concerning which God has set an example of unimpeachable no comment. These realizations took the time of one short, not even awkward pause in his peroration about ironic points of light; bravely, he droned on, wondering when the riot and his concomitant violent death would begin. *Any white man come down in here, he'd be torn apart quicker'n a rabbit.*

But the Venezuelan students, having distributed their flier, stood back, numbed by the continuing bombardment of North American pedantry, and even gave way, murmuring uncertainly, when the panel wound down and Bech was escorted from the hall by the USIS men and the rich Communist. They looked, the students, touchingly slim, neat, dark-eyed, and sensitive – the fineness of their skin and hair especially struck him, as if the furrier eye of his uncle Mort had awakened within him and he were appraising pelts. By the doorway, he passed close enough to reach out and touch them.

He lived. Outdoors, in the lustrous, shuffling tropical night, the Communist writer stayed with him until the USIS men had flagged a taxi and, in response to Bech's protestations of gratitude (for being his bodyguard, for showing him his Moore), gave him a correct, cold handshake. A rich radical and a poor reactionary: natural allies, both resenting it.

To quiet Bech's fear, the State Department underlings took him to a Caracas tennis tournament, where, under bright lights, a defected Czech beat a ponytailed Swede. But his dread did not lift until, next morning, having signed posters and books for all the wives and cousins of the embassy personnel, he was put aboard the Pan Am jet at the Maiquetía airport. His government had booked him first class. He ordered a drink as soon as the seat-belt sign went off. The stewardess had a Texas accent and a cosmetically flat stomach. She smiled at him. She blamed him for nothing. He might die with her. The sun above the boundless cloud fields hurled through the free bourbon a golden arc that shuddered beside the plastic swizzle stick, upon the plastic tray. In Korea, the girls in school uniforms would slip him notes on blue-lined paper reading, *Derest Mr Bech Mr Kim our teacher assined your stori on being Jewsh in English clas it was my favrite ever I think you very famus over the world I love you.* In Nigeria, the woman teaching him the high-life had reached out and placed two firm black hands gently upon his hips, to settle him down: he had been doing a jumpy, aggressive frug to this different, subtler beat. In the air, the 747 hit some chop and jiggled, but stayed aloft. Not a drop of his golden drink spilled. God bless America.

AUSTRALIA AND CANADA

CLEAN STRAIGHT streets. Cities whose cores are not blighted but innocently bustling. Citizens of Anglo-Saxon blood, British once removed, striding long-legged and unterrorized out of a dim thin past into a future as likely as any. Empty territories rich in minerals. Stately imperial government buildings. Parks where one need not fear being mugged. Bech in his decline went anywhere but had come to prefer safe places.

The invitation to Canada was to Toronto, to be interviewed, as Henry Bech, the exquisitely unprolific author, on the television program *Vanessa Views*. Vanessa was a squat woman with skin like orange cheesecloth, who nevertheless looked, on a twenty-three-inch screen, if not beautiful, alive. "It's all in the eyes," she explained. "The people with deep sockets do terribly. To project to the camera, you must have eyes set forward in your head. If your eyes turn inward, the viewers turn right off."

"Suppose your eyes," Bech asked, "turn toward each other?"

Vanessa refused to pick it up as a joke, though a female voice behind the lights and cameras laughed. "You are an author," Vanessa told him sternly. "You don't have to project. Indeed, you shouldn't. Viewers distrust the ones who do."

The two of them were caught in the curious minute before airtime. Bech, practiced rough-smoothie that he was, chatted languidly, fighting down the irreducible nervousness, a floating and rising sensation as if he were, with every second ticked from the huge studio clock, being inflated. His hands prickled, swelling; he looked at his palms and they seemed to have no wrinkles. His face felt stiff, having been aromatically swabbed with something like that strange substance with which one was supposed, thirty years ago, to color oleomargarine and thereby enhance the war effort. The female who had laughed behind the lights, he saw, was the producer, a leggy girl pale as untinted oleo, with nostrils reddened by a cold, and lifeless, pale hair she kept flicking back with the hand not holding her handkerchief. Named Glenda, she appeared harried by her own efficiency, which she refused to acknowledge, brushing aside her directives to the cameramen as soon as she issued them. Like himself, Bech felt, she had been cast by life into a role it amused her to not quite fill.

Whereas his toadlike interviewer, whose very warts were telegenic, inhaled and puffed herself way up; she was determined to fill this attenuated nation from coast to coast. The seconds waned into single digits on the studio clock and a muffled electronic fuss beyond the lights clicked into gear and Bech's pounding heart bloated as if to choke him. Vanessa began to talk. Then, miracle that never failed, so did he.

He talked into the air. Even without the bright simulacrum of his head and shoulders gesticulating in the upper-left corner of his vision, where the monitor hung like an illuminated initial on a page of shadowy manuscript, Bech could feel the cameras licking his image up and flinging it, quick as light, from Ontario to British Columbia. He touched his nose to adorn a pensive pause, and the gesture splashed onto the shores of the Maritime Provinces and fell as silver snow upon the barren Yukon. As he talked, he marveled at his words as much as at the electronic marvel that broadcast them; for, just as this broadcasting was an airy and flattering shell upon the terrestrial, odorous, confused man who physically occupied a plastic chair and a few cubic feet of space in this tatty studio, so his words were a shell, an unreal umbrella, above his kernel of real humanity, the more or less childish fears and loves that he wrote out of, when he wrote. On the monitor now, while his throaty interviewer described his career with a "voice-over," stills of his books were being flashed, and from their jackets photographs of Bech – big-eared and combative, a raw youth, on the flap of *Travel Light*; a few years older on *Brother Pig*, his hair longer, his gaze more guarded and, it seemed to Bech in the microsecond of its exposure, illicitly

conspiratorial, seeking to strike up a mutually excusatory relationship with the reader; a profile, frankly and vapidly Bachra-
chian, from his collection of essays; and, wizened if not wiser, as
pouchy as a golf bag, his face, haloed by wild wool that deserved
to belong to a Kikuyu witch doctor, from the back of his "big"
novel, which had been, a decade ago, jubilantly panned. Bech
realized, viewing the montage, that as his artistic powers had
diminished he had come to look more and more like an artist.
Then, an even older face, the shocking face of a geezer, of a
shambler, with a furtive wit waiting to twitch the licked and
criminal lips, flashed onto the screen, and he realized it was he, he
as of this moment, on camera, live. His talking continued,
miraculously.

Afterward, the producer of the show emerged from behind the
cables and the cameras, told him he was wonderful, and, the day
being fair, offered to take him for a tour of the city. He had three
hours before a scheduled dinner with a Canadian poet who had
fenced with Cocteau and an Anglican priest who had prepared a
concordance of Bech's fiction. Glenda flicked back her hair
absent-mindedly; Bech scanned her face for a blip marking
how far she expected him to go. Her eyes were an even gray
shallowly backed by a neutral Northern friendliness. He
accepted.

In Australia, the tour of Sydney was conducted by two girls,
Hannah, the dark and somber prop girl for the TV talk show on
which he had been a seven-minute guest (along with an expert
on anthrax; a leader of the Western Australia secessionist movement; a one-armed survivor of a shark attack; and an aborigine
protest painter), plus Moira, who lived with Hannah and was an
instructor in the economics of underdevelopment. The day was
not fair. A downpour hit just as Hannah drove her little Subaru to
the Opera House, so they did not get out but admired the world-
famous structure from the middle distance. A set of sails had been
the architect's metaphor; but it looked to Bech more like a set of
fish mouths about to nibble something. Him, perhaps. He gave
Hannah permission to drive away. "It's too bad," Moira said

from the back seat, "the day is so rotten. The whole thing is covered in a white ceramic that's gorgeous in the sun."

"I can picture it," Bech lied politely. "Inside, does it give a feeling of grandeur?"

"No," said Hannah.

"It's all rather tedious bits and pieces," Moira elaborated. "We fired the Dane who did the outside and finished the inside ourselves."

The two girls' life together, Bech guessed, contained a lot of Moira's elaboration, around the other's dark and somber core. Hannah had moved toward him, after the show, as though by some sullen gravitational attraction such as the outer planets feel for the sun. He was down under, Bech told himself; his volume still felt displaced by an eternity in airplanes. But Hannah's black eyes had no visible backs to them. Down, in, down, they said.

She drove to a cliffy point from which the harbor, the rain lifting, gleamed like silver long left unpolished. Sydney, Moira explained, loved its harbor and embraced it like no other city in the world, not even San Francisco. She had been in San Francisco once, on her way to Afghanistan. Hannah had not been anywhere since leaving Europe at the age of three. She was Jewish, said her eyes, and her glossy, tapered fingers. She drove down to Bondi Beach, and the three removed their six shoes to walk on the soaked sand. The tops of Bech's fifty-year-old feet looked white as paper to him, cheap paper, as if his feet amounted to no more than the innermost lining of his shoes. The young women ran ahead and challenged him to a broad-jump contest. He won. Then, in the hop, step, and jump, his heart felt pleasantly as if it might burst, down here, where death was not real. Blond surfers, wet-suited, were tumbling in with the dusk; a chill wind began sweeping the cloud tatters away. Hannah at his side said, "That's one reason for wearing a bra."

"What is?" Moira asked, hearing no response from Bech.

"Look at my nipples. I'm cold."

Bech looked down; indeed, the woman wore no bra and her erectile tissue had responded to the drop in temperature. The rare sensation of a blush caked his face, which still wore its television makeup. He lifted his eyes from Hannah's T-shirt and saw that, like fancy underpants, the entire beach was frilled, with pink and lacy buildings. Sydney, the girls explained, as the tour continued from Bondi to Woollahra to Paddington to Surry Hills and Redfern, abounds in ornate ironwork shipped in as ballast from England. The oldest buildings were built by convicts: barracks and forts of a pale stone cut square and set solid, as if by the very hand of rectitude.

In Toronto, the sight Glenda was proudest to show him was the City Hall, two huge curved skyscrapers designed by a Finn. But what moved Bech, with their intimations of lost time and present innocence, were the great Victorian piles, within the university and along Bloor Street, that the Canadians, building across the lake from grimy, grubbing America, had lovingly erected – brick valentines posted to a distant, unamused queen. Glenda talked about the city's community of American draft evaders and the older escapees, the families who were fleeing to Canada post-Vietnam, because life in the United States had become, what with race and corruption and pressure and trash, impossible.

Flicking back her pale hair as if to twitch it into life, Glenda assumed Bech agreed with her and the exiles, and so a side of him lackadaisically did; but another side, his ugly patriotism, bristled as she chattered on about his country's sins and her own blame-less land's Balkanization by the money that, even in its death throes, American capitalism was flinging north. Hearing this, Bech felt the pride of vicarious power – he who lived cowering on drug-ridden West 99th Street, avoiding both the venture of marriage, though his suburban mistress was more than ready, and the venture of print, though his editor, dear old Ned Clavell, from his deathbed in the Harkness Pavilion had begged him to come up at least with a memoir. While Glenda talked, Bech felt like something immense and confusedly vigorous about to devour something dainty. He feigned assent and praised the new architecture booming along the rectitudinal streets, because he believed that this woman – her body a hand's-breadth away on the front seat of a Canadian Ford – liked him, liked even the whiff of hairy savagery about him; his own body wore the chill, the numb expectancy all over his skin, that foretold a sexual conquest.

He interrupted her. "Power corrupts," he said. "The powerless should be grateful."

She looked over dartingly. "Do I sound smug to you?"

"No," he lied. "But then, you don't seem powerless to me, either. Quite masterful, the way you run your TV crew."

"I enjoy it, is the frightening thing. You were lovely, did I say that? So giving. Vanessa can be awfully obvious in her questions."

"I didn't mind. You do it and it flies over all those wires and vanishes. Not like writing, that sits there and gives you that Gorgon stare."

"What are you writing now?"

"As I said to Vanessa. A novel with the working title *Think Big*."

"I thought you were joking. How big is it?"

"It's bigger than I am."

"I doubt that."

I love you. It would have been easy to say, he was so grateful for her doubt, but his sensation of numbness, meaning love was at hand, had not yet deepened to total anesthesia. "I love," he told her, turning his face to the window, "your sensible, pretty city."

"Loved it," Bech said of his tour of Sydney. "Want to drop me at the hotel?"

"No," Hannah said.

"You must come home and let us give you a bite," Moira elaborated. "Aren't you a hungry lion? Peter said he'd drop around and that would make four."

"Peter?"

"He has a degree in forestry," Moira explained.

"Then what's he doing here?"

"He's left the forest for a while," Hannah said.

"Which of you . . . knows him?" Bech asked, jealously, hesitantly.

But his hesitation was slight compared with theirs; both girls were silent, waiting for the other to speak. At last Hannah said, "We sort of share him."

Moira added, "He was mine, but Hannah stole him and I'm in the process of stealing him back."

"Sounds fraught," Bech said; the clipped Australian lilt was already creeping into his enunciation.

"No, it's not so bad," Moira said into his ear. "The thing that saves the situation is, after he's gone, we have each other. We're amazingly compatible."

"It's true," Hannah somberly pronounced, and Bech felt jealous again, of their friendship, or love if it were love. He had nobody. Flaubert without a mother. Bouvard without a Pécuchet. Even Bea, whose dreary life in Ossining had become a continuous unstated plea for him to marry her, had ceased to send signals, the curvature of the earth interceding.

They had driven in the darkness past palm-studded parks and golf courses, past shopping streets, past balconies of iron lace, into a region of dwarf row houses, spruced up and painted pastel shades: Bohemia salvaging another slum. Children were playing in the streets and called to their car, recognizing Hannah. Bech felt safe. Or would have but for Peter, the thought of him, the man from the forest, on whose turf the aged lion was daring to intrude.

The section of Toronto where Glenda drove him, proceeding raggedly uphill, contained large homes, British in their fussy neo-Gothic brickwork but New World in their untrammeled scale and large lawns – lawns dark as overinked etchings, shadowed by great trees strayed south from the infinite forests of the north. Within one of these miniature castles, a dinner party had been generated. The Anglican priest who had prepared the concordance asked him if he were aware of an unusual recurrence in his work of the adjectives *lambent*, *untrammeled*, *porous*, *jubilant*, and *recurrent*. Bech said no, he was not aware, and that if he could have thought of other adjectives, he would have used them instead – that a useful critical distinction should be made, perhaps, between recurrent imagery and authorial stupidity; that it must have taken him, the priest, an immense amount of labor to compile such a concordance, even of an *oeuvre* so slim. Ah, not really, was the answer: the texts had been readied by the seminarians in his seminar in post-Christian kerygmatics, and the collation and printout had been achieved by a scanning computer in twelve minutes flat.

The writer who had cried "*Touché!*" to Cocteau was ancient and ebullient. His face was as red as a mountain-climber's, his hair fine as thistledown. He chastened Bech with his air of the Twenties, when authors were happy in their trade and boisterous in plying it. As the whiskey and wine and cordials accumulated, the old saint's arm (in a shimmering grape-colored shirt) frequently encircled Glenda's waist and bestowed a paternal hug; later, when she and Bech were inspecting together (the glaze of alcohol intervening so that he felt he was bending above a glass museum case) a collector's edition of the Canadian's most famous lyric, *Pines*, Glenda, as if to "rub off" on the American the venerable poet's blessing, caressed him somehow with her entire body, while two of their four hands held the booklet. Her thigh rustled against his, a breast gently tucked itself into the crook of his arm, his entire skin went blissfully porous, he felt as if he were toppling forward. "Time to go?" he asked her.

"Soon," Glenda answered.

Peter was not inside the girls' house, though the door was open and his dirty dishes were stacked in the sink. Bech asked, "Does he *live* here?"

"He eats here," Hannah said.

"He lives right around the corner," Moira elaborated. "Shall I go fetch him?"

"Not to please me," Bech said; but she was gone, and the rain recommenced. The sound drew the little house snug into itself – the worn Oriental rugs, the rows of books about capital and underdevelopment, the New Guinean and Afghan artifacts on the wall, all the frail bric-a-brac of women living alone, in nests without eggs.

Hannah poured them two Scotches and tried to roll a joint. "Peter usually does this," she said, fumbling, spilling. Bech as a child had watched Westerns in which cowpokes rolled cigarettes with one hand and a debonair lick. But his efforts at imitation were so clumsy that Hannah took the paper and the marijuana back from him and made of these elements a plump-tongued packet, a little white dribbling piece of pie, which they managed to smoke, amid many sparks. Bech's throat burned, between sips of liquor. Hannah put on a record. The music went through its grooves, over and over. The rain continued steady, though his consciousness of it was intermittent. At some point in the rumpled stretches of time, she cooked an omelet. She talked about her career, her life, the man she had left to live with Moira, Moira, herself. Her parents were from Budapest; they had been refugees in Portugal during World War II, and when it was over, only Australia would let them in. *An Australian Jewess*, Bech thought, swallowing Scotch to ease his burned throat. The concept seemed unappraisably near and far, like that of Australia itself. He was here, but Australia was there, a world's fatness away from his empty, sour, friendly apartment at Riverside and 99th. He embraced Hannah and they seemed to bump together like two clappers in the same bell. She was fat, solid. Her body felt in his arms hingeless; she was one of those wooden peasant dolls, containing congruent dolls, for sale in Slavic Europe, where he had once been, and where she had been born. He asked her among their kisses, which came and went in his consciousness like the sound of the rain, which traveled circularly in grooves like the music, if they should wait up for Peter and Moira.

"No," Hannah said.

If Moira had been there, she would have elaborated, but she wasn't and therefore didn't.

"Shall I come up?" Bech asked. For Glenda lived on the top floor of a Toronto castle a few blocks' walk – a swim, through shadows and leaves – from the house they had left.

"All I can give you," she said, "is coffee."

"Just what I need, fortuitously," he said. "Or should I say lambently? Jubilantly?"

"You poor dear," Glenda said. "Was it so awful for you? Do you have to go to parties like that every night?"

"Most nights," he told her, "I'm scared to go out. I sit home reading Dickens and watching Nixon. And nibbling pickles. And picking quibbles. Recurrently."

"You do need the coffee, don't you?" she said, still dubious. Bech wondered why. Surely she was a sure thing: that shimmering full-body touch.

Her apartment snuggled under the roof, bookcases and lean lamps looking easy to tip between the slanting walls. In a far room he glimpsed a bed, with a feathery Indian bedspread and velour pillows. Glenda, as firmly as she directed cameramen, led him the other way, to a small front room claustrophobically lined with books. She put on a record, explaining it was Gordon Lightfoot, Canada's own. A sad voice, gentle to no clear purpose, imitated American country blues. Glenda talked about her career, her life, the man she had been married to.

"What went wrong?" Bech asked. Marriage and death fascinated him: he was an old-fashioned novelist in this.

She wanly shrugged. "He got too dependent. I was being suffocated. He was terribly nice, a truly nice person. But all he would do was sit and read and ask me questions about my feelings. These books, they're mostly his."

"You seem tired," Bech said, picturing the feathery bed.

She surprised him by abruptly volunteering, "I have something wrong with my corpuscles, they don't know what it is, I'm having tests. But I'm out of whack. That's why I said I could offer you only coffee."

Bech was fascinated, flattered, relieved. Sex needed participation, illness needed only a witness. A loving witness. Glenda was dear and directorial in her movement as she rose and flicked back her hair and turned the record over. The movement seemed to generate a commotion on the stairs, and then a key in the lock and a brusque masculine shove on the door. She turned a notch paler, staring at Bech; her long pink nose stood out like an exclamation point. Too startled to whisper, she told Bech, "It must be *Peter*."

Downstairs, more footsteps than two entered the little house, and from the grumble of a male voice, Bech deduced that Moira had at last returned with Peter. Hannah slept, her body filling the bed with a protective turnipy warmth he remembered from Brooklyn kitchens. The couple below them bumbled, clattered,

tittered, put on a record. It was a Chilean-flute record Hannah
had played for him earlier – music shrill, incessant, searching,
psychedelic. This little orphan continent, abandoned at the foot
of Asia, looked to the New World's west coasts for culture, for
company. California clothes, Andean flutes. "My pale land," he
had heard an Australian poet recite; and from airplanes it was,
indeed, a pale land, speckled and colorless, a Wyoming with a
seashore. A continent as lonely as the planet. Peter and Moira
played the record again and again; otherwise, they were silent
downstairs, deep in drugs or fucking. Bech got up and groped
lightly across the surface of Hannah's furniture for Kleenex or
lens tissue or anything tearable to stuff into his ears. His fingers
came to a paperback book and he thought the paper might be
cheap enough to wad. Tearing off two corners of the title page,
he recognized by the dawning light the book as one of his own,
the Penguin *Brother Pig*, with that absurdly literal cover, of a
grinning pig, as if the novel were *Animal Farm* or *Charlotte's
Web*. The paper crackling and cutting in his ears, he returned
to the bed. Beside him, stately Hannah, half-covered and unconscious, felt like a ship, her breathing an engine, her lubricated
body steaming toward the morning, her smokestack nipples
relaxed in passage. The flute music stopped. The world stopped
turning. Bech counted to ten, twenty, thirty in silence, and his
consciousness had begun to disintegrate when a man harshly
laughed and the Chilean flute, and the pressure in Bech's temples, resumed.

"This is Peter Syburg," Glenda said. "Henry Bech."

"*Je sais, je sais bien*," Peter said, shaking Bech's hand with the
painful vehemence of the celebrity-conscious. "I saw your gig on
the tube. Great. You talked a blue streak and didn't tip your hand
once. What a con job. Cool. I mean it. The medium is *you*, man.
Hey, that's a compliment. Don't look that way."

"I was just going to give him coffee," Glenda interposed.

"How about brandy?" Bech asked. "Suddenly I need my
spirits fortified."

"Hey, don't go into your act," Peter said. "I *like* you."

Peter was a short man, past thirty, with thinning ginger hair and a pumpkin's gap-toothed grin. He might have even been forty; but a determined retention of youth's rubberiness fended off the possibility. He flopped into a canvas sling chair and kept crossing and recrossing his legs, which were so short he seemed to Bech to be twiddling his thumbs. Peter was a colleague of sorts, based at the CBC office in Montreal, and used Glenda's apartment here when she was in Montreal, as she often was, and vice versa. Whether he used Glenda when she was in Toronto was not clear to Bech; less and less was. Less and less the author understood how people lived. Such cloudy episodes as these had become his only windows into other lives. He wanted to go, but his going would be a retreat – Montcalm wilting before Wolfe's stealthy ascent. He had a bit more brandy instead. He found himself embarked on one of those infrequent experiments in which, as dispassionate as a scientist bending metal, he tested his own capacity. He felt himself inflating, as before television exposure, while the brandy flowed on and Peter asked him all the questions not even Vanessa had been pushy enough to pose ("What's happened to you and Capote?" "What's the timer makes you Yanks burn out so fast?" "Ever thought of trying television scripts?") and expatiating on the wonders of the McLuhanite world in which he, Peter, with his thumb-like legs and berry-bright eyes, moved as a successful creature, while he, Bech, was picturesquely extinct. Glenda flicked her pale hair and studied her hands and insulted her out-of-whack corpuscles with cigarettes. Bech was happy. One more brandy, he calculated, would render him utterly immobile, and Peter would be displaced. His happiness was not even punctured when the two others began to talk to each other in Canadian French, about calling a taxi to take him away.

"*Taxi, non*," Bech exclaimed, struggling to rise. "*Marcher, oui. Je pars, maintenant. Vous le regretterez, quand je suis disparu. Au revoir, cher Pierre.*"

"You can't walk it, man. It's miles."

"Try me, you post-print punk," Bech said, putting up his hairy fists.

Glenda escorted him to the stairs and down them, one by one;

at the foot, she embraced him, clinging to him as if to be rendered fertile by osmosis. "I thought he was in Winnipeg," she said. "I want to have your baby."

"Easy does it," Bech wanted to say. The best he could do was, "*Facile le fait.*"

Glenda asked, "Will you ever come back to Toronto?"

"*Jamais,*" Bech said, "*jamais, jamais,*" and the magical word, so true of every moment, of every stab at love, of every step on ground you will not walk again, rang in his mind all the way back to the hotel. The walk was generally downhill. The curved lights of the great city hall guided him. There was a forested ravine off to his left, and a muffled river. And stars. And block after block of substantial untroubled emptiness. He expected to be mugged, or at least approached. In his anesthetized state, he would have welcomed violence. But in those miles he met only blinking stop lights and impassive architecture. *And they call this a city,* Bech thought scornfully. *In New York, I would have been killed six times over and my carcass stripped of its hubcaps.*

The cries of children playing woke him. The sound of the flute at last had ceased. Last night's pleasure had become straw in his mouth; the woman beside him seemed a larger sort of dreg. Her eyelids fluttered, as if in response to the motions of his mind. It seemed only polite to reach for her. The children beneath the window cheered.

Next morning, in Toronto, Bech shuffled, footsore, to the Royal Ontario Museum and admired the Chinese urns and the totem poles and sent a postcard of a carved walrus tusk to Bea and her three children.

Downstairs, in Sydney, Moira was up, fiddling with last night's dishes and whistling to herself. Bech recognized the tune. "Where's Peter?" he asked.

"He's gone," she said. "He doesn't believe you exist. We waited up hours for you last night and you never came home."

"We *were* home," Hannah said.

"Oh, it dawned on us finally." She elaborated: "Peter was so moody I told him to leave. I think he still loves *you* and has been leading this poor lass astray."

"What do you like for breakfast?" Hannah asked Bech, as

wearily as if she and not he had been awake all night. Himself, he felt oddly fit, for being fifty and on the underside of the world. "Tell me about Afghanistan – should I go there?" he said to Moira, and he settled beside her on the carpeted divan while Hannah, in her lumpy blue robe, shuffled in the kitchen, making his breakfast. "Grapefruit if you have it," he shouted to her, interrupting the start of Moira's word tour of Kabul. "Otherwise, orange juice." *My God*, he thought to himself, *she has become my wife. Already I'm flirting with another woman.*

Bech boarded the plane (from Australia, from Canada) so light-headed with lack of sleep it alarmed him hardly at all when the machine rose into the air. His stomach hurt as if lined with grit, his face looked gray in the lavatory mirror. His adventures seemed perilous, viewed backward. Mysterious diseases, strange men laughing in the night, loose women. He considered the nation he was returning to: its riots and scandals, its sins and power and gnashing metal. He thought of Bea, his plump suburban softy, her belly striated with fine silver lines, and vowed to marry her, to be safe.

THE HOLY LAND

I NEVER should have married a Christian, Bech thought, fighting his way up the Via Dolorosa. His bride of some few months, Beatrice Latchett (formerly Cook) Bech, and the Jesuit archaeologist that our Jewish-American author's hosts at the Mishkenot Sha'ananim had provided as guide to the Christian holy sites – a courtly Virgil to Bech's disbelieving Dante – kept getting ahead of him, their two heads, one blond and one bald, piously murmuring together as Bech fell behind in the dusty jostle of nuns and Arab boys, of obese Protestant pilgrims made bulkier still by airline tote bags. The incessant procession was watched by bored gaunt merchants with three-day beards as they stood before their souvenir shops. Their dark accusing sorrow plucked at Bech. His artist's eye, always, was drawn to the irrelevant: the overlay of commercialism upon this ancient sacred way fascinated him – Kodachrome where Christ stumbled, bottled Fanta where He thirsted. Scarves, caftans, olive-wood knickknacks begged to be bought. As a child, Bech had worried that merchants would starve; Union Avenue in Williamsburg, near where his uncles lived on South Second Street, had been lined with disregarded narrow shops, a Kafka world of hunger artists waiting unwatched in their cages. This was worse.

Père Gibergue had confirmed what Bea already knew from her guidebooks: the route Jesus took from Pilate's verdict to Golgotha was highly problematical, and in any case, all the streets of first-century Jerusalem were buried under twelve feet of rubble and subsequent paving. So they and their fellow pilgrims were in effect treading on air. The priest, wearing flared slacks and a short-sleeved shirt, stopped to let Bech catch up, and pointed out to him overhead a half-arch dating, it seemed certain, from the time of Herod. The other half of the arch was buried, lost, behind a gray façade painted with a polyglot array in which Bech could read the word GIFTS. Bea's face, beside the tanned face of the archaeologist, looked radiantly pale. She was lightly sweating. Her guidebook was clutched to her blouse like a missal. "Isn't it all wonderful?" she asked her husband.

Bech said, "I never realized what a big shot Herod was. I thought he was just something on the back of a Christmas card."

Père Gibergue, in his nearly flawless English, pronounced solemnly, "He was a crazy man, but a great builder." There was something unhappy about the priest's nostrils, Bech thought; otherwise, his vocation fit him like a smooth silk glove.

"There were several Herods," Bea interposed. "Herod the Great was the slaughter-of-the-innocents man. His son Herod Antipas was ruling when Jesus was crucified."

"Wherever we dig now, we find Herod," Père Gibergue said, and Bech thought, *Science has seduced this man. In his archaeological passion, he has made a hero of a godless tyrant.* Jerusalem struck Bech as the civic embodiment of conflicted loyalties. At first, deplaning with Bea and being driven at night from the airport to the Holy City through occupied territory, he had been struck by the darkness of the land, an intended wartime dark such as he had not seen since his GI days, in the tense country nightscapes of England and Normandy. Their escort, the son of American Zionists who had emigrated in the Thirties, spoke of the convoys that had been forced along this highway in the '67 war, and pointed out some hilly places where the Jordanian fire had been especially deadly. Wrecked tanks and trucks, unseeable in the dark, had been left as monuments. Bech remembered, as their car sped vulnerably between the black shoulders of land, the rapt sensation (which for him had been centered in the face, the mouth more than the eyes – had he been more afraid of losing his teeth than his sight?) of being open to bullets, which there was no dodging. Before your brain could register anything, the damage would be done. Teeth shattered, the tongue torn loose, blood gushing through the punctured palate.

Then, as the car entered realms of light – the suburbs of Jerusalem – Bech was reminded of southern California, where he had once gone on a fruitless flirtation with some movie producers, who had been unable to wrap around his old novel *Travel Light* a package the banks would buy. Here were the same low houses and palm fronds, the same impression of staged lighting, exclusively frontal, as if the backs of these buildings dissolved into unpainted slats and rotting canvas, into weeds and warm air: that stagnant, balmy, expectant air of Hollywood when the sun goes down. The Mishkenot – the official city guesthouse, where this promising fifty-two-year-old writer and his plump Protestant wife were to stay for three weeks – seemed solidly built of the same stuff of cinematic illusion: Jerusalem limestone, artfully pitted by the mason's chisel, echoing like the plasterboard corridors of a Cecil B. De Mille temple to the ritual noises of weary guests unpacking. A curved staircase of mock-Biblical masonry led up to an alcove where a desk, a map, a wastebasket, and a sofa awaited his meditations. Bech danced up and down these stairs with an enchantment born in cavernous movie palaces; he was Bojangles, he was Astaire, he was George Sanders, wearing an absurd headdress and a sneer, exulting in the captivity and impending torture of a white-limbed maiden who, though so frightened her jewels chatter, will not forswear her Jahweh. Israel had no other sentimental significance for him; his father, a 47th Street diamond merchant, had lumped the Zionists with all the *Luftmenschen* who imagined that mollifying exceptions might be stitched into the world's cruel and necessary patchwork of competition and exploitation. To postwar Bech, busy in Manhattan, events in Palestine had passed as one more mop-up scuffle, though involving a team with whom he identified as effortlessly as with the Yankees.

Bea, an Episcopalian, was enraptured simply at being on Israel's soil. She kept calling it "the Holy Land." In the morning, she woke him to share what she saw: through leaded windows, the Mount of Olives, tawny and cypress-strewn, and the silver bulbs of a Russian church gleaming in the Garden of Gethsemane. "I never thought I'd be here, *ever*," she told him, and as she turned, her face seemed still to brim with reflected morning light. Bech kissed her and over her shoulder read a multilingual warning not to leave valuables on the window sill.

"Why didn't you ask Rodney to bring you," he asked, "if it meant so much?"

"Oh, Rodney. His idea of a spiritual adventure was to go backpacking in Maine."

Bech had married this woman in a civil ceremony in lower Manhattan on an April afternoon of unseasonable chill and spitting snow. She was the younger, gentler sister of a mistress he had known for years and with whom he had always fought. He and Bea rarely fought, and at his age this appeared possibly propitious. He had married her to escape his famous former self. He had given up his apartment at 99th and Riverside – an address consecrated by twenty years of *Who's Who*s – to live with Bea in Ossining, with her twin girls and only son. These abrupt truths, still strange, raced through his mind as he contemplated the radiant stranger whom the world called his wife. "Why didn't you tell me," he asked her now, "you took this kind of thing so much to heart?"

"You knew I went to church."

"The *Epis*copal church. I thought it was a social obligation. Rodney wanted the kids brought up in the upper middle class."

"He thought that would happen anyway. Just by their being his children."

"Lord, I don't know if I can hack this: be an adequate step-father to the kids of a snob and a Christian fanatic."

"Henry, this is your Holy Land, too. You should be thrilled to be here."

"It makes me nervous. It reminds me of *Samson and Delilah*."

"You *are* thrilled. I can tell." Her blue eyes, normally as pale as the sky when the milkiest wisps of strato-cirrus declare a storm coming tomorrow, looked up at him with a new, faintly forced luster. The Holy Land glow. Bech found it distrustworthy, yet, by some twist, in some rarely illumined depth of himself, flattering. While he was decoding the expression of her eyes, her mouth was forming words he now heard, on instant replay, as "Do you want to make love?"

"Because we're in the Holy Land?"

"I'm so excited," Bea confessed. She blushed, waiting for his response. Another hunger artist.

"Wouldn't it be blasphemous?" Bech asked. "Anyway, we're being picked up to sight-see in twenty minutes. What about breakfast instead?" He kissed her again, feeling estranged. He was too old to be on a honeymoon. His marriage was like this Zionist state they were in: a mistake long deferred, a miscarriage of passé fervor and antiquated tribal righteousness, an attempt to be safe on an earth where, for Jews, there was no safety.

Their quarters in the Mishkenot included a kitchen. Bea called from within it, "There's two sets of silver. One says Dairy and the other says Meat."

"Use one or the other," Bech called back. "Don't mingle them."

"What'll happen if I do?"

"I don't know. Try it. Maybe it'll trip the trigger and bring the Messiah."

"Now who's being blasphemous? Anyway, the Messiah *did* come."

"We can't all read His calling card."

Her only answer was the clash of silver.

I'm too old to be married, Bech thought, though he smiled to himself as he thought it. He went to the window and looked at the view that had sexually stimulated his wife. Beyond the near, New Testament hills, the color of unglazed Mexican pottery, were lavender desert mountains like long folds in God's comfortless lap.

"Is there anything I should know about eggs and butter?" Bea called.

"Keep them away from bacon."

"There isn't any bacon. There isn't any meat in the fridge at all."

"They didn't trust you. They knew you'd try to do something crummy." His Christian wife was thirteen years younger than he. Her belly bore silver stretch marks from carrying twins. She made gentle yipping noises when she fucked. Bech wondered whether he had ever really been a sexy man, or was it just an idea that went with bachelorhood? He had been a satisfactory sprinter, he reflected, but nobody up to now had challenged his distance capacity. At his age, he should be jogging.

The first sight they were taken to, by a Jewish archaeologist in rimless glasses, was the Wailing Wall. It was a Saturday. Sabbath congregations were gathered in the sun of the limestone plaza the Israelis had created by bulldozing away dozens of Arab homes. People were chanting, dancing; photographs were forbidden. Men in sidelocks were leaning their heads against the wall in prayer, the broad-brimmed hats of the Hasidim tipped askew. The archaeologist told Bech and Bea that for a millennium the wall could not be seen from where they stood, and pointed out where the massive, characteristically edged Herodian stones gave way to the smaller stones of Saladin and the Mamelukes. Bea urged Bech to walk up to the wall. The broad area in front of it had been designated a synagogue, with separate male and female sections, so they could not pass in through the fence together. "I won't go where you can't go," he said.

Bech's grandfather, a diamond-cutter and disciple of Spinoza, had come to the United States from the ghetto of Amsterdam in 1880; Bech's father had been an atheistic socialist; and in Bech socialist piety had dwindled to a stubborn wisp of artistic conscience. So there was little in his background to answer to the unearthly ardor of Bea's urging. "I want you to, Henry. Please."

He said, "I don't have a hat. You have to have a hat."

"They have paper yarmulkes there. In that basket," the archaeologist offered, pointing. He was a short bored bearded man, whose attitude expressed no wish, himself, to approach the wall. He stood on the blinding limestone of the plaza as if glued there by his shadow.

"Let's skip it," Bech said. "I get the idea from here."

"No, Henry," Bea said. "You must go up and touch it. You must. For me. Think. We may never be here again."

In her plea he found most touching the pronoun "we." Ever since his honorable discharge from the armed forces, Bech had been an I. He picked a black paper hat from the basket, and the hat was unwilling to adhere to his head; his hair was too woolly, too fashionably full-bodied. Graying had made it frizzier. A little breeze seemed to be blowing outward from the wall and twice threatened to lift his yarmulke away. Amid the stares of congregated Hasidic youth, their side curls as menacing as lions' manes, he held the cap to the back of his skull with his hand and approached, step by cautious step, all that remained of the Temple.

It was, the wall, a Presence. The great rectangular Herodian stones, each given a shallow border, like a calling card, by the ancient masons, were riddled with paper lice. Into the cracks of erosion, tightly folded prayers had been stuffed – the more he looked, the more there were. Bech supposed paper lasted forever in this desert climate. The space around him, the very air, felt tense, like held breath. Numbly he reached out, and, as he touched the surprisingly warm sacred surface, an American voice whined into his ears from a small circle of Hasidim seated on chairs nearby. "Who is this God?" the voice was asking loudly. "If He's so good, why does He permit all the pain in the world? Look at Cambodia, man...." The speaker and his audience were undergoing the obligatory exercise of religious debate. The Jewish tongue, divinely appointed to be active. Bech closed his ears and backed away rapidly. The breeze made another grab at his paper yarmulke. He dropped the flimsy thing into the basket, and Bea was waiting on the other side of the fence.

She was beaming, proud; he had been attracted to that in her which so purely encouraged him. Amid many in this last, stalled decade of his who had wished to reshape, to activate him forcefully, she had implied that his perfection lay nowhere but in a deepening of the qualities he already possessed. Since he was Jewish, the more Jewish he became in her Christian care, the better.

"Wasn't it wonderful?" she asked.

"It was something," was all he would grant her. Strange diseases, he thought, demand strange remedies: he, her. As they linked arms, after the separation imposed by a sexist orthodoxy, Bech apprehended Bea with refreshed clarity, by this bright, dry light of Israel: as a creature thickening in the middle, the female of a species mostly hairless and with awkward gait, her flesh

nearing the end of its reproductive capacity and her brain possessed by a bizarre creed, yet pleasing to him and asking for his
loyalty as unquestioningly, as helplessly as she gave him hers.

Their guide led them up a slanted road, past an adolescent
soldier with a machine gun, to the top of the wall. On their left,
the faithful continued to circle and pray; on their right, a great
falling off disclosed the ugly results of archaeology, a rubble
of foundations. "The City of David," the archaeologist said
proudly, "just where the Bible said it would be. Everything,"
he said, and his gesture seemed to include all of the Holy City,
"just as it was written. We read first, then we dig." At the Gate of
the Moors, their guide yielded to a courtly Arab professor –
yellow face, brown suit, Oxford accent – who led them in
stockinged feet through the two mosques built on the vast platform that before 70 A.D. had supported the Temple. Strict Jewish
believers never came here, for fear of accidentally treading upon
the site of the Holy of Holies, the Ark of the Covenant. Within
the Aqsa Mosque, Bech and Bea were informed of recent violence: King Abdullah of Jordan had been assassinated near the
entrance in 1951, before the eyes of his grandson the present King
Hussein; and in 1969, a crazed Australian had attempted to set the
end nearest Mecca afire, with considerable success. Craziness,
down through history, has performed impressively, Bech thought.

They were led past a scintillating fountain, up a few marble
stairs, to the Dome of the Rock. Inside an octagon of Persian tile,
beneath a dizzyingly lavish and symmetrical upward abyss, a spine
of rock, the tip of Mount Moriah, showed where Abraham had
attempted to sacrifice Isaac and, failing that, had founded three
religions. Here also, the professor murmured amid the jostle of
the faithful and the touring, Cain and Abel had made their fatally
contrasting offerings, and Mohammed had ascended to Heaven
on his remarkable horse Burak, whose hoofprints the pious claim
to recognize, along with the fingerprints of an angel who
restrained the Rock from going to Heaven also. For reasons
known best to themselves, the Crusaders had hacked at the
Rock. Great hackers, the Crusaders. And Suleiman the Magnificent, who had wrested the Rock back from the (from his
standpoint) infidels, had his name set in gold on high, within

the marvelous dome. The King of Morocco had donated the green carpets, into which Bea's stockinged feet dug impatiently, aching to move on from these empty wonders to the Christian sites. *Sexy little feet*, Bech thought. From boyhood on, spying his mother's shoeless feet flitting by, he had responded to the dark band of reinforcement that covers half of a woman's stockinged toes, giving us eight baby cleavages.

"Do you wish to view the hairs from the Beard of the Prophet?" the professor asked, adding, "There is always a great crowd around them."

Hairs of the Prophet were the kind of sight Bech liked, but he said, "I think my wife wants to push on."

They were led down from Herod's temple platform along a peaceable path beside an Arab cemetery. Their guide suddenly chuckled; his teeth were as yellow as his face. He gestured at a bricked-up portal in the Old City wall. "That is the Golden Gate, the gate whereby the Messiah is supposed to come, so the Ommiads walled it solid and, furthermore, put a cemetery there, because the Messiah supposedly is unable to walk across the dead."

"Hard for him to go anywhere if that's the rule," Bech said, glancing sideways to see how Bea was bearing up under these malevolent overlays of superstition. She looked pink, damp, and happy, her Holy Land glow undimmed. At the end of the pleasant path, at the Lion's Gate, they were passed into the care of the debonair Jesuit and embarked upon the Via Dolorosa.

Lord, don't let me suffocate, Bech thought. The priest kept leading them underground, to show them buried Herodian pools, Roman guardrooms that the sinkage of centuries had turned into grottoes, and paving stones scratched by the soldiers as they played a time-killing game – proof, somehow, of the historical Jesus. Père Gibergue knew his way around. He darted into the back room of a bakery, where a dirty pillar of intense archaeological interest stood surrounded by shattered crates. By another detour, Bech and Bea were led onto the roof of the Church of the Holy Sepulcher; here an ancient company of Abyssinian monks maintained an African village of rounded huts and sat smiling in the sun. One of them, standing against a cupola, posed for Bea's camera. Below the cupola, Père Gibergue zealously explained, was the crypt where Saint Helena, mother of Constantine, discovered in the year 327 the unrotted wood of the True Cross. To the Jesuit's sorrow, the young Russian Orthodox priest (his face waxen-white, his thin beard tapered to a double point: the very image, as Bech imagined it, of Ivan Karamazov) who answered their ring at the door of the Alexandra Hostel refused to admit them, this being a Sabbath, to the excavated cellar wherein had been found, Père Gibergue excitedly explained, a worn threshold beyond doubt stepped upon by the foot of God Incarnate.

So this is what's been making the goyim tick all these years. All these levels – roofs coterminous with the street, sacred footsteps buried meters beneath their own – afflicted Bech like a sea of typographical errors. Perhaps this was life: mistake heaped upon mistake, one protein molecule entangled with another until the confusion thrived. Except that it smelled so fearfully dead. The Church of the Holy Sepulcher was so needlessly ugly that Bech said to Bea, "You should have let the Arabs design it for you."

Père Gibergue overheard and said, "In fact, an Arab family has been entrusted with the keys for eight hundred years, to circumvent the contention among the Christian sects." Inside the hideous edifice, the priest, too, seemed overwhelmed; he sat on a bench near some rusting pipe scaffolding and said, "Go. I will pray here while you look." He hid his face in his hands.

Undaunted, Bea with her guidebook led Bech up a marble staircase to the site of the Crucifixion. This turned out to be a great smoke-besmirched heap or fungus of accreted icons and votive lamps. Six feet from the gold-rimmed hole where Christ's cross had supposedly been socketed, a fat Greek priest, seated in his black muffin hat at a table peddling candles, was taking a swig from a bottle in a paper bag. At Bech's side, Bea did a genuflective dip and gazed enthralled at this mass of aesthetic horrors. German tourists were noisily shuffling about, under a barrage of exploding flashbulbs.

"Let's go," Bech muttered.

"Oh, Henry, why?"

"This frightens me." It had that alchemic stink of medieval basements where vapors condensed as demons and pogroms and autos-da-fé. Torquemada, Hitler, the czars – every despot major or minor who had tried to stunt and crush his race had inhaled these Christly vapors. He dragged Bea away, back down to the main floor of the church, which her guidebook itself admitted to be a *conglomeration of large and small rooms, impossible to consider as a whole.*

Père Gibergue unbowed the tan oval of his head. He asked hopefully, "Enough?"

"More than," Bech said.

The Jesuit nodded. "A great pity. This should be Chartres. Instead . . ." He told Bea, "With your camera, you should photograph that, what the Greeks are doing. Without anyone's permission, they are walling up their sector of the nave. It is barbarous. But not untypical."

Bea peered through a gilded grate into a sector of holy space crowded with scaffolding and raw pink stone. She did not lift her camera. She had been transported, Bech realized, to a realm beyond distaste. "We cannot go without visiting the Sepulcher of Christ," she announced.

Père Gibergue said, "I advise against it. The line is always long. There is nothing to see. Believe me."

Bech echoed, "Believe him."

Bea said, "I don't expect to be here ever again," and got into line to enter a little building that reminded Bech, who joined her, of nothing so much as those mysteriously ornate structures that used to stand in discreet corners of parks in Brooklyn and the Bronx, too grand for lawn mowers but unidentified as latrines; he had always wondered what had existed inside such dignified small buildings – mansions in his imagination for dwarfs. The line moved slowly, and the faces of those returning looked stricken. *Impossible to consider as a whole.*

There were two chambers. The outer held a case containing a bit of the stone that the Angel is said to have rolled away from the mouth of the tomb; a German woman ahead of Bech in line kissed the cracked glass top of the case and caressed herself in an elaborate spasm of pious gratification, eyeballs rolling, a dovelike moan bubbling from her throat. He was relieved that Bea was better behaved: she glanced down, made a mental note, and passed by. She had pinned up her fine blond hair and hid it under a kerchief like an Arab woman. As she bowed her head he glimpsed the damp nape of her neck as if seeing it for the last time. They were about to be separated by an infamous miracle.

The inner chamber was entered by an opening so small Bech had to crouch, though the author was not tall. Within, as had been foretold, there was "nothing to see." Smoking lamps hanging thick as bats from the low ceiling. A bleak marble slab. No trace of the original sepulcher hewn from the rock of Golgotha. In the confines of this tiny space, elbow to elbow with Bech, another stocky Greek priest, looking dazed, was waving lighted tapers held cleverly between his spread fingers. The tapers were for sale. The priest looked at Bech. Bech didn't buy. With a soft grunt of irritation, the priest waved the lighted tapers out. Bech was fascinated by this sad moment of disappointed commerce; he imagined how the wax must drip onto the man's fat fingers, how it must hurt. A hunger artist. The priest eyed Bech again. The whites above his dolefully sagging lower lids were very bloodshot. Smoke gets in your eyes.

Back in their room at the Mishkenot, he asked Bea, "How's your faith?"

"Fine. How's yours?"

"I don't know much about places of worship, but wasn't that the most God-forsaken church you ever did see?"

"It's history, Henry. You have to see through external accidents to the things of the spirit. You weren't religiously and archaeologically prepared. The guidebook warns people they may be disappointed."

"Disappointed! Disgusted. Even your poor Jesuit, who's been there a thousand times, had to hide his face in his hands. Did you hear him complain about what the Greeks were doing to their slice of the pie? Did you hear his story about the Copts swooping down one night and slapping up a chapel that then couldn't be taken away for some idiotic superstitious reason?"

"They wanted to be close to the Holy Sepulcher," Bea said, stepping out of her skirt.

"I've never seen anything like it," Bech said. "It was garbage, of an ultimate sort."

"It was beautiful to be there, just beautiful," Bea said, skinning out of her blouse and bra in one motion.

How, Bech asked himself, out of a great materialist nation containing one hundred million fallen-away Christians had he managed to pick this one radiant aberration as a bride? *Instinct*, he answered himself; his infallible instinct for the distracting. At the height of the lovemaking that the newlyweds squeezed into the dusky hour before they were due to go out to dinner, the bloodshot eyeball of the unsuccessful taper-selling priest re-appeared to him, sliding toward Bech as toward a demon brother unexpectedly encountered while robbing the same tomb.

The dinner was with Israeli writers, in a restaurant staffed by Arabs. Arabs, Bech perceived, are the blacks of Israel. Slim young men, they came and went silently, accepting orders and serving while the lively, genial, grizzled, muscular intellectuals talked. The men were an Israeli poet, a novelist, and a professor of English; their wives were also a poet, a novelist, and a professor, though not in matching order. All six had immigrated years ago and therefore were veterans of several wars; Bech knew them by type, fell in with their chatter and chaffing as if back into a party of uncles and cousins. Yet he scented something outdoorsy, an unfamiliar toughness, a readiness to fight that he associated with Gentiles, as part of the psychic kit that included their indiscriminate diet and their bloody, lurid religion. And these Jews had the uneasiness, the slight edge, of those with something to hold on to. The strength of the Wandering Jew had been that, at home nowhere specific, he had been at home in the world. The poet, a man whose face appeared incessantly to smile, broadened as it was by prominent ears and a concentration of wiry hair above the ears, said of the Wailing Wall, "The stones seem smaller now. They looked bigger when you could see them only up close."

The professor's wife, a novelist, took fire: "What a reactionary thing to say! I think it is beautiful, what they have done at the Kotel Ha. They have made a sacred space of a slum."

Bech asked, "There were many Arab homes?"

The poet grimaced, while the shape of his face still smiled. "The people were relocated, and compensated."

The female novelist told Bech, "Before '67, when the Old City was theirs, the Jordanians built a hotel upon the Mount of Olives, using the old tombstones for the soldiers' barracks. It was a vast desecration which they committed in full view. We felt very frustrated."

The male novelist, whose slender, shy wife was a poetess, offered as a kind of truce, "And yet I feel at peace in the Arab landscape. I do not feel at peace in Tel Aviv, among those Miami Beach hotels. That was not the idea of Israel, to make another Miami Beach."

"What was the idea, then?" asked the female novelist, teasing – an overweight but still-dynamic flirt. There is a lag, Bech thought, between the fading of an attractive woman's conception of herself and the fading of the reality.

The male novelist, his tanned skin minutely veined and ponderously loose upon his bones, turned to Bech with a gravity that hushed the table; an Arab waiter, ready to serve, stood there frozen. "The idea," it was stated to Bech in the halting murmur of an extreme confidence, "is not easy to express. Not Freud and Einstein, but not Auschwitz, either. Something . . . in between."

Bech's eye flicked uneasily to the waiter and noticed the name on his identification badge: SULEIMAN.

The poetess, as if to lighten her husband's words, asked the American guests, "What have been your impressions so far? I know the question is foolish, you have been here a day."

"A day or a week," the female novelist boisterously volunteered, "Henry Bech will go back and write a best-selling book about us. Everyone does."

The waiter began to serve the food – ample, deracinated, Hilton food – and while Bech was framing a politic answer, Bea spoke up for him. He was as startled as if one of his ribs had suddenly chirped. "Henry's in raptures," she said, "and so am I. I can't believe I'm here, it's like a dream."

"A costly dream," said the professor, the youngest of the men and the only one wearing a beard. "A dream costly to many men." His beard was as red as a Viking's; he stroked it a bit preeningly.

"Vision and reality," the male novelist pronounced. "Here, they come together and clash."

"The Holy Land," Bea went on, undeterred, her voice flowing like milk poured from above. "I feel I was born here. Even the air is so *right*."

Her strangeness, to her husband at this moment, did verge on the miraculous. At this table of Jews who, wearied of waiting for the Messiah, had altered the world on their own, Bea's voice with its lilt of hasty good news came as an amazing interruption. Bech answered the poetess as if he had not been interrupted. "It reminds me of southern California. The one time I was there, I felt surrounded by enemies. Not people like you," he diplomatically amended, "but up in the hills. Sharpshooters. Agents."

"You were there before Six-Day War," joked the female professor; until then, she had spoken not a word, merely smiled toward her husband, the smiling poet. It occurred to Bech that perhaps her English was insecure, that these people were under no obligation to know English, that on their ground it was his obligation to speak Hebrew. English, that bastard child of Norman knights and Saxon peasant girls – how had he become wedded to it? There was something diffuse and eclectic about the language that gave him trouble. It ran against his grain; he tended to open books and magazines at the back and read the last pages first.

"What shall we do?" the flamboyant female novelist was urgently asking him, evidently apropos of the state of Israel. "We can scarcely speak of it anymore, we are so weary. We are weary of war, and now we are weary of talk of peace."

"The tricky thing about peace," Bech suggested, "is that it doesn't always come from being peaceable."

She laughed, sharply, a woman's challenging laugh. "So you, too, are a reactionary. Myself, I would give them anything – the Sinai, the West Bank. I would even give them back East Jerusalem, to have peace."

"*Not* East Jerusalem!" the Christian in their midst exclaimed. "Jerusalem," Bea said, "belongs to everybody."

And her face, aglow with confidence in things unseen, became a cause for wonder among the seven others. The slim, shy poetess, whose half-gray hair was parted in the exact center of her slender skull, asked lightly, "You would like to live here?"

"We'd love to," Bea said.

Bech felt he had to step on this creeping "we" of hers. "My wife speaks for herself," he said. "Her enthusiasm overwhelmed even the priest who took us up the Via Dolorosa this afternoon. My own impression was that the Christian holy sites are hideously botched. I liked the mosques."

Bea explained with the patience of a saint, "I said to myself, I've waited for this for thirty-nine years, and I'm not going to let anybody, even my husband, ruin it for me."

Sunday-school pamphlets, Bech imagined. Bible illustrations protected by a page of tissue paper. Bea had carried those stylized ochre-and-moss-green images up from infancy and, when the moment had at last arrived, had placed them carefully upon the tragic, eroded hills of Jerusalem and pronounced the fit perfect. He loved her for that, for remaining true to the little girl she was. In the lull of silence her pious joy had induced, Suleiman came and offered them dessert, which the sated Israelis refused. Bech had apple pie, Bea had fig sherbet, to the admiration of their hosts. Young in marriage, young in appetite.

"You know," he told her in the taxi back to the Mishkenot, "the Holy Land isn't holy to those people tonight the way it is to you."

"I know that, of course."

"To them," he felt obliged to press on, "it's holy because it *is* land at all; after nineteen hundred years of being pushed around, the Jews have a place where they can say, O.K., this is it, this is our country. I don't think it's something a Christian can understand."

"I certainly can. Henry, it saddens me that you feel you must explain all this to me. Rodney and I once went to a discussion group on Zionism. Ask me about Herzl. Ask me about the British Mandate."

"I explain it only because you've surprised me with your own beliefs."

"I'll keep them to myself if they embarrass you."

"No, just don't offer to immigrate. They don't want you. Me, they wouldn't mind, but I have enough problems right now."

"I'm a problem."

"I didn't say that. My work is a problem."

"I think you'd work very well here."

"Jesus, no. It's depressing. To me, it's just a ghetto with farms. I *know* these people. I've spent my whole life trying to get away from them, trying to think bigger."

"Maybe that's your problem. Why try to get away from being Jewish? All those motorcycles, and Cincinnati, and Saint Bernard – you have to make it all up. Here, it'd be real for you. You could write and I could join a dig, under Father Gibergue."

"What about your children?"

"Aren't there kibbutz schools?"

"For Episcopalians?"

She began to cry, out of a kind of sweet excess, as when angels weep. "I thought you'd like it that I love it here," she got out, adding, "with you."

"I *do* like it. Don't you like it that I like it in Ossining, with you?" As their words approached nonsense, some dim sense of what the words "holy land" might mean dawned on him. The holy land was where you accepted being. Middle age was a holy land. Marriage.

Back in their room in the Mishkenot, a calling card had been left on a brass tray. Bech looked at the Hebrew lettering and said, "I can't read this."

"I can," Bea said, and turned the card over, to the Roman type on the other side.

"What does it say?"

Bea palmed the card and looked saucy. "My secret," she said.

I never should have married a Christian, Bech told himself, without believing it. He was smiling at the apparition of his plump Wasp wife, holding a calling card shaped like a stone in Herod's wall.

Wifely, she took pity. "Actually, it's somebody from *The Jerusalem Post*. Probably wanting an interview."

"Oh God," Bech said.

"I suppose he'll come again," Bea offered.

"Let's hope not," Bech said, blasphemously.

MACBECH

BEA on her mother's side was a Sinclair, and a long-held dream of hers had been to visit the land of her ancestors – the counties of Sutherland and Caithness in the eastern Scots Highlands. Bech, now legally established in the business of making her dreams come true, and slightly enriched by the sale of a forgotten *Collier's* chestnut to a public-television series promoting Minor Masters of the American Short Story, volunteered to take her there, as a fortieth-birthday present. They parked their crumbling mock-Tudor manse in Ossining and its three juvenile inhabitants with a house-sitting young faculty couple from Mercy College and flew that May to London, entraining north to Edinburgh and thence to Inverness. Bech liked Great Britain, since its decline was as notorious as his, and he liked trains, for the same reason. The farther north they went, the strangely happier he became.

His happiness first hit him in Edinburgh, as he lugged their suitcases up a mountainous flight of stairs from the sunken glass-and-iron sheds of Waverley Station. As he turned onto North Bridge, at the far end of which their hotel waited, his eyes confronted not metropolitan rectangles but a sweeping green shoulder of high and empty land named, Bea read aloud at his side from out of her blue guidebook, Arthur's Seat. Burdened by baggage as he was, Bech felt lifted up, into the airy and the epic. Scotland seemed at a glance ancient, raw, grimy, lush, mysterious, and mannerly. Like Bech, it was built solid of disappointments. Lost causes abounded. Defenders of the Castle had been promptly hanged outside the Portcullis Gate, witches were burned in bundles, Covenanters were slaughtered. In Holyrood Palace, the red-haired Queen of Scots, taller than Bech had expected, slipped in her brocaded slippers down a spiral stone staircase to visit the handsome boy Darnley, who, devoid of all common sense, one evening burst into her little supper room and, with others, dragged off her pet secretary David Rizzio and left him in the audience chamber dead of fifty-six stab wounds. *The alleged indelible stain of blood, if it exists, is concealed by the floor covering. Jealousy of Rizzio's political influence, and perhaps a darker suspicion in Darnley's mind, were the probable motives for the crime.* Dried blood and dark suspicions dominated the Caledonian past; nothing in history sinks quicker, Bech thought, than people's actual motives, unless it be their sexual charm. In this serene, schizophrenic capital – divided by the verdant cleavage of a loch drained in 1816 – he admired the biggest monument ever erected to an author, a spiky huge spire sheltering a statue of Sir Walter Scott and his dog. He glanced, along the slanting Royal Mile, down minuscule alleys in the like of which Boswell had caught and clipped his beloved prostitutes. "Heaven," Bech kept telling Bea, who began to resent it.

But Bech's abrasive happiness grew as, a few days later, the windows of their next train gave on the gorse-blotched slopes of the Grampians, authentic mountains green and gray with heather and turf. In Inverness, they rented a little cherry-red car in which everything normally on the right was on the left; groping for the gear-shift, Bech grabbed air, and, peering into the rearview mirror, saw nothing. Bea, frightened, kept reminding him that she was there, on his left, and that he was driving terribly close to that stone wall. "Do you want to drive?" he asked her. At her expected answer of "Oh, no," he steered the short distance to Loch Ness; there they stood among the yellow-blooming bushes on the bank, hoping to see a monster. The water, dark even in the scudding moments of sunlight, was chopped into little wavelets each shadow of which might be a fin, or a gliding plesiosaur nose. "It's possible," Bech said. "Remember the coelacanth."

His fair wife touched his arm and shivered. "Such dark water."

"They say the peat, draining into it. Tiny black particles suspended everywhere, so all these expensive cameras they lower down can't see a thing. There could be whales down there."

Bea nodded, still staring. "It's much bigger than anybody says."

Married peace, that elusive fauna swimming in the dark also, stole back upon them at the hotel, a many-gabled brick Guests beside the pretty river Ness. After dinner, in the prolonged northern light, they wandered across a bridge and came by chance upon a stadium where a show for tourists was in progress: Scots children in kilts performed traditional dances to the bag-pipes' keening. The couple loved, when they travelled, all chil-dren, having none of their own. Their marriage would always be sterile; Bea had been willing, though nearing the end of her fourth decade, but Bech shied from paternity, with its over-whelming implication of commitment. He aspired to be no more than one of mankind's uncles, and his becoming at a blow stepfather to Bea's twin adolescent girls, Ann and Judy, and to little Donald (who had at first called him "Mr. Bech" and then "Uncle Henry"), was bliss and burden enough, in the guardianship line. His books and in his fallow years his travels were his children, and by bringing Bea along he gave her what he could of fresh ties to the earth. Some of the Scots performers were so small they could barely hop across the swords laid flat on the grass, and some had to be tugged back and forth in the ritual patterns by their older sisters. Watching the trite, earnest rou-tines, Bea beside Bech acquired a tranced smile; tears had appeared in her blue eyes without canceling the smile, an unsur-prising combination in this climate where sun and shower and rainbow so swiftly alternated. In the sheltered bleachers where they sat they seemed the only tourists; the rest were mothers and fathers and uncles, with children's raincoats in their laps. As Bech and Bea returned to their hotel, the still-twilit sky, full of hasten-ing clouds, added some drops of silver to the rippling river that looked as pure as soda water, though it was fed by the black loch.

Next day they dared drive left-handedly along the crowded coast road north, through Dingwall and Tain, Dornoch and Golspie. At Dunrobin Castle, a downpour forbade that they descend into the famous formal gardens; instead they wandered

unattended through room after paneled room, past portraits and
stag horns and framed photographs of turn-of-the-century weekends – the Duke of Sutherland and his guests in white flannels,
holding tennis rackets like snowshoes. "*Its name,*" Bech read to
Bea from the guidebook, "*may mean 'Robin's Castle,' after Robert,
the sixth Earl of Sutherland, whose wife was a daughter of the barbarous
Alexander, Earl of Buchan, a younger son of King Robert II and known
as 'The Wolf of Badenoch.*' Now there's *his*tory," he said. " 'The
barbarous Alexander.' The third Duke of Sutherland," he went
on, paraphrasing, "was the largest landowner in Western Europe.
Almost the whole county of Sutherland, over a million acres. His
father and grandfather were responsible for the Clearances. They
pushed all these poor wee potato farmers out so they could graze
sheep – the closest thing to genocide in Europe up to Hitler,
unless you count the Armenians in Turkey."

"Well, don't blame me," Bea said. "I was just a Sinclair."

"It was a man called John Sinclair who brought the Cheviot
sheep north into Caithness."

"My mother's branch left around 1750."

"The Highlanders were looked at the same way the Victorians
saw the Africans – savage, lazy, in need of improvement. That's
what they called it, kicking the people out and replacing them
with sheep. Improvement."

"Oh look, Henry! Queen Victoria slept in this bed. And she
left her little lace gloves."

The bed had gilded posts but looked hard and small. Bech told
Bea, "You really don't want to face it, do you? The atrocities a
castle like this is built on." He heard his sore-headed father in
him speaking, and closed his mouth abruptly.

Bea's broad maternal face was flustered, pink, and damp in the
humidity as rain slashed at the leaded windows overlooking the
North Sea. "Well I hadn't thought to face it *now*, just because I'm
a little bit Scotch."

"Scots," he corrected.

"The Sinclairs didn't order the Clearances, they were victims
like everybody else."

"They had a castle," Bech said darkly.

"Not since the seventeenth century," Bea said back.

"I want to see the Strath Naver," he insisted. "That's where the worst of the Clearances were."

Back in the car, they looked at the map. "We can do it," Bea said, her wifely composure restored. "Go up through Wick and then around John o'Groats and over through Thurso and then down along the Strath Naver to Lairg. Though there won't be much to see, just empty land."

"That's the point," Bech said. "They moved the poor crofters out and then burned their cottages. It was the women, mostly, who resisted. The sheriff's men got drunk and whacked them on the head with truncheons and kicked them in their breasts."

"It was a terrible, terrible thing," Bea said, gently outflanking him. Her face looked luminous as harsh rain drummed on the roof of their little red English Ford, where everything was reversed. Her country, his patriotism. Her birthday, his treat. How strange, Bech bothered to notice, that his happiness in Scotland should take the form of being mean to her.

The Sinclairs had farmed, and perhaps a few did still farm, these great treeless fields of Caithness whose emerald sweep came right to the edge of the perilous cliffs. The cliffs, and the free-standing towers the sea had created from a millennial merging of those eroded ravines called gills, were composed of striations of gray sandstones as regular as the pages of a book. Down on the shore, vast, slightly tilted flagstones seemed to commemorate a giant's footsteps into the sea, or to attest to the ruin of a prodigious library. No fence prevented a tourist or a cow from toppling off and hurtling down the sheer height composed of so many accreted, eroding layers; paths had been beaten raggedly parallel to the cliff edge, leading to cairns whose explanatory legend was obscured by lichen and to, in one spot, an unofficial dump, where newspapers and condensed-milk cans had been deposited upon the edge of the precipice but had not all fallen in. Gulls nested just underneath the lip of the turf and in crannies straight down the cliff face; their white bodies, wings extended in flight, speckled the windy steep spaces between the surface of the twinkling sea and the edge where Bech and Bea stood. The plunging perspectives made her giddy, and she shrieked when, teasing, he took a few steps forward and reached down as if to steal a gull egg. The mother gull tipped her head and peered up at him with an unimpressed pink eye. Bech backed away, breathless. For all his boyish bravado, his knees were trembling. Heights called to him. *Fall. Fly.*

The wind so fierce no trees spontaneously grew in this northernmost county of Britain was a bright May breeze today, setting a blush on Bea's cheeks and flaring Bech's nostrils with the scent of salt spray. The Vikings had come to this coast, leaving ruin behind, and flaxen-haired infants. The houses of the region were low, with roofs of thatch or slate, and squared slabs of its ubiquitous flagstone had been set upright and aligned into fences along field boundaries. But the primary feel of this land was of unbounded emptiness, half-tamed and sweet, with scarce a car moving along the A9 and not another walking man or woman to be seen this side of the green horizon, beyond which meadows gave way to brown moors where peat was dug in big black bricks out of long straight trenches, and the emptiness began in earnest. Every cemetery they stopped at had its Sinclairs. Bea was excited to be on ancestral territory, though less ecstatic than she had been in Israel. Bech had felt crowded there, and here, in the many-pocketed tweed jacket he had bought along Princes Street and the droop-brimmed plaid bog hat purchased just yesterday in Wick, he felt at home. "This is my kind of place," he told Bea from the cliff edge, his breath regained and his knees again steady.

"You're just paying me back," she said, "for liking the Holy Land so much."

"That was overdeveloped. This is just right. Thousand-acre zoning."

"You look ridiculous in that hat," she told him unkindly, uncharacteristically. The wind, perhaps, had whipped a shine into her eyes. "I'm not sure the jacket suits you, either."

"They feel great. 'Blow, winds, and crack your cheeks!' "

"They give you that troll look."

"What troll look?"

"That troll look that —"

He finished for her. "That Jews get in tweeds. Shit. I've really done it. I've married an anti-Semite."

"I wasn't going to say that at all." But she never did supply what she had been going to say, and it was not until they were snuggled in their bed on the musty third floor of the Thurso Arms that the monsters in the deep space between them stopped shifting. The brown brick city fell away beneath the gauze curtains at their windows like a town in one of the drabber fairy tales. They made love dutifully, since they had been given a double bed. There was no doubt, Bea did resent his taking Scotland so readily – so greedily – into himself. The stones and grass of this place, its pinnacles and cobbles and weatherswept grays, its history of constant, though turbulently contested, loss in relation to the cushioned green land to the south . . . weren't the Scots one of the ten lost tribes of Israel? Like the Jews, the Celts had been pushed aside from the European mainstream yet not thrown quite free of it: permitted, rather, to witness closely its ruthless forward roar and to harbor in wry hearts and pinched lives the unblinkered knowing of Spinoza and Hume, Maxwell and Einstein. Or so it seemed while Bea slept and Bech lay awake relishing the sensation of being, on the northern edge of this so thoroughly annotated Great Britain, in a kind of magical margin, the sky still white though the time approached midnight. From beneath his window arose the unexpected sound of raucous teen-age horseplay, a hungry scuffling and hooting that further enriched his mystical, global sensations. For surely, if Bech's own narrow and narcissistic life was miracle enough to write about, an interlocked miracle was the existence, wherever you went on a map, of other people living other lives.

Except, it seemed, in the Highlands. Often where a place name sprouted on the dotted red line of the road, there seemed to be nothing, not even the ruined walls of a single house. Nothing was left of men but this name on the map, and the patches of brighter green where, over a century ago, potato patches had been fertilized. Otherwise, mile after mile of tummocky brown turf unrolled with no more than an occasional river or lake for punctuation, or one of those purple-green protuberances, neither mountain nor hill, for which the name was "ben." Bech and Bea had driven west from Thurso above the sea and turned south along the Strath Naver, scene of the most infamous of the Clearances. Atrocity leaves no trace on earth, Bech saw. Nature shrugs, and regroups. Perhaps in Poland there were stretches made vacant like this. There seemed no trace of man but the road itself, which was single-track, with widened spots at intervals where a car could pull over to let another pass. The game did not take long to learn: when two vehicles approached, the drivers accelerated to reach the farthest possible turnout short of collision. Bea maintained that that wasn't the way the game was played at all; rather, drivers courteously vied for the privilege of pulling over and letting the other driver pass with a wave of cheerful gratitude. "Do you want to drive?" he asked her.

"Yes," she answered, unexpectedly.

He stopped the car and stepped out. He inhaled the immaculate Highland air. Small white and pink flowers starred the violet reaches of moor. The clouds leaned in their hurry to get somewhere, losing whole clumps of themselves. There were no sheep. These, too, had been cleared away. As Bea drove along, her chin tipped up with the mental effort of not swerving right, he read to her about the Clearances. "*We have no country to fight for. You robbed us of our country and gave it to the sheep. Therefore, since you have preferred sheep to men, let sheep defend you!*" he read, a lump in his throat at the thought of an army of sheep. Jewish humor. "That's what they said to the recruiters when they tried to raise an army in the Highlands to help fight the Crimean War. The lairds were basically war chieftains, and after the Scots were beaten at Culloden and there was no more war, the crofters, who paid their rent mostly with military service, had nothing to offer. The lairds had moved to London and that nice part of Edinburgh we saw and needed money now, and the way to get money was to rent their lands to sheep farmers from the south."

"That's sad," Bea said absently, pulling into a patch of dirt on the left and accepting a grateful wave from the driver of a rattling old lorry.

"Well, there's a kind of a beauty to it," Bech told her. "The Duke of Sutherland himself came up from London to see what was the matter, and one old guy stood up in the meeting and told him, *It is the opinion of this county that should the Czar of Russia take possession of Dunrobin Castle and of Stafford House next term we couldn't expect worse treatment at his hands than we have experienced in the hands of your family for the last fifty years.*" Bech chuckled; he thought of his own ancestors, evading enlistment on the opposite side of that same war. His mother's people had come from Minsk. History, like geography, excited and frightened him with the superabundance of life beyond his dwindling own.

Bea blinked and asked, "Why are you so enthusiastic about all this?"

"You mean you aren't?"

"It's sad, Henry. You're not looking at the scenery."

"I am. It's magnificent. But misery must be seen as part of the picture."

"Part of *our* picture, you mean. That's what you're rubbing my nose in. You bring me here as a birthday present but then keep reminding me of all these battles and evictions and starvation and greed, as if it applies to *us*. All right. We're mortal. We're fallible. But that doesn't mean we're necessarily cruel, too." One of the leaning, hurrying clouds was darker than the others and suddenly it began to rain, to hail, with such ferocity that Bea whimpered and pulled the car to a halt in a wide spot. The white pellets danced upward from the red hood as if sprung from there and not the sky; the frown within the air was like what the blind must confront before the light winks out entirely. Then the air brightened. The hail ceased, and through the luminous mist of its ceasing a rainbow appeared above the shadows of a valley where a cultivated field formed a shelf of smooth verdure. They had come down from the remotest Highlands into an area where cultivation began, and telephone wires underlined the majesty of the sub-arctic sky. They both climbed out of the little car, to be nearer the rainbow, which, longer in one leg than the other, receded from them, becoming a kind of smile upon the purple-green brow of a ben. Bech luxuriated in the wild beauty all around and said, "Let's buy a castle and murder King Duncan and settle down. This is where we belong."

"We do *not*," Bea cried. "It's where *I* belong!" He was startled; fear must have shown on his face, for an anxious wifely guilt blurred hers as, close to tears, she still pressed her point: "That's so *typ*ical of you writers – you appropriate. My own poor little Scottishness has been taken from me; you're more of a Scot now than I am. I'll have nothing left eventually, and you'll move on to appropriate somebody else's something. Henry, this marriage was a horrible mistake."

But the sheer horror of what she was saying drove her, her blurred round face pink and white like that of a rabbit, into his arms. He held her, patting her back while her sobs moistened his tweed shoulder and the rainbow quite faded in the gorse-golden sun. She was still trying to explain herself, her outburst. "Ever since we got married –"

"Yes?" he encouraged, noting above her sunny head that the lower slopes of the mountain, for aeons stark moor, had been planted in regiments of fir trees to feed the paper mills of the south.

"– I've felt myself in your mind, being di*gest*ed, becoming a *char*acter."

"You're a very real person," Bech reassured Bea, patting mechanically. "You're my Christian maiden." In deference to the spine of feminist feeling that had stiffened beneath his hands, he quickly amended this to: "God's Christian maiden."

BECH WED

THE HOUSE in Ossining was a tall mock-Tudor with an incon-
gruous mansard roof, set on a domed lawn against a fringe of
woods on an acre and a half tucked somewhere between the
Taconic State and the Briarcliff-Peekskill parkways. Its exterior
timbers were painted the shiny harsh green of park benches and
its stucco had been aged to a friable tan; the interior abounded in
drafty wasteful spaces – echoing entrance halls and imperious
wide staircases and narrow windowless corridors for vanished
servants to scuttle along. Bea and Rodney while their marriage
thrived had fixed it up, scraping the white paint and then, next
layer down, the dusty-rose off the newel posts and banisters until
natural oak was reached; they had replaced all the broken glass
and fragmented putty in the little greenhouse that leaned against
the library, retiled the upstairs bathrooms, replastered the back-
stair walls, and laid down a lilac hedge and a composition tennis
court. As their marriage ran into difficulties, the scraping stopped
halfway up the left-hand banister and the tennis court was taken
over by the neighborhood children and their honey-limbed
baby-sitters. Now Bech was installed in the mansion like a hermit
crab tossed into a birdhouse. The place was much too big; he
couldn't get used to the staircases and the volumes of air they
arrogantly commandeered, or the way the heat didn't pour
knocking out of steam radiators from an infernal source concealed many stories below but instead seeped from thin pipes
sneaking low around the baseboards, pipes kept warm by per-
sonalized monthly bills and portentous, wheezing visits from the
local oil truck. In the cellar, you could see the oil tanks – two
huge rust-brown things greasy to the touch. And here was the

furnace, an old converted coal-burner in a crumbling overcoat of plastered asbestos, rumbling and muttering all through the night like a madman's brain. Bech had hardly ever visited a basement before; he had lived in the air, like mistletoe, like the hairy sloth, Manhattan subgenus. Though he had visited his sister in Cincinnati, and written his freshest fantasy, *Travel Light*, upon impressions gathered during avuncular visits there, he had never in his bones known before what America was made of: lonely outposts, log cabins chinked with mud and moss.

Insulation was a constant topic of conversation with the neighbors, and that first winter Bech dragged his uprooted crab tail back and forth to the building-supply center along Route 9 and hauled home in Bea's sticky-geared Volare station wagon great rolls of pink insulation backed by silver paper; with a hardening right hand he stapled this cumbersome, airy material between the studs of an unused and unplastered third-floor room, intended for storage, and made himself, all lined in silver imprinted with the manufacturer's slogans, a kind of dream-image, a surreal distillation, of his cloistered, forsaken apartment high above the windswept corner of 99th and Riverside. Here, his shins baking in the intersecting rays of two electric heaters, he was supposed to write.

"Write?" he said to Bea, who had proposed this space allocation. "How do you do that?"

"You know," she said, not to be joshed. "It'll all come back to you, now that you're settled and loved."

His heart, which had winced at "settled," fled from the word "loved" so swiftly that he went momentarily deaf. These happy conditions had nothing to do with writing. Happiness was not the ally but the enemy of truth. Dear Bea, standing there in her slightly shapeless housedress, her fair hair straggled out in the dishevelment of utter sincerity, seemed a solid obstacle to the translucent on-running of the unease that was Bech's spiritual element, his punctilious modernist diet. Too complacent in her seventh-hand certainty, descended from Freud, that she held between her soft thighs the answer to all his questions, Bea assumed that the long sterile stretch of his unwed life before her had been, simply, a mistake, a wandering in a stony

wilderness cluttered with women and trips. He doubted it was
that simple. Being an artist was a matter of delicate and prolonged
maneuver; who could tell where a false move lay? Think of
Proust's, think of Rilke's, decades of procrastination. The
derangement of the senses, Rimbaud had prescribed. Didn't all
of Hart Crane's debauchery find its reason in a few incandescent
lines that burned on long after the sullen waves had closed upon
his suicide?

"What you must do," Bea told him, even as her blue Scots
eyes slid sideways toward some other detail of housekeeping, "is
go up there first thing every day and write a certain number of
pages – not too many, or you'll scare yourself away. But do that
number, Henry, good or bad, summer or winter, and see what
happens."

"Good or bad?" he asked, incredulous.

"Sure, why not? Who can tell anyway, in the end? Look at
Kafka, whom you admire so much. Who cares now, if *Amerika*
isn't as good as *Das Schloss*? It's all Kafka, and that's all we care
about. Whatever you produce, it'll be Bech, and that's what
people want out of you. *Mehr Licht; mehr Bech!*"

He hadn't known she knew all this German. "I don't admire
Kafka," he grumbled, feeling a child's pleasurable restiveness. "I
feel him as an oppressive older brother. He affects me the way his
father affected him."

"What you're doing," Bea told him, "is punishing us. Ever
since *The Chosen* got panned, you've been holding your breath
like an angry baby. Enough now. Finish *Think Big*."

"I was thinking of calling it *Easy Money*."

"Good. A much better title. I think the old one intimidated
you."

"But it's about New York. How can I write about New York
when you've taken me away from it?"

"All the better," Bea briskly said, patting her hair in closer to
the luminous orb of her face. "New York was a terrible place for
you, you were always letting yourself get sidetracked."

"Who's to say," he asked, giving his old aesthetic one more
try, "what a sidetrack is?"

"Simple. It's the track that doesn't lead anywhere. Do what

you want with your talent. Hide it under a bushel. I can't stand here arguing forever. From the sounds out back, Donald and his friends are doing something terrible to the dog."

It was true, Donald and two pals from a house across the lane were trying to play rodeo with Max, a sluggish old golden retriever that Rodney and Bea had bought as a puppy. He had yelped when lassoed and then, as the boys were being scolded, hung his tail, ashamed of having tattled. Bech had never lived in close conjunction with a dog before. He marveled at the range of emotion the animal could convey with its tail, its ears, and the flexible loose skin of its muzzle. When he and Bea returned from the supermarket or an expedition to the city, old Max in his simple-minded joy would flog the Volare fenders with his tail and, when his new master bent down to pat his head, would slip Bech's hand into his mouth and try to pull him toward the house – retrieving him, as it were. The grip of the dog's teeth, though kindly meant, was firm enough to give pain and to leave livid marks. Bech had to laugh, trying to pull his hand free without injury. Max's muzzle rumpled with fond determination as he kept tugging the stooping, wincing man toward the back door; his ears were rapturously flattened, and cats slid off the porch to rub at Bech's ankles jealously. Cats came with this house, and rodent pets of Donald's that died of escaping from their cages. The three children all had noisy friends, and Bea herself would spend many a morning and afternoon entertaining housewives from the neighborhood or from Briarcliff Manor or Pleasantville – old friends from the Rodney days, curious perhaps to glimpse the notorious author (in the suburbs, at least since *Peyton Place*, all authors are *sui generis* notorious) whom Bea – *Bea*, of all people – had somehow landed. If these visitors were there for morning coffee, they gave Bech little more than bright-eyed, wide-awake smiles above the crisp dickies stuck in their cashmere sweaters; but if he came upon them amid the lengthening shadows of the cocktail hour, slouched around second drinks in a murky corner of the timbered living room, these Gentile housewives would dart toward him blurred, expectant glances and, merriment wax-ing reckless, challenge him to "put" them "in" a book. Alas, what struck him about these women, in contrast to the women of his travels and of Manhattan, was just their undetachability from these, to him, illegible Westchester surroundings.

Without so many inducements to flee upstairs, Bech might never have settled into his silver room. But it was the one spot in the vast house where he did not seem to be in the middle of a tussle, or a party, or a concert. The twin girls especially could not bear to be out of range of amplified music. They were fifteen when Bech became their stepfather – rather bony, sallow girls with Rodney's broad forehead and solemn, slightly bulging gray eyes. They lolled on the sofa or upstairs in their room reading fat novels of witchcraft and horror in Maine while bathed in the clicking thud and apocalyptic lyrics of reggae. Donald, who had inherited more of Bea's curves and shades of humid pink, was ten, and for a time carried everywhere with him a battery-powered CB unit on which he attempted to chat with truckers rolling north beyond the woods. The sound of traffic, though kept at a distance, nevertheless permeated Westchester County, its pitch more sinister, because concealed by greenery, than the frank uproar of Manhattan. Marrying Bea, who had drifted into his life in the wake of her stormy sister, Bech had ignorantly climbed aboard an ark of suburban living whose engines now throbbed around him like those of a sinking merchant ship in Conrad. There was no ignoring noise in these environs. In New York, there were walls, precincts, zones and codes of avoidance; here in Ossining every disturbance had a personal application: the ringing phone was never in someone else's apartment, and the child crying downstairs was always one's own. A kind of siege crackled around the gawky half-green house, so conspicuous on its hillock of lawn – a siege of potentially disastrous groans in the plumbing and creaks in the woodwork, while the encircling animal world gnawed, fluttered, and scrabbled at the weakened structure. Invisible beetles and ants powdered the basement floor with their leavings, and Bech was astonished at how much infiltrating wildlife lurked in even a thoroughly tamed and mortgaged stretch of woods. Squirrels – or was it bats? – danced over his head in the silver room, above the ceiling with its fantasy map of stains, within those dusty constructional gaps that merged with the teeming treetops via holes he could never spot from the

ground or a ladder. Even in the summer he kept his room's one
window closed against the distracting variety of birdcalls. That
second spring, a colorless small bird had built a nest in a chink
of the eaves of the mansard roof and bewitched Bech with the
incessancy of its trips to the nest. A fluffy beating of wings, an
arousal of tiny cheeping, a momentary silencing of the cheeping
with wriggling food, and then a beating of the wings away again.
So much fanatic labor, to add a few mousy birds to the world's
jungle. One morning, suddenly, there was silence from the nest;
the fledglings had flown. A loneliness enveloped the writer's
aerie, with its old army-green desk from Ninety-ninth Street,
its tinny electric heaters, its bookshelves of raw pine attached to
the studs with screwed-in L-brackets, its cardboard boxes of
dishevelled but accumulating manuscript. For Bech had, even
before their Scots trip, taken root in his birdhouse; he had
accepted Bea's advice and was pecking his way steadily through
the ghostly tangle of *Think Big*.

Bech's fourth and, as critical diction has it, "long-awaited"
novel existed in several spurts, or shoals, of inspiration. The first
had come upon him in London, during a brief fling with a petite
heiress and gossip columnist named Merissa, and took the envisioned form of an ambitious and elegiac novel directed, like *Anna
Karenina* and *Madame Bovary*, toward the heroine's suicide. The
heroine was to have Merissa's exquisite small bones and feline
adaptability but to be squarely, winsomely, self-ruinously American. Her name came to him, with an oddness bespeaking a profoundly subconscious imperative, as Olive. Bech managed about
sixty handwritten pages, dealing mostly with Olive's education at
a Southern girls' college where the stench of horse manure
incongruously swept through the curried green campus and the
idyllic vista of young women of good family striding to class in
smart skirts and high heels. But when it came time in the novel to
bring her to that capital of ruined innocence, New York City, he
was at a loss for what professional field he should mire her in.
The only one he knew first-hand, that of publishing, inspired
great distaste in our author when encountered in published

fiction; he did not much like involution, whether met in Escher prints, iris petals, or the romantic theme of incest. Yet all those glass boxes weighing on the heart of the city – what was done inside them, what empires rose and fell? He could not imagine. Stalled, Bech let a year slide by as he responded to invitations and filled out questionnaires from doctoral candidates. Then, one iron-cold winter afternoon, with steam pouring lavishly from the radiator valves, Bech to counter his claustrophobia turned on television, and met there a young actress's face uplifted beseechingly toward that of an aseptic-capped doctor, whose soothing baritone yet had a menacing rumble to it. Turning the channel, Bech eavesdropped upon the staccato conversation of two vexed women as they swiftly circulated among the furniture of a Texas-scale living room. Clicking past a channel of electronic ticker tape and another of Spanish sitcom, he found on the third major network a teen-aged girl screaming and snuffling about an abortion while California cliffs soared past the windows of her convertible. Here, Bech realized, was an empire, a kingdom as extensive and mystically ramified as a Chinese dynasty; the giant freckled figure of boyish, ruthless Tad Greenbaum swam into his cerebrum, trailing those of pliant, pill-popping Thelma Stern, Tad's mistress; her diabolical ex-husband, the enigmatic Polonius Stern; and her unscrupulous though insouciant lawyer-brother, Dolf Lessup. A world of searingly lighted soundstages and intimately dark cutting rooms, of men frantically reaching out from within a closed expensive world of wide desks and deep carpets and dim French restaurants toward the unseen millions sitting lonely in shabby rooms, offered itself to Bech as a wilderness sufficiently harsh to memorialize, and one wherein all his ignorances could be filled in with bits from those old Hollywood movies about making Hollywood movies. For some pages, his path lit alternately by klieg lights and *crêpes flambées*, the author moved through this luminous maze, until all lights failed and he went dry again. For the fact was that power, and the battle for it, utterly bored Bech. Then he met Ellen, a Steiner School teacher, and by the glow of her intelligent, unsmiling moon face he revised some of the yellowing old shoals. Olive, his heroine, became Lenore, and less vulnerable and innocent than when she had been conceived, toward the end of the still-sexist Sixties. Today's young woman would as soon commit murder as suicide. And television soap opera had become, disconcertingly, the rage, a cliché. More trips mercifully intervened. Bech had passed fifty, and his hair had become a startling blob of white in the publicity photographs, and his work in progress, *Think Big*, had been so often mentioned in print that collectors wrote him in some exasperation over their inability to procure a copy. It was this mess of hopeful beginnings, it was this blasted dream, that Bea now ordered him to make come true.

What did she know of art? She had been an honors student at Vassar, majoring in economics. Her father, old Judge Latchett, recently dead, had run the quickest docket in the East. Her sister, the difficult Norma, ill-disguised prototype of Thelma Stern, had had a testy and judgmental tongue. Bea's softness, which had lured him, sheathed an instinctive efficiency; at heart she was still that good child who would check off Toothbrushing, Breakfast, and Toidy on the chart provided before going off each day to school. "Writing isn't like that," he protested.

"Like what?"

"Like toothbrushing and breakfast and doing toidy. The world doesn't need it that way."

She thought, her face in repose round and unsmiling, like that of his character Lenore. "*You* do, though," she said. "Need it. Because you're a writer. At least that's what you told me you were."

Bech ignored the suggestion that he had deceived her, for the many years of their courtship. He pursued his argument: "To justify its existence writing has to be extraordinary. If it's ordinary it's less than worthless; it's clutter. Go into any bookstore and try to breathe. You can't. Too many words produced by people working every morning."

"You know," Bea told him, "Rodney wasn't that crazy about being a bond analyst, either. He would have loved to play tennis all day, every day. But up he got, to catch that 7:31, rain or shine; it used to break my heart. I'd hide in bed until he was gone, it made me feel so guilty."

"See," Bech said. "By marrying me, you've freed yourself

from guilt." But every time she brandished Rodney's example at him, he knew that he had given the world of power a hook into his flesh.

"Donald keeps asking me what you *do*," Bea went on. "The girls were asked at school if it was true you were insane. I mean, thirteen years without a word."

"Now you're hurting me."

"You're hurting *us*," she said, her face going pink in patches. "Rodney feels sorry for me, I can tell over the phone."

"Oh *fuck* Rodney. What do I care about the Rodneys of the world? Why'd you ever leave him if he was so great?"

"He was a pill; but don't make me say it. It's you I love, obviously. Forget everything I said, I *love* it the way you keep yourself pure by never putting pen to paper. There's just one little thing."

"What's that?"

"Never mind."

"No, tell me." He loved secrets, had loved them ever since his father whispered to him that his mother was bad-tempered that day for a reason that had nothing to do with them, and that some day when Henry grew up he would understand. It was not until Bech was about thirty-eight, and lying in bed beside a lovely sleeping girl called Claire, that Bech realized his father had been referring to menstruation.

"We need the dough," Bea said.

"Oho. Now you're really talking."

"This is a big house to heat, and they say fuel oil's going to go to a dollar a gallon. And some slates fell off the north side after that big wind last week."

"Let's sell this barn and move back to the Apple, where the living is easy."

"You know I would, if it weren't for the children."

He knew nothing of the kind, but enjoyed making her lie. He enjoyed, indeed, these contentious conversations, bringing out the Norma in Bea, and would have continued had not the front-door bell rung. It was Marcie Flint, another driven veteran of the suburban quotidian, come to compare second marriages over coffee. Bech fled upstairs, past all the tumbled toys and blankets of the children's bedrooms, to his third-floor retreat. He scratched out *Think Big* on page one of his mauled manuscript and penned the words *Easy Money*. He changed his heroine's name back to Olive. Ripe with reckless scorn, he began anew.

As Bech typed, countering with his four-finger syncopation the nervous rustling of the Rodentia overhead, and as spring's chartreuse buds and melting breezes yielded to the oppressive overgrowth of summer, in turn to be dried and tinted according to the latest fall fashions and returned to the frostbound earth, memories of Manhattan weather washed through him unpredictably, like pangs of bursitis. There, the seasons spoke less in the flora of the hard-working parks than in the costumes of the human fauna, the furs and wool and leather boots and belts and the summer cotton and clogs and in these recent condition-conscious years the shimmering tanktops and supershorts of the young women who rose up from the surfaces of stone as tirelessly as flowers out of mud. New York was so *sexy*, in memory: the indoorness of it all, amid circumambient peril, and the odd good health imposed upon everyone by the necessity of hiking great distances in the search for taxis, of struggling through revolving doors and lugging bags heavy with cheesecake and grapefruit up and down stairs, the elevator being broken. On this island of primitive living, copulation occurred as casually as among Polynesians, while Scarlatti pealed from the stereo and the garbage truck whined its early-morning song two blocks away. Bech remembered, from that cozy long decade of his life before the onset of Claire, how he had gone home from a publishing party with a *Mademoiselle* editor and how in her narrow kitchen her great creamy breasts had spilled from her loosened Shantung dress into his hands as simultaneously their mouths fused in the heat of first kiss and his eyes, furtively sneaking a look at his surroundings, filled with the orbs of the glossy scarlet onions hung on a jutting nail above this overflowing lady's sink. He remembered how Claire, slender as a fish, would flit naked through the aquarium light of his own rooms as a short winter day ended outside in a flurry of wet snow collecting flake by flake on the ridges of the fire escape. She had been studying dance in those remote days, and as Ravel latticed the snow-darkened air with rhythm could have been practicing in a flesh-colored leotard but for the vertical smudge of her pubic hair; unlike the dark triangle that was standard, her pussy formed a gauzy little column as of smoke. Of the mistress succeeding Claire, Bech entertained fewer nostalgic memories, for she had been Norma Latchett, now his sister-in-law. Norma occasionally visited them, dirtying every ashtray in the house with a single lipsticky cigarette each and exuding a rapacious melancholy that penetrated to Bech even through the dungeon walls of the kinship taboo that now prevailed between them. Judge Latchett, having sent so many to their reward, had gone to his, and the sisters' mother was legally incompetent; so Norma now faintly stank to Bech of family depressingness, as Wasps know it. It was the romantic period before Norma that with a sweetness bordering on pain welled up to flood the blank spaces in his ragged manuscript; it now seemed a marvel worth confiding that through those publicly convulsed years under two lugubrious presidents the nation had contained catacombs of private life. Bech at his green steel desk retrieved that vast subterrain detail by detail and interwove the overheard music of a buried time with the greedy confusion his characters bred. They were, but for Olive and some lesser shiksa mistresses, Jewish, and here, in this house built and repeatedly bought by Protestants, and presently occupied save for himself by blonds, and haunted by the tight-lipped ghost of Rodney Cook, Jewishness too became a kind of marvel – a threadbare fable still being spun, an energy and irony vengefully animating the ruins of Christendom, a flavor and guile and humor and inspired heedlessness truly superhuman, a spectacle elevated the promised Biblical notch above the rest of the human drama. His own childhood, his Brooklyn uncles and West Side upbringing, he now saw, through the precious wrong end of the telescope, to be as sharp and toylike as once the redneck motorcyclists of the Midwest had seemed, when the telescope was pointed in the other direction. Day by day his imagination caught slow fire and reduced a few pages to the ash-gray of typescript. He had determined not to rewrite, in his usual patient-spider style, or even to reread, except to check the color of a character's hair or sports car. Where the events seemed implausible, he reasoned that a novel about Greenbaum Productions might legitimately have the texture of a soap opera; where a character seemed thin and unformed, he reassured himself that later episodes would flesh him out; where a gap loomed, Bech enshrined yet another erotic memory from that past enchanted by the removes of time and his Ossining exile. He cast off as spiritual patrons finicky Flaubert and Kafka and adopted the pragmatic fatalism of those great native slapdashers Melville and Faulkner. Whatever faults he was bundling pell-mell into his opus he saw as deepening his revenge upon Bea. For his uncharacteristic gallop of activity was among other things spiteful – fulfillment of a vow to "show" her. "I'll show you!" children would sometimes shout, near tears, beneath his window.

Downstairs, when the day's dizzying flight with the smirched angels of his imagining was over, a brave new domestic world awaited Bech. For lunch he might eat several drying peanut-butter-and-jelly sandwich halves that Donald and a playmate had spurned an hour before. As summer ripened, vegetables from Bea's garden – beans, broccoli, zucchini – might be lying on the butcher-block kitchen counter and could be nibbled raw. That there was great nutritional and moral benefit in raw, home-grown vegetables was one of the Christian notions he found piquant. If Bea was around, she might warm him soup from a can and sit at the round kitchen table and sip some with him. Luncheon meat might be in the refrigerator or not, depending upon the vagaries of her shopping and the predations of Ann's and Judy's boyfriends. It was a chaotic contrast to the provender of Bech's bachelor days, when the stack of delicatessen salami occupying in lonely splendor the second shelf of his refrigerator went down at the inexorable rate of three slices a day, like a book being slowly read through. Dinner in those days he usually ate out; or else, in the emergency of a blizzard or an irresistible TV special, he heated up a frozen Chinese meal, a nugget of ice remaining at the heart of the egg roll. Here, wed, he confronted great formal meals planned by Bea as if to fatten him up for the kill, or else fought for scraps with barbaric adolescents.

Ann's and Judy's boyfriends struck him as a clamorous and odorous swarm of dermatological disasters, a pack of howling

wolves clad in the latest style of ragbag prep, their clothes
stretching and ripping under the pressure of their growing
bodies, their modes of courtship uniformly impossible to ignore,
from the demonstrations of football prowess arranged on the
September lawn to the post-midnight spinouts of their parents'
Mercedeses on the gravel drive after some vernal dance. The
twin girls themselves – Ann a touch more pensive and severe
than Judy, Judy the merest shade more womanly than Ann, as if
the fifteen minutes by which she had preceded her into the world
insured an everlasting edge of maturity – were much at school.
Bech was irritably conscious of their presence most during those
evenings when, bored by homework, they would collapse
together into whispering and giggles, making in the house an
everywhere audible, bottomless vortex of female hilarity that fed
endlessly upon itself and found fresh cause wherever it glanced.
Bech could only imagine that he was somehow the joke, and
feared that the entire house and his life with it would be sucked
down into their insatiable mirth, so sinisterly amplified by twin-
nishness. Whereas little Donald, his companion in the error of
being male, stirred in him only tender feelings. In the child's
clumsy warrior energy he saw himself at heart; standing above
the sleeping boy's bed at night, he took the measure of his own
grotesque age and, by the light of this dream-flushed, perfect
cheek, his own majestic corruption. Donald returned on the
pumpkin-colored school bus around four, and sometimes
he and Bech would play catch with a baseball or football, the
forgotten motions returning strangely to Bech's shoulders, the
rub and whack of leather to his hands. Or, before the fall chill
caused the backyard pools to be drained and the tarpaulins tugged
into place, the two of them and Bea might go swimming at a
neighbor's place to which Bea's old friendship gave them access,
and where the hostess would emerge to keep them company and
offer them a drink. These old friends of Bea's, named Wryson or
Weed or Hake or Crutchman – sharp English names that might
have come off the roster of a Puritan caravel – had their charms
and no doubt their passions and disappointments and histories,
but seemed so exotic to Bech, so brittle and pale and complacently situated amid their pools and dogwoods and old Dutch

masonry, that he felt like a spy among them and, when not a silent spy, a too-vigorous, curly-haired showoff. Exquisite and languid as a literary practitioner, he was made to feel among Bea's people vulgar and muscular, a Marx brother about to pull up a skirt or grind out a cigar in a finger bowl. An evening amid such expectations wearied him. "I don't know," he sighed to Bea. "They're just not my crowd."

"You don't give them a chance," she said, driving him home along the winding lanes. "You think just because they don't live in apartment houses and have metal bookcases crammed to the ceilings and grandparents that came from a *shtetl* they're not people. But Louise Bentley, that you met tonight, had something really terrible happen to her years ago, and Johnny Hake, though I know he can get carried away, really *did* pull himself back from the abyss."

"I don't doubt," Bech said. "But it isn't my abyss." Money, for example, as these Wasps possessed it, seemed something rigid and invisible, like glass. Though it could be broken and distributed, acquired and passed on, it quite lacked organic festiveness. Whereas money under Jewish hands was yeasty; it grew and spread and frolicked on the counting table. And their bizarre, Christmassy religion: many of Bea's crowd went to church, much as they faithfully played tennis and golf and attended rallies to keep out developers. Yet their God, for all of His colorful history and spangled attributes, lay above Earth like a whisper of icy cirrus, a tenuous and diffident Other Whose tendrils failed to entwine with fibrous blood and muscle; whereas the irrepressible Jewish God, the riddle of joking rabbis, playing His practical jokes upon Job and Abraham and leading His chosen into millennia of mire without so much as the promise of an afterlife, this hairy-nostrilled God beside Whom even the many-armed deities of the Hindus appeared sleek and plausible, nevertheless entered into the daily grind and kibitzed at all transactions. Being among the goyim frightened Bech, in truth; their collective chill was the chill of devils.

He felt easier in downtown Ossining, with its basking blacks and its rotting commercial streets tipped down sharply toward the Hudson and its chunky Gothic brick-and-cornice architecture whispering to Bech's fancy of robber barons and fairy tales and Washington Irving. Washington Heights, he supposed, once looked much as Ossining did now. He had not expected such a strong dark-skinned presence on the streets so far up the Hudson, or the slightly sleepy Southern quality of it all – the vacant storefronts, the idle wharfs, the clapboarded shacks and rusting railroad spurs and Civil War memorials. Throughout the northeastern United States, he realized, there were towns like this, perfected long ago, topped with a band pavilion and a squat civic library, only to slide into sunstruck somnolence, like flecks of pyrite weeping rust stain from the face of a granite escarpment. Ossining, he learned, was a euphemism; in 1901, the village fathers had changed the name from Sing Sing, which had been pre-empted by the notorious prison and long ago had been stolen from the Indians, in whose Mohican language "Sin Sinck" meant "stone upon stone." Stone upon stone the vast correctional facility had arisen; electrocutions here used to dim the lights for miles around, according to the tabloids Bech read as a boy. The coarsely screened newspaper photos of the famed "hot seat" at Sing Sing, and the movie scene wherein Cagney is dragged, moaning and rubbery-legged, down a long corridor to his annihilation, had told the young Bech all he ever wanted to know about death. He wondered if denizens of the underworld still snarled at one another, "You'll fry for this," and supposed not. The lights of Ossining no longer flickered in sympathy with snuffed-out murderers. The folks downtown looked merry to Bech, and the whole burg like a play set; he had the true New Yorker's secret belief that people living anywhere else had to be, in some sense, kidding. On that sloping stage between Peekskill and Tarrytown he enjoyed being enrolled in the minor-city minstrelsy; he often volunteered to run Bea's errands for household oddments, killing time in the long dark unair-conditioned drugstore, coveting the shine on the paperbacks by Uris and Styron and marveling at the copious cosmetic aids of vain, anxious America. His light-headedness on these away-from-home afternoons strengthened him to burrow on, through that anfractuous fantasy he was tracing among the lost towers of New York.

He remembered the great city in the rain, those suddenly thrashing downpours flash-flooding the asphalt arroyos and over-whelming the grated sewer mains, causing citizens to huddle – millionaires and their mistresses companionable with bag ladies and messenger boys – under restaurant canopies and in the recessed marble portals of international banks, those smooth fortresses of hidden empery. In such a rain, Tad Greenbaum and Thelma Stern are caught without their limousine. For some time, remember, Thelma has been resolved to leave Tad but dreads and postpones the moment of announcement. The taxis splash past, their little cap lights doused, their back seats holding the shadowy heads of those mysterious personages who find cabs in the worst of weathers: when the nuclear bombs begin to fall, those same shadows will be fleeing the city in perfect repose, meters ticking. Thelma's dainty Delman's – high gold heels each held to her feet by a single gilded ankle strap – become so soaked as she wades through the gutter's black rivulet that she takes them off, and then scampers across the shining tar in her bare feet. No, cross that out, her feet are not bare, she would be wearing pantyhose; with a madcap impulse she halts, beneath the swimming DONT WALK sign, and reaches up into her Shantung skirt and peels herself free, disentangling first the left leg, then the right. Now her feet are truly bare. Tomboyishly she, who as the lithe Lessup girl had run wild in the hills of Kentucky, wads the drenched nylon and chucks it overhand into one of those UFO-like trash barrels the filth-beleaguered metropolis provides. Tad, catching up to her, his size thirteen iguana-skin penny loafers still soggily in place, laughs aloud at her reckless gesture. Her gold shoes follow into the bin; his immense freckled bari-tone rings out into the tumult of water and taxi tires and squeal-ing hookers caught loitering in their scarlet stretch pants a few doors up Third Avenue with no more for shelter than a MASSAGE PARLOR sign. "I – want – out," she suddenly shouts up at him. Her raven hair is pasted about her fine skeletal face like the snake-ringlets of Medusa.

"Out – of – what?" Tad thunders back.

Still the pedestrian sign says DONT WALK, though the traffic light on the avenue has turned red. The ghostly pallor of her face, upturned toward his in the streaming rain, takes on an abrupt greenish tinge. "Out – of – *you*," she manages to shout at last, the leap of her life, her heart falling sickeningly within her at the utterance; Tad's face looms above her like a blimp, bloated and unawares, his chestnut mop flattened on his wide freckled brow and releasing down one temple a thin tan trickle of the color-freshener his hair stylist favors. He is just a boy growing old, she thinks to herself, with a boy's warrior brutality, and a boy's essential ignorance. Without such ignorance, how could men act? How could they create empires, or for that matter cross the street?

Their sign has changed from red to white, a blur spelling perilously WALK. Tad and Thelma run across Third Avenue to take refuge in the shallow arcade of a furrier. The street surface is a rippling film; wrappers are bunched at the clogged corner grate like bridesmaids' handkerchiefs. Feeling tar on the soles of her feet and being pelted by rain all the length of her naked calves has released in Thelma an elemental self which scorns Tad and his charge cards and his tax breaks. He, on the other hand, his Savile Row suit collapsed against his flesh and an absurd succession of droplets falling from the tip of his nose, looks dismal and crazed. "You bitch," he says to her in the altered acoustics of this dry spot. "You're not going to pull this put-up-or-shut-up crap on me again; you know it's just a matter of time."

Meaning, she supposes, until he leaves Ginger – Ginger Greenbaum, that stubborn little pug of a wife, always wearing caftans and muu-muus to hide her thirty pounds of overweight. Thelma marvels at herself, that she could ever sleep with a man who sleeps with that spoiled and pouting parody of a woman, whose money (made by her father in meatpacking) had fed Tad's infant octopus. It seems comic. She laughs, and prods with a disrespectful forefinger the man's drenched shirtfront of ribbed Egyptian cotton. His stomach is spongy; there comes by contrast into her mind the taut body of her slender Olive, their gentle mutual explorations in that exiguous, triangular West Side apartment where the light from New Jersey enters as horizontally as bars of music and thus provides accompaniment for the breathing silence of the two intertwined women.

Tad slugs her. Or, rather, cuffs her shoulder, since she saw it coming and flinched; the blow bumps her into a wire burglar-guard behind which a clay-faced mannequin preens in an ankle-length burnoose lined with chinchilla. The rain has lessened, the golden taxis going by are all empty. "You were thinking of that other bitch," Tad has shrewdly surmised.

"I was not," Thelma fervently lies, determined now to protect at all costs that slender other, that stranger to their city; she has remembered how the subtle crests of Olive's ilia cast horizontal shadows across her flat, faintly undulant abdomen. "Let's go back to your place and get dry," she suggests.

And Henry Bech in his mind's eye saw the drying streets, raggedly dark as if after a storm of torn carbon paper, and each grate exuding a vapor indistinguishable from leaks of municipal steam. And the birds, with that unnoticed bliss of New York birds, have begun to sing, to sing from every pocket park and potted curbside shrub, while sunlight wanly resumes and Thelma – all but her sloe eyes and painted fingernails hidden within the rustling, iridescent cumulus of a bubble bath in Tad's great sunken dove-colored tub – begins to cry. It is a good feeling, like champagne in the sinuses. His own sinuses prickling, Bech lifted his eyes and read the words *Apply this side toward living space* on the aluminum-foil backing of his room's insulation. He turned his attention out the window toward the lawn, where little Donald and a grubby friend were gouging holes in the mowed grass to make a miniature golf course. Bech thought of yelling at them from his height but decided it wasn't his lawn, his world; his world was here, with Tad and Thelma. She emerges from the bathroom drying herself with a russet towel the size of a Ping-Pong-table top. "You big pig," she tells Tad with that self-contempt of women which is their dearest and darkest trait, "I love your shit." He in his silk bathrobe is setting out on his low glass Mies table – no, it is a round coffee table with a leather center and a stout rim of oak, and carved oaken legs with griffin feet – champagne glasses and, in a little silver eighteenth-century salt dish bought at auction at Sotheby's, the white, white cocaine. Taxi horns twinkle far below. Thelma sits – whether in bald mockery of the imminent fuck or to revisit that sensation of

barefoot mountain-girl uncontrollability she experienced on
the rainswept street – naked on an ottoman luxuriously covered
in zebra hide. Each hair is a tiny needle. Bech shifted from
buttock to buttock in his squeaking chair, empathizing.

By such reckless daily fits, as seven seasons slowly wheeled by
in the woods and gardens of Ossining, the manuscript accumulated: four emptied boxes of bond paper were needed to contain
it, and still the world it set forth seemed imperfectly explored,
a cave illumined by feeble flashlight, with ever more incidents
and vistas waiting behind this or that stalagmite, or just on the
shadowy far shore of the unstirring alkaline pool. At night sometimes he would read Bea a few pages of it, and she would nod
beside him in bed, exhaling the last drag of her cigarette (she had
taken up smoking, after years on the nicotine wagon, in what
mood of renewed desperation or fresh anger he could not
fathom), and utter crisply, "It's good, Henry."

"That's all you can say?"

"It's loose. You're really rolling. You've gotten those people
just where you want them."

"Something about the way you say that –"

"What am I supposed to do, whoop for joy?" She doused her
butt with a vehement hiss in the paper bathroom cup half-full
of water she kept by her bedside in lieu of an ashtray, a trick
learned at Vassar. "All those old sugarplums you fucked in New
York, do you really think I enjoy reading about how great they
were?"

"Honey, it's *fan*tasy. I never knew anybody like these people.
These people have money. The people I knew all subscribed to
Commentary, before it went fascist."

"Do you realize there isn't a Gentile character in here who
isn't slavishly in love with some Jew?"

"Well, that's –"

"Well, that's life, you're going to say."

"Well, that's the kind of book it is. *Travel Light* was *all* about
Gentiles."

"Seen as hooligans. As barbaric people. How can you think

that, living two years now with Ann and Judy and Donald? He just adores you, you know that, don't you?"

"He can beat me at Battleship, that's what he likes. Hey, are you crying?"

She had turned her head away. She rattled at her night table, lighting another cigarette with her back still turned. The very space of the room had changed, as if their marriage had passed through a black hole and come out as anti-matter. Bea prolonged the operation, knowing she had roused guilt in him, and when she at last turned back gave him a profile as cool as the head on a coin. She had a toughness, Bea, that the toughness of her sister, Norma, had long eclipsed but that connubial privacy revealed. "I've another idea for your title," she said, biting off the words softly and precisely. "Call it *Jews and Those Awful Others*. Or how about *Jews versus Jerks?*"

Bech declined to make the expected protest. What he minded most about her in these moods was his sense of being pro-grammed, of being fitted tightly into a pattern of reaction; she wanted, his loving suburban softy, to *nail him down*.

Frustrated by his silence, she conceded him her full face, her eyes rubbed pink in the effort of suppressing tears and her mouth a blurred cloud of flesh-color sexier than any lipstick. She put an arm about him. He reciprocated, careful of the cigarette close to his ear. "I just thought," she confessed, her voice coming in little heated spurts of breath, "your living here so long now with me, with *us*, something nice would get into your book. But those people are so vicious, Henry. There's no love that makes them tick, just ego and greed. Is that how you see us? I mean us, people?"

"No, no," he said, patting, thinking that indeed he did, indeed he did.

"I recognize these gestures and bits of furniture you've taken from your life here, but it doesn't seem at all like me. This idiotic Ginger character, I hate her, yet sometimes whole sentences I know I've said come out of her mouth."

He stroked the roundness of the shoulder that her askew nightie strap bared, while her solvent tears, running freely, released to his nostrils the scent of discomposed skin moisturizer.

"The only thing you and Ginger Greenbaum have in common," he assured her, "is you're both married to beasts."

"You're not a beast, you're a dear kind man —"

"Away from my desk," he interjected.

"— but I get the feeling when you read your book to me it's a way of paying me *back*. For loving you. For marrying you."

"Who was it," he asked her, "who told me to do a few pages a day and not worry about *le mot juste* and the capacity for taking infinite pains and all that crap? Who?"

"Please don't be so angry," Bea begged. The hand of the arm not around his shoulders and holding a cigarette, the hand of the arm squeezed between and under their facing tangent bodies, found his dormant prick and fumblingly enclosed it. "I love your book," she said. "Those people are so silly and wild. Not like us at all. Poor little Olive. She had to end it herself."

His voice softened as his prick hardened. "You talk as though this was the first time I've ever written about Jews. That's not so. *Brother Pig* had that union organizer in it, and there were even rabbis in *The Chosen*. I just didn't want to do what all the others were doing, and what Singer had done in Yiddish anyway."

She snuffled, quite his Christian maiden now, and burrowed her pink nose deeper into the grizzly froth of his chest while her touch lower down took on a quicksilver purity and slidingness. "I have a terrible confession to make," she said. "I never got through *The Chosen*. It was assigned years ago in a reading group I belonged to up here, and I tried to read it, and kept getting interrupted, and then the group discussed it and it was as if I *had* read it."

Any guilt Bech might have been feeling toward her eased. Claire had read *The Chosen*; it had been dedicated to her. Norma had read it twice, taking notes. He rolled across Bea's body and switched off the light. "Nobody who did read it liked it," he said in the dark, and kneeled above her, near her face.

"Wait," she said, and dunked her cigarette with a sizzle. Something like a wet smoke ring encircled him; tightened, loosened. What beasts we all are. What pigs, Thelma would say. *I love your shit.*

Bea found him a typist — Mae, a thirty-year-old black woman

with an IBM Selectric in a little ranch house the color of faded raspberries on Shady Lane; there was a green parakeet in a cage and a small brown child hiding behind every piece of furniture. Bech was afraid Mae wouldn't be able to spell, but as it turned out she was all precision and copyediting punctilio; she was in rebellion against her racial stereotype, like a Chinese rowdy or an Arab who hates to haggle. It was frightening, seeing his sloppily battered-out, confusingly revised manuscript go off and come back the next weekend as stacks of crisp prim typescript, with a carbon on onionskin and a separate pink sheet of queried corrigenda. He was being edged closer to the dread plunge of publication, as when, younger, he would mount in a line of shivering wet children to the top of the great water slide at Coney Island – a shaky little platform a mile above turquoise depths that still churned after swallowing their last victim – and the child behind him would nudge the backs of his legs, when all Bech wanted was to stand there a while and think about it.

"Maybe," he said to Bea, "since Mae is such a whiz, and must need the money – you never see a husband around the place, just that parakeet – I should go over it once more and have her retype."

"Don't you dare," Bea said.

"But you've said yourself, you loathe the book. Maybe I can soften it. Take out that place where the video crew masturbates all over Olive's drugged body, put in a scene where they all come up to Ossining and admire the fall foliage." Autumn had invaded their little woods with its usual glorious depredations. Bech had begun to work in his insulated room two springs ago. Spring, summer, fall, winter, spring, summer, fall: those were the seven seasons he had labored, while little Donald turned twelve and Ann, so Judy had tattled, lost her virginity.

"I loathe it, but it's you," Bea said. "Show it to your publisher."

This was most frightening. Fifteen years had passed since he had submitted a manuscript to The Vellum Press. In this interval the company had been sold to a supermarket chain who had peddled it to an oil company who had in turn, not liking the patrician red of Vellum's bottom line, managed to foist the firm

off on a West Coast lumber-and-shale-based conglomerate
underwritten, it was rumored, by a sinister liaison of Japanese
and Saudi money. It was like being a fallen woman in the old
days: once you sold yourself, you were never your own again.
But at each change of ownership, Bech's books, *outré* enough to
reassure the public that artistic concerns had not been wholly
abandoned, were reissued in a new paperback format. His longtime editor at Vellum, dapper, sensitive Ned Clavell, had succumbed to well-earned cirrhosis of the liver and gone to that
three-martini luncheon in the sky. Big Billy Vanderhaven, who
had founded the firm as a rich man's plaything in the days of the
trifling tax bite and who had concocted its name loosely out of
his own, had long since retired to Hawaii, where he lived with
his fifth wife on a diet of seaweed and macadamia nuts. A great
fadster, who had raced at Le Mans and mountain-climbed in
Nepal and scuba-dived off Acapulco, "Big" Billy – so called sixty
years ago to distinguish him from his effete and once socially
prominent cousin, "Little" Billy Vanderhaven – had apparently
cracked the secret of eternal life, which is Do Whatever You
Damn Well Please. Yet, had the octogenarian returned under
the sponsorship of that Japanese and Saudi money to take the
helm of Vellum again, the effect could have been scarcely
less sensational than Henry Bech turning up with a new manuscript. Bech no longer knew the name of anyone at the
firm except the woman who handled permissions and sent
him his little checks and courtesy copies of relevant anthologies,
with their waxen covers and atrocious typos. When at last,
gulping and sitting down and shutting his eyes and preparing to slide, he dialed Vellum's number, it was the editor-
in-chief he asked for. He was connected to the snotty voice of
a boy.

"You're the editor-in-chief?" he asked incredulously.

"No I am not," the voice said, through its nose. "This is her
secretary."

"Oh. Well could I talk to her?"

"May I ask who is calling, please?"

Bech told him.

"Could you spell that, please?"

"Like the beer but with an 'h' on the end, 'h' as in 'Heineken.' "

"Truly? Well aren't we boozy this morning!"

There was a cascade of electronic peeping, a cup-shaped silence, and then a deep female voice saying, "Mr. Schlitzeh?"

"No, no. Bech. B-E-C-H. Henry. I'm one of your authors."

"You sure are. Absolutely. It's an honor and a pleasure to hear your voice. I first read you in Irvington High School; they assigned *Travel Light* to the accelerated track. It knocked me for a loop. And it's stayed with me. Not to mention those others. What can I do for you, sir? I'm Doreen Pease, by the way. Sorry we've never met."

From all this Bech gathered that he was something of a musty legend in the halls of Vellum, and that nevertheless here was a busy woman with her own gravity and attested velocity and displacement value. He should come to the point. "I'm sorry, too," he began.

"I *wish* we could get you in here for lunch some time. I'd love to get your slant on the new format we've given your reprints. We're just crazy about what this new designer has done, she's *just* out of the Rhode Island School of Design, but those stick figures against those electric colors, with the sateen finish, and the counterstamped embossing –"

"Stunning," Bech agreed.

"You know, it gives a *uni*ty; for me it gives the shopper a handle on what *you* are all about, you as opposed to each individual title. The salesmen report that the chains have been really enthusiastic: some of them have given us a week in the window. And that ain't just hay, for quality softcover."

"Well, actually, Mrs. – Miss? – Miz? –"

"Doreen will do fine."

"It's about a book I'm calling."

"Yess?" That was it, a single spurt of steam, impatient. The pleasantries were over, the time clock was running.

"I've written a new one and wondered whom I should send it to."

The silence this time was not cup-shaped, but more like that of a liqueur glass, narrow and transparent, with a brittle stem.

She said, "When you say you've written it, what do you mean

exactly? This isn't an outline, or a list of chapters, you want us to bid on?"

"No, it's finished. I mean, there may be some revisions on the galleys –"

"The first-pass proofs, yess."

"Whatever. And as to the bid, in the old days, when Big – when Mr. Vanderhaven was around, you'd just take it, and print it, and pay me a royalty we thought was fair."

"Those *were* the old days," Doreen Pease said, permitting herself a guffaw, and what sounded like a puff on her cigar. "Let's get our pigeons all in line, Mr. Bech. You've finished a manuscript. Is this the *Think Big* you mention in interviews from time to time?"

"Well, the title's been changed, tentatively. My wife, I'm married now –"

"I read that in *People*. About six months ago, wasn't it?"

"Two and a half years, actually. My wife had this theory about how to write a book. You just sit down –"

"And do it. Well of course. Smart girl. And you're calling me to ask who to send it to? Where's your agent in all this?"

He blushed – a wasted signal over the phone. "He gave up on me years ago. That was fine. I hate people reading over my shoulder."

"Henry, I'm cutting my own throat saying this, but if I were you I'd get me one. Starting now. A book by Henry Bech is a major development. But if you want to play it your way, send it straight here to me. Doreen Pease. Like the vegetable with an 'e' on the end."

"Or I could bring it down on the train. I seem to live up here in Westchester."

"Tell me where and we'll send a messenger in a limo to pick it up."

He told her where and asked, "Isn't a limo expensive?"

"We find it cuts way down on postage and saves us a fortune in the time sector. Anyway, let's face it, Henry: you're top of the line. What'd you say the title was?"

"*Easy Money.*"

"Oh yesss."

The hiss sounded prolonged. He wondered if he was tiring

her. "Uh, one more thing, Miss Pease, Doreen. If it turns out you like it and want to print it –"

"Oh, Christ, I'm sure we'll want to, it can't be that terrible. You're very sweetly modest, Henry, but you have a name, and names don't grow on trees these days; television keeps coming up with so many new celebrities the public has lost track. The public is a conservative animal: that's the conclusion I've come to after twenty years in this business. They like the tried and true. You'd know that better than I would." She guffawed; she had decided that he was somehow joshing her, and that all her worldly wisdom was his also.

"What I wanted to ask," Bech said, "was would I be assigned an editor? My old one, Ned Clavell, died a few years ago."

"He was a bit before my era here, but I've heard a ton about him. He must have been a wonderful man."

"He had his points. He cared a lot about not splitting infinitives or putting too much vermouth into a martini."

"Yess. I think I know what you're saying. I'm reading you, Henry."

She was? He seemed to hear her humming; but perhaps it was another conversation fraying into this line.

"I think in that case," Doreen decided, "we better give you over to our Mr. Flaggerty. He's young, but very brilliant. *Very*. And sensitive. He knows when to *stop*, is I think the quality you'll most appreciate. Jim's a delicious person, I *know* you'll be *very* happy with him."

"I don't have to be *that* happy," Bech said, but in a burble of electronic exclamations their connection was broken off. Neither party felt it necessary to re-place the call.

The limo arrived at five. A young man with acne and a neo-Elvis wet look crawled out of the back and gave both Ann and Judy, who crowded into the front hall, a lecherous goggle eye. Bech began to fear that he was guarding treasure, in the form of these blossoming twins. Rodney, their biological father, after a period of angry mourning for his marriage, had descended into the mid-Manhattan dating game and exerted an ever feebler paternal presence. He showed up Sundays and took Donald to the Bronx Zoo or a disaster movie, and that was about it. The only

masculine voices the children heard in the house belonged to
Bech and the old man who came in a plastic helmet to read the
water meter. But now that Bech's book was submitted and, as of
November, "in the works," the homely mock-Tudor house
tucked against the woods no longer felt like a hermitage. Calls
from Vellum's publicity and production departments shrilled at
the telephone, and a dangerous change in the atmosphere, like
some flavorless pernicious gas, trickled through the foundation
chinks into the heated waste spaces of their home: Bech, again a
working author, was no longer quite the man Bea had married,
or the one his stepchildren had become accustomed to.

Vellum Press (the "The" had been dropped during a stream-
lining operation under one of its former corporate owners) had
its offices on the top six floors of a new Lexington Avenue
skyscraper the lacteal white of ersatz-ivory piano keys; the architect, a Rumanian defector famous in the gossip press for squiring
the *grandes dames* of the less titled jet set, had used every square
inch of the building lot but given the skyline a fillip at the top,
with a round pillbox whose sweeping windows made the publisher's offices feel like an airport control tower. When Bech had
first published with Vellum in 1955, a single brownstone on East
67th Street had housed the operation. In those days Big Billy
himself, ruddy from outdoor sport, sat enthroned in a leather
wing chair in what had been two fourth-floor maid's rooms, the
partition broken through. He would toy with a Himalayan
paper-knife and talk about his travels, his mountain-climbing
and marlin-fishing, and about his losing battle with the greed
and grossly decayed professional standards of printers. Bech
enjoyed these lectures from on high, and felt exhilarated when
they were over and he was released to the undogmatic, ever fresh
street reality of the ginkgos, of the polished nameplates on the
other brownstones, of the lean-legged women in mink jackets
walking their ornamentally trimmed poodles. Ned Clavell's
office had been a made-over scullery in the basement; from its
one narrow window Bech could see these same dogs lift a fluffy
hind leg, exposing a mauve patch of raw poodle, and daintily
urinate on the iron fencing a few yards away. Ned had been a
great fusser, to whom every page of prose gave a certain pain,

which he politely tried to conceal, or to voice with maximum politeness, his hands showing a tremor as they shuffled sheets of manuscript, his handsome face pale with the strain of a hangover or of language's inexhaustible imperfection. His voice had had that hurried briskness of Thirties actors, of Ronald Colman and George Brent, and meticulously he had rotated his gray, brown, and blue suits, saving a double-breasted charcoal pinstripe for evening wear. A tiny gold rod had pressed the knot of his necktie out and the points of his shirt collar down; he wore rings on both hands, and had never married. Bech wondered now if he had been homosexual; somehow not marrying in those years could seem a simple inadvertence, the oversight of a dedicated man. "Piss off, you bitch!" he used to blurt out, from beneath his pencil-line mustache, when one of the poodles did its duty; and it took years for Bech to realize that Ned did not mean the dog but the woman with taut nylon ankles who was overseeing the little sparkling event. Yet Ned had been especially pained by Bech's fondness for the earthier American idioms, and they spent more than one morning awkwardly bartering tits, as it were, for tats, the editor's sharpened pencil silently pointing after a while at words he took no relish in pronouncing. Dear dead Ned: Bech sensed at the time he had his secret sorrows, his unpublished effusions and his unvented appetites, but the young author was set upon his own ambitions and used the other man as coolly as he used the mailman. Now the man was gone, taking his decent, double-breasted era with him.

Through the great bowed pane of Mr. Flaggerty's office the vista of the East River and of Queen's waterfront industrial sheds was being slowly squeezed away by rising new construction. Flaggerty also was tall, six three at least, and the hand he extended was all red-knuckled bones. He wore blue jeans and an open-necked shirt of the checkered sort that Bech associated with steelworkers out on their bowling night. He wondered, *How does this man take his authors to restaurants?* "It's super Doreen is letting me handle you," Flaggerty said.

"I've been told I'm hard to handle."

"Not the way I hear it. The old-timers I talk to say you're a pussycat."

This young man had an uncanny dreamy smile and seemed content to sit forever at his glass desk smiling, tipped back into his chair so that his knees were thrust up to the height of his heaped In and Out baskets. His lengthy pale face was assembled all of knobs, melted together; his high brow especially had a bumpy shine. His desk top looked empty and there was no telling what he was thinking as he gazed so cherishingly at Bech.

Bech asked him, "Have you read the book?"

"Every fucking word," Flaggerty said, as if this was unusual practice.

"And – ?"

"It knocked me out. A real page-turner. Funny *and* gory."

"You have any suggestions?"

Flaggerty's wispy eyebrows pushed high into his forehead, multiplying the bumps. "No. Why would I?"

"The language didn't strike you as – a bit rough in spots?" One of Ned Clavell's favorite phrases.

This idea seemed doubly startling. "No, of course not. For me, it all worked. It went with the action."

"The scene with Olive and the video crew – "

"Gorgeous. Raunchy as hell, of course, but with, you know, a lot of crazy tenderness underneath. That's the kind of thing you do so well, Mr. Bech. Mind if I call you Henry?"

"Not at all. Sock it to me, Jim." Bech still had not got what he wanted – an unambiguous indication that his manuscript had been pondered. He had the strange sensation, talking to Flaggerty, that his editor had not so much read the book as inhaled it: that Bech's book had been melted down and evaporated in these slice-of-pie-shaped offices and sent into the ozone to join the former contents of aerosol cans. Here, in Vellum's curved and pastel halls, languidly drifting young women in Vampira makeup outnumbered any signs of literary industry; the bulletin boards were monopolized by tampon and lingerie ads torn out of magazines, with all their chauvinistic implications underlined and annotated in indignant slashing felt-tip. Flaggerty's walls were white and mostly blank, but for a grainy blowup of Thomas Wolfe about to board a trolley car. Otherwise they might be sitting in a computer lab. Bech asked him, "How do you like the title?"

"*Easy Money?*" So he had got that far. "Not bad. Might confuse people a little, with all these how-to-get-rich-in-the-coming-crash books on the market."

"The original title was *Think Big*, but I found it hard to work under. It weighed on me. I couldn't get going really until my wife told me to scrap the title."

"*Think Big*, huh?" Flaggerty's eyes, deep in their sockets of bone, widened. "I like it." They were beryl: an acute pale cat color. "Don't you?"

"I do," Bech admitted.

"It comes at you a little harder somehow. More *zap*. More subliminal leverage."

Bech nodded. This tall fellow for all his languor and rural costume talked Bech's language. They were in business.

BECH IS BACK! was to be the key of the advertising campaign. Newspaper ads, thirty-second radio spots, cardboard cutouts in the bookstores, posters showing Bech as of over a decade ago and Bech now. *Fifteen Years in the Making* was a subsidiary slogan. But first, nine months of gestation had to be endured, while proofs languished in the detention cells of book production and jacket designs wormed toward a minimum of bad taste. Back in Ossining, Bea was frantic over the loss of Ann's virginity. Judy had squealed on her younger sister. If only it had been Judy, Bea explained, she wouldn't be so shocked; but Ann had always been the good one, the A student, the heir to Rodney's seriousness.

"Maybe that's why," Bech offered. "It takes some seriousness to lose your virginity. Always flirting and hanging out with the cheerleaders like Judy, you get too savvy and the guys never lay a glove on you."

"Oh, what do you know? You've never had daughters."

"I had a sister," he said, hurt. "I had a twenty-one-year-old mistress once."

"I bet you did," Bea said. "Typical. You're just the kind of thing Rodney and I hoped would never happen to our girls."

The twins were seventeen. They would be eighteen on Valentine's Day. The deflowerer, if Judy could be believed, was one of the preppy crowd crunching around in the driveway with their fathers' cars. "I don't see that it's any big deal," Bech said. "I mean, it's a peer, it's puppy love, it's not rape or Charles Manson or anybody. Didn't I just read in a survey somewhere that the average American girl has had intercourse by around sixteen and a half?"

"That's with everybody figured in," Bea snapped. "The ghettos and Appalachia and all that. If I'd wanted my girls to be ghetto statistics I would have moved to a ghetto."

"Listen," Bech said, hurt again. "Some of my best ancestors grew up in a ghetto."

"Don't you *understand*?" Bea asked, her face white, her lips thinned. "It's a de*file*ment. A woman can never get it *back*."

"What would she do with it if she could get it back? Come on, sweetie. You're making too fucking much of this."

"Easy for you to say. Easy for you to say anything, evidently. Do you think this would have happened if that book of yours hadn't been in the house, all that crazy penthouse sex you cooked up out of your own sordid little flings?"

"I didn't know Ann had read it."

"She didn't have to. She heard us talking about it. It was in the air."

"Oh, please. It doesn't take a book of mine to put sex in the air."

"No of course not. Don't blame books for anything. They just sit there behind their authors' grins. You act as though the world is one thing and art is another and God forbid they should ever meet. Well, my daughter's virginity has been sacrificed, as I see it, to that damn dirty book of yours."

Bech had never seen Bea like this before, raging. What frightened him most were her eyes, unseeing, and the mouth that went on, a machine of medium-soft flesh that could not be shut off. This face that had nested in every fork of his body floated like some careening gull in the wind of her fury, staring red-rimmed at him as if to swoop at the exposed meat of his own face. "Jesus," he offered with mild exasperation. "The kid is seventeen. Let her experiment if that's what she wants."

"It's *not* what she wants, how could she want one of those awful boys? She *doesn't* want it, that's the point; what she wants is to show *me*. Her mother. For leaving her father and screwing you."

"I thought it was Rodney who left."

"Oh, don't be so literal, you know how these things are. It takes two. But then my taking up with you, so quickly really, in that house on the Vineyard that time, and the way we've been here, so h-happy with each other" – her face was going from white to pink, and drifting closer to his – "I never thought of how it must look to them. The children. Especially the girls. Don't you see, I've made them confront what they shouldn't have had to so early, their own mother's" – now her face was on his shoulder, her breath hot on his neck – "s-sexuality! And of *course* they're appalled, of *course* they want to do self-destructive things out of spite!" He was in her grip, no less tight for her being grief-stricken. As her storm of remorse worked its way through Bea's fragile, Christian nervous system, tough, Semitic Bech, dreamer and doer both, author of the upcoming long-awaited *Think Big*, pondered open-eyed the knobbed and varnished and lightly charred mantel of their fieldstone fireplace. Above it there was an oil painting, with a china-blue, single-clouded sky, of a clipper ship that Bea's maternal great-grandfather had once captained, depicted under full sail and cleaving a bottle-green sea as neatly crimped by waves as an old lady's perm. Upon the mantel stood two phallic clay candlesticks, one by Ann and one by Judy, executed by the twins in some vanished summer's art camp at Briarcliff and now by consecrated usage set on either end of the mantelpiece; beside it leaned a fishing rod with broken reel that Donald had chosen to abandon in the corner where the fieldstones met the floral-wallpapered wall. Bourgeois life: its hooks came in all sizes.

He patted Bea's back and said, "And for all this you blame me?"

"Not you, *us*."

Like Adam and Eve. The first great romantic image, the Expulsion. The aboriginal trinity of producer, advertiser, and consumer. This woman's fair head was full of warping myths. Her sobbing had become its own delicious end, a debauchery of sorts, committed not with him but with Rodney's ghost, to the accompaniment of spiritual stride piano played by that honorary member of many a Jew–excluding organization, Judge R. Austin Latchett.

Tad slugs her. Bech looked around for cold water, and threw some. "What about birth control?" he asked.

Bea looked up out of her tear-mottled face. "What about it?"

"If the kid's humping, she better have it or you'll really have something to cry about."

Bea blinked. "Maybe it was only one time."

Bech flattened a tear at the side of her nose, tenderness returning. "I'm afraid it's not something you do only once. You get hooked. Have you ever talked to the girls about all this?"

"I suppose so," Bea said vaguely. "I know at school they took hygiene. . . . It's *hard*, Henry. For a long time they're so young it wouldn't make any sense and then suddenly they're so old you assume they must know it all and you'd feel foolish."

"Well, there're worse things than feeling foolish." It was hard for him, on his side, to believe that Bea needed his advice, his wisdom. Female mockery and its Southern cousin female adulation had played in his ears for five decades, so it was hard for him to hear this shy wifely tune, this halting request for guidance in a world little more transparent in its fundamental puzzles to female intuition than to male. "You must talk to her," Bech advised firmly.

"But how can I let her know I know anything without betraying Judy?"

The prototypical maze, Bech remembered reading somewhere, was the female insides. He tried to be patient. "You don't have to let her know. Just tell her as an item of general interest."

"Then I should be talking to them both at the same time."

She had a point there, he admitted to himself. Aloud he said, "No. In this area being a twin doesn't count anymore. You can imply to Ann you've had or will have the same conference with Judy, but for now you want to talk privately with *her*. Listen. The girl must know she's gotten in deep, she *wants* to hear from her mother. She's not going to grill you about what you know or how you know."

The more persuasively he talked, the more slack and dismayed her expression grew. "But what do I say ex*act*ly, to start it off?"

"Say, 'Ann, you're reaching an age now when many girls in our society enter into sexual relations. I can't tell you I approve, because I don't; but there are certain medical options you should be aware of.'"

"It doesn't sound like me. She'll laugh."

"Let her. She's a little girl inside a woman's body. She's suddenly been given the power to make a new human life out of her own flesh. It's more frightening than getting a driver's license. She's more frightened than you are."

"How do you know so much?"

"I'm a man of the world. People are my profession."

A new thought struck Bea. "Don't boys like that use things?"

"Well, they used to, but in this day and age I expect they're too spoiled and lazy. They don't like that snappy feeling."

"But if I begin to talk contraception with her so calmly, it amounts to permission. I'm saying it's *fine*." Panic squeezed this last word out thin as a wire.

"Well, maybe it is fine," he said. "Think of Samoa. Of Zanzibar. Western bourgeois civilization, don't forget, is a momentary episode in the history of *Homo sapiens*."

She heard the impatience of his tone, his boredom with wedded worry and wisdom. "Henry, I'm sorry. I'm being stupid. It's just I'm so scared of doing the wrong thing. For some reason I can't think."

"Well," he began in a deep voice, for the third time. "It's easy to give advice where it's not your own life and death. On the matter of my book, you were very hard-headed."

"And you resent it," she pointed out, dry-eyed at last.

After this fraught discussion of sexuality, it seemed to Bech, Bea pulled back, she who had once been so giving and playful, so honestly charmed to find this new, hairier, older, more gnarled and experienced man in her bed. Now when at night, finished reading, he turned off his light and experimentally caressed her, she stiffened at his touch, for it interrupted her inner churning. Even under him and enclosing him, she felt absent. "What are you thinking about?" he would ask.

It would be as if he had startled her awake, though the whites of her eyes gleamed sleeplessly in the Ossining moonlight. Sometimes she would confess, blaming herself for both the girl's sin and this its frigid penance, "Ann."

"Can't you give it a rest?"

"God in Heaven I wish I could."

At Vellum, lanky, laconic Flaggerty had a young female assistant, a quick black-haired girl fresh from Sarah Lawrence, and Bech wondered if it was her hands that appeared in the Xeroxes the firm sent him of his galley sheets. Whoever it was had held each sheet flat on the face of the photocopier, and in the shadowy margins clear ghosts of female fingers showed, some so vivid a police department could have analyzed the fingerprints. Bech inspected these parts of disembodied hands with interest; they seemed smaller, slightly, than real hands, but then womanly smallness, capable of Belgian embroidery and Rumanian gymnastics, is one of the ways by which the grosser sex is captivated. He looked through the photocopied fingers for the hard little ghost of a wedding or engagement ring and found none; but then she might have been employing only her right hand.

At last Bea did take Ann aside, on an evening when Judy was working late on the senior yearbook, and they had their conversation. "It was just as you predicted," Bea told Bech in their bed. "She wasn't angry that I seemed to know, she seemed relieved. She cried in my arms, but she wouldn't promise to stop doing it. She isn't sure she loves the boy, but he's awfully sweet. We agreed I'd make an appointment with Doctor Landis to get her fitted for a diaphragm."

"Well then," he said. "After all that fuss."

"I'm sorry," Bea apologized. "I know I've been distracted lately. You want to make love now?"

"In principle," Bech said. "But in practice, I'm beat. Donald made me bowl six strings with him over at Pin Paradise and my whole shoulder aches. Also I thought I'd take the train into town tomorrow."

"Oh?"

"There're some things I want to go over on the galleys with Flaggerty. It's better if we can hash it out right there, and I want to be sharp. He's deceptive – all lazy and purring and next thing he's at your throat."

"I thought you said he never had any suggestions. Unlike that other editor you had years ago."

"Well, he didn't, but now he's developing some. I think he was babying me before, since I'm a living legend."

"O.K., dear. If you say so. Love you."

"Love you," Bech echoed, preparing to fold his mind into a dark shape, a paper airplane to be launched with a flick from the crumbling cliff of consciousness.

But Bea broke into his dissolution with the thought, spoken aloud toward the ceiling, "I worry now about what Judy will say. Somehow I don't think she'll approve. She'll think I've been too soft."

His sweet suburban softy, Bech thought sibilantly, and slept.

At his suggestion next day Flaggerty introduced him to his assistant. "Arlene Schoenberg," Flaggerty said, stooping in his shirt of mattress ticking like some giant referee overseeing a jump-off between two opposing players at a midget basketball game. The girl was small, slender, and sleek, with hair in a Lady Dracula fall and sable eyes fairly dancing, in their web of sticky lashes, with delight at meeting Henry Bech.

"Mr. Bech, I've admired you for *so* long – "

"I feel like old hat," Bech finished for her.

"Oh, *no*," the girl said, aghast.

"So you tote bales for Massah Jim here," Bech said.

"Arlene has all the moves," Flaggerty said, shuffling, about to blow the whistle.

Bech had held on a half-second longer than necessary to her hand. Her dear small busy clever hand. It was much whiter than in the Xeroxes, and decidely pulsing in his.

He glided back to Ossining as the early-winter dusk was bringing to a glow the signal lights, the grudged wattage of the station platform, the vulnerable gold of the windows of homes burning in the distance, all softened by the tentative wet beginnings of a snowfall. His head and loins were light with possibility merely, for Flaggerty had taken him to lunch at a health-food restaurant where no liquor was served and, when they had returned, Arlene Schoenberg was absent on a crosstown errand. Bech drove his old Ford – only thirty-three thousand miles in eighteen years of ownership – home through the cosmic flutter. He was met by a wild wife. Bea pulled him into the downstairs bathroom so she could impart her terrible new news. "Now Judy wants one too!"

"One what?" Bea's eyes, after his brooding upon Arlene's dark, heavily lashed ones all through the lulling train ride, looked so bald and blue, Bech had to force himself to feel there was a soul behind this doll's stare.

"One *di*aphragm!" Bea answered, putting the lid hard on her desire to scream. "I asked her if she was making love to anybody and she said No and I told her they couldn't fit one in with her hymen intact and she said she broke hers horseback-riding years ago, and I just have no idea if she's lying or *not*. She was *aw*fully cocky, Henry; I know now I did the wrong thing with Ann, I *know* it." Bea uttered all this in a choked tearful rush; he had to hug her, there in the downstairs bathroom, the smallest room in the big house.

"You did the right thing," he had to say, for she had followed his advice.

"But why did Ann have to run right away and *tell* her?" Bea asked.

"Bragging," Bech offered, already bored. He felt this woman's mind narrowing in like the vortex in a draining bathtub toward an obsession with her daughters' vaginas. There must be more to life than this. He asked Bea, "What would Rodney have done in this situation?"

It was the wrong name to invoke. "This situation wouldn't have *hap*pened if Rodney were still here," Bea said, making little fists and resting them on Bech's chest in lieu of thumping him.

"Really?" he asked, wondering whether this could be so. Rodney had gone from being a pill and a heel to become *in absentia* the very principle of order – the clockwork God of the Deists, hastily banished by the Romantic rebellion. "Could he really have stopped the girls from growing up?"

Bea's face was contorted and clouded by a rich pink veil of mourning for Rodney. Beyond a certain age, women are not enhanced by tears. Bech shrugged off her absent-minded grip upon him and snapped, "Here's a simple solution. Tell Judy she has to go out and get fucked first before you'll buy her a diaphragm."

Get a diaphragm the old-fashioned way, ran through his mind. *Earn it*. He left Bea weeping in the tiny room, with its honorable, solid turn-of-the-century plumbing, and surveyed the weather from the bay windows. It was snowing hard now, thick as a ticker-tape parade. The mass of woods behind the house was toned down almost out of sight; in the near foreground the spherical aluminum bird-feeder suspended from the old grape arbor swung softly back and forth like a bell buoy in a whispering white sea. Donald was outside trying to toboggan already on the fresh-fallen inch, and the twin girls were huddled giggling on the long orange sofa in the TV den, which had been intended a hundred years ago as a library. On its shelves Bech's books still waited to be integrated with the books already there. Rodney had been a history buff, and collected books on sailing. The girls' faces looked feverish with secrets. Their giggles stopped when Bech loomed in the doorway. "Why don't you two little angels," he asked them, "stop giving your mother a hard time with your nasty little cunts?"

"Screw you, Uncle Henry," Judy managed to get out, though their four gray eyes stared in fright.

Rather than wax more ogreish, he climbed the stairs to his silver room and read proof for the hour before dinner. Mortimer Zenith, a minor character who took on an unexpected menace and dynamism in the third chapter, was outlining to poor fat, battered, snuffly, alcholic Ginger Greenbaum the potential financial wonders of a divorce. Mortimer, too, has his designs on the lovely Olive, once he gets his own game show, which he is hoping Ginger will back, once she gets her chunk of Tad's money. Ginger, muddled and despairing though she is, cannot quite imagine life without Tad, whose scorn and long absences are somewhat mitigated by the afternoon consolations of Emilio, the young Filipino horsetrainer on their newly acquired Connecticut estate. What caught Bech's eye as he wrote, and now as he rewrote on proof, was the light at the great windows of the

Greenbaum penthouse, while Mort and Ginger murmur and car horns – he crossed out "twinkle" – bleat ever more urgently ten stories below. The sky has sifted out of its harsh noon cobalt a kind of rosy brown banded behind the blackening profiles of the skyscrapers, here and there a cornice or gargoyle flaming in the dying light from the west. Rush hour, once again. Bech in his mind's eye sees a pigeon scrabblingly alight on the sill outside, causing both scheming, curried heads to turn around simultaneously. At his own window, the outdoors was an opaque gray blanket. Individual pellets of snow ticked at the icy panes, like a tiny cry for help. Downstairs, a trio of female voices was lifted in pained chorus, chanting the scandal of Bech's brief exchange with the twins. The front door slammed as Donald came in frozen, his voice loud with complaint at the toboggan's perfor- mance. Happiness was up here, as the tendrils of emendation thickened along the margins and the electric heaters glazed Bech's shins with warmth. He glanced again at his window and was surprised not to see a pigeon there, with its cocked head and Chaplin-tramp style of walking, its beady eye alert for a handout. *Tick. Tick.* Blizzards are ideal for doing proof, he thought. Socked in. Byrd at the South Pole. Raleigh in the Tower.

The storm felt sexy, but beneath the goosedown puff Bea whimpered to him, "I'm sorry, sweetie. This thing with the girls has exhausted me. Judy and Ann and I had a big cry about everything but it still all feels so up in the air." Wind softly whirred in the chimney of their bedroom fireplace, with its broken damper. Gently his hand sought to tug up the flannel of her nightie. "Oh, Henry, I just *can't*," Bea pleaded. "After all this upset I just feel *numb* down there." When her breathing slowed to a sleeper's regularity, and the house sighed in all its walls as the storm cuffed its frame with rhythmic airy blows, Bech in his meteorological rapture masturbated, picturing instead of his own thick hand that small, dark, dirty Xeroxed one.

The snow descended for forty-eight hours, and they were snowbound for another two days. The pack of pimply wolves attracted to this house by Ann and Judy's pheromones assembled now not in their fathers' cars but on cross-country skis and, in one specially well equipped case, on a Kawasaki snowmobile; the boys, puffed up by parkas to the size of that cheerful monster made out of Michelin tires, clumped in and out of the front hall, tracking snow and exhaling steam. Bea's immediate neighbors, too, tracked in and out, swapping canned goods and tales of frozen pipes and defrosted food lockers. The oral tradition in America was not quite dead, it seemed, as sagas of marooned cars, collapsed gazebos, and instant Alps beside the plowed parking lots downtown tumbled in. The worst privation in Ossining appeared to be the three days' non-delivery of *The New York Times*; withdrawal symptoms raged at breakfast tables and beset stolid bankers as they heaved at the snow in their driveways, recklessly aware of bubbles of ignorance in their bloodstreams that might reach their hearts. All day long, while feathers whipped from the spines of drifts and children dug tunnels and golden retrievers bounded up and down in the fluff like dolphins, people discussed in hushed tones the scandal of it, of being without the *Times*. Television stations flashed pictures of the front page, to reassure outlying districts that it was still being published, and the *Citizen Register* (serving Ossining, Briarcliff, Croton, Buchanan, Cortlandt) expanded its World/Nation section, but these measures only underlined the sense of dire emergency, of being cut off from all that was real. Bech retreated from the *Times*less hubbub to his silver-lined room, adding tendrils to his proofs like a toothpicked avocado pit sending down roots into a water glass. For the first time, he began to think he might really have something here. Maybe he really was back.

The gestation period of nine months dictated that *Think Big* be a summer book, and that helped it; it didn't have to slug it out with that musclebound autumnal crowd of definitive biographies or multi-generational novels with stark titles like *Lust* or *Delaware* and acknowledgment pages full of research assistants, nor with their hefty spring sisters, the female romancers and the feminist decriers of the private life. *Think Big* in its shiny aqua jacket joined the Popsicles and roller coasters, baseball games and beach picnics as one of that summer's larky things; "it melts in your mouth and leaves sand between your toes," wrote the reviewer for *The East Hampton Star.* "The squalid book we all deserve," said Alfred Kazin in *The New York Times Book Review.* "A beguilingly festive disaster," decreed John Leonard in the daily *Times.* "Not quite as *vieux chapeau* as I had every reason to fear," allowed Gore Vidal in *The New York Review of Books.* "Yet another occasion for rejoicing that one was born a woman," proclaimed Ellen Willis in *The Village Voice.* "An occasion for guarded celebration," boomed Benjamin De Mott in *Partisan Review,* "that puts us in grateful mind of Emerson's admonition, 'Books are the best of things, well used; abused, among the worst.'" "An occasion," proposed George Steiner in *The New Yorker,* "to marvel once again that not since the Periclean Greeks has there been a configuration of intellectual aptitude, spiritual breadth, and radical intuitional venturesomeness to rival that effulgence of middle-class, *Mittel*-European Jewry between, say, Sigmund Freud's first tentative experiments with hypnosis and Isaac Babel's tragic vanishing within Stalin's Siberian charnel houses."

People simply opined, "A blast, if you skip the scenery," and featured Bech and Bea repairing their grape arbor in his-and-hers carpenter coveralls. Even before the foam-topped notices came rolling in, the fair-weather flags had been up. Bech was photographed by Jill Krementz, caricatured by David Levine, and interviewed by Michiko Kakutani. The Book-of-the-Month Club made *Think Big* its Alternate Alternate choice for July, with a Special Warning to Squeamish Subscribers. Bantam and Pocket Books engaged in a furious bidding of which the outcome was a well-publicized figure with more zeroes than a hand has fingers. "Bech Is *In!*" *Vogue* splashed in a diagonal banner across a picture of him modeling a corduroy coat and a ribbed wool turtleneck. "Bech Surprises" was *Time*'s laconic admission in a belated follow-up piece, they having ignored *Think Big* during publication week in favor of a round-up of diet cook books. What surprised Bech, that remarkably fair summer, was seeing his book being read, at beaches and swimming pools, by lightly toasted teen-agers and deep-fried matrons and even by a few of his male fellow commuters during his increasingly frequent trips to New York. To think that those shuttling eyes were consuming the delicate, febrile interplay of Tad and Thelma, or of Olive and Mort, or of Ginger and her Filipino while lilacs droopy with bloom leaned in at the open upper half of the stable door and the smell of oats mingled with human musk – the thought of it embarrassed Bech; he wanted to pluck the book from its readers' hands and explain that these were only his idle dreams, hatched while captive in Sing Sing, unworthy of their time let alone their money.

Having taken Donald swimming one day at the pool of Bea and Rodney's old club, Bech saw a bronze and zaftig young woman on a plastic-strap chaise holding the book up against the sun, reading it through her rhinestone-studded sunglasses. "How's it going?" he asked aloud, feeling guilty at the pain he must be giving her – the squint, the ache in her upholding arm. She lowered the book and stared at him, dazed and annoyed; it was as if he had awakened her. He saw from the tightening of her zinc-white lips that she made no connection between the world she had been immersed in and this stocky, woolly male intruder in outmoded plaid trunks, and that if he did not instantly move away she would call for the lifeguard. Yet she had an appealing figure, and must have an emptiness within, which his book was in some sense filling. He was his own rival. He came to flinch at the sight of his aqua jackets; they were as vivid to his sensitized sight as swimming pools seen from an airplane. He had filled the world with little distorting mirrors. *Think Big* was in its sixth printing by September, and Big Billy telegraphed in congratulation from Hawaii, GROW OLD ALONG WITH ME THE BEST IS YET TO COME.

He couldn't even take Arlene Schoenberg to lunch in an unprestigious Italian restaurant without some nitwit asking him to sign a scrap of paper – usually one of those invitations to a "health club" staffing topless masseuses that are handed out all over our sordid midtown. Every time an autograph-seeker approached, it put more stardust in Arlene's eyes and set seduction at another remove. The world, by one of those economic balancings whereby it steers, had at the same time given him success and taken from him the writer's chief asset, his privacy.

Her little fascinating hands enticingly fiddled with her knife and fork, caressed her Campari-and-soda, and dropped to her lap. After a moment, like an actress taking a curtain call, one of them returned into sight to scratch with a fingernail at an invisible itch on the side of her high-arched nose. She asked him where he got his ideas, from real life or out of his imagination. She asked him if he thought a writer owed anything to society or just to himself. She asked him if he had always been such a neat typist and good speller; now, her little brother and sisters, none of them could spell, it was really shocking, you wonder if there will be any books at all in twenty years, the terrible way it's going. Bech told her that credit for his typing and spelling should go to Mae, a genius his wife had found for him in Ossining. In an attempt to steer Miss Schoenberg's fascination away from his professional self, he talked a good deal about his wife. He gave Bea credit for finally settling him down in front of a typewriter and getting him to finish his book. He further confessed, putting the intimacy level up a notch, that when he had married her he had not realized what a worrier she was: she had seemed, in contrast to her difficult sister, Norma, so calm and understanding, so, well, motherly. And indeed she had proved motherly: she thought about her kids all the time, and nearly went wild when one of her daughters began to – Bech hesitated, for this starstruck minx was also somebody's daughter, and the word "fuck" or "screw," running ahead as a kind of scout, might startle her into a defensive posture – "misbehave," he said. As he spoke, the house in Ossining, with its dome-shaped lawn and coarse green exoskeleton and cool silver-lined retreat, became uncomfortably real. The storm windows were only half up. Some insulation in his study needed to be taped and restapled. Bech wondered if the magic appeal of those Xeroxed hands, haunting the edges of his duplicated galleys, might not have been a mirage peculiar to that silver-lined environment. Certainly Miss Schoenberg, as she sat perkily across from him in her sparrow-colored sweater, gave signs of being common.

"It must be terribly exciting to be a writer's wife," she said. "I mean, she must never know what you're thinking."

"Oh, I expect she knows as much as she wants to."

"I mean, when you look at her, she must feel she's being X-rayed. You write about women so well, she must feel naked."

Campari-and-soda always gave Bech the same sensation as swallowing aspirin: that burny feeling at the top of the esophagus. Thinking of naked, he stared glumly at Arlene's thready sweater and found it utterly opaque. Did she have breasts in there, or typewriter spools? She was wearing a thin gold chain which nobody had ripped off her neck yet. And she was going on, "Writers have such rich fantasy lives, I think that's what makes them so fascinating to women."

"Richer, you think, than, say, Mr. Flaggerty's fantasy life?"

It was an inspired stab. She said petulantly, "Oh *him*, all he fantasizes about is the Mets and then the Jets. Really. And where to get good Mexican brown like they used to groove on at college when he was picketing the ROTC and marching with Dylan and all that."

"You seem," Bech ventured, "to know him pretty well."

For the first time, her eyes lost their starry celebrity shine and submitted to an amused and sexual narrowing. "Well enough. He's a good boss. I've had worse."

Bech nostalgically wished he were back home raking the lawn. But Arlene Schoenberg was just getting relaxed, her shapely hands deftly twirling spaghetti onto a fork. The restaurant skills of New York women: like praying mantises roving the twigs of a creosote bush. He should have had more Gothamesque eating-out in his book. And the way the tables are inching out into the streets, into the soot. His silence brought a slow smile to Arlene's face, showing a provocative rim of gum and a fleck of tomato sauce. "See," she said. "I have no idea what you're thinking."

"I was wondering," he told her, "if there was a way we could get Vellum to pay for this lunch. Can you forge Flaggerty's signature, or aren't you that friendly yet?"

Her eyes became solemn bright circles again. "Oh, no."

"O.K., then. On me. What else can I do for you?"

"Well" – she absent-mindedly, tuggingly fiddled up a loop into her gold chain and squeezed her finger in it so that the tip turned bright red – "that brother I was telling you about, you know, *did* want me to ask you if you could possibly come talk to his seventh-grade class, it's a special school for dyslexics out toward Glen Cove, they'd be *so*, you know –"

Bech saw his opportunity and took it. He patted her bare hand as it lay distracted on the checked tablecloth. "I'd like to," he told her, "but I can't. The last time I spoke in a school I got involved in a disastrous affair with a woman who only cared about the literary me. She spurned the man. Wasn't that rotten of her?"

"I'd have to know the circumstances," Arlene Schoenberg prudently said, as if there had never been a sexual revolution, and pulled back her hand to cope further with the spaghetti.

On the walk from the restaurant back to the Vellum offices, they passed the Doubleday window, which held a pyramid of *Think Big*s. Bech always pitied his books, seen in a bookstore; they looked so outnumbered. He had sent them forth to fight in inadequate armor, with guns that jammed. These unbought copies were beginning to fade and warp in the daily slant of sun. On the train home, he saw how many of the yellowing trees were already bare. Soon it would be a year since he had finished the book Bea had got him to sit down and write. Their household had changed: the girls were off at college, Ann at M.I.T. and Judy at Duke, and little Donald no longer wanted his stepdad to take him places. Each fall they used to go to one Ossining High School football game together, played by mostly black players on a field where you could smell the torn earth and hear each cheerleader's piping voice fragile against the sky. This year the boy, newly thirteen, had looked disdainful and begged off. His father's snobbery was welling up through his genes. Rodney had taken Donald instead to the Harvard–Princeton game, at Palmer Stadium.

The house crackled in its timbers and joints, now that the furnace was on again and a heat differential applied torque. Workmen were busy inside the house and out; since Bech's book had made a million dollars, the north face of the mansard roof was being given new slates and the grand front staircase was being fully refinished, after ten years of a half-scraped left-hand banister. The television crew of *Sixty Minutes* had come and rearranged all the furniture, exposing how shabby it was. Within the many rooms Bech had been somewhat avoiding Bea; she wanted mostly to talk about their household expenditures, or to complain that Donald kept climbing on the roofers' scaffolding after they had gone for the day. "He has these horrible new delinquent friends, Henry. With Ann and Judy off I thought we'd be so relaxed now."

"How did that ever work out, by the way, with the diaphragms?"

She looked blank. If there was one thing Bech resented about women, it was the way they so rapidly forgave themselves for the hysteria they inflicted on others. He prompted, "You remember, Judy wanted one too, but she was still a virgin...."

"Oh. Yes. Didn't I tell you? It was very simple, I don't know why we didn't think of it. Doctor Landis fitted Ann for one, and then gave me a prescription for two the same size. After all, they *are* twins."

"Brilliant," Bech sighed.

"Sweetie, could you spare a minute and look at these Sloane's catalogues with me? What I'd like to do around the fireplace is get sort of a conversation-pit feeling without having it look like a ski lodge. Do you think boxy modern looks silly on a big Oriental?"

The hinges of his jaw ached with a suppressed yawn. "I think," he said, "the room looks nice enough now."

"You're not focusing. The staircase being all new and shiny shows everything else up. If it's the cost you're worried about, Sheila Warburton says with things so unsettled in the Middle East *any* Oriental you buy is a better investment than stocks, than gold –"

"I love those old wing chairs," Bech said. In the evenings he would sit in one, his feet up on an inverted bushel basket that was meant to hold wood, and read; he was reading Thomas Mann on Goethe, Wagner, Nietzsche, Schopenhauer, and Freud these nights. What chums they all turned out to have been!

"Those chairs were Rodney's mother's, and he really should have them back now that he has a bigger apartment."

"Bea, you know we don't *have* the million dollars yet, it's just a bunch of bits in Vellum's computer. I won't get my first royalties till next August."

"That was another thing Sheila Warburton said: you were crazy not to ask for a whopping advance, with inflation the way it is."

"*Damn* Sheila Warburton, and that pompous Paul as well. Nobody knew the book would take off like this. In the old days a respectable author *nev*er asked for an advance; that was strictly for the no-talents starving down in the Village."

Standing contemplative in her room of imagined furniture, Bea was hard to rattle. She slowly woke to his tone of indignation and came and embraced him. She had been raking leaves in an unraveling ski sweater that smelled muskily of leaf mold and lank autumn grass. "But these aren't the old days, Henry," she said, tickling his ear with her breath. "It costs a fortune to live down in the Village now. And you aren't the old Henry, either." She shuddered in happiness, and in her spasm gave him a squeeze. "We're all so *proud* of you!"

If there was another thing Bech resented about women it was the way they enveloped – the way they yearned, at moments of their convenience, to dissolve the sanitary partition between I and Thou. Assimilation, the most insidious form of conquest. He was becoming a shred of leaf mold. "I don't know about that book," he began.

"The book is wonderful," she interrupted, with breathy impatience. "When do we do another?"

"Another?" The thought sickened him. A whole new set of names to invent, a theme to nurture within like a tumor, a texture to maintain page after page ... His suburban softy, his plot of earth, was insatiable.

"Sure," Bea said briskly, backing off. "The storm windows are up, you've done all the publicity the media can stand, you've said the same things to twenty different interviewers, what are you going to do with your days?"

"Well, there've been some invitations to read at colleges. Some little agricultural college in West Virginia sounded interesting, and an Indian school in South Dakota – "

"Oh you've *done* all that," Bea said. "You don't need to go expose yourself for peanuts anymore, or fuck those little coeds in the Ramada Inn. Don't think I don't know really why you did all that speaking." Her sideways glance was both hostile and flirtatious, a common marital combination.

And he resented female knowingness, its coy invasion, its installation of an *Oberführer* in every province of his person. His mind, body, mouth, genitals – Bea had possessed them all and set up checkpoints along every escape route. His "triumph" (to quote *Vogue* again) was more deeply hers than his; that night in bed, when she insisted on copulating, it was, he felt, with the body of her own triumphant wifeliness that she came to climax, cooing above him and then breaking into that ascending series of little yips that had the effect, on this occasion at least, of reducing his own climax to something relatively trivial. More and more Bea favored the female-superior position. As the air in the bedroom seasonally cooled, she kept on her nightie, becoming in the dark a tent of chiffon and lace and loose blond hair, an operatic apparition whose damp grip upon him was swaddled and unseen as she pulled him up forcefully into manhood, into achievement, into riches and renewed fame, into viscid fireworks and neural release. She collapsed onto his chest panting.

"I feel so satisfied with you," she confided.

"And I with you," he responded, trusting the formal grammar to shade his inevitable and as it were pre-shaped rejoinder.

She heard the shadow. "Aren't you pleased?" she asked. "Not only about the book but about *us*? Tell me."

"Yes, I'm pleased. Of course."

"You were such a sad person then, Henry." Then. Before their marriage had infiltrated every cell and extracted daily wordage and nightly semen.

"I was?"

"*I* thought so," Bea said. "You used to frighten me. Not just sad. Other things, too. A lovely man, but, I don't know, sterile. You're so sweet with Donald."

Her arm across his chest was wonderfully heavy. He felt pegged down, and the image of Donald was another luminous nail. "We get along," he admitted. "But the kid's growing up."

Bea would not allow even so faint a discord to be the final note. "He loves you," she uttered, and as she slept he could see by moonlight that a smile remained on her face, rounding the cheek not buried in the pillow.

In his dream he is free. The landscape seems European – low gray sky, intense green fields, mud underfoot, churned and marked by tire treads and military boots. He has escaped from somewhere; fear is mixed sourly with his guilt, guilt at having left all those others behind, still captive. Yet in the meantime there are the urgencies of escape to cope with: dogs pursuing him are barking, and a hedge offers a place to hide. He squeezes in, his heart enormous and thumping. Candy wrappers litter the ground underfoot. The hedge is too wintry and thin; he will be discovered. In that thick gray European wool overhead, a single unseen bomber drones. It is, he instinctively knows, his only hope, though it will bring destruction. He awakes, and recognizes the drone as the furnace floors below. The neighborhood dogs have been harrying something, a raccoon perhaps, and downstairs Max had sleepily joined in with a gruff bark or two. Yet terror and guilt were slow to drain from Bech's system.

That afternoon, Bea had to pick up Donald after school and take him to the orthodontist and then to buy some school clothes; he had outgrown last year's. The child's smile had sprouted touching silver bands, and the first few pimples, harbingers of messy manhood, marred the skin once as perfect as a girl's. They would not be home until six at the earliest. Bech roamed the great house with a vague sense of having lost something, a Minotaur restless in his maze. Around four, the doorbell rang. He expected to open it upon a UPS deliveryman or one of Bea's Ossining sipping companions; but the woman on the porch was Bea's sister, Norma Latchett.

Where middle age had brought out Bea's plumpness, it had whittled Norma down, making her appear even more stringy, edgy, and exasperated than formerly. Her dark hair was turning gray and she was not dyeing it but pulling it back from her brow severely. Yet her black silk suit was smart, her lipstick and eye shadow were this fall's correct shade and amount, and across her face, when it proved to be he who opened the door, flickered all

the emotions of a woman first alarmed by and then standing up
to a former lover. "Where's Bea?" she asked.

Bech explained, and invited her in to wait until six or so.

Norma hesitated, holding a big calfskin briefcase and looking
slightly too trim, like the Avon lady. "I'm heading north to give a
talk in Poughkeepsie and thought I'd say hello. Also I have some
papers for Bea to sign. You two never come to the city anymore."

"Bea hates it," Bech said. "What are you giving your talk
about? Come in, for heaven's sake. Just me and Max are here,
and we aren't biting today."

"Oh, the usual thing," Norma said, looking vexed but entering the great varnished foyer. Since the workmen had done the
refinishing it gleamed like the cabin of a yacht. "Those awful
icons." For years, Norma had held jobs off and on in museums,
and in these last ten years, as hope of marriage faded, had put
herself seriously to school, and become an expert on Byzantine
and Russian Orthodox art. Icons becoming ever more "collect-
ible," she included bankers as well as students in the audience for
her expertise. She lit a cigarette whose paper was tinted pale
green, and looked switchily about for an ashtray.

"Let's go into the living room," Bech said. "I'll build a fire."

"You don't have to entertain me, I could push on to Vassar
and have the art department chairman give me dinner. Except
I hate to eat before I talk, the blood all rushes to your stomach
and makes you very stupid."

"I don't think anything could make you *very* stupid," he said
gallantly, remembering as he followed her in past the pompous
staircase how her body had concealed surprising amplitudes – her
hips, for instance, were wide, as if the pelvic bones had been
spread by a childbirth that had never occurred, so that her thighs
scarcely touched, giving her a touching knock-kneed look,
naked or in a bathing suit. He took three of the logs he had
split last winter in hopes that the exercise would prolong his life,
and laid a fire while she settled into one of the wing chairs, his
favorite, the one covered in maroon brocade, that he usually read
in. The match flared. The crumpled *Times* caught. The pine
kindling began to crackle. He stood up, asking, "Tea?" His

heart was thumping, as in last night's dream. The house in all its
rooms held silent around them like the eye of a storm. Max
padded in, claws clicking, and dropped himself with a ponderous
sigh on the rug before the quickening flames. One golden eye
with a red lower lid questioned Bech before closing. "Or a real
drink?" Bech pursued. "I'm not sure we have white crème de
menthe. Bea and I don't drink that much." Norma had, he
remembered, a fondness for vodka stingers, for Black Russians,
for anything whose ingredients he was likely not to have.

"I never drink before I talk," she said sharply. "I'm wondering,
if I'm going to stay, if I should bring my slides in from the car.
You leave them in a cold car too long, they sometimes crack in
the heat of the projector."

As Bech retrieved the gray metal box from the trunk of her
car, Max trotted along with him, letting one of Norma's tires
have his autograph and running a quick check on the wood-
chuck trying to hibernate underneath the porch. In returning,
Bech closed the front door on the dog's rumpled, affronted face.
Three's a crowd.

The slides tucked safely beneath her chair, beside her swollen
briefcase, Norma asked, "Well. How does it feel?"

"How does what feel?" This time her cigarette was violet in
tint. They must come mixed in the box, like gumdrops.

"Having pulled it off."

"What off?" The nylon sheen of her ankles picked up an
orange glimmer from the fireplace flames; her eyes held wet
and angry sparks.

"Don't play dumb," she said. "That book. She got you to
make a million. Busy Bea, buzz, buzz."

"She didn't get me to do anything, it just happened. Is happening. They say there's going to be a movie. Sure you don't
want any tea?"

"Stop being grotesque. Sit down. I have your chair."

"How can you tell?"

"The look on your face when I sat here. It *didn't* just happen,
she's bragging all the time about how she got you your little *room*,
and told you to write a few pages every *day*, and keep going no
matter how *rotten* it was, and how now the money's rolling in.

How does it feel, being a sow's ear somebody's turned into a silk purse?"

He had thought they might trade a few jabs with the big gloves on; but this was a real knife fight. Norma was furious. The very bones in her ankles seemed to gnash as she crossed and recrossed her legs. "Did you read the book?" Bech mildly asked her.

"As much as I could. It's lousy, Henry. The old you would never have let it be published. It's slapdash, it's sentimental, it's *cozy*. That's what I couldn't forgive, the coziness. Look how everybody loves it. You know that's a terrible sign."

"Mm," he said, a syllable pressed from him like a whistle from the chimney, like a creak from the house.

"I don't blame you; I blame Bea. It was she who forced it out of you, she and her cozy idea of marriage, to make a monument to herself. What if the monument *was* made of the bodies of all your old girlfriends, *she's* the presiding spirit, she's the one who reaps the profit. Top dog. Bea always had to be top dog. You should have seen her play tennis, before she got so fat." Norma's eyes blazed. The demons of vengeance and truth had entered this woman, a dazzling sight.

"Bodies of old girlfriends – ?" Bech hesitantly prompted.

"Christ, Henry, it was a pyre. Smoke rising to heaven, to the glory of big fat Bea. Thanks by the way for calling me Thelma, so all my friends can be sure it's me."

"Thelma wasn't exactly . . ." he began. And, thinking of Bea herself, her soft body in bed, the way her eyelids and nose looked rubbed and pink when she was sad or cold, he knew that the rebirth and growth of *Think Big* weren't quite as Norma had described them, making something sudden and crass out of all those patient months spent tapping away amid the treetops and the flying squirrels. Still, she put the book in a fresh harsh light, and a fresh light is always liberating. "Bea *is* pleased about the money," he admitted. "She wants to refurnish the entire house."

"You bet she does," Norma said. "You should have seen the way she took over the dollhouse my parents had meant for both of us. She's greedy, Henry, and materialistic, and small-minded. Why does she keep you out here with these ridiculous commuters? The real question is, Why do you permit it? You've always been weak, but weak in your own way before, not in somebody else's. I guess I better have tea after all. To shut me up." She pinched her long lips tight to dramatize and turned her head so her profile looked pre-Raphaelite against the firelight. Some strands of her hair had strayed from severity, as if a light wind were blowing.

He perched forward on the lemon-colored wing chair and asked, "Didn't you at least like the part where Mort Zenith finally gets Olive alone in the beach cabaña?"

"It was cranked out, Henry. Even where it was good, it felt cranked out. But don't mind me. I'm just an old discarded mistress. You've got Prescott and Cavett with you and they're the ones that count."

In the barny old kitchen, its butcher-block countertops warping and its hanging copper pans needing Brillo, the tea water took forever to boil: Bech was burning to get back to his treasure of truth, arrived like an arrow in Ossining. He was trembling. Dusk was settling in outside. Max woofed monotonously at the back door, where he was usually at this hour let in and fed. When Bech returned with the two steaming cups and a saucer of Ritz crackers to the living room, Norma stood up. Her wool suit wore a fuzzy corona; her face in shadow loomed featureless. He set the tray down carefully on the inverted bushel basket and, giving the response that seemed expected, held and kissed her. Her mouth was wider and wetter than Bea's and, by virtue of longer acquaintance, more adaptable. "I have a question for you," he said. "Do you ever fuck before you talk?"

They were so careful. They let Max in and closed the kitchen door. Upstairs, they chose Donald's bed because, never made, it would not show mussing. The boy's shelves still held the stuffed toys and mechanical games of childhood. A tacked-up map of the world, in the projection that looks like a flattened orange peel, filled Bech's vision with its muted pinks and blues when his eyelids furtively opened. *So this is adultery*, he thought: this homely, friendly socketing. An experience he would have missed, but for marriage. A sacred experience, like not honoring your father and mother. Good old Norma, she still had a faintly sandy texture to her buttocks and still liked to have her nipples endlessly, endlessly flicked by the attendant's tongue. She came silently, even sullenly, without any of Bea's angelic coos and yips. They kept careful track of the time by the clown-faced plastic clock on Donald's maple dresser, and by five-thirty Bech was downstairs pouring Kibbles into Max's bowl. The dog ate greedily, but would never forgive him. Bech cleared away the telltale untasted tea, washed and dried the cups, and put them back on their hooks. What else? Norma herself, whom he had last seen wandering in insouciant nudity toward the twins' bathroom for a shower, was maddeningly slow to get dressed and come back downstairs; he wanted her desperately to go, to disappear, even forever. But she had brought in her briefcase some documents connected with old Judge Latchett's estate – the release of some unprofitable mutual-fund shares – that needed Bea's signature. So they waited together in the two wing chairs. Bech took the maroon this time. Max went and curled up by the front door, pointedly. Norma cleared her throat and said, "I *did*, actually, like that bit with Zenith and your heroine. Really, it has a lot of lovely things in it. It's just I hate to see you turn into one more scribbler. Your paralysis was so beautiful. It was . . . statuesque."

Her conceding this, in softened tones, had the effect of making her seem pathetic. A mere woman, skinny and aging, hunched in a chair, his seed and sweat showered from her. In praising his book even weakly she had shed her dark magic. Bad news had been Norma's beauty. She was getting nervous about the talk she had to give. "If they aren't back by six-fifteen, I really *will* have to leave."

But Donald and Bea returned at six-ten, bustling in the door with crackling packages while the dog leaped to lick their faces. Donald's face had that stretched look of being brave; he had been told he must keep wearing retainers for two more years. Bea was of course surprised to find her sister and her husband sitting so primly on either side of a dying fire. "Didn't Henry at least offer you a drink?"

"I didn't want any. It might make me need to pee in the middle of my lecture."

"You poor thing," Bea said. "I'd be impossibly nervous." She knew. Somehow, whether by the stagy purity of their waiting or the expression of Max's ears or simple Latchett telepathy, she knew. Bea's blue eyes flicked past Bech's face like a piece of fair sky glimpsed between tunnels high in the mountains. And little Donald, he knew too, looking from one to the other of them with a wary brightness, feeling this entire solid house suspended above him on threads no more substantial than the invisible currents between these tall adults.

WHITE ON WHITE

NO SOONER had the great success of *Think Big* sunk into the Upper East Side's social consciousness than engraved invitations had begun to arrive at the Bechs' Ossining house. After Bech moved out, Bea in her scrupulous blue handwriting would forward these creamy stiff envelopes, including those addressed to "Mr. and Mrs.," to Bech's two drab sublet rooms on West 72nd Street. Many of the invitations he dropped into the plastic wastebasket, after lovingly thumbing them as examples of the engraver's art and the stationer's trade; but he tended to accept those that carried with them a shred of old personal connection. His marriage having dissolved around him like the airy walls of a completed novel, anyone who knew Bech "when" interested him, as a clue to his past and hence to his future.

Mr. and Mrs. Henderson Hyde, III
and
Colortron Photographics, Inc.
request the pleasure of your company
at a party, honoring the publication of

White on White

by Angus Desmouches, esquire
on Friday, the thirteenth of April
at six o'clock

R.s.v.p.
12-7777

Suggested dress
All white

Bech remembered being photographed by the young and eager Angus Desmouches for *Flair*, long defunct, in the mid-Fifties, when *Travel Light* was coming out, to a trifling stir. The youthful photographer had himself looked at first sight as if seen through a wide-angle lens, his broad, tan, somehow Aztec face and wide head of wiry black hair dwindling to a pinched waist and tiny, tireless feet; clicking and clucking, he had pursued Bech up and down the vales and bike paths of Prospect Park, and then for contrast had taken him by subway to lower Manhattan and posed him stony-faced among granite skyscrapers. Bech had scarcely been back to the financial district in the decades since, though now he had a lawyer there, who, with much well-reimbursed head-wagging, was trying to disentangle him and his recent financial gains from Bea and her own tough crew of head-waggers. In a little bookshop huddled low in the gloom of Wall Street Bech had flipped through a smudged display copy of *White on White* ($128.50 before Christmas, $150 thereafter): finely focused platinum prints of a cigarette butt on a plain white saucer, a white kitten on a polar-bear rug, an egg amid feathers, a naked female foot on a tumbled bedsheet, a lump of sugar held in bared teeth, a gob of what might be semen on the margin of a book, a white-hot iron plunged into snow.

Bech went to the party. The butler at the door of the apartment looked like a dancer in one of the old M-G-M musical extravaganzas, in his white tie, creamy tails, and wing collar. The walls beyond him had been draped in bleached muslin; the apartment's regular furniture had been replaced with white wicker and with great sailcloth pillows; boughs and dried flowers spray-painted white had been substituted for green plants; most remarkably, in the area of the duplex where the ceiling formed a dome twenty feet high, a chalky piano and harp shared a platform with a tall vertical tank full of fluttering, ogling albino tropical fish. Angus Desmouches bustled forward, seemingly little changed – the same brown pug face and gladsome homosexual energy – except that his crown of black hair, sticking out stiff as if impregnated with drying paste, had gone stark white. So stark Bech guessed it had been dyed rather than aged that color; his eyebrows matched, it was too perfect. The years had piled celebrity and wealth upon the little photographer but not added an inch to his waist. He looked resplendent in a satin plantation suit. Bech felt dowdy in an off-white linen jacket, white Levi's, and tennis shoes he had made a separate trip out to Ossining to retrieve.

"Gad, it's good to press your flesh," Desmouches exclaimed, seeming in every cubic centimeter of his own flesh to mean it. "How long ago was that, anyway?"

"Nineteen fifty-five," Bech said. "Not even twenty-five years ago. Just yesterday."

"You were such a sweet subject, I remember that. So patient and funny and wise. I got some delicious angles on especially the downtown take, but the foolish, *fool*ish magazine didn't use any of it, they just ran a boring head-and-shoulders under some weeping *wil*low. I've always been afraid you blamed *me*."

"No blame," Bech said. "Absolutely no blame in this business. Speaking of which, that's some book of yours."

The other man's miniature but muscular hands fluttered skyward in simultaneous supplication and disavowal. "The idea came to me when I dropped an aspirin in the bathtub and couldn't find it for the longest time. The idea, you know, of exploring how little contrast you could have and still have a photograph." His hands pressed as if at a pane of glass beside him. "Of taking something to the *li*mit."

"You did it," Bech told the air, for Desmouches like a scarf up a magician's sleeve had been whisked away, to greet other guests in this white-on-white shuffle. Bech was sorry he had come. The house in Ossining had been empty, Donald off at school and Bea off at her new job, being a part-time church secretary under some steeple up toward Brewster. Max had been there, curled up on the cold front porch, and had wrapped his mouth around Bech's hand and tried to drag him in the front door. The door was locked, and Bech no longer had a key. He knew how to get in through the cellar bulkhead, past the smelly oil tanks. The house, empty, seemed an immense, vulnerable shell, a *Titanic* throttled down to delay its rendezvous with the iceberg. Its emptiness did not, oddly, much welcome him. In the brainlessly short memories of these chairs and askew rugs he was already forgotten; minute changes on all sides testified to his absence. Bea's clothes hung in her closet like cool cloth knives seen on edge, and in the way his remaining shoes and his tennis racket had been left tumbled on the floor of his own closet he read a touch of disdain. He turned up the thermostat a degree, lest the pipes freeze, before sneaking back out through the cellar and walking the two miles to the train station, through the slanting downtown, where he had always felt like a strolling minstrel. His West 72nd Street rooms had been rented in haste from a disreputable friend of Flaggerty's, and though Bech deplored the tattered old acid-trip decor – straw mats, fringed hassocks – he was surprised by how much better he slept there than in bucolic splendor, surrounded by cubic yards of creaking space for whose repair and upkeep he had been, those Ossining years, at least half responsible.

The drinks served at this party were not white, nor was the bartender. An ebony hand passed him the golden bourbon. The host and hostess came and briefly cooed their pleasure at Bech's company. Henderson Hyde may have been a third but he came from some gritty town in the Midwest and had the ebullient urbanity of those who have wrapped themselves in Manhattan as in a sumptuous cloak. His wife, too, was the third – a former model whose prized slenderness was with age becoming gaunt. Her great lip-glossed smile stretched too many tendons in her neck; designer dresses hung on her a trifle awkwardly, now that they were truly hers; her tenure as wife had reached the expensive stage. Tonight's gown, composed of innumerable crescent slices as of quartz, suggested the robe of an ice-maiden helper that Santa had taken on while rosy-cheeked Mrs. Claus looked the other way. Until he had married Bea, Bech had imagined that Whitsuntide had something to do with Christmas. Not at all, it turned out. And there was an entire week called Holy Week, corresponding to the seven days of Pesach. They were in it, actually.

"Smash of a book," said Hyde, giving the flesh above Bech's elbow a comradely squeeze as expertly as a doctor taps the nerves below your kneecap.

"You got through it?" Bech asked, startled. His funny bone tingled.

Mrs. Hyde intervened. "I told him all about it," she said. "He couldn't get to sleep for all my chuckling beside him as I read it. That scene with the cameramen!"

"It's top of the list I'm going to get to on the Island this summer. Christ, the books keep piling up," Hyde snarled. He was wearing, Bech only now noticed in the sea of white, a brilliant bulky turban and a caftan embroidered with the logo of his network.

"It's hard to read anything," Bech admitted, "if you're gainfully employed."

Somebody had begun to tinkle the piano: "The White Cliffs of Dover." *There'll be bluebirds over . . .*

"So sorry your wife couldn't be with us," Hyde's wife said in parting.

"Yeah, well," Bech said, not wanting to explain, and expecting they knew enough anyway. "Easy come, easy go." He had meant this to be soothing, but an alarmed look flitted across Mrs. Hyde III's gracious but overelastic features.

The harp joined in, and the melody became "White Christmas." *Just like the ones we used to know . . .* A man of his acquaintance, a fellow writer, the liberal thinker Maurie Leonard, came up to him. Maurie, though tall, and thick through the shoulders and chest, had such terrible, deskbound posture that all effect of force was limited to his voice, which emerged as an urgent rasp. Metal on metal. Mind on matter. "Some digs, huh?" he said. "You know how Hyde made his money, don'tcha?" More than a liberal, a radical whose twice-weekly columns were deplored by elected officials and whose bound essays were removed from the shelves of public-school libraries, Maurie yet took an innocent prideful glee in the awful workings of capitalism.

"No. How?" Bech asked.

"Game shows!" Maurie ground the words out through a mirth that pressed his cheeks up tight against his eyes, whose sockets were as wrinkled as walnuts. "*Hyde-Jinks, Hyde-'n'-seek.* Haven't you heard of 'em? Christ, you just wrote a whole book about the TV industry!"

"That was fiction," Bech said.

Maurie, too, exerted pressure on the flesh above Bech's elbow, muttering confidentially, "You wouldn't know it to look at the uptight little prick, but Hyde's a genius. He's like Hitler – the worst thing you can think of, he's there ahead of you already. Know what his latest gimmick is?"

"No," Bech said, beginning to wish that this passage were not in dialogue but in simple expository form.

"Mud wrestling!" Maurie rasped, and a dozen wrinkles fanned upward from each outer corner of his Tartarish, street-wise eyes. "In bikinis, right there on the boob tube. Not your usual hookers, either, but the girl next door; they come on the show with their husbands and mothers and goddamn gym teachers and talk about how they want to win for the hometown and Jesus and the American Legion and the next thing you see there they are, slugging another bimbo with a fistful of mud and taking a bite out of her ass. Christ, it's wonderful. One or two falls and they could be fucking stark naked. Wednesdays at five-thirty, just before the news, and then reruns Saturday midnight, for couples in bed. Bech, I defy you to watch without getting a hard-on."

This man loves America, Bech thought to himself, *and he writes as if he hates it.* "Easy money," he said aloud.

"You can't imagine how much. If you think this place is O.K., you should see Hyde's Amagansett cottage. And the horse farm in Connecticut."

"So what I wrote was true," Bech said to himself.

"If anything, you understated," Leonard assured him, his very ears now involved in the spreading folds of happiness, so that his large furry lobes dimpled.

"How sad," said Bech. "What's the point of fiction?"

"It hastens the Revolution," Leonard proclaimed, and in farewell, with hoisted palm: "Next year in Jerusalem!"

Bech needed another drink. The piano and harp were doing "Frosty the Snowman," and then the harp alone took on "Smoke Gets in Your Eyes." The room was filling up with whiteness like a steam bath. At the edge of the mob around the bar, a six-foot girl in a frilly Dior nightie gave Bech her empty glass and asked him to bring her back a Chablis spritzer. He did as he was told and when he returned to stand beside her saw that she had on a chocolate-brown leotard beneath the nightie. Her hair was an unreal red, and heavy, falling to her shoulders in a waxen Ginger Rogers roll; her bangs came down to her straight black eyebrows. She was heavy all over, Bech noticed, but comely, with a greasy-lidded humorless gaze. "Whose wife are you?" Bech asked her.

"That's a chauvinistic approach."

"Just trying to be polite."

"Nobody's. Whose husband are you?"

"Nobody's. In a way."

"Yeah? Tell me the way."

"I'm still married, but we're split up."

"What split you up?"

"I don't know. I think I was bad for her ego. Women now I guess need to do something on their own. As you implied before."

"Yeah." Her pronunciation was dead level, hovering between agreement and a grunt.

"What do *you* do, then?"

"Aah. I been in a couple a Hendy's shows."

Ah. She was a mud wrestler. Maurie Leonard in his enthusiasm for the Revolution sometimes got a few specifics wrong. The mud wrestlers *were* hookers. The give-away-nothing eyes, the calm heft held erect as a soldier's body beneath the frills. "You win or lose?" Bech asked her. He had the idea that wrestlers always proceeded by script.

"We don't look at it that way, win or lose. It's more like a dance. We have a big laugh at the end, and usually dunk the referee."

"I've always wondered, what happens if you get mud in your eyes?"

"You blink. You the writer?"

"One of the many."

"I saw you on Cavett. Nice. Smooth, but, you know, not too. You gonna stick around here long?"

"I was wondering," he said.

The girl turned her face slightly toward him – a thrilling sight, like the soft sweep of a lighthouse beam or the gentle nudging motion of a backhoe, so much smooth youth and health bunched at the base of her throat, where her nightie's lace hem clouded the issue. He felt her heavy gaze rest on the top of his head. "Maybe we could go out get a snack together afterward," she suggested. "After we circulate. I'm here to circulate."

"I am too, I guess," Bech said. Men and women: what a grapple. New terminology, same old pact. "Name's Lorna," his mud wrestler told him, and moved off, her leotard suspended like a muscular vase within the chiffon of her costume. He remembered Bea's soft nighties, and the bottom dropped out of his excitement, leaving an acid taste. Better make the next drink weak, it looked like a long night.

"Shine On, Harvest Moon" had become the tune, and then one he hadn't heard since the days of Frankie Carle, "The Glow Worm." *Glimmer, glimmer.* The music enwrapped as with furling coils of tinsel ribbon the increasingly crowded room, or rooms; the party was expanding in the vast duplex to a boundary whereat one could glimpse those rooms stacked with the polychrome furniture that had been temporarily removed, rooms hung with paintings of rainbows and flayed nudes, bursts of color like those furious quasars hung at the outer limits of our telescopes. In the mass of churning whiteness the mud wrestlers stood firm, big sturdy girls wearing silver wigs and rabbit-fur vests and shimmery running shorts over those white tights nurses wear, or else white gowns like so many sleepwalking Lady Macbeths, or the sterilized pajamas and boxy caps of laboratory workers dealing with bacteria or miniaturized transistors; in the pallid seethe they stood out like caryatids, supporting the party on their heads.

Bech had to fight to get his bourbon. The piano and the harp were jostled in the middle of "Stardust" and went indignantly silent. Like a fuzzy sock being ejected by the tumble-dryer there was flung toward Bech the shapeless face of Vernon Klegg, the American Kafka, whose austere minimalist renderings of kitchen spats and dishevelled mobile homes were the rage of writers' conferences and federal and state arts councils. There was at the heart of Klegg's work a haunting enigma. Why were these heroines shrieking? Why were these heroes going bankrupt, their businesses sliding from neglect so resistlessly into ruin? Why were these children so rude, so angry and estranged? The enigma gave Klegg's portrayal of the human situation a hollowness hailed as quintessentially American; he was published with great faithfulness in the Soviet Union, as yet another illustrator of the West's sure doom, and was a pet of the Left intelligentsia everywhere. Yet one did not have to be a very close friend of Klegg's to know that the riddling texture of his work sprang from a humble personal cause: except for that dawn hour of each day when, pained by hangover and recommencing thirst, Klegg composed with sharpened pencil and yellow-paper pad his few hundred beautifully minimal words – nouns, verbs, nouns – he was drunk. He was a helpless alcoholic from whom wives, households, faculty positions, and entire neighborhoods of baffled order slid with mysterious ease. Typically in a Klegg *conte* the hero would blandly discover himself to have in his hands a butcher knife, or the broken top fronds of a rubber plant, or the buttocks of a pubescent babysitter. Alcohol was rarely described in Klegg's world, and he may himself not have recognized it as the element that kept that world in perpetual centrifugal motion. He had a bloated face enlarged by a white bristle that in a circle on his chin was still dark, like a panda marking. In this environment he seemed not unsober. "Hear you turned down Dakota Sioux Tech," he told Bech.

"My wife advised me to."

"Didn't know you still had a wife."

"My God, Vern, I don't. I plumb forgot."

"It happens. My fourth decamped the other day, God knows why. She just went kind of crazy."

"Same with me," Bech said. "This modern age, it puts a lot of stress on women. Too many decisions."

"Lord love 'em," Klegg said. "Who are all these cunts standing around like cops?"

"Mud wrestlers. The newest thing. Wonderful women. They keep discipline."

"About time somebody did," Klegg said. "I've lost the bar."

"Follow the crowds," Bech told him, and himself rotated away from the other writer, to a realm where the bodies thinned, and he could breathe the intergalactic dust. A stately creature swaddled in terrycloth attracted him; her face was not merely white, it was painted white, so that her eyes with their lashes stared from within a kind of mask. She smiled in welcome, and her red inner lips and gums seemed to declare an inner face of blood.

"Hey man."

"Hey," he answered.

"What juice *you* groovin' on?"

"Noble dispassion," he answered.

Her hands, Bech saw, were black, with lilac nails and palms. She was black, he realized. She was truth. The charm of liquor is not that it distorts perceptions. It does not. It merely lifts them free from their customary matrix of anxiety. America at heart is black, he saw. Snuggling into the jazz that sings to our bones, we feel that the Negro lives deprived and naked among us as the embodiment of truth, and that when the castle of credit cards collapses a black god will redeem us. The writer would have spoken more to this smiling apparition with the throat of black silk beneath her mask of rice, but Lorna, his first mud wrestler, sidled up to him and said, "You're not circulating." Her wig was as evenly, incandescently red as the glowing coil of the hot plate he cooked his lonely breakfasts on.

"Is it time to go?" he asked, like a child.

"Give it another half-hour. This is just fun for you, but Hendy makes us girls toe the line. If I skip off early it could affect my match-ups."

"We don't want that."

"No we don't, ol' buddy." Before she went off again her body purposely and with only peripheral menace brushed Bech's; in the lightness of the contact her breast felt as hard as her hip. A dangerous word from Bech's linguistic past, spoken rarely even by his uninhibited uncles, occurred to him. *Kurveh.* The stranger who comes close.

The piano and harp were interrupted again, this time in the middle of "Stars Fell on Alabama." Henderson Hyde was up on the piano bench, making a speech about Angus Desmouches's extraordinary book. "... horizons. . . . not since Atget and Stei-

chen . . . rolling back the limits of the photographic universe . . . "
The albino fish in the vertical tank flurried and goggled, alarmed
by the new vibrations. They were always in profile. On edge
they looked like knives, like Bea's clothes in the closet. *Why is a
fish like a writer?* Bech asked himself. *Because both exist in a different
medium.* Since seeing through the black woman's white paint and
obtaining for himself a fourth bourbon (neat: the party was
running out of water), Bech felt the gift of clairvoyance growing
within him. Surfaces parted; he had achieved X-ray vision. The
white of this party was a hospital johnny beneath which lungs
harbored dark patches and mud-packed arteries sluggishly pulsed.
Now Angus Desmouches was up on the piano bench, saying he
owed everything to his mother's sacrifices and to the nimbleness
and sensitivity of his studio assistants too numerous to name. Not
to mention the truly wonderful crew at Colortron Photographics. A limited number of signed copies of *White on White*
could be purchased in the foyer, at the pre-Christmas price.
Thank you. You're great people. Really great. The albino
crowd flared and fluttered, looking for its next crumb. In the
mass of white, heads and shoulders floated like photos on the
back flaps of dust jackets. Bech recognized two authors, both
younger than he, more prolix and better publicized, and saw
right through them. Elegantly slim, pearl-laden Lucy Ebright, she
of dazzling intellectual constructs and uncanny six-hundred-page
forays into the remoter realms of history: in her work a momen-
tous fluency passed veils of illusion before the reader's eyes
everywhere but when, more and more rarely, her own threadbare Altoona girlhood was evoked. Then as it were a real cinder
appeared at the heart of a great unburning fire of invention. For
the one thing this beautiful conjurer of the world's riches truly
understood was poverty; the humiliation of having to wear
second-hand clothes, the inglorious pain of neglected teeth, the
shame of watching one's grotesque parents grovel before the
distributors of jobs and money – wherever such images arose,
even in a psychoallegorical thriller set in the court of Kublai
Khan, a jarring authenticity gave fluency pause, and the reader
uncomfortably gazed upon raw truth: *I was poor.* Lucy was chat-
ting, the sway of her long neck ever more aristocratic as her

dreams succeeded in print, with the brilliant and engaging Seth Zimmerman, whose urbane comedies of sexual entanglement and moral confusion revealed to Bech's paternal clairvoyance a bitter, narrow, insistent message. *I hate you all,* Seth's comedies said, *for forsaking Jesus.* A Puritan nostalgia, an unreasonable longing for the barbaric promise of eternal light beyond the slate-marked grave, a fury at all unfaith including his own gave Zimmerman's well-carpentered plots their uncentered intensity and his playful candor its hostile cool. Both rising writers came up to Bech and in all sincerity said how much they had adored *Think Big.*

"I just wished it was even longer," Lucy said in her lazy, nasal voice.

"I wished it was even dirtier," Seth said, snorting in self-appreciation.

"Bless you both," said Bech. Loving his colleagues for having, like him, climbed by sheer desperate wits and acquired typing skill up out of the dreary quotidian into this alabaster apartment on high, he nevertheless kept dodging glances between their shoulders to see if his new friend in her nightie and fiery wig were approaching to carry him off. The piano and harp, running out of white, had turned to "Red Sails in the Sunset" and then "Blue Skies." Radiant America; where else but here? Still, Bech, sifting the gathering with his liquored gaze, was not quite satisfied. Another ancestral word occurred to him. *Trayf,* he thought. Unclean.

BECH AT BAY
(1998)

CONTENTS

Something of the unreal is necessary to fecundate the real.

—WALLACE STEVENS, in his preface
to William Carlos Williams'
Collected Poems 1921–1931 (1934)

BECH IN CZECH

THE AMERICAN AMBASSADOR'S RESIDENCE in Prague has been called the last palace built in Europe. A rich Jewish banker, Otto Petschek, built it; within a decade of its construction, he and his family had to flee Hitler. The Americans had acquired the building and its grounds after the war, before Czechoslovakia went quite so Communist. The whole building gently curves – that is, it was designed along the length of an arc, and a walk down its long corridors produces a shifting perspective wherein paintings, silk panels, marble-topped hall tables, great metallicized oaken doors all slowly come into view, much as islands appear above the horizon to a ship at sea and then slowly sink behind it, beyond the majestic, roiling, pale-turquoise wake.

Henry Bech, the semi-obscure American author, who had turned sixty-three in this year of 1986, felt majestic and becalmed in the great Residence, where, at one end, he had been given a suite for the week of his cultural visit to this restive outpost of the Soviet empire. As a Jew himself, he was conscious of the former owners, those vanished plutocrats, no doubt very elegant and multilingual, who with such pathetic trust, amid the tremors of the Diaspora's Middle-European golden age (not to be confused with the golden age in Saracen Spain, or the good times under the Polish princes), had built their palace on the edge of an abyss. For a Jew, to move through postwar Europe is to move through hordes of ghosts, vast animated crowds that, since 1945, are not there, not there at all – up in smoke. The feathery touch of the mysteriously absent is felt on all sides. In the center of old Prague the clock of the Jewish Town Hall – which, with the

303

adjacent synagogues, Hitler intended to preserve as the relic of an exterminated race – still runs backwards, to the amusement of tourists from both sides of the Iron Curtain. The cemetery there, with its four centuries of dead crowded into mounds by the pressures of the ghetto, and the tombstones jumbled together like giant cards in a deck being shuffled, moved Bech less than the newer Jewish cemetery on the outskirts of town, where the Ambassador felt that the visiting author should see Kafka's grave.

The Ambassador was an exceptionally short and peppy man with sandy thin hair raked across a freckled skull; he was an Akron industrialist and a Republican fund-raiser who had believed in Reagan when most bigwig insiders still laughed at the notion of a movie actor in the White House. For his loyalty and prescience the Ambassador had been rewarded with this post, and there was an additional logic to it, for he was Czech by ancestry; his grandparents had come to Pittsburgh from the coalfields of Moravia, and the language had been spoken in his childhood home. "They love it when I talk," he told Bech with his disarming urchin grin. "I sound so damn old-fashioned. It would be as if in English somebody talked like the King James Bible." Bech fancied he saw flit across the Ambassador's square face the worry that Jews didn't have much to do with the King James Bible. The little man quickly added, for absolute clarity, "I guess I sound quaint as hell."

Bech *had* noticed that the Czechs tended to smile when the Ambassador talked to them in their language. It was all the more noticeable because Czechs, once a wry and humorous race, found rather little to smile about. The Ambassador made Bech smile, too. Having spent most of his life in the narrow precincts of the Manhattan intelligentsia, a site saturated in poisonous envy and reflexive intolerance and basic impotence, he was charmed by the breezy and carefree ways of an authentic power-broker, this cheerful representative of the triumphant right wing. In entrepreneurial style, the Ambassador was a quick study, quick to pounce and quick to move on. He must have skimmed a fact sheet concerning his cultural guest, and it was on the basis of this information that he took Bech – freshly landed that morning, jet throb still ringing in his ears – to Kafka's grave. "It's the kind of thing that'll appeal to you." He was right.

The official limousine, with its morosely silent and sleepy-eyed chauffeur, wheeled along steep cobblestoned streets, past the old parapets and trolley tracks of Prague, and came, in what had once been outskirts, to a long ornate iron fence. The tall gate was locked and chained. The Ambassador rattled at the chains and called, but there was no answer. "Try the flag, honey," said the Ambassador's wife, a leggy blonde considerably younger than he.

Bech, who had traveled in Africa and Latin America and seen the Stars and Stripes attract rocks and spittle, winced as the Ambassador plucked the little American flag from the limousine's front fender and began to wave it through the gate, shouting incomprehensibly. He noticed Bech's wince and said in quick aside, "Relax. They love us here. They love our flag." And indeed, two young men wearing plaster-splattered overalls shyly emerged, at the patriotic commotion, from within a cement-block shed. The Ambassador talked to them in Czech. Smiling at his accent, they came forward a few steps and spoke words that meant the cemetery was closed. The flag was given a few more flutters, but the boys continued, bemusedly, to shake their heads and pronounce the soft word *"ne"*. The Ambassador, with a playful and shameless aggressiveness that Bech had to admire even as he blushed for it, wielded a new inspiration; in his next spate of words Bech heard his own name, distinct in the rippling, Stygian flow of the opaque language.

The politely denying smiles on the faces of the young men gave way to open-eyed interest. They looked away from the Ambassador to the American author on the other side of the bars.

"*Travel Light*," the taller one said in halting English, naming Bech's first novel.

"*Big Idea*," said the other, trying to name his last.

"*Think Big*," Bech corrected, his blush deepening; he wouldn't have guessed he had left in him so much spare blood as was making his cheeks burn, his palms tingle. This was absolutely, he vowed, his last appearance as a cultural icon.

"Ahhhh!" the two boys uttered in unison, enraptured by

the authentic correction, out of the author's mouth. With cries of jubilation from both sides, the locks and chains were undone and the three Americans were welcomed to the Strašnice cemetery.

It was an eerie, well-kept place. Impressive and stolid black tombstones stood amid tall trees, plane and ash and evergreen, and flourishing ivy. The vistas seemed endless, lit by the filtered sunlight of the woods, and silent with the held breath of many hundreds of ended lives. Most of the inhabitants had been shrewd enough to die before 1939, in their beds or in hospitals, one by one, before the Germans arrived and death became a mass production. The visitors' party walked along straight weeded paths between grand marble slabs lettered in gold with predominantly Germanic names, the same names – Strauss, Steiner, Loeb, Goldberg – whose live ranks still march through the telephone directories of New York City. The Ambassador and the two young workmen led the way, conversing in Czech – rather loudly, Bech thought. To judge from the Ambassador's expansive gestures, he could be extolling the merits of the free-enterprise system or diagramming the perfidy of Gorbachev's latest arms-reduction proposal.

"I find this very embarrassing," Bech told the Ambassador's wife, who walked beside him in silence along the lightly crunching path.

"I used to too," she said, in her pleasantly scratchy Midwestern voice. "But, then, after a couple of years with Dick, nothing embarrasses me; he's just very outgoing. Very frontal. It's his way, and people here respond to it. It's how they think Americans ought to act. Free."

"These young men – mightn't they lose their jobs for letting us in?"

She shrugged and gave a nervous little toss of her long blond hair. It was an affecting, lusterless shade, as if it had been washed too often. Her lips were dry and thoughtful, with flaking lipstick. "Maybe they don't even have jobs. This is a strange system." Her eyes were that translucent blue that Bech thought uncanny, having seen it, through his youth, mostly in toy polar bears and mannequins on display in Fifth Avenue Christmas windows.

"How well," Bech said, looking around at the elegant and silent black stones, "these people all thought of themselves."

"There was a lot of money here," the Ambassador's wife said. "People forget that about Bohemia. Before the Communists put an end to all that."

"After the Germans put an end to all *this*," Bech said, gesturing toward the Jewish population at rest around them. There were, curiously, a few death dates, in fresh gold, later than 1945 – Jews who had escaped the Holocaust, he supposed, and then asked to be brought back here to be buried, beneath the tall straight planes with their mottled trunks, and the shiny green ivy spread everywhere like a tousled bedspread. Burial plots, records, permits – these things persisted.

"Here he is, your pal," the Ambassador loudly announced. Bech had seen photographs of this tombstone – a white stone, relatively modest in size, wider at the top than at the bottom, and bearing three names, and inscriptions in Hebrew that Bech could not read. The three names were those of Dr. Franz Kafka; his father, Hermann; and his mother, Julie. In his last, disease-wracked year, Kafka had escaped his parents and lived with Dora Dymant in Berlin, but then had been returned here, and now lay next to his overpowering father forever. A smaller marker at the foot bore the names of his three sisters – Elli, Valli, Ottla – who had vanished into concentration camps. It all struck Bech as dumbfoundingly blunt and enigmatic, banal and moving. Such blankness, such stony and peaceable reification, waits for us at the bottom of things. No more insomnia for poor hypersensitive Dr. Franz.

Bech thought he should try a few words with their young hosts, who had shown some knowledge of English. "Very great Czech," he said, pointing to the grave.

The broader-shouldered young man, who had wielded the key that let them in, smiled and said, "Not Czech. Žid. Jude."

It was a simple clarification, nothing unpleasant. "Like me," Bech said.

"You" – the other boy, more willowy, with plaster even in his hair, pointed straight at him – "vonderful!"

The other, his eyes merry at the thought of talking to an

internationally famous writer, made a sound, "R-r-r-r-rum, *rrroom*," which Bech recognized as an allusion to the famous rubber-faced motorcyclists of *Travel Light*, with its rapes and rumbles and its desolate roadside cafés on their vast gravel parking lots – Bech's homage, as a young Manhattanite, to the imaginary territory beyond the Hudson. "Very *americký, amerikanisch*," the young man said.

"*Un peu*," Bech said and shrugged, out of courtesy abandoning English, as his conversational companions had abandoned Czech.

"And *Big Thinking*," the shorter boy said, emboldened by all this pidgin language to go for an extended utterance, "we love very much. It makes much to laugh: TV, skyscrapes." He laughed, for absolute clarity.

"Skyscrapers," Bech couldn't help correcting.

"I loved Olive in that novel," the Ambassador's wife said huskily at his side.

This, Bech felt, was a very sexy remark: Olive and the entire television crew, under the lights; Olive and her lesbian lover Thelma, in the West Side apartment as the tawny sun from New Jersey entered horizontally, like bars of music. . . .

"Kafka more *Schmerz*," his Czech fan was going on, as if the buried writer, with his dark suit and quizzical smile, were standing right there beside the still-erect one, for comparison. "You more *Herz*. More – " He broke down into Czech, turning to face the Ambassador.

"More primitive energy," the Ambassador translated. "More raw love of life."

Bech in fact had felt quite tired of life ever since completing his last – his final, as he thought of it – and surprisingly successful novel, whose publication coincided with the collapse of his one and only marriage. That was why, he supposed, you traveled to places like this: to encounter fictional selves, the refreshing false ideas of you that strangers hold in their minds.

In Czechoslovakia he felt desperately unworthy; the unlucky country seemed to see in him an emblem of hope. Not only had his first and last novels been translated here (*Lekhá cesta, Velká myšlenka*) but a selection of essays and short fiction culled from *When the Saints* (*Když svatí*). All three volumes carried opposite the title page the same photo of the author, one taken when he was thirty, before his face had bulked to catch up to his nose and before his wiry hair had turned gray; his hair sat on his head then like a tall turban pulled low on his forehead. The rigors of Socialist photogravure made this faded image look as if it came not from the 1950s but from the time before World War I, when Proust was posing in a wing collar and Kafka in a bowler hat. Bech had ample opportunity to examine the photo, for endless lines formed when, at a Prague bookstore and then a few days later at the American Embassy, book-signing sessions were scheduled, and these Czech versions of his books were presented to him over and over again, open to the title page. His presence here had squeezed these tattered volumes – all out of print, since Communist editions are not replenished – up from the private libraries of Prague. Flattered, flustered, Bech tried to focus for a moment on each face, each pair of hands, as it materialized before him, and to inscribe the difficult names, spelled letter by letter. There were many young people, clear-eyed and shy, with a simple smooth glow of youth rather rarely seen in New York. To these fresh-faced innocents, he supposed, he was an American celebrity – not, of course, a rock star, smashing guitars and sobbing out his guts as the violet and magenta strobes pulsed and the stadium hissed and waved like a huge jellyfish, but with a touch of that same diabolic glamour. Or perhaps they were students, American-lit majors, and he something copied from a textbook, and his signature a passing mark. But there were older citizens, too – plump women with shopping bags, and men with pale faces and a pinched, pedantic air. Clerks? Professors? And a few persons virtually infirm, ancient enough to remember the regime of Tomáš Masaryk, hobbled forward with a kindly, faltering expression like that of a childhood sweetheart whom we cannot at first quite recognize. Most of the people said at least "Thank you"; many pressed a number of correctly shaped, highly complimentary English sentences upon him.

Bech said *"Děkuji"* and *"Prosím"* at random and grew more and more embarrassed. Across the street, Embassy underlings gleefully whispered into his ear, Czech policemen were photographing the line; so all these people were putting themselves at some risk – were putting a blot on their records by seeking the autograph of an American author. Why? His books were petty and self-indulgent, it seemed to Bech as he repeatedly signed them, like so many checks that would bounce. In third-world countries, he had often been asked what he conceived to be the purpose of the writer, and he had had to find ways around the honest answer, which was that the purpose of the writer is to amuse himself, to indulge himself, to get his books into print with as little editorial smudging as he can, to slide through his society with minimal friction. This annoying question did not arise in a Communist country. Its citizens understood well the heroism of self-indulgence, the political grandeur of irresponsibility. They were voting, in their long lines, for a way out, just as Bech, forty years before, stuck on Manhattan like archy the cockroach, had composed, as a way out, his *hommages* to an imaginary America.

The Ambassador and his minions arranged for Bech to attend a party of unofficial writers. "Oh, those sexy female dissidents," the Ambassador's wife softly exclaimed, as if Bech were deserting her. But she came along. The party, and the apartment, somewhere off in the unscenic suburbs that visitors to historic Prague never see, and that Bech saw only that one night, by the veering, stabbing, uncertain headlights of the Ambassador's private little Ford Fiesta, were reminiscent of the Fifties, when Eisenhower presided over a tense global truce and the supreme value of the private life was unquestioned. Bookshelves to the ceiling, jazz murmuring off in a corner, glossy-haired children passing hors d'oeuvres, a shortage of furniture that left people sprawled across beds or hunkered down two to a hassock. The hostess wore a peasant blouse and skirt and had her hair done up in a single thick pigtail; the host wore a kind of dashiki or wedding shirt over blue jeans. Bech felt taken back to the days of relative innocence in America, when the young were asking only for a little more freedom, a bit more sex and debourgeoisation, a whiff of pot and a folk concert in a borrowed meadow. These people, however, were not young; they had grown middle-aged in protest, in dissidence, and moved through their level of limbo with a practiced weariness. Bech could see only a little way into the structure of it all. When husbands could not publish, wives worked and paid the bills; his hostess, for instance, was a doctor, an anesthesiologist, and in the daytime must coil her bulky pigtail into an antiseptic cap. And their children, some of them, were young adults, who had studied in Michigan or Iowa or Toronto and talked with easy American accents, as if their student tourism were as natural as that of young Frenchmen or Japanese. There was, beyond this little party flickering like a candle in the dark suburbs of Prague, a vast dim world of exile, Czechs in Paris or London or the New World who had left yet somehow now and then returned, to visit a grandmother or to make a motion picture, and émigré presses whose products circulated underground; the Russians could not quite seal off this old heart of Europe as tightly as they could, say, Latvia or Kazakhstan.

The wish to be part of Europe: the frustration of this modest desire formed the peculiarly intense Czech agony. To have a few glass skyscrapers among the old cathedrals and castles, to have businessmen come and go on express trains without passing through pompous ranks of barbed wire, to have a currency that wasn't a sham your own shop owners refused, to be able to buy fresh Sicilian oranges in the market, to hang a few neon signs in the dismal Prague arcades, to enrich the downtown with a little pornography and traffic congestion, to enjoy the harmless luxury of an anti-nuclear protest movement and a nihilist avant-garde – this was surely not too much to ask after centuries of being sat on by the Hapsburgs. But it was denied: the Czechs and the Slovaks, having survived Hitler and the anti-Hussites, had fallen into the Byzantine clutches of Moscow. Two dates notched the history of dissidence: 1968, the year of "Prague Spring" (referred to so often, so hurriedly, that it became one word: "Pragspring") and of the subsequent Russian invasion; and 1977, when Charter 77 was promulgated, with the result that many of its signatories went into exile or to jail.

Jail! One of the guests at the party had spent nearly ten years in prison. He was dapper, like the café habitués in George Grosz drawings, with a scarred, small face and shining black eyes. He spoke so softly Bech could hardly hear him, though he brought his ear close. The man's hands twisted under Bech's eyes, as if in the throes of torture. Bech noticed that the fingers were in fact bent, and some were without nails. How would he, the American author asked himself, stand up to having his fingernails pulled? He could think of nothing he had ever written that he would not eagerly recant.

Another guest at the party, wearing tinted aviator glasses and a drooping, nibbled mustache, explained to Bech that the Western media always wanted to interview dissidents and he had become, since released from his two years in prison, the one whom the avid newsmen turned to when needing a statement. He had sacrificed not only his safety but his privacy to this endless giving of interviews, which left him no time for his own work. Perhaps, he said with a sigh, if and when he was returned to jail, he could again resume his poetry. His eyes behind the lavender lenses looked rubbed and tired.

What kind of poetry did he write, Bech asked.

"Of the passing small feelings," was the considered answer. "Like Seifert. To the authorities, these little human feelings are dangerous like an earthquake; but he became too big, too big and old and sick, to touch. Even the Nobel could not hurt him."

And meanwhile food was passed around, the jazz was turned up, and in the apartment's other room the Ambassador and his wife were stretched out on the floor, leaning against a bookcase, her long legs gleaming, in a hubbub of laughter and Czech. To Bech, within his cluster of persecuted writers, the sight of her American legs seemed a glint of reality, something from far outside yet unaccountably proceeding, as birds continue to sing outside barred windows and ivy grows on old graves. The Ambassador had his coat off, his tie loosened, a glass in his hand. His quick eyes noticed the other American peering at his wife's legs and he shouted out, in noisy English, "Show Bech a book! Let's show our famous American author some *samizdat!*"

Everyone was sweating now, from the wine and pooled body heat, and there was a hilarity somehow centered on Bech's worried, embarrassed presence. He feared the party would become careless and riotous, and the government police surely posted outside the building would come bursting in. A thin young woman with frizzy black hair – a sexy dissident – stood close to Bech and showed him a book. "We type," she explained, "six copies maximum; otherwise the bottom ones too blurred. Xeroxing not possible here but for official purposes. Typewriters they can't yet control. Then bound, sometimes with drawings. This one has drawings. See?" Her loose blouse exposed, as she leaned against Bech to share the book with him, a swath of her shoulders and a scoop of her bosom, lightly sweating. Her glazed skin was a seductive tint, a matte greenish-gray.

Bech asked her, "But who binds them so nicely? Isn't that illegal?"

"Yes," was her answer. "But there are brave men." Her reproachful, inky eyes rolled toward him, as she placed the book in his hands.

The page size was less than that of American typewriter paper; small sheets of onionskin thickness, and an elite typewriter, had been used, and a blue carbon paper. The binding was maroon leather, with silver letters individually punched. The book that resulted was unexpectedly beautiful, its limp pages of blue blurred text falling open easily, with an occasional engraving, of Picassoesque nudes, marking a fresh chapter. It felt lighter, placed in Bech's hands, than he had expected from the thickness of it. Only the right-hand pages held words; the left-hand held mirrored ghosts of words, the other side showing through. He had been returned to some archetypal sense of what a book was: it was an elemental sheaf, bound together by love and daring, to be passed with excitement from hand to hand. Bech had expected the pathos, the implied pecking of furtive typewriters, but not the defiant beauty of the end result. "How many such books exist?"

"Of each, six at least. More asks more typing. Each book has many readers."

"It's like a medieval manuscript," Bech said.

"We are not monks," said the young woman solemnly. "We do not enjoy to suffer."

In the Ford Fiesta, the Ambassador's wife teased him, saying to

her husband, "I think our celebrated author was rather taken
with Ila."

The Ambassador said nothing, merely pointed at the ceiling of
the car.

Bech, not understanding the gesture, repeated, "Ila?" Ila; Elli,
Kafka's sister. "Is she Jewish?" The bushy hair, the sallow matte
skin, the tension in her slender shoulders, the way she forced
meaning through her broken English.

The Ambassador's wife laughed, with her scratchy light-
hearted voice. "Close," she said. "She's a Gypsy."

"A Gypsy," Bech said, as if he and she were playing a game,
batting words back and forth in the car's interior. He was sitting
in the back seat, and the Ambassador's wife in the front. Feeble
Socialist streetlight intermittently shone through her straw-pale
hair, which had been fluffed up by the fun of the dissident party.
"They have those here?" he asked.

"They have those here of course," she said, her tone almost
one of rebuke. "The French word for Gypsy is 'bohémien.' Many
are assimilated, like your new lady friend. Hitler killed quite a
few, but not all."

Hitler. To come to Europe is somehow to pay him a visit. He
was becoming a myth, like the Golem. Bech had been shown the
Old-New Synagogue, where the cabalist and alchemist Rabbi
Loew had read from the Talmud and concocted a Golem whose
giant clay remains still wait in the synagogue attic to be revived.
And the Pinkas Synagogue, its walls covered with the names of
seventy-seven thousand concentration-camp victims. And the
nearby hall filled with the drawings Jewish children drew while
interned at the camp at Terezín, houses and cows and flowers
such as children draw everywhere, holding their crayons tight,
seizing the world with stubby beginner's fingers. Communists
can always say in their own defense that at least they're not
Hitler. And that *is* something.

In alternation with the light on the filaments of the American
woman's hair, a vague black dread penetrated Bech's stomach, a
sudden feeling he used to get, when six or seven, of being in the
wrong place, a disastrously wrong place, even though he was
only three blocks from home, hurrying along upper Broadway in

a stream of indifferent strangers. "Those poor guys," he abruptly said. "The one with the slicked-down hair had been ten years in jail, and I glanced at a couple of his stories he showed me. They're like Saki, harmless arch little things. Why would they put him in jail for wanting to write those? I was looking at him, trying to put myself in his shoes, and he kept giving me this sweet smile and modest little shrug. You know the one I mean – old-fashioned suit and vest, one of those names full of zizzes –"

The Ambassador cleared his throat very noisily and pointed again at the low ceiling of the little car. Bech understood at last. The car was bugged. They spoke hardly a word all the rest of the way back to the Residence, through the gabled and steepled pro-file of midnight Prague. There was never, it seemed to Bech, any moon. Did the moon shine only on capitalism?

At the Residence, in the morning, it was nice to awake to the sound of birds and of gardeners working. One crew was raking up the winter leaves; another crew was getting the tennis court ready for the summer. Bech's bathroom lay many steps from his bed, through the sunny parqueted living room of his suite, with its gently curved walls. Mammoth brass fixtures, the latest thing in 1930, gushed water over Art Deco shower tiles or into por-celain basins big enough to contain a fish pond. Otto Petschek had bought only the best. Breakfast appeared at a long table in a dining room next door, where timid women fetched Bech what he had checked off on a printed form the night before. "*Prosím*," they said, as Italians say "*Prego*."

"*Děkuji*," he would say, when he could think of the word, which he found an exceptionally difficult one. *Jakui* is how the Ambassador's wife pronounced it, very rapidly. She was never at breakfast; Bech always ate alone, though sometimes other place settings hinted at other guests. There *were* others: a suave plump Alsatian photographer, with a slim male assistant, was photo-graphing the place, room by room, for *Architectural Digest*, and some old friends from Akron had come by on the way to Vienna, and the Ambassador's wispy daughter by a former marriage was taking school vacation from her Swiss *lycée*. But in the mornings all this cast of characters was invisible, and Bech in lordly solitude took his post-breakfast stroll in the garden, along the oval path whose near end was nestled, like an egg in a cup, into the curve of the palace and its graceful flagstone patio, past the raking gardeners and the empty swimming pool, around to where three men in gray workclothes were rolling and patting flat the red clay of the tennis court, just the other side of the pruned and banked rose garden, from which the warming weather had coaxed a scent of moist humus. He never met another stroller. Nor did he ever see a face – a princess, gazing out – at any of the many windows of the Residence.

It seemed that this was his proper home, that all men were naturally entitled to live in luxury no less, amid parquet and marquetry, marble hall tables and gilded picture frames, with a young wife whose fair hair would flash and chiffon-veiled breasts gleam when, in an instant, she appeared at a window, to call him in. As on a giant curved movie screen the Residence projected the idea of domestic bliss. What a monster I am, he thought – sixty-three and still covetous, still a king in my mind. Europe and not America, he further thought, is the land of dreams, of fairy-tale palaces and clocks that run backwards. Hitler had kissed the princess and made her bad dreams come true. But, then, there have been many holocausts. Bech had been shown the window of Hradčany Castle from which the Defenestration of Prague had occurred; though the emissaries defenestrated had landed unharmed on a pile of manure, the incident had nevertheless commenced the Thirty Years' War, which had decimated Central Europe. Bech had seen the statue of Jan Žižka, the one-eyed Hussite general who had piously slaughtered the forces of the Pope and Holy Roman Emperor for five years, and the statue in the baroque Church of St. Nicholas that shows a tall pope gracefully, beatifically crushing with the butt of his staff the throat of a pointy-eared infidel. For centuries, conquest and appropriation piled up their places and chapels on the crooked climbing streets of Prague. The accumulation remained undisturbed, though the Nazis, ever faithful to their cleansing mission, tried to blow things up as they departed. The mulch of history, on these moist mornings when Bech had the oval park to himself, was deeply peaceful. The dead and wronged in their multitudes are mercifully quiet.

A young citizen of Prague had thrust himself upon the cultural officers of the Embassy and was conceded an appointment to meet Bech. He bravely came to the Embassy, past the U.S. Marine guards and the posters of the dismantled Statue of Liberty, and had lunch with Bech in the cafeteria. He was so nervous he couldn't eat. His name was unpronounceable, something like Syzygy – Vítěslav Syzygy. He was tall and dignified, however, and less young than Bech had expected, with a dusting of gray in his sideburns and that pedantic strict expression Bech had come to know as characteristically Czech. He could have worn a pince-nez on his high-bridged narrow nose. His English was impeccable but halting, like a well-made but poorly maintained machine. "This is very strange for me," he began, "physically to meet you. It was twenty years ago, just before Pragspring, that I read your *Travel Light*. For me it was a revelation that language could function in such a manner. It is not too much to say that it transformed the path of my life."

Bech wanted to say to him, "Stop sweating. Stop trembling." Instead he dipped his spoon into the cafeteria *bramborovka* and listened. Syzygy, officially silenced as translator and critic since his involvement nearly two decades ago in "Pragspring," had spent these past years laboring upon an impossibly good, dizzyingly faithful yet inventive translation into Czech of a Bech masterwork, *Brother Pig*, not yet favored by a version into his language. *Bratr vepř* was at last completed to his satisfaction. Never, in his severely, precisely stated opinion, has there been such a translation – not even Pasternak's of Shakespeare, not Baudelaire's of Poe, constituted such scrupulous and loving *hommage*. The difficulty…

"Ah," Bech said, wiping his lips and, still hungry, wondering if it would be gross etiquette to dip his spoon into Syzygy's untouched bowl of milky, spicy *bramborovka*, "so there is a difficulty."

"As you say," Syzygy said. Bech now knew the code: the lowered voice, the eyes darting toward the ubiquitous hidden bugs – as great an investment of intramural wiring here as of

BECH AT BAY

burglar alarms in the United States. "Perhaps you remember, in the middle chapter, with the amusing title 'Paradoxes and Paroxysms,' how the characters Lucy and Marvin in the midst of the mutual seduction of Genevieve make passing allusions to the then-new head of the Soviet state, a certain Mr. —" Syzygy's eyes, the gentle dull color of the non-inked side of carbon paper, slid back and forth helplessly.

"Begins with 'K,'" Bech helped him out.

"'X,' in Russian orthography," Syzygy politely corrected, making a soft hawking sound. "A guttural letter. But exactly so. Our friends, how can I say — ?"

"I know who your friends are."

"Our friends would never permit such an impudent passage to appear in an official publication, even though the statesman in question himself died in not such good official odor. Yet I cannot bring myself to delete even a word of a text that has become to me, so to speak, sacred. I am not religious but now I know how certain simple souls regard the Bible."

Bech waved his hand magnanimously. "Oh, take it out. I forget why I popped it in. Probably because Khrushchev struck me as porcine and fitted the theme. Anything for the theme, that's the way we American writers do it. You understand the word, 'porcine'?"

Syzygy stiffened. "But of course."

Bech tried to love this man, who loved him, or at least loved an image of him that he had constructed. "You take anything out or put anything in that will make it easier for you," he said. But this was bad, since it implied (correctly) that how Bech came across in Czech couldn't matter to him less. He asked, apologetically, "But if you are in, as we say, not such good odor yourself with our friends, how do you expect to get your translation published?"

"I *am* published!" Syzygy said. "Often, but under fictitious names. Even the present regime needs translations. You see," he said, sensing Bech's wish to peer into the structure of it all, "there are layers." His voice grew more quiet, more precise. "There is inside and outside, and some just this side of outside have friends just on the inside, and so on. Also, it is not as if —" His very white hands again made, above his untouched soup, that curt helpless gesture.

"As if the present system of government was all your idea," Bech concluded for him, by "your" meaning "Czechoslovakia's."

The Ambassador, as they walked along cobblestones one night to a restaurant, felt free outdoors to express his opinion on this very subject. "Up until sixty-eight," he said in his rapid and confident entrepreneurial way, seeing the realities at a glance, "it was interesting to be an intellectual here, because to a degree they had done it to themselves: most of them, and the students, were for Gottwald when he took over for the Communists in *for*ty-eight. They were still thinking of *thir*ty-eight, when the Germans were the problem. But after *six*ty-eight and the tanks, they became an occupied country once more, with no responsibility for their own fate. It became just a matter of power, of big countries versus little ones, and there's nothing intellectually interesting about that, now is there, professor?"

Addressed thus ironically, Bech hesitated, trying to picture the situation. In his limited experience – and isn't all American experience intrinsically limited, by something thin in our sunny, democratic air? – power was boring, except when you yourself needed it. It was not boring to beat Hitler, but it had become boring to outsmart, or be outsmarted by, the Russians. Reagan was no doubt President because he was the last American who, imbued with the black-and-white morality of the movies, still found it exciting.

"I mean," the Ambassador said impatiently, "I'm no intellectual, so tell me if I'm way off base."

Bech guessed the little man simply wanted flattery, a human enough need. Bech sopped it up all day in Czechoslovakia while the Ambassador was dealing with the calculated insults of European diplomacy. "You're right on, Mr. Ambassador, as usual. Without guilt, there is no literature."

The Ambassador's wife was walking behind, with the wife of the Akron couple and the fashionable photographer's young assistant; their heels on the cobbles were like gunfire. The wife from Akron, named Annie, was also blonde, scratchy-voiced, and sexy with that leggy flip shiksa sexiness which for Bech was the glowing center of his American patriotism. *For purple mountain majesties* raced through his mind when the two women laughed, displaying their healthy gums, their even teeth, *for amber waves of grain.*

He was happy – so happy tears crept into his eyes, aided by the warm wind of this Prague spring – to be going out to a restaurant without having to sign books or talk to students about Whitman and Melville, the palefaces and red men, the black-humor movement, imperial fiction, and now the marvelous minimalists, the first wave of writers raised entirely within the global village, away from the malign influences of Gutenbergian literacy. Idolized Bech loved, at the end of a long day impersonating himself, being just folks: the shuffle around the table as he and his fellow Americans pragmatically tried to seat themselves, the inane and melodious gabble, the two American women sinking their white teeth into vodka fizzes, the headwaiter and the Ambassador enjoying their special, murmurous relationship. The husband from Akron, like the Ambassador a stocky business-man, sat nodding off, zombified by jet lag. They had flown from Cleveland to New York, New York to London, London to Frankfurt, rented a Mercedes, driven through the night, and been held six hours at the Czech border because among their papers had been discovered a letter from their hostess that included a sketchy map of downtown Prague. Communists hate maps. Why is that? Why do they so instinctively loathe anything that makes for clarity and would help orient the human individual? Bech wondered if there had ever before been regimes so systematically committed to perpetuating ignorance. Then he thought of another set: the Christian kingdoms of medieval Europe.

The Ambassador announced, "My friend Karel here" – the headwaiter – "informs me that several busloads of Germans have made reservations tonight and suggests we might want to move to the back room." To Bech he explained, "This is the only country in Europe both West Germans and East Germans have easy access to. They get together in these restaurants and drink pilsner and sing."

"Sing?"

"Oh boy, do they sing. They crack the rafters."

"How do the Czechs like that?"

"They hate it," the square-faced man said with his urchin smile.

The restaurant was in a vast wine cellar once attached to somebody's castle. They woke up the dozing Akron husband and moved to a far recess, a plastered vault where only the Ambassador could stand upright without bumping his head. Whereas Mr. Akron kept falling asleep, his wife was full of energy; she and the Ambassador's wife had sat up till dawn catching up on Ohio gossip, and then she had spent the day seeing all the available museums, including those devoted to Smetana and Dvořák and the one, not usually visited by Americans, that displayed the diabolical items of espionage confiscated at the border. Now, exhilarated by being out of Akron, Annie still maintained high animation, goading the Ambassador's wife into a frenzy of girlish glee. They had gone to the same summer camp and private school, come out at the same country-club cotillion, and dropped out the same year of Oberlin to marry their respective Republican husbands. Bech felt it a failing in himself, one further inroad of death, that he found there being *two* of them, these perfect Midwestern beauties, somehow dampening to his desire: it halved rather than doubled it. The thought of being in bed with four such cornflower-blue eyes, a quartet of such long scissoring legs, a pair of such grainy triangular tongues, and two such vivacious, game, fun-loving hearts quailed his spirit, like the thought of submitting to the gleaming apparatus in Kafka's story about the penal colony. Annie, on her second vodka fizz, was being very funny about the confiscated devices displayed in the border museum – radio transmitters disguised as candy bars, poison-dart fountain pens, *Playboy*s from the era when pubic hair was still being airbrushed out – but gradually her lips moved without sound emerging, for the Germans had begun to sing. Though they were out of sight in another part of the subterranean restaurant, their combined voices were strong enough to make the brickwork vibrate as the little low nook cupped the resonating sound. Bech shouted in the Ambassador's ear, "What are they singing about?"

"Der Deutschland!" the answer came back. "Mountains! Drinking!"

When the united German chorus began to thump their beer mugs on the tables, and then thump the tables on the floor, circular vibrations appeared in Bech's mug of pilsner. The noise was not exactly menacing, Bech decided; it was simply unconsciously, helplessly large. The Germans in Europe were like a fat man who seats himself, with a happy sigh, in the middle of an already crowded sofa. The Czech waiters darted back and forth, wagging their heads and rolling their eyes in silent protest, and a Gypsy band, having made a few stabs at roving the tables, retreated to a dark corner with glasses of brandy. Gypsies: Bech looked among them for the curly head, the skinny sallow shoulders of his dissident friend, who had talked so movingly about books, but saw only mustachioed dark men, looking brandy-soaked and defeated.

Next day – there seemed to be endless such days, when Bech awakened at his end of the palatial arc, shuffled in his bare feet across the parquet, through a room in which fresh flowers had always been placed, to the brassy, rumbling bathroom, and then breakfasted in enchanted solitude, like a changeling being fed nectar by invisible fairies, and took his proprietorial stroll along the oval path, bestowing terse nods of approval upon the workmen – the next day brought an appointment to meet some literary officials, the board of the publishing house that dealt with foreign translations. Out of loyalty to the dissidents he had met earlier in his visit, Bech expected to be scornful of these apparatchiks, who would no doubt be old, with hairy ears and broad Soviet neckties. But in truth they were a young group, younger by a generation than the aging dissidents. The boy who seemed to be chairman of the board had been to UCLA and spoke with an oddly super-American accent, like that of a British actor playing O'Neill, and his associates, mostly female, stared at Bech with brighter eyes and smiles more avidly amused than any that had greeted him among the dissidents – to whom he had been, perhaps, as curious in his insignificant freedom as they to him in their accustomed state of danger and melancholy indignation. These young agents of the establishment, contrariwise, were experts in foreign literature and knew him and his context well. They boasted to him of American writers they had translated and published – Bellow, Kerouac, Styron, Vidal – and showed him glossy copies, with trendy covers.

"Burroughs, too, and John Barth," a young woman proudly told him; she had a mischievous and long-toothed smile and might, it seemed to Bech, have Gypsy blood. "We like very much the experiment, the experimental. William Gaddis, Joan Didion, the abrupt harsh texture. In English can you say that? 'Abrupt texture'?"

"Sure," said Bech. "In English, almost anything goes." It embarrassed him that for these young Czechs American writing, its square dance of lame old names, should appear such a lively gavotte, prancing carefree into the future.

"Pray tell us," another, pudgier, flaxen-haired young woman said, "of whom we should be especially conscious among the newer wave."

"I'm not sure there is a new wave," Bech admitted. "Just more and more backwash. The younger writers I meet look pretty old to me. You know about the minimalists?"

"And how," the chairman of the board said. "Abish, Beattie, Carver – we're doin' 'em all."

"Well," Bech sighed, "you're way ahead of me. Newer wave than that, you'll have to dig right down into the fiction workshops. There are thousands of them, all across the country; it's the easiest way to get through college."

"*Less Than Zero*," the blonde pronounced, "was evidently composed in one such class of instruction."

The chairman laughed. "Like, really. He does a fantastic job on that sick scene."

"Good title," Bech admitted. "After the minimalists, what can there be but blank paper? It'll be a relief, won't it?"

The long-toothed woman laughed, sexily. "You talk the cynic, in the fashion of Mortimer Zenith in *Velká myšlenka*. Perhaps, we think here, this novel, with its ironical title *Think Big*, departs your accustomed method. Is your first attempt at post-literary literature, the literature of exhaustion."

"It seemed that bad to you?" Bech asked.

"That *good*, man," interposed the chairman of the board.

"Whereas *Travel Light* was your experiment in the Beatnik school," pursued the mischievous dark woman, "and *Brother Pig* your magic realism."

"Speaking of *Brother Pig* —"

"Is ready to print!" she interrupted gaily. "We have fixed the pub date — that is the expression? — for this autumn that is coming."

Bech continued, "I've met a man, a translator —"

The next interruption came from a slightly older man, with a square pragmatic head like that of the American Ambassador, at the far end of the table. Bech had not hitherto noticed him. "We know and value the work," he smoothly said, "of your friend Comrade Syzygy."

Bech took this to mean that they were using Syzygy's labor-of-love translation, and the Pragspring lambs were lying down with the Husák lions, and the levels of this mysterious fractured society were melding and healing beneath his own beneficent influence. With so pleasant a sensation warming Bech's veins, he was emboldened to say, "There's one novel of mine you never mention here. Yet it's my longest and you could say my most ambitious — *The Chosen*."

The members of the board glanced at one another. "*Vyvolení*," the sexy long-toothed girl, dropping her smile, explained to the square-faced man, who nodded. He had very thin skin; a nerve jumped at the corner of one eye.

In the face of their collective silence, Bech blushed and said, "Maybe it's a terrible book. A lot of American critics thought so."

"Oh, no, sir," the little blonde said, her own color rising. "Henry Bech does not produce terrible books. It is more a matter —" She could not finish.

The dark one spoke, her smile restored but the sparkle banished from her eyes by a careful dullness. "It is that we are feeling *Vyvolení* is for the general Czech reader too –"

"Too special," the chairman of the board supplied, quite pleased at having found the exact shade of prevarication within the English language.

"Too Jewish," Bech translated.

In chorus, somewhat like the Germans singing, the board reassured him that nothing could be too Jewish, that modern Czechoslovakia paid no attention to such things, that the strain of Jewish-American literary expression was greatly cherished in all progressive countries. Nevertheless, and though the meeting ended with fervent and affectionate handshakes all around, Bech felt he had blundered into that same emptiness he had felt when standing in the crammed Old Jewish Cemetery, near the clock that ran backwards. He knew now why he felt so fond of the Ambassador and his wife, so safe in the Residence, and so subtly reluctant to leave. He was frightened of Europe. The historical fullness of Prague, layer on layer, castles and bridges and that large vaulted hall with splintered floorboards where jousts and knightly elections used to be held; the museums with their halls of icons and cases of bluish Bohemian glass and painted panoramas of the saga of the all-enduring Slavs; the tilted streets of flaking plasterwork masked by acres of scaffolding; that clock in Old Town Square where with a barely audible whirring a puppet skeleton tolls the hour and the twelve apostles and that ultimate bogeyman Jesus Christ twitchily appear in two little windows above and, one by one, bestow baleful wooden stares upon the assembled tourists; the incredible visual pâtisserie of baroque church interiors, mock-marble pillars of paint-veined gesso melting upward into trompe-l'oeil ceilings bubbling with cherubs, everything gilded and tipped and twisted and skewed to titillate the eye, giant wedding-cake interiors meant to stun Hussite peasants back into the bosom of Catholicism – all this overstuffed Christian past afflicted Bech like a void, a chasm that he could float across in the dew-fresh mornings as he walked the otherwise untrod oval path but which, over the course of each day, like pain inflicted under anesthesia, worked terror upon his subconscious. The United States has its rough spots – if the muggers don't get your wallet, the nursing homes will – but it's still a country that never had a pogrom.

More fervently than he was a Jew, Bech was a writer, a literary man, and in this dimension, too, he felt cause for unease. He was a creature of the third person, a character. A character suffers from the fear that he will become boring to the author, who will simply let him drop, without so much as a terminal illness or a dramatic tumble down the Reichenbach Falls in the arms of Professor Moriarty. For some years now, Bech had felt his author wanting to set him aside, to get him off the desk forever. Rather frantically hoping still to amuse, Bech had developed a new set of tricks, somewhat out of character – he had married, he had written a best-seller. Nevertheless, and especially as his sixties settled on him, as cumbersomely as an astronaut's suit, he felt boredom weighing from above; he was – as H. G. Wells put it in a grotesquely cheerful acknowledgment of his own mortality that the boy Bech had read back when everything in print impressed him – an experiment whose chemicals were about to be washed down the drain. The bowls in his palace bathroom had voracious drains, gulping black holes with wide brass rims, like greedy bottomless bull's-eyes. *Ne, ne!*

Around him in Czechoslovakia things kept happening. Little Akron Annie returned from a shopping expedition in the countryside with an old-fashioned sled, of bright-yellow wood, with the fronts of the runners curved up like a ram's horns. Her children back in Ohio would love it. The photographer and his assistant had a fearful spat in French and German, and the boy disappeared for a night and came creeping back to the Residence with a black eye. The Ambassador, taking his wispy daughter with him, had to drive to Vienna for a conference with all the American Ambassadors of Central Europe for a briefing on our official stance in case Kurt Waldheim, a former assistant killer of Jews, was elected President of Austria. There was, in his un-avoidable absence, a reception at the Residence; Bech gave a talk, long scheduled and advertised, on "American Optimism as

Evinced in the Works of Melville, Bierce, and Nathanael West,"
and the Ambassador's wife introduced him.

"To live a week with Henry Bech," she began, "is to fall in
love with him."

Really? he thought. Why tell me now?

She went on quite brightly, leaning her scratchy voice into the
mike and tripping into spurts of Czech that drew oohs and ahs
from the attentive audience; but to Bech, as he sat beside her
watching her elegant high-heeled legs nervously kick in the
shadow behind the lectern, came the heavy, dreary thought
that she was doing her job, that being attractive and vivacious
and irrepressibly American was one of the chores of being an
American ambassador's wife. He stood blearily erect in the warm
wash of applause that followed her gracious introduction. The
audience, lit by chandeliers here in the palace ballroom, was all
white faces and shirtfronts. He recognized, in a row, the young
board of the publishing house for translations, and most of
the crowd had a well-groomed, establishment air. Communists,
opportunists, quislings.

But afterwards it was the dissidents, in checked shirts and
slouchy thrift-shop dresses, who came up to him like favored
children. The scarred man, his shiny black eyes mounted upon
the curve of his face like insect eyes, shook Bech's hand, clinging,
and said, apropos of the speech, "You are naughty. There is no
optimism."

"Oh, but there is, there is!" Bech protested. "Underneath the
pessimism."

The Gypsy was there, too, in another loose blouse, with her
hair freshly kinked, so her sallow triangular face was nested as in a
wide pillow, and only half-circles of her great gold earrings
showed. "I like you," she said, "when you talk about books."

"And I you," he answered. "That was *such* a lovely book you
showed me the other night. The delicate thin paper, the hand-
done binding. It nearly made me cry."

"It makes many to cry," she said, much as she had solemnly
said, *We are not monks. We do not enjoy to suffer.*

And a blond dissident, with plump lips and round cheeks, who
looked much like the blonde at the publishing house except that

she was older, and wiser, with little creased comet's tails of
wisdom trailing from the corners of her eyes, explained, "Václav
sends the regrets he could not come hear your excellent talk. He
must be giving at this same hour an interview, to very sympathetic West German newspaperman."

Syzygy, dark-suited and sweating as profusely as a voodoo
priest possessed by his deity, could not bear to look at Bech.
"Not since the premiere of *Don Giovanni* has there been such a
performance in Prague," he began but, unable out of sheer
wonder to continue, shudderingly closed his eyes behind the
phantom pince-nez.

At last Bech was alone in his room, feeling bloated by the
white wine and extravagant compliments. This was his last night
in the last palace built in Europe. Tomorrow, Brno, and then the
free world. The moon was out, drenching in silver, like the back
of a mirror, the great oval park – its pale path, its bushes with
their shadows like heaps of ash, the rectilinear unused tennis
courts, as ominous as a De Chirico. Where had the moon been
all week? Behind the castle. Behind Hradčany. Bech moved back
from the window and got into his king-size bed. From afar he
heard doors slam, and a woman's voice cry out in ecstasy: the
Ambassador returning to his bride, having settled Waldheim's
hash. Bech read a little in Hašek's *Good Soldier Schweik*, but even
this very tedious national classic did not soothe him or allay his
creeping terror.

He lay in bed sleepless, beset by panic. *Jako by byl nemocen,
zjistil, že může ležet jen v jedné poloze, na zádech. Obrátit se na druhý
bok znamenalo nachýlit se nad okraj propasti, převrátit se na břicho
znamenalo riskovat, že utone ve vodách věčného zapomnění, jež bublaly
ve tmě zahřívané jeho tělem.* A single late last trolley car squealed
somewhere off in the labyrinth of Prague. The female cry greeting the Ambassador had long died down. But the city, even
under its blanket of political oppression, faintly rustled, beyond
the heavily guarded walls, with footsteps and small explosions of
combustion, as a fire supposedly extinguished continues to
crackle and settle. *Zkoušel se na tyto zvuky soustředit, vymačkat z
nich pouhou silou pozornosti balzám jejich nepopiratelnosti, nevinnost,
která byla hlavním rysem jejich prosté existence, nezávisle na jejich*

dalších vlastnostech. Všechny věci mají tutéž existenci, dělí se o tytéž atomy, přeskupují se: tráva v hnůj, maso v červy. Temnota za touto myšlenkou jako sklo, z něhož se stírá námraza. Zkoušel si příjemně oživit svůj večerní triumf, předčítání odměněné tak vřelým potleskem.

He thought of the Gypsy, Ila, Ila with her breasts loose in her loose blouse, who had come to his lecture and reception, braving the inscrutable Kafkaesque authorities, and tried to imagine her undressed and in a posture of sexual reception; his creator, however, was too bored with him to grant his aging body an erection and by this primordial method release his terror, there in the Ambassador's great guest bed, its clean sheets smelling faintly of damp plaster.

Becha to neuspalo. Jeho panika, jako bolest, která sílí, když se jí obíráme, když jí rozněcujeme úpornou pozorností, se bez hojivého potlesku jitřila; nicméně, jako rána, zkusmo definovaná protiinfekčním a odmítavým vzepřením těla, začala nabírat jistou podobu. His panic felt pasty and stiff and revealed a certain shape. That shape was the fear that, once he left his end of the gentle arc of the Ambassador's Residence, he would – up in smoke – cease to be.

BECH PRESIDES

HENRY BECH had reached that advanced stage of authorship when his writing consisted mostly, it seemed, of contributions to Festschrifts – slim volumes of tributes, often accompanied by old photographs and an uneasy banquet at the Century Club or Lutèce or Michael's Pub, in honor of this or that ancient companion in literature's heady battles. These battles, even for their most enthusiastic veterans, took the form of a swift advance achieved in the dawn dimness of youthful ignorance, the planting of a bright brave flag in some momentary salient of the avant-garde's wavering front line, and then a sluggish retreat back through the mud of a clinging fame, sporadically lit by flares of academic exegesis. Such an honorable retreat could go on virtually forever, thanks to modern medicine, which keeps reputations breathing right through brain death.

Dear Mr. Bech:
   As you doubtless are aware, Isaiah Thornbush will turn seventy in 1991. We of the Aesop Press, casting about for a suitable commemoration of this significant milestone, came up with the idea of a Festschrift volume, in a boxed limited edition, with marbleized endpapers and a striped linen headband, to be made available only to his inner circle of friends and disciples. Our enthusiasm for this project is matched and heartily seconded by our parent firm, Grigson-Kawabata Corporation Ltd., and by Mr. Thornbush's longtime literary agent Larry "Ace" Laser, and by those of his seven children whom we have been able to trace and contact. Two of his three ex-wives have even agreed to write brief memoirs and to "vet" the text overall for accuracy!

We very much hope you will supply a contribution. Almost anything will do – a reminiscence, a poem, a photograph in which the two of you appear, a shared perception as to where Isaiah Thornbush's sterling example has been most helpful in your own artistic or personal development. Your considerable stylistic debt to him has been often remarked by critics and, though you did not mention him by name, was plainly hinted at in one of your wonderful autobiographical essays. (Exactly which one escaped all of us here at Aesop, though we spent hours this morning racking our brains!)

But anything, Mr. Bech, even the most informal sort of salute, will be gratefully received – the more "unbuttoned" the better, up to a point of course. Contributors will be invited to a festive occasion at the Thornbush Manhattan residence, hosted by his lovely wife Pamela, this fall, and we know you wouldn't want to be a missing face there. We eagerly await hearing from you.

Sincerely yours,
Martina O'Reilly
Associate Editor
Trade Division, Aesop Press

Like an irritatingly detailed fleck in the vitreous humor, Izzy Thornbush's all-too-familiar face floated in Bech's inner eye as he read: the lewdly bald head with its thrusting wings of white gossamer, the bulbous little nose decorated by a sprinkle of blackheaded pores, the wide fleshy mouth that ambitious dental work of recent years had pushed forward into an eerie simulacrum of George Washington's invincible half-grimace. He was two years older than Bech, and ever since the late Forties the two had been espying each other around Manhattan, two would-be lions in too populous a Serengeti. In his younger days Izzy had sported a Harpoesque mop of curly strawberry-blond hair; always he was brain-vain. He tried to write books with his head – heavy, creaking historical allegories, with Aristotle and William of Occam and Queen Nefertiti as historical characters, debating in a fictional auditorium surrealistically furnished with modern appliances. It all seemed rather lumbering to Bech – giant watchworks hacked out of wood – and quite lacking in what he, stylistically, prized: the fuzzy texture of daily life, that gray felt compacted of a thousand fibers, that elusive drabness containing countless minute scintillae. Bech's own tremulous, curvaceous early prose, kept supple by a reverent and perhaps cowardly close attentiveness to the subjective present tense, was at the opposite aesthetic pole from Thornbush's dense and angular blocks of intellectual history; yet both appeared in the short-lived literary journal *Displeasure* (1947–1953), and they could not help meeting at those Village cocktail parties and Long Island cookouts with which the postwar intelligentsia had hoped to restore, after the austerities of the duration, the bootlegged gemütlichkeit of the Twenties.

America's imperium, having strangled two snakes, was still a burly infant in those years. As the Forties shed their honest khaki for the peacock synthetics of Fifties populuxe, Bech and Thornbush oozed upward into eminence – Bech's breakthrough being the Kerowacky novel *Travel Light* (1955), and Izzy's his bawdy thousand-page saga, in mock-Chaucerian English, on the vicissitudes of philosophical realism in the Middle Ages, culminating in its destruction by the centripetal forces of nominalism and the bubonic plague (*Occam's Razor*, 1954). The analogies to McCarthyism, atomic fallout, and gray-suited conformity scarcely needed to be underlined, but the reviews underlined them nevertheless, and perhaps political awareness went to Izzy's head, which was stocked not just with highbrow erudition but with low mercantile cunning.

During the succeeding decades the two writers met at handsomely financed cultural symposiums in Aspen and Geneva, on quasi-ambassadorial forays to Communist countries, at sickeningly sweet prize-bestowing ceremonies, and, as the Sixties took hold, in the midst of protest marches and rallies. Izzy blossomed, in bell-bottoms and love beads, while his hair simultaneously thinned and lengthened, into a guru of the young. His double-column travesty of the Bible, *The LB-Bull*, setting forth with gory detail and unmistakable analogic resonance the anti-Mexican atrocities of the nineteenth-century war that followed upon the American annexation of Texas, all in a twangy slang that plainly aped the accents of the current President, became a

sacred text to college youth, an impressively erudite encouragement to indignation and revelry. For Bech, the Sixties were a
somewhat recessive time; a lungful of the mildest marijuana made
him sick, and draft evasion disgusted him, whether a war was
"good" or not. This veteran of the Bulge and the Rhine crossing
found it hard to cheer the American flag's being burned. His
magnum opus of domestic, frankly Jewish (at last) fiction, published in late November 1963, was buried under the decade's
unraveling consensus. His ironical title, *The Chosen*, turned out
to be ill-chosen, since Chaim Potok wrote a thumping best-seller
with the same title, used unironically, in 1967, and within a few
years the novel's sauciest, most Freudian bits were made to seem
tame by the more furious revelations of Philip Roth and Erica
Jong.

In the Seventies, however, it was Izzy's star that dimmed. His
massive *Nixoniad*, written in intricately "rhymed" couplets of
prose chapters, came out, though the printer rushed, six months
after its subject, apotheosized as a stumble-tongued Lord of
Misrule, had resigned and dragged his shame into the shadows
of San Clemente. Nixon-bashing had become obsolete, and
students, in an economy hungover from its own binge, were
more concerned about getting jobs than with exploring the
pleasures of an archly erudite anti-establishment romp weighing
in at half a million words. When, as the decade ended, Bech
startled himself and the world by outflanking a writer's block and
publishing a commercially successful novel for television-heads
called *Think Big*, Thornbush's sour grapes spilled over into print,
in a *Commentary* review ("Le Penseur en Petit") whose acid
content was left undiluted by his alligator tears of professed
prior admiration.

Not that Bech had ever liked Izzy's stuff. In fact, at bottom, he
didn't like any of his contemporaries' work. It would have been
unnatural to: they were all on the same sinking raft, competing
for dwindling review space and demographic attention. Those
that didn't appear, like John Irving and John Fowles, garrulously,
Dickensianly reactionary in method seemed, like John Hawkes
and John Barth, smugly, hermetically experimental. O'Hara,
Hersey, Cheever, Updike – suburbanites all living safe while

art's inner city disintegrated. And that was just the Johns. Bech would not have minded if all other writers vanished, leaving him alone on a desert planet with a billion English-language readers. Being thus unique was not a prospect that daunted him, as he sat warming his cold inspirations, like a chicken brooding glass eggs, in the lonely loft, off lower Broadway, to which he had moved when his suburban marriage to his longtime mistress's sister had been finally dissolved. Solipsism was the writerly condition; why not make it statistical? Certainly the evaporation of Izzy Thornbush was a pleasing fancy. Those protruding eyes and hair-wings; those oversize, over-white capped teeth; that protruding intellect, like the outthrust boneless body of a poisoned mollusc whose shell has fatally relaxed – *pffft!* Bech's disrespect had intensified when, in the flat wake of the miscalculated *Nixoniad*, Thornbush, whose three previous wives had been muscular, humorous, informal women of Jewish ancestry and bohemian tastes, had bolstered his ego by capturing the hand of a shiksa heiress – apple-cheeked, culturally ambitious Pamela Towers, whose father, the infamous Zeke Towers, a New Jersey cement mixer, had made good on his family name by becoming, as vertical plate-glass replaced stepped-back brick in the skyline, one of Manhattan's real-estate magnates. In the luxury of Park Avenue, Palm Beach, and East Hampton residences Izzy, the former artificer, maker of mazy verbal Pyramids, need build no more; a magnificently kept man, he need oversee only the elaborate buttressing of his crumbling reputation. Nevertheless:

Dear Ms. O'Reilly:
    The voice of praise, rising in my throat to do justice to my dear old friend Isaiah Thornbush, is roughened by the salty abrasions of affection and nostalgia. How different the map of postwar American fiction would be without the sprawling, pennanted castles of his massive, scholastically rigorous opuses – intellectual *opera* indeed! "Here be dragons" was the formula with which the old cartographers would mark a space fearsomely unknown, and my own fear is that, in this age of the pre-masticated sound-bite and the King-sized gross-out, the vaulted food court where Thornbush's delicacies are served is too little patronized – the demands that they, pickled in history's brine and spiced with

cosmology's hot stardust, would make upon the McDonaldized palate of the reader, to whom, were he or she ideal, every linguistic nuance and canonical allusion would be mentally available, have become, literally (how else?), unthinkable. Not that my delicious old friend Izzy ever betrays by any slackening of his dizzying pace the slightest suspicion of being cast by fate in the role of a wizard whose tricks are beyond his audience's comprehension, or, like those of a magician on doctored film, too easily accounted for. *Au*, as the well-worn phrase runs, *contraire*: he continues to bustle – there is no other word – hither and yon on errands of literary enterprise, judging, speaking, instructing, introducing, afterwording, suffering himself to be impaneled and honored to the point where we shyer, less galvanic of his colleagues vicariously sag under the tonnage of his medals and well-weighed kudos. Soldier on, comrade, though the plain where ignorant armies clash is more darkling than ever; sail on, Izzy, and remind all those who glimpse your bellying spinnaker upon the horizon that there was once such a thing as Literature!

Ms. Reilly, the above is for publication and oral recitation – what follows is for your eyes and no doubt dainty ears only. You may not think it unbuttoned enough. If you deign to use it, don't, I repeat DO NOT, change my punctuation or break up the continuous rhapsodic exhalation of my paragraph. By the way, Aesop is good to undertake this; the commercial houses are conspicuously sitting on their hands in the case of serious writers like Thornbush. I understand his last romp through the stacks (Middle Kingdom, pre-Marco Polo, right?) saw seven publishers before the eighth, who printed it only with extensive cuts and elimination of all passages not in Roman typeface and the English language. Also by the way, how did a maiden called Martina meet a man called O'Reilly? Or are you the product of a tempestuous mating between a Communist expat and an IRA gunrunner?

Your nosy pal,
Henry Bech

The Festschrift party was held in the Thornbush penthouse, the fifteenth and sixteenth floors of a chaff-colored brick building on Park. Sharp-edged minimalist statuary was dangerously scattered about on veneered French antiques. Moonlighting young actresses and actors in all-black unisex outfits passed, with the eerie schooled grace and white-faced expressionlessness of mimes, slippery hors d'oeuvres besprinkled with scallion snips. High on the two-story wall of the duplex, above a circular spiraling glass stairway, a huge Tibetan banner, a *thang-ka*, suspended above the heads of the living a tree, a *tshog shing*, of rigid, chalk-colored, but basically approachable deities. In the vast living room that yet was too small for this gabbling assemblage, cigarette smoke, that murderous ghost of the past, was briefly thick again. Bech saw around him dozens of half-forgotten faces, faces of editors and agents and publicists and publishers who had moved on (fired and rehired, sold out to a German conglomerate, compelled to scribble news briefs for a Stamford cable station) yet remained eerily visible within the gabby industrial backwater of New York publishing. And there were painters – hawk-nosed, necktieless, hairy, gay – because Izzy was among his other accomplishments a reviewer for *ARTnews* and an expert on Persian miniatures, Quaker furniture, misericords, and so on. And there were composers – smooth, barrel-chested party animals in double-breasted suits, their social skills brought to a high polish by lives of fine-tuning students and buttering up patrons – because Izzy was himself an accomplished amateur violinist who, had not his big brain dragged him away from his finger exercises, might have had a concert career and who, it was said, contributed not just the words but the melody line of several crowd-pleasing songs in the musical comedy, *Occam!*, based upon his first novel, as well as several of the numbers in the bawdy review, *Nefertiti Below the Neck*, loosely derived from his second. And there were history professors Izzy had befriended in the course of his researches, including the famously tall one and the famously short one, who insisted on huddling *tête-à-tête*, like the letter "f" ligatured to the letter "i," and, finally, there were writers – in a single glance Bech spotted Lucy Ebright with her shining owl eyes and swanlike neck, and Seth Zimmerman with his self-infatuated giggle, and Vernon Klegg in his alcoholic daze. But it was Pamela Thornbush, Lady Festschrift herself, who came up to Bech, her rosy cheeks echoed by the freckled pink breasts more than half exposed by the velvet plunge of her plum-colored Prada. She had another woman in tow, a firm-bodied young woman dressed in mousy gray, with the dull skin and militant, faintly angry bearing that Bech associated with the beauties of Eastern Europe, those formerly Communist hussies whose attractions had been at the service of the Stasi, the ÁVÓ, the KGB. "Dear Henry," Pamela said, though they had not met many times previously, "Izzy was just touched to tears by what you wrote about him; I never have seen him so moved, honestly. And this is our beautiful Martina, who pulled the whole project together. She still talks about your fresh letter."

Bech grasped the slim cool hand proffered, which mustered a manly squeeze while her eyes leveled into his own. She was his height, perhaps an inch less. Her eyes were a grave shade of hazel. "At my age," he told her, "it's either fresh or frozen."

How strangely, unironically *there* this Martina was, though not quite beautiful; she had no sheen of glamour. She was all business. "I hope you noticed," she said, "that I defended your paragraph from the copyeditors. As you predicted, they wanted to break the flow." She spoke with the easy quickness of a thoroughly naturalized American, yet the words had an edge of definiteness, as if she did not quite trust them to convey her full meaning – a remnant, Bech guessed, of her immigrant parents' accents.

"Copyeditors do hate flow," he said. "I haven't looked into the book yet, actually. I thought it might make me too jealous. I'm all of sixty-eight, and nobody fests my schrift."

"You're too young, Mr. Bech. You must reach a round number."

"I'm not sure," he said, seriously – this steady-eyed woman was an invitation, received however late in life, to be serious; he checked their vicinity to verify that Pamela, the freckled, fabulous, still-girlish heiress, had moved on, having made this little conversational match – "that I have Izzy's gift for round numbers. Look at the bastard. The perfect host, lapping up homage. He should have been a Roman emperor."

Thornbush, with the sixth sense that the literary jungle breeds, intuited from far across the room that Bech was talking about him; his protuberant eyes, with their jaundiced whites, slid toward his old colleague, even as a ring of adorers exploded into laughter at his most recent witticism, hot from his fat and flexible tongue.

In response to Bech's mustered seriousness, Martina intensified her own. For emphasis she rested her cool fingers on the back of his hand, where it clasped a drink at his chest, a bourbon getting watery as he radiated heat. "People are afraid of you," she said in a scallion-scented gust of sincerity that tingled the hairs in his avid nostrils. "You're so pure. I think they think you'd laugh at the idea of a Festschrift. You'd scoff at the concept that people love you."

He considered the possible truth of this, as he contemplated the waxy white crimps of her ear. This ear was bared beneath a taut side of sensible brown hair, and was, as he had hazarded in their only previous communication, dainty. Fancy anticipates reality. He liked the old-fashioned severity of her hairdo, pulled back into a ponytail secured by a ringlet of silk, a pink cloth rose – an appealing cheap touch. He liked thrift in a woman, an ascetic self-careless streak; it showed the fitness needed to travel even briefly with him on his rocky road. "They're right, I would," Bech answered. "Praise that you squeeze out of people is worth about ten cents on the dollar. Enough about me. Tell me about you."

She let her level gaze drop while her sallow cheek, above her firm, excitingly antagonistic jaw, resisted a blush. "You had it only slightly wrong. My parents got out in '68, when I was three years old. My husband wasn't a gunrunner but in mergers and acquisitions, if you can see the difference."

"Was? Was in mergers and acquisitions, or was your husband?"

"The latter. I'm sorry I wrote 'unbuttoned.' I was nervous. Pamela was frantic to have you in the Festschrift. I thought you'd spit on it. I was both grateful and disappointed when you didn't."

This, again, took them to a level of seriousness where neither was quite prepared to breathe. "I succumbed," he admitted. "To your blandishments. I've been to Czechoslovakia," he added.

"Of course. Everybody goes now. It's cheap, and Prague is raunchy."

"I was there when it was still real. Still Communist. That huge statue of Stalin. Those aging hippieish dissidents. It seemed like a very lively, tender place. Vulnerable."

"Yes, we are. The Czechs were put too close to fiercer peoples. Even when we broke free, we smiled our way out."

"Nothing wrong with that. Would that we all could."

Her hands were clutched in front of her, one cupping the other, which held a glass of red wine tipped at a dangerous angle. He dared reach out and touch her. Her hand had seemed cooler when she had touched him. "Watch your back," he said. "Here comes the birthday boy."

Izzy Thornbush, the few hairs on his head sprung upright in party excitement, toddled to the duo. Standing beside Martina as if in military formation, he squeezed her shoulders hard enough to make her snicker in surprise. But she kept her wine from sloshing out. "She's some tootsie, huh, Henry, like we used to say?"

"The term hadn't occurred to me," said Bech gallantly.

"She's been my best buddy at Aesop," the much-honored scrivener went on. "The rest of those young slobs over there now are computerniks who think the written word is obsolete junk. They don't care about grammar, they don't care about margins. This young lady is a real throwback, to the age of us dinosaurs."

"I have always loved books," Martina said, with a little wriggle that loosened the wordmaster's bearlike grip. "I like the way," she said, "the reader can set his or her own pace, instead of some director on speed or Prozac, who sets it for you." Did Bech imagine it, or did her lips threaten a stammer, as her almost-native English stiffened on her tongue? Bech was annoyed to think that she was impressed, or intimidated, by Izzy.

The novelist's massive eyebrows – thickets wherein russet sparks struggled to stay alight amid wands from which all color and curl had been extracted – lifted in appreciation of this bulletin from the pharmaceutical generation. "There's never been enough organized thought," he announced, "on how a reader's input helps create the book. We have no equivalent to the art installation, where the viewer is also the orderer."

"Well, there was *Hopscotch*," Bech said. "And Barthes somewhere writes about how he always skips around in Proust."

"A computer system," Izzy was wool-gathering on, his eyes popping and bubbles of saliva exploding between his lips, "say, *À la Recherche* on CD-ROM, could generate a new path, an infinite series of new paths, through it, making a new novel every time – there could be one in which Jupien is the hero, or in which Albertine becomes Odette's lover!"

"A reader doesn't want decision-making power," Martina said, a bit testily, in the face of Thornbush's eminence. Perhaps she was showing Bech she was less intimidated than he, onlooking, had thought. "You read because no decisions are asked of you, the author has made them all. That is the luxury."

"But isn't this," Izzy said, displaying that he was not too old to have developed a Derridean streak, "a mode of tyranny? Isn't a traditional author the worst sort of maniacal Yahweh, telling us how everything must be?"

Bech glanced upward, wondering if Yahweh, who used to consider it a dreadful uncleanness to have His name in a mortal mouth, would strike Thornbush dead. Or had Izzy through marriage and promiscuously roving the world of ideas become so little a Jew as to enjoy a goyish immunity? A cool hard pressure on his hand recalled Bech to earth; Martina, formal and mannish, was shaking his hand goodbye. "I'll leave you two to settle these great matters," she said. "A pleasure to meet you, Mr. Bech. Thank you again for your wonderful contribution."

"Goodbye so soon? Perhaps," he ventured, "when and if I get my own Festschrift . . ."

Her serious deepset eyes met his; no smile crimped her unpainted lips. "Or sooner," she said sternly.

Sooner? Bech scented sex, that hint of eternal life. Her face, unadorned, held a naked promise that her body did not deny. Izzy rotated his great neckless head to watch her gray-clad derrière, firm but a touch more ample than was locally fashionable, disappear into a smoky wall of animated cloth. "Cute," he muttered. "Bright. Knock the Commies all you want, they put some backbone into their brats you don't see in American kids that age – gone limp in front of the damn television."

"She came here when she was three, she told me," Bech said.

"You learn more by three than all the rest of your life," Thornbush rebutted. "Read Piaget. Read Erikson. Read anybody, for Chrissake – what the hell do you do all day in that empty loft downtown? Nobody can figure it out."

But he had an agenda. Now it was Bech's turn to feel the force of Izzy's grip, on his upper arm, through a patched tweed sleeve. "Henry, listen. How'd you like to head up the Forty? Do us all a favor and be the next president. Von Klappenemner's term's up, and it's time we got a younger guy in there, somebody from the literary end. These composers, they look good presiding, but they have no head for facts, and a few facts come up from time to time, even there."

The Forty – its number of members a wistful imitation of the French Academy – was one of the innumerable honorary organizations that the years 1865–1914, awash in untaxed dollars, had scattered throughout Manhattan. It was housed in a neoclassical, double-lot brick-front in the East Fifties, near the corner of Third Avenue, where the glass boxes – Citicorp! the Lipstick Building! – were marching north. An unwed heiress, Lucinda Baines, who, like Pamela Thornbush, fancied herself a patroness of the arts, had left her grand townhouse, with a suitable endowment, to serve as the gracious gathering-place of the hypothetical forty best artists – painters, writers, composers, sculptors – in the country. Her fortune had stemmed from a nineteenth-century nostrum called Baines' Powders, a fraud taken off the market by the Pure Food and Drug Act of 1906, but not before its illusory powers of palliation had eased many a rough-hewn death; the powders were gone but the fortune rolled on, keeping the mansion in heat and repair, feeding the faithful at the Forty's half-dozen ceremonial dinners a year, and funding a clutch of annual awards to the possibly deserving with which the organization preserved its tax-exempt status. A small paid staff fulfilled the daily duties, but by a romantic provision of Lucinda's will the membership itself owned the building and controlled the endowment. "How come you're involved?" Bech asked, perhaps rudely.

When Izzy blinked, massive lashless eyelids had to traverse nearly a full hemisphere of yellowing eyeball. "I'm on the board."

"What about *you* for president? Isaiah the prez: that has a ring to it."

"You schmo, I *was* president, from '81 to '84. Where were you? Try to pay attention – you never come to the dinners."

"I'm watching my figure. Don't you find, once you pass sixty-five –"

"Yeah, yeah. Listen, I got to circulate. The wife is giving me the evil eye. But think of Edna – she'd love it. She's dying for you. I'm asking on behalf of Edna." Edna was the directress, a wiry little white-haired spinster from Australia. "Don't make her beg, at her age. The whole board is crazy about the idea. They delegated me, since they thought we were friends."

"Izzy, we *are* friends. Read your fucking Festschrift."

"People can be friends. Writers, no. Writers are condemned to hate one another, doesn't Goethe somewhere say? *Mit der Dummheit kämpfen Götter....* Or was that Schiller? Forget it. I'm putting this forward as a person. Loosen up. Remember the good times we had in Albania? We were the first Western writers in over the top."

"Slovenia, *not* Albania. Nobody got into Albania. Ljubljana World Writers for Peace, in the Carter years. How could you have forgotten, Izzy – that frisky little blond poet from the Ukraine we had to do everything with in fractured French? Remember how she showed us the trick with a little tomato, biting it after tossing down a shot of vodka?"

It had been Bech, though, and not Thornbush that she had taken back with her to her cell of a room in the people's hotel. But much of the fervor of the encounter had been wasted in a breathless whispered discussion, in uncertain French, of birth control. She had kept rolling her eyes toward the corners of the room, indicating, as if he didn't know, that the walls were bugged. He knew but as an American didn't care. Perhaps she had been risking the gulag for him. How lovely in its childlike skinniness her naked body had been! Her pubic hair much darker than the hair on her head. The acid aftertaste of cherry tomato fighting with the sweetness of vodka in his mouth. She had halted him halfway in, with a stare of those wide scared eyes, eyes a many-petaled Ukrainian blue. For all the liquor she had consumed, she had been tight in the cunt, but he pushed on. She seemed relieved when he came, too soon. He had tried to wait, staring at a painting above the headboard. Shabby as the furniture was, the walls held real paintings, rough to the touch: the Socialist state supporting its hordes of collaborationist daubers.

As if he had accompanied Bech in his swift dip into memory, Thornbush sighed heavily and said, "They gave us a good time, the Commies. We're going to miss 'em."

"They soured me on writers' organizations. I don't want to be president of the Forty."

"Is that what you want me to tell Edna? You think I can go to her and tell her that? She's getting on, Henry. She's going to retire one of these days. Why break her heart? Be a pal. Be a *chaver*."

"Out of thirty-eight members not you or me," Bech patiently said, "there must be somebody else who can do it. How about a woman? Or a black?"

Once you start to argue with somebody like Thornbush, it becomes a negotiation. His painful grip on Bech's arm resumed. "There aren't forty of us, we're four or five short of the full body. Those that can do it have all done it. We're all old as bejesus. Any time a slot opens up in the membership, one old bastard puts up another, even older. As the Forty goes, you're a *kid*. Come *on*; I've done it; there's nothing to it. Two meetings a year, spring and fall; you can skip some of the dinners. All you've got to do is preside. Just *sit* there on your famous *tochis*."

Martina O'Reilly had emerged from the smoky wall of cloth, wearing an olive-drab loden coat, looking inquisitively everywhere but toward him. She was going to leave, Bech saw, and was giving him a chance to leave with her. If he missed this boat, who knew when there would be another? The docks were crumbling, like those off the West Fifties that had bustled with tugs and toughs when he was boy. "I'm not a presider," he told Izzy, more sharply, "I'm a — "

A learner rather, Stephen Dedalus had said, but Bech didn't finish, stricken by the way that Martina, resolving now to leave alone, glancing about with the reckless quickness of a woman in tears, reached up with both hands and lightly brushed back, in a symmetrical motion, some long strands straying from her severe hairdo.

"Cop-out," Izzy finished for him. "Above-it-all. That's the beauty of you for this post – you don't dirty yourself, generally, with being a nice guy. That's why we especially need you, after a string of these twelve-tone gladhanders. *Edna* needs you; she's got a bunch of senile fogeys on her hands."

"Izzy, let me think about it. I got to go."

"The fuck you'll think about it. Your check is in the mail, too. I know a brush-off." He had grabbed both Bech's forearms and the (slightly) younger author feared that he would have to wrestle the powerful older to escape. Martina was receding in the corner of Bech's squeezed field of vision. She was hatless, hurrying.

"O.K.," Bech said, "I'll *do* it. I'll do it, maybe. Have Edna call me and tell me the duties. Tell Pamela for me it was a great party, a great coronation."

"What's your rush? There's real eats coming. I wanted you to meet Pam's brother, he's a hell of a good egg, a genius in his line – moves real estate around like a chess player. And Pam wanted to talk to you about one of her pets, some benefit up at the Guggenheim."

"I bet she did. Another time. Izzy" – he found himself giving the man a hug, Communist-style, Brezhnev to Chou En-lai – "they don't make bullshitters like you any more."

He hustled through a scrum of late arrivals in the foyer, whose walls were hung with silk prayer rugs from Kazakhstan, and saw ahead of him a pink cloth rose about to disappear. "Hey," he called. "Hold the elevator!"

Once they were sealed in together, softly plunging the fifteen stories down, he saw from the satisfied set of Martina's unpainted lips that she was not surprised by his pursuit; she had hoped for it. "Thanks," he said to her. "For holding the door." She had thrust her bare hand into its rubber-edged jaws. "Getting hot in there," he nervously added. "*Trop de fest*." He did feel warm, across his chest and under his arms: his exertions in coping with Izzy and escaping the party, but also a curious nagging satisfaction, a swollen sense of himself. President Bech. He had made, for wrong enough reasons, the right decision.

He rather liked presiding. Perhaps seven or eight of the Forty attended the biannual meetings. In what had been the solarium of the dainty Baines mansion, Bech sat at the massive president's desk – mahogany, with satinwood inlay – and in a facing row of leather wing chairs some of the most distinguished minds of his generation feigned respectful attention. Edna slipped the agenda to him beforehand on a sheet of paper and sat at his side with a tape recorder, taking notes on the proceedings. There might be a matter of repairs to the exquisitely designed building; or of the salary of Gabriel, the Hispanic caretaker who lived in the basement with his wife and three children; or of the insurance on the paintings and drawings that Reginald Marsh, John Sloan, William Glackens, William Merritt Chase, and the like had casually bestowed, as gentlemanly pleasantries, upon the place, and that by now had grown so in value that the insurance was prohibitive. And then there was the matter of new members – in the past two years death had opened up six new vacancies, and of thirty-four nomination requests mailed out this year only three had been returned. The array of sage and even saintly old faces confronting Bech politely, inscrutably listened. Edna adjusted the volume of her tape recorder and placed it closer to the edge of the desk, to catch any utterance from the quorum of the Forty. The quorum had once been ten but in response to poor attendance had been reduced to five. The meetings were held at dusk, before one of the dinners, so rush traffic was roaring north on Third Avenue, buses chuffing, trucks shifting down, taxis honking. It was hard to hear, even for those not hard of hearing. Across the street, trailer tractors moved in and out, laboriously backing, of a nameless bleak building that took up a third of the block.

J. Edward Jamison, whose novels of city manners had been thought sparklingly impudent as late as 1962, quaveringly spoke up: "There's this fellow Pynchon appears to be first-rate. At least, my grandsons adore his stuff. Computers is what they mostly care about, though."

"He'd never accept," croaked Amy Speer deLessups, one of the few female members and faithful in her attendance, perhaps because she lived in Turtle Bay, a modest hop to the south. Her rhyming confessions of her many amours had once created a sensation, thanks to her strict metrical defiance of the prevailing vers-libre mode. Now it was the amours themselves that seemed scandalous, in connection with this shriveled, wispy body, lamed by arthritic joints. She walked with a cane, wore black velvet bell-bottoms, and carried her little wrinkled round face tipped up, a flirtatious habit left over from her days of comeliness. She went on, creakily turning in her chair to address Jamison and almost shouting in her pain, "He turns down *ev*erything. These younger ones are like that. They think it's *smart*, not to belong. I was the same at their age."

Jamison perhaps had failed to hear her despite her effort, or had grasped only the most general import of her words, for he replied ambiguously, "Not a bad idea. Then there's this Salinger my grandsons used to talk about. Not so much lately; now they've discovered the Internet, and girls."

"He won't accept either," Amy shouted.

This exchange awoke Aaron Fisch, a small and gnomish painter whose peculiar enameled, fine-focus style of surrealistic political allegory had peaked in the late Thirties, plateaued for four popular years as war propaganda (no one could do Mussolini as he could, with five-o'clock shadow and jutting lower lip, and Hirohito in all his military braid, and Hitler's burning black eyes in a lean white poisoned-looking face), and then had, postwar, fallen swiftly into abysmal unfashionability, though Aaron himself lived on. A decade or more ago his work resurfaced in the art magazines as an anticipation of photorealism, but his recent paintings, as his eyes and fine motor control failed, were increasingly rough, more and more like Soutine. Blinking, repeatedly pushing his thick black-framed spectacles back on his small nose, he looked toward Bech and asked, "Mr. President, have we ever given consideration to Arshile Gorky? Or did he never become an American citizen?"

"Aaron, he's *dead*," the other painter present, Limbaugh Seidensticker, gloomily erupted. "He committed suicide."

"Who?" the little surrealist asked, looking about in alarm, and almost piteously returning his pink-lidded gaze to the president, for guidance.

"Arshile Gorky, Mr. Fisch," Bech said.

"Oh, of course. I knew that. A wonderful sensibility. His onions and bulb-forms; very organic. He never understood why the Abstract Expressionists took him up."

This may have been deliberately tactless, since Seidensticker was an adamantly abstract painter, who worked entirely with commerical paint rollers and latex colors straight from the hardware-store can. Not since his moment of revelation in 1947 had he deviated from his faith that painting's subject was painting, pure paint itself, and even the rectangular shape of the canvas was an embarrassing outworn tie with the picture/window fallacy. There were almost none like him left; the resurgence of figuration, among young artists who had no training in how to draw, had left him sputtering on his flat fields of chaste monochrome. "It's a scandal," he said now, "that Donald Judd isn't a member."

"Oh, Limby, don't you think if you've gone and seen one aluminum box you've seen them all?" Amy intervened, tipping up her wrinkled face to him like a round dish to be filled with sunlight, as the last rays of the spring afternoon bounced off the blank side walls of the truck depot across the street and sidled into Lucinda Baines' old solarium. Once plants had flourished under its greenhouse dome; the faces of the Forty seemed to Bech flowers, yellowish blooms of ancient flesh suspended against the Rembrandtesque gloom of the dark leather chairs.

"It would be a scandal if he were," said Aaron Fisch. "What about Andy Wyeth? He's been coming along lately. Those Helga things weren't as bad as people said."

Limbaugh Seidensticker snorted. "Oh, all that *hu*man interest! All those half-rotting fenceposts and flowering weeds, stalk by stalk! *Yukk*, as the young people say." Rage was galvanizing his body, lifting his head into the declining light so that his rimless glasses formed ovals of blind brightness. "Next we'll be entertaining purveyors of pictotrash like David Hare."

"He's dead," someone in the chairs said.

"He was just a boy," another softly exclaimed.

Edna cleared her throat and whispered something to Bech.

Bech said, "The directress informs me that Andrew Wyeth is already a member, though he rarely attends."

"In that case," Seidensticker rather boomingly announced, "I resign." But he did not get up from his chair.

Bech asked the group, "Is there any more discussion of possible new members?"

Silence.

"Does anyone wish to second the nomination of Donald Judd?"

Again, silence.

"Mr. President." Another old, especially dignified voice quavered into audibility, above the whir of Edna's tape recorder and the muffled rumble of traffic.

"Yes, Mr. MacDeane?" Amory Henry MacDeane was a historian, an avid chronicler of the dowdy, unsatisfactory stretches of national government between Jackson and Lincoln, when the United States, its founding successfully consolidated, ineffectually sought a compromise that would hold the South in the Union without giving everything, including all the West, over to the proponents of black slavery. MacDeane, the son of an Ohio Scots-Irish factory owner, had several times abandoned the halls of academe for those of Washington, where he had advised Democratic administrations in their own compromises as they sought to contain Communism without engaging it in nuclear war. MacDeane knew Russian, French, German, and Italian, and had acted as ambassador to several ticklish, demonstration-prone countries; he wrote his histories and memoirs in elegiac Victorian periods imbued with the sadness of an advisory realism, this consideration always balancing that. Bech admired him, as an intellectual who had willingly dirtied himself with decision-making in the realm of real, as opposed to coveted, power. Now he was old, over eighty, and scoop-faced, with a mustache the same faded tint as his gray skin, and lived in New York only because he had lost the way back to Ohio, the vanished Ohio of his youth. He spoke in quavery, fine-spun sentences. "The difficulty of obtaining nominations, so that the functioning membership of the so-called Forty is actually thirty-four, of whom the meagre quorum I count here as seven – eight, with the president – leads me to wonder, Mr. President, if our beloved institution, so benignly conceived and pleasantly housed, is not perhaps destined to join those other institutions whose historical moment is past. One thinks, on a far larger scale of course, of the Grand Army of the Republic, so mighty and influential in its time, and the Industrial Workers of the World, known as the Wobblies. There is no disgrace in death," the old diplomat went on in his faint, husky, but still superbly controlled voice. "The disgrace comes in prolonging life with artificial and unseemly means."

"I agree," Isaiah Thornbush announced from the end of the row, with uncharacteristic brevity. His position surprised Bech. Izzy soaked up honors and loved clubs; Bech had always rather despised him for it.

Eric Von Klappenemner, tall and bald and with a piercing flutelike delivery, said, "Oh, all my friends, it's so *bor*ing, they say they don't want this and they don't want that, they don't want oxygen and they don't want electronic resuscitators or whatever they are; I say to them, Why not? I want it *all*! Oxygen and IVs and bloody livers and bone marrow and all of it! What's the purpose of science, if not to prolong human life?"

"Klappy, you're so *greedy*!" Amy deLessups flirted. How did so addictively heterosexual a woman, Bech wondered, view a homosexual like Von Klappenemner? Fondly, it seemed. As a fellow caster of the pearl of oneself before male swine.

"It's not *me*, it's not any senseless *hun*ger for my personal existence, there's nothing I'd like better than a good long afternoon *nap*, a nap that never ends, it would be *splen*did. It's what I can still *give* people, all that beauty and majesty still locked up in me – suppose Beethoven had thrown it all in after that rather piffling Eighth Symphony; we'd have never had the glorious *Ninth*!"

Von Klappenemner had reached that stage of mental deterioration when verbal inhibitions lift, though the old habits of syntax are still intact. He had been, with his gleaming head and those curling Nordic lips spouting wicked drolleries from beneath his Saracen curve of a nose, a universal charmer; now the dimming solarium held, like a sound-swallowing baffle of nippled black foam rubber, the hush of his charm falling on deaf ears. The melody was still there, but the body's aged instrument could no longer play it. Bech felt he was coming to the babbling composer's rescue, saying, "Perhaps we're straying from the topic."

"What is the topic?" Aaron Fisch unabashedly asked.

"Isn't it time for cocktails?" J. Edward Jamison seconded.

"The topic is the dearth of new members," Bech told one, and then the other: "It is only ten minutes to six, Mr. Jamison. Let me say, before we proceed to the last item of the agenda" – Edna had cleared her throat and placed, suppressing a stab of impatience, a supremely sharp pencil-point upon the item still to be discussed – "that I am surprised to hear talk of dissolution, if that is what I have just heard. The purposes for which Miss Baines made her generous bequests are still valid. American society has not been so transformed since 1902 that the arts need no longer be honored, nor is there, to my knowledge, any other organization quite like ours – so purely and disinterestedly honorary. Are any of you suggesting that the artistic spirit – the appetite for truth and beauty – has suddenly died? If so, I missed the obituary in the *Times*. Many worthy prospective members exist, to fill up the spaces in our ranks; a meeting such as this serves, primarily, as an occasion to vent our views. Nominations should be submitted in writing, with the signature of one other member as a second. Then, in due course, we will vote, as our predecessors always have and our successors always will."

"Well said, Henry," Edna murmured at his side.

Indeed, his firmness in defending an organization he in fact viewed as superfluous surprised Bech. The words came out of him as crisply as if Teletyped; the president within, whom he had never suspected was there, had spoken. And the elderly bodies seated before him – inspiration-scarred warriors in the battle for precision and harmony, for order in a world where the concept of divine order had become an obscene joke – fell silent under his conservative barrage, his rattling salute to continuity. "The last item on the agenda," Bech announced, his eyes bent on Edna's pencil-point, "is less existential and more practical. Gabriel Mendez, who, as you all know, lives in our basement as caretaker and watchman, has told Edna that he and his family must have more nearly adequate health benefits. Their youngest child evidently needs a great deal of specialized care."

Once it was ascertained that the endowment, benefiting from the steady rise in stock prices since the crash of October '87, could foot the bill, the benefits were voted, eight to none. A good deed done, with money not theirs. Yet, rising from his heady session of presiding, Bech felt the floor under him tip, the long dark desktop curve downward at both edges, and the emptying wing chairs defy perspective. The president was somehow on a slippery slope. Wasn't the Forty from its turn-of-the-century founding based on a false belief that art naturally kept company with gentility, both gracefully attendant on money – that money and power could be easily transmuted into truth and beauty, and that a club of the favored could exist, ten brownstone steps up from the pitted, filthy, sorely trafficked street? What was he doing here, presiding?

He lived on the west side of Crosby Street, that especially grim cobbled canyon of old iron-façaded industrial structures running south from Houston, one block east of lower Broadway. He occupied a loft so vast he had been able, finally, to get his books into a single set of shelves, a ramshackle rampart of pine planks on cinder blocks, Marx next to Marvell, Freud in all his frowning paperbacks between the slim poems of Philip Freneau and the leather-swaddled chronicles of Jean Froissart – picked up for four dollars when Bech was a GI-Bill student at NYU.

Bech could be said to be both a keen reader and the opposite; he nervously plucked at any journal or newspaper within reach of his hand, often leafing through back to front, a habit left over from his childhood, when mass magazines ran their cartoons toward the back. He pulled books from his shelves fitfully, quickly pleased or bored by a page, but he rarely settled to read a book through. This browsing was selfish and superstitious: he was looking for clues that would help him turn his own peculiar world into words, and he resisted submitting for long to another author's spell. After half an hour of reposing in his antique beanbag chair, in the carpeted island in the center of his single great room furnished in scattered islands, he would need to go outside, where the dour but populated streets fed another kind of scanning. Running-shoe-shod tourists cruising the galleries; art salesmen lugging wrapped rectangles; a fork-bearded, red-shirted geezer fresh, it seemed, from the hills of Kentucky; a young man with bleached-blond ponytail flying by on an absurdly small motorized scooter; a pair of young women totally in black prolongedly embracing, either in passionate reunion or determined demonstration of gay pride, the shorter of them wearing thrillingly brutal square-heeled black boots dotted with silver studs; a plump social worker leading on a knotted cord a quartet of the blind, with their sunken sockets and undirected smiles – all such bits of street theatre excited Bech with a sense of human life, a vast inchoate atmosphere waiting, like the lead-gray sky seen through the fire escapes overhead, to be condensed and experienced as drops of rain or as letters of type.

For years he had lived at 99th Street and Riverside Drive, before a romantic excursion into marriage had taken him to a Westchester suburb and another excursion (into the body of his wife's sister) had brought him ingloriously back to the city. Within its confines, he had headed south, off the numbered grid. Here in SoHo the flash and glitter of youthful aspiration mingled with the clangor of old warehouse enterprise. There were cobblestones and elaborate dirty ironwork; there were still greasy bicycle shops and men in bloody butchers' aprons. The area below Houston – that light-filled slash in Manhattan's close-woven fabric – had once been known as Hell's Hundred Acres, because of its infernal sweatshops and frequent fires. Long black limousines out of Little Italy prowled between aisles of graffiti-sprayed metal shutters. Signs in Chinese popped up on its south-eastern edge. From spots on Broome and Spring Streets Bech could see both the gleaming needle of the Chrysler Building and the looming outcrop of the financial district, topped by the twin spireless World Trade towers, box cathedrals. In the lowlands of SoHo Bech experienced an oddly big sky and a sensation – important, he felt, for an artist – of the disreputable, if not (there were too many art galleries and cappuccino joints) of the proletarian.

Martina earnestly considered his confessed queasiness in regard to the Forty. She brought to every issue he raised an intent, unsmiling consideration he associated with Communist peace conferences, of which he had attended a few. "What is the point, again," she asked, "of the Forty?"

"To exist, simply. A city on a hill, sort of. A mountain seen from the *plains*. This woman, Lucinda *Baines*, left her dandy townhouse and a lot of ill-gotten *gains* for a kind of French Academy, though we have none of their responsibilities. They keep working away at a French dictionary, for one thing, and have uniforms with braid."

The long-dead Lucinda, he realized, had become one of his love objects, and little efficient Edna another. His imagination bred a needy flock he lived to serve and placate – ewes who gave him an identity as shepherd. He was an old-fashioned gallant, Henry Bech; in all the women of his life he was seeking truth and goodness. A great reservoir of both must lie, he reasoned, with an entity able to take his sexual agitation and turn it into a limpid, post-coital peace. Martina moved around the carpeted island, set in a sea of boards splintered by vanished industrial machinery, on solid bare feet, in a white terrycloth robe that an inamorata of Bech's, the volatile Claire Hoagland, had stolen long ago from their room in the Plaza, in one of her caprices. There was little capriciousness in Martina; she took literary giants seriously, even in their underwear.

"I wonder," she mused, "if it wasn't a dead idea even then. I mean, old guys sitting around drinking port and smoking cigars and telling each other what fine fellows they are – how William Dean Howells can you get?"

"Poor Howells," Bech said. "Everybody thinks of him as a toastmaster. In fact, the older he got, the more radical he became. I can't say the same for myself. You should have seen Edna's face when I defended the Forty so stoutly – her jaw dropped nearly back to Alice Springs."

It was charming when Martina laughed, the cautious dimpling and half-smothered eruption, her Socialist conscience checking her acquired American freedom to mock. "It is unlike you," she said. "You usually scoff at pomp and pretension."

"But the Forty is not pompous, it's *touch*ing. Almost nobody comes. Those that do are deaf or senile. The place has paintings on the wall we can't afford the insurance on. Everything inside is so exquisite and Grecian – high sculpted plaster ceilings and no two fireplaces carved alike – and across the street squats this huge uncaring flank of some building where dozens of trailer trucks seem to live."

"New York is full of uncaring buildings," she solemnly said. "What does your friend Isaiah Thornbush think about this anachronistic Forty?"

"Who knows? He got me into the presidency, and then at the spring meeting he hardly spoke up. At one point he announced he agreed with MacDeane about something, but it could have been about dying, preventing extraordinary measures. We got onto that somehow. The discussion rambled."

"Why do you like presiding?"

Martina had spent the night, and so was there to greet the mid-morning sun as it threw golden rhomboids of warmth into the loft. She had curled her body in one of them, on a sofa opposite Bech's beanbag, across his glass coffee table and striped Peruvian rug. Bea, Bech's nicely domestic ex-wife, had covered a cracked old leather sofa of his with nubbly beige wool; nestled upon it, with her bare feet palely protruding from her robe, Martina suggested a big blintz – the terrycloth the enfolding crepe, her flesh the pure soft cheese. Her sunstruck toes wiggled in idle pleasure, and her hair swirled in a loose tangle all about her broad face. Her brows, usually thick and straight and stern, were interrogatively arched.

How good it was of women, Bech thought, not for the first time, to allow you intimacy with them, sharing their pleasure in the simplest elements of life. You can, through chinks in the male armor, feel a fraction of the bliss that must tumble in upon them all day long. "I suppose I like having the attention," he answered, "even as a formality, of men and women whose accomplishments I respect. Old poops now, it may be, they once put their minds and hearts on the line and tried to make something decent.

Think of all that MacDeane knows about Millard Fillmore. Think of how he's made himself care about Calhoun. Even Von Klappenemner – all the Beethoven he's passed through his head and his arms, he's earned the right to call one of the symphonies piffling. I find that moving."

"I find it rather shocking," Martina said, "and likewise that you're so impressed. You saw the Writers' Unions perform their thuggery in Communist countries – why isn't the Forty more of the same?"

"Well, those were closed shops, and the politicians were pulling the strings. We're above politicians, or beneath their notice. Mailer a couple of years ago had George Shultz, when he was Reagan's Secretary of State, address a PEN conference, and everybody jumped all over him."

"And you didn't like that?"

"I didn't like the jumping, no. Free speech ought to be Shultz's right too. He gave a rather nice speech, but nobody listened. All that mob of intelligentsia cared about was hissing Reagan and the contras."

Martina slowly uncurled, pressing her feet into the cushion against the sofa's far arm. "Wasn't that clever of Izzy," she purred, "to know that you were presidential timber? Under that curly head of hair, behind those rumpled eyes, such a true-blue conservative."

"Oh, Izzy," he said, offended by her familiar reference to the old phony. "He gives intelligence a bad name." Was she, he wondered in his most paranoid moments, a tool of Izzy's Stasi? His fingerprints were all over her.

She put her feet down, so for a moment they were viewed by Bech as if in a glass case, through the coffee-table top, their yellow heels and pink toes and blue instep veins displayed on red-and-black Peruvian stripes, and then she sidestepped languidly around the coffee table, her hands on the loose knot of her terrycloth robe. "Henry, I think it's so darling, that you have all these traditional sentiments. What did people used to say? Corny. It's a real turn-on." She lightly undid the belt. From within the parted folds of her robe, her naked body, displayed inches from his face, emitted the warmth and scent of food, a

towering spread of it, doughy-pliant yet firm, lustrous, with
visible mouthable details, tits pussy hips navel armpits, each
with its flavor, its glaze, its tang of overwhelming goodness.
Martina fucked administeringly, amused from a small distance
and then the distance diminishing until she was lost in its absence.
The Forty and its dainty mansion could not hold a candle to
this.

The fall meeting was better attended than the spring's had
been. Of the faithful, little Aaron Fisch had died; there would
be no more nominations for Arshile Gorky. Seidensticker,
MacDeane, Jamison, Von Klappenemner, Izzy, and Amy deLessups were there, along with six or seven more, not all of whom
Bech knew. There were: Jason Marr, one of the two African-
Americans among the Forty, a pale and suave preacher's son
whose essays, long-lined poems, and surrealistic fictions were
unremittingly full of rage and dire prophecy; X. I. Fong, a
refugee from Mao's China whose large pale penciled abstractions
thrillingly approached invisibility; Isabella Úrsula "Lulu" Buendía
Fleming, a Venezuelan diplomat's daughter whose many years as
a girl and then young woman in Washington had led to fluent
English, an American marriage, and a remarkable graft of magic
realism upon the humdrum substance of suburban Maryland; and
three or four others in the back row, probably composers, wearing dark suits. Edna read the minutes of the last meeting, which
were approved. How could Edna's meticulous handiwork ever
be disapproved? Several special repair requests – the copper
flashing on the slate roof over the front portal had buckled in
last summer's heat wave, and a bronze sundial, in the shape of a
rampant griffin, donated by the late Paul Manship to stand in the
ivy bed in the rear garden, had been bent and spray-painted by
vandals – were passed. A tribute to Aaron Fisch was read,
surprisingly, by Lulu Fleming; that was why, Bech realized, she
had made the trip up from Bethesda. She found in Fisch's work a
worthy Lower East Side equivalent of the idealistic mural art of
Rivera and Siqueiros, with something of Salvador Dalí's hal-
lucinatory high finish, itself derived from the ardent literalism

of Catholic altar painting; it was in this broad and bloody stream of anonymous popular style that our deceased friend and colleague Aaron Fisch, she asserted, ultimately stood.

The report on election results was discouraging. None of the four candidates duly nominated and seconded over the course of the summer received a majority of the votes cast by mail ballot or the ten-vote minimum established by the by-laws. Oral nominations to fill the now seven new vacancies came sluggishly and begrudgingly. The name of William Gaddis, put forward by Thornbush, was batted aside with the phrase "Joycean gibberish" by J. Edward Jamison, and that of Jasper Johns met unenthusiasm in Seidensticker's summation of "Pop tricks and neo-figurative doodles – he had an abstract phase, but it turned out to be insincere." When MacDeane mentioned Susan Sontag, Amy pertly shot out her chin and said, "*Sonntagskind ist Montags Mutter*," which made several of the shadows in the back – polyglot composers – laugh out loud.

Bech announced, rather desperately, "If we don't ever manage to elect anybody, the institution will dwindle to nothing."

The venerable MacDeane, his distinguished hangdog face tinged by the lingering tan of a Nantucket summer, pronounced in faint and quavery syllables, "As I took the liberty of suggesting at our last meeting, Mr. President, would that be an entirely unfortunate development? Perhaps our institutional body is trying to tell us something – that the moment for *gloire* is by. War ceased, in the trenches of 1914–1918, to be a means of *gloire* that any civilized man could condone, and now I wonder, with the passing of the Cold War, if *gloire* by even peaceful means is not an idle hope, a misbegotten vision based upon dissolved intellectual conventions. I raise this possibility quite without joy; but it is often a historian's duty to describe that which gives him – or her, of course – no joy."

Glwaar, Bech thought to himself, trying to wrap his mind around the juxtaposed consonants. Had it been to *glwaar* that he had been enslaved, denying himself a paying job, a spread of progeny, a life that was more than an excuse for those few minutes of each day when he was secreting words that might, possibly, harden to become, if not imperishable diamond, translucent amber, holding in it a captured moment like an extinct bug? An abyss of wasted minutes opened beneath Bech and Edna, Edna his sterile partner in immortality management, Edna his presidential bride, here at the great dark desk whose satinwood-rimmed top stretched toward the horizon like the flight deck of an aircraft carrier. In her neat but jagged hand, relentless as a cardiograph, Edna was etching notes on yellow legal paper, while the tape recorder at her angular elbow purred. Beneath its top the desk had a portly bowed shape, as if its sides were bending outward under invisible pressure from above.

A shadowy man in the back row half-stood, waving his hands like a conductor during an allegro movement. "There are no more composers!" he called. "There is only electronic tapes! That is all the young musicians care about! To elect one of them would be to elect a machine!"

Seidensticker growled in agreement, "Painting now is all crap – victim art with stick figures. Ever since Kiefer and Kienholz hit it big, atrocities are all you get – the Holocaust, the slave trade, rape, ecology, blah blah. Everything is a protest poster. Always excepting my distinguished colleague here." X. I. Fong, who never spoke at meetings, managed a beaming little kowtow without leaving his seat. Seidensticker went on, trying now to be gracious to the dead, "At least Aaron had the excuse of when he was born, back in those American Scene dark ages – the kids now have no excuse, and they know it. It's all gallery politics, and who are the gallery customers? New York liberals soaking up guilt, or else Japanese and Arabs wanting some soft porn for their dens."

"Shit," announced Eric Von Klappenemner, six months further gone into the de-inhibitions of dementia. "What they call art now is shit, smeared on the wall, smeared into your ears. Where is beauty? Trashed underfoot. Where is grace, discipline, self-denial? All gone up the boob tube. My young friends say, Watch TV, it's American meditation. But I say it's shit, I don't mince my words. They don't either. They tell me, You are a fucking old fool."

"Klappy, why do you have such rude young friends?" Amy deLessups asked, rolling her eyes roguishly at the composer, who was staring above her head to one side of Bech's head, where the tricolor (maroon, gold, and indigo) flag of the Forty hung limp on its standard, next to a portrait of Clarence Edmund Stedman, its first president, a Wall Street broker and a poet with a fleecy, trapezoidal beard. Not even Yahweh had had a whiter beard.

Bech, perched in Stedman's seat like a rat on a throne, surveyed the leather arc of immortals, looking for a friend. "We've heard from an artist, a composer, and a historian; how do the poets and novelists among us feel?"

"How do *you* feel, Bech?" J. Edward Jamison asked in peppery rejoinder. "Can you read any of these kids? I mean, the ones under sixty?"

"There is no magic," Lulu Fleming volunteered, with her enchanting small trace of Spanish singsong. "There are these facts, this happened and then that happened, all told in this killingly clean prose. They have advanced degrees in creative writing; they go to these workshops and criticize each other, there is nothing left to criticize, but something is missing, I don't know what it is – a love of the world, some hope beyond the world."

"I read these younger women poets," Amy deLessups said, "and it seems they've slept with the same men I did, or the same women, but they came to it ironically, wrapped in irony for protection, and knew ahead of time it wouldn't work. Perhaps," she admitted, her little round face seductively dimpling, "they had read my poems."

"I confess, ladies and gentlemen," Bech told the chairs, "that new fiction makes me tired. All that life that isn't mine. All that clamoring 'Look at me!' But I thought the fault might be mine, the effect of age. Izzy, what do you think? You still read everything, you have the digestion of an ox. When and where these days is fiction not weary?" Izzy attended these meetings in a kind of watchful sulk, ever since Bech had become president; he deserved being put on the spot.

Slumped in the second row, Thornbush roused, and pronounced, "If you'd asked me in the Seventies, I would have said Latin America; in the Eighties, Eastern Europe. Now, with the Nineties, the whole globe seems on hold. Maybe the great stuff is all on the Internet and we don't know how to access it yet. Mr. President, I'd like to propose a moratorium on new members until after the millennium clears the air."

"Second," said one of the composers in the back row.

There were a number of other seconds.

"Motion made and seconded," Bech had to say, though he knew it was all mischief. "Discussion?"

Edna cleared her throat beside him and said, in her thrilling Anglo-Australian twang, "If I may make a point. The by-laws are very clear about our electing new members. It's our main responsibility, virtually our *only* responsibility. I'm not sure we wouldn't be forfeiting our charter, and the endowment with it, if such a motion passed." Her white hair, cut in Prince Valiant fashion, trembled at the thought. Discreetly she bent her gaze back to her yellow pad, where she noted her own remarks. Bech fought an urge to pat her sleek head comfortingly.

"But we can't seem to find anybody," Amy sang out sweetly, "as wonderful as ourselves."

"We must *try*," Bech said, in his most severe presidential voice. "We must think back, to when we were on the outside, looking in. Suppose the then members had been as fastidious as we seem to be now?"

"Times are different," Seidensticker said. "Money and the media hadn't hopelessly corrupted everything yet. You heard Eric say it — it's all shit."

"*Please*," the president said primly.

X. I. Fong spoke up, smiling. "Lim, Lim, not that bad. Like always — some O.K., some not O.K. Things go in seasons. Change, never change."

Izzy Thornbush's stentorian voice cut across these melodic formulations. "Mr. President, there is a motion on the floor."

"We're discussing it, aren't we?"

"I move the question."

Bech was taken aback. He had forgotten the motion. Seeing this, Thornbush said, "The question is, Shall we declare a moratorium on new members until the millennium?"

"A lot can happen between here and the millennium," Bech observed. "It's eight years away. We could all be dead."

"The question, the question!" the dark suits in the back row insisted. Bech had always had a slight fear of composers. He couldn't understand what was in their heads – those key changes, those dominants and progressions and intervals, what did it all mean? They were men from outer space, and yet worldly, allied with money-men, artistic lawyers of a sort, so much of what they offered as created really mere boilerplate, the repeat sign saying *Here we go again.* . . .

"Our directress says we might forfeit our charter and the endowment," he pointed out to the membership.

"*Ayyye,*" Izzy thundered, and the back row choroused, and Seidensticker that puritanical prick also, and Von Klappenemner in his dementia, so Bech had to say, "The question has been moved. All those in favor of the moratorium raise your hands." Three from the back row, and Izzy and Seidensticker, but Von Klappenemner perhaps thought he had already voted. Mac-Deane, Bech was sorry to see, after a moment's thought raised his hand, perhaps acting on an old Cold Warrior's instinct that time gained is a victory, and any moratorium is a good one. That made six for. "Those opposed?" Bech asked, and his own hand went up. The writers, bless them, stuck with him – Jamison, Amy, Lulu, and Marr, who Bech might have thought would welcome damage inflicted on such a white man's club. But his brown hand was in the air, and so was the delicate yellow hand of X. I. Fong, master of pencil on paint. That made six against. In his confusion as to what was being decided, or perhaps captivated by a bygone ecstasy, Von Klappenemner made a flowery conductor's gesture, and Bech counted him in. "The motion fails," he announced, "seven to six. Membership in the Forty is still open."

Order had collapsed, everyone was jabbering; the hubbub subsided when Jason Marr indicated he would speak. "What this outfit needs," he said, "is a little affirmative action. Its spectrum needs to be broadened. I would like to nominate Toni Morrison, Henry Louis Gates, Cornel West, Albert Murray, and Lanford Wilson, right off the top of my head."

"I second them all," Amy exclaimed.

Edna interposed, "Toni Morrison is already a member."

"Then I nominate Rita Dove," said Marr suavely.

"Yes, women!" Amy cried. "There are so many these days! Wise women! Elaine Pagels! Ellen Zwilich! Eudora Welty! We no longer need swim on our backs, turning our foolish broken hearts into song, that was what we did in my day. Babies and songs – nothing else mattered enough. Even Dorothy Thompson and Martha Gellhorn, they thought they should be in love. I knew them both."

"Miss Welty is already a member," said Edna.

"I loved Gellhorn," Lulu interposed. "Even just the name. *Como una matadora.*"

"They were never members," Edna felt obliged to point out. She was getting tired. Her little cardiographs were trailing off into weak, irregular beats, and the tape recorder, if Bech read its little red light aright, was spinning a spool empty of tape. He was beginning to feel rescued, free. In his biggest, most presidential voice he announced, "These are all excellent nominations. We'll put them into writing. Send in any others to Edna, with seconds. We will get ballots in the mail by Christmas." One of Edna's young minions had come in, attractively breathless; her whispered secret was imparted from Edna to Bech. "I am informed," he announced, "that the caterer downstairs says the hot hors d'oeuvres are getting cold. Does anyone except me want a drink? If the answer is aye, I propose we adjourn. Thank you all for coming. It was an exceptional turnout." In the absence of a gavel, he rapped his knuckles on the wood, and the hollow, bow-sided desk resounded sonorously, like an African drum.

As the little elderly mob, growling and quarreling and laughing, pressed toward the stairs, Edna at his side put down her pencil. "That was a bit of a scrape," she muttered, pronouncing it "scripe."

"Yeah, what's going on? What's eating Izzy? He twisted my arm to take this job, and now he gives off nothing but negative vibes."

"Deep waters, Henry," she said. He looked at her; she had never before employed a tone this intimate. His *éminence grise.* His First Lady. She was prim and efficient but with a lurking antipodean strangeness, an occasional hoot of laughter out of the outback. Her profile was a cameo, in eighteenth-century English style – precise pursed mouth, high-bridged Romneyesque nose. The white wings of her short page boy swung forward as she fussed, motherly, with the recording device and her yellow pad of jagged notes. While they all played at being the Forty, she *worked*. She was sixtyish, but, then, he was a year short of seventy. Spinsters preserve themselves, he figured. The buds of passion remain coiled tight. He had once been to Australia, and sampled the handsome native women there, but had never talked to Edna about it – the pale parched land, the alkaline sky, the lacy iron balconies in Sydney, the opera house like a ship under full sail. An America without Calvinism or Judaism, just sunny brown space and the rough male humor of a penal colony. He found himself, in the wake of the battle they had breasted together, quite close to Edna. What was it Izzy had told him? *She's dying for you*. His dying for her wouldn't be the worst fate. She had the requisite severity, a cameo purity.

His relationship with Martina was deteriorating. Behind that Communist innocence lurked a Nineties American woman – canny, ambitious, condition-conscious, self-preserving. Bech could hardly blame her for seeing men younger than himself (she would need the exercise, the multiple orgasms he could no longer provide), but the suspicion that she and Izzy had something going nagged. That polymathic slob, that kept man, that pseudo-Talmudic maze-maker. Bech had an opportunity to spy on the situation when Pamela invited him and, separately, Martina, to a Christmas party in her penthouse. The artistic crowd that had shrouded the Festschrift gala in smoke and stale rivalries was in attendance only spottily – a plump Princeton savant who believed that Genesis was written by a woman; Vernon Klegg celebrating his latest dryly written, alcohol-soaked *succès d'estime*; and a skinny, bespectacled poet whose poems all dealt, in cindery glints, with Great Lakes industrial depression. "I had pictured your husband as looking different," Bech confided to the poet's iron-haired but still-lissome wife.

"Oh? How?" she responded, too brightly. There was something giddy, on the edge of naughty, about this woman that Bech wearily ascribed to his ancient roguish reputation, which had preceded him.

"More blue-collar," he said. "He's always doing sestinas and pantoums about rusty I-beams and how he scrubbed out vats of acid in a rubber suit."

"That was his brother who did the vats. Jim worked in the mills only summers; he was the family dreamer. They all sacrificed so he could go to college."

"And is he grateful?"

"Very," she said. "But they hate his poems. They want him to write about higher things, not about *them*, and the mills."

Across the round table, delicate, pampered Jim in his rimless glasses nodded and cringed beneath the chattery, fluttery attentions of his hostess. He had won prizes, and Pamela liked that. But she noticed Bech noticing, and accosted him after dessert. The shining skin exposed by her low-cut Herrera gown of watered silk flashed like a breastplate; she pressed him into a conversational corner. He wanted, under the stimulus of the three colors of wine served with the meal, to reach down and fish up one of her tits, to see if her freckles extended to the nipple. Did she go topless, that is, in her and Izzy's privacy beside their East Hampton pool? As a girl she had surely sunbathed with minimum coverage on the salty, rainbow-ridden foredeck of her father's yachts as they plowed the Sound and the turquoise Caribbean. She read these thoughts, or sensed their heat, and pressed her freckled décolletage two inches closer to his already rumpled shirtfront. "Henry, what's happening between you and Martina? She seems so distracted and sour."

"She does?" He searched out where in the little crowd of penthouse visitants Martina and her dull charcoal dress had lodged. She was, his secret garden fragrant of spices and overripe, leaf-embowered fruits, in close conversation with the blue-collar poet; without doubt Jim was the hero of the evening. "Well, maybe she doesn't like the way the Communist countries have adopted capitalism," Bech suggested. "They've taken the gangsters and the exploitation of the masses and left out all the rest."

"Henry, darling" – the "darling" meant that she knew he wanted to fish up her tits; she too had imbibed a tricolor of wine – "only you think of Martina as a Communist. She left Czechoslovakia when she was a toddler."

"As the twig is bent," Bech said.

"Isaiah and I thought you two were perfect for each other. Lately she has dropped to him one or two hints that we were wrong."

"Being perfect for each other is itself an imperfection, don't you think, in the murky sexual arena? I mean, sadomasochism has to have some room for exercise. How do you and Izzy handle perfection, may I ask?"

Pamela tapped him on the sternum, deftly mirroring his desire to touch her in the corresponding, but naked, spot. Perky shiksa tits, without that sallow Jewish heaviness, that nagging memory of a lactating mother. Pam's apple cheeks glowed; her teeth, small and round and tilted inwards like a baby's, were exposed by a flirtatious laugh back to the molars, which lacked a single metal filling. Had they been crowned? What is natural and what is not? With rich women one never knows. Were Pamela's eyes so wide-open because he was fascinatingly provocative, or because she had had a lid lift? He peered at the delicate circumocular skin, looking for tiny scars. "We share interests," she told him. "And we adore the children we've had by other marriages."

"Ah, children," Bech said, numbed by his memory of the three children of Bea Latchett's with whom he had for a time shared a Westchester County domicile – three little quick stabs, followed by a throb of loss. Ann and Judy, the twins, had married away from the East Coast, but Donald, their little brother, lived in New York, as a fashion photographer's assistant. Once a year he and his former stepfather had lunch. Donald was – to judge by his tight but tinted haircut and right-eared earring and failure ever to mention a girlfriend – gay, but Bech never inquired. If the boy had been warped, Bech blamed himself; when he and Bea had split up, Donald had been ten, and heartbreakingly willing to love them both.

"And on the rare occasions when we don't agree," Pamela was explaining, "we know how to fight healthily."

"Yes, I can see health written all over you. But sedentary old Izzy? Pamela, tell me" – he touched her bare arm, just under the freckled ball of her shoulder, a compromise – "don't you find him sometimes terribly, how can I say this, oppressive?"

Her face stiffened, intensifying Bech's suspicions of plastic surgery. She said, "Isaiah is the most sensitive and quick-witted man I have ever met. Don't be jealous, Henry. You have your own style. There's room enough in the world for both epic poets and writers of haiku."

"Is that what I write? Haiku? Even *Think Big*?"

Pamela, like many a woman before her, saw that it had been a mistake to get him on the subject of his writing: he took it too seriously, more seriously than sex or money. You cannot flirt with a writer about his books. She changed the subject: without even a shift of those wide-open eyes of hers, she grabbed a bulky man passing by in a double-breasted blue blazer. "Henry, I don't think you met my brother when you were here before. Zeke loves your books. He says you write rings around my darling husband."

"He's just teasing you," Bech assured her, shaking the big puffy hand extended toward his. Zeke Towers, Jr., had one of those practiced handshakes that don't quite come into your grip but somehow withhold the palm, giving you just the fingers. The family freckles covered his big face so thickly he looked diseased, or clad in a Tom Sawyer mask.

"*The Travellers*," young Zeke pronounced, his boyish face betraying a deep mnemonic effort. "It knocked me out, back when I was in college. It was assigned in two different courses."

"*Travel Light*, I think you must mean. About a motorcycle gang cruising from town to town in the Midwest, raping and pillaging."

The fascinating face, which, like a plate of *nouvelle cuisine*, was bigger than it needed to be to contain what was on it, lit up with relief. "Yeah, terrific – I'd never been hardly west of the Hudson, and here was all this sex and violence."

"All made up," Bech assured him.

"And then that other one, set in New York, with the scene where the television crew –"

"*Think Big*. I've always been kind of embarrassed about that book – it became a best-seller."

"And that was bad?" Zeke Jr. asked in genuine puzzlement. Bech gathered that the man's brother-in-law didn't talk this perverse way. For Izzy, worldly success was a legitimate goal.

"Pretty bad. And then it ruined my perfectly fine marriage. My wife's sister was so indignant I had written a best-seller and appeared in *People* that she seduced me and her sister kicked me out." He confessed all this partly to interest and offend Pamela; but she, as was her way, had ducked off, leaving him with the conversational companion of her choosing.

It was hard to tell with Wasp males how old they were; they don't stop being boys. Zeke Jr. must have been fifty or so, and he blinked as if he had never heard self-deprecating doubletalk before. "That sounds rough," he said. "Say, Mr. Bech, I bet you've been asked this before, but what I've always wondered about you writer types is, Where the hell do you get your ideas?"

More and more, as Bech went out to parties, he found himself being interviewed. It was a mode of conversation he disliked but had become hardened to. "A good question," he said firmly, repeating it: "Mr. Bech, where do you get your ideas?" Having given himself a moment to think, he now answered: "Your ideas are the product, generally, of spite. There is somebody you want to get even with, or some rival you want to outdo. The fiction then is what the psychiatrists call a working out. Or is it an 'acting out'?"

"You'd have to ask Pam about that. Until she got linked up with Izzy, she was on the couch five days a week."

"But she's the picture of health now. She and I were just discussing it." Rosy cheeks, buoyant dappled breasts, seamless plastic surgery. Was Bech falling in love yet again?

"Izzy's done wonders for her, I can tell you. My dad died happy, seeing his daughter in good hands at last."

"He sounds like an easy man to make happy."

Zeke Jr. was again puzzled, but had already built puzzlement into his expectations of Bech, and was determined to be polite. Why? Uneasily the unprolific author wondered what charm he held for this financial buccaneer, this boyish wielder of air rights and metropolitan acreage. "My dad had been lucky in life," young Zeke said reverently, as if reciting a frat pledge, "and nothing was too good for his family. He would have spoiled the hell out of us, if he hadn't also exemplified the work ethic."

Before such piety, Bech was almost silent. "*My* father," he confessed, "thought nothing could be too bad for us. He was a spoiler. He managed to die in the subway at rush hour."

"My dad came from Queens," said Zeke Jr., taking the high road. "He began with just a couple of vacant lots, and then in the Depression he'd assume the mortgages of bankrupt commercial property, stuff nobody else'd touch. He never looked back. Even into his eighties he was working ten, twelve hours a day. 'I love the hassle and the wrassle,' he'd say."

What was this kid – kid, he could be sixty, if you factor in the rejuvenating effects of gym workouts and winter visits to the Fountain of Youth – trying to sell him? Maybe an earnest, innocent selling manner had become his only style, just like Bech could only do prose haiku. He wasn't used to such friendly attention from men in such expensive blazers, with a silk hand-kerchief tumbling from the breast pocket like a paisley orchid. "Where do you get *your* ideas?" Bech asked him.

"Ideas?"

"For deals."

Zeke Jr.'s candid eyes narrowed; the skin beneath them took on a crêpey pallor, a tinge of corruption. "Oh – they just develop. It's a team effort. Not like what you do – think up all this stuff out of nowhere. That to me is awesome."

Thank God, Izzy came up to them, bringing the fresh air of familiar rudeness. "Henry *is* awesome," he said. "Especially in the sack."

"Who says?" Bech asked.

"Rumor hath it," said Thornbush smugly. "Henry, you are talking here to one of your foremost fans. Though it galls me to admit it, my main distinction in this lad's eyes is having a claim to your acquaintance."

"Not just a claim. You've done the mining."

"And pure gold it was. Is." The tenacious Izzy grip had closed around Bech's upper arm, which became a kind of tiller in these choppy currents. Bech found himself being steered toward a wall where an ice bucket and a militant array of bottles were being tended by a slender young mime sporting a nostril-ring.

"A privilege and pleasure to meet you, Mr. Bech," his alleged admirer's voice called after them.

Izzy turned in stately, politic fashion. "Zeke," he said, "I'd invite you to join us for brandy and cigars but I know you never let yourself be contaminated. Your better half was making noises in the dining room about the long ride back to Greenwich."

"You really feel at home with a *shaygets* like that?" Bech had to ask when he and the other writer were alone in a corner – the only such corner – containing bookshelves. Bech vainly scanned them for one of his own books; he knew their spines better than his past mistresses' faces. Pamela must keep them in her bedroom.

"Don't underrate the boy," Izzy assured him. "He may not look it, but he's a genius at what he does. New York real estate has been rocky lately, but young Zeke never gets caught holding the bag. He's as ruthless as his old man, and smoother. You can be glad old Zeke isn't here any more. A fucking monster – never got past eighth grade, and with every prejudice in the book. Came out of the South Jersey pine woods – Appalachia without the mountain air. He would have blocked the marriage if I hadn't told him I would rescue his daughter from Jewish shrinks. Takes a Jew to chase a Jew, I knew he'd think."

Izzy had lit up a cigar, a smuggled Havana, and Bech was holding the brandy. His third sip of the raw cognac put him in touch, via a knight's move of the consciousness, with the volatile essence of truth. "How would he have blocked it?" he asked.

"Disinherit," Izzy said.

"But surely," Bech protested, "you didn't marry Pamela for her money?"

"It was part of the picture. Just like her tits. Would you want to marry a woman if they sawed off her tits? Stick with her, sure – but take her on? Hey, what's with you and La O'Reilly?"

"She's souring on me. She ever talk to you about it?"

Under those prodigious eyebrows the old wizard's blood-shot optical organs veiled meretriciously. "She and I don't talk romance, just the word business. I was surprised you put such a move on her. You don't generally go for bluestocking, methodical types; you like destructive."

"Martina has her sweet destructive side," Bech said. He must not finish this brandy, he vowed to himself.

"I think she's jealous of Edna," Thornbush volunteered.

"Edna? Dear little birdy, virginal Edna?" Yet the very name had conjured up the chaste inner spaces of the Forty's mansion, and the distinguished dim visages over whom he now and then presided as if over a congress of the ghosts of the dignity, the integrity, the saintly devotion that had once attached to the concept of the arts in the American republic.

"She says you talk about her. You talk about the Forty all too tenderly, in Martina's view. She thinks you've gone establishment. I tell her, 'Not Bech. He's the last of the desperadoes. *Dérèglement de tous les sens*, that's his motto.'"

"Well, thanks. I guess. You and Martina have these intimate consultations about me often?"

"No, just at lunch the other day. We had business. Aesop is bringing out a collection of my out-of-print essays, including a bunch I did for *Displeasure*. Remember *Displeasure*?"

"How could I forget?" For all his egregious faults, Izzy had what few people left in the world had: he remembered *Displeasure*. Its crammed second-floor offices in Chelsea, its ragged right margins, its titles in lower-case sans. The long-haired internes from the Village, girlfriends of associate editors, who helped out, their triangular brows furrowed by the search for typos, which tended to multiply when corrected.

"Old Tim Egle in his bedroom slippers," Izzy was saying, "with that funny sweet smell around his head all the time. We were so frigging innocent we didn't know he was sucking opium. We thought it was his hair tonic. The whole shebang riding on Arnie Tompkins's money, and then the *yentz* get bored."

"How big is the collection?" Bech was jealous. The Vellum Press had let his miscellany *When the Saints* go out of print, and his second novel, *Brother Pig*, existed only in quality paperback, available, maybe, at college bookstores. He used to see himself on drugstore racks and in airports, but no more. If he wasn't assigned in a college seminar on postwar anti-realism, he wasn't read.

"Too big," Thornbush allowed with mock modesty. "Over a thousand pages, unless they cheat me on the leading. These young editors keep asking for this and that favorite they remember, and Aesop doesn't want to leave out any real gem."

"Heaven forbid," Bech said, and decided to see the brandy through after all. He swirled the dark-amber residue in the bottom of the snifter and dizzily reflected that no doubt there were strict laws, known to mathematicians and specialists in the study of chaos, to describe exactly its elliptical gyrations. Then he tossed it down. It burned, lower and lower in his esophageal tract. "Listen, Izzy," he said. "You got me into being president of the Forty, it's not something I was dying to do. Now you're acting like there's something dirty about it. At the fall meeting, when MacDeane began to talk about what sounded like dissolution, you egged it on: you proposed that moratorium on new members that just about would have scotched the whole institution. Who of us is going to be around in the year 2000? Edna was horrified. So was I."

"I was saving the situation," Izzy suavely said. "Those goons from music were out for blood."

"Yeah, why?"

"You heard them. They don't like the electronic crowd that might get elected. Seidensticker doesn't like representational revisionism. MacDeane doesn't like the revisionist historians that label us the bad guys in the late Cold War. Also, he's out of the Washington power loop and it hurts."

"So, kill the whole thing. The whole idea of the Forty, never mind what Forty. Is that what the arts in America have come to? Is that what Lucinda Baines laid down her fortune for? A lot of people died, taking Baines' Powders, so the Forty could exist."

Izzy with his clownish side-wings of snowy hair was playing an imaginary violin, so convincingly that his jaw sprouted multiple chins. Bech could see the strings, hear the vibrato. "You're breaking my heart," Izzy said. "Anyway, my motion saved the situation. Glad I could help out. You can thank me later."

"If that was help, I'll take opposition. Hey," Bech said, "I got to go. Martina's making motions of her own." She was, as over a year ago, moving about in her loden coat, preparing to leave without him.

Izzy was enjoying the conversation. "It's like prizes and prize committees," he said. "Do *you* want to be a literary judge? Reading all that crap, and then getting no thanks?"

"No," Bech admitted. "I always duck it."

"Me, too. So who accepts? Midgets. So who do they choose for the prize? Another midget."

There was an analogy there, but Bech felt he was missing it. He knew that Thornbush hadn't won a prize since a Critics Circle for *The LB-Bull* in 1971. Sour grapes, the champagne of the intelligentsia. Martina had put on that shapeless green coat over her gray wool dress and as she bent forward to give Pamela an unsmiling kiss, a peck on each cheek European-style, she seemed to brandified Bech a schoolgirl refugee from those pre-war public-school classrooms where he had sat learning the rudiments of history, biology, and mathematics. P.S. 87, at 77th and Amsterdam, had been staffed in that laggard time mostly by unmarried Christian women who, hindsight told him, were very young. Girls, really. They had seemed enormously tall and mature and wise. They had taught him to read, and that had been the making and unmaking of him. "I feel like my feet are stuck in buckets of brandy," he told Izzy, trying to break free of the other writer's powerful gravitational field.

But Martina moved across his field of vision, green, a bit of Birnam wood removing to Dunsinane. *I say, a moving grove*, the messenger told Macbeth. The power of sexual attraction snapped Bech loose from Izzy's spell; he sailed across the room and came up against Martina with a bump. "What are you doing?" he asked.

"Going."

"Without me?"

"Why not? You've ignored me all night."

"I didn't want to cramp your style."

"I have no style, Henry. I'm just a lowly copyeditor, correcting the mistakes of famous writers and getting small thanks."

Small thanks seemed to be a theme of the evening. "That's not

true. You have tons of style. You're Colette in a loden coat.
Listen, you. We may not have come together, but we go
together. That's how we do it." His stomach sagged and burned
beneath the brandy-soaked possibility of losing this fragrant,
solid, slightly un-American woman. He was bad at the business
of life, which is letting go. In the elevator he pleaded, "Come
back to the loft. We got to work on our relationship."

"Ha," Martina said. "Relating to you is like wallpapering an
igloo."

"That bad?" The phrase didn't sound like her; it was too good,
too bookish, too Thornbushian.

Martina went on, "I saw you with our hostess, trying to crawl
down the front of her dress. She's all show, Henry, I tell you this
as a friend. All show and no performance. Like any rich bitch.
She fucks badly."

"How do you know that? Let me guess. The husband. Holy
Isaiah, with his suction-cup mouth. At age seventy-one, he wants
performance?"

The plunging elevator hiccuped to its stop, and they put on
straight faces for the doorman, who warned them, in his jolly
Russian-refugee accent, that it was cold outside – calder than
vitch's teet.

When Bech lived up on West 99th Street, he would feel,
heading across West End Avenue toward Riverside Drive and
the Hudson, safe at last; now he felt that way when the taxi
crossed Houston's rushing river of cars. The industrial streets
reflected scattered wan lights on their old paving-stones; the
incidence of habitation here reverted to prehistoric times, when
man was outnumbered by lions and timber wolves, and his lonely
fires flickered at the backs of caves halfway up iron-stained cliffs.
Bech's second-floor loft lay in the rickety block between Prince
and Spring. His neighbors were, below him, a struggling gallery
of Sahel art and crafts, and, above him, a morose little sweatshop
where a pack of Filipinos wove and bent baskets, rope sandals,
floor mats, and rattan animals. At night his nearest active neighbor was a jazz club at the back of a building up the block; its

weakly applauded riffs and cymbal-punctuated climaxes filtered through his walls. Bech, a bit sickened by the cognac and the sweet smell of Izzy Thornbush's sell-out to the rich, poured himself a cleansing Pellegrino, but Martina decided to stick with white wine. She found some recorked Chardonnay in the back of his refrigerator. "Henry," she said, settling into the exact center of the little sofa opposite his beanbag chair, so that there was no space for an amorous drunk on either side of her, "I don't intend to quarrel or make love. We've done both for all they're worth."

"Done and done? Isn't there a recurrent need? Pamela thought you seemed distracted and sour lately."

"Oh, Pamela. Those wide-open little-girl eyes. Unlike her, I have more in life than to play. All my books at work are problem books. A lot of necessary revision, fighting prima-donna authors, and not much payoff on the bottom line likely."

He thought of sawing away at an imaginary violin, but instead asked, "What do you and Izzy talk about all the time? He said you're bringing out a collection of all the essays he's ever written. That's some load."

"Some of them are quite amazing," she said, tucking her stocking feet up under her solid haunches on the old leather sofa that Bea in Ossining had covered in nubbly almond-colored wool before she sent both Bech and the sofa back to New York. Strange, but, thinking of fabrics, Bech perceived that Martina had managed to find in the United States pantyhose of the less-than-fine, gray-brown knit that Communist women used to wear. "Such intellectual curiosity!" she was going on, of the deplorable Thornbush's written effusions. "There was nothing he wouldn't tackle – chess, the international meaning of Ping-Pong, Adlai Stevenson as Hamlet versus Eisenhower's Fortinbras, these Persian and Chinese and Ethiopian novelists nobody else has heard of or read –"

"Wonderful, wonderful. The walking brain, later to be known as Mr. Potato-Head. What did you mean when you told him at lunch that you thought I was going establishment?"

Her face – the deepset eyes, the unplucked brows, the no-collagen-added lips – was startled by the betrayal. A clarinet swooped up an octave in the jazz club many walls away, then slippingly descended the scale via flats and sharps. "I didn't say it exactly like that. I'm surprised he told you."

"That's how Izzy is. A communicator. If you thought you and he had any secrets, forget it."

The restless, slightly guilty way she adjusted her stocking feet under her haunch's warm weight was driving him tenderly wild. "What I may have said was that ever since you became president of the Forty you've been acting a little different. Not self-important, exactly, but . . . more declarative. Dictatorial, even. When you come back from meeting all afternoon privately with Edna you're quite impossible – I don't think you're aware of it."

"Well, yes, I dictate. I've never had the use, before, of a secretary, to take down my words and type them all up on cream-colored stationery. For the first time I see what all these men with power are clinging to."

"And you've never had a professional harem before, possibly," she said, working on it with him therapeutically. "They all grovel when you show up, Edna and her help. You're the catch, the living immortal."

"Author of prose haiku," he said. It still rankled.

"What do you care what a flutterbrain like Pamela Thornbush says? How greedy you are, Henry, to have every woman in the world on her knees in front of you."

The image was pure blue movie. Now the drummer, his brushes and high-hat cymbals tingling, had launched a solo, coaxing a spatter of applause from the desultory little crowd. "Flutterbrain," he said. "Is that a word you made up, or what the smart young people now are all saying?"

"You know what I meant. Birdbrain. Don't deflect. I think it's sad, that an absolutely meaningless organization like the Forty, just because it has some endowment to play with and the staff flatters you, would take up any of your time and energy. In the days when you had integrity, you would have sneered at it. It is decadent capitalism at its most insidious."

"Don't you mean triumphant, not decadent? Read the papers."

"It's just not *real*," Martina said. "A bunch of mostly New York City has-beens electing each other. It's worse than the Writers' Unions – at least they had a kind of policing function. They could reward and punish."

"What do you want me to do, get it to dissolve?"

"Yes." The simple syllable was paired with a distant collapse of multiple instruments into the climactic, finalizing set of chords. "It's pointless," she said, "and an insult to young artists. The only positive thing it does is make work for Edna and her sleek little lackeys."

How did she know the assistants were sleek? Their brushed hair, their respectful smiles, their little golden granny glasses. As in some ceiling vision by Tiepolo they ministered, bare legs dangling, to the arc of befuddled old faces, faces shiningly clean from their lifelong bath in the higher verities. "Imagine the Forty," he told Martina, "as a Festschrift all year long."

"That was my job. I thought you were stupid, contributing to it, by the way. I thought it was beneath you. And your irony didn't save it."

"Then why was your letter so seductive?"

She took her feet out from under her haunch and sat up as if to go somewhere. "Was it?"

"I thought so."

"My pantyhose feel hot."

"They look heavy. You should break down and buy the finer gauge."

"Those run," she told him, pushing her pelvis toward the loft ceiling to hook her thumbs around the pantyhose's waist-band.

"You've said," he pointed out, "unforgivable things to me."

Her voice was milder, though she still didn't smile. "Just that you're silly to be seduced by something like the Forty. You scorn Izzy and his rich wife, but you're knocked silly by this dead woman's money, what was her name, Lucinda Baines?" In stripping off her pantyhose she had flashed old-fashioned plain white non-bikini underpants; the old-fashionedness hit Bech hard, hurtling him back to boyhood glimpses of underpants at P.S. 87. Did his memory betray him, or did wisps of pubic fuzz peek out of the loose legholes, the elastic limp in the Depression?

"You should see the house Lucinda gave us," he boasted. "So lovely – no two mantelpieces alike, and a solarium that's like a high oval birdcage. We meet in there. The president's desk has bowed-out sides like a Spanish galleon, and upstairs, there is this terrific library with carved animal heads, lions alternating with lambs, full of everybody's books, which nobody reads."

She was stuffing her pantyhose into her purse and perching forward on the sofa to leave. "I'm sorry," she said, "I just cannot sleep with a man who takes a birdcage or dollhouse or whatever like that so seriously. Who would care about becoming a member except midgets?"

"Midgets," he said. "There's a word I've heard already to-night. According to Izzy, we're all midgets, except him."

"Not you, Henry." She seemed sincere. Her serious eyes, shadowed by the lateness of the hour, bored into his. "You can do magical things Izzy can't. You can make characters breathe and walk on their own. His, he has to move them around himself; all their energy is his."

"Really?" he said. Was it he or the brandy blushing? He was deeply gratified. Farther along in the drab recesses of Crosby Street, the jazz group took up another set, with a tenor sax laying out the tune – "April in Paris" – in halting, introspective phrases. "You believe that?"

She stood loomingly above him, the little fuzzy pills of wear on her gray skirt a more appealing texture to him than the most shimmering watered silk: the homely texture of virtue. "Everybody knows it," she said, and he could hear her voice resonate in her belly. He leaned his face, his ear against that flat belly. It was warm through the worn wool. Skin and hair were within kissing distance.

"You're right," he said. "The Forty is a farce. It just seems to me a harmless farce."

"Nothing is harmless," said Martina sternly, "if it takes up space. Mental and spiritual space. You must get it out of your mind."

"I will. It is. Out." He struggled up from the clammy grip of the beanbag chair to wrap his arms around her thickest part, the haunch and rump whose muscle and fat were braced by the flaring pelvis. He thought of all her layers, bones out to clothes, and foresaw a profound satisfaction in removing just the outermost ones. They hadn't made love for weeks, because of this edgy political tension always between them. "Do stay tonight," Bech begged, hoarsely. "I'll swear off presiding forever." Did he imagine it, or was the scent of musk pressing through the wool lap of the skirt, along the horizontal seam where, if Martina were a mermaid, her fishy half would begin?

"You can preside," Martina said. She made an impatient motion within his arms, of wanting to be free. "Just don't be so proud of it. It makes you absurd, like some poltroon."

"Now there's a word you must have got from one of your prima-donna authors," he said, sinking back into the beanbag. He was tired, but he just had to relax and it would all happen, as water flows downhill; already she was out of her jacket and undoing the little pearly buttons of her blouse. *Chestnuts in blossom*, the saxophone was repeating. "Do you really think I'm a better writer than Izzy?"

"Better *writer*," Martina said, shedding her clothes and slowly filling the loft with her scents, as apples rotting in the long wet grass perfume an entire orchard. "He's the better *thinker*. Most of the time, Henry dearest" – she was drawing closer – "you don't seem to be thinking at all."

The spring meeting of the Forty, though the day turned out to be a rainy one, attained an all-time high: twenty-three members were in attendance. The buzz was up; the white-haired old heads bobbed one toward another as the rain drummed on the panes of the solarium, arching above their heads in a high half-shell. Over the winter, the stately MacDeane had died and also, her avidly flirtatious heart unexpectedly giving out after one last poetry reading at the 92nd Street "Y," Amy Speer deLessups. Bech would miss them both. He had read them when young; they took with them some of the glamor of the postwar years, when the New York School was outpainting Paris, and at any minute the new *Farewell to Arms* would appear, and it seemed everything would pick up and go on as it had before the war, only better, without the poverty and racial cruelty. You ate lunch in drugstores, and books cost two dollars, and college students wore neckties, and typewriters were the most advanced word processors there were. Amy had been smart and slender and wore big straw hats and slept with Delmore Schwartz and Philip Rahv in rumored conjunctions as exalted and cloudily chaste as the copulations of the Olympian gods. She was gone now, with Schwartz and Rahv and Wilson and Trilling and all those other guardians of Bech's youthful aspirations.

When the rudimentary business of announcements and minutes was over with, the shapely brown hand of Jason Marr was lifted for recognition. Bech imagined he would be commenting on the unprecedented number of African-American candidates brought forth into nomination. But no, it was on a graver, more general matter that Marr spoke. "Mr. President," he said, in his rich slow voice reminiscent of the pulpit, "as we discovered at our last meeting, there is an element within this institution that for unfathomable reasons of their own wishes to see it dissolved. I would like to give expression to my righteous horror at this development. Since I was a boy on the mean streets well north of here, I had heard of the Forty; the streets were not so mean, nor was our ignorance so complete, that word was denied to the least of us that somewhere on this rocky island the pinnacle of artistic accomplishment could be located – as it turned out, in the very building where I am now privileged, unto my everlasting wonder and gratitude, to sit. I have often heard the other members complain that this institution serves no distinct purpose, save that of self-glorification. But of how many institutions can it be said that, even if their distinct good deeds do not make a legion of headlines, they do symbolize in their very being something eternal and unquestionably to be valued? Are love and respect for the arts so dead – are we so far gone in electronic degradation and the lust for monetary profit – that we can seriously contemplate writing 'finis' to a dream born at the outset of this cruellest of centuries, in the heart of a refined lady of means, one Lucinda Baines, who dared hope to redeem her drug-peddling family's unsavory fortune by devoting a fraction of it to the establishment of a golden hill, a hill to be set before the eyes of the nation's young as a Mount Sinai, a Mount Olympus, a Mount Everest of the spirit existing to be climbed by them? Mr. President, I would welcome a comment from the chair, and an endorsement or a refutation of these sentiments." He sat down.

Bech's head spun a little; there was more going on here than he knew. What did "the lust of monetary profit" have to do with it? He said cautiously, "Mr. Marr, your sentiments endorse themselves, by virtue of the eloquence of their expression. But someone playing the devil's advocate could ask, Might we not embody an idea whose time has come and gone, with its distinct savor of elitism and of outmoded establishment values? Values, I need not tell you, established by a white male hierarchy whose comfortable idealism rested on the unconfessed exploitation of women, workers, and people of color." Martina, he felt, would have especially liked the insertion of "workers" in the litany of abused minorities.

Marr was on his feet indignantly. "Mr. President, I did not speak as a person of color. I spoke as a person of sensibility, one elected to this body on the strength of my work. If the content of my work is rage, black rage, its form is timeless, of the ages. As a poet I claim fellowship with Sappho, with Whitman, with Shakespeare – yea, with Kipling and Tennyson and the singers of the white empire of their day. If the Forty is disbanded, I will be denied one of the few venues in which I can express that everlasting fellowship – I, and all my brothers and sisters of color. We are set to climb the golden hill; now some would take the golden hill away!"

"But," Bech pointed out, "there is no motion to disband the Forty."

"I so move, Mr. President," a voice boomed from within the several rows of heads, shadowy beneath the thrumming rain. Bech recognized the voice of Isaiah Thornbush, its topping of English accent on a base of local gravel. There was a host of eager seconds.

"Would Mr. Thornbush," Bech asked, striving to keep a level head, "like to speak to the motion?"

"You've already nailed it, Henry," Izzy said with impudent coziness. "Elitist. Edwardian. Establishment. Extinct. You're either in the march of progress or you're obstructing it. This luxurious, idle, *honorary*" – scornfully emphasized and prolonged – "organization is an obstruction. It's cultural clutter, if I may coin a virtual anagram."

At Bech's elbow Edna's pencil was stabbing frantically on her yellow pad. *Charter by-laws don't provide for dissolution*, he made out. The spinning in his head had increased; he was feeling helicoptered high above the fray. The members' heads looked like eggs in a carton. His desk looked the size of a shoebox. "The directress," he stated to the meeting from on high, "informs me that the by-laws have no provision for dissolution."

"Laws are for men, not men for laws," one of the composers in the back row shouted.

Seidensticker in his vast abstract irritability announced, "Don't elect anybody, don't elect the crap artists, that's the way to end this boondoggle. Bad as the NEA, supporting all this performance art, some woman shaving her cunt in public, smearing herself all over with chocolate pudding, all this so-called earth art, some big ditch bulldozed in the desert, who needs it? Photorealism – what a crock. Any fool with a Polaroid and an enlarger can do it! That's not drawing, it's *tracing!*"

Others, too, vented the injustices and slights endured in a lifetime of practicing the arts. Frauds, phonies, pedants, narcissists – that had been the competition, garnering prizes and acclaim. Izzy's orotund voice rolled through the hubbub: "Could the directress kindly answer a simple question: Who owns this building?"

Bech glanced aside at Edna; color was high in her cameo profile. A raspberry tinge had crept up, like a stain in litmus paper, to color her throat. The membership grew quiet. "The terms of the will," she said, her upper lip lifting in disdain at this invasion of institutional privacy, "are somewhat imprecise. The lawyer who drew it up was a close friend of Miss Baines who himself administered the trust until he died a good many years later; since then his Wall Street firm, Briggs, Parsons, and Traphagen, has acted as trust officers and overseen the financial details."

"But in trust," Izzy pressed, "for whom?"

"Well," Edna admitted, her throat slowly regaining its white-ness, her upper lip now stiffening as if frosted, "it would seem from the phrasing that Miss Baines was leaving it directly to the Forty, as the group would be constituted after her death. But this is a legal impossibility."

"I don't see why," Izzy said. He no longer had to raise his voice to be heard; such an alert silence had fallen over the solarium that the caterers could be heard downstairs setting up their bottles and slamming the stainless-steel doors of their steam cabinets. "The Forty owns the building, with the endowment for its upkeep, and if there were a dissolution, the proceeds would be divided among the forty members. Since – how many member-ships are open now, Edna?"

"Nine, actually."

"Since nine are open, among a mere thirty-one. A pretty penny, I would estimate – way uptown in Lucinda's day, this lot has come to be prime midtown real estate. And let's not forget the pictures on our walls. Chase and Sloan ain't exactly chopped liver."

An excited furor ensued; Bech faced it, but with an irresistible sense of drifting away, of being disconnected. Halfway through his three-year term, he was tired of presiding. J. Edward Jamison spoke with quivering outrage of breaking with tradition; his gray smudge of a Brian Aherne-style mustache seesawed as he sneer-ingly mouthed his opinion of those who would sell their father's mansion for a mess of pottage; Jason Marr had set a convenient Biblical tone. Von Klappenemner, his bald head ridged like a quartz hatchet-head, stood and enunciated thoughts upon group euthanasia that had become, in his advanced dementia, totally unintelligible, though all of his compellingly graceful conductor's gestures remained. Lulu Fleming said that in her opinion all of the little nobility that was left in the United States was right here in this room; disbanding would be an atrocity, though since she was also an honorary member of the Academia Brasileira de Letras and the Academia Venezolana it wouldn't really be the end of her world.

The antis, the pros, they sounded alike – the same stridency,

the same ready recourse to the first person singular, the same
defensive encirclement of imaginary prerogatives. Bech thought
of Martina opening her bathrobe to release zephyrs of carnal
odor, her face stern and unsmiling atop her sturdy nudity;
everything else seemed vanity and maya. His quiescence, his
psychological absence during the rhetorical storm, was slowly
sensed as an insult by the agitated members. Izzy called,
"Mr. President, I move the question."

"What is the question, Mr. Thornbush?"

"To be or not to be, that is the question. Whether or not the
Forty should disband, sell the mansion, and divide the proceeds
among the members as an encouragement to the living best in
American art."

"Second!" snorted Seidensticker.

The vote was eleven to disband, eleven to continue as before.
Bech himself had not voted. All eyes turned on him. Edna's were
alarmed, above her suddenly hectic cheeks. She was pure nerves,
and Bech had always vibrated in response to the nervousness of
women, their iridescent aura of potential hysteria. Adrift, he tried
to haul himself in and to dock at the distasteful and awkward
matter at hand. "Well, you do wonder," he began, "if half of an
organization is willing to sell itself out, what purpose there is in
the other half denying them the pleasure. I would like to resign,
and let my esteemed old friend and colleague Isaiah Thornbush
come preside in my stead. He seems to be running things anyway, from the back bench."

Edna wrote on her pad, in handwriting that seemed to be
tracing a cardiac seizure, "Can't be done. New elections necessary."

Bech regained a presidential timbre: "But since it can't, evidently, be done, I will stay in my chair and vote against the
motion and propose that our able directress consult Briggs,
Parsons, and Traphagen as to the financial and legal parameters
of the case and give us a full report at the fall meeting."

Von Klappenemner's long waving arms were unignorable,
and he was getting to his feet whether or not Bech recognized
him. "Oh no you don't, Mr. sassy Presi–dent," he fluted in that
demented but still musical voice. "Oh no you don't, you literary

wiseacre. You're not cheating me out of my share of this mansion – we're talking millions, all my fellow composers have just assured me. Millions for everybody! I change my vote. I vote Yes, yes, let's for common decency's sake put ourselves out of our misery and disband. Die, everybody! This place has been on life supports for years. No intubation, no respirator, no plastic hearts, no liver and lung transplants. Let's all die! Die rich!!"

Bech asked Edna quietly, "Did he vote against it before?"

"I'm afraid he did, Henry."

"Ah," he announced, with an unconscionable relief. "Very well. With Mr. Von Klappenemner's change of vote, the motion then stands twelve to eleven for disbandment and liquidation and division of the spoils. On such a drastic decision, however, the entire membership must be notified and the matter put to a paper ballot. The lawyers must be consulted. The U.S. Congress should be consulted, since they granted us our charter in 1904. All this will take time. Now is the time, however, ladies and gentlemen, for us to go downstairs and drink and dine. *Carpe diem*, the night is coming." Still lacking a gavel, he rapped his knuckles several times on the resounding desk.

"Well said, Mr. President," Edna murmured as the jostling, thirsty, hungry shards of the dissolving organization filed out.

"But, Edna, it doesn't look good. Once word gets out that there's money to be had ... "

She hooted: a brawling, what-the-hell noise emerged from her refined small face, a sort of a snort confessing that the two of them had been, as it were, in bed together. An aboriginal wilderness lurked in that hoot. Then her face snapped shut again, upon its own composure. A decisive fatigue veiled the chalk-blue eyes and pursed the chiseled lips. "I've been thinking of retirement, Henry. This has been a long haul, thirty-five years with the Forty. I came to Manhattan when I was twenty-two – graduate work at Columbia in anthropology of all things – and never intended to stay. You were born here, I believe; it doesn't sit on your chest the way it does on mine. For years, when I woke up, I felt I was caught in some enormous machine rattling all around me. Grace Paul took me on as an assistant when I was at loose ends and she was growing dotty, and the year to get out

never quite came. I was well enough paid. I enjoyed the building; I liked as well as admired the members, and, the oddest
thing, I think I fell in love with Lucinda Baines. You've seen the
portraits and photographs of her that we have about the place;
poor thing, she was terribly plain. I pitied her, fancying myself *not*
plain, but, looking back on my life, I see that I might as well have
been. I've led the life of a very plain woman. Anyway, love,
don't mean to be bending your ear."

"Bend away. The sphinx speaks."

"You're a good sort. Most of you are. You all have to be self-
centered, I realize that, if you're going to do anything worth-
while."

From downstairs arose the din of the members talking and
wolfing down the free drinks and watercress sandwiches. The
nearly deserted solarium was gathering the spring dusk in its high
inverted bowl of leaded panes. Pollen and pale-green catkins
tinted the gutters and car roofs, in the Manhattan spring, and
the smell of tar underfoot intensified. *Pollen and catkins/tint gutters
and car roofs green./Underfoot, sweet tar.*

Edna touched a spot below one eye, and then looked at her
fingertip to see if it were wet. "Sorry, old Henry. This is an
emotional moment for me, evidently. My widowed sister has an
enormous spread in the hills north of Adelaide. For years she's
been wanting me to come and help her manage the vineyards.
And the sheep." She brushed back a silken strand of white hair
and returned to stroking the spot below her eye, as if she were
reawakening to simple sensation. "It will be a strange thing, after
New York, being able to see the horizon. My memory of it is,
there's a dreadful amount of horizon."

It has been said – meaning no derogation, of course – that Henry
Bech writes American haiku. But, though some of his precious
paragraphs, distilled molecule by molecule like dewdrops, give
the studied impression of his having counted the syllables, I do
not see Bech as belonging to the company of Bashō, Buson, and
Issa. *Travel Light*, the novel with which he burst upon the mid-
Fifties like a leather-jacketed biker into a party of gray suits, surely

finds its affinity in the tales of the raffish demimonde of the compassionate and uninhibited Ihara Saikaku, and his next, *Brother Pig*, in the grotesque fantasy of the splendid Ueda Akinari. *The Chosen*, with its undercurrent of moralism no less irresistible for its being saline with sardonic irony, evokes yet another Tokugawa master, the copious yet high-minded Takizawa Bakin, and *Think Big*, if not quite Bech's *Genji monogatari* (to give the famous tale its precise title), certainly contains scenes that, in their easy warmth of stylization and elegant candor, might not have embarrassed Lady Murasaki. But it is to a poet far too little known, Tachibana Akemi, who was born the year when Napoleon was defeated and died the year in which Ulysses Grant was elected President, that Bech has his closest affinities, so powerful they are foreshadowed anagrammatically. For it was, of course, Tachibana, along with Ōkuma Kotomichi and the Buddhist priest Ryōkan, who wrested the tanka – a form two lines more capacious than the haiku – away from court poets and wrought it into a vehicle for describing not just the autumn moon and cherry blossoms but the ineluctable details of daily happenstance, including political developments and otherwise unheard rumblings within the sealed room of the Tokugawa era. This is the Bech of inestimable value – he who hustles toward us like a waiter laden with not just the tureen of soup made from the tortoise upon whose back the universe legendarily rests but the meat, potatoes, and peas of quotidian fare, transformed into ambrosia by its painstaking cookery. If Bech had taken less pains, the shelf of his books would be thrice as long, but we might be but a third as grateful for his exquisite *yugen*, to use the Japanese term most easily translated "mystery and depth." Congratulations, indispensable Henry – seventy is but a number to conjure with, for those who still possess the conjuror's boyish spirit!

Thus read Isaiah Thornbush's cagey contribution to Henry Bech's Festschrift volume, which had been assembled, over Bech's objections, by the assistant to his editor, Jim Flaggerty. The assistant that Bech had first known, petite, black-haired Arlene Schoenberg, with the shadow of whose fine female hands on the photocopying machine he had briefly fallen in love, had long since moved on, to a line of online cookbooks; her latest replacement, with the New Age name of Crystal, had done an adequate job assembling the volume, but the overall production values, not to mention the fervor of the tributes, fell considerably short, Bech felt, of what Thornbush had received two years earlier. The Festschrift party, instead of being held in a Park Avenue penthouse, was held in some back rooms of Michael's Pub. A pianist and bassist mutteringly played, but Woody Allen, though invited, had declined to sit in. Nor did Donald Trump come, though Pamela Thornbush had extracted from him and Marla what she had thought had been a promise.

Thornbush himself was trying to ease his bulk inconspicuously through the Bech-oriented crowd, but his reflective bald head, winged like a swan alighting on a pond, was hard to miss. Bech swiftly sidled over to him, knifing through a trio of Armani-clad agents. "Izzy, I didn't know you knew Japanese," he said.

"I don't. I consulted the *Britannica*. The '69 edition, the last solid one before they ruined it with that micro/macro crap. Pam had told me you seemed offended when she told you you wrote haiku."

"Am I that kind of sorehead? Have I ever even complained about the vile way you panned *Think Big* in *Commentary*? At the age of three score and ten, who should hold a grudge? Where *is* Pam? I'll give her a hug that'll make her tits squeak."

Izzy seemed a shade depressed. "She couldn't come — some Christian good cause her brother got her on the board of. Canned milk for starving Ethiopians — who knows? Zeke Jr. turns out to be a kind of holy Joe. She said she'd hope to drop by but these do-gooder meetings go on forever."

"No Pam, huh? Well, how about Martina?"

Thornbush looked distinctly frayed. There were yellow bags under his eyes, and beneath his outspread wings of hair his ears were red as stoplights. *Eyes with yellow bags./Beneath wings of hair outspread,/ears red as stoplights.*

"Haven't you heard?" he asked Bech. "She's left Aesop to help get out the bimonthly newsletter of a conservative Washington think tank. They offered her more money than she'd known existed and a crack at the editorship in two years, if she learns to sing their neocon tune. This with my mega-collection of criticism and opinion pieces still up in the air. I kidded her about becoming an apologist for capitalism but she got very solemn, the way she can, and said, 'What else is there left to believe in?' But you must have heard all this from her."

"No. As *you* must have heard, we broke up when the Forty began to come apart. I know I shouldn't have blamed her, but I did. I saw her as a temptress. It got worked around in my mind that Edna stood for everything noble and she'd been raped. That made Martina the rapist. And you, of course."

"Me? *Me*? I was the least of it. It was the composers and artists, they can't stand anybody's dreck but their own. I could have swung either way. The Forty was a fun place to go now and then, but, frankly, Edna always struck me as a bit out of her depth. How's she doing, have you heard?"

"She dropped me a postcard. She says the sheep seem pretty sensible, after all those years with us."

The ballot by mail in the summer past had totaled up five against, six not voting, and twenty for disbandment and dispersement of the realized assets. The Baines heirs – a flock of distant cousins resident in Indiana and Oklahoma – had filed motions contesting the interpretation of Lucinda's will, demanding that all the proceeds not consumed by lawyers' fees be distributed to living Baineses. It would be years, if ever, before the matter was legally settled. The fall meeting consisted of Bech announcing these developments and that a specially struck gold-alloy medal, bearing her own profile, was being awarded to Edna for her decades of service. At dinner there were spontaneous toasts and even some singing; several members said it was the best dinner for ages and they certainly looked forward to next year's. They didn't understand that there would be no next year's. Bech had served for only two of the three years of a president's usual term. He was the end of a list of which Clarence Edmund Stedman, hand-picked by the dying Lucinda, was the first. The mansion had already found a buyer, for something in a hearty eight figures. The lawyers on all sides had agreed to let the sale go through, rather than have the upkeep whittle at the endowment.

Izzy asked him, "How do you like *Summa Saeculorum* for a title?"

"For what?"

"For my book, you *farmishter*. See, it's my summing up, and *saeculum* means an age, our age, as well as world, worldly, you know, as opposed to *theologica*."

"You and Aquinas, together again. You don't think it's a little, how can I say, grandiose?"

"Thus speaketh the old haikumeister. But listen, seriously" – here was that grip on the tender part of the arm again – "you did a great job with the Forty. A number of us saw the demise coming, and you gave it dignity; I figured you would. Edna agreed."

"She saw it coming too?"

"Maybe not consciously, but in her gut. You know women. Hey, who's this little mother's joy?"

A girl in a very short silver dress, with platinum hair a nappy half-inch long covering her beautifully ovoid skull, had appeared at Bech's side. "Izzy," he said, "I'd like you to meet Crystal Medford, Jim Flaggerty's assistant over at Vellum and the editor and organizer of my Festschrift volume. It offended my modesty, but nothing I said could dissuade her from her salaried duty."

"Crystal," Izzy repeated. "Of course. *Adored* your letter; you got me to do something I swore I never would – heap more praise on this bastard's swelled head. So your mother called you Crystal. I bet it came to her in a vision."

"My parents told me it was my dad's idea," said the assistant editor politely, her little hand lost and evidently forgotten within the old maze-maker's heavy grip. "He's the one more into extra dimensions."

"Yes, those extra ones. Still with us, is he, your dad? On our earthly plane?"

"Oh yeah, he's doing real well. He makes these special birdhouses in Vermont. They're like apartment buildings, for the purple martins, to put out in the marshes and on golf courses, to keep the bugs down without chemicals."

"Enchanting," Izzy said, and Bech could feel his old rival's creative gears turn a worn cog or two – birds, a city of such apartment houses, a mock epic satirizing modern society, feather by feather. A muscle in Bech's jaw ached from suppressing an anticipatory yawn.

"Crystal has both feet on the ground," he said protectively.

"Not, I hope, every single hour of the day," Izzy said with roguish gallantry, releasing her hand from his enveloping grip as if slowly disclosing a humid secret.

Crystal gazed at her creased palm and told Bech nervously, "Mr. Flaggerty says there are some German bookclub people here he'd like you to meet." As they threaded their way toward these sacred guests, Bech tried to comfort her; her hand was bright pink from the prolonged pressure. "That's America's most portentous writer," he said. "Didn't they assign you some Thornbush in college?"

"Something about Nixon," she said. "Or was that Philip Roth? I didn't get very far in it. Is Nixon the President who kept hitting people with golf balls?"

"Try Izzy when you're older. He's what is called professionally *un monstre sacré. Guten Abend, meine Herren,*" he smoothly continued, they having arrived at the smiling Germans, who spoke English so beautifully that it seemed to Bech that a polished metal language-machine hung in front of their faces.

With the help of two old-fashioneds and a frequently refilled wineglass, he felt the party as an enormous success, a spontaneous outpouring of love for his person and of respect for his slim but agile oeuvre. Even those who were not here were here: his mother, dead nearly a half-century ago but her faith in him still a live goad, and Norma Latchett, his mistress and fruitful irritant for many years, and Bea Latchett, his wife and mollescent muse for, alas, too brief a period, and all the women he had burningly coveted and (a much smaller number) fleetingly possessed, and, having joined the piano and the bass, Woody Allen himself, hitting one high note after another on the old licorice stick, as we used to call it. In his imagination Bech presided over this gathering – "*Dies ist mein Endfest,*" he had told the Germans, to their puzzled, civil guffaws – with superhuman energy and charm, gliding from one conversational knot to another, intruding the deft words which let each guest know that his or her presence was especially meaningful. Each brought to him, as the worms brought Badroulbadour up from her tomb in the Wallace Stevens poem, a piece of himself, from his scampish boyhood on the Upper West Side to his heady days as a negotiable item of

American cultural exchange abroad. Skip Reynolds was there, now retired from the State Department and the president of a bankrupt Long Island college, and Angus Desmouches, the ubiquitous fashion photographer, whose wide head of wiry black hair had turned as white as coal in a negative, and Lucy Ebright, who had put Bech into one of her innumerable novels but he could never find the one, and Tad Greenbaum, the six-foot-four, highly personable hero of *Think Big*, Bech's lone best-seller. Even Pamela Thornbush showed up, as she had promised but Bech had not dared hope, on the arm of her boyish brother, Zeke Towers, Jr.

Bech hugged Pamela but her breasts did not squeak. Her cheek under his kiss was like an upstate apple, cool and smooth from the refrigerator truck. "Has Izzy been misbehaving?" she murmured breathlessly, flirtatiously into his ear.

"Sugar, when isn't he?" He loved that in himself, how smoothly corrupt he could sound.

"Who's the girl in the silver dress he's got cornered?"

"Her name is Crystal, but relax. He's cruising not for nooky but for some gullible slave to edit the biggest book since the dictionary. *Summa Summorum*. Why don't you tell him to think small for a change? It would be good for his cardiovascular system."

"Henry, please – you're manicky. My brother has something serious he wants to say to you."

Young Zeke looked Bech straight in the eyes, lovingly, and said, "Now, Mr. Bech, I really want to thank you for all you did to help make the Baines property available."

"The Baines property? Oh. I didn't do a thing, did I?"

"It's not something to kid about, sir. My brother-in-law says you're the only one who could have swung it, with the requisite sensitivity and tact. We've been needing that piece for five years, to complete our parcel. Now we have the whole half-block and if the city goes along we'll be putting up a building ten feet taller than the Citicorp."

"Ten feet?" Bech felt as if his two feet had been dragged down from twinkling like Tinker Bell's through his party and abruptly dressed in concrete.

"That's not counting the flagpole and airplane-warning lights. The Towers Building – the dream of my dad's lifetime. We'll have our own tunnel into both the Fifty-third Street station on the Queens line and the Fifty-first Street on the Lex. Some day, when they renovate, we might even get the name of a station. Think of it, Mr. Bech: as you pull in you'll see TOWERS spelled out in tiles on the wall."

Pamela broke in, adding, "We're all so thrilled and grateful, Henry." Her blue eyes were bright as amethysts; the freckles on her bosom danced; her round cheeks flamed. Money does that, he thought – promotes health and strong family feeling.

"We're going to express our appreciation some way, you can count on that," Zeke assured the septuagenarian author. Bech winced under the glare of that frat-boy sincerity, that dazzling Wasp blankness which comes of never having been scorned and persecuted.

"I don't deserve a thing, honest Injun," Bech protested, at the same time wondering, with a tingle that spread from his scalp to the soles of his concrete shoes, what this expression of plutocratic appreciation might consist of. A Mercedes? A cottage in the Hamptons? *After a lifetime/of dwelling among fine shades/a payoff at last.*

BECH PLEADS GUILTY

NOW, AND ONLY NOW, can it be told. Until recently, possible legal ramifications have laid a seal of silence on the three weeks that Bech once spent in Los Angeles, being sued for libel. The year was 1972. Vietnam was winding down, and the seeds of Watergate were nestled warm within Nixon's paranoia. Bech was a mere forty-nine, wallowing in the long trough between the publication, in 1963, of his rather disappointingly received chef d'oeuvre, *The Chosen*, and, sixteen years later, the triumphantly sleazy best-seller *Think Big*. He lived in dowdy bachelor solitude in his apartment at West 99th Street and Riverside, and, though continuing royalties from his 1955 semi-Beat near-classic *Travel Light* dribbled in, along with other odd sums, his need for money was acute enough to drive him out into the sunlit agora of a wider America: he went around impersonating himself at colleges and occasionally accepted a magazine assignment, if it seemed eccentric enough to be turned, by a little extra willful spin, into art. Art – as understood in the era of his boyhood, which extended through the Depression and ended in 1941 – was his god, his guiding star.

When a new New York biweekly called *Flying Fur*, in hopeful echo of *Rolling Stone*, asked him to write an "impressionistic sort of piece" on the new, post-studio Hollywood, he consented, imagining that he would be visiting the site of the black-and-white melodramas that had entranced his adolescence. Alas, he found instead a world in full and awful color, like reels of fermenting, bleached Kodachrome stock – cans and cans of worms, of agents and manipulators voraciously trying, in the absence of the autocratic old studios, to assemble

393

blockbuster-potential "packages" within the chaotic primal soup of underemployed actors, directors, stuntmen, and all such other loose hands once kept busy within the film industry when its assembly lines moved and television hadn't yet kidnapped its mass audience. Bech had described what he saw and felt, and got sued for his trouble. Admirer of Hollywood melodrama though he had been, he couldn't believe it. "You mean I actually have to go out there again, to sit in a courtroom and be sued for just writing the truth?"

"What is truth?" his New York lawyer asked over the phone, each syllable ticking into the meter running at, in those days, $110 an hour.

Bech had been paid $1,250 for the article, plus the expenses of his week on the West Coast doing research. In the two years since it had appeared, *Flying Fur* had gone belly-up. Its editors and layout artists had dispersed to other frontiers, and its old offices on East 17th Street – canary-yellow walls hung with Pop Art prints – were given over to a team of young tooth-implant specialists. This lawsuit, however, survived, an unkillable zombie stalking its prey through the mists.

"You'll love our West Coast team," the lawyer said, mollifyingly. "Tom Rantoul may not look it, Henry, but he is a legal wizard. I don't know when he last lost a case; my memory doesn't go back that far."

Rantoul proved to be a huge and hearty former athlete of Southern background, with an inward slope to the back of his head and meaty though manicured hands. At a lawyer-client luncheon on Bech's fourth day in Los Angeles, Rantoul announced, "Well, lady and gents, it looks like we done finally got ourselves a judge." He gestured with one of those manicured hands toward the browned filet of sole on the defendant's plate. "He's about the color of that there fish."

Bech hesitated with his fork, then stabbed and parted the white meat. Racial issues did not seem, offhand, to be at stake. He was being sued because he called the plaintiff, a venerable Hollywood agent named Morris Ohrbach, an "arch-gouger" who for "greedy reasons of his own rake-off" had "widened the prevailing tragic rift between the literary and cinematic arts." He knew the phrases by heart, since they had been the subject of fitful and increasingly dire communications ever since his article had appeared, under the title (supplied by a vanished sub-editor) "The Only Winners Left in Tinseltown." Ohrbach was claiming that he had suffered five million dollars in personal distress and humiliation, and another five million in loss of professional credibility. In the course of Bech's week, two years before, of bilious-making lunches and pay-phone calls and hot waits in the nightmarishly constant California sun, Ohrbach's name had repeatedly surfaced, with a spume of that mingled outrage and admiration with which the carnivores of the film world hail an especially spectacular predator. It was Ohrbach who had invented the 15-percent agent's fee, with a non-returnable down payment by the client; it was Ohrbach who had devised a discretionary clause whereby, above the 15 percent, up to half of the client's earnings was to be invested at the agent's discretion, with a 3-percent investment commission withdrawn semi-annually from the capital. It was related to Bech how, having bled the great pop singer Lanna Jerome and her gullible husband at the time (a former pet hairdresser, famous for his poodle cuts) of millions of her earnings, Ohrbach demanded a half-million more to prop up the teetering edifice of porkbelly options and dry oil wells he had constructed, and promptly sued her when she and her new husband (a former disco bouncer) at last moved to stop the bleeding. Ohrbach was lightning-quick to sue. He would even, as a scorpion when aroused will supposedly sting itself, sue his own lawyers, if he felt a suit had been inadequately prosecuted.

As to Bech, he had a soft spot for Lanna Jerome. He and Claire Hoagland, a skittish blond love object he had romanced when his heart was relatively young and uncallused, had met to the background music of Lanna's first hit, "Comin' On Strong," and had separated, four years later, while the singer's "Don't Send Me Back My Letters" ("Keep them in their envelopes / Holding my forsaken hopes") dominated the airwaves. This soft spot of Bech's, painfully touched by the tales of Ohrbach's predatory inroads into Lanna Jerome's sentimentally generated fortune, may have been what landed him here, in the iron grip of lawyers. Even when he wrote the word, "arch-gouger" seemed a touch extreme, with a bit of extra, private spin. But hardly, he thought, actionable. A creeping sense of unreality enveloped him as, bit by bit, the certified letters on legal stationery piled up, and a lawyer of his own had to be obtained, and depositions were taken in an awkward atmosphere blended of jollity and menace, and various forestalling actions and moves for dismissal from his side were consumed in an inexorable munching process on the other side. Finally the legalities required Bech to make another continent-spanning visit to Los Angeles, the capital of organized unreality. The law, with its slow motion and spurious courtesy, was at home here, in a world of pretend where amid the plaster pillars and masked trapdoors the unpredictable imps of fantasy roamed. Rantoul, having raised the spectre of race, now touched upon the hazards of regional prejudice, allowing solemnly that there was no telling how the jury might respond to Bech's reputation as a sophisticated Easterner.

"Ohrbach is a Westerner, then? Some cowboy," Bech said. His lawyer only slowly smiled.

"Yes, in a way, Morris is one of ours," he conceded. His was a hybrid accent wherein Georgia still controlled the vowels.

"So are the rats in the Santa Monica dump," Bech snapped; a long buildup of indignation lay repressed in him. "He's the kind of vulture that's drowning Hollywood in crassness and cocaine." Even as he spoke, he wondered if he hadn't, finding boyish refuge each Saturday afternoon and many a weekday evening in the hypertrophied cinema palaces of upper Broadway, ideal-ized the old Hollywood, the Dearborn of tintype dreams.

The lawyer's assistant spoke up. He was named Gregg Nunn, and wore a Dutch-boy haircut and thick aviator-style glasses. His voice had an irritating timbre, a near-squeak, like the semi-musical sound produced by rubbing the rims of a glass with a wet finger. "Oh, I think he's quite a puritan," he said. "He works these incredibly long hours and lives quite modestly, over in Westwood, behind the university. In his own image of himself, he's a conscientious slave to his clients' interests."

Irritated by this underling's elfin shine of perverse admiration, Bech said to Rantoul, "To get back to your point: I can't believe a jury of L.A. working men and women is going to identify that much with a ruthless Hollywood wheeler-dealer."

"Oh, they identify," was the drawled answer. "Everybody thinks movies out here. They're as proud of their local product as the good folks in Iowa are of corn. The opposition is sure as shooting going to present this as an effete Eastern smart-aleck maligning a worker in the fields. What you call gouging the plaintiff will endeavor to construe as the going rate and simple honorable enterprise."

Bech's voice, after Rantoul's, sounded rather anxious and hurried in his own ears – effetely Eastern. "But what about what he did to poor Lanna Jerome? He absolutely disem*bow*eled her money." Violent gory images – buzz-saws ripping through stacks of dollar bills, vultures and hyenas tugging at the ribbed carcass of a succulent chanteuse beneath a blazing desert sun – assaulted the defendant's head. Perhaps the lawsuit was right; he was too suggestible to be a trustworthy journalist. His father, as hard as diamonds, had always scoffed at Bech's dreams of being a writer. Writing a hard-boiled exposé like "The Only Winners Left in Tinseltown" for a fly-by-night rag like *Flying Fur* had been an attempt, perhaps, to convince the old man that he could turn a dollar when he needed it. Abraham Bech had died last year, in the subway, under the sliding filth of the East River. At least he hadn't lived to crow over this debacle.

"Now you're talking the local language," the lawyer said, his eye moving from his very clean plate to Bech's half-eaten sole. "You get Lanna Jerome up on the stand, the jury's yours. But she's hiding out in Palm Springs and has dodged every summons we've put out on her."

"Anyway," said Gregg Nunn, "there's no telling how the jury would react. That long affair she had with the governor of Nevada didn't sit too well with a lot of fundamentalists."

Rantoul explained, "L.A.'s a lot like Iran these days; everybody's either a fundamentalist or a whore. And then there's this: if we seem to have Lanna on our side, the jury may figure there's tons of money and why not throw poor old Morris the sop of a million or so?"

My non-existent million, Bech thought. The fish he had swallowed bit the tender lining of his stomach, and he devoutly wished he were back in the twelve-table Italian restaurant he knew, just off upper Broadway on 97th, sitting solitary with a plate of spinach fettuccine and that afternoon's *Post*. Not even in his idealistic postwar *Partisan Review* and *Accent* stage had he dreamed that words, mere words, had so much power – the power to pull him across the continent and dump him in this sumptuous restaurant with these three expensive strangers. The restaurant was wide and deep and dark, in that heavy baronial style that had possessed Hollywood at the height of its grandeur. There were carved dadoes and corbeled stones and leaded windows with Gothic arches. Errol Flynn and the sheriff of Nottingham (played by Basil Rathbone) might stroll in at any minute.

The fourth person at the table, the "lady" of Rantoul's jocular announcement, was a female paralegal named Rita: tightly pulled-back long black hair, carmine lips, hoop earrings, and an unsmiling Latina intensity. On a blue-lined pad beside her plate she sporadically took rapid notes.

Flying Fur had carried some libel insurance but bankruptcy had canceled it. If the jury found for the defense, Rantoul planned to countersue for legal expenses. In the meantime, Bech had drawn out his savings and borrowed from his publisher on a novel he felt much too distracted and put-upon to write. Four pricey days had already been spent waiting for the Los Angeles legal system to find a judge with space on his docket for this case. Ohrbach's attorneys had asked for a jury trial and that would take more days. Biting, nibbling, churning hatred of Morris Ohrbach robbed Bech of his appetite, and he asked his lawyer if he'd like to try his sole. "Just a taste," the big man obligingly drawled, reaching with his fork. "There was quite a to-do in the Food Section of the L.A. *Times* when they hired this chef all the way from Grenoble, France, and Ah confess Ah couldn't much tell from my pork chop what the fuss was all about."

* * *

The judge was really more the color of a pale briefcase, and surprisingly young, and amazingly, Bech thought as the days in court wore on, patient. The judge sat for hours without saying a word, leaning a bit to his left, as if away from the winds of justice blowing out of the slowly filling jury box. When he did speak, it was firmly and softly, with an excessive fairness, Bech felt, to the inept, time-wasting shenanigans of Ohrbach's counsel, a short and excitable man called Ralph Kepper. The defense team named him Sergeant Kepper. He always wore khaki pants and baggy sports jackets, which amounted to a statement: he was no fancy-Dan pinstriped Eastern-establishment cat's-paw, he was an honest workaday legal man.

In questioning the prospective jurors, Kepper would ask them if they had ever read a magazine called *Flying Fur* (they answered, invariably, no) and if they had any prima-facie prejudice against "sophisticated, cynical, New York-style journalism." Sometimes he would ask them if, when they heard the words "Hollywood agent," they suffered any "pejorative input." Language did strange things in Kepper's mouth, and he frequently announced himself as having "misspoke" – "Yeronner, I misspoke myself."

Nevertheless, this rumpled clown was regarded by the pale-brown judge with unwinking gravity, and his endless peremptory challenges caused juror after juror to leave the box, humiliated. The tactic, Bech's team explained to him, was merely to prolong the proceedings and make the defendant all the more willing to offer a settlement as the cheapest way out.

"Well?" Bech asked. "Would it be? The cheapest way out."

Rantoul was stunned enough to stop chewing. He swallowed and rested a thick hand on Bech's sleeve. "Even if it were," he said, "this team won't let you. Now, don't tell me that you lack team spirit."

A spacious cafeteria occupied the top floor of the Los Angeles Courthouse, and here the defense team gathered for lunch every day, during the long recesses. Protocol dictated that, but for curt, prim nods of recognition, they ignore Kepper as he ate in morose solitude, gnawing at a sandwich that kept getting lost under sheaves of legal paper. Ohrbach, over a week into the proceedings, had not deigned to appear yet. Rantoul thought the jury, when at last in place, would resent this show of indifference, whereas Nunn thought it might, on the contrary, signify an impressively crowded schedule and enhance his eventual appearance. "Not being here," Nunn fancifully continued, his little hands flickering and his elfin face gleaming under the tidy pale Dutch bangs, "makes him the central figure of our drama, the awaited Godot, whose minions carry on in his behalf. Absence is an awesome statement, as the world's religions demonstrate."

"He lets hisself get arrogant," Rantoul allowed, shifting in his chair before engulfing a thick wedge, topped with whipped cream, of cafeteria pecan pie. "That's come out in some of his other trials. He goes along real smooth on the stand, and then he gets cute. He stops minding the store. It's hurt him before, and it'll hurt him again."

The description touched a furtive chord of sympathy in Bech. "Cute" and "not minding the store" were phrases his late father would have used for what his only son had chosen to do in life. Young Bech didn't have his feet on the ground, he didn't know his ass from his elbow. It was true. Just writing "arch-gouger" showed a kind of dreaminess; he should have let the facts and the percentages speak for themselves. He had been inflamed by misplaced love for Lanna Jerome, confusing her with dear lost Claire. He had tried to get her attention with the fervor of his denunciation of her despoiler. But how could Lanna Jerome care about him and what he wrote in a doomed 17th Street rag? She received three million plus some points of the unadjusted gross for a feature film, and her last album went platinum within a week of issue.

Outside the cafeteria, the roof held an open-air promenade, from which one could see vast hazed tracts of pastel housing, glass skyscrapers, merging ribbons of freeway, and far hills dried to the gold of the southern-California winter. On a near hill perched the shiny blue stadium where the once-Brooklyn Dodgers played, and, down below, across the street, stood a gold-trimmed opera house, with a small green park around it. Though it all looked nothing like his idea of a metropolis, Bech felt at home on this roof. When he was an awkward thirteen his family moved from the Upper West Side to Brooklyn. The West Side was getting too full of blacks and spics, his father felt, and Brooklyn was where two of Abe Bech's brothers, Ike and Joe, had lived for years. His father was a dealer in diamonds and precious metals on West 47th Street. Though the materials were precious, the competition was stiff and the profit margin ever more finely shaved. Life was a struggle. Even in Brooklyn, it turned out, it was a struggle. The kids weren't necessarily tougher than those on the Upper West Side, but they were provincial – intolerant of outsiders, un-understanding of nuances. Henry was already a creature of nuances. For fresh air the easiest thing for him, rather than walking the eight blocks to Prospect Park and risking getting hassled by bigger teenagers, was to go up on the roof of their Ninth Street brownstone. The other rooftops of Brooklyn spread out in a vast dark plain thickly planted with chimney pots; on one edge of the plain, like a rectilinear mountain hazed by carbon dioxide, Manhattan rose. Now, on the opposite side of the continent, Bech found himself remembering those monotonous tarpaper vistas and again, as when an adolescent, yearning to fly away, to launch himself from the roof into another life, an airy, glamorous life of literature.

The trial finally got under way. The plaintiff's side had exhausted all its challenges. Rantoul tried to expedite matters by challenging almost nobody: only one old dignified Chicano gardener, whose command of English appeared halting (he was insulted; he protested, "I understand good, I am citizen since twenty years!"), and a snappily dressed Bel Air matron who had once been married to a lawyer. "You never know how she might react," Rantoul explained. "Ex-wives just aren't rational where the law is concerned."

The solemnly impaneled twelve jury members, with the two alternates, sat on the left of the courtroom. Bech and what spectators there might be – a stray street person; a courthouse office worker taking a break – faced the judge's high desk across an area of chairs and tables; here the lawyers, the agonists, performed and the court stenographer, like an unspeaking

Greek chorus, rippled out yards and yards of typed notes. The paper folded itself, accordion-style, into a cardboard box on the far side of his shorthand machine. The stenographer was a thin pale bald man with a yellow toothbrush mustache and an unfocused blue gaze. He dressed like the old vaudeville comedians, in checked suits and polka-dot ties. When the lawyers held a conference with the judge, he hurried with his machine to eavesdrop and kept on tapping. When the judge declared some passage of procedure off the record, his tireless long white fingers dropped to his lap and his glazed stare rested on a blank wall near the American flag. He was the only person in the room who seemed to Bech not to be wasting his time.

Though by modernist prescription artists live on the edge of respectability, in a state of liberating derangement, Bech had never before been hauled into court. He had heard that the wheels of justice ground fine, but he had not expected those wheels to be so wobbly, so oddly swiveled in every direction but that of the simple truth.

The first witness for the plaintiff was a mincing professor of English at Southern Cal who responded at length to Sergeant Kepper's questions about the words involved. The prefix "arch," by way of Anglo-Saxon and Old French, derives from a Greek verb meaning "to begin, to rule," and signifies either the highest of its type, as in "archbishop" or "archangel" or, to quote Webster, "most fully embodying the qualities of his or its time." Mr. Bech's article asserted, then, that Mr. Ohrbach was the chief, or most fully developed, gouger in the entire Los Angeles area. "Gouge," authorities tend to agree, is a word of Celtic origin, by way of Late Latin, referring to a chisel of concave cross section. Had the word Mr. Bech chosen been "chiseler," it was interesting to note, the implication of wrongdoing would have been more distinct, and the connotation of brute strength rather less. The phrase "greedy reasons of his own rake-off" is less easy to decipher, and for a time the expert thought there might be a typographical error or an editorial slip involved. The expression "rake-off," of course, stems from the old practice in gambling houses of the croupier with his rake taking the house's percentage out of the chips on the table.

"Widened the prevailing tragic rift between the literary and cinematic arts" is also far from clear, since the two arts have never been close and the tragedy of their separation would seem to lie only in the eye of the beholder, in this case a writer of modestly paid fiction and journalism who might have had in mind the much greater financial rewards of film work.

"Objection: conjecture," Rantoul automatically growled.

"Sustained," the judge as automatically responded.

All this semantic disquisition was putting the jury to sleep. They sat there, in their two sextuple rows (five men, seven women; five whites, four blacks, two Asian-Americans, and a part-Cherokee) plus the two alternates, who sat beside but not in the elevated jury box, all hoping to see Lanna Jerome, with her rice-powder makeup, her artificial mole, her slinky, slimmed-down figure, her hair dyed soot-black and moussed into short spikes. "Slinky, slimmed-down": as was common knowledge among her millions of fans, Lanna had a weakness for Dr Pepper and junk snacks. After her relationship with the governor of Nevada had broken up, she put on thirty pounds in mournful bingeing. Bech had loved her all the more for that vulnerable, blubbery side of her.

Rantoul and the word-expert batted the prefix "arch" around, the latter finally conceding, mincingly, that its use here might signify merely a relatively high standing as a gouger, not a supreme and ruling status in an organized group of them.

The next witness for the prosecution, a self-styled "expert in media," discoursed on the circulation figures of *Flying Fur* during its eighteen months of existence. Though the subscriptions in southern California were only forty-two in number, of which eighteen went to libraries, the influence of those few copies would be hard to overestimate; the magazine, as the latest "hip" word from New York City, was avidly read by agents, actors, producers, and other persons active in Mr. Ohrbach's business, and an adverse reference in its pages would certainly do him substantial professional damage.

Rantoul had a field day with that witness, and ate an especially hearty lunch in the sky-view cafeteria. The trial was under way, and still Ohrbach had not showed up. However, Bech did have a glimpse, one afternoon, of the judge out by the elevators, going home. He was wearing a denim suit the tasty shade of honeydew melon, with bell-bottom pants and a lapel-less jacket. Out of his robes, he was a smooth young dude heading into the pleasures of the evening. He studiously avoided Bech's eye.

In the legal world, eye avoidance is an art. Morris Ohrbach turned out to be a master of it. When, the next day, he at last appeared, he entered the courtroom bobbing and smiling in all directions, but his smiles landed nowhere, like the fist-flurry of a boxer warming up. His gaze, as benign and generalized as that of a Byzantine icon, flicked past Bech's face. One of Ohrbach's well-known eccentricities was a virtually religious avoidance of being photographed, so Bech had had no idea of his archenemy's appearance. The elderly plaintiff, of middle height, hunched over like a man about to break into a run; he had this vaguely smiling mouth, a large nose, and a shock of wavy white hair thrust forward by a cowlick that reminded Bech of his own stiffly curly, hard-to-control hair. Bech's hair was still basically dark, and his posture had not yet acquired an elderly stoop, but the resemblance was nevertheless strong. Ohrbach looked enough like him to be his father.

The jury stirred, excited by the presence of someone who, if not exactly famous, had bilked the famous. The judge moment-arily sat up straight, and paid scrupulous attention to the morning's witnesses, a series of character witnesses on Ohrbach's behalf. They were women, Hollywood hostesses, who, at first timidly and then irrepressibly, testified to the plaintiff's humanity – his courteous manners, his unfailing good humor and even temper, his personal and financial generosity to a host of causes ranging from the state of Israel to a little-league baseball team of impoverished Mexican-American youngsters.

"Morrie Ohrbach is a superb human being!" one especially pneumatic widow cried, in an abrupt release of pressure; she had been previously stifled by Rantoul's objections to her breathy account of how, during her bereavement some years before, the agent had been assiduously attentive and beautifully considerate. Further, she added defiantly, as Rantoul half-stood to object again, *all* the investments he had talked *her* into had made money – *scads* of it.

Another woman, squarish and brown and bedecked with Navajo jewelry, testified that when she heard that her dear friend Morris had been called a gouger in one of these snide Eastern magazines she broke down and cried, off and on, for days. He would drop by the house in the late afternoon and looked an absolute wreck – he got so thin she was afraid he'd sink, just a bundle of bones, in her swimming pool and drown. Morrie himself, poor soul, didn't have a swimming pool any more; he lived in this tiny two-bedroom condo in Westwood and had had to sell all but one of his sports cars, that's how much of a gouger he was.

Rantoul in cross-examination elicited that the move to Westwood and the sale of his sports cars had followed the adverse legal judgment in the Lanna Jerome case. "Oh, that *hid*eous woman!" was the unabashed response. "Everybody knows how she chased after the governor of Nevada until she broke up his lovely home and absolutely *wrecked* his career! He could have been *Pres*ident!"

At lunch, Bech confessed he was getting scared. Ohrbach was being painted as a saint, and in fact he did look awfully sweet, and rather touchingly shabby. He had worn a linen suit with a yellow sheen, and a sad little bow tie that called attention to his neck wattles.

Rantoul snorted, "And Ah bet you think a Gila monster has a friendly face." He had taken off his coat and turned back his sleeves to dig into some cafeteria corn on the cob. Flecks of starch dotted his jaw.

"There *is* something friendly about his face. Something sensitive and shy. When he came in, he seemed so outnumbered. Just poor old Sergeant Kepper and him, against all of us."

"Us-all ruthless Eastern-establishment types," Rantoul filled in. "You got the message he was sending. Ah'm sure glad, Henry, you ain't on that there jury."

Rita laughed, showing dazzling sharp teeth. "It is you who are

sweet, Henry, to see in such a way." Like Lanna Jerome, she had
a mole near her chin. In Rita's case, it looked genuine.

"To me," said Gregg Nunn, "his face is weird. I get queasy and
dizzy, looking at it. There's no center. It's like he's a hologram.
And his eyes. What color are his eyes? Nobody knows – we're all
too spooked to look, and if you notice, even when he seems to
be smiling at you, his eyes are downcast, like he's trying to see
through the lids. He's an alien – he can see through his eyelids!"
As the boy expanded on his fantasy, his small round hands made
wider and wider circles, and his voice attained so excited a pitch
that several heads in the cafeteria turned around.

Kepper and his client were not here; they were off, perhaps
hatching more character witnesses. Or witnesses to expose Bech,
his whole discreditable career. His refusal to learn the diamond
trade at his father's knee. His restless resistance to his mother's
intrusive love. His failure to become a poet, like Auden and
Delmore Schwartz, both of whom he had met in his postwar
phase of haunting the Village, or a critic, like Dwight Macdonald
and Clement Greenberg, who also had been caught in his skein
of acquaintance. He had felt that what critics did was too pat, too
dictatorial; he preferred, lazily, to submit to his subjective ink-
lings and glimpses, and to turn these into epiphanies briefer than
Joyce's and less grim than Kafka's. He had failed his publisher,
hearty, life-loving, travel-tanned Big Billy Vanderhaven, by
refusing to deliver, in the wake of *Travel Light*'s mild *succès
d'estime*, the "big" novel just sitting there, in the realm of Platonic
ideas, waiting to take the public and the book clubs by storm; he
had failed his first editor, dapper, fastidious Ned Clavell, by
refusing to remove from the sprawling text of *The Chosen* all
those earthy idioms and verbal frontalia that chilled, in still-prissy
1963, the book's critical and popular reception. Bech had just
refused to pan out, as author, son, and lover. One woman after
another, having given her naked all, stridently had pointed out
that he was unable to make a commitment. Behind him stretched
a chain of disappointments going back to his grade-school
teachers at P.S. 87 – kindly Irish nuns *manquées*, most of them –
and his professors at NYU, whom he felt he had usually wound
up disappointing, after a flashy first paper. He failed, or declined,

to graduate. He was not a superb human being. He was a vain, limp leech on the leg of literature as it waded through swampy times. In the courthouse cafeteria, he lost his appetite, and left half of his tuna-salad sandwich untouched, and all of the butter-almond ice cream he had taken for dessert, homesick for the Italian restaurant's spumoni. Rantoul, having consumed a platter of meatloaf, gravy, mashed potatoes, and peas, delicately inquired after these remnants, and made them disappear.

The next character witnesses were other agents, who praised Ohrbach as their mentor and inspiration, as an immensely creative and concerned thinker on behalf of the film industry. It was Ohrbach, claimed one rough beast in a tieless silk shirt and a number of gold chains, who had originated the valuable concept of total agent involvement – no longer could one rest content with forging advantageous deals for the client, but one should follow up and make sure that the rewards, in the always uncertain and sometimes abbreviated career of a performing artist, were secure and themselves performing up to capacity. Not just career management, but total life-assets management was the basis of the concept, traceable (in the rough beast's view, his ringed hands chopping the air and chest hair frothing from between his chains) to the genius of Morris Ohrbach. Then secretaries – ex-bimbos with plastic eyelashes and leathery, bone-deep tans – testified to Ohrbach's generosity as a boss, and told of days off granted with pay when a mother died, of bonuses at both Christmas and Passover, of compassionate leaves of absence during spells of health or man trouble. Clients – sallow, slightly faded and off-center male and female beauties – confided how Morris would tide them over, would reduce his cut to $12\frac{1}{2}$ percent, would give them fatherly advice for free, out of his own precious time.

Throughout this torrent of homage, its object, who sat beside Sergeant Kepper at a table six feet in front of Bech, actively pursued his good works, scribbling away on pieces of paper and annotating small stacks of correspondence and financial statements and occasionally dashing off and sealing a letter, with a licking and thumping of the envelope so noisy as to cause the court stenographer to glance around and the judge to direct a disciplinary stare. Was the judge, from his angle, receiving the same piteous impression, of vulnerable elderliness, that Bech was gathering from behind? The cords of Ohrbach's slender neck strained, the shirt collar looked a size too big and not entirely fresh, the overgrown ears had sprouted white whiskers. The frail skull gently wagged in decrepitude's absent-minded palsy.

Abe Bech had not allowed himself to appear old, though he had been seventy-six when he died. He had used a rinse to keep his hair dark, sat in the winter under a sun lamp, and gone off to the diamond district each day in a crisp white shirt laundered at a place that handed them back to you uncreased, on hangers. Like most salesmen, he gave his best self to his prospective customers, and saved his rage, sarcasm, and indifference for his family. Though circulatory problems had for some time been affecting his legs and hands, his cerebral hemorrhage had come out of the blue. In death as in life he had been abrupt and hard to reach. His last impact upon the metropolis – the only one to make the newspapers – was a half-hour delay underground at rush hour, inconveniencing thousands. Since the service elevator at the Clark Street station in Brooklyn Heights was out of commission, the stretcher bearers had brought Abraham Bech's blanketed body up all those dirty tile steps, through the flood of exasperated commuters. In his son's mind it had the grandeur of a pharaoh's funeral procession up from the Nile, into the depths of a Pyramid where the mighty soul's embalmed shell would lie forever intact.

By leaning forward and reaching with his arm, Bech could have tapped Ohrbach's thin, hunched shoulder and asked his forgiveness for calling him an arch-gouger. But the gesture would have admitted ten million dollars' worth of guilt, and betrayed his team.

The team was less impressed by the plaintiff's accumulating case than Bech was. Rantoul even rose to indignation about Ohrbach's chiropractor, an autocratically bald man who from the witness stand claimed to have observed a marked psychosomatic deterioriation in his patient immediately after the *Flying Fur* article had appeared. Solemnly turning over leaves from his files, in a cumbersome ring binder, the chiropractor described lower-back spasms and attendant pain that incapacitated the sensitive agent for months thereafter and perhaps permanently impaired his professional effectiveness. Rantoul had asked to examine the pages that the chiropractor consulted, and he spotted terms like "mental-stress-induced" and "spastic depression" inserted in a smaller handwriting, in a fresher ink, into the records of two long years ago, when "The Only Winners Left in Tinseltown" had appeared. At lunch, the attorney boasted, "Ah asked the judge to admit the file in evidence and Kepper turned pale as a goose's belly. He withdrew the testimony. We would have had 'em for perjury sure as sugar."

The last word was a modification, in Southern-courtly fashion, for Rita's benefit. As his stay in Los Angeles moved into its third week, Rita had become clearer to Bech. Her Hispanic rat-tat-tat way of thinking and talking, he saw, had been softened by North American entrepreneurism, its willingness to smile and to explore possibilities. One day when Rantoul and Nunn had some other legal fish to fry, Bech and she had gone out to lunch at a Mexican restaurant a few blocks from the courthouse. To her he had unburdened himself of his qualms, his growing sympathy and pity for the plaintiff, who seemed to be the defendant. "I feel so *guilty*," he said.

"That is a luxury you are allowing yourself," Rita explained. "Some kind of Jewish thing, identifying with the people trying to destroy you. A way of making yourself superior to a fight. That's fine, Henry. That's very lovable. That's why you have us, to do the fighting for you."

"Ohrbach's Jewish, too. Maybe he feels the same way about me."

"Don't you wish."

"How do you think it's going?"

She shrugged, making her hoop earrings wobble. "Their case is *basura*, but that doesn't mean the jury won't buy it. Juries go for underdogs and you haven't yet established yourself as one. Ohrbach is doing that. We think he's buying his shirts with the collar a size too big deliberately, and has developed on purpose that piteous head-waggle."

"Really? Then that does make me mad. Rita, let's nail the slippery bastard. May I call you Rita? Tell me, what do you do nights?"

His own nights stretched long and empty, moseying about his skyscraper hotel – a futuristic round tower arisen where two freeways met – with its many levels of underpatronized restaurants. One night he would sit at a counter watching nimble Japanese in chef hats slice steak and vegetables into a kind of edible origami; the next night he patronized the Chinese in their trickling grotto, with its small arched bridge guarded by a silk-clad hostess. He tried walking out into the night, but the downtown was eerily empty, and felt dangerous. There was only the rustle of palm trees and the roar of freeway traffic. He could never figure out where the movie houses were, or the little Italian restaurants, or the corner newsstands so ubiquitous in New York. In the mornings, however, as Bech climbed up a concrete hill above a chasm where cars vibratingly pummeled the earth and made the air quiver with carbon monoxide, he could feel in the fresh sunlight, faithfully delivered from a cloudless sky, what had fetched and held millions here: a desert clarity, a transparency that ascended from the fragile panorama of pastel buildings to the serene glassy nothingness at the heart of the heavens. No amount of reckless development and ruthless exploitation could hopelessly besmog such sublime air. This was the Promised Land; this was what Israel should have been, not some crabbed, endlessly disputed sliver of the Arab world. The Spanish had been ousted, yet remained, in the architecture, the place names, the ochre tint, the fatalism of this splendid mirage. He would arrive at the courthouse steps with a light sweat started across his shoulder blades, and a faint breathlessness of expectation.

"Oh, you don't care," Rita told him. "You must have a lot of girls back east, terribly clever and attractive East Coast girls."

"I care," he assured her.

"I do legal homework and cook for my parents and take care of my sister's kids," Rita answered. "She performs nude water ballet in a big tank at a businessmen's bar over in Venice."

"How about my taking you out to dinner, some night when she's drying off?"

"Henry, let's wait until after the verdict. You may not have enough left to pay for a single taco."

Back in court, the plaintiffs had produced their most amusing witness, who had the jury laughing until tears came; he even elicited a smile from the court stenographer as he pattered away, his fingers falling – like a pianist's more than a regular typist's – in chords. The witness was an enormously fat and beautifully spoken process server, a virtuoso of court testimony who, in attempting to subpoena Lanna Jerome, had hid in the bushes and howled outside her condo wall in Palm Springs like a dog, mewed like a kitten, and chirped like a wounded bird. The singer and screen star was notoriously fond of animals, and he had thought thus to create a window of opportunity and slap the papers at her over the sill. No soap. She never stuck her head out. He demonstrated the howl, the mew, and the chirp.

"What is the relevance of all these sound effects?" the judge asked, when the jury's laughter – slightly forced and sparse at the end, like canned laughter – had died down.

Sergeant Kepper was on his feet. "We have reason to believe, yeronner, that Ms. Jerome has changed her mind and now harbors a more favorable opinion of Mr. Ohrbach's professional services on her behalf than she did at the time wherein on advice of her unscrupulous counsel he sued her. I mean *she* sued *him*. I misspoke myself, yeronner."

"Objection. Irrelevant and immaterial and unproven hearsay," Rantoul said.

"Sustained." The judge directed the jury to forget the exchange they had just heard, and the process server pulled himself from the witness chair with the practiced skill of a wine steward easing out a champagne cork.

Up in the cafeteria, Rantoul was jubilant. "They keep opening up that Jerome can of worms like dogs returning to their mess," he gloated. "She shows up, their case is *toast*."

Gregg Nunn said excitedly, "Did you all notice how through that whole fantastic performance, with the animal noises and everything, Morrie never looked up and kept scribbling notes to himself? He's given up on this one and is working on his next finagle. The guy never rests; he's a spider, he spins lawsuits!"

Bech was grateful to Nunn for voicing his own sense of the plaintiff as a transcendent phenomenon. At night, lying unsleeping and agitated in his hotel room, he felt Ohrbach enclosing him suffocatingly. This room was in the shape of a slice of pie. Bech's head lay in the narrow end, near the shaft at the core of the round tower, in which elevators throbbed and hummed at all hours: high-priced hookers riding up with their junketing clients from the Pacific Rim, and then riding down alone. Beyond Bech's twitching feet, gold curtains hid a forest of other glass skyscrapers, in L.A.'s eerily empty and abstract downtown. Ohrbach and his implacable lawsuit had brought Bech here, wedged into this unreal corner of the continent, just as his father had irascibly moved him, on the delicate cusp of puberty, to Brooklyn. The parallel made Ohrbach seem vast, and somewhat benign, as all the forces that create us must, in our instinctive self-approval, seem benign. In spite of his legal team's warrior spirit, Bech harbored the sneaking suspicion that he and his enemy could strike a deal — indeed *were*, beneath all the vapid legal machinations, invisibly striking a deal. Ohrbach, Bech knew from the way the elderly man's misty, evasive gaze tenderly flicked past the defendant's face every morning, loved him; his apparent mercilessness hid a profound, persistent mercy.

Sure enough, the white-haired agent, brought to the stand to testify, oddly dissolved. He scotched his own case. In Rantoul's phrase, he stopped minding the store. His eyes were now as shy of the jury as they had been of the defense team; he kept gazing down at some three-by-five cards he had brought to the stand, and as the lawyers and the judge sought to resolve some question of procedure, he would compulsively begin annotating them, with an old-fashioned fountain pen that audibly scratched. Kepper tried to lead him through the mental agony of being libeled in *Flying Fur*, but Ohrbach seemed no longer much interested; rather, he wanted to speak of Lanna Jerome, how much he had loved her and her then husband for the many years of their association, how wounded he had been when she inexplicably sued him at the instigation of her new, bouncer husband, and how entirely his affection and admiration for her had survived the mere "legal wars" that he and she had been obliged to wage.

He would lay down his life for her, Ohrbach confided to the jury, and down deep he was sure that she felt the same about him.

Had she ever, Kepper asked him, sweatily trying to keep the testimony on track, called him a "gouger"?

"Oh, she might have, but only in fun. In affectionate fun. Exaggeration was her style – a performer's stock in trade."

Kepper blanched. Had any of his clients, he asked Ohrbach, ever accused him of gouging, to the best of his recollection?

"There's always a discussion," Ohrbach smilingly allowed, "before the exact terms of any arrangement are ironed out. Things are said in heat that neither party actually means."

Had anybody in his entire life, Kepper asked, almost shouting in exasperation, ever called him a "gouger," let alone an "arch-gouger"?

These were creampuff pitches, Bech could see, meant to be knocked out of the park; but Ohrbach was letting them pop into the catcher's mitt.

His waggling white-crowned head thrust even lower from his oversize collar as the talent agent said, in a shaky, slanting voice that still kept an edge of New York accent, "Well, in fifty years of working the Hollywood mills I've been called any number of things. I don't recall ever seeing it in print, though, until the article by this nice young man." And his shifty eyes dared follow his withered hand, for a second, in its shy gesture toward the place where Bech had been sitting and stewing day after day. Ohrbach was reaching out. David and Absalom. Joseph and his brothers. The Prodigal Son. Forgiveness, the patriarchal prerogative. Bech fought an impulse to leap up and go kneel before the witness and bow his head for the touch of the blessing that his own father had denied.

"Shit," said Sergeant Kepper. His stubby arms lifted from his sides and slapped back down, like a penguin's flippers. "I give up." To the electrified court he apologized, "Sorry, yeronner. I misspoke myself."

"Didn't that break your heart?" Bech asked Rita that Saturday night, at a Polynesian restaurant in Venice Beach, where great flaming things were hurried back and forth on platters that sounded wired to amplify the sizzle. "His own lawyer giving up on him."

"No, Henry," she said. "My heart is as fragile as any other woman's, but that did not break it. One shabby performer crossing up another, it happens all the time. I think our plaintiff's brain has been scrambled by too many years of *escamoteo*."

"He seemed to miss Kepper's signals entirely."

"Your pet gouger is not in his prime – why should that sadden you so?"

The restaurant door was open to the soft California twilight, its pacific silence gashed by the grating sound of skateboards and roller skates hurtling muscular young bodies along.

"Speaking of people in their primes," he said, "where is the place where your sister does her underwater act?"

"Far from here, in terms of both distance and ambiance. I did not want you to ogle my sister. I want you all for myself, Henry. I am more jealous than your New York sophisticated girls." With a volcanic burst of flame and a thunderous cascade of scalding fat, their appetizer, Pork Strips à la Molokai, arrived. A pack of Rollerbladers cascaded past. Bech saw, with a simultaneous rising and sinking sensation, that his date had primed herself to go all the way.

The case for the defense was brisk and anticlimactic. Rantoul had found more witnesses than he needed to swear that Ohrbach was no angel. A revered octogenarian mogul from the old studio days, crowned by even more snowy hair than the plaintiff, answered, when asked what Ohrbach's reputation was in the industry, with a single phrase, "The pits." Another witness, an actress whose smooth, almond-eyed face was vaguely familiar to millions for having played female co-pilots, androids, and extraterrestrial princesses in low-budget space movies, wept as she described the shockingly fractional fortune left to her after Ohrbach's ministrations.

Bech found her performance a bit overwrought, but it froze all the profiles of the jury – compacted, from his angle, like one of those patriotic posters Norman Rockwell had crammed with a cross-section of Americans. Not quite all profiles, actually, because one of the two alternates, a large round-faced woman in a series of unfortunate pants suits, had taken to staring at him. Her luminous moon face bothered the corner of his eye all day. Whenever he happened to glance toward her, she gave him a wink. He would have been more heartened by this if she hadn't been only an alternate. It was a sign, he supposed, of habituation when a locality's females began to zero in. He had been out here nearly three weeks, at the cost of a thousand or more a day. If he winked back at the alternate juror, the judge might declare a mistrial. Bech determinedly refocused on the back of Ohrbach's head, and noticed a pathetic little bald spot, a peek of defenseless pink amid the snowy waves, where a cowlick swirled. When he had viewed his father at the Brooklyn morgue, Bech had been struck by how thin his hair had become; as long as Abe Bech was alive, the Grecian Formula, the year-round tan, and his ferocious will had enforced the illusion of a full and bristling head.

At the end of that day's testimony, when the plaintiff quaveringly stood near the door and let his cloudy, sad, reflexive smile skid here and there across the courtroom faces, Bech accidentally caught his eye and, with winks on his mind, gave him one.

Or did he? He couldn't believe he would do a thing so disastrous. His enemy's eyes filmed over with fishiness; they were virtually colorless, dragged up from some depth of the sea where light made no difference. Bech blushed in embarrassment, and tried to picture ten million dollars, stacked up in bundled tens and twenties. That's what that wink could cost him. Recalled to the stand, Ohrbach could testify, "Your honor, and ladies and gentlemen of the jury, the defendant winked at me. Surely that proves beyond the shadow of a doubt, if further proof were needed, that he views me as a pal, a fellow spirit and soulmate, and by no means as an arch-gouger!"

But Ohrbach, instead of pressing his sudden advantage, reverted to not showing up in court. Bech's imprudent wink, if it occurred, had perhaps mortally offended him. The old finagler had felt mocked; the machinations of the law were not to be winked at. In his absence the trial dragged in a trance toward its termination. Circlets of gray hair had begun to appear in the judge's Afro, and his list to the left approached the supine. Lanna

Jerome did not come out of hiding in Palm Springs, but an accountant and a lawyer in her employ testified with a stultifying double-entry particularity as to financial wrongs and half-wrongs she had suffered. Her relationship with Morrie Ohrbach had begun with "Comin' On Strong" and had ended with "Don't Send Me Back My Letters, My Lawyer Will Be in Touch with Yours."

Bech himself took the stand. The courtroom, seen at last from so different an angle, had a surreal pop-up quality – the judge looming close, the jury fanned out like a grandstand viewed from the playing field, the scattered marks on the court stenographer's spewing paper almost legible. In his old high-school debating voice, as clear as footprints in the mud, Bech testified that the epithet in question had seemed to him, after much time spent gathering evidence from responsible sources, both apt and fair. He had meant "arch" in its second, more common dictionary sense of "extreme: most fully embodying the qualities of his or its kind."

He had always imagined that it would be very difficult to lie in court, after taking an oath on the Bible, but nothing, he discovered, would be easier. One becomes an actor, a protagonist in a drama, and words become mere instruments of the joust. Words: how could he have dedicated his life to anything so flimsy, so flexible, so ready to deceive? Asked by Rantoul if he had meant to express it as his *opinion* that Ohrbach was an arch-gouger or as a *fact*, he said that he had meant to express it as his *opinion*. Bech had been amply coached in this legal distinction, upon which mighty First Amendment matters somehow hinged, though it made no real sense to him. What good is an opinion if it doesn't express a fact? But he refrained from saying this, and his thick-necked lawyer gave him an approving grimace.

Sergeant Kepper rose to cross-examine. "Would you describe yourself, Mr. Bech, as infatuated with Lanna Jerome?"

The little courtroom went so quiet Bech heard a juror's shoe scrape; the stenographer's machine tapped what seemed two measures of skeletal melody. "No," he lied. "I admire her talents, of course, but so do millions."

"Never mind the millions," Kepper said raspingly. "The tone

of your description of her relations with the plaintiff reminded me, may I say, of a jealous would-be lover."

"Objection," Rantoul cried. "Conjecture. Irrelevant."

"Overruled," the judge said quietly. "It could be relevant. Proceed, counselor."

"Might it be fair to say," Kepper proceeded, "that your infatuation with Miss Jerome led you to show, in print, hatred, ill will, and spite toward Mr. Ohrbach?"

Bech recognized the legal language, the poison on the tip of the lance. "Not at all," he said, with an invincible sincerity. "I feel now and felt then no ill will toward Mr. Ohrbach. I have never met him, and have had no dealings with him." He suppressed the insane urge to confess that, far from ill will, he had come in these days in court to feel a filial affection.

He was ready to plead guilty, had they only known it. But Sergeant Kepper's pokes toward the chinks in the defendant's armor became listless, and Bech was soon allowed to step down. There were no more witnesses.

Next day, Kepper's summation of Ohrbach v. Bech was distracted and jerky, with much misspeaking and idle oratory about the dangers of unbridled media. He spoke of east and west coasts, the West being the open-hearted seat of creativity and entertainment, and the East of caviling, negativistic criticism. Who is this Henry Bech, a modestly paid litterateur (with emphasis on the last syllable, pronounced *toor*), to understand the ins and outs of agent-client relations in a vastly successful popular art? Yet, though his stubby arms sawed up and down, his heart and mind seemed to have moved on. In Rantoul's opinion, Kepper had been persuaded to take Ohrbach's case on a contingency basis, and knew the jig was up when no out-of-court settlement was reached beforehand. All this — all this expense and terror — had been simply going through the motions.

Ohrbach had absented himself from the denouement. The ghost had evaporated from the machine.

Rantoul, striving to rouse the case from its torpor, drawled out almost a comically eloquent word-picture of the preposterous injustice of this claim of libel, in view of the plaintiff's notorious reputation; if in this great country an honest opinion, supported by a rich array of evidence, that a man is an arch-gouger can't be expressed in a journal of information, what is the point of the Constitution and all the wars fought to defend it against tyrannies of both the fascist and Communist persuasion?

It took the jury, though, four whole hours, while caterpillars becoming butterflies chewed at the lining of Bech's stomach, to arrive at the verdict of not guilty. One of the Asian-Americans, Gregg Nunn later discovered and confided in a gossippy letter to Bech, thought *Flying Fur* was a pornographic publication, and as a born-again Christian he wasn't so crazy about Lanna Jerome's affair with the governor of Nevada either, or her well-publicized statements in defense of abortion rights and single motherhood.

Abraham Bech had had terrible varicose veins in the last decade of his life, symptomatic of the circulatory difficulties that eventually killed him. Nevertheless, he walked off to the subway each morning, the Atlantic Avenue station, and stood on his feet in the gloomy, glittering diamond store all day, when he wasn't limping up and down 47th Street looking for a deal. Dealing is what fathers do, so that sons can disdain it and try to fly away, over the rooftops. But in the end we are brought back to reality and find ourselves tossing a man and his whole life of dealing – doing the necessary, by his own lights – into the hopper for the sake of a peppy phrase. For $1,250 plus expenses. "I feel so guilty," Henry Bech told Rita.

"Why on earth why? The plaintiff, he was one *podrido* son of a bitch."

Her voice had lost its paralegal primness and relaxed back toward a maternal Latina rhythm. They were naked in his bed in the futuristic hotel, side by side, sharing a joint. She had biscuit-brown shoulders and spiraling dark down on her fore-arms and a tousled short hairdo just like the pre-punk Lanna Jerome's. They had been discussing Bech's countersuit, not only for the legal expenses but for his mental anguish and time lost and the inestimable damage to his professional reputation. Tom Rantoul was licking his chops. "We'll nail that turkey," he vowed, "so he'll never gobble again." The case, to be financed on a contingency basis, would take months to prepare, and it seemed that Bech's life was here now, on this coast. He had been asking around, looking up the contacts he had made two years before, and even got a few nibbles. Could he do TV scripts? A lot of the sitcoms take place in the Northeast, because of the audience demographics, and yet there was a whole generation of Hollywood writers to whom New York was just a fable, an Old World from which their fathers and grandfathers had emigrated. The fee named for a trial script equaled half of Bech's earnings for all last year. He said he'd have to think it over.

"I loved him," he told Rita. "The stooped way he moved and kept bobbing his head, asking everybody's pardon and not expecting to get it. When my father died," he went on, "we found in his bureau drawers these black elastic stockings I had bought him, so his legs wouldn't hurt so much. He had never worn them. They still had the cardboard in them. Pieces of cardboard shaped like feet."

"Sweetheart, O.K. I see it. The cardboard feet. Dying down in the subway. Life is rough. But that other *judío* was trying to eat you. You eat him, or he eats you. Which would you rather?"

"Hey, I don't know," the defendant responded, touching two fingers to the erectile tip – the color of a sun-darkened, un-sulphur-treated apricot – of her nearer breast. "Neither seems ideal."

And neither coast is ideal; Bech in a few more weeks of consultation and courtship returned to our own, while on that far shore a broken female heart slowly mended, and legal wheels, like masticating jaws, ground on and on and then, one day when nobody was looking, stopped.

BECH NOIR

BECH HAD A NEW SIDEKICK. Her monicker was Robin. Rachel "Robin" Teagarten. Twenty-six, post-Jewish, frizzy big hair, figure on the short and solid side. She interfaced for him with an IBM PS/1 his publisher had talked him into buying. She set up the defaults, rearranged the icons, programmed the style formats, accessed the ANSI character sets – Bech was a stickler for foreign accents. When he answered a letter, she typed it for him from dictation. When he took a creative leap, she deciphered his handwriting and turned it into digitized code. Neither happened very often. Bech was of the Ernest Hemingway save-your-juices school. To fill the time, he and Robin slept together. He was seventy-four, but they worked with that. Seventy-four plus twenty-six was one hundred; divided by two, that was fifty, the prime of life. The energy of youth plus the wisdom of age. A team. A duo.

They were in his snug aerie on Crosby Street. He was reading the *Times* at breakfast: caffeineless Folgers, calcium-reinforced D'Agostino orange juice, poppy-seed bagel lightly toasted. The crumbs and poppy seeds had scattered over the newspaper and into his lap but you don't get something for nothing, not on this hard planet. Bech announced to Robin, "Hey, Lucas Mishner is dead."

A creamy satisfaction – the finest quality, made extra easy to spread by the toasty warmth – thickly covered his heart.

"Who's Lucas Mishner?" Robin asked. She was deep in the D section – Business Day. She was a practical-minded broad with no experience of culture prior to 1975.

"Once-powerful critic," Bech told her, biting off his phrases.

"Late *Partisan Review* school. Used to condescend to appear in the *Trib Book Review*, when the *Trib* was still alive on this side of the Atlantic. Despised my stuff. Called it 'superficially energetic but lacking in the true American fiber, the grit, the wrestle.' That's him talking, not me. The grit, the wrestle. Sanctimonious bastard. When *The Chosen* came out in '63, he wrote, 'Strive and squirm as he will, Bech will never, never be touched by the American sublime.' The simple, smug, know-it-all son of a bitch. You know what his idea of the real stuff was? James Jones. James Jones and James Gould Cozzens."

There Mishner's face was, in the *Times*, twenty years younger, with a fuzzy little rosebud smirk and a pathetic slicked-down comb-over like limp Venetian blinds throwing a shadow across the dome of his head. The thought of him dead filled Bech with creamy ease. He told Robin, "Lived way the hell up in Connecticut. Three wives, no flowers. Hadn't published for years. The rumor in the industry was he was gaga with alcoholic dementia."

"You seem happy."

"Very."

"Why? You say he had stopped being a critic anyway."

"Not in my head. He tried to hurt me. He did hurt me. Vengeance is mine."

"Who said that?"

"The Lord. In the Bible. Wake up, Robin."

"I thought it didn't sound like you," she admitted. "Stop hogging the Arts section. Let's see what's playing in the Village. I feel like a movie tonight."

"I'm not reading the Arts section."

"But it's under what you are reading."

"I was going to get to it."

"That's what I call hogging. Pass it over."

He passed it over, with a pattering of poppy seeds on the polyurethaned teak dining table Robin had installed. For years he and his female guests had eaten at a low glass coffee table farther forward in the loft. The sun slanting in had been pretty, but eating all doubled up had been bad for their internal organs. Robin had got him to take vitamins, too, and the calcium-reinforced o.j. She thought it would straighten his spine. He was in his best shape in years. She had got him doing sit-ups and push-ups. He was hard and quick, for a man who'd packed away his Biblical three score and ten. He was ready for action. He liked the tone of his own body. He liked the cut of Robin's smooth broad jaw across the teak table. Her healthy big hair, her pushy plump lips, her little flattened nose. "One down," he told her, mysteriously.

But she was reading the Arts section, the B section, and didn't hear. "*Con Air, Face/Off*," she read. This was the summer of 1997. "*Air Force One, Men in Black*. They're all violent. Disgusting."

"Why are you afraid of a little violence?" he asked her. "Violence is our poetry now, now that sex has become fatally tainted."

"Or *Contact*," Robin said. "From the reviews it's all about how the universe secretly loves us."

"That'll be the day," snarled Bech. Though in fact the juices surging inside him bore a passing resemblance to those of love. Mishner dead put another inch on his prick.

A week later, he was in the subway. The Rockefeller Center station on Sixth Avenue, the old IND line. The downtown platform was jammed. All those McGraw-Hill, Exxon, and Time-Life execs were rushing back to their wives in the Heights. Or going down to West 4th to have some herbal tea and put on drag for the evening. Monogamous transvestite executives were clogging the system. Bech was in a savage mood. He had been to MoMA, checking out the Constructivist film-poster show and the Project 60 room. The room featured three "ultra-hip," according to the new *New Yorker*, figurative painters: one who did "poisonous portraits of fashion victims," another who specialized in "things so boring that they verge on non-being," and a third who did "glossy, seductive portraits of pop stars and gay boys." None of them had been Bech's bag. Art had passed him by. Literature was passing him by. Music he had never gotten exactly with, not since USO record hops. Those cuddly little WACs from Ohio in their starched uniforms. That war had been over too soon, before he got to kill enough Germans.

Down in the subway, in the flickering jaundiced light, three competing groups of electronic buskers – one country, one progressive jazz, and one doing Christian hip-hop – were competing, while a huge overhead voice unintelligibly burbled about cancelations and delays. In the cacophony, Bech spotted an English critic: Raymond Featherwaite, former Cambridge eminence lured to CUNY by American moolah. From his perch in the CUNY crenelations, using an antique matchlock arquebus, he had been snottily potting American writers for twenty years, courtesy of the ravingly Anglophile *New York Review of Books*. Prolix and *voulu*, Featherwaite had called Bech's best-selling comeback book, *Think Big*, back in 1979. Inflation was peaking under Carter, the AIDS virus was sallying forth unidentified and unnamed, and here this limey carpetbagger was calling Bech's chef-d'oeuvre prolix and *voulu*. When, in the deflationary epoch supervised by Reagan, Bech had ventured a harmless collection of highly polished sketches and stories called *Biding Time*, Featherwaite had written, "One's spirits, however initially well-disposed toward one of America's more carefully tended reputations, begin severely to sag under the repeated empathetic effort of watching Mr. Bech, page after page, strain to make something of very little. The pleasures of microscopy pall."

The combined decibels of the buskers drowned out, for all but the most attuned city ears, the approach of the train whose delay had been so indistinctly bruited. Featherwaite, like all these Brits who were breeding like woodlice in the rotting log piles of the New York literary industry, was no slouch at pushing ahead. Though there was hardly room to place one's shoes on the filthy concrete, he had shoved and wormed his way to the front of the crowd, right to the edge of the platform. His edgy profile, with its supercilious overbite and artfully projecting eyebrows, turned with arrogant expectancy toward the screamingly approaching D train, as though hailing a servile black London taxi or a gilded Victorian brougham. Featherwaite affected a wispy-banged Nero haircut. There were rougelike touches of color on his cheekbones. The tidy English head bit into Bech's vision like a branding iron.

Prolix, he thought. *Voulu*. He had had to look up *voulu* in his

French dictionary. It put a sneering curse on Bech's entire oeuvre, for what, as Schopenhauer had asked, isn't willed?

Bech was three bodies back in the crush, tightly immersed in the odors, clothes, accents, breaths, and balked wills of others. Two broad-backed bodies, padded with junk food and fermented malt, intervened between himself and Featherwaite, while others importunately pushed at his own back. As if suddenly shoved from behind, he lowered his shoulder and rammed into the body ahead of his; like dominoes, it and the next tipped the third, the stiff-backed Englishman, off the platform. In the next moment the train with the force of a flash flood poured into the station, drowning all other noise under a shrieking gush of tortured metal. Featherwaite's hand in the last second of his life had shot up and his head jerked back as if in sudden recognition of an old acquaintance. Then he had vanished.

It was an instant's event, without time for the D-train driver to brake or a bystander to scream. Just one head pleasantly less in the compressed, malodorous mob. The man ahead of Bech, a ponderous black with bloodshot eyes, wearing a knit cap in the depths of summer, regained his balance and turned indignantly, but Bech, feigning a furious glance behind him, slipped sideways as the crowd arranged itself into funnels beside each door of the now halted train. A woman's raised voice – foreign, shrill – had begun to leak the horrible truth of what she had witnessed, and far away, beyond the turnstiles, a telepathic policeman's whistle was tweeting. But the crowd within the train was surging obliviously outward against the crowd trying to enter, and in the thick eddies of disgruntled and compressed humanity nimble, bookish, elderly Bech put more and more space between himself and his unwitting accomplices. He secreted himself a car's length away, hanging from a hand-burnished bar next to an ad publicizing free condoms and clean needles, with a dainty Oxford edition of Donne's poems pressed close to his face as the news of the unthinkable truth spread, and the whistles of distant authority drew nearer, and the train refused to move and was finally emptied of passengers, while the official voice overhead, louder and less intelligible than ever, shouted word of cancelation, of disaster, of evacuation without panic.

Obediently Bech left the stalled train, blood on its wheels, and climbed the metallic stairs sparkling with pulverized glass. His insides shuddered in tune with the shoving, near-panicked mob about him. He inhaled the outdoor air and Manhattan anonymity gratefully. Avenue of the Americas, a sign said, in stubborn upholding of an obsolete gesture of hemispheric good will. Bech walked south, then over to Seventh Avenue. Scrupulously he halted at each red light and deposited each handed-out leaflet (GIRLS! COLLEGE SEX KITTENS TOPLESS! BOTTOMLESS AFTER 6:30 P.M.!) in the next city trash receptacle. He descended into the Times Square station, where the old IRT system's innumerable tunnels mingled their misery in a vast subterranean maze of passageways, stairs, signs, and candy stands. He bought a Snickers bar and leaned against a white-tiled pillar to read where his little book had fallen open,

> *Death, be not proud, though some have callèd thee*
> *Mighty and dreadful, for thou art not so;*
> *For those whom thou think'st thou dost overthrow*
> *Die not, poor Death, nor yet canst thou kill me.*

He caught an N train that took him to Broadway and Prince. Afternoon had sweetly turned to evening while he had been underground. The galleries were closing, the restaurants were opening. Robin was in the loft, keeping lasagna warm. "I thought MoMA closed at six," she said.

"There was a tie-up in the Sixth Avenue subway. Nothing was running. I had to walk down to Times Square. I *hated* the stuff the museum had up. Violent, attention-getting."

"Maybe there comes a time," she said, "when new art isn't for you, it's for somebody else. I wonder what caused the tie-up."

"Nobody knew. Power failure. A shootout uptown. Some maniac," he added, wondering at his own words. His insides felt agitated, purged, scrubbed, yet not yet creamy. Perhaps the creaminess needed to wait until the morning *Times*. He feared he could not sleep, out of nervous anticipation, yet he toppled into dreams while Robin still read beneath a burning light, as if he had done a long day's worth of physical labor.

ENGLISH CRITIC, TEACHER DEAD/IN WEST SIDE SUBWAY MISHAP,
the headline read. The story was low on the front page and
jumped to the obituaries. The obit photo, taken decades ago,
glamorized Featherwaite — head facing one way, shoulders
another — so he resembled a younger, less impish brother of
George Sanders. High brow, thin lips, cocky glass chin. . . . *according to witnesses appeared to fling himself under the subway train as it
approached the platform . . . colleagues at CUNY puzzled but agreed he
had been under significant stress compiling permissions for his textbook of
postmodern narrative strategies . . . former wife, reached in London,
allowed the deceased had been subject to mood swings and fits of creative
despair . . . the author of several youthful satirical novels and a single
book of poems likened to those of Philip Larkin . . . Robert Silvers of The
New York Review expressed shock and termed Featherwaite "a valued
and versatile contributor of unflinching critical integrity" . . . born in
Scunthorpe, Lincolnshire, the third child and only son of a greengrocer
and a part-time piano teacher . . .* and so on. A pesky little existence.
"Ray Featherwaite is dead," Bech announced to Robin, trying
to keep a tremble of triumph out of his voice.

"Who was he?"

"A critic. More minor than Mishner. English. Came from a
grocery store, just like Thatcher — I had never known that. Went
to Cambridge on a scholarship. I had figured him for inherited
wealth; he wanted you to think so."

"That makes two critics this week," said Robin, preoccupied
by the dense gray pages of stock prices.

"Every third person in Manhattan is some kind of critic," Bech
pointed out. He hoped the conversation would move on.

"How did he die?"

There was no way to hide it; she would be reading this section
eventually. "Jumped under a subway train, oddly. Seems he'd
been feeling low, trying to secure too many copyright permissions or something. These academics have a lot of stress. It's a
tough world they're in — the faculty politics is brutal."

"Oh?" Robin's eyes — bright, glossy, the living volatile brown
of a slick moist pelt — had left the stock prices. "What subway
line?"

"Sixth Avenue, actually."

"Maybe that was the tie-up you mentioned."

"Could be. Very likely, in fact. Did I ever tell you that my father died in the subway, under the East River in his case? Made a terrible mess of rush hour."

"Yes, Henry," Robin said, in the pointedly patient voice that let him know she was younger and clearer-headed. "You've told me more than once."

"Sorry."

"So why are your hands trembling? You can hardly hold your bagel." And his other hand, he noticed, was making the poppy seeds vibrate on the obituary page, as if a subway train were passing underneath.

"Who knows?" he asked her. "I may be coming down with something. I went out like a light last night."

"I'll say," said Robin, returning her eyes to the page. That summer the stock prices climbed up and up, breaking new records every day. It was unreal.

"Sorry," he repeated. Ease was beginning to flow again within him. The past was sinking, every second, under fresher, obscuring layers of the recent past. "Did it make you feel neglected? A young woman needs her sex."

"No," she said. "It made me feel tender. You seemed so innocent, with your mouth sagging open."

Robin, like Spider-man's wife, Mary Jane, worked in a computer emporium. She not so much sold them as shared her insights with customers as they struggled in the crashing waves of innovation and the lightning-swift undertow of obsolescence. The exorbitant memory demands of Microsoft's Windows 95 had overflowed two-year-old 4-RAM and 8-RAM IBMs and Compaqs. Once-mighty Macintosh had become a mere tidal pool, crawling with slowly suffocating Apple addicts. Simply holding one's place in cyberspace required more and more megabytes and megahertzes. Such pell-mell dispensability uncomfortably reminded Bech of his possible own, within the cultural turnover. Giants of his youth – A. J. Cronin, Louis Bromfield, John Erskine, Pearl Buck – had slipped over the horizon of living

readership into the limbo of small-town book sales. Like a
traveler in one of Einstein's thought experiments, he could be
rapidly shrinking in such a recession and be the last to know it.
Bech found himself described in scholarly offprints as "Early
Postmodern" or "Post-Realist" or "Pre-Minimalist" as if, a narrowly configured ephemerid, he had been born to mate and die
in a certain week of summer.

Nevertheless, it pleased him to view Robin in her outlet – on
Third Avenue near 27th Street, a few blocks from Bellevue –
standing solid and calm in a gray suit whose lapels swerved to
take in her bosom. Amid her array of putty-colored monitors and
system-unit housings, she received the petitions of those in thrall
to the computer revolution. They were mostly skinny young
men with parched hair and sunless complexions. Many of them
forgot, Robin confided, to sleep or to bathe, in the intensity of
their keyboard communions. She spoke their foreign language.
It seemed exotic to Bech, erotic. He liked to stare in the display
windows at her, while she was copulating, mentally, with a rapt
customer. She had a rough way of seizing her own hair, bushy as
it was, and pulling it back from her face for a moment, before
letting it spring back again around her features, which were
knotted in earnest disquisitions on the merits, say, of upgrading
a modem from 14.4 kilobytes per second to 33.6 kbps. Sometimes Bech would enter the store, like some grizzled human
glitch, and take Robin to lunch. Sometimes he would sneak
away content with his glimpse of this princess decreeing in her
realm. He marveled that at the end of the day she would find her
way through the circuitry of the city and return to him. The
tenacity of erotic connection presaged the faithful transistor and
trustworthy microchip.

Bech had not always been an evil man. He had dedicated
himself early to what appeared plainly a good cause, art. It was
amusing and helpful to others, he imagined as he emerged from
the Army, to turn contiguous bits of the world into words, words
which when properly arranged and typeset possessed a gleam that
in wordless reality was lost beneath the daily accretions of habit,
worry, and boredom. What harm could there be in art? What
enemies could there be?

But he discovered that the literary world was a battlefield – mined with hatred, rimmed with snipers. His first stories and essays, appearing in defunct mass publications like *Liberty* and defunct avant-garde journals like *Displeasure*, roused little comment, and his dispatches, published in *The New Leader*, from Normandy in the wake of the 1944 invasion, and then from the Bulge and Berlin, attracted little notice in a print world drenched in war coverage. But, ten years later, his first novel, *Travel Light*, made a small splash, and for the first time he saw, in print, spite directed at himself. Not just spite, but a willful mistaking of his intentions and a cheerfully ham-handed divulgence of all his plot's nicely calculated and hoarded twists. A New York Jew writing about Midwestern bikers infuriated some reviewers – some Jewish, some Midwestern – and the sly asceticism of his next, novella-length novel, *Brother Pig*, annoyed others: "The contemptuous medieval expression for the body which the author has used as a title serves only too well," one reviewer (female) wrote, "to prepare us for the sad orgy of Jewish self-hatred with which Mr. Bech will disappoint and repel his admirers – few, it is true, but in some rarefied circles curiously fervent." And his magnum opus, *The Chosen*, in which he tried to please his critics by facing the ethnicity purposefully sidestepped in *Brother Pig*, ran into a barrage of querulous misprision, not a barbed phrase of which had failed to stick in his sensitive skin. "Ignore the cretins," his avuncular acquaintance Norman Mailer had advised him. "Why do you even read the drivel?" Joseph Heller sagely asked. Bech had tried to take their advice, and in mid-career imagined that he had developed, if not the hide of a rhinoceros, at least the oily, resplendent back of a duck. He thought the reviews ran off him, chilly droplets swallowed in Lethe's black waters.

However, as he aged into the ranks of the elderly, adverse phrases from the far past surfaced in his memory, word for word – "says utterly nothing with surprising aplomb," "too toothless or shrewd to tackle life's raw meat," "never doffs his velour exercise togs to break a sweat," "the sentimental coarseness of a pornographic valentine," "prose arabesques of phenomenal irrelevancy," "refusal or failure to ironize his reactionary positions," "starry-eyed sexism," "minor, minorer, minormost" – and clamorously rattled around in his head, rendering him, some days, while his brain tried to be busy with something else, stupid with rage. It was as if these insults, these hurled mud balls, these stains on the robe of his vocation, were, now that he was nearing the end, bleeding wounds. That a negative review might be a fallible verdict, delivered in haste, against a deadline, for a few dollars, by a writer with problems and limitations of his own was a reasonable and weaseling supposition he could no longer, in the dignity of his years, entertain. *Any* adverse review, even a single mild phrase of qualification or reservation within a favorable, indeed an adoring notice, stood revealed as the piece of pure enmity it was – an assault, a virtual murder, a purely malicious attempt to unman and destroy him. What was precious and potentially enduring about Bech was not his body, that fraternal pig with its little scared oink of an ego, but his oeuvre. Any slighting of his oeuvre attacked the self he chiefly valued. After fifty years of trying to rise above criticism, he liberated himself to take it personally. A furious lava – an acidic indignation begging for the Maalox of creamy, murderous satisfaction – had secretly become Bech's essence, his angelic ichor.

The female reviewer, Deborah Frueh, who had in 1957 maligned *Brother Pig* as a flight of Jewish self-hatred lived far from New York, in the haven of Seattle, amid New Age mantras and medicinal powders, between Boeing and Mount Rainier. He could not get her ancient review out of his aging mind – the serene inarguable *complacency* of it, the certainty that she grasped the ineffable reality of being "covenanted" and he, poor pseudo-Jew, did not. He began to conceive of a way to reach her with the long arm of vengeance. She was still alive, he felt in his bones. She had been young when she dealt the young Bech her savage blow, but had emerged in 1979 to write, for the *Washington Post*, a stinging, almost pathologically sour review of *Think Big* beginning, "Somehow, I have never been persuaded to hop onto the Bech bandwagon. Even (or maybe especially) at its flashiest, his prose seems flimsy, the nowhere song of a nowhere man, devoid of any serious ethnic identification and stimulated by only the most trivial, consumeristic aspects of what we used to call, in

braver days, Amerika. . . ." She, the spot bio accompanying this
onslaught revealed, taught English poetry and the post-colonial
novel at the University of Washington. From this remove her
dismissive, pompous criticism ever more rarely reached the
book-review columns of the Northeast Corridor. Perhaps academia had seduced her into Derridean convolution, culminating
in self-erasure. But she could not hide from him, now that he had
been aroused and become, on the verge of dotage, a man of
action.

   Though she was grit too fine to be found in the coarse sieve of
Who's Who, he discovered her address in the *Poets & Writers'*
directory, which listed a few critical articles and her fewer books,
all children's books with heart-tugging titles like *Jennifer's Lonely
Birthday* and *The Day Dad Didn't Come Home* and *A Teddy Bear's
Bequest*. These books, Bech saw, were her Achilles' heel.

   The renovated old factory where he lived assigned each of its
tenants a storage room in the basement. But these partitioned,
padlocked chambers by no means included all the basement
space: exploration discovered far, dim-lit, brick-walled caverns
that harbored rusted stitching machines and junked parts whose
intricate shape defied speculation as to their mechanical purpose
at the other, clanking end of the century. In a slightly less
neglected recess, the building's management – a realty corporation headquartered in New Jersey – kept some shelved cans of
paint and, hung on pegboard, plumbing supplies and carpentry
tools and other infrequently wielded implements of upkeep. The
super had about a dozen SoHo buildings in his care and was
seldom in the basement, though a split, scuffed Naugahyde armchair, a stack of musty *Hustler*s, and an antique, gray-encrusted
standing ashtray, long ago lifted from a hotel lobby, testified to a
potential presence capable of, in the era before downsizing, an
idle hour or two. In one of his furtive forays into these lower
levels of Manhattan's lost Industrial Age, Bech found around a
grimy corner a narrow wooden closet fitted between waste pipes
and an abandoned set of water meters. The locked door was a
simple hinged frame holding, where glass might have been,
chicken wire rusted to a friable thinness. Peering inside, he saw
a cobwebbed cache of dried dark jars, nibbled cardboard boxes,

and a time-hardened contraption of rubber tubing with a tin hand-pump, coiled and cracked and speckled with oxidation. His attention fastened on a thick jar of brown glass whose label, in the stiff and innocent typographic style of the 1940s, warned POISON and displayed along its border an array of dead vermin, roaches and rats and centipedes in dictionary-style gravure. Snapping the frail brown wire enough to admit his hand, Bech lifted the bottle out. The size of a coffee can, it sloshed, half-full. In the dusty light he read on the label that among the ingredients was hydro-cyanic acid. Fearful that the palms of his hands might become contaminated, Bech carried the antique vermicide up to his loft wrapped in a *News* the super had tossed aside (headline: KOCH BLASTS ALBANY) and did not unscrew the rusty lid until he had donned Robin's mint-green rubber kitchen gloves. He exerted his grip. His teeth ground together; his crowns gnashed on their stumps of dentine. The lid's seal snapped a second before his carotid artery would have popped. Out of fifty intervening years of subterranean stillness arose the penetrating whiff, cited in many a mystery novel, of bitter almonds. The liquid, which was colorless, seemed to be vaporizing eagerly, its ghostly essence rushing upward from the gaping mouth of the jar.

He replaced the lid. He hid the jar in the drawer of his filing cabinet where he kept his old reviews. He did some research. Hydrocyanic, or prussic, acid was miscible with water, and a minute amount – a few drops of even a mild solution – would slow the heart, inhibit breathing, dilate the pupils, promote violent convulsive movements, cause loss of consciousness, and asphyxiate the victim with a complete loss of muscular power. Cyanides act within seconds, halting tissue oxidation and sus-pending vital functions. The victim's countenance turns a bluish color, not to be confused with Prussian blue, an inert precipitant of the poison.

Bech wrote Deborah Frueh a fan letter, in a slow and childish hand, in black ballpoint, on blue-lined paper. "Dear Debora Freuh," he wrote, deliberately misspelling, "You are my very favrite writer. I have red your books over 'n' over. I would be greatful if you could find time to sign the two enclosed cards for me and my best frend Betsey and return them in the inclosed envelop. That would be really grate of you and many *many* thanx in advance." He signed it, "Your real fan, Mary Jane Mason."

He wrote it once and then rewrote it, holding the pen in what felt like a little girl's fist. Then he set the letter aside and worked carefully on the envelope. He had bought a cheap box of one hundred at an office-supply store on lower Broadway and destroyed a number before he got the alchemy right. He put on the rubber gloves. They made his hands sweat. With a paper towel he delicately moistened the dried gum on the envelope flap – not too much, or it curled. Then, gingerly using a glass martini-stirring rod, he placed three or four drops of the colorless poison on the moist adhesive. Lest it be betrayingly bitter when licked, and Deborah Frueh rush to ingest an antidote, he sweetened the doctored spots with some sugar water mixed in an orange-juice glass and applied with an eye-dropper. Several times he stopped himself from absent-mindedly licking the flap to test the taste. He recoiled; it was as if he had been walking the edge of a cliff and nearly slipped and fell off, down into a Prussian-blue sea of asphyxia and oblivion. In the midst of life, death is a misstep away.

The afternoon waned; the roar of tunnel-bound traffic up on Houston reached its crescendo unnoticed; the windows of the cast-iron façade across Crosby Street went blind with the blazing amber of the lowering sun. Bech was wheezily panting in the intensity of his concentration. His nose was running; he kept wiping it with a trembling handkerchief. His littered desk – an old army-surplus behemoth, with green metal sides and a black plastic top – reminded him of art-class projects at P.S. 87, before his father heedlessly moved him to Brooklyn. He and his peers had built tiny metropolises out of cereal boxes, and butterflies out of colored papers and white paste. They had scissored into being red valentines and black profiles of George Washington, and even paper Easter eggs and Christmas trees, under their young and starchy Irish and German instructresses, who without fear of protest swept their little Jewish-American pupils into the Christian calendar. Back then, the magazine covers on the newsstand rack, the carols on the radio, the decorations on the school windowpanes all bespoke one culture, in which children still celebrated with paper, cardboard, and paste the tired legend of that cryptic young Jew who had made his way from Bethlehem to Golgotha.

Bech thought hard about the return address on the envelope, which could become, once its fatal bait was taken, a dangerous clue. The poison, before hitting home, might give Deborah Frueh time to seal the thing, which in the confusion after her death might be mailed. That would be perfect – the clue consigned to a continental mailbag and arrived with the junk mail at an indifferent American household. In the Westchester directory he found a Mason in New Rochelle and fistily inscribed the address beneath the name of his phantom Frueh fan. Folding the envelope, he imagined he heard a faint crackling – microscopic sugar and cyanide crystals? His dried-up conscience undergoing a reaction? He slipped the folded envelope with the letter and four (why not be generous?) three-by-five index cards into the envelope painstakingly addressed in the immature, girlish handwriting. As he licked the stamp he thought of the Simpson trial and the insidious intricacy of DNA evidence. Semen, blood, saliva – all contain the entire person, coiled in ribbons of microscopic code. Everywhere we dabble or dribble or spit, we can be traced. Bech stuck the tongue-licked stamp thriftily on a blank envelope and moistened the one for Frueh with a corner of paper towel held under a running faucet, then squeezed.

The tall old wobbly windows across Crosby Street cast a sketchy orange web of reflected light into his loft. Before Robin could return from work and express curiosity about the mess on his desk, he cleaned it up. The paper towel and spoiled stationery went into the kitchen trash, and the lethal jar into the back of the cabinet drawer with the old reviews, which only he cared about – only he and a tiny band of Bech scholars, who were dying off and not being replaced by younger recruits. Even the caretaker of his archives at NYU had expressed a lack of interest in his yellowing clippings – which included such lovingly snipped tidbits as Bech sentences cited in the *Reader's Digest* feature "Picturesque Speech and Patter" – claiming that old newsprint posed "a terrible conservancy problem."

Bech took off the rubber gloves and hurried downstairs, his worn heart pounding, to throw Mary Jane Mason's fan letter into the mailbox at Broadway and Prince. A lurid salmon-striped sunset hung in the direction of New Jersey. The streets were crammed with the living and the guiltless, heading home in the ghostly natural light, blinking from the subway's flicker and a long day spent at computer terminals. The narrow streets and low commercial buildings imparted the busy intimacy of a stage set, half lit as the curtain goes up. Bech hesitated a second before relinquishing his letter to the blue, graffiti-sprayed box, there in front of Victoria's Secret. A middle-aged Japanese couple in bulbous sightseer's sneakers glanced at him timidly, a piece of local color with his springy white hair, his aggressively large nose, his deskworker's humped back. A snappy black woman, her beaded cornrows bristling and rattling, arrived at his back with an armful of metered nine-by-twelve envelopes, impatient to make her more massive, less lethal drop. Bech stifled his qualm. The governmental box hollowly sounded as its lid like a flat broad tongue closed upon the fathomless innards of sorting and delivery to which he consigned his missive. His life had been spent as a votary of the mails. This was but one more submission.

Morning after morning, the *Times* carried no word on the demise of Deborah Frueh. Perhaps, just as she wasn't in *Who's Who*, she was too small a fish to be caught in the *Times*' obituary net. But still, it reported at respectful length the deaths of hundreds of people of whom Bech had never heard. Former aldermen, upstate prioresses, New Jersey judges, straight men on defunct TV comedies, founders of Manhattan dog-walking services – all got their space, their chiseled paragraphs, their farewell salute. Noticing the avidity with which he always turned to the back of the Metro section, Robin asked him, "What are you looking for?"

He couldn't tell her. His necessary reticence was poisoning their relationship. We are each of us sealed containers of gaseous fantasies and hostilities, but a factual secret, with its liquid weight, leaks out, if only in the care with which one speaks, as if around a pebble held in the mouth. "Familiar names," he said. "People I once knew."

"Henry, it seems morbid. Here, I'm done with Arts and Sports."

"I've read enough about arts and sports," he told this bossy twat, "to last me to the grave." Mortality was his meat now.

He went to the public library, the Hamilton Fish Park branch over on East Houston, and in the children's section found one of Deborah Frueh's books, *Jennifer's Lonely Birthday*, and checked it out. He read it and wrote her another letter, this time in blue ballpoint, on unlined stationery with a little Peter Max-ish elf-figure up in one corner, the kind a very young girl might be given for her birthday by an aunt or uncle. "Dear Deborah Frueh," he wrote, "I love your exciting work. I love the way at the end of *Jennifer's Lonely Birthday* Jennifer realizes that she has had a pretty good day after all and that in life you can't depend on anybody else to entertain you, you have to entertain and pre-occupy your own mind. At the local library I have *The Day Dad Didn't Come Home* on reserve. I hope it isn't too sad. I liked the positive ending to *Jennifer's Lonely Birthday*. They never heard of *A Teddy Bear's Bequest* at the library. I know you are a busy celebritty and are working on more really swell books but I hope you could send me a photograph of you for the wall of my room or if your too busy to do that please sign this zerox of the one on the cover of *Jennifer's Lonely Birthday*. I like the way you do your hair, it's like my Aunt Florence, up behind. Find enclosed a stamped envelope to send it in. Yours most hopefully, Judith Green."

Miss Green in Bech's mind was a year or so older than Mary Jane Mason. She misspelled hardly at all, and had self-consciously converted her grammar-school handwriting to a stylish printing, which Bech slaved at for several hours before attaining the proper girlish plumpness in the "o"s and "m"s. He tried dotting the "i"s with little circles and ultimately discarded the device as unper-suasive. He did venture, however, a little happy-face, with smile and hair ribbon. He intensified the dose of hydrocyanic acid on the envelope flap, and eased off on the sugar water. When Deborah Frueh took her lick – he pictured it as avid and thorough, not one but several swoops of her vicious, pointed tongue – the bitterness would register too late. The covenanted bitch would never know what hit her.

The postmark was a problem. Mary Jane up there in New Rochelle might well have had a father who, setting off in the morning with a full briefcase, would mail her letter for her in New York, but two in a row from Manhattan and Frueh might smell a rat, especially if she had responded to the last request and was still feeling queasy. Bech took the ferry from the World Financial Center to Hoboken, treating himself to a river ride. He looked up Greens in a telephone booth near the terminal. He picked one on Willow Street to be little Judy's family. Hoboken made him nostalgic for the Depression. In this densely built port from the past, lacy with iron balustrades, he went into an old-fashioned greasy spoon on Washington Street; there were wooden booths and stools at a counter and the selections and prices up in movable white letters on a grooved blackboard. He sat in a booth. He needed a table to write the return address on. In case he spoiled one envelope he had brought a spare, with a pastel elf in the lower left corner. But the address went well, it seemed to him. For a flourish he added a smiley face underneath the zip code.

Art excited his appetite. He ordered liver and onions from the lunch menu, a dish he hadn't had for years. The fried slab of gut came framed in oblong bubbles of blood-tinged grease. He ate it all, burped, and tasted the onions again. He deposited his letter in a small box on a concrete post – he hadn't known boxes like that still existed – and took the ferry back to lower Manhattan. His nerves hummed. His eyes narrowed against the river glare. The other passengers, too, felt the excitement of waterborne transition; they chattered in Spanish, in Chinese, in ebonics. What did Whitman write of such crossings? *Flood-tide below me! I see you face to face!* And, later on, speaking so urgently from the grave, *Just as you are refresh'd by the gladness of the river and the bright flow, I was refresh'd, / Just as you stand and lean on the rail, yet hurry with the swift current, I stood yet was hurried.* That "yet was hurried" was brilliant, with all of Whitman's brilliant homeliness. Soon, Bech reflected, he too

would be dead, looking up through the flowing water to the
generations as yet unborn, his bloodless visage sadder than Whitman's, because for all his striving and squirming he had – according to Lucas Mishner, himself recently enrolled in the underworld's
eddying throng – never been touched by the American sublime.

The fuck he hadn't. Bech's hurried heart hummed all the way
up Church Street to Warren, then over to City Hall and on up
Broadway and home. *I too walk'd the streets of Manhattan island . . .
/ I am he who knew what it was to be evil, / I too knotted the old knot of
contrariety, / Blabb'd, blush'd, resented, lied, stole, grudg'd . . .*

A week went by. Ten days. The death he desired was not
reported in the *Times*. He wondered if a boy fan might win a
better response, a more enthusiastic, heterosexual licking of the
return envelope. "*Dear Deborah Freuh,*" he typed, using the
clunky Script face available on his IBM PS/1:

> *You are a great writer, the greatest as far as I am
> concerned in the world. Your book titled "The Day Dad
> Didn't Come Home" broke me up, it was so sad and true.
> The way little Katrina comforts her baby brother Sam and
> realizes that they all will have to be Dad for each other
> now is so true it hurts. I have had a similar experience.
> I bet thousands of your readers have. I don't want to
> waste any more of your time reading this so you can get
> back to writing another super book but it would be
> sensational if you would sign the enclosed first-day
> cover for Sarah Orne Jewett, the greatest female
> American writer until you came along. Even if you have a
> policy against signing I'd appreciate your returning
> it in the enclosed self-addressed stamped envelope
> since I am a collector and spent a week's allowance for
> it at the hobby shop here in Amityville, Long Island,
> NY. Sign it on the pencil line I have drawn. I will erase
> the line when you have signed. I look forward to hearing
> from you soon.*
>
> > *Yours very sincerely,
> > Jason Johnson, Jr.*

Boys did seem a bit more adventurous and thrusting in their thinking than girls, Bech discovered through this act of ventriloquism. Maybe he should cut down on Jason's verbal braggadocio. The word processor, its frictionless patter, encouraged, as academics had been complaining for years, prolixity. But Featherwaite had pronounced Bech prolix when he was still using a manual, a Smith-Corona portable. He decided to let the boy have his say.

It was a pleasant change, in the too-even tenor of Bech's days, to ride the Long Island Rail Road out to Amityville and mail Jason Johnson's letter. Just to visit Penn Station again offered a fresh perspective – that Roman grandeur from Bech's youth, that onetime temple to commuting Fortuna, reduced to these ignoble ceilings and beggarly passageways. And then, after the elevated views of tar-roofed Queens, the touching suburban stations, like so many knobbed Victorian toys, with their carefully pointed stonework and gleaming rows of parked cars and stretches of suburban park. Each stop represented happiness for thousands, and reminded him of his own suburban days in Ossining, married to Bea, stepfather to female twins and a small boy. He had felt uneasy, those years, a Jew with three acres and a dog and a car, as though occupying someone else's dream; but wasn't America after all the place to live in a dream, a dream determined not by your own subconscious but the collective unconscious of millions? He had not been unhappy, until the bubble was pricked and New York's leaden gravity sucked him back. In Amityville, he found a suitable Johnson – on Maple Drive – and mailed Jason's letter and had a lettuce-and-cucumber sandwich at a salad bar full of suburban women and their fidgety little sprouts. Then he headed back to town, each station more thickly surrounded by shabbier, more commercial constructions and the track bed becoming elevated and then, with a black roar, buried, underground, underriver, undercity, until the train stopped at Penn Station again and the passengers spilled out into a gaudy, perilous mess of consumeristic blandishments, deranged beggars, and furtive personal errands perhaps as base as his own.

Four days later, there it was, in eight inches of *Times* type: the death of Deborah Frueh. Respected educator was also a noted critic and author of children's books. Had earlier published scholarly articles on the English Metaphysicals and Swinburne and his circle. Taken suddenly ill while at her desk in her home in Hunts Point, near Seattle. Born in Conshohocken, near Philadelphia. Attended Barnard College and Duke University graduate school. Exact cause of death yet to be determined. Had been in troubled health lately – her weight a stubborn problem – colleagues at the University of Washington reported. But not despondent in any obvious way. Survived by a sister, Edith, of Ardmore, Pennsylvania, and a brother, Leonard, of Teaneck, New Jersey. Another ho-hum exit notice, for every reader but Henry Bech. He knew what a deadly venom the deceased had harbored in her fangs.

"What's happened?" Robin asked from across the table.

"Nothing's happened," he said.

"Then why do you look like that?"

"Like what?"

"Like a man who's been told he's won a million dollars but isn't sure it's worth it, what with all the tax problems."

"What a strange, untrammeled imagination you have," he said. "I wonder if selling computers does justice to all your talents."

"Let me see the page you're reading."

"No. I'm still reading it."

"Henry, are you going to make me stand up and walk around the table?"

He handed her the creamcheese-stained obituary page, which was toward the end of Section C today, this being Saturday and the paper the Weekend Edition. Robin, while the rounded masseters of her wide jaw thoughtfully clenched and unclenched on the last milky crumbs of her whole-bran flakes, flicked her quick brown eyes up and down the columns of print. Her eyes held points of red like the fur of a fox. Morning sun slanting through the big loft window kindled an outline of light, of incandescent fuzz, along her jaw. Her eyelashes glittered like a row of dewdrops on a spider-strand. "Who's Deborah Frueh?" she asked. "Did you know her?"

"A frightful literary scold," he answered. "I never met the lady, I'm not sorry to say."

"Did she ever review you or anything?"

"I believe she did, once or twice."

"Favorably?"

"Not really."

"Really unfavorably?"

"It could be said. Her reservations about my work were unhedged, as I vaguely recall. You know I don't pay much attention to reviews."

"And that Englishman last month, who fell in front of the subway train – didn't you have some connection with him, too?"

"Darling, I've been publishing for over fifty years. I have slight connections with everybody in the print racket."

"You've not been quite yourself lately," Robin told him. "You've had some kind of a secret. You don't talk to me the breezy way you used to. You're censoring."

"I'm not," he said, hating to lie, standing as he was knee-deep in the sweet clover of Deborah Frueh's extermination. He wondered what raced through that fat harpy's mind in the last second, as the terrible-tasting cyanide tore into her esophagus and halted the oxidation process within her cells. Not of him, certainly. He was but one of multitudes of writers she had put in their places. He was three thousand miles away, the anonymous progenitor of Jason Johnson, Jr. *Sic semper tyrannis*, you unctuous, hectoring, covenanted shrew.

"Look at you!" Robin cried, on so high a note that her orange-juice glass emitted a surprised shiver. "You're triumphant! Henry, you killed her."

"How would I have done that?"

She was not balked. Her eyes narrowed. "At a distance, some-how," she guessed. "You sent her things. A couple of days ago, when I came home, there was a funny smell in the room, like something had been burning."

"This is fascinating," Bech said. "If I had your imagination, I'd be Balzac." He chattered on, to deflect her terrifying insights, "Another assiduous critic of mine, Aldie Cannon – he used to be a mainstay of *The New Republic* but now he's on PBS and the Internet – says I can't imagine a thing. And hate women."

Robin was still musing, her smooth young mien puzzling at

the crimes to which she was an as yet blind partner. She said, "I guess it depends on how you define 'hate.'"

But he loved *her*. He loved the luxurious silken whiteness of her slightly thickset young body, the soothing cool of her basic- ally factual mind. Beauty, the newspapers were saying that summer, is a matter of averaging out – babies and adults alike are more attracted to photographs of a morphed combination of faces than to the image of any specific one. What we desire is supernormality, a smooth statistical average; yet inevitably it comes in a package unique, fragile, precious. He could not long maintain this wall between them, this ugly partition in the light-filled loft of their intimacy.

The next day, the *Times* ran a little follow-up squib on the same page as the book review and the book ads. The squib was basically comic in its tone, for who would want to murder an elderly, overweight book critic and juvenile author? It stated that the Seattle police had found suspicious chemical traces in Frueh's autopsied body. They were closing in. Bech panicked. He was going to fry. The lights would dim in Ossining when they pulled the switch. He confessed to Robin. The truth rose irrepressible in his throat like the acid burn of partial regurgitation. Pushing the large black man who pushed a body that pushed Feather- waite's. Writing Deborah Frueh three fan letters with doped return envelopes. His belief, possibly delusionary, that before he died he had a duty to rid the world of critics, or at least of conspicuously malignant ones. Robin listened while reposing on his brown beanbag chair in Claire Hoagland's old terrycloth bathrobe. She had taken a shower, so her feet had babyish pink sides beneath the marble-white insteps with their faint blue veins. It was Sunday morning. The bells in that sinister walled convent over at Prince and Mulberry had sounded their unheeded call. Robin said when he was done, "Henry, you can't just go around rubbing out people as if they existed only on paper."

"I can't? And who says they don't? That's where they tried to eliminate me, on paper. They tried to put me out of business. They preyed on my insecurities, to shut off my creative flow.

They nearly succeeded. I haven't written nearly as much as I could have."

"Was that their fault?"

"Partly," he estimated. Maybe he had cooked his own goose, spilling his guts to this chesty kid. "O.K. Turn me in. Go to the bulls."

"The bulls?"

"The police – haven't you ever heard that expression? How about 'the fuzz'? or 'the pigs'?"

"I've never heard them called that, either."

"My God, you're young. What have I ever done to deserve you, Robin? You're so pure, so straight. And now you loathe me."

"No, I don't, actually. I might have thought I would, but in fact I like you more than ever." She never said "love," she was too post-Jewish for that. "I think you've shown a lot of balls, frankly, translating your resentments into action, for once, instead of sublimating them into art."

He didn't much like it when young women said "balls" or called a man "an asshole," but today he was thrilled by the cool baldness of it. They were, he and his mistress, in a new realm, a computer universe devoid of blame or guilt, as morally null as an Intel chip. There were only, in this scannable universe, greater or lesser patches of electricity, and violence and sex were greater patches. She stood and opened her robe. When Martina had done that, in this same loft, a few years ago, a nutritious warm-dough smell had spilled forth; but Robin had no strong smell, even between her legs. She gave off a babyish scent, a whiff of sour milk; otherwise her body was unodoriferous, so that Bech's own aromas, the product of over seven decades of marination in the ignominy of organic life, stood out like smears on a white vinyl wall. Penetrated, Robin felt like a fresh casing, and her spasms came rapidly, a tripping series of orgasms made almost pitiable by her habit of sucking one of his thumbs deep into her mouth as she came. When that was over, and their pulse rates had leveled off, she looked at him with her fox-fur irises shining expectantly, childishly. "So who are you going to do next?" she asked. Her pupils, tiny inkwells as deep as the night sky's zenith, were dilated by excitement. He pushed back her hair from her face, and let the wiry mass spring forward again.

"Well," Bech reluctantly allowed, "Aldie Cannon *is* very annoying. He's a forty-something smart-aleck, from the West Coast somewhere. Palo Alto, maybe. He has one of these very rapid agile nerdy minds – whatever pops into it must be a thought, he figures. He began by being all over *The Nation* and *The New Republic* and then he moved into the *Vanity Fair/GQ* orbit, writing about movies, books, TV, music, whatever, an authority on any sort of schlock, and then got more and more on radio and TV – they love that kind of guy, a thirty-second opinion on anything, bing, bam – until now that's basically all he does, that and write some kind of junk on the Internet, his own Web site, I don't know – people send me printouts whenever he says anything about me, I wish they wouldn't."

"What sort of thing does he say?"

Bech shifted his weight off his elbow, which was hurting. Any joint in his body hurt, with a little use. His body wanted to retire but his raging spirit wouldn't let it. He rested his head on the pillow beside Robin's pillow and stared at the ceiling, which had been recently fabricated of polystyrene acoustical tiles perforated by dots. The dots were distributed with a studied irregularity that suggested the mountains and valleys of a shallow safe country as yet uncoagulated into cities. This bedroom had been carved, with wallboard and lumber, out of the loft's great space, complete with ceiling, like a cage within a circus tent. "He says I'm the embodiment of everything retrograde and unenlightened in pre-electronic American letters. He says my men are sex-obsessed narcissistic brutes and all my female characters are just anatomic-ally correct dolls."

"*Ooh*," murmured Robin, as if softly struck by a bit of rough justice.

Bech went on, aggrieved, "For twenty years he's been getting a cheap ride hitchhiking on feminism, saying, 'Tut tut' and 'Too bad' to every novel by us older guys that isn't about an all-male platoon in World War Two being saved by a raft of angelic Red Cross nurses. He's been married, but never for long, and the word on the street is the jury's still out on his sexual orientation. Physically, he's a wimp – a pair of thick hornrims and a haircut like a toothbrush. He never got over George Gobel on television. You're too young to remember George Gobel."

"But he's clever," Robin prompted. "Clever enough to get under your skin."

"He's clever if glib cheap shots and a souped-up pseudo-show-biz lingo are clever, yeah."

"What else has he said about you?"

"He says I have no imagination. He says things like, and I quote, 'Whenever Bech attempts to use his imagination, the fuse blows and sparks fall to the floor. But short circuits aren't the same as magic-realist fireworks.' End quote. On top of being a smart-aleck he's a closet prude. He hated the sex in *Think Big*; he wrote, as I dimly remember, 'These tawdry and impossible wet dreams tell us nothing about how men and women really interact.' Implying that he sure does, the creepy fag. He's never interacted with anything but a candy machine and the constant torrent of cultural crap."

"Henry, his striking you as a creepy fag isn't reason enough to kill him."

"It is for me. He's a local blot on the universe."

"How would you go about it?"

"How would *we* go about it, maybe is the formula. What do we know about this twerp? He's riddled with insecurities, has all this manicky energy, and is on the Internet."

"You *have* been mulling this over, haven't you?" Robin's eyes had widened; her lower lip hung slightly open, looking riper and wetter than usual, as she propped herself above him, bare-breasted, livid-nippled, her big hair tumbling in oiled coils. Her straight short nose didn't go with the rest of her face, giving her a slightly flattened expression, like a cat's. "My lover the killer," she breathed.

"My time on earth is limited." Bech bit off his words. "I have noble work to do. I can't see Cannon licking return envelopes. He probably has an assistant for that. Or tosses them in the wastebasket. He thinks he's big-time, the little shit." Bech stared at the ceiling's unearthly geography. He averted his eyes from

Robin's bared breasts, their gleaming white weight like that of gourds still ripening, snapping their vines.

She said, "So? Where could I come in?"

"Computer expertise. You have it, or know those that do. My question of you, baby, is, Could we break into his computer?"

Robin's smooth face, its taut curves with their invisible fuzz, hardened in intellectual engagement. "If he can get out," she said, "a smart cracker can get in. The Internet is one big happy family, like it or not."

The Aldie Cannon mini-industry was headquartered in his modest Upper East Side apartment. Even the most successful operatives in the post-Gutenbergian literary world lived modestly, relative to the arriviste young wizards of electronic software, pop music, fashion design, and hair styling, not to mention the thousands of the already rich, whose ancestors or earlier, shrewder selves had scooped up a fortune from some momentary turn in the evolution of a rural democracy into a capitalist powerhouse. In recent years they had all needed to do nothing but watch their investments double and redouble in a stock market that, under the first baby boomer to be President, knew no downside. Cannon lived, with his third wife and two maladjusted small children, not on one of the East Sixties' genteel, ginkgo-shaded side streets but in a raw new blue-green skyscraper, with balconies like stubby daisy petals, over by the river. His daily Internet feature, *Cannon Fodder*, was produced in a child-resistant study on a Compaq PC equipped with Windows 95. His opinionated claptrap was twinkled by modem to a site in San Jose, where it was checked for obscenity and libel and misspellings before going out to the millions of green-skinned cyberspace goons paralyzed at their terminals. E-mail sent to **fodder.com** went to San Jose, where the less inane and more provocative communications were forwarded to Aldie, for possible use in one of his columns.

Robin, after consulting some goons of her acquaintance, explained to Bech that the ubiquitous program for E-mail, Sendmail, had been written in the Unix ferment of the late 1970s, when security had been of no concern; it was notoriously full of bugs. For instance, Sendmail performed security checks only on a user's first message; once the user passed, all his subsequent messages went straight through. Another weakness of the program was that a simple |, the "pipe" symbol, turned the part of the message following it into input, which could consist of a variety of Unix commands the computer was obliged to obey. These commands could give an intruder log-in status and, with some more manipulation, a "back-door" access that would last until detected and deleted. Entry could be utilized to attach a "Trojan horse" that would flash messages onto the screen, with subliminal brevity if desired.

Bech's wicked idea was to undermine Cannon's confidence and sense of self – fragile, beneath all that polymathic, relentlessly with-it bluster – as he sat gazing at his monitor. Robin devised a virus: every time Aldie typed an upper-case "A" or a lower-case "x," a message would flash, too quickly for his conscious mind to register but distinctly enough to penetrate the neuronic complex of brain cells. The subversive program took Robin some days to perfect; especially finicking were the specs of such brief interruptions, amid the seventy cathode-ray refreshments of the screen each second, in letters large enough to make an impression that could be read unawares by a modern mind habituated to the lightning message, the commercially loaded seme, the come-hither flutter of sexually loaded images. She labored while Bech slept; half-moon shadows smudged and dented the silken smoothness of her face. Delicately she strung her contingent binaries together. They could at any moment be destroyed by an automatic "sniffer" program or a human "sysadmin," a systems administrator. Federal laws were being violated; heavy penalties could be incurred. Nevertheless, out of love for Bech and the fascination of a technical challenge, she persevered and, by the third morning, succeeded.

Bech began, once the intricate, illicit commands had been lodged, with some hard-core Buddhism. BEING IS PAIN, the subliminal message read; NON-BEING IS NIRVANA. The words invisibly rippled into the screen's pixels for a fifteenth of a second – that is, five refreshments of the screen, a single one being,

Robin and a consulted neurophysiologist agreed, too brief to register even subliminally. After several days of these basic equations, Bech asked her to program the more advanced, NO MISERY OF MIND IS THERE FOR HIM WHO HATH NO WANTS. It was critical that the idea of death be rendered not just palatable but inviting. NON-BEING IS AN ASPECT OF BEING, AND BEING OF NON-BEING: This Bech had adapted from a Taoist poem by Seng Ts'an. From the same source he took TO BANISH REALITY IS TO SINK DEEPER INTO THE REAL. With Aldie's manicky productiveness in mind, he dictated, ACTIVITY IS AVOIDANCE OF VICTORY OVER SELF.

Together he and Robin scanned Cannon's latest effusions, in print or on the computer screen, for signs of mental deterioration and spiritual surrender. Deborah Frueh had taken the bait in the dark, and Bech had been frustrated by his inability to see what was happening – whether she was licking an envelope or not, and what effect the much-diluted poison was having on her detestable innards. But in the case of Aldie Cannon, his daily outpouring of cleverness surely would betray symptoms. His review of a Sinead O'Connor concert felt apathetic, though he maintained it was her performance, now that she was no longer an anti-papal skinhead, that lacked drive and point. His roundup of recent books dwelling, with complacency or alarm, upon the erosion of the traditional literary canon – cannon fodder indeed, the ideal chance for him to do casual backflips of lightly borne erudition – drifted toward the passionless conclusion that "the presence or absence of a canon amounts to much the same thing; one is all, and none is equally all." This didn't sound like the Aldie Cannon who had opined, of Bech's collection *When the Saints*, "Some of these cagey feuilletons sizzle but most fizzle; the author has moved from not having much to say to implying that anyone's having anything to say is a tiresome breach of good taste. Bech is a literary dandy, but one dressed in tatters, plucked up at the thrift-shop bins of contemporary ideation."

It was good for Bech to remember these elaborate and gleeful dismissals, lest pity bring him to halt the program. Where the celebrant of pop culture would once wax rapturous over Julia Roberts' elastic mouth and avid eyes, he now dwelt upon

her ethereal emaciation in *My Best Friend's Wedding*, and the
"triumphant emptiness" of her heroine's romantic defeat and
the film's delivery of her into the arms of a confirmed homosexual. Of Saul Bellow's little novel, he noticed only the "tha-
natoptic beauty" of its culmination in a cemetery, where the
hero's proposal had the chiseled gravity of an elegy or a death
sentence. The same review praised the book's brevity and confessed – this from Aldie Cannon, Pantagruelian consumer of
cultural produce – that some days he just didn't want to read
one more book, see one more movie, go to one more art show,
look up one more reference, wrap up one more paragraph with
one more fork-tongued aperçu. And then, just as the Manhattan
scene was kicking into another event-crammed fall season, *Cannon Fodder* now and then skipped a day on the Internet, or was
replaced, with a terse explanatory note, by one of the writer's
"classic" columns from a bygone year.

Sometimes, as Bech and his accomplice sat together monitor-
ing Aldie Cannon's Web page, Robin's eyes in their gelatinous
beauty glanced away from the plastic screen into Bech's face, but
saw no more mercy in one than the other. His once rugged,
good-humored features were shrinking with age, expelling their
water, like a mummy's, becoming an overlapping bundle of
leathery scraps all seam and pucker and coarse stitch. NON-
BEING IS BLISS, he told her to make the Trojan horse spell, and
SELFHOOD IS IMPURITY, and, at ever-faster intervals, the one word
JUMP. JUMP, the twittering little pixels cried, and JUMP YOU
BABBLING FOOL, giving a dangerously (in case an investigation
were to reconstruct these smuggled commands) personal voice to
Bech's subliminal barrage, which was varied by JUMP YOU TWIT
or JUMP YOU HOLLOW MAN or DO THE WORLD A FUCKING FAVOR
AND JUMP but always came back to the monosyllabic imperative
verb. JUMP.

Bech had made a pilgrimage to the blue-green skyscraper near
the river to make sure a suicide leap was feasible. Its towering
mass receded above him like giant railroad tracks – an entire
railroad yard of aluminum and glass. The jutting semicircular
petals of its balconies formed a scalloped dark edge against the
clouds as they hurtled in lock formation across the china-blue

late-summer firmament. It always got to the pit of Bech's
stomach, the way the tops of skyscrapers appeared to lunge across
the sky when you looked up, like the prows of ships certain to
crash. The building was fifty-five stories high. Its windows were
sealed but the balconies were not caged in, as more and more
high spaces were, to frustrate pathological Icaruses dying to test
the air. The top of the Empire State Building was now caged in;
in Bech's boyhood it had not been, and when he was eight or so
his father had held his ankles while he rested his chest on the
broad parapet and looked straight down. Bech had never forgotten that dizzying moment of risk and trust, nor a photograph
he had once seen in the old *Life*, of a beautiful young woman
who had jumped and whose body lay as tranquilly intact on the
dented top of a parked car as on a bier banked with flowers.

Within Bech a siren wailed, calling Aldie out, out of his cozy
claustral nest of piped-in, faxed, E-mailed, messengered, videoed
cultural fluff and straw – culture, that tawdry, cowardly anti-
nature – into the open air, the stinging depths of space, cosmic
nature pure and raw. Bech envisioned Manhattan yawning below
the hesitating suicide – a crammed clutter of wooden water tanks
and turbanned ventilators and tarred rooftops marked with coded
letters in whitewash addressed apparently to God's eye. Let go,
Aldie, sky-dive, jump, merge your nasty little self with the vasty
scribbled earth.

"I can't believe this is you," Robin told him. "This killer."

"I have been grievously provoked," he said.

"Just by reviews? Henry, nobody takes them seriously."

"I thought I did not, but now I see that I have. I have suffered a
lifetime's provocation. My mission has changed; I wanted to add
to the world's beauty, but now I merely wish to rid it of ugliness."

"Poor Aldie Cannon. Don't you think he means well? Some
of his columns I find quite entertaining."

"He may mean well but he commits atrocities. His facetious
half-baked columns are crimes against art and against mankind.
He has crass taste – no taste, in fact. He has a mouth to talk but
no ears with which to listen." Liking in his own ear the rhythm
of his tough talk, Bech got tougher. "Listen, sister," he said
to Robin. "You want out? Out you can have any time. Walk

down two flights. The subway's over on Broadway or up on Houston. I'll give you the buck-fifty. My treat."

She appeared to think it over. She said what women always say, to stall. "Henry, I love you."

"Why the hell would that be?"

"You're cute," Robin told him. "Especially these days. You seem more, you know, *together*. Before, you were some sort of a sponge, just sitting there, waiting for stuff to soak in. Now you've, like they say on the talk shows, taken charge of your life."

He pulled her into his arms with a roughness that darkened the fox-fur glints in her eyes. A quick murk of fear and desire blurred her features. His hoary head cast a shadow on her silver face as he bowed his neck to kiss her. She made her lips as soft as she could, as soft as the primeval ooze. "And you like that, huh?" he grunted. "My becoming bad."

"It lets me be bad." Her voice had gotten small and hurried, as if she might faint. "I love you because I can be a bad girl with you and you love it. You eat it up. *Yum*, you say."

"Bad is relative," he informed her, from the height of his antiquity. "For my purposes, you're a good girl. The worse you are the better you are. So it excites you, huh? Trying to bring this off."

Robin admitted, "It's kind of a rush." She added, with a touch of petulance as if to remind him how girlish she was, "It's my project. I want to stick with it."

"Now you're talking. Here, I woke up with an inspiration. Flash the twerp this." It was another scrap of Buddhist death-acceptance: LET THE ONE WITH ITS MYSTERY BLOT OUT ALL MEMORY OF COMPLICATIONS. PLEASE JUMP.

"It seems pretty abstract."

"He'll buy it. I mean, his subconscious will buy it. He thinks of himself as an intellectual. He majored in philosophy at Berkeley, I read in that stuff you downloaded from the Internet."

While she was at the terminal pattering through the dance of computer control, he found in the same ancient text – Seng Ts'an's "Poem on Trust in the Heart" – a line that greatly moved him. *Space is bright, but self-illumined; no power of mind is exerted*. Self-illumined: that was what he in his innocence had once hoped to be. *Nor indeed could mere thought bring us to such a place*, the text went on, comfortingly. Yes. Mere thought was what he was done with. *It is the Truly-so, the Transcendent Sphere, where there is neither He nor I*. Neither He nor I.

Robin came back to him. "It went through, but I wonder."

"Wonder what?"

"Wonder how much longer before they find us and wipe us out. There's more and more highly sophisticated security programs. Crackers are costing industry billions; the FBI has a whole department now for computer crime."

"The seed is sown," Bech said, still somewhat in Buddhist mode. "Let's go to bed. I'll let you suck my thumb, if you beg nicely. You bad bitch," he added, to see if her eyes would darken again. They did.

But the sniffers were out there, racing at the speed of light through the transistors, scouring the binary code for alien configurations and rogue algorithms. Now it was Robin who each morning rushed, in her inherited terrycloth robe, on her pink-sided bare feet, down the two flights to the ground-floor foyer and seized the *Times* and scanned its obituary page. The very day after her Trojan horse, detected and killed, failed to respond to her typed commands, their triumph was headlined: ALDOUS CANNON, 43, CRITIC, COMMENTATOR. Jumped from the balcony of his apartment on the forty-eighth floor. No pedestrians hurt, but an automobile parked on Sutton Place severely damaged. Distraught wife alleged the writer and radio personality, whose Web site on the Internet was one of the most visited for literary purposes by college students, had seemed preoccupied lately, and confessed to sensations of futility. Had always hoped to free up time to write a big novel, possibly concerning the American Civil War. In a separate story in Section B, a wry collegial tribute from Christopher Lehmann-Haupt.

Bech and Robin should have felt jubilant. They had planted a flickering wedge of doubt beneath the threshold of consciousness and brought down a wiseguy, a media-savvy smart-ass. But it became clear after their initial, mutually congratulatory embrace, there above the sweating carton of orange juice and the slowly

toasting bagels, that they felt stunned, let down, and ashamed.
They avoided the sight and touch of each other for the rest of the
day, though it was a Saturday. They had planned to go up to the
Metropolitan Museum and check out the Ivan Albright show and
then try to get an outdoor table at the Stanhope, in the deliciously
crisp September air. But the thought of art in any form sickened
them – sweet icing on dung, thin ice over the abyss. Robin went
shopping for black jeans at Barneys and then took a train to visit
her parents in Garrison, while Bech in a stupor like that of a snake
digesting a poisonous toad sat watching two Midwestern college-
football teams batter at each other in a screaming, chanting stadium far west of the Hudson, where life was sunstruck and clean.

Robin spent the night with her parents, and returned so late
on Sunday she must have hoped her lover would be asleep. But
he was up, waiting for her, reading. First some Froissart, on the
Battle of Crécy ("the bodies of 11 princes, 1200 knights, and
about 30,000 common men were found on the field"), and then a
dip into the little volume of Donne:

> License my roving hands, and let them go,
> Before, behind, between, above, below.
> O my America! my new-found land . . .

His eyes kept sliding off the page. The day's lonely meal had
generated a painful gas in his stomach. His mouth tasted chemi-
cally of nothingness. Passive consumption, moral insufficiency.
The alleged selflessness of the artist – what a crock. All was
vanity, a coy dance of veils grotesque in a septuagenarian.
Robin's key timidly scratched at the lock and she entered; he
met her near the threshold and they gently bumped heads in a
show of contrition. They had together known sin. Like playmates who had mischievously destroyed a toy, they slowly
repaired their relationship. As Aldie Cannon's surprising but
not unusual (John Berryman, Jerzy Kosinski) self-erasure slipped
deeper down into the stack of used newspapers, and the obligatory notes of memorial tribute tinnily, fadingly sounded in the
PEN and Authors Guild newsletters, the duo on Crosby Street
recovered their dynamism and a fresh will to adventure, in the
quixotic cause of ridding literary Gotham of villains.

* * *

Bech bought himself a cape and Robin a mask. A black mask, covering half her tidy white bobbed nose and framing her warm, intricate eyes in a stiff midnight strangeness. It turned him on; he made her wear it during lovemaking. "I feel so dirty," she confessed. "I feel like one of those corrupted countesses in French pornography. I feel like O."

Bech was good in bed but impotent elsewhere. "I can't sit at a desk any more," he said. "I want to get out and *do* something," he said. "Ever since Aldie jumped, it's like I've got St. Vitus' dance."

"Let's walk up to Washington Square. We'll cruise the remaining bookstores on Eighth Street."

"They were right, the bastards," Bech fumed, "I have nothing to say. I just wanted to pose, and print was the easiest place for a shy guy. I'm an elderly useless *poseur*."

Out walking, he wore, with trepidation at first, his cape – a shiny blue satin, a shade lighter than navy, with a comforting lining of red lamb's wool, and a gold-plated clasp in the shape of a talon. He thought people would stare if not laugh, but he had underestimated the commonplace *bizarrerie* of Manhattan street theatre – the love-starved throngs, the poignant chorus of vain attention-getting. Hair dyed pastel colors, see-through blouses, lovely young shoulders blotched by tattoos, chalk-white black-lipped vampire makeup, the determinedly in-your-face costumes of the proclaimedly gay, the secret oddities of *Psychopathia Sexualis* turned inside out and put on show, like the convolute, inviting forms of flowers. Such exhibitionists denied Bech a single sideways glance at his cape as it swirled dramatically around him. Their eyes went to Robin – the candid purity of her face, boyish in its fashionable short haircut, formal like a waxen seal set on the untold pleasures of her body, curvaceous in its mauve catsuit.

To go with his cape Bech affected stovepipe trousers and narrow black slipperlike shoes, with rippled rubber treads. In these shoes he moved stealthily across pavements, lightly climbed stairs to bright gatherings – gallery openings, poetry readings – of tufted young aspirants to artistic fame who were startled to see that he, who had haunted, for a truncated page or two, their laborious double-columned high-school readers, was still alive. He slit his eyes against the glaze of their winey sweat and shuttling banter; he lifted his nose to scent evil and detected only the mild aroma of an illiterate innocence. These pretty children did not read, not in the old impassioned, repressed way, scouring print for forbidden knowledge, as his generation had done. Nietzsche, Marx, Freud, Joyce – the great God-killers. His enemies breathed his own air and lurked in lairs, in shadowy corners. His slippers carried him one night up the fire escape of a four-story red-brick building on Christopher Street, in the slant reaches, junglelike with ailanthus, of the West Village.

Robin in her mask followed him up, across the rusty iron slats. Tall old sash windows revealed roach-ridden kitchens and book-lined walls crawling with the wires of outmoded stereo sets. Noises could be heard through these windows, cries of emotion and laughter, whether in reality or on television was not perfectly clear. Bech climbed on, up the spindly metal welded by work-men long dead, toward a fourth-floor apartment where thirty years ago he had been a guest. He had been in his forties; his host in his fifties. The fire-escape slats threw diagonal harps of shadow across the crumbling bricks. One landing, seen downward through another, made a shimmering pattern located, like the elusive effects of Op Art, in no particular space. The fourth-floor windowpanes were dark, but held oily orange traces of a reading lamp dimly burning several rooms away. Bech tested the sash but it was shut. The loathsome bookworm inside had barricaded himself against the warm October night – its cries of human intercourse, its garbage smells of life.

From beneath his cape, Bech whipped out a strip of duct tape, attached it to a lower pane of the upper sash, deftly struck it with the stock of a glinting pistol. The muffled sound of fracture suggested that of a single ripe fruit falling. Swiftly his gray-gloved hand was in, twisting the worn window lock, and the weathered sash eased up on its rotten cords. He slithered over the sill, Robin as close behind him as a shadow. Inadvertently her hand on the sill caught his trailing cape. With a silent, predatory gesture, the silhouetted avenger tugged the lined satin free.

They were in a kind of pantry. Shelves designed for pans and crockery were filled with books, a lot of them bound galleys for review, stashed sideways and two deep, yellowing, collecting dust. Stealthily the intruders passed through an exiguous kitchen, scrubbed and bare, as a daytime caretaker would leave it. Three apples in a wooden bowl were the only visible food. *Judgment of Paris*, Bech thought. *Venus the winner. Trouble in Troy.* The apples imparted to his nostrils the faint tang of orchards gone under to malls. Then came a small dining room, its walls hung with spidery engravings of what seemed conferences – men in white wigs and black knickers plotting revolutions. They were making sweeping gestures. Kill the King, *écrasez l'infâme*, make it new. A half-open door led to a small bedroom, a single bed made up taut as a hospital bed, with a number of upright pillows. Sleeping upright. Buried alive. Bech's own breath empathetically grew short.

The sallow light dimly perceived from the fire escape strengthened. Bech and Robin found themselves in a room lined with books, books piled to the ceiling, disorder upon order, uniform sets submerged under late arrivals, biographies and commentaries and posthumous volumes, the original organization overwhelmed, torn bookmarks and offprints chaotically interleaved. An arid smell, as of man-made desert, seeped from so much paper. Dust mites, spilling allergens, rustled underfoot.

Beyond this room, glimpsed through a doorway carved in the sepulchrally thick wall of books, an underfurnished living room bared itself to the streetlight, to the scattered glimmer of lower Manhattan and the sullen gap of the Hudson. Nobody was there.

The occupant of this Village apartment, the mastermind behind its parched accumulations, sat behind the intruders, in a corner of the library, reading and sniffing oxygen. A baby-blue plastic tube led from a cylindrical tank beside his armchair up to his nose, where it forked to take in both nostrils. The man had advanced emphysema, from a lifetime of contented smoking while he read. A gooseneck lamp looked over his shoulder. His black-stockinged feet were up on an old-fashioned ottoman, with tassels and rolled seams and a top of multicolored leather sliced like a pie. His body, boneless and amorphous, merged with that of his creased leather armchair, tucked like a kind of shroud around him. Time had nearly ceased to flow here. Nothing moved but the invalid's limp, flat-ended fingers as he turned a page. He looked up blinking, resenting the interruption of his reading. "Bech," he said at last. "My God. Climbing fire escapes now. Why the crazy get-up? I thought you were a madman, breaking in."

"Get real, Cohen," Bech snapped. "Capes are coming back. They *are* back. Monocles, next."

"Or a dope addict," the invalid wheezily continued, in Skeltonic gasps. "I get about one a week. They diss me because . . . there's nothing to steal. Just old books. Kids today have no idea . . . of the value of books. And who's your little sidekick? *Zaftig*, I can see . . . but so young, to get mixed up in . . . old men's quarrels." Cohen had taken off his reading glasses, to focus on the incursion from beyond the printed page. His eyes were pinched in folds of collapsing lids and puckered socket-skin. Seeing that Bech would not perform introductions, he said, in a mockery of politeness, "I almost liked your last book. The one about . . . the Korean War orphan. At least you weren't trying . . . to pass off your feeble fantasies . . . as any country we know."

Cohen had barely the breath to blow out a candle. His utterances resembled sentences lifted from book reviews and peppered with ellipses to make them more favorable. His reference was to *Going South* (1992), a tender, well-researched novella imagining the adventures of a parentless nine-year-old girl, Hang Kim, from a village near Huichon, caught up in the routed American armies retreating from the waves of Chinese troops all the way to Taejon. As Bech aged, his thoughts turned to war. He had fought in one over a half-century ago. At the time, and for most of the time since, he had thought of war as an aberration, a dehumanizing episode to be gotten through and forgotten. But lately he had begun to wonder if Hemingway and Tolstoy weren't right: war was truth, in an unbearably pure state. It has shaped the map and spawned the most vigorous moral principle, that of tribal loyalty.

Bech swirled his cape, performing, with an ironic bow, the courtesies Cohen had requested. "Rachel, meet my nemesis, Mr. Orlando Cohen, the arch-fiend of American criticism. Orlando, this is Ms. Rachel Teagarten, who helps me out in my work. She understands computers, copulation, and elementary cooking."

"I suppose computers," the old magus wheezed, "are worth understanding. I always think in this connection . . . of the chess-playing automaton . . . who turned out to be . . . a dwarf. The board had to be transparent, so he . . . could follow the moves. Imagine . . . following the moves upside down . . . crouched in a little airless box. And winning sometimes. He didn't always win, actually – that is a myth. There was a series of dwarfs . . . some of whom were undoubtedly . . . more skillful than others."

This long speech left Cohen utterly breathless. He inhaled prolongedly through his nose. His nose and ears had enlarged with age, or had remained the same while the rest of him shrunk. He had been a handsome man, once, and women had been tantalized and maddened by their failure to distract him from his chaste ambition to be the ultimate adjudicator of literature – all literature, but specializing in American. He had steadfastly refused to grant Bech a place, even a minor place, in the canon. In review after review he had found Bech's books artificial, hollow, dandyish, lame. His review of *Going South*, in *The New Criterion*, had been jeeringly titled "Halt and Lame."

"Don't try to buy time with gabble," Bech advised him. "The jig is up."

"What jig?" Cohen managed to get out. The tip of his nose looked blue with anoxia. He had a strange contemplative habit of twitching his nose, of swinging its tip from side to side, rapidly.

"The jig of trashing me. What did I ever do to you?"

"You failed to write well."

"How could that be? It was all I cared about, writing well."

"You cared too much. You let the words hold you back . . . from descending into yourself. You were Jewish . . . and tried to pretend . . . you were American."

"Can't you be both?"

"Bellow can. Salinger could, once. Mailer, alternately . . . never both at once. Malamud . . . I don't know. He lost me in those last

books . . . *Dubin's Lives* and the one about the monkeys. He
wanted credentials. Jews can't get credentials. Not in a world
run by goyim. Israel is a credential. It's not a good one. The
Arabs won't stamp it."

"You're stalling, Orlando. See this? What is it?" Bech delved
beneath his beautiful, midnight-blue cape and brandished the
steel weapon he came up with. It felt heavy, heavier than it
looked, so exquisitely machined of black stealth metal.

"A gun," Orlando Cohen said. His spatulate fingers adjusted
the plastic leech whispering into his nostrils.

"A gat," Bech corrected. "A rod. With a silencer. Not even
the people downstairs are going to hear when I plug you. They'll
think it's your dishwasher kicking into the next part of the
cycle."

The sick man's eyes left Bech's face. "Rachel," he said. "How
long has he . . . been like this?"

"Don't answer the scumbag," Bech commanded her. "The
prick, he sucks up to Wasps. The stiff-necked old establishment.
The more anti-Semitic they were – the Jameses, the Adamses,
the Holmeses – the more he loves them. Hemingway, Fitzgerald
– never mind their snide cracks. He even praised Capote, can
you imagine? Praised Capote and panned me."

Cohen replied, so faintly the duo had to strain to listen, picking
up all sorts of muttered street noise and radio music in the process.
"Capote . . . descended into himself. In *In Cold Blood* . . . he hit his
vein. He wanted to be hung with Perry. He hated himself . . . the
little squeaky monster he was. He worked his self-hatred . . . into
an objective correlative. He made us care. Bech . . . you . . . you
missed your vein. You were squeamish . . . and essentially lazy.
You missed . . . the boat. The boat . . . to America."

"I am going to shut you up," Bech told him. "I am going to
squeeze this fucking trigger and rub you out. Don't think I'm too
squeamish. I've killed before." In the war. There was no knowing how many. With a Browning automatic rifle you poured lead
into a thicket or Belgian farm shed that had been sheltering
enemy fire or took on a flak-wagon or machine-gun emplace-
ment and at the end there was no telling how many of the bodies
were yours, these German bodies that after a few freezing days in

their piles looked like cordwood or enormous purple-and-green vegetables. In the Ardennes, in December of '44, in the Twenty-eighth Infantry, in the bitter cold: the German soldiers were specks in the snow, distant, running, toward him or away from him wasn't easy to tell in the snow glare; you squeezed, you squeezed the icy trigger of the M1, metal so cold the oil would freeze and jam the bolt, you squinted into the glare and squeezed through the crumbling GI gloves whose fraying olive threads grew little balls of frozen snow, cold to the bones from the night in the wet foxhole, huddled with O'Malley and Perera and Lundgren, the loved strangers whose bodies were life's warmth, up to your knees in icy water in the trench, the physical misery great enough and so incessant you could get light-hearted about the death that might hide behind the next tree, as you scuttled along, hump-backed with your pack; thick ancient beeches the trees were, their gray lines rounded and graceful like those of women in the snow. Country like a Christmas card, great Kraut-killing country, the men joked, the bleary heartless boy-men, and it was true, the Ardennes counteroffensive brought the Heinies up out of their bunkered, Kraut-trim emplacements into the open, upright, trying to advance, under Hitler's mad orders. You squeezed and the distant scurrying dot dropped and you felt a spurt of warmth inside, a surcease in the misery, a leak of satisfaction and pride from some other, impossible world, a world at peace. He would pot a few more, like ducks against a white sky, before the platoon fell back and he got his feet out of ice water. If he had killed for his country, he could kill for his art.

"Go ahead," Cohen breathlessly urged him. "Pull it. Do it. I'm eighty-two and . . . can't take five steps . . . without suffocating. Do me the favor." Yet the old creep didn't mean it; he was cunning; he was crazy to live. Cannily, Cohen went on, "What about your young friend here? Rachel. Think she'll like it . . . the rest of her days in the pen? They execute . . . women these days. Seems a heavy price to pay for . . . your demented boyfriend's vanity."

"She chose to come along. I didn't drag her."

"I love seeing Henry so energized," Robin told Cohen.

"He should have put his energy . . . into his work. *Travel*

Light . . . Think Big . . . stunts. You can't believe a word. I ignore *The Chosen* because everybody agreed . . . it was an embarrassment."

"Not Charles Poore in the daily *Times*. He loved it."

"Poore, that old lady. What did he know? You tried to con us. You thought you could skip out . . . of yourself and write American. Bech . . . let me ask you. Can you say the Lord's Prayer?"

Bech didn't dignify his inquisitor with an answer, just laid the pistol – a 9-mm Luger, a war souvenir lifted from the body of a dead officer, a gun that may well have killed Jews before – a little off from pointing, with its elongating silencer, at his enemy's heart. He laid it sideways in air, giving Cohen's struggling, insatiable tongue permission to continue.

"Well, ninety percent of the *zhlubs* around you can. It's in their heads. They can rattle . . . the damn thing right off . . . how can you expect to write about people . . . when you don't have a clue to the *chozzerai* . . . that's in their heads? The Holy Ghost . . . These goyim came here thinking . . . the Holy Ghost had them by the hand. The Holy Ghost. Who the hell is that? Some pigeon, that's all . . . anybody knows. Those first winters . . . they'd never seen anything like it . . . back in England. They stuck it out . . . but that God-awful faith . . . Bech . . . when it burns out . . . it leaves a dead spot. Love it or leave it . . . a dead spot. That's where America is . . . in that dead spot. Em, Emily, that guy in the woods . . . Hem, Mel, Haw . . . they were there. No in thunder . . . the Big No. Jews don't know how to say No. All we know is Yes. Yes, I'll kill Isaac . . . Yes, let's wrestle. That's why you're lousy, Bech. You gave it a shot . . . some say a good shot . . . but not me. For me it fell flat. You aimed away . . . from the subject you had . . . into the one no one has . . . except the people who can inhabit nowhere. America, opportunity, jazz, O.K. . . . but it's a nowhere. A coast-to-coast nowhere. You thought . . . like those Hollywood *meshuggeners* . . . Jews slap-happy with getting out of the ghetto . . . you could tickle it into becoming . . . a *place*, with cute people. Mickey Rooney, Lewis Stone . . . Jesus. James, Twain, Adams, those mean old boys . . . you got to love them. You, Bech, I don't have to love. You are a phony. You made yourself up . . . *worse* even than

Capote. Go ahead. Pull it. I'm dying for it, no kidding. I can't breathe, can't talk, can't fuck, can't eat . . . can't even sleep more than an hour at a time. Pull it. Look the other way, Rachel. Death's not as pretty . . . as you kids these days seem to think. You think it's nothing . . . but it's still . . . something." The revered critic's nose twitched, its blue tip swinging back and forth for perhaps the last time.

Bech uncertainly glanced sideways at Robin. He admired, in her profile, the emphatic black eyebrow, a boldface hyphen, stark and Mediterranean in feeling. Iphigenia and Esther, Electra and Delilah had possessed such fatal unflinching eyebrows. If he wanted to shoot, she would watch him shoot. She was the best sidekick a man could have.

"Robin," he told her. "Go pull the tube out of the slimeball's nostrils."

She quickly did as she was told, padding forward in her catsuit, thinking perhaps this was a preliminary courtesy, when one old man killed another after decades of enmity.

Bech explained, lowering the gun, "Let's see if he can breathe on his own."

Cohen had steeled himself, but panic was creeping up, from his lungs to his face. The tip of his nose was revolving in continuous motion, tracing a tiny circle. He strained forward, to unpinch his lungs, and scrabbled at the side of his chair for the whispering oxygen tube. His words were mere husks, in clumps of two or three. "Not like this. Use the gat. Bech . . . believe me . . . your stuff . . . won't last. It's . . . upper-middlebrow . . . schlock. Not even upper. Middle-middle."

"You fetid bag of half-baked opinions," Bech snarled. "You rotten spoiler. You've been stealing my oxygen for years."

"Your stuff . . . it's . . . it's . . ." Cohen had slumped sideways in the chair. The book he had left on the arm (Walter Benjamin, *Selected Writings, Volume I, 1913–1926*) hit the floor with a thud. His complexion approached the tint of a fish, his throat puffing like stifled gills. "Fifties!" he concluded with a triumphant leer. "You're Fifties!" His yellow eyeballs rolled upward and his reading glasses flopped into his lap.

"Let's blow this joint," Bech told Robin. "I smell escaping gas."

"But –" He knew what she meant. If he wasn't going to shoot him, wasn't it cruel to let him asphyxiate? Or was this rough justice, on the anoxic literary heights?

"Listen, doll. We're doing him a favor, just like he asked. The poor sap is addicted. Nobody likes air after they've tasted pure oxygen. How does he breathe when he goes to the john? When he grabs his hour of sleep? Between us, I bet he socks in a solid seven, eight hours a night, with maybe one trip to the hopper to take a piss."

Orlando Cohen, fabled maker and destroyer of reputations, lay crumpled in his chair like a baby transfixed in the mystery of crib death. Robin whimpered and took a step toward the unconscious dotard. Bech's steely gray-gloved hand on her arm restrained her impulsive motion.

"Don't let that dickhead manipulate you," he told his companion. "You're like any broad. You're too soft. A cold-hearted *k'nocker* like that, he takes advantage. He'll get it together as soon as he hears us out the window and down the fire escape. Did you dig that canned lecture on American lit? He's given it a thousand times."

Off in the city, a police siren began to ululate; not for them on this caper, but perhaps the next. Clatteringly, the duo descended into the weedy dark back garden, where the shadows of ailanthus leaves restlessly stabbed. Robin brushed up against Bech in these shadows, her face, without its mask, startlingly white. "I want a baby," she said softly.

"Hey," Bech said. "I said broads were soft-hearted, I didn't say they had to act on it."

"I want to bear your child," she insisted.

"I'm seventy-four," he said. "I'm past my 'sell by' date."

They made their stealthy way out, past overflowing trashcans and dying rosebushes, onto Christopher Street, where they became, in the early-evening lamplight, another discreetly quarreling couple. "I felt scared," Robin confessed, "when I thought you were going to shoot that wheezy old man."

"I should have shot the *putz*," Bech responded morosely. "He's done me a world of woe. He's tried to negate me."

"Why didn't you then?" Her hand tugged on his arm like another question, there under the red-lined cape, which lifted a little behind them, as a breeze from Bleecker Street conveyed an ozone suggestion of a thunderstorm before midnight.

"I believed him; it was worse for him to live."

"You know what I think?"

She waited, irritating Bech, for the thousandth time, with the playful, self-pleasuring expertise with which women work the relational game. "What?" he had to respond, gruffly.

"I think," she said, "you're a bit soft-hearted yourself."

"I was," he allowed, "but they beat it out of me. They nagged and nitpicked and small-minded me out of it."

"They couldn't," she said. "They're just critics, but you –"

Once again, her artful pause forced him to make a response: "Yes?"

"You're you."

"And who isn't?"

"Everybody is, but few take it as much to heart as you have. Henry –"

"*What?* Cut it out with the dialogue!"

"Do you think maybe we've rid the world of enough evil for now?"

"There's plenty left. There's a guy who teaches at Columbia, Carlos something-era, an English professor, or whatever they call it now, who really got my goat in the *Book Review* the other week. He said I lacked *duende*. *Duende!* I looked it up in the Spanish dictionary and it said 'ghost, goblin, fairy.' And then there's Gore Vidal, who – And Garry Wills, who –"

"Darling."

"What now?"

"You're sputtering. Let's think about our baby."

"I can't bring a baby into a world as polluted by wicked criticism as this one."

"Nobody criticizes a baby."

"They would any of mine. Robin, we were just getting going as a duo."

"Were?"

"I want to wreak more vengeance."

"No you don't," Robin told him. "What a duo wants is to become a trio. Here's a deal: knock me up, or I go to the cops. The bulls."

"And tell them what?"

"Everything."

"This is blackmail."

"I'd call it devotion. To your best interests." They turned right on Bedford, to cut through to Houston, to walk on to Crosby. The city hung around them like an agitprop backdrop, murmurous and surreal, perforated by lights and lives in the millions. A bat-colored cloud bank gathered in the east, trailing wisps, above the saffron dome of the city's glow. Rachel Teagarten snuggled closer, complacently, under his cape. Bech wondered if this little tootsie wasn't getting to be a bit of a drag.

BECH AND THE BOUNTY OF SWEDEN

A STORM OF PROTEST greeted the announcement that Henry Bech had won the 1999 Nobel Prize for Literature. Fumed a *New York Times* editorial:

> The Swedish Academy's penchant for colorful nonentities and anti-establishment gadflies as recipients of its dynamite-based bounty has surpassed mere caprice and taken on, in this latest selection, dimensions of wantonness. If the time for an American winner had at last come round again, then a deliberate affront must be read in this bypassing of solid contenders like Mailer, Roth, and Ozick, not to mention Pynchon and DeLillo, in favor of this passé exponent of fancy penmanship, whose skimpy oeuvre fails even to achieve J. D. Salinger's majestic total abstention from publication.

The *Post* quoted Isaiah Thornbush as saying, "With all respect to my dear colleague and old friend Henry, this turns the Prize into a prank. I was, quite frankly, stunned." BECH? WHODAT??? was the *Daily News*'s front-page headline, and *People* ran as its cover the least flattering photo they could find on file, showing Bech and his then wife, Bea, in bib overalls feigning repairs to the grape arbor of their mock-Tudor, mock-Edenic residence in Ossining. *New York* rose to the occasion with a languidly acid John Simon retrospective entitled "The Case (Far-Fetched) for Henry Bech."

Meanwhile, the phone in his Crosby Street loft kept ringing, sometimes interrupting the septuagenarian winner in the midst of changing diapers for his eight-month-old baby, Golda (when it came to naming her daughter, Rachel Teagarten was not so post-Jewish after all), so that the spicy smell of ochre babyshit and the shrilling of the phone became the two sides of one exasperating experience. Golda was sturdy and teething and had her mother's challenging calm stare, not fox-colored thus far but an infant's contemplative, unblinking slate blue. She was old enough to think there was something fishy about this knobby-handed old man groping about in her crotch and bottom crack with chilly baby wipes, and then too firmly pressing the adhesive fasteners in place upon her glossy, wobbly belly. Golda would tease him and show off her strength by twisting on the changing towel, cork-screwing like a baroque putto. She preferred her mother's cool quick touch, or the light brown hands of Leontyne, the lilting au pair from Antigua by way of Brooklyn's Crown Heights.

The voice on the phone was usually that of Meri [sic] Jo Zwengler, Vellum Press's leather-clad chief of publicity. "But I don't want to go on 'Oprah,'" he would tell her. "I hate that hooting audience of Corn Belt feminists she has."

Meri Jo would sigh. "It's expected, Henry. It would be considered an insult to two-thirds of America if you don't deign to appear."

"Yeah, the illiterate two-thirds. Where were they when *Going South* sold less than twenty thousand copies?"

Meri Jo was stagily patient with him. "You're a Laureate now, Henry. You're not free to pull that Henry Bech reclusive don't-bother-me-I'm-having-a-writer's-block act."

"'Bech, whodat?'" he quoted.

"Nobody's asking that any more. You're hot, Henry. I'm sorry. But the spike in sales should put your little girl through college, if you help nurse it along. We're thinking of even bringing *When the Saints* back into print."

"Why did you let it go out of print?"

"Don't be difficult, Henry. Warehousing costs have been sky-rocketing. We have a big overhead in our new quarters."

Meri Jo's annual salary, he estimated, would loom above a year's worth of his royalties like a sequoia above a bonsai cherry tree. "Did I ask you," he asked her, "to build yourselves a sky-scraper, just because McGraw-Hill had one?"

"Hon, please be an angel and stop giving me a hard time," she said. He imagined he could hear the squeak of leather and the

click of studs on metal as she shifted her heft in her personally
molded swivel chair. "You were wonderful on 'Charlie Rose.'"

"*Char*lie was wonderful," Bech protested. "I hardly said a
word." The interviewer's long face, tinted the color of a salmon,
loomed in memory; Rose had leaned forward ominously close,
like an Avedon portrait of himself, and urged, "Tell me honestly,
Henry, aren't you *embarrassed*, to have won this Prize when so
many other writers haven't?" And the culture-purveyor's eyes
protruded toward him inquisitorially, so that he resembled Dick
Van Dyke in Disney animation.

These professional personalities operated at an energy level
that stretched Bech's brain like chewing gum on the shoe of a
man trying to walk away. Terry Gross, in her beguilingly adolescent and faintly stammery voice, had put it to him more
brutally yet: "How can you explain it? It must feel like a weird
sort of miracle, I mean, when Henry James and Theodore
Dreiser and Robert Frost and Vladimir Nabokov didn't..."

"I'm not a Swedish mind-reader," was all Bech could manage
by way of apology. "I'm not even a Swedish mind."

This seemed to him a pretty good quip, which he had prepared in the reveries of insomnia, but which, on its occasion for
utterance, lacked the lilt of spontaneity. The short, short-haired
interviewer's giggle was perfunctory, and then like a dingo
worrying the throat of a lamed kangaroo she went back to the
attack: "No, but seriously..."

This was on a radio swing down through Megalopolis, from
Christopher Lydon in a dismal stretch beyond Boston University
to Leonard Lopate in the dingy corridors of the Municipal
Building to Philadelphia's "Fresh Air" in a canister-lined chamber of WHYY and on to Diane Rehm's WAMU aerie on
Brandywine Street, in the bosky midst of American University
in Washington, D.C. She had fascinatingly blued hair and a
crystalline, beckoning voice – as if from another room she
were calling some sorority girls to dinner – and in this particular
chain of interviewers put Bech least on the defensive. Why, of
course, she seemed to be saying, Mr. Bech has won the Nobel
Prize for Liter-a-ture. Who better? Listeners, you tell *us*.

The very first caller-in, whose sugary Southern accent buzzed in Bech's earphones like tinnitus, wanted to know if it was true, as she had read in the *National Enquirer*, that Mr. Bech had recently fathered a baby out of a young lady a *thuuhd* of his age?

"I suppose it's not untrue," Bech grudged into the microphone. Robin had blackmailed him into it, he resisted explaining. It was become either a father or an accused serial killer.

"Mah questi-yun is, sir, do you think that such behavior is fay-yer to either the young lady or that little helpless baby, when, begging your pardon, you might drop daid any taahm?"

"Fair?" It was a concept he hadn't encountered lately. As a child he would protest to his playmates that something wasn't *fair*, but as the inexorable decades had washed over him, his indignation had been slowly leached away.

"And thet million dollars you've gone and won – do you intend to do any *goood* with it?"

He had repeatedly explained to interviewers and crasser talk-show hosts that by the time his taxes were paid to state, city, and nation it wouldn't be anything like a million. It would be less than half a million. Counting the hours of his time and ergs of his energy the Prize had taken, and the universal consensus that he now owed the world something, he had come to figure it as a net financial loss. And, anyway, what does half a million dollars get you in New York City these days? A Jeff Koons statuette, or a closet in a Fifth Avenue co-op. He began to explain all this, but the caller, who had come to inhabit Bech's head like an incurable parasite, steadily maintained her investigative line: "And is it true, suh, as I have read in *sev*eral reputable sources, that, whaal traveling in the Communist world under the sponsorship of our U.S. government, you did enjoy a lee-ay-son with a certain famous Bulgarian poet and had a chaald by that lady whom you have never officially acknowledged? A chaald brought up under strict Communist doctrines until he was a grown may-yun, never knowing who his father was, while you enjoyed a capitalist laaf-staahl?"

The strange images and lies were coming so fast, and so winsomely, he could scarcely speak, though he had been speaking steadily since the Prize had been announced. His mouth opened, two inches from the sponge-muffled mike – like a miniature boxing glove, or an inedible all-day sucker – but only a scraping noise emerged. Hating even a half-second of dead air, Diane Rehm melodiously enunciated, "Perhaps our guest does not care to answer?"

The voice in Bech's head burrowed deeper, working its jaws faster and showing a rough underbelly of Christian resentment. "Well now Diane, if this may-yun doesn't care to answer, what's he doin' sittin' on your show? If he's gone to jest clam up, maybe he shouldn't hev accepted the Praahz."

"I have never been a father before," Bech brought out. "Just like I have never won the Nobel Prize before."

"Well, if you've never been a father before," the voice said, "from all that I've read you should be teachin' these black teen-agers birth control."

"Thank you for your call, Maureen," Diane Rehm said firmly, and pressed a switch that eliminated Maureen from the airways. "Next," she announced to the nation, "Betty Jean, from Greens-boro, North Carolina."

But Betty Jean was no better. She said, "Speaking of black teenagers, I don't think all you celebrities' having babies out of wedlock is setting any kind of example, now is it?"

"But," Bech said, at bay, "I wasn't a celebrity until I won the Prize. I was just a writer, off in a corner. Anyway, I'd be delighted to marry the mother of my child, but she's still mulling my offer over. She's very modern."

"If you ask me," said Betty Jean, in the instant before her electronic execution, "all you Yankees are too damn modern."

Bech in his heart agreed. *Moral insufficiency.* Lying awake in his loft, while Rothkoesque rectangles of incidental city light vibrated around him on the walls, he listened for his baby to peep and reflected back upon his life and work, his daily, ever briefer earthly existence. A few countries, a few women. There were many countries he would never visit, some even now being born, younger than Golda, from the wrecks of condemned old empires. The women – he supposed they had been the point of it all, the biologically ordained goal of male existence, nearing and looming and then receding. They had been sufficient in number. He could not count them up or recall all their names, though he could always retrieve at least a face, a glimmer of pallor in a darkened room, an uncertain, fetching smile and eye-pits of warm, wild shadow. Still, it had been a frightfully curtailed minority of all the appropriate-aged women that had been available, globally. Likewise, his works, the seven volumes* (not counting the British anthology, *The Best of Bech*, long out of print), seemed remarkably few, considering the possibilities, and as mysteriously contingent as the major turnings of his life. Seven stages, seven branches on the menorah, seven tones to the scale. He had never quite understood why the black piano keys, the half-tones, had those two gaps within an octave. It enabled the pianist to find his way, he supposed. Bech's seven books glimmered in his backward glance like fading trail-marks in a dark wood, *una selva oscura*, the tangled wilderness where his consciousness intersected with the universe. He rarely looked into their parched pages, his books seemed to have so perilous a connection with the giant truth of the matter: his arbitrary identity arisen, like the universe, out of darkness and silence. First, the slimy preconscious miracle, in velvety uterine darkness, of repeated prenatal mitosis, keyed to viable complexity by unfathomable signals among the chromosomes and proteins. Then, the harsh eruption into the icy hospital light and the fragrant, noisy Freudian triangle, with its oppressive yet nurturing atmospheres of kitchen, bedroom, and bathroom. Then, the long monitored stairways of schooling, class after class, teacher after teacher, and his abrupt graduation, in the year of Pearl Harbor, into war and the inconclusive trials of adulthood, of which his present sardonic, Prize-bothered decrepitude was the latest if not quite the last. *And one man in his time plays many parts, / His acts being seven ages.*

Golda whimpered in her crib, which they had placed just outside their flimsily partitioned-off bedroom. In the day, they

---

* *Travel Light*, a novel (1955); *Brother Pig*, a novella (1957); *When the Saints*, a miscellany (1958); *The Chosen*, a novel (1963); *Think Big*, a novel (1979); *Biding Time*, sketches and stories (1985); *Going South*, a novella (1992)

moved her crib into this shelter of two-by-fours and wallboard, a box within the loft – a kind of jewelbox when Golda was napping within it. Robin would be off at Computer Crossroads, on Third Avenue; Bech would scribble softly, writing and scratching out, while Leontyne tiptoed through the breakfast dishes and the laundry. Two adults, he marveled, held in thrall by eighteen pounds of guileless ego. When the baby awoke, the cocoa-colored au pair, cooing in Caribbean, would feed her fragments of toast and chicken, gleefully chewed though Golda still had fewer teeth than fingers. What teeth she had were big and hard-earned, having given her much grief pushing up through the gums. Then a bottle was administered on the sofa, Golda blindly sucking while Leontyne's eyes lapped up *Days of Our Lives*. At two, Leontyne switched channels to *One Life to Live*, and Bech, if the pesky demands of the Prize allowed him, indulged her addiction and himself pushed the stroller to a playground. There was a sad, bare little one at Spring and Mulberry, and one even more exiguous on Mercer above Houston, beside an NYU recreation building. When feeling ambitious, he would push Golda all the way across the Bowery to the several in the long park named after Roosevelt's overprotective mother, Sara. The ginkgoes and sycamores were dully turning and dead leaves were blossoming underfoot. Bech trussed his wriggling daughter in one of those black rubber diapers that do for swing-seats now and pushed her back and forth until the gravity-teasing wonder of it wore thin. She was still too young to dare alone the heights and swinging walkways of the plastic castle at the playground's rubber-paved center, but he entrusted her sometimes to the spiral slide, allowing her, a slippery missile in her padded playsuit, to swoop out of his hands for a swerve or two, before he grabbed her at the bottom. And he let her crawl up the slide stairs, mounting upward on her own motor drives, his hands hovering inches behind her back in case she toppled when she unsteadily turned to share with him her pride of ascension. He saw a father's role, while he was here to enact it, as empowering her to skirt danger more closely than either Robin or Leontyne would have allowed – to introduce into her life a particle of the male love of risk.

On the level loft floor, Golda was a muscular, unstoppable crawler, moving across toys, adult feet, scattered books, and slippery sheaves of the Sunday *Times* in her tank-like progress. At night, though, when her whimper brought Bech to hover over her crib, her muscularity had been shed with her playsuit and she seemed all spirit, a well of inarticulate need he strained to peer into, as they both sought the source of her unease. In the first six months, he would simply lift her up and take her in to his soundly sleeping young mate, who would drowsily fumble a stunningly large, green-veined white breast into the little mouth and stifle discontent. But Robin, wearying of milk stains on the trim bodices of her work outfits, and of this tyrannical physical tie to another's innards, had weaned Golda, so that Bech, lifting the whimpering little body into his arms, had the option of changing her diaper or warming up a bottle, or both. These fumbling communions with his infant daughter at ungodly hours, while yet some traffic – gangster limousines from Little Italy, yellow cabs to and from SoHo's dance-to-dawn clubs – trickled by on Crosby Street, were unlike any other of the fleeting relationships life had brought him: he was clearly, by virtue of his size, dominant, and yet tenderness and an atavistic animal protectiveness tilted the balance in favor of the helpless one.

On the edge of language – she could say "Hi," and wave bye-bye – Golda communicated with what the King James Bible called her bowels, not just the spicily fragrant movements but the interior mysteries, the thirst or pain or bad dream or existential loneliness that had driven her soul out of sleep into the teeming world in search of consolation. He tried to provide it; some nights Robin awoke, too, and with a mother's primal flesh swamped the infant's irritation. Beside them on the bed, Bech enjoyed the wash of warmth as the two young female bodies softly collided. He felt relieved when Robin intervened, but also cheated, of perhaps his last opportunity to satisfy another – to find the biological key that turned a lock outside of himself, in this case that of an ego implausibly extended from his own. "*You* are my prize," he would murmur into Golda's dulcet little ear as, waiting the sixty seconds for the bottle to warm in the microwave, he held her by the window, both of them gazing down upon the yellow top of a single cab as it hurtled rumbling over the rough cobblestones toward some dubious haven of mirrors, drugs, strobe lights, and spastic dancing. "You are good, good, *good*," Bech told Golda, her appraising eyes attracted to his face by the desperate hoarseness of his whisper. "You are a truly outstanding person."

They were two of a kind – irregular sleepers, stubborn crawlers. "Oh, you are your daddy's girl," Leontyne would coo to the child in the daytime, so Bech at his desk could hear. "You have his frisky looks and his stand-up hair."

"Leontyne," he would ask, "do you think this is a terrible mistake? My having a child at my age?"

"Babies are the gifts of God," she said, in that gently rocking voice of hers. "They come when He wants them coming. The mommy and the daddy may think not yet, not yet, but He knows when a blessing due. You loves that little girl so much I can't stand some time to watch. And the mommy, too, you loves for sure, but you two have your settled ways, your paths in the world. My parents the same way, my daddy come and go. Nine children they manage to make, when he coming and going. I was the second youngest. My little brother come when Mother forty-two. She used to joke when he got born she had to put on eyeglasses to be seeing him."

Leontyne's confident acceptance of the world as a divine cradle in which they were all rocking soothed Bech during the day, but unsettled him at night, when it appeared so clearly a delusion. In his wakefulness he was alone on a pillar, a saint torn from the safe quotidian. His winning the Prize had unleashed a deluge of letters that battered him like hostile winds. *You would think now they could give it to some American who wasn't a kike or a coon or an immigrant who can't even speak English right . . . I have been struggling to complete my novel while holding down two jobs to pay for my wife's prohibitive chemo treatments plus the child care and just one percent of the enormous amount you have so deservedly in my opinion won would enable me . . . you have probably forgotten me but I sat in the row behind you at P.S. 87 over on 77th and Amsterdam and though you*

never paid me any attention I always knew that some day you . . . celeb-
rity auction even the tiniest personal item last year we had remarkable
good success with Mariah Carey's toenail clippings and a used paper
towel from Julia Child's kitchen . . . well Hank I guess you got them all
fooled now except me I still have your number jewboy and it isn't number
one or even one thousand and one . . . Temple Emmanuel our reading
circle can offer not even a modest honorarium but your cab fare would be
covered and there are home-prepared refreshments beforehand . . . my son
is going to be two this December and a friendly note from you on your
personal letterhead copying out a favorite passage from your own work or
that of another great writer and dated month and date and year . . . you
seemed uneasy with Charlie Rose but you have nothing to be ashamed of
or do you? . . . I enclose my own privately printed book setting out in
irrefutable detail the means whereby God will bring about His kingdom
first in the Middle East and then on the other six continents in rapid
succession . . . help a signed photograph help a one-page statement to one
in need in the battle to win young minds back to reading a modest check a
quotation we could use in our promotion no automated signatures
please . . . happy to come and share with you our professional investment
advice and expertise in estate planning . . . I try to get on top of my fury
but after forty years of writing rings around you in not just my own
opinion but that of most critics who aren't total shmucks I can't inter-
nalize what seems to me a savage and pointed rejection of me, me, I
know it's absurd dear Henry I know life to you is and always has been
the fabled bowl of cherries . . . Envy and resentment poured toward
Bech out of the American vastness, from every state including
Hawaii and Alaska, a kind of lateral sleet rattling on the tin roof
of his rickety privacy. He tried to utilize his insomnia by com-
posing the lecture which Nobel laureates were obliged to give.
He had received wads of information from Sweden, much of it
on those long European sheets of paper impossible to fit into
American filing systems. His speech was to be three days before
the ceremony, at the Swedish Academy. Who would attend? He
couldn't imagine. *Your Royal Highnesses, Mr. Lord Mayor of Stock-*
holm, Members of the Academy, distinguished guests both foreign and
domestic: The Nobel Prize has become so big, so rich and famous, such a
walloping celebrity of a prize, that no one is worthy to win it, and the
embarrassed winner can shelter his unworthiness behind the unworthiness

of everyone else. It lifts us up, this Prize, to a terrible height, a moment of global attention, and tempts us to pontificate. Looking down upon our planet, I see a growing gap between those who ride airplanes and those who do not; those who have taken wing into the cyberspace of the information age and those who are left behind on the surface of the earth, to till the soil, fish the seas, and perform the necessary tasks that once formed the honored substance of all lives but a few. No. What did he know of any lives but his eremitic own and the smattering of others he had tangled with? His point about airplanes was obsolete. He could remember when getting on a plane was an adventure for the elite, dressed in suits and cocktail dresses, the chic of it intensified by the air of danger as they bounced around among silvery, Art-Deco thunderheads, an air to which free champagne and duck or steak dinners served on real china added an elegance not unworthy of the *Titanic*. But now the sort of people swarmed aboard who used to go by bus. They wore shorts and blue jeans and even what appeared to be their pajamas, a scrum of sweaty bodies taking a thousand-mile hop as casually as a drive to the 7-Eleven. Flight was no more a miracle to them than their daily bread. They crammed their duffel bags and scuffed laptops into the overhead bins and didn't even bother to look out the windows, from six death-defying miles up. So capitalism, our creed triumphant, was right: the masses are brought along, pulled in their hundreds of millions up the ladder of prosperity built by enterprise and technology. *The telephone and radio, cinema and television, internal combustion and jet propulsion – mankind has absorbed them as readily as Native Americans took to guns, horses, and firewater. As it happened in the valleys of the Ruhr and the Merrimac, so it will happen in Malaysia and Mali – everybody rich, civilized, neurotic, and unhappy.* No. Avoid economic geopolitics. Who could say whither the wonderful world in all its multitudinous adaptations? Strike a personal note, as Ōe and Heaney had done. West Side/Brooklyn boyhood. The experience of war. GI Bill, NYU. Village in the Forties, 99th Street in the Fifties and thereafter. *Books, to me when young, were rectangular objects seen in department stores, stationery shops, and, without their shiny jackets, in the public library. There, their dusty spines, decimally numbered in white ink, seemed feathers on a dark and protective wing;*

their aroma of dried glue mingled with the decaying wistful smells of old men, called "bums" in my youth and "the homeless" in these more enlightened times. What did these books mean? Who made them? Well, men in tweed jackets, smoking pipes, who lived in Connecticut, made them. And women only a shade less glamorous than movie stars, draped in chiffon or else, like Dorothy Thompson and Martha Gellhorn, dressed like men, and even like men in battle dress. No. The Swedes and the world don't want to hear of these virtually forgotten authors who once were stars in Bech's eyes. He must speak instead of the timeless bliss when pencil point touches paper and makes a mark. *But isn't this atomic moment much too small to mention, in so vast an auditorium of attention? In a world of suffering, of famine and massacre, wasn't aesthetic bliss obscene? And now?* he must ask aloud. *The printed word? The book trade, that old carcass tossed here and there by its ravenous jackals? Greedy authors, greedy agents, brainless book chains with their Vivaldi-riddled espresso bars, publishers owned by metallurgy conglomerates operated by glacially cold-hearted bean-counters in Geneva. And meanwhile language, the human languages we all must use, no longer degraded by the barking murderous coinages of Goebbels and the numskull doublespeak of bureaucratic Communism, is becoming the mellifluous happy-talk of Microsoft and Honda, corporate conspiracies that would turn the world into one big pinball game for child-brained consumers. Is the gorgeous, fork-tongued, edgy English of Shakespeare and Gerard Manley Hopkins, of Charles Dickens and Saul Bellow becoming the binary code for a gray-suited empire directed by men walking along the streets of Manhattan and Hong Kong jabbering into cell phones? Who is going to stop the world from evolving? Poets? Dilettantes like yours truly? Don't make me laugh, Your Highnesses and assorted dignitaries. As a dear old friend of mine kindly informed the American press recently, your Prize is a prank.*

"I can't do it," he told Robin. "I can't say anything important enough. The essence of what I do is that it isn't important, or at least doesn't *come on* as important. Importance is not important, that's what I've been trying to say all my life."

"Well," she said, "try saying that."

"But that's *really* unimportant," he protested. "And egotistical. I don't want to be egotistical. I don't want to seem to be trying to get *on top of* the Prize, if you know what I mean."

"I think you're outsmarting yourself," Robin offered, primarily concerned with persuading Golda of the nutritional worth of the diced carrots the child kept picking up from her high-chair tray with curly slimy tiny fingers and dropping carefully on the floor. "All the Swedes want is a little relaxed gratitude –"

"You don't understand. You give a little bow when the King hands it all to you – the medal, the certificate, the week's pass on the Stockholm transit system. You say thanks at the banquet after the ceremony. The lecture comes earlier in the week. It's the lecture that's killing me. My chance at last to make a statement, after seventy-six years of nobody listening. Well, I guess my mother listened, for the first five years or so."

"– a little gratitude and a half-hour's intellectual entertainment. Think of *them*," Robin said. "They've been sweating over these prizes all year, neglecting their own work and their families. Swedes have feelings, too – look at those Ingmar Bergman movies."

"The *women* in those movies have feelings; the men don't. They're *frozen*. Leontyne" – Leontyne was folding little dresses and playsuits, at the new washer and drier they had installed beside the refrigerator, there in the loft's once-primitive kitchen – "what should I tell the people of the world?"

"You go tell them," Leontyne readily advised, "that you been wanting to make people happy ever since you been a little boy. That the Lord be telling you what to say, and you just writing it down."

"I don't think God plays well in Sweden," he said. "God sticks pretty close to the equator."

That did make Leontyne laugh; he was never quite sure what would. Her shy pealing seemed to pull itself back on every note, into her supple throat, as if laughter were a sin to be retracted. Her eyes looked lacquered by merriment; her solemn brief bangs, a straightened fringe, came less than halfway down her brow. Her twelve-year-old daughter, Emerald, Bech knew from snapshots, had hair done in beaded corn-rows, the maternal work of hours.

He wondered if he could work God's favoring the peoples of the equator into his Nobel lecture; perhaps he was wrong to ignore the world's lurking ethnic sores. *Your Highnesses, Lord*

Mayor, and welcome guests: the Prize is a fine bauble upon the pale chest of Western civilization, but as a Jew let me wonder aloud, What has this civilization, this Christendom, meant to my people? It has meant ghettos, pogroms, verbal and physical abuse, unappealable injustice, exclusionary laws, yellow stars, autos-da-fé, scapegoating whenever disaster threatened a Christian society, and a collective helplessness at the whim of every petty Christian ruler and government. One nation to whose glory and prosperity we had contributed, as artisans and merchants and moneylenders, for hundreds of years, Spain, rewarded us with unconditional expulsion in the very year in which America was discovered. Germany and Austria, where Jews had seen their talents ripen into genius, wealth, and an apparent bourgeois security – those very nations instituted a systematic plan for the extermination of the Jews, a plan whose all but completely successful execution remains the astonishment of this century, the final refutation of any European claims to signal virtue and wisdom. Even in my own country, thought by many to be too indulgent of its Jews, swastikas are spray-painted upon synagogues. In Sweden, I have read, one out of three teenagers doubts that the Holocaust ever took place. And so, Your Highnesses, I find that as a Jew I cannot accept this sop, this pathetic attempt to paper over the smoking pit, the thousands of gas ovens in which thousands of greater gifts and purer hearts than my own . . . What was he doing? Turning the Prize down had made Sartre look like a fool, and Pasternak like a Soviet slave.

"Meri Jo, I'm panicked," he told her, over a lunch at Four Seasons he had invited her to give him. "Find me a speech."

"Henry, an old Spielmeister like you? Tell them what you told Oprah; that was charming."

"I forget what I say on these damn talk shows. I try to suppress it as soon as I say it."

"You told her you didn't write pornography, you just tried to give the sexual component of our lives a fair shake. Or something like that."

"The Swedes don't care if I write pornography. It's all legal there. It's part of their healthy pagan outlook."

Meri Jo was mellowing out; she reminisced, "I'll never forget you on 'Donahue' when *Think Big* was fresh out. I was a sophomore at Barnard, and my roommate and her boyfriend were channel-surfing – you had to twist the dial in those days

– and I said, 'No, wait, that man is saying something.' You were younger then, and your hair filled the whole top half of the screen. You were so calm and understated, not letting him bully you, and only lightly but sweetly letting the audience know you thought he *was* a bully. . . ."

"That was his job. Highly paid bully. Bully of the people, for the people. What did I *say*, though?"

Meri Jo's round face – in which a pertly pointed chin still tried to assert itself above a set of others, like ghosts in New York television before cable came in – was flushed, either from empathy with his plight or from the two pint-sized glasses of white wine that she had drunk with the meal, or else from the compressing effects of her leather jacket, its zipper as wide as a yardstick and its brass studs the size of gumdrops. "It wasn't what you *said*, it was the way you said it. You were sincere without being *heavy*. You were funny without being the least bit, you know, Catskills. Six months later, when I read in *People* that you and your wife had broken up, I remember – I shouldn't be telling you this, I shouldn't have had that second glass of Chardonnay – I was delighted; I thought, Maybe he'll meet *me*. So I went into publishing, but you weren't there. Or there very rarely. You were one of our invisible authors. Never mind, Henry; it's been a good life, P.R. I guess I was naïve, but I was only a sophomore, remember, and my guy of the time, I've forgotten everything about him except the way his fingernails were never clean, was having some potency issues. Pardon me for blushing."

"Meri Jo, you'll have me blushing myself. Tell me, would it help for me to see a tape of that Donahue show? Did Publicity keep one?"

"To be honest, Henry, we might have, but a ton of that stuff got tossed when we moved to the new building. Can't you just talk about the future of the written word or something?"

"Look, this Prize comes but once a lifetime, and everybody says it was a miracle I got it. I hate to pollute the occasion with idle prattle."

"Oh, hon, don't badmouth prattle," she said. Her chin, the top one, firmed up and pointed at him. "I have a raft of requests for you to consider. They keep coming in. We said yes, you remember, to a print interview with the Washington *Post*, and if you say yes to the *Post* you can't say no to the Atlanta *Constitution*, it's a booming market down there, ever since air-conditioning. Then there's the Minneapolis *Star Tribune*, the books editor has been terribly good to Vellum over the years, and we're trying to do more with the Northwest, so there's this smart new arts editor at the Tacoma *News Tribune* . . ."

"I *hate* print interviews," Bech said. "They take forever, they get you all relaxed and gabby, and then they crucify you, writing down whatever they please. There's no evidence of what you really said except their tape, and they keep the tape. No. No more print. Print is dead."

"Each one will come to your apartment –"

"It will ruin Golda's nap."

"And take no more than an hour and a half, with some time before or after for the photographer. Only Annie Leibovitz is apt to ask you to put on makeup. Maybe with her you can get away with just a funny hat."

"Meri Jo, why are you doing this to me? Is it my fault you liked me on 'Donahue'? I didn't like *myself* on 'Donahue.'"

She put her hand, still remarkably dainty, on his gnarled, hairy-backed one, as he struggled with his green fettuccine. The oiled strips eluded the tines of his fork like eels wriggling out of a trap. "People want you, dear, and it's my job to facilitate access."

"It's not my fault they want me. I don't want them. I want peace. I vunt to be alone, and to vatch Golda grow. She can almost say words. She says 'Hi.'"

"I'm not asking for myself, or for yourself, even. I'm asking for the *in*dustry. There's such a thing – you've never learned this, darling, your mother obviously spoiled you rotten – as responsibility to others. With prizes come responsibilities, didn't Delmore Schwartz say that? You're making me seriously think about a third glass of wine."

"Think about it all you want. I'm saying no to any more interviews."

"But you don't mean no." Her sea-green eyes must once have been lovely and big; now they were small in her face, little sinister bits of buried beach glass.

He didn't have the heart not to be seduced by her. He grumbled by way of caving in, "They won't want me once I botch this lecture."

"You won't botch it. You can't botch it. Faulkner wrote his on the airplane with a hangover and read it in a mumble and now it's a document like the Gettysburg Address. Think Gettysburg Address. Henry: Do you want to have some chocolate cheesecake with me, or do you want me to feel depraved all by myself?"

Stockholm, scattered on its Baltic archipelago, shone with the cold. The Swedish women sported blood-bright cheeks above their collars of wolf and ermine as they carried their golden heads along the trendy streets, lined with restaurants and antique stores, of Gamla Stan, the Old Town. Bech was taken to lunch at the venerable gathering-spot for writers, the Källaren Den Gyldene Freden, with a few impish members of the Swedish Academy. "It looked like a deadlock," confided one of them, a small bald twinkling man known for his Värmland tales in the tradition of Selma Lagerlöf, "between Günter Grass and Bei Dao, with Kundera the dark horse. You were in the final selection because some were afraid a stronger American might actually win. And then, you rascal, you won! The votes for you, in my view, constituted an anti-Socialist protest. As you can see, we live well here, but the taxes strike some as very burdensome."

"Do not let Sigfrid fill you with his amiable nonsense," intervened a female member of the Academy, a gracile poet and the biographer of such Nordic classics as the short-lived, tormented Erik Johan Stagnelius and the eventually mad Gustaf Fröding. "You are much esteemed in Scandinavia, for your ruthless clarity. You rape your women as you describe them. I myself prefer to read you in French, where I think your style is even more clean and – how do you say? – starkers?"

"When your names from the basket were counted," volunteered a lyric feuilletonist of prodigious bulk and height, "I was surprised but not astounded. It is as if, recently, there are others voting, ghostly presences, around the table. The results are mysterious!"

"As you may know," his first informant, his spectacles and mobile lower lip glinting, "the Academy is not at our full strength of eighteen. There have been resignations, and yet the members cannot be replaced. Once a member, the only way out is death."

"Like being a member of the human race," Bech ventured, diplomatically. He was nervous. Robin and Golda were back alone in the hotel suite. They had not brought Leontyne, for this week of festivity and formality. Bech was afraid the cold might blast her, like a jasmine blossom. He wanted her to spend more time with her husband, a security guard who left for the night shift as she arrived home. Bech felt that he and Leontyne were drawing too close in the loft, yoked together to a baby's body. He was getting to lean on her otherworldly wisdom and to think in her voice. He wanted to shut down, at this terminal stage of his life, his rusted but still-operative falling-in-love apparatus.

As for Robin, she was not used to being with Golda all day. She missed her computers, and the authority they gave her, her site in the Web. She found Sweden not for her. "Oh, it's great for *you*," she complained, "all you do is go out being wined and dined and interviewed, and go to receptions for the fun-loving biology winners, while I'm cooped up in this so-called Grand Hotel with a crying kid and a lot of pompous furniture. It's too cold to go out and too hot to stay in. When I try to order room service, the people in the kitchen only speak Turkish."

"Inger has said they'd get us all the babysitters we want." Inger Wetterqvist was their Nobel attendant; every winner got one. She was lovely, efficient, and in constant attendance. Her statuesque neck, with wispy flaxen tendrils in the hollows of the nape, fascinated Bech.

But Golda had problems with the Swedes. Whenever she saw a big blond woman, she stuck the central two fingers of her left hand into her mouth and hid her face against her mother's thigh. When she realized, on the first full day of their stay, that her parents were about to leave her alone with a golden-haired babysitter, she screamed in a panicked fury Bech had never heard before. The child feared these tall, shining Aryans.

Inger was, in her splendor, frightening. The world seemed to hold, Bech had noticed, more and more young women over six feet in height – whole clusters of them, whole basketball teams, striding through airports or down Fifth Avenue together – as if Nature, no longer designing women close to the ground for purposes of childbearing and domestic labor, were launching them toward some function as yet unknown.

Robin, embarrassed, told the helpless girl who, it had been arranged, would care for Golda during the official lunch at the American Embassy, "Our au pair back home is black – you know, Negro? I guess she's used to her." Golda would not stop shrieking. In the end, Robin and Bech took their daughter to the Ambassador's lunch; it included little carrots, which the infant carefully dropped one by one on the floor.

It was true, Bech was having fun, though his lecture was still unwritten, a fact that he tried all day to forget and which gave him the horrors when he awoke at night, his temples aching with an excess of convivial aquavit and congratulatory champagne. To him, Sweden was a stupefying Heaven. He liked the quick arc of daylight, like cold crystal, and the giant Nikki Ste.-Phalle sculptures at the Moderna Museet – women! more power to them! Greta! Ingrid! from Stockholm their beauty, tinged with melancholy as beauty must be, had come forth to flood the filmstruck world – and a certain pastel lightness to the city, under its close sub-arctic sky. It reminded him of Leningrad, as it had appeared to him in 1964, when he was but forty-one, and susceptible to the charms of a stony-faced *apparatchika* in a military jacket, and thrilled to be breathing Tolstoyan air. Now an old man, he saw through dimmed eyes. He had done what he could; he had tried to write his own books rather than books others wanted him to write; he had come to this Northern fastness to put his pen to rest. He gave interviews to the *Svenska Dagbladet*, *Expressen*, *Damernas Värld*, *Dagens Nyheter*, *Västerbottens-Kuriren*. The interviewer from *Svenska Dagbladet* asked Bech what he thought of the future of Socialism. He answered that he thought it was in a down phase, but would be back, as an alternative; the world was a sick man turning over and over in bed. The weak must always be protected somewhat from the strong, but not so satisfactorily that no incentive remains to become strong. Failure must have real penalties, or there will be no striving for success. Man is in the awkward position of being kinder than Nature.

The *Svenska Dagbladet* interviewer, an alert unbarbered lad in grape-colored jeans, asked him if these insights were to be the burden of his Nobel lecture.

"If they were," Bech asked, "why would I be giving them away to you and your readers now? But tell me, what is a Nobel lecture about, usually?"

The young man thought. His eyelashes were white, which gave him, with his clever thin mouth, a delicately clownish look. "Oh, the importance of writing. And how the winner came to write."

"Do those seem to you worth talking about?"

The interviewer, interviewed, shrugged evasively. "It is the custom."

"Sweden is a land of customs, yes?"

The young man, his reddish fair hair straight in his beard but tangled in curls on his head, smiled hesitantly. His English was not quite good enough to be certain if he was being teased. "You could say so," he replied.

"I understand that at some point angels will break into our hotel room."

"Singers heralding the advent of St. Lucia, patroness of our festival of light." The interviewer was still worrying over Sweden's being a land of customs – America, by implication, being a land devoid of customs. "Our winters are long," he said, "with very short days, so there is perhaps a Swedish need to be festive – to have festivities. We light many candles, many torches – you will see. Nobel Week is more a holiday now than Christmas."

The Swedes had provided on their long pieces of paper a minute-by-minute forecast of what would happen at the ceremony – the music to be played; the order of procession; the seating on the stage, amid the many Academies, with Prize-winners arrayed facing the King and Queen; the braided arrangement of flowers to mark the edge of the stage – and at the banquet afterwards, in the vast Blue Hall of Stockholm's red-brick City Hall, thirteen hundred guests eating from special Nobel dinnerware (*Nobelservisen*) while the Uppsala male choir sang and young women in blue peasant outfits danced down the broad stairs and streams of waiters bore aloft torrents of softly flaming platters of dessert. But to earn his place in such grand procedures Bech had to deliver his lecture.

"My God, what I am going to do?" he asked Robin back in the hotel room. "I have to give the damn thing in two days, and I have no time to write it, there are all these receptions, all this champagne I have to keep drinking."

"Henry, I hate to see you rattled like this. I have a feminine need to think of you as debonair."

"Nothing I can say will be good enough. I'm unworthy."

"They already know that. You told me the Academy didn't mean to elect you, they were casting protest votes against each other."

"My informant might have been pulling my leg. They have this weird Viking sense of humor. Ho, ho, have a smash on the noggin."

"Did you know," Robin asked him, "that during the war they weren't so neutral? I was reading on the Internet how the Sapo, their secret police, turned over Norwegian resistance fighters to the Nazis. And a lot of Swedish-Jewish businessmen got mysteriously fired. Hitler *loved* the Swedes; they were his idea of a real *Volk*."

"Stop scaring me. You and Golda, you have all this racial prejudice."

"She's not so dumb. Here. Focus on your daughter for once." She thrust Golda into his arms. The infant's bottom felt damp. When she grinned, with her scattered teeth, she drooled. Another tooth coming. Her slimy little curious hand reached out and grabbed a piece of Bech's cheek and squeezed.

"*Ow*," he said.

"She's so used to being with me all day she doesn't understand your whiskers. I'm putting on a cocktail dress and getting out for an hour. A nice young accountant in the office downstairs offered to show me the hotel computer system, and then take me for a drink to some American-style skyview place along the waterfront. He was shocked when I told him I hadn't seen anything of Stockholm. He couldn't believe I was so neglected."

"Did you tell him it's mostly your choice? Inger offered to find us an African sitter, though it isn't easy up here."

"They're all these Senegalese brand-name-pocketbook ripoff peddlers. She said there are some dark-skinned Turks, but I said no Moslems, thanks."

"There you go. More prejudice. Until Israel, Moslems were much better to Jews than Christians."

Robin read the anxiety, the potential defeat, on his face and said, "Henry, I'm young. I'm stir-crazy. I'll be back in time for you to go to the official concert at eight. Golda needs some daddy magic. You and she can write your lecture together."

"Members of the Academy, distinguished guests both foreign and domestic," Bech began his lecture. "The Nobel Prize has become so big, such a celebrity among prizes, that no one is worthy to win it, and the embarrassed winner can shelter his unworthiness behind the unworthiness of everyone else." The audience packed the chairs set out in the long and tawny main salon of the Swedish Academy, a room a-brim with pilasters and archways like a Renaissance fantasy, a Michelangelesque vision of human form turned into architecture. The King – tall and studious-looking, wearing glasses whose rims were of a regal thinness – was not there, nor his beautiful black-haired Queen. Bech had been foolish to think of himself as speaking from the top of the world. He was speaking to a dutiful audience of pale polite faces, in an overheated space on the northern edge of Europe, a subcontinent whose natives for a few passing centuries had bullied and buffaloed the rest of the world. Among the faces he recognized few. Meri Jo Zwengler and lanky, shaggy, laid-back Jim Flaggerty, his editor, grayer-headed than twenty years ago but still ruminating on a piece of phantom gum in his mouth, had flown over from Vellum to hold his hand. Some pinstriped minions from the Ambassador's staff had been delegated to attend. Robin perched in the front row, her face a luminous pearl of warmth in the frosty jumble of alien visages. The audience as a whole had stirred in surprise when Bech, following his crisp if less than enthusiastic introduction by Professor Sture

Allén, had come to the lectern carrying a baby. But, being in the main Swedish, the audience suppressed its titters, as if this living child were an eccentricity of ethnic costume, like Wole Soyinka's African robes of a few years ago.

"It lifts one up, this Prize," Bech continued his lecture, Golda wriggling and threatening to corkscrew in his crooked right arm, "to a terrible height, a moment of global attention, and tempts one to pontificate. I could talk to you about the world," he said, "as it exists in this year of 1999, waiting for the odometer to turn over into a new millennium, watching to see if Islamic militants will lock ever more of its surface into a new Dark Age, or if China will push the United States aside as top superpower, or Russia will spit out capitalism like a bad fig, or the gap between those who ride in airplanes and those who drive ox-carts will widen to the point of revolution or lessen to the point of Dis-neyfied, deep-fried homogeneity – but what, my distinguished friends, do I know of the world? My life has been spent attending to my inner weather and my immediate vicinity." In that vicin-ity, Golda was getting impatient. She had that solemn look which, combined with a spicy nether smell, signaled a develop-ment that would soon need tending to. Meri Jo and Robin were right; he could spiel on forever, once given a podium and a captive audience. It was something about himself he would have preferred never to have discovered. "Or," Bech went on, "I could talk to you about art, in the spasmodic, distracted practice of which I have spent my finest and most valuable hours. Is art, as the ancients proposed, an imitation of life, or is it, as the moderns suggest, everything that life is not – order instead of disorder, resolution rather than inconclusiveness, peace and harmony in preference to our insatiable discontent and, at the bottom of our souls, as Kierkegaard and Strindberg and Munch teach us, our terror? Our dread – dread at being here, on this planet that appears lonelier and more negligible with each new revelation from astronomy. Or is art *both* duplication and escape – life tweaked, as it were, into something slightly higher, brighter, other? We feel it to be so, as it is engendered at the end of a pencil point or on a computer screen. Art is somehow *good*, if only for the artist."

Golda wriggled more strenuously, straining his venerable armature of bone and muscle. Bech studied the audience, a sea of white visages dotted here and there with a black or yellow face. To Golda's short-sighted, slate-blue eyes — two shades of blue, actually: a darker ring and a paler, more skyey iris inside — the crowd must recede endlessly, out the back wall into the entire rest of the Earth. "I represent," Bech could not resist going on, "only myself; in citizenship I am an American and in religion a non-observant Jew, but when I write I am nothing less than a member of my triumphant but troubled species, with aspirations it may be to speak for the primates, the vertebrates, and even the lichen as well. *Life!* the toast in Hebrew cries — *L'Chaim!* — in salute at least to the molecular amazingness of it, regardless of whatever atrocities appetitive or brainwashed organisms visit upon one another. I came here, ladies and gentlemen, deter-mined not to generalize away the miracle, the quizzical quiddity, of the specific, that which is 'the case,' as Wittgenstein put it, and in honor of the majesty of my task developed an absolute writer's block in regard to the lecture I am now audibly failing to deliver. So I (just a minute more, sweetie) invoke the precedent of my predecessor Nobel Laureate in Literature Naguib Mahfouz — a writer, by the way, who was knifed in the throat for his efforts to describe the life of his Egypt with accuracy and equanimity, a true hero in a field, literature, rife with false heroics — and have asked my daughter to speak for me. She is ten months old, and will enjoy her first birthday in the new millennium. She belongs to the future. The topic we have worked out between us is, 'The Nature of Human Existence.' " Bech repeated, in his presidential voice: "The Nature of Human Existence."

He and Golda had rehearsed, but there was no telling with infants; the wiring of their minds hadn't yet jelled. If she had begun, with her loaded diaper and confining paternal arm, to scream, that would have been a statement, but an overstatement, and not her father's sort of statement. She did not let him down. She had her young mother's clear mind and pure nature, purged of much of the delusion and perversity whose devils had tor-mented the previous two thousand years, or should one say previous 5,760 years? In the audience, wide-jawed, luminous

Robin parted her lips in maternal and wifely concern, as if to intervene in a rescue. He shifted their child to his other arm, so that her little tooth-bothered mouth came close to the microphone – state-of-the-art, a filigreed bauble on an adjustable stem. She reached out with the curly, beslobbered fingers of one hand as if to pluck the fat metallic bud. He felt the warmth of her skull, an inch from his avid nose; he inhaled her scalp's powdery scent. Into the dear soft warm crumpled configuration of her ear he whispered, "Say hi."

"Hi!" Golda pronounced with a bright distinctness instantly amplified into the depths of the beautiful, infinite hall. Then she lifted her right hand, where all could see, and made the gentle clasping and unclasping motion that signifies bye-bye.

HIS OEUVRE
(1999)

HIS OEUVRE

HENRY BECH, the aging American author, found that women he had slept with decades ago were showing up at his public lectures. He could sense them in the auditorium even when it was dark. Clarissa Tompkins, for instance, slipped in late at a reading in New Jersey, in an old suburban movie theatre converted to cultural uses, after the house lights were dimmed and he had already launched himself into one of the prose poems from his miscellany *When the Saints* (1958), evoking an East Village junk shop. Lifting his head to project the phrase "a patina of obscure former usage annealing a contemporary application of very present dust," savoring the sibilance in that clinching duet of words, he saw her silhouette against the dull glow cast by the old-fashionedly ornate sign to the movie house's ladies' room. Clarissa glided out of the island of amber light into the dark rows at the back, but there had been no mistaking the upswept hairdo, taffy-colored in his memories, that enlarged her already sizable head, a head poignantly balanced on her petite, breastless frame. After lovemaking in the Tompkinses' splendid Fifth Avenue apartment, with its view of the Reservoir, they would have a naked picnic on the deep-napped Oriental at the center of the living room, a little further burst of taffy color innocently flared as she sat cross-legged, devouring her half of the turkey sandwich that her cook had made before leaving for the afternoon. Amidst the opulence of her apartment Clarissa was thrifty. One sandwich was cut in two, one teabag served two cups. Her face beneath all that bouffant hair looked tiny, and as she scrunched it into her half-sandwich it almost disappeared – the small straight nose, the myopic green eyes usually straining to see but now swimming out of focus in her orgasm's aftermath. At each bite, her plump upper lip would leave a cerise blur at the rim of white bread. Her lipstick was messy and indelible; Bech usually needed a full cleanup, not with just a washrag but with paper towels dabbed in vodka, before he dared confront the elevator, the doorman, the avenue.

What had led her to show up in New Jersey, at this community college wedged in the suburban wastes north of Newark? How had she known of his reading? He lost his place, wondering, and a silence stretched above the faces listening in the shadows before he found his spot on the page and went on: "One warily inspects, bending forward, a mostly wooden apple-corer, a piece of carved intricacy suggesting a torturer's device out of Borges or Kafka, that has somehow, through a chain of canny and, one hopes, profitable transactions made its way from an underheated Vermont attic to this stuffy, jumbled trading post in southerly Gotham." He disliked the sentence, more wordy than he had ever noticed before.

Mr. Tompkins had been a patron – the chief patron, indeed – of an avant-garde publication with the austere name of *Displeasure*, to which Bech had been a faithful contributor. Clarissa had seen in him, perhaps, a noble savage – a woolly-haired, thick-bodied bohemian beyond all bourgeois scruples. The Fifties had been a boom time for noble savages, more or less modeled on Henry Miller, before the Sixties brought in such a slew of them that they became a politically demanding mob. But Bech had a tender regard, if not for wealth as a Marxian steamroller, a brute mass of blind numbers, then for the delectable artifacts wealth could purchase – for Tompkins's lush carpets, for his gilt-brushed Oriental prints, for his kitchen gleaming with brass Swiss fixtures and green marble countertops, for his king-size bed and its sheets of sea-island cotton. The couple was childless; these possessions were their helpless children. Each tryst in the luxurious duplex – the maid and the cook tactfully dismissed by the mistress but retaining who knew what low suspicions – had made Bech morally queasy. Tompkins patronizes art; the literary artist pays him back by screwing his wife. Is this justice?

Clarissa, to do her credit, felt that the situation was somehow sensitive for her lover. She pressed her physical claims as if upon an invalid, with the soft yet unretreating voice of a hospital visitor, coaxing him into vigor; she led him as if he had been a teen-ager into certain byways of gratification that left her lipstick stains passed back and forth between their bodies like the rico-chet marks in a squash court. The route to her orgasms could be tortuous. A yoga adept, she liked being bent backward over a silk-cushioned stool so that her head rested on the floor a foot below her hips, her green eyes groping for his face and the rug's swirling pattern showing through her teased, expanded hair. She did not mind, she led him to slowly understand, certain Hindu variations on the standard positions, and with wordless hints drew his masculine force out of its shell of shyness. His very reserve and hesitation enabled her, it seemed, to break some seal on her own inhibitions.

Still, she could not hold him. His sense of himself as a violator of Arnold Tompkins's posh apartment, its blameless silks and unstained satins, led him to write Clarissa a letter of withdrawal, pleading, not falsely, a desire to leave her ensconced among treasures whose beauty and worth, though negligently dismiss-able by her, were not so by him. In short, he did not want by any consequence of scandal to become responsible for a rich woman's upkeep, ardent for debasement though she had shown herself to be.

As he read at the tippy, ill-lit lectern, plowing on with these forty-year-old prose poems, which suddenly seemed fatally man-nered as well as badly dated, and then launching himself into the well-worn anthology piece, the truck-stop brawl in his road novel, *Travel Light*, he scanned the audience between sentences, looking for a stray glimmer from the high airy crown of her hair. She had shifted in the darkness, as best he could make out, from her initial perch in the back row, near the glowing amber sign that was, he squintingly perceived, a kind of magic lantern, a metal box cut, in one of the elegancies common in the old movie-palaces, so as to form against its light bulb the silhouette of a pompadoured eighteenth-century woman at her toilet, above the cut-out script spelling *Mesdames*.

And when the house lights came up, for the apple-corer

torture of the question-and-answer period, Clarissa was quite gone, sunk forever beneath the smiling sea of middle-aged – more than middle-aged, elderly – female book-lovers and author groupies. How mischievous of her to show up so magically and then vanish! Had it been a reprimand for his disappearance from her life, to which he had been granted such unstinting entry? They had not met again, even at an office party, for Tompkins had shortly thereafter withdrawn his patronage from *Displeasure*, and the magazine had limped along a while and then collapsed.

At the West Side "Y" – so much cozier a venue than the more heavily publicized East Side forum at 92nd Street – Bech sought for a friendly face in the audience upon which to pin his reading. He was trying, for far from the first time, to pump life into that scene from his novel *Think Big* wherein Olive, having discovered herself at last to be a lesbian, confesses her previous amours while lying in the arms of Tad Greenbaum's discarded mistress, Thelma, in the orange sunset light that enters the room horizontally, like bars of music, from beyond the Palisades. This passage, with its shuffling back and forth between two love-drugged female voices, was a precarious one to animate aloud, and needed the encouragement of a willing smile from some female auditor. Tonight the smile, so radiant – luscious, even, in its wide white face – did not have to be sought out; rather, it seemed to have sought him out. As he read aloud, murmuring into the rustling, sometimes woofing microphone, he was nagged by the notion that he had known this encouraging face before. The smile, outlined in a lipstick so dark it appeared black in the auditorium half-light, had a sweet, forgiving tuck on one side that implied former acquaintance, an insight into him that bypassed his theatrical attempt to breathe life into the drowsy confidences of two imaginary daughters of Bilitis. The only thing real in what he was reading was the room itself, an exact transcription of the Riverside Drive apartment he had lived in for years, before his ill-fated marriage to Bea Latchett, Norma Latchett's relatively sweet-tempered sister.

Wait, he thought even as he kept his voice working. There

was a cranny, a niche in the era of his life dominated by the
Latchett sisters where this disembodied smile fit. Burgundy-lip-
sticked mouth, long-lashed purple-irised eyes, straight black hair
falling to glossy wide shoulders, a vivid black arrowhead centered
between white, well-cushioned pelvic crests. A woman encountered at widely scattered intervals, a woman a touch too fleshy
and dogmatic for him, but whose amazing waxen pallor, lighting
up rooms otherwise dim, drew him back, now and again, as he
glancingly, skittishly moved through downtown literary circles in
those slovenly Sixties. *Gretchen*. Gretchen Folz, the would-be
poet. Her pathetic cubbyhole on Bleecker Street, its narrow
bed snug against a parsley-green wall, access to its other side
limited by tilting stacks of New Directions and Grove Press
paperbacks. The bed had an Amish bedspread whose pattern of
triangular patches reminded him of stars of David, and an iron
head whose vertical pipes dug grooves into his back when
Gretchen, in the woman-couchant position, straddled him and
teased his mouth with her livid nipples.

The thrill of recovered memory made his voice boom inap-
propriately as he read Olive's tender summing up to Thelma: "It
was all, you know, like Snow White's forest on the path to *you*."
Decades ago, he remembered, he had vacillated between "path"
and "way" and had rejected "way" as a word with too many
meanings and too evocative of Proust, but now "way" seemed
the more natural expression, though less incidentally evocative of
entangling sexual grapples, with leering male faces on the Dis-
neyesque tree trunks.

Gretchen's poems had wispily trailed down the page, making
elliptical jumps that he had taken to be faithful to the way her
mind worked, her erratic inner connections. Her orgasms did not
come easily either. She had been flustered at first by Bech's rather
burly determination to work on the problem with her. "Slam,
bam, thank you ma'am is really often the most satisfying," she
told him.

"What a cop-out," he said. "Think what an exploitative heel
that makes me."

"But what . . . ? I mean how . . . ?"

How lovely, how adorably alight her wide, avidly intellectual face – had been in its girlish confusion, its pre-feminist reluctance to think of her genitals in detail. He had piqued her interest, and they clambered together over the pillars of Pound and Burroughs, Céline and Genet, Anaïs Nin and Djuna Barnes, which spilled like a row of dominoes, the topple reaching the center of the tiny room.

Why had his contacts with Gretchen been so scattered, so infrequent, as willing and, gradually, responsive as she had been? Her writing, perhaps, had offended him: his erotic drive generally steered clear of literary women, who might compete or try to touch the aloof, unspeakable heart of his raison d'être. Also, she was large, not lithe and little as he liked females; he distrusted the luxury of her spilling flesh, the creamy slowness of her laboring, amid the swelling smells of brine and estrus, toward sexual release. If she had lost a little weight, if there had been a little less flesh to move, she might have found the way – the path – easier. His ministrations felt awkwardly close to those of a doctor rather than those of a lover, with a therapeutic focus that diluted his own excitement. Also, descending into the cramped quarters and futile literary ambitions of Bleecker Street struck him – already faintly famous, with all four of his titles, up to 1963, having achieved mention in the *New York Times Book Review*'s Christmas list of Notable Books – as slumming. And she was Jewish, which wasn't what he needed at the time. He felt Jewish enough for two. He had something she strongly needed, his sexual patience, and this naked need of hers disgusted, it could have been, his fastidious side. Though he neglected her for weeks at a time, she was never indignant for long when he coasted back into her orbit.

Tonight, too, after he had doggedly, absent-mindedly completed his reading, and taken half-hearted swings at a few of the puffball questions the audience tossed up, Gretchen met him with no shadow of resentment for his fitful wooing and unapologetic fading-away, but instead with a matured form of her old wistful glee, her girlish hope of fulfillment at his hands. Her kiss of greeting claimed him with a new authority; her bohemian diffidence was gone. "Henry, I'd like you to meet my husband," she said.

He was a substantial red-faced fellow, sixty or so, dignified but not unfriendly, wearing a pinstriped suit that was more accustomed to board meetings than prose readings. "Good stuff," he said gamely, guessing why he had been brought here. To be shown off.

"Henry, how you still do go on," Gretchen said. "A lesbian is the last thing you want to be. You'd have to give up your balls."

"I don't know. I'm still evolving," he said, regretting that her peck to one side of his mouth had been so brief, so dry. She looked fulfilled. Her wide-hipped weight, next to the bulk of her spouse, was no problem, and she had had her hair cut raggedly short and tinged with a metallic cinnabar red, giving her a rather ravishing futuristic look.

"What ever happened to your poems?" he asked. He never knew quite what to say to these women who showed up.

"Privately printed," she answered. The sharp dark corners of her mouth tucked into her creamy cheeks with the only hint of revenge that her forgiving nature would allow itself. "*Beau*tifully printed. Bob *loves* them."

"Bob," Bech said, prolonging the vowel as if to taste her once again, "is obviously a discerning critic. He likes both our stuff. Stuffs."

You don't expect much to happen in Indianapolis, once you've seen the Hoosier Dome and the Soldiers' and Sailors' Monument. Their pairing reminded Anglophilic Bech of the closer coupling, in London, of the Royal Albert Hall – round and capacious and rosy – and the phallic spike of the Albert Memorial across Kensington Road. Perhaps the world can be deconstructed into these two basic shapes, everywhere seeking the other. Just before his reading at the Marion County Public Library, while he was standing idle and momentarily unchaperoned on one side of the steps to the stage, a crisp, short, pleasant-looking woman in a magenta tweed suit came up to him starry-eyed.

He had encountered starry eyes before, in the visages of women who had read too much into one of his novels, casting themselves as his sketchy script's heroine. This woman's approach, however, was not that of a fan. "Henry Bech," she said, in the fearless flat accent of the great American inland. "I am Alice Oglethorpe. You may not remember, but we once traveled from New York to Los Angeles on the same train."

Her handshake was like her voice, firm, and neither cold nor warm, but he detected a slight tremble. Then, her identity dawning, Bech's heart surged forward in his chest and he, the professional spielmeister, felt his mouth open and nothing come out. Her blue eyes, with their uncanny silvery backing, clung to his attentively while his brain groped. He would not have recognized her at all. She seemed too young to be his Alice. Though his blood had bounded toward her, he was ashamed to have become, since they had last been together, an old man. "Oh my God," he brought out at last. "You. Of course I remember. The Twentieth Century Limited."

"Just as far as Chicago," she corrected him. "After that, it was the Santa Fe Super Chief."

His left hand, holding the book that he was to read from tonight, clumsily tried to caress the hand, the precious piece of her, that he was holding in his right. "How are you?" he asked. "*Where* are you? What happened next?"

Bech's confusion gratified her, and calmed her. She withdrew her hand, with its tremble. Her eyes did not leave his, but her mouth, tense at first, settled into a smile. She had been recognized. "I'm here," she answered. "Or, rather, in Bloomington. I'm well. Still married. I got over it."

She had oddly little aged, just broadened a bit. Her hair was the same light-brunette shade, too nondescript to be a tint – "dishwater blonde" was the phrase his mother used to use – and her wool suit was scarcely saved by its bold magenta from verging on dowdy. Her disguise as an ordinary, respectable woman was intact.

Her husband, he remembered, had been some sort of financial analyst, a middle-level money man. She had been traveling to L.A. to join him at the end of a weeklong conference sponsored by the southern-California defense industry, then in its hearty youth. Oh, she could have gone with Tad and stayed in the hotel, but what would she have done all day – take bus tours to the homes of the stars? Her silvery eyes and dry intonation told Bech that she considered herself, at some level, as much of a star as they. At least she was a proximate presence, talking only to him. She had always wanted to travel across the country, she told him, and hated to fly, though she *could* do it, with a couple of stiff drinks inside her. Bech was going to the far coast on what he intuited would be a futile exploration of the cinematic possibil- ities of his first, somewhat sensational novel, *Travel Light*. He, too, would rather ride the rails than entrust his body to the bumpy, propeller-driven flights of the late Fifties, before the onset of the big jets. The dashing transcontinental trains were on the way out, and by taking one Alice and he disclosed a kindred romantic streak. All this emerged in their first conversa- tion, they having been seated together, two singles, in the crowded dining car.

The shiver of their cutlery on the vibrating tablecloth. The reassuring, fairy-tale solidity of the heavy-bottomed cups and coffeepots, bearing the New York Central's logo. The theatri- cally deferential black waiters in a world where happy black servitude was also on the way out. Bech sensed as soon as she was ushered to his tingling table that she would sleep with him. There was that pale light in her eyes, a slightly loud shimmer in her teal-blue gabardine suit, an eager electricity in the way she moved and, with a little wine in her, talked. Women who were talkative, the sexual lore of his youthful Brooklyn buddies had reported and his limited experience tended to verify, "put out" in other respects. He and this woman were as alone on that speed- ing train, clicking north beside the blue autumnal Hudson, as on a desert island.

His chaperone, the head librarian of Indianapolis, reclaimed him; it was time to go onstage and earn his fee. Alice Oglethorpe said, warmly but formally, that it had been good to see him after all these years.

"You look wonderful – wonderful!" was all he could bring out. She turned away, he turned away. How stupid he had been! No blushing schoolboy could have been more tongue-tied. That clumsy scraping caress he had tried to deliver with a book in his hand. His failure to ask any searching questions. His body felt like a struck gong, swollen by its reverberations. To think that she was near, that she had come to find him! As he dizzily plowed through his reading, the questions he should have asked her flocked to his mind. Where did she live, exactly? Was she happy? Would she run away with him now, now that her motherly duties were done? There had been small children, he remembered, whom she had left with her husband's parents in the Bronx. But she was not from New York City, her journey had begun upstate, and that made her seem even more of a gift from beyond. Beyond all reason. Beyond all expectations. Under the lectern light his hands looked strange and withered, but for all that rather beautiful. Articulated masses, with fine hairs on the backs of his fingers. He had once been beautiful.

She did not sleep with him the first night. She stood up after coffee and firmly said good night. In those days the Pullman sleepers with green-curtained upper and lower berths had become antiques; the sleeper cars on the Twentieth Century Limited were divided into roomettes, each measuring seven feet by three. Bech scarcely slept, knowing that she was but a few steps away, in another roomette. Perhaps like him she was writhing between the too-tight sheets and flipping the pillow over to its cool side in the vain hope that blessed oblivion would rise from it, mixed with the tireless thud of the rail joints. Toward dawn there was a prolonged bright ruckus that must have been Buffalo.

They found each other at breakfast, in the dining car as it swayed and chimed through Ohio. "How did you sleep?" he asked.

"Terribly."

"Maybe we were lonely."

"I never sleep well on trains, thanks," she said. Her sleepless pallor and the unforgiving morning sunlight as it bounced up from the glittering stubble of the cornfields brought out a slight roughness, a constellation of tiny nicks as if from an adolescent storm of acne, below her cheekbones. The harsh slant sunlight betrayed her and then was slapped down by intervening poles, brick gables, rail-side warehouses. Makeup hadn't quite covered this touching flaw. He had forgotten it, he had forgotten to look for it in the few amazing moments when she had appeared again before him. She had once asked him if he would ever forget her. He had scorned the idea.

He turned the slightly abrasive page under the lectern light. He had chosen – God knows why, perhaps because he believed Indianapolis to be a pious place – that passage from *Brother Pig* where the Trappist monks, loosely based on what he had read of Thomas Merton, silently plot, with hand signals and written slips, to smuggle in a Jewish reporter from a New York tabloid – a "scandal sheet," one would call it now – to expose the abbot's tyranny and pederasty. How did he, Henry Bech, get caught in this embarrassing tangle of far-fetched, decadent motifs when the most marvelous lay of his life was out there among the shadowy, offended heads of devout Quaylites and Butler University evangels?

Alice and he had breakfasted together, and sat dozily with books in the club car. Other travelers spoke to them, and they were inveigled into a game of bridge, of which he scarcely knew the rules, squinting at his cards beside the sun-slapped windows, trying to decipher her bids, all the time feeling her with him in a dream world of insomniac yearning and wordless anticipation of the night. When, in late afternoon, they pulled into Chicago, for a half-hour shuffle of cars and locomotives, Bech dashed out of the great barrel-vaulted station to buy, in that era just before the Pill's liberating advent, a three-pack of Trojans at a Rexall's on Jackson Boulevard. His heart thrummed as if to break his ribs. The sly, blond-mustached clerk tried to talk him into an entire tin of fifty instead of the pack of three – "You'll use 'em," he promised, on no more basis than Bech's flushed, panting face – and with spiteful slowness, the economy size declined, counted out Bech's change. Suppose the train pulled out without him?

Now, in Indianapolis, he was compelled to make his way through pages he had felt obliged, decades ago, to write, in order to give his scabrous, irreligious journalist a family background and a professional history satiric of postwar New York literary circles. Had ever a selection been more ill-chosen, more maddeningly prolonged? A few nervous titters in the audience tried to rise to the cultural occasion. Did he hear Alice's laugh? She had laughed, telling him once, "You're safe."

At dinner, as the train hurtled into the darkness of flat farmland where a few distant houses pricked the night, she rose unsteadily from her coffee, smoothing some crumbs from her lap, and said, "I must lie down. I feel sick."

"Oh dear, why?"

His new friend smiled. "The constant motion. The long day. Not you. I like you." She hesitated, fighting a bit for balance as the Super Chief slammed over a patch of rocky roadbed. She bent toward him above the chattering silverware and said, softly but matter-of-factly, "Give me an hour. I must rest a little. Roomette sixteen. Knock twice."

"'Klein found himself fascinated by the Trappists,'" he heard himself reading. "'Like Hasidim, they seemed to possess an archaic secret of joy, a secret coded in their grotesque hairdos. The monks' tonsures framed a pink circle of scalp, and their faces had a childish sheen polished to a bright daze by the cruel hours of their devotions and their dawn rising to the dreary duties of farmers.'" Too many dentals, Bech thought. And then his captive tongue was launched into a long and dated description of Klein's brother, a labor organizer when such men still wielded a power that could bring the country to a halt.

After an hour of staring at the flat, loam-black land – were they still in Illinois? – Bech had had the porter make up his roomette, number 5. In pajamas and pinstriped cotton robe he ventured out into the carpeted aisle, alone with its rigid, retreating, vibrating perspective. He feared she would be asleep, but her answer to his two knocks was quick. Her hair pulled back, her face clean of makeup – his impression was of a nun or a prisoner in her cell – she was kneeling in a nightgown on the bed; there was nowhere else in the tiny cell to be. So that twenty-four roomettes could be fitted into the length of a car, they were dovetailed, with two steps' difference in height between each adjacent pair; the bed of the slightly lower chamber slid in daytime under the floor of the raised room beside it, and the feet of its occupants extended under an overhang which somewhat inhibited their movements.

But Alice was small and flexible and he not tall, and at times they seemed to stretch their allotted space to the size of a ballroom. Between times they raised the shade, gingerly, as if watchdogs of Midwestern puritanism might be posed in the black air streaming outside. The vast sleeping landscape would be shattered by a rapid garble of silhouetted architecture, or by lowered crossing gates where headlights patiently burned, or a local station platform like a suspensefully empty stage set. The small towns with their neon signs and straight strings of streetlamps wheeled and fell away to reveal the main visual drama, the abysmal void of farmland. Low streaks of cloud hung in a faint phosphorescence, like a radioactive aftermath.

They must be in Missouri now, if not Kansas. Her pliant nakedness, unified to his senses of touch and smell, flickered in curved short circuits as the train roared past lights defending a water tower or a set of grain silos. When the train hissed and slid to a stop, at a platform holding only a bare baggage-wagon and one loudly reuniting family, he raised the stiff green shade a few inches so he could ponder his companion's supine beauty as a continuous, calm, exultant entity, with rises and swales and dulcet shadowed corners. The curious silvery light of her eyes now lived all along her skin. In the small space carved from the surrounding, upholding clatter and mutter of the rushing train, she was a giantess who met him, his sensation was, wherever he thrusted, with an embracing cavity. She did it all, and had to keep suppressing moans which would disturb the unknown fellow-passengers presumably sleeping an arm's length away. "Will you forget me?" she at one point whispered, a cry come from afar, softly. There were fits of dozing amid a constant rejoining. The sly druggist had been right: Bech had underbought. The couple's closet of satisfied desire became nicely rank with a smell that was neither him nor her. "We're all mixed up together," she whispered, after she had swallowed his semen and caught her breath. The heartland they endlessly poured through seemed no vaster than territories laid open within them. "You're *per*fect," she sighed toward morning, sadly, like a distant train whistle, in his ear. She was not quite perfect, he had observed by the hard morning light in the dining car. In the dark he touched her cheeks, which had looked abraded with tiny nicks. A miracle. They were perfectly smooth. "So are you," he told her. It was the truth.

As he read aloud, he kept remembering that it was his unhappy sister's boss, a self-important thug in a double-breasted camel-hair topcoat, who had reluctantly filled in the young author with details of how labor unions operated. At the time, Bech thought he could, in the long future before him, assemble all America as a mosaic of such research. Now these details, as they passed through the microphone into the air, seemed worked-up and tinny, and his antihero Klein's cynical take on the Trappists – misfits, defectives, cop-outs – adolescently callous. With relief he at last ended the reading; but there were still the questions from the audience to face. Do you use a word processor and, if so, what kind? What authors influenced you in your youth? Why did they never make a movie of *Travel Light?* It would have been great with Sal Mineo. What – his least favorite question – is your personal favorite of your books? The auditorium lights had been turned up, so he could see the waving hands, the eager respectful aggressive faces. He scanned them for Alice, and failed to spot her, but the crowd was large, with restless, ill-lit edges over by the walls, and there was nothing about her, not even the magenta suit, to keep her from blending in.

Dawn had brought them into gauntly irrigated land yielding, mile by mile, to desert. He had scuttled out of her roomette like a gopher, and snatched a few hours of sleep in his own. The Pullman car had an ecology they were fitting into. The other passengers accepted them, by now, as a couple. They were invited again to play bridge – Bech timidly failed to bid a small slam though Alice had given clear signals that her hand was loaded – and a beefy pair of middle-aged Iowans sat down at their table for dinner, not appearing to notice that the other couple was too groggy to make small talk and conversationally lacked a common past to draw upon. At some ten-minute stop, where the Spanish adobe architecture squatted as if stunned under a sky full of vaporous thunderheads, Bech ran off the train to find a drugstore and replenish his supply of Trojans. He saw nothing near the station but pottery and buckskin souvenirs of the West, and heard the conductor call "All aboard." The train had become a conscience to him, a home he hurried back to in a panic that, huge as the thing was, it would disappear.

"That's all right," Alice said that night, of his Trojan failure. "I wouldn't mind having a baby of yours."

"But —" he began, thinking of her unsuspecting husband. Tad. The name suggested an insecure glad-hander, with an affected clipped accent.

"It's my body," she said, a woman ahead of her time. He wondered if inside every conventional housewife there was such a sexual radical. She took mercy on him: "Don't worry — I'm about to have my period. You're safe." She laughed then, a brief tough snicker, as if her voice had been lowered by moment-ary empathy with a man's point of view.

After sleepwalking through the day, they gained a second wind when night fell on the duned, saguaro-dotted desert. "Your place, or mine?" he had asked.

"Yours," Alice said. Having a choice — a little play in their situation — amused her. "I hate that nasty little overhang; my feet get claustrophobic." His slightly higher roomette had no such feature. They could spread out, relatively. Having mounted the two steps, they felt on top of the world. Their three days, he often reflected, had composed a courtship, a honeymoon, and a marriage. You fuck at first to stake a claim, and afterwards to keep the claim staked. They were less ravenous this second night together, and tender in their genitals, and slept for several stretches of an hour or more. They could hear, in the sudden gulp and changed pitch, as of a great musical instrument, the train entering tunnels, and feel its wheels carefully fumble over the switch points at some crucial junction. They could feel the train climb and sinuously labor through some pass, on a canyon's curved edge, beneath the unseen stars hanging cold and close above the desert mountains. As he sensed the night tilting and slowly swerving toward its end, Bech in his sexual hysteria and exhaustion began to cry, smearing his tears with his face, like a deer marking a tree, across her belly, her breasts, a kind of spiritual semen, leaving its own slimy glitter. As she submitted to this, she patted and tugged his thick, resilient hair.

The line of people with books to sign had no end in sight. "Would you just make this one 'To Roger'? He's my grandfather, he loves your work, he says you've really spoken for his generation." "Could you personalize this one 'For the Inimitable Lyndi'? That's 'L,' 'Y,' 'N,' 'D,' 'I.' No 'E.' Perfect. Thanks so much. It's wonderful to have you here in the Hoosier State."

By daylight the Mojave Desert yielded, an oasis at a time, to the California paradise. Pastel houses and palm trees multiplied to make a horizontal city, oddly colorless under a sky as blue and unflecked as a movie-set backdrop. The train crept to a final bump in mission-style Union Station, and there fell upon all its length the flurry and sudden hustle of a little world coming apart, with some porters to tip and others to beckon, with farewells to be said or avoided, with baggage to be gathered and safeguarded. Alice, at Bech's side all morning in the club car, sleeping with her head on his shoulder, had squeezed his hand and stood up and said, "I'll be back." The sun beating through the window put him in a doze. The train bumped. Where was he? Where was she? He went onto the platform, into the unreally benign air. She had put the distance of two or three cars between them when he spotted her, leading a porter with a trolley, down beside the locomotive, where the engineer, his task completed, traded guffaws with a uniformed station official. She merged with a man in a gauche brown outfit – slacks one shade, jacket another – and melted into the crowd, Tad's claim reclaimed. Bech had the impression that Oglethorpe was tall and bald. What happened next? Over the years he forgot why, whenever he saw a woman with a touch of rash or roughness on her cheeks, intended by nature to be silken, he was saddened and stirred.

He had imagined he would somehow see her again. The universe, having witnessed so sublime a coupling, would arrange it. And so it had, in its unsatisfactory fashion. The last fan in line went away with his authentic Henry Bech signature, that tiny piece of him chipped from his dwindling life span, and there was no one left in the auditorium lobby but the bookstore staff, packing all his unsold books into boxes, and the tired but cheery local matron, perhaps herself a secret sexual radical, who had chaired the committee that had arranged to get him here. Alice had vanished, and the librarian of Indianapolis had also gone home.

The sight of his books, the seven thin, passé titles, being briskly stashed in boxes disgusted Bech. No matter how many he sold and signed, there were always bushels left, representing tons of wasted paper. These women who showed up at his readings did it, it seemed clear, to mock his books – clever, twisted, false books, empty of almost everything that mattered, these women he had slept with were saying. We, *we* are your masterpieces.